***** T H E   C O V E R *****

Peter lifted the painting from its makeshift tripod on the table. "White Fang?" His mind asked as he looked at brush strokes in shades of greys and white that looked like fur. From a distance it looked like an animal; like a wolf or dog, but close up it looked different. What would be the eye made it difficult to know for sure. The eye was odd. Peter studied it and then realized that the glare of light in the eye took on a definite form and shape. It looked like it was someone dancing,, a girl. "Yes." Peter thought, looking at it closely, "That's her long hair flowing behind her in the wind" The sentence caused his mind to flash the image of Jeneil on the beach the first time he saw her there. He touched the glare on the painting gently with the tips of his fingers. "That's how she looked." His heart skipped a beat. He studied the painting for a name even turning it over and checking the back of it. There wasn't one. As he turned the canvas to the painted side again, the eye suddenly looked Asian to him. "Soul?" His mind questioned. "Is someone painting soul?" He asked himself. The woman in charge of the table joined him. "I'll take this one," Peter said, taking out his wallet.

"Isn't that odd? I felt the eye looked Asian and here you are buying it. I love art and sometimes I wish paintings could talk. What a fascinating story they could tell."

"I know what you mean." Peter replied, wondering about this new painting of White Fang, a girl dancing in the wind, and soul. "She's been married for almost three months," He thought, "if it is her painting, why did she paint it?" Peter wondered as he gave the girl the money.

"Oh this is generous." The woman smiled looking at what he gave.

"I like the painting." Peter answered quietly.

This is a "Author's Edition" of "The Songbird / Volume Four" This "unedited" version of the story is complete just as Beverly intended it to be read.

Only a limited number will be printed for family and friends. "The Songbird / Volume Four" is the fourth of a five volume series. This should make this a treasured keepsake for those friends who have continued to support our efforts to bring recognition to a truly gifted writing talent. Your help is so very essential to "The Songbird" success.

Beverly Louise Oliver-Farrell was never given the opportunity to show her incredible writing and storytelling gift to the world. She represents all of those with exceptional talent who are bypassed in life simply because the every-day existence of life's struggles never affords that opportunity to be recognized and showcased. Beverly talks about this "Conveyor Belt" of responsibility in "The Songbird".*(Page 4 / Volume 1)* To all gifted talents out there who never get the opportunity to jump off the "Conveyor Belt". This is for you.

The original manuscript was handwritten in twelve five-subject notebooks over an twelve year period. I just couldn't allow such talent to be lost in a box in the attic.

Thank you so very, very, very much for supporting "The Songbird."

Brian B. Farrell

2/10/2014

Brian B. Farrell

The Songbird

Volume Four

By

Beverly Louise Oliver-Farrell

***** A C K N O W L E D G E M E N T S *****

Getting "The Songbird" Published would never have happened had it not been for the efforts of some very special people. They make up "The Songbird" team. It took me two weeks to type the first twenty-nine pages into the computer. I hit the wrong button and lost it all. I realized then that I couldn't do this myself. I'll be eternally grateful for each of their contributions.

A "Very Special Thank You" to "The Songbird" Editorial team.

Brian J. Farrell
Benjamin G. Farrell
Amber Massie
Karalee Shawcroft
Lisa Cramer
Kimberly Niven
Virginia Rabun

*****

I have had fantastic support from some very learned technical people. The patience and efforts they have shown in dealing with such a computer klutz as me and keeping my equipment running and meeting the needs of "The Songbird" project is greatly appreciated by all of us.

A "Very Special Thank You" To "The Songbird" Technical team

Benn Farrell at Dockrat Entertainment (Website)
Lee Sanchez at PC & Mac Repairs (Computers)
Bill & Sharon Price at Laserpro II (Printers)
Jean-Claude Picard at Microcrafts (Lamination)
Jaime Smith (Graphic Designer/Cover Assembly)
Wishing Well Glass Blowers (Unicorns)

***** A C K N O W L E D G E M E N T S *****

Every Wednesday night I go to an "Independent/Assisted Living" facility and read and share "The Songbird" with a group of "Very Special" people who have become my close friends.
I don't think they will ever fully understand how much they have taught me and caused me to grow.   I thank them so very much for their support and encouragement.

A "Very Special Thank You" to "The Songbird Book Club"
at "Viewpointe"

Virginia Rabun	Harriet Spangenberg
Ruth Goetzman	Susie Glidden
Chet Derezinski	Gary Bleckert
Bertha Lang	Carol Barrett
Gladys Mercier	Beverly Osbum
Ruth Dougherty	Liz Nichols
Albert and Trudy Luigi	

*****

A "Very Special Thank you" to members of the Viewpointe Staff for their valuable assistance in gathering our group together each Wednesday night.

Judine Carkner   Natalie Mutch   Peggy Striplin   Patty Wright
*****

One person deserves "Special Recognition."   His encouragement and living example has shown me that "you never give up your dreams."

A "Very Special Thank You" to my "Best Friend"

Robert Louis Tyler

***** S Y N O P S I S *****

"The Songbird" is a love story about a young woman named Jeneil who believed in fairy tales, a prince charming, and happy endings. She goes on a quest to find herself before the "conveyor belt" of responsibility forces her to accept a lesser existence. In her quest for superlative, she almost destroys herself and the lives of some of those people around her.

Jeneil, a white girl from Nebraska, finds her Prince Charming in Peter, a Chinese gang kid from the streets of New York's Chinatown, who is in his last year as a residence in a New England hospital where they meet. "The Songbird" is their story. Add Steve, Peter's best friend, whose life began as a baby left on the doorsteps of an upper New York state orphanage, to the mix and life will never be the same for this triad of friends
.

It is a story of love, communication, murder, mystery, danger, betrayal, suspense, honesty and dignity, personal achievements, and a look at life which covers the trials of human relationships. It is steeped in a reality that will cause everyone who reads "The Songbird" to identify with their own life experiences.

COMMENT: *The complete story of the "The Songbird" is a five volume series. Beverly Louise Oliver-Farrell has laid out "The Songbird" from beginning to end, stacking one incident on top of another like a set of logo blocks, carefully interlocking the past, present, and future together in a not-so-perfect world. Beverly holds the reader's interest by leaving clues and dangling unanswered questions throughout "The Songbird" and just when you think you have it all figured out....... She is very successful tying it all together and being able to keep the end of the story a secret until the closing pages.*

I love you, Baby

I'm going to miss you

Beverly wrote The Songbird between 1985 to 1995. The storyline of The Songbird takes place during the 1980's. The 1980's while having it's share of sensationalism, was a period of peaceful co-existence as a nation attempted to heal itself from the ravages of an unpopular Vietnam war. It can best be described as the "Reagan Years." Prosperity reigned and after the turbulent years of the 60's and 70's was a welcomed change. There were some events that left there mark on history such as the ending of the "Cold War" with Russia and the tearing down of the Berlin wall, the pandemic introduction of the "Aids" virus, the mid-air explosion of the space shuttle "Challenger", the nuclear meltdown of the Russian atomic reactor at Chernobyl, the attempted assassination of President Reagan, and the senseless mass killing and injuries of students at Columbine High School in Denver were just some of the events that reminded us that no decade is devoid of a place in history. The 80's can be likened to the 'calm before the storm' for the events in the 90's would bring changes to the human existence the likes of which man had never before seen and will probably never be matched in this generation and many generations to come. It was the "Technology Explosion" of the 90's which took computers and all it's data-collecting abilities out of the hands of corporate giants (*the only ones who could afford them*) and into the hands of the common citizenry, including a bunch of young entrepreneurs led by Microsoft's Bill Gates and Apple's Steve Jobs who created software programs in almost every field of endeavor. These young challengers of the status quo produced a new bred of young million/billionaires. Changes erupted so fast that in many cases throughout the 90's, the new technology was obsolete before it could be introduced.

As Beverly struggled to complete The Songbird during the first half of the 1990's, she ran headlong into this new technology and it concerned her thinking it would make some of the medical procedures she had used in The Songbird to build her story obsolete. Some small things like the use of the mobile/cell phone started to replace the land line telephones and slowly brought about the demise of the long lines of telephone booths that would line the corridors or halls of many of our public buildings. The fact that Peter was vacationing in Europe and couldn't be reached because the cell phone, while being talked about, had not yet been developed to be the world-wide communication tool it was to become. It was only when Beverly realized that her book was a period piece, similar to the roaring twenties, the depression thirties, world war two forties, the flower children of the sixties, etc, and the "Reagan" eighties, (*A term I have given the decade to identify it. Time may offer up a more eloquent description in later years.*) that she was able reconcile her thoughts with facts and complete her story.

*****

I have often thought that The Songbird could be read starting at Volume Three because that is where the story really starts to unfold. The Songbird / Volume One and The Songbird / Volume Two give explanations and understanding of the main characters Jeneil, Peter and Steve and creates a path to Volume Three, and it adds so much to Beverly's writing. Some people who have read The Songbird / Volume One and Two have gone back and read it a second time, and yes a third time. These people who have done that have told me that they have so much more insight into the characters and also they found The Songbird to be just plain good reading. If you started the reading at Volume Three, I hope you'll make a date to go back and read what has gone on before. You will not be disappointed and be glad you did.

Brian B. Farrell

The Songbird

One

Jeneil opened a small picnic cooler and took out a lemon. Slicing two pieces, she handed one to Dennis who looked stunned. "Jeneil, I can't. That's awful, eating a lemon."

She snipped through the rind on her piece and pulled the yellow strip flat causing the pulp to form triangles. "It's easy. Think of something pleasant and slip the fruit from the membrane," she said, showing him how.

His face contorted just watching her eat it. "Jeneil, I've been on your herbal drinks and vitamin kick for a few days now and I admit I feel better, but honey, give me a break. You've gotten me to drink grapefruit juice; please, I can't eat a lemon."

"Bite the bullet and at least try a wedge just to prove to yourself that you can. I'm afraid of water and I've decided to come to grips with that this summer. I'm going to meet that fear on my terms and see what I learn about myself."

Dennis smiled. "Your fire for things makes me crazy. Here, give me a slice." He took a slice of lemon and bit it, keeping it on his tongue.

"Swallow it quickly, Dennis, don't punish yourself."

He laughed and it slipped down his throat. "Where the hell do you get these phrases? I think you hang off my sofa too much."

She smiled. "I hang my head off your sofa for blood circulation because I can't do yoga handstands, my arms are too weak. Peter is incredible. He can stand on his hands steadily for a full minute." She finished her lemon slice. "Maybe it's genetic. The Chinese have a history of being great acrobats."

Dennis looked at her. "When are you going to be free of him, honey? It's over."

She pierced the yellow lemon peel with her fingernail releasing the scented oil. "I love the smell of fresh lemons."

Dennis grinned and kissed her cheek gently. "Ignore me if you want to but at least start speaking about him in the past tense. Peter *used* to stand on his hands."

"I'm sure he still can even though I can't see him do it," she said, grinning.

Dennis chuckled and put his arms around her. "You're so damn cute."

"Oh, cuddle and snuggle time," Robert said walking into the room. "I love the theatre; you people have great coffee breaks. Where's the hug line forming on this beautiful sea urchin? I want my turn, too." He smiled, squeezing the back of Jeneil's neck gently.

Dennis continued holding her. "Where do you get off calling her a sea urchin? They're tough and bristly, she's soft and smooth and she smells good, too."

Robert laughed. "Oh yeah, make a pass at her and pop instant sea urchin."

Dennis looked at Jeneil. "Is he giving you trouble?"

"You mean sexual harassment? It's one of his less decadent habits," she replied, smiling at Robert.

"Ooo," Dennis laughed, "bullwhip attack, Robert."

Robert grinned. "Dennis, how come with you the oyster opens and exposes the smooth pearl but with me its sea urchin?"

"That's a good question, Jeneil, answer it," Karen said, standing at the door with a coffee mug. They all turned as she shuffled into the room. "Why is that, Jeneil? Explain why."

"Karen," Dennis cautioned.

"Because he's married to you, Karen, so I know his hugs are just hugs. Robert's hugs are passion," Jeneil replied.

Dennis scowled at Karen. "Sounds innocent enough to me."

"Don't you like passion?" Karen asked.

"She's healing, Karen," Robert said.

Dennis let go of Jeneil and put his arm around Karen's shoulder. "You'll have to excuse Karen everyone, she has trouble hugging lately. Her arms aren't long enough."

Dennis moved to kiss Karen's cheek but she pulled away. "For a man who makes a living using words you sure stumble over them around me. Here, I brought you coffee. I'm fresh out of guava juice but Jeneil probably brought some for your lunch along with her other health tricks." She put the mug on his desk and shuffled to the door. "Thank you for the spa membership, Jeneil. I'm going there now and maybe when I get back I'll be soft and smooth and smell good, too."

"Dennis, she's hurt," Jeneil said, as Karen left. "Go walk her to her car and be nice."

"No," he snapped. "She's on a steady diet of self-pity lately. Let her get fat on it."

Jeneil frowned. "It looks like you're chewing on some yourself right now."

Robert smiled and put his arm around her shoulder, squeezing her to him. "Go walk her to the car, Dennis, before I kick your ass," Robert said matter-of-factly. "Or you'll have trouble you know where."

Dennis sighed. "Shit," he said, going to the door, "this is possibly the worst summer I've ever lived through."

"Nah," Robert answered, "the worst one was when you were fourteen at sleep away camp and caught poison ivy over ninety percent of your body on the week the buxom blonde said it was your turn for some fun and you developed acne just thinking about it."

Dennis laughed. "You're right, that would be worse. I'll be right back. I've got to see a lady about an apology." He left quickly to catch up to Karen.

Jeneil sighed. "This is a trying summer, isn't it?"

"Well I'll keep trying." Robert grinned and kissed her lips lightly.

Jeneil smiled and shook her head. "I think I need a therapist, Robert. Your decadence is becoming charming."

"Try a sex therapist," he answered, and moved out of her arm range quickly.

"Now that's enough!" she snapped. "I am not frigid!"

"Whoa!" He laughed. "I knew that remark would pop the sea urchin."

"You're exasperating," she said, going to her desk. "But, you know, I like that name, *Sea Urchin*. I think that's what I'll call my boat. What kind of paint should I use?"

Robert sat on her desk and folded his arms. "Well now, that's a professional question for an artist. I'd have to charge you a fee or go to your place and paint it for you in exchange for some of that dead chicken on coals."

"I'll pay your fee," she said, teasing him.

He leaned across the desk on one elbow before her and smiled enticingly. "Are you sure you're ready to pay my fee, spitfire?"

She sighed and shook her head wearily. "You wear me out."

He laughed. "Hell, that's my problem then. I'm trying to wear you down, not wear you out."

She covered her eyes. "I give up. How do you manage to bring everything I say around to sex?"

"Look in the mirror," he said, lying on his back across her desk.

She got up and paced. "Have you decided how you want the sections of backdrop fastened yet?"

"They're done. I did them this morning before I started on Section 10-4 in Scene Three."

"Did you?" she asked, smiling. "That's great. You do work fast."

"How do you know?" he asked, grinning slyly.

"Robert!" she yelled. "Get off my desk; I need to get under…I mean I need to get my work list that's under you. I have work to do." He laughed as he watched her fumble.

"What are you doing to my assistant, Robert?" Dennis asked, returning and going to his desk.

"Not what I want to do, that's for sure."

"Robert, stop, please," Jeneil pleaded, tears rolling down her cheeks.

"Hey!" he said, sitting up quickly and jumping off her desk. "I'm sorry, sweetheart." He kissed her temple gently. "I overwhelmed you, didn't I?" Dennis watched them together, studying Jeneil.

She pushed away gently, smiling as she wiped her tears. "I'm okay, Robert. I cry when I'm overwhelmed. Don't worry about it. You're good for me in a way; you're like my boat and my fear of water."

"Are you sure you're okay?" Robert asked.

She nodded. "I'm fine, tantrum is over."

Robert touched her cheek tenderly. "Hell, sweetheart, if you did that in a board meeting I'd give you whatever you were asking for."

She laughed. "You were wise to avoid going into business then, but that's why you're a great artist. Your intense feelings show up in your work."

"I think you're terrific," he said, kissing her tenderly. "I'll let you get back to work. Can I paint the *Sea Urchin*?" he asked, and she nodded and he kissed her again and headed for the door. "Dennis, you'll have Act Two Scene Three by four-thirty today." Robert pointed at Dennis and strode confidently out of the room.

Jeneil shook her head. "He's incredible. He makes me hyperventilate from his wild energy. I can't control him and it infuriates me."

"Do you like to control your men?"

"What?" She turned, surprised by the question. "Well no, but Robert isn't my man. I just realized Robert and I had an arrangement. He wasn't supposed to kiss me, but he's always kissing me. He doesn't listen to me and I get swept up as he thrashes about. It's hard to explain."

"You're both wildfire," Dennis said, smiling.

Jeneil chuckled. "Well, how do you stand the two of us in your life?"

"I find you both interesting. I come alive around you and I'm glad you're both on my staff, I just sort of breeze along like the wind. Did Peter overwhelm you?"

"He does, in a different way, but I can maintain my equilibrium with Peter."

Dennis frowned. "Did Jeneil, he did. Past tense, honey; remember that or you won't heal."

"Right," she answered quietly, embarrassed she was living a lie. "Dennis, can I tell you something in confidence?"

"Sure."

"I hate to keep lying to you. Peter isn't past tense."

"What!" He sat forward in his chair. "Maybe you'd better explain that because it sounds like you're telling me you're his mistress."

She shook her head. "No, I'm waiting for him. The baby isn't his and after he proves it, we're going to be married."

"Baby? His wife's pregnant?"

"She isn't his wife. Well she is legally, but that's all."

He stared at her. "Jeneil, did I grasp this all straight? Peter married a girl because she said he got her pregnant. He told you he didn't, but he's been married to her a few months now and you think he's not sleeping with her?"

"He's not," Jeneil insisted.

Dennis covered his face and sighed. "That son-of-a-bitch."

Jeneil was stunned and disappointed. "I'm sorry, forget I told you. I know it's hard to believe."

Dennis got up slowly. "Forget you told me? Jeneil, honey, wake up. How long has he been married?"

"Almost six months," she answered. "Why?"

Dennis held her tightly in his arms. "Honey, no. No, no, no. Don't wait."

She pushed away. "What do you mean? I hear something else in your words, what is it?"

He touched her cheek gently. "Oh, baby, six months and…no, sweetheart. Look, I'll even give Peter the benefit of the doubt and buy the story he told you, but after six months…honey, maybe he doesn't want out now."

The words struck Jeneil with force. She had never thought of that. "That's not true," she gasped, tears stinging her eyes. "Don't say that! Don't, it's not true!" She wiped her tears away with her fingertips.

"I'm sorry," Dennis said, seeing the hurt he had caused and he put his arms around her again. "You know him better than I do. Don't listen to me."

His words sounded empty and she knew he didn't believe her. She leaned against him wishing she hadn't admitted the truth to him. At that moment, she missed Steve. He was her steadying force. He understood the whole situation. He gave her comfort and hope. She pushed away gently and smiled at Dennis. "You're a good friend. You're worried about me. I can see that. I guess you'll have to trust my judgment."

He nodded. "Yeah, I guess I'll have to."

"Boy, I'm sure weepy today." She went to her desk and picked up her purse. "I'm going to fix my face, I'll be right back."

"Okay," he said, watching her leave. That bastard barbarian, he thought, how the hell could he do that on her first time out or any time? He sat at his desk angrily thumping a pencil. Oh, Jeneil, wake up. Maybe the tears were from a struggle between her head and her heart. Maybe one of them was trying to get her to listen to the truth. Shit, he should have pushed and split the two of them up. But no, he hadn't wanted to hurt her. He hadn't wanted to take advantage of their friendship. Now look at them. What a mess. Throwing his pencil on the desk, he got up and paced thinking how annoying it was when life played dirty tricks on people.

*****

Steve began calling Jeneil every night after hearing about the surveillance camera. It made him feel better knowing she was safe. In talking every night, he uncovered a lot of little details as he looked for conversation and had learned that lightning struck the utility pole opposite her driveway several times which amazed her, but she had passed it off and installed lightning rods on both the house and garage. He also discovered that she rarely saw anyone in the neighborhood except for the workman who came once a week to check the pole. Again she mentioned how odd the situation was but not having any reason to be suspicious she simply ignored it. Under the guise of wondering if the utility company had hired minorities for overtime, Steve had asked if the workman was a minority and was told he was white. Peter and Steve assessed all the information and decided the camera was on the pole and was the reason lightning kept striking it. The fact that the same workman came every week was a puzzle but they felt Uette was the key. As long as she and Peter were getting along, they believed Jeneil would be safe.

Steve hadn't been able to see Jeneil during the week living so far from each other and he was looking forward to seeing her on the weekend. He gritted his teeth as she excitedly told him that Robert had helped her with the boat now called *Sea Urchin*. A stake had been installed and she had attached a long tow rope that allowed her to drift out past the inlet and even into the mouth of the bay. She felt that would be her limit though. Her fear of the water had disappeared, she could deal with it on her terms now and that allowed her a lot of fun on the water. Robert had also built a small dock and the boat had become their favorite past time when he was at Wonderland.

After finishing his call, Steve decided that nothing would interrupt his weekend with her. It sounded like Robert was getting too close. He was glad it was Thursday and he made sure his schedule at the office and hospital allowed him to leave early Friday. Things at the hospital were getting almost silly as he began getting dinner invitations for both him and Jeneil. They were a couple according to the gossip even though Steve kept insisting they were just dating and he wondered how Peter could stand hearing about him and Jeneil. He thought how much better for her Peter was since in thinking about it he knew he wouldn't allow Jeneil half the freedom Peter did. He was convinced that she was too deadly and he'd keep her very close to home on a tow rope just like her boat where she would be miserably unhappy.

*****

Uette had resisted all of Peter's efforts to get her into counseling and insisted she didn't need drug rehabilitation since she wasn't hooked. She had been contrite about the incident in his bedroom and thanked him for not overreacting. The baby was beginning to grow and her stomach began to protrude making her miserable. She lived on diet drinks and iced tea and rarely left the apartment. She refused to buy maternity clothes and spent most of her time in revealing negligees, again refusing to attend her graduation ceremony.

Peter was discouraged not having heard from Lin Chi. He called from time to time to make sure they were all right by asking for a particular sandwich to-go using the name of Barr. It was Lin Chi's idea as a cover and Peter began to see exactly how scared she was. They were being very careful who they talked to every step of the way. He sighed as he went home for dinner. He was tired of living in fear that some good people would be hurt and his panic that Jeneil was being watched made him feel choked most of the time. He longed for peace and contentment.

The heat had been oppressive on the drive home reminding him of the heat wave that had sent him and Jeneil to camp out a year earlier when they had begun their physical relationship. He arrived at the apartment missing her like crazy and resenting Uette for the turmoil in his life. She was in her room when he walked in. Not being very hungry, he checked the refrigerator and chose a few cold items to eat. Checking the freezer, he noticed the frozen dinner supply wasn't moving too fast. He turned to see Uette at the kitchen door in what looked like a mean mood.

"What happened, did your mother-in-law stop by?" he asked, assessing her mood.

"Of course," she snapped, "she brought her supply of throw away from China Bay and she cleaned up the apartment. Can you believe that? What colossal nerve!"

"She likes you, Uette. Is that so hard to take?"

She watched him steadily. "I found out today that you and Steve are still very good friends. Isn't that awfully odd? He steals your woman and you're not mad at him. And the mouse, you're not mad at her either." She shook her head. "Do you really think I'm that stupid? Very cozy, Steve visits Jeneil in your place. Think you're clever, huh? Well now the rule is that you stay away from Steve too, and I know you'll do that because now I know why you're civil to me. You're afraid of my friends. Well shape up or they'll do more than just watch Jeneil. Is that clear? I'm so sick of her that I'd like to erase her." She stomped out of the kitchen and slammed the bedroom door.

Peter was drained of feeling as he sat at the kitchen table. The frustration of trying to protect Jeneil added to his discouragement. "Where is Lin Chi?" he asked. "Is this crazy bitch bluffing?" Resting his head back, he sighed.

Peter reported Uette's new order to Steve after surgery Friday morning. Steve refused to be reassured that Jeneil would be safe and left for the weekend feeling very strongly that he should tell Jeneil everything, convinced the only one who could protect Jeneil was Jeneil. The exact words wouldn't form in his mind even after the drive. Pulling into the driveway, he sighed and realized he must be appearing on video. Getting out of the car, he crossed the road and avoided looking at it directly. He could tell there was no camera on the pole and he wondered what that meant. He walked back to the driveway and headed to the house. It was empty but Jeneil's car was in the driveway.

Going back outside and down to the water, he smiled as he noticed the taut rope tied to the stake. He tugged gently at it so she'd feel the pull and then he began to pull the rope in while standing on the dock, thinking his grey suit wasn't exactly the right outfit for water fun. He wondered why she was taking so long to come back; the mouth of the bay wasn't far from her yard. Looking over the top of the marsh, he tried to see the boat. He thought he glimpsed it coming into the marsh but he couldn't see her. He watched, pulling the rope more quickly. The boat pulled into the marsh opening and Steve's heart stopped, seized by fear. Jeneil was draped across the front of the boat, her head hanging in the water. The boat under her was red in spots.

"Jeneil!" he shouted. "Jeneil!" His voice cracked as panic seized him. He pulled desperately at the rope working faster and faster as he became concerned that she wasn't responding. No, he shouted in his mind, and he jumped off the dock and splashed through the water toward the boat as quickly as he could. "Jeneil!" he called, as panic raced through him. He pulled furiously at the rope as he ran through the water as his worst fear reached his mind. He'd kill that bitch himself. He choked up and pulled furiously at the rope. His clothes were wet and held him back from moving quickly. She was still and lifeless as the boat moved through the water. She was almost to him and he lunged.

"Gotcha!" she said, lifting herself up quickly. Her face showed shock as she looked at him. "Your suit," she screamed, "your good suit!" He put his arms around her trying to calm down. No words would form. He held her tight, glad it was a joke and he kept swallowing to make the lump in his throat disappear. "Steve, are you okay?" she asked, holding onto him. He nodded but didn't answer. He couldn't. Realizing the joke wasn't funny she clung to him and stroked his hair. "I'm really sorry, Steve. You've ruined your good suit because of me. I'm so sorry. Now that I see it from your side, it wasn't funny."

"Jeneil," he whispered hoarsely, "Jeneil, you scared the hell out of me."

"I know. It was a sick joke now that I think about it." She kissed his cheek gently.

He pulled away from her slightly and looked at the boat wondering what the red had been. *Sea Urchin* was painted on in red paint. He took her hands in his. "Jeneil, I want to tell you something," he said seriously, and she watched him with concern. "I have to tell you this, Jeneil. It's serious." He kissed her fingertips.

"What is it?" she asked, and he yanked her hard catching her off balance. She screamed as she went under the water and stood up sputtering and gasping for air.

"You're a bitch. I have to tell you that," he shouted, "a crazy bitch." He grabbed her shoulders and pushed her backwards down into the water again. He watched smiling, feeling justified as she struggled to stand up, taking huge gulps of air. He walked toward her and she backed away rubbing her eyes.

"No," she pleaded, "I'm sorry! I am! I'm really sorry!" He grabbed her wrist and she grabbed him around the neck as he was about to push her causing them both to lose their footing. They struggled to stand up, gasping for air. "I deserve all this," she said, breathing hard as she tried to stand up. They leaned on each other for support but were unsteady from the weight of their water-soaked clothes. Jeneil began to giggle as she saw how ruined Steve's suit was. "I'm sorry. I know it isn't funny but I can't help it," she said, trying to fix his lapels.

He put her arms around her and held her close to him. "Jeneil, you don't know what happened to my stomach when I saw you like that. I was a wreck." She leaned against him enjoying his strength and the comfort and peace he brought to her life.

"Steve, I missed you," she said, clinging to him.

Her words spun through him like high voltage power. Their closeness at the moment and his relief that she hadn't been hurt rushed at him. He had wanted to kiss her when he found she was all right but hadn't. All those emotions had accumulated and he didn't want to hide or pretend anymore. He wanted her to know how he felt. He wanted her to know how much he really loved her. Courage welled up in him with a determination to be honest and open with her.

"Steve, I've realized this week how important you are to me and Peter. I know I couldn't live without him and I'll get through this nightmare because of you. I will always be in your debt for what you're doing for us," she said, hugging him tightly. He held her and felt her words sting, cutting through his courage and determination like a swift, sharp blade, leaving a deep wound inside of him.

"It's okay, kid," he answered sadly.

They got changed and comfortable on the cushions in the air-conditioned living room. Steve was stunned by the stacks of books she was reading and laced throughout were ones about China and Chinese culture. Reality loomed clearly before him. She belonged to Peter and if he was going to have her in his life it would either be as a friend or not at all. He realized the damage his confession would cause to their friendship. He watched her lying on the cushions thinking and the reality that she'd never be his filled him. Sadness settled within him again. He felt lost not knowing where he was in her life and confused by the gnawing feeling that she belonged to him. He looked at the ceiling wishing he could regain his control. Her prank had uncovered his deepest feelings for her and he struggled against them now. He repeated her words, '*I know I couldn't live without Peter,*' over and over in his mind hoping the pain would push his feelings back into the recesses of his inner being so objectivity would surface and he could be the good friend she believed he was. He loved her with everything that was in him. Her prank had shown him that and he wondered if he would find anyone else he cared for as much.

Jeneil turned onto her side to face him. "Steve," she faltered, her tone reaching him as she struggled with something.

"What?" he asked, propping himself up on his elbow.

She bit her lower lip and swallowed. "Is it possible that Peter...well, do you think he wants to be married to Uette now?"

Steve was dumbstruck by the question and he stared at her in disbelief. "Jeneil, are you crazy? The guy is only half alive without you. He's a complete wreck," he said, and tears rolled down Jeneil's cheeks. "Why would you even think that?"

"I didn't, someone asked me about it. Not seeing him, not talking to him, it's difficult to understand why this is taking so long. Why is she accepting such a pathetic life? Where's the baby's father? Didn't she love him? She got pregnant." She sighed. "I don't know, I guess the longer this continues the less clear everything seems to be. I'm frightened."

He slid his cushions across the hardwood floor to her and he kissed her forehead tenderly. "Everything Pete's doing, he's doing for you."

She cried softly. "I miss him so much. Everything in my life feels so foreign right now." Seeing her pain was exactly what he needed to restore his objectivity. She belonged to Peter and the separation was hurting her. He wanted her happiness. His place in her life was clear; she needed him and his friendship. He could give her that. He wanted to give her that.

"Come here, kid," he said softly. She looked at him as he held his arm out to her. She slipped beside him and felt herself begin to relax as his arm encircled her, bringing a sense of comfort and peace, and she was filled with love for him at that moment.

"Steve, you'll never know how much this moment means to me. Just to feel your caring and concern. I need that right now and I can relax knowing you don't expect anything from me," she said, sighing contentedly. He smiled and kissed her forehead understanding what she was feeling. He understood being deadly wasn't easy for her and he doubted she knew she was. She didn't like the noise and the raging of the stampede. The battle of the sexes wasn't a war she was well equipped to fight, but she was in it. He knew why Peter hovered over her; she needed a rest stop and protection to survive.

"Who's handing you the line of shit, honey? Danzieg?"

"No, Dennis just made the comment. Our situation doesn't stand up to real scrutiny. I know that now. It's better if I keep the truth to myself. No one seems to want to hear it," she said, and Steve squeezed her and she smiled at him. "You know, I'm finding that life is a very singular experience. No one but you knows you as well. How things feel to you, what they mean, you can try to describe thoughts and feelings, but then there are times when certain magic happens where the singularity is shared." She paused and smiled at him again. "You are really special to me."

Steve saw the look in her eyes. She loved him and he knew it, and he was really glad he hadn't confessed his deeper feelings earlier or this moment wouldn't be happening and he wouldn't have felt the magic that she was talking about. They were silent as the magic of the moment and their special love filled them both.

Two

Jeneil was awake and dressed when Steve walked out of his bedroom. "Come on, kid. I'll take us to breakfast."

"I can't, Steve," she said, standing near the kitchen window drinking juice.

"Why?" he asked, getting a glass and going to the fridge.

"I have to handle something here this morning. You won't believe what I found. We're putting a new security system into Fairview Apartments and I've been looking through catalogs of surveillance equipment. Yesterday, I realized the pole across the street had a box on it that looked like a camera I'd seen in the catalogs," she said, and Steve turned quickly to look at her. "The workman usually comes around this time every Saturday. I had my staff remove it." She patted the box next to her on the counter. "I want him to tell me what this is all about." Steve was frozen where he stood. "Here he is!" Jeneil picked up the box and Steve dropped his glass and ran after her.

"No, Jeneil! No!" He grabbed her arm. "You can't."

"Steve, I have to know what this camera means." She ran down the deck stairs and around the house. He wished he had a gun and he panicked at the thought of her facing the muscle unarmed and unprepared. He couldn't think of anything else to do but go with her and face whatever they found. Jumping the deck railing, he caught up with her and headed to the workman who had gotten out of his truck and was looking up at the empty pole. "Are you looking for this?" Jeneil asked, holding the camera in her hand.

The workman turned around surprised by her voice. Steve was shocked as he recognized the detective he had hired to find Jeneil. Steve went to him and grabbed his shirt with two hands. "What the hell kind of game are you playing?"

"You know him?" Jeneil asked, her turn to be shocked.

"Yes, this bastard is the private detective I hired to find you."

"What is this all about?" she asked angrily, staring at the man. "I'd like to hear your story before taking legal action. I think you've violated a few rules and government property to say nothing about my privacy. Who's behind this? Are you sure you're watching the right person? Who'd be interested in me?"

The man wrenched himself from Steve's grasp. "Aren't you Jeneil Alden-Connors?"

"Yes," Jeneil answered, not believing he was actually looking for her. She had thought the surveillance camera was a mistake. "Who hired you?"

The man fidgeted. "Look, this is harmless enough, do we have to make a federal issue out of it?"

"Harmless!" Jeneil shouted. "You're spying on me and using public property. Who's hired you? I have the film as proof."

"This was the last week," the man said. "The cost has been too high from lightning damage. Can't we just let this pass?"

"Who hired you?" Jeneil demanded, getting really annoyed. "Tell me or you won't get a job anywhere close to this field of work again. If you're out of prison that is. I want to know who hired you before we talk about negotiating."

Steve had never seen Jeneil do business before. He watched her and smiled. Uette called her a mouse. Not hardly. She had courage and strength that were beyond belief.

The man fidgeted, embarrassed having been caught. "Mrs. Peter Chang."

The name confused Jeneil for a second because it was her name and then she realized who he meant "Uette!" she gasped in disbelief. "Why?" she asked, almost shrilling.

"I don't know, lady. I've never collected so much useless tape in my life. I've thrown whole cassettes out because they had nothing on them to splice. So now can we negotiate?"

Jeneil rubbed her temple confused by the revelation. "What kind of reports have you given her?" she asked sternly. "You must have given reports or the tapes are worthless to her."

"Just the names of all the people who visit you. What about negotiating?"

Jeneil thought for a moment. "I want copies of all the reports and tapes you've sent her."

"But lady, that'll eat into my profits. The lightning damage has nearly killed me as it is."

"Court costs and a prison sentence will eat into your profits even worse. So make your choice," Jeneil countered, and Steve smiled as he watched the tough mouse work.

"That's it?" the man asked. "That's all you want? No money?"

"How would you finish up this case?" Jeneil asked.

The man looked puzzled. "I'd splice this film and send her a written report like all the others. It's a weird case, lady. She's Chinese and at first I thought it was a straying husband case, but nobody looking like a Chang has shown up on the tape so I'm not sure what her problem is. Then I get hired to find you by him." He pointed to Steve. "Two clients for one person, that's odd, too."

Jeneil shook her head, confused. "What good is a tape of a driveway? That's hardly incriminating."

The man nodded agreeing. "That's what I thought too, but she was happy to see the list of names." He paused and fidgeted. "Because you're being so decent about this I'm going to tell you something. Being so isolated here I couldn't put the camera in too many places where it wouldn't be spotted. The lightning damage cost her plenty and she ran out of money just as she asked me to sight your bedroom."

"Oh shit," Steve gasped, and turned away disgusted.

Jeneil was shocked but recovered. "Well that wouldn't have been incriminating either unless she likes soliloquies."

"What are soliloquies?" the man asked.

"Long dialogues by one person," Jeneil answered and sighed, and the man smiled. "I've already spliced your tape," she continued, and the man looked surprised. "I removed the footage of me climbing a ladder to get a better look. I couldn't believe it was a camera. We can close this deal if you give her this tape and not mention that I know. I want copies of the past tapes and reports before I give you this one and the camera. It's still evidence."

The man shrugged. "Sounds okay; she gets what she paid for, I'm still ethical and you can buy my silence. I'm getting off easy. I know it."

Jeneil smiled. "Ethical. The word doesn't seem to fit this situation."

"In your case, I can see that," the man said. "But I do help society, lady. There are women out there who'd get shafted by cheating husbands looking to kick them out cheap and cheating wives doing their husbands dirty, too."

Jeneil sighed. "I suppose you can call it help. It's exposing truth in a society that doesn't understand it or live it. Maybe our civilization is a very low degree of civilization. What's lower; isolationism then mob rule and back to tribes until we bay at the moon like animals?"

The man shrugged. "I don't know, lady. I don't judge life, I just record it. I'm not a philosopher, I'm only a detective."

Jeneil smiled at his honesty and humility. "And you didn't create the need you're only supplying the demand."

"You're okay," the man said, smiling at her. "I think I'd understand a straying husband in your case." Steve smiled watching as she worked her deadly magic.

"Okay," Jeneil took control, "stop at my office before ten any weekday morning and we'll close our deal." She handed him her business card.

"Thanks again." The man smiled, taking it. "When I saw the camera was missing, I felt the hangman's noose around my neck. I owe you big," he said, heading for his truck. "Collect on it anytime."

Jeneil was quiet as they walked back to the house, tears starting to fall by the time they reached the deck. Going into the screened section, she sat on the bench. Steve joined her, rubbing her back gently. "This feels so cheap and sordid, I feel dirty." She sighed and wiped her tears. "I've been asking myself what she does with the tapes and I'm afraid the answer is that she shows them to Peter, and my mind is panicked wondering if Robert has kissed me while standing in the driveway. He can't remember he's not supposed to. Poor Peter. What the tapes must do to him."

"Honey, he understands."

Jeneil looked up quickly, shocked. "You know about him seeing the videos? You knew there was a camera here?" she asked, and he nodded. "Why didn't you tell me?" she asked, sounding hurt.

Steve realized it was time for truth. He stood up and took her hand. "Come on, kid. We've got to make a phone call."

Steve waited while the hospital located Peter. "This is Dr. Chang."

"Pete, it's Steve."

"What is it?" Peter asked, surprised to hear from Steve on a Saturday morning.

"Plenty," Steve answered. "Jeneil found the camera and confronted the man who showed up to collect the film."

"Oh my gosh!" Peter gasped with his stomach in a knot. "Is she hurt?"

"No, the guy is a private detective the bitch hired. This is the last film. She was going to have the bedroom videotaped but ran out of money. He and Jeneil worked out a package deal, but it's time for truth, Pete. Jeneil's confused."

Peter rubbed his forehead. "Okay, maybe you're right."

"Any word on your end?" Steve asked.

"No, but it's serious. Lin Chi is scared."

"Damn it!" Steve exhaled. "Do you want to tell Jeneil?"

"Yes," Peter answered quietly, "but Steve, since I can't be sure Uette had access to muscle, I want to keep away from you and Jeneil until I'm sure where the guns are pointed."

"Okay," Steve replied, "I can understand that. Here, talk to Jeneil."

She took the receiver quickly. "Peter, what's happening? Why is everything so crazy?"

Peter sighed hearing the confusion in her voice and feeling the electricity it caused to race through him. "Honey, things are very serious. Lin Chi found out that Uette was private stock to the scum who took over the Dragons."

"Oh no!" Jeneil said, covering her mouth.

"Lin Chi hasn't been able to find out who it is. It's so dangerous she has to work slowly."

"Oh, Peter." Jeneil choked up. "Peter, it's somebody at the top, the very top."

"How do you know?" Peter asked, surprised.

"Because Uette is desperate, she's too desperate. It has to be somebody with power. This is the piece that was missing. This is why she'd risk anything. You were her ticket out."

"Honey, we don't know that yet."

"It has to be, Peter. What else would do it?"

"Right now, baby, I've got to tell you something. Uette's been making threats against you saying she'd use muscle."

"She's revealed that much about her past?" Jeneil asked, leaning against the counter.

"Honey, listen to me. I can't contact you at all anymore and now she wants me to stay away from Steve, too. She knows he's the one taking messages back and forth. I have to go along with it. I don't know how much she's bluffing. I told her that you broke off our relationship and were dating Steve, and it worked until she found out Steve and I are still friends. I have to stay away from both of you now, honey. This is a dangerous mess. I'm really worried about you. She'll panic if I threaten to leave. I'm caught." He paused and then chuckled. "Keep those ninja moves handy. They looked pretty good."

"Oh gosh, you saw that?" she asked, embarrassed.

"You're tough, baby. Ki would've made you the first skirt he ever had as a guard."

She laughed and then became serious. "Peter, I miss you and now I'm scared."

"Don't panic, honey."

"Maybe you should just get a divorce," she suggested.

"No," Peter answered emphatically. "Uette panics every time I threaten to leave. No, I'm not going to face Hollis with this baby against me. I'll hang in until I get what I'm after. If I can't clear my name, I might as well stay married to the bitch. I couldn't face Hollis."

Jeneil was stunned. "Peter, don't say that! Don't even think that!"

"Count on it, honey. I'll clear my name. The baby isn't mine and I'll face the Chuns myself if I have to."

Jeneil's heart trembled at his words. "Peter, that's crazy. You don't sound like yourself anymore. You're so angry. This isn't going according to plan. It's crazy. I don't like it."

"Don't panic, honey. I'm sorry you even had to know this much. Let me handle it. Just understand why I can't talk about you to Steve. Okay?"

"Okay," she agreed, sighing.

"Hey, Jeneil?"

"What?"

"Is Irish okay?"

She smiled. "Irish is fine, very okay."

"Good. And what about us, are we okay, too?"

"Very okay, I love you."

He sighed. "Jeneil, I love you, too. I miss our life and Camelot like crazy."

Jeneil choked up and tears filled her eyes. "Me too, Chang."

"I'd better go, honey."

"Okay, Peter. Whenever things are settled, call me at my office."

"I will, baby. Watch yourself, please."

"You too, Peter. You're in more danger than I am. I understand Uette now."

"Well, you're a majority of one then, honey. Take care and thank Steve for me."

"I will, Peter. Goodbye." She heard the click and the dial tone and they vibrated through her with a thread of finality. She struggled with the feeling she wouldn't hear from him again. The thought panicked her and she hung up sobbing. Steve held her and she clung desperately to him. "I'm scared," she sobbed.

"Don't be, the bitch doesn't have muscle. I know that now. She had to hire a detective."

"The Dragons!" She tried to breathe deeply to get herself under control. "Life doesn't mean a thing to them. I'm afraid for Peter." She wiped her tears. "Peter is way past saving face. This was a detail nobody expected." She paced and wrung her hands.

Steve cleaned up the broken glass then made her sit down. "We'll take each day and get through it. Pete can handle himself," he reassured her.

"He's so changed, so rigid and hostile. I could feel his anger," Jeneil said, sighing sadly as tears worked slowly down her cheeks.

*****

Their Saturday went more pleasantly than Steve expected and Sunday brought visitors to Wonderland. Steve noticed that people who stopped by never turned their visits into riotous parties. Wonderland was no-fuss, a rest stop, and people visited for that reason. Standing on the deck waiting for Jeneil, Steve watched three people from the theatre sitting in the screen house talking and laughing. They had come to rest and Jeneil didn't fuss; no one expected her to. She had fashioned barbeque pans from anything she thought would tolerate the heat and there were several of them around. An institution-sized metal can had become a stove that kept a coffee pot hot most of the morning. The buddy burners she had made for cooking looked crazy and visitors were dumbfounded when she taught them to make bacon and eggs in a brown paper bag or burgers in foil. It was a crazy break from the stampede and everyone loved it. Steve smiled surveying the small groups of people hanging loose.

"Ain't this something," Charlie commented, walking by with a garden hose over his shoulder. "If the parks department hears about this, they'll make her take out a license." Steve laughed and Charlie shook his head. "What amazes me is they all like the quiet. I ain't heard anything noisier than a laugh. Chess, checkers, backgammon, soft music, picnic lunches, camp-overs; it's terrific and have you ever seen grownups have so much fun as they have in the wooden raft Robert made?"

Steve saw a lot of evidence of Robert Danzieg around and was glad Robert had a job that took him to New York every weekend. At least Steve could count on Jeneil being alone from Thursday night to Monday. She had bought a one-man boat for Karen and hidden it in the garage. Karen and Dennis would arrive early Saturday mornings so Karen could float on the water for hours to relieve her back pain. It was comical to watch Dennis take the long-pole and get aboard the wooden raft, stroking out to the mouth of the bay with Karen in tow in the one-man boat. Steve worried about Dennis, too. Something was happening between him and Jeneil; there was a closeness he didn't like at all. Adrienne had told him that Jeneil was helping Dennis put a play together and that he shouldn't worry, but he bordered on panic whenever Jeneil and Dennis were around each other. Dennis was looking at her differently and Jeneil was in awe of him. It was all too obvious. Even Karen was angry and seemed just as panicked, pushing Steve and Jeneil at each other, treating them as a couple in a desperate attempt to protect her marriage.

Steve sighed as he wondered what the summer was going to do to people's lives. He was angry, too; angry for Peter and as he examined his feelings closely knew he was really angry for himself. He felt betrayed and knew it was a result of the deeply rooted feeling that she was his. It was more than a feeling now, it was a conviction, and he had to watch himself so he wouldn't act like a jealous husband. He stood on the deck thinking about all of it as Jeneil came out of the house wearing the softest-looking dress he had ever seen. Electricity spread through him. It was becoming more and more difficult for him to maintain objectivity in Peter's absence.

"Sorry to be so long," Jeneil said, smiling as she struggled with a small pearl button on the back of her dress, "the more delicate the material, the smaller the buttons."

Steve smiled and moved behind her, doing the button. Looking up, he noticed Dennis watching them. Jeneil's dress skimmed her body softly and her perfume smelled clean and fresh. At that moment, he wished he had Robert's flair so he could feel comfortable grabbing her shoulders and kissing the back of her neck as a way to strike out at Dennis and because he wanted to. And he knew he wanted to far too much.

"All set, kid," he said, stepping to her side, resenting being the good friend she thought he was.

"Thanks," she said, smiling as she picked up the purse she had set on the railing earlier. "Are you sure you won't mind a chamber music concert?"

"Don't know, we'll find out," he answered, grinning.

"It's Franklin's group so you realize Sienna might sit with us. Does that bother you?"

"Who's Sienna?" he teased.

Jeneil had been right; Sienna was there and had sat with them. Steve witnessed another of Jeneil's struggles as she answered Sienna's questions about Peter. Sienna was stunned to hear he was married insisting it didn't make sense since Peter had seemed so deeply committed to Jeneil. Steve could see that Jeneil was tempted to tell Sienna the truth but instead simply answered, "Se la vie." Steve wanted to tell Sienna to shut up as she replied that it wasn't 'such is life' as Jeneil had said, insisting that if anyone looked like they'd be married and living happily ever after it was her and Peter. Jeneil had just shrugged and remained silent, and Steve was glad when Sienna went to talk to people she knew.

Jeneil turned to Steve. "You look very nice in your summer suit. You're lucky you can wear something off the rack like that. Are you finding this all too stodgy yet?"

"No, I'm fine. In fact, I have to thank you. Drs. Sprague, Young, and Fisher just walked in. This will make them think I've got good taste."

Jeneil looked at him curiously. "Why do you feel like you have to prove yourself?"

He chuckled. "Jeneil, I arrived at med school a pain in the ass. I was me and it was too bad if they didn't like it. But there's this nudging you get as part of your training to become classy and dignified. It's hard to fight. I was from an orphanage; I got branded the White Stallion and put on probation. That makes you feel low class. I've come to realize I'm going to spend my life stuffing myself into an image. I did it to be a successful pickpocket and now a doctor."

She nodded understandingly. "It's the conveyer belt, Steve. They're everywhere. But maybe we could still have some real fun here. Training is a terrible thing to waste. Teach me the rudiments of picking pockets and maybe during intermission we'll mingle. I'll go for watches since I'm a beginner and you try for wallets to see if you still have the right touch." Steve looked shocked and then, realizing she was joking, he laughed. She took his arm and smiled. "Why are you laughing? You lack confidence in my ability?"

"You're crazy," he said, chuckling. "That's a fun idea though."

"Oh, please teach me," she pleaded, tugging at his wrist.

"You're crazy," he repeated, and then he saw Mrs. Sprague wave to him. "Maybe I should go over and say hello. Want to come with me?"

"Sure," she said, grinning, "and you'd better be sure you have the right time in case they ask."

"What?" he asked, looking at his wrist as a natural reaction to her comment and was stunned to find his watch was gone. Puzzled, he looked at her and she winked and handed him his watch. He shook his head not believing she had snookered him. "Where the hell did you learn that?" he asked, laughing as he put his watch back on.

"In some movie. I know the secret is to distract the victim."

"I'm sure you're crazy," he said, and laughed as he took her arm.

"Youz probably right, Mac. Dis crowd looks like they ain't got nuttin green, just plastic. Why risk your job with the knife over it. Come on," she said, smiling, "I got taught real good on one of my conveyor belts. Watch me; I learned all kinds of couth things."

Steve smiled and hoped he wouldn't laugh as they approached the group of doctors. "Don't make me laugh, Jeneil, please," he mumbled under his breath.

"Right, Mac, trust me."

Steve groaned. "Oh geez, don't go into tilt, honey."

"Gotcha, Mac. I can read your riot. Don't worry about dis kid."

Mrs. Sprague smiled as she extended her hand to Steve. "How are you?" she asked, kissing his cheek and smiling at Jeneil.

"Mrs. Sprague, this is Jeneil Alden-Connors."

"Hi," Mrs. Sprague said, smiling warmly. Jeneil liked her in spite of the tightness she saw in the woman's eyes.

"It's very nice to meet you, Mrs. Sprague. I worked at the hospital so I know your husband."

"You've cut your hair. I thought you looked different," Dr. Sprague said. "You look well. How are you doing?"

"Just fine," Jeneil answered, smiling.

"Where are you working now?"

"The family business," Jeneil replied, not elaborating. Steve introduced her to Dr. and Mrs. Young and to Dr. Fisher.

"You don't need to introduce us," Mrs. Fisher remarked. "I know Jeneil from my auxiliary job. She's a contributor herself as well as being connected to the Mandra Foundation." Steve smiled warmly with pride as all the doctors' eyes opened wide at hearing a name that caused red carpets to roll out.

"Well, we all know that name," Dr. Young said, smiling warmly as he looked at Steve. Steve felt the feeling of pride spread through him. He had always felt that he never measured up enough for Dr. Young who was the most dignified doctor of the associates, but now Dr. Young's attitude toward him seemed different as he stood there with Jeneil by his side. "And how are you connected to the Mandra Foundation?"

"She was a close family friend and after my parents passed away she looked after me," Jeneil answered simply in her understated tone. They all quickly glanced at each other with looks of shock done in good taste but shock nonetheless that the girl from Records had such a background. Steve felt nearly hysterical from the look on Dr. Sprague's face; Jeneil had slipped past his radar scope of personnel.

Dr. Fisher recovered quickly. "At the risk of sounding very rude, I'd like to ask why you were in our records department then."

"That's really her business, dear!" Mrs. Fisher said aghast, and then she smiled at Jeneil apologetically. Steve saw how much power Jeneil had behind her and it surprised him even more in that moment.

"That's not very rude, Dr. Fisher. It is odd I guess, but I was simply floating in life at that time and resisting the idea of going back home. The job kept me here and I fell in love with the ocean."

Dr. Young smiled. "That's right; the Mandra Foundation is in the Midwest."

"But I thought you said you were working in the family business," Mrs. Young said.

"I opened a branch office here and I commute once a month or more if needed. Actually, Amanda Pike taught me her approach to business. She was a clever woman. It's all in your management team and I've done very well finding very good people. My love is theatre and I'm on staff at the playhouse this season."

"You want to be an actress?" Mrs. Young asked in a snobbish, matronly tone, clearly shocked.

Jeneil smiled patiently. "No, I'm interested in the mechanics of the arts, not the delivery."

Mrs. Fisher looked at Mrs. Young nervously. "She's interested in all the arts, Clarisse. She's involved with the International Arts League and the Soho Group." Steve noticed the inflection in Mrs. Fisher's voice. She was clearly telling Mrs. Young to button her lip because the young woman standing before them clearly outranked them all.

Mrs. Young raised her eyebrows. "How absolutely wonderful that young blood is involved, good for you." Steve could see that it was difficult for her to relinquish control, but her attitude was quite different. Steve watched Dr. Sprague as the information poured over him and he stood there nearly drowning in shock, staring at Jeneil intently.

Dr. Young was staring, too. "It seems to me I remember the foundation's board of directors has a woman chairing it and I'm told she has a lot of clout. I remember thinking how ultra-modern that was. Are you a field representative for them?"

Jeneil fidgeted as she hesitated. "No sir, I'm the chairperson," she said quietly, wishing she didn't have to. All the doctors stood at attention and Dr. Sprague adjusted the knot in his tie. Steve stared at Jeneil quite in shock himself. Jeneil added quietly, "But I should mention the board consists of some dynamic men and women who are indispensable. Their training and expertise have been invaluable at all levels. And Mandra taught me that clout is a nickname for serious responsibility. The other voices on that board are why I can sleep well at night, besides the team of analysts, accountants, and lawyers."

"That's remarkable. How old are you?" Dr. Young asked, clearly impressed. Mrs. Fisher covered her eyes completely embarrassed.

Mrs. Sprague smiled. "Richard, really, any woman who answered that would betray anyone." Everyone laughed and Mrs. Fisher breathed again.

"Join us in our box," Mrs. Young said, smiling.

Steve looked at Jeneil. "It's up to you."

Jeneil smiled warmly. "I certainly appreciate the invitation but I have a subscription too and today I have guests in my box. The flutist and his fiancee are friends of mine and we're all having a picnic dinner by the lake after the performance with the violinist and his wife. But thank you for asking. I'm sorry to miss spending more time with you. It was very nice to have met you, all of you." The chamber group was warming up and Jeneil excused herself to find the other women, telling Steve she would meet him at their seats.

"Well done, Bradley," Dr. Young said, smiling. "What a fine young woman. She'll round out your life. I've appreciated Clarisse for dragging me to these things. We need to keep in touch with the poetic side of life." Steve smiled, silently wishing Jeneil really was his. He excused himself and headed to his seat.

"Oh, Warren, this one looks serious. He's taken with her. There's electricity there, too," Mrs. Sprague whispered, as they walked toward their own seats. "She's a very nice girl."

Dr. Sprague nodded. "Yes, she is, and she seems to undo my outstanding surgeons for some reason," he replied, thinking of Peter and Jerry Tollman.

"What do you mean?" Mrs. Sprague asked.

"I'm not sure but don't get too excited about those two yet. Steve said they're just dating."

"Well, she's special to him. I've watched him with other girls I've introduced him to. Jeneil has caught his attention." She looked to where Steve was taking his seat. "Oh my gosh! Isn't that Sienna sitting with Jeneil and Steve?"

"Yes, it is," Dr. Sprague answered.

Mrs. Sprague tried to act casual. "But she was dating Steve. Isn't that awfully sophisticated?"

"Don't ask me. Lately, I can't figure out that group and the quiet girl from Records is the biggest shock yet."

"Well good for her," Mrs. Sprague said, smiling, "she made Warren Sprague lose control of the jigsaw puzzle he calls life."

Dr. Sprague looked across at the box having to admit that his wife was right. Steve was definitely very taken with Jeneil, too taken, and he wondered why Steve was so closely involved with Jeneil with his feelings for her being so deep. It worried him since in his weekly meetings with Peter he was being told that she was waiting for him and he marveled at how such a quiet, well-mannered girl of refined tastes had managed to tame both the Chinese Stud and the White Stallion. That was the biggest puzzle. He watched as Jeneil sat next to Steve and wondered what the future held for them. It reminded him of the story of Camelot and he thought it was a troublesome mess. It had to divide into two in the end. It always did so no matter how one looked at it somebody was going to be hurt. He sighed and forced himself to focus on the concert.

With the exception of Sienna, Steve enjoyed the concert as well as the picnic. It was romantic to spread a quilt out near a cool lake and share a light dinner with Jeneil's friends. They were serious people who talked to each other and he thought there must be something exhilarating about performing in a concert because both Franklin and the violinist were snuggling closely with their women. He envied the playfulness they seemed to enjoy. It was a luxury he couldn't afford in relationships because it was always taken as meaning more than he really meant, playful causing a more serious reaction in women for him. He watched Jeneil and smiled thinking that with her he could mean more but she'd probably ninja him right into the lake. He wondered how Robert Danzieg got away with it.

They left the group with promises of more moonlit dinners and Steve got the feeling that the lakeside party wasn't over at all. It was with great reluctance that he left Jeneil at her house and drove home. He began to miss her a mile away from her driveway and he knew he could very easily enjoy being married to her. The thought surprised him since he had always worried about settling down and getting married. It had seemed like such a strangling and stifling idea until Jeneil. It wasn't all physical which really surprised him; he found that he really just enjoyed having her around. Her chatter was even pleasant; he usually hated when women chattered. He smiled thinking about her and then sighed as reality infiltrated his thoughts and how lucky Peter was to have her in his life. The doctors from his group had been impressed with her and he sighed again thinking she would make a great doctor's wife.

Three

Jeneil drove north on the nearly deserted highway at five forty-five in the morning bracing herself for another Monday. The lakeside dinner had made her miss Peter. The romantic mood had been lovely, but it had been embarrassing to share it with Steve. She felt sorry for him thinking he was entitled to do some snuggling of his own. The fact that he was babysitting her on weekends made her feel even worse. He needed a life of his own and shouldn't be in a holding pattern because of her. She sighed wishing the situation would end. She thought of Peter and the danger he was in and again a sense of panic returned. She concentrated on her work agenda instead. The corporation had her tangled until almost one and then it was back to the playhouse. She smiled as she thought of the evening ahead. She and Dennis were staying late and the work was so satisfying that she always went home on an incredible high, which caused her to miss Peter to the point of tears and bleak emptiness.

As she drove, she thought of her summer and the deep conflicting emotions she was dealing with. She felt lost without Peter and safe with Steve, exhilarated and comfortable with Dennis and insecure and overwhelmed with Robert. Gosh, she had a lot of men in her life. Then she laughed; too bad she didn't care how things looked to narrow-minded people. She had spent too many years trying to appease gossips and now she was way behind schedule in understanding herself for all her effort and they were still gossiping about her. Talk for all she cared, these men were important in her life. They were good friends and friends were valuable in life. She wasn't going to run from gossip anymore.

She missed Peter; he was her anchor and made life make sense. She knew being without him was causing her to be emotional. Her feelings were more easily sorted through with him around. He was her rock. Life was steady and structured with him; life was nearly complete. She thought about him and sighed.

"Be safe, Peter. You carry my life so deeply in yours that I feel my own vulnerability and it scares me. Without you, my life wouldn't make sense." She felt herself choke up. "Nice positive thoughts for a Monday morning, Nebraska."

Again she forced herself to think about her day's agenda and smiled to herself as the excitement of the play filled her as she thought about it and Dennis's incredible talent. There was magic in that one, too.

*****

Jeneil got through the day feeding on anticipation. Arriving at the theatre, she was met with chaos. There were mishaps involving scenery for the play currently in production, Robert couldn't be located, and Dennis was stomping through in a low mood. Jeneil handled the mail on the desk which had piled up and reassigned the volunteer group while avoiding Dennis as much as possible. The telephone rang and she answered it, immediately wishing she hadn't. The supporting actress had a bad sunburn and cancelled. Deciding to find the stand-in before telling Dennis, she went to the mess hall where the group was rehearsing. It was named appropriately. By the end of the season, order was a rare commodity, if it existed at all, as vacations and accidents took their toll on the theatre group leaving one main room where the cast congregated in a frenzy of activity.

Jeneil admired the actors and actresses whom were constantly learning lines and rehearsing. She couldn't understand how they kept it all straight, but they did as the supporting player on one play rehearsed for the lead in the next. To her it was madness, to them it was show biz and they endured bravely. Jeneil had found that being around all of it as a regular was quite different from her experience as a part-timer. It was all too easy now to be drawn into the madness as everyone looked for able bodied hands and she found herself working on projects way out of her job description. It was a test of a clear head to maneuver through it all and still help alongside the rest of the team. Delivering the message to the stand-in who took it in stride, Jeneil went to find Dennis.

"Megan called in with a bad sunburn. Sheila says she's ready to go on. I thought I should let you know," Jeneil said, finding Dennis in the scenery garage.

Standing up from a crouching position where he was checking a shattered corner of scenery, Dennis sighed. "Thanks. Did you let Line know?"

"He's at The Rep borrowing some props, remember?"

"Oh, that's right then who's in the group?"

"They're directing themselves."

Dennis closed his eyes and sighed again. "I'm afraid to ask how it's going."

"It was peaceful," Jeneil reassured him. "The temperature's too high for egos."

He looked at her outfit. "You never changed from your office clothes."

Jeneil shrugged. "I got drawn into the bedlam and kept going."

Dennis smiled. "You've got grease paint in your veins, honey. You hold together pretty well around here."

Jeneil looked at the shattered scenery. "How are you going to deal with that?"

"In absence of a magic wand, I don't know. No luck finding Robert?" he asked, and Jeneil shook her head. "Par for the course," he replied, putting both hands in his back pockets. "It's the end of the production; this is going to require time and money."

"Can you treat it like a defect in an apartment wall that the landlord drags his feet to fix?"

Dennis smiled. "You mean like hanging a picture over it?"

Jeneil nodded. "At least it's damaged at the base and not the more obvious middle or top."

Watching her as he rolled the thought around in his head, he smiled, pleased with her suggestion. "Are you staying tonight?"

"Yes, are Derek and Line?"

"No, it's just us tonight."

"Want to cancel?" she asked, waiting for his answer before leaving.

He folded his arms and thought. "Actually no, I'd really like just us. My fears of a committee are surfacing. Collaborating with you would be good for me."

She nodded. "We'll work in the office that way we don't waste time traveling to my place and settling in."

"Jeneil," he called, as she headed to the door, "do you have any guava juice?"

She smiled. "I'll be right back."

Karen was leaning against the wall in the hallway holding a tall glass of iced coffee. Jeneil could tell from her expression that her back was causing her trouble from her protruding belly.

"Painful today?" Jeneil asked.

Karen nodded with discouragement and discomfort. Jeneil went into a room and returned placing a chair near Karen. She dropped into it sighing with relief. "This is Dennis's coffee."

"You've read his mind. He's thirsty."

Karen rested her head against the wall. "I read Dennis well, too well. Would you tell him I'm going home?" She sighed. "And I think I'll stay there. My being here won't change a damn thing. I can see that, so I might as well be comfortable and worry there."

Jeneil smiled, impressed with Karen's devotion. "You're right; you being here won't stop broken scenery and other accidents. It'll be September in another month. That's the end, it'll be baby time. Would you like me to drive you home? You look so uncomfortable."

Karen watched as Jeneil missed all her pointed comments. "Jeneil, I wish you were easy to dislike."

"Why?" Jeneil asked, surprised.

Karen smiled wearily. "Nothing, my claws are showing."

Jeneil stooped before her. "Karen, you're pregnant and your belly is in the way of your view. He's yours Karen, yours."

Karen stared at Jeneil. "You're sharper than you let on."

Jeneil grinned. "It takes me awhile, but I tortoise my way through eventually. I'll take this coffee to Dennis and come back to drive you home."

"Thanks," Karen said, sighing. "Driving isn't easy anymore either."

Jeneil squeezed her hand. "You're so fragile-looking that the baby seems almost two-thirds of you. It hardly seems fair that your first pregnancy should be so large!"

Karen smiled, cheered by their brief talk. "I like you, Jeneil," she replied, "and I'd like you even more if I weren't so selfish."

"I'm not listening," Jeneil sang, as she stood up. What a summer, she thought, as she headed back to the scenery garage. Everything seemed to have been set adrift by life.

"Thanks," Dennis said quietly, studying her as he took the coffee. Jeneil wanted to hug him, he seemed so surrounded by all life's demands, but Karen's concern about her and Dennis made her hold back so she turned to leave. "Hey," he said, and Jeneil stopped and looked back. "I felt a hug in that scene, where is it?" She smiled and he put his arms around her. "Thanks for being you, honey," he said, and kissed her cheek. She nodded, embarrassed by the moment. Dennis watched her walk away, aware of the high voltage electricity racing through him.

*****

The deluge of minor accidents didn't ease up and Dennis poured himself onto the office sofa, glad for a break at the end of the day. Resting his head back, he rubbed his face with both hands. Jeneil watched feeling deep compassion for him and the struggles that seemed so much a part of his chosen field of art.

"Maybe we should cancel so you can go home for some rest. The havoc seems to have backed off."

"No, please, Jeneil. I'd like to spend tonight with you." He continued staring at the ceiling, too weary to look up. "Let's get some dinner though, I missed lunch, I'm starved."

Jeneil went to the corner of the office and picked up a picnic cooler. "I picked up something when I took Karen home."

"Make it three of whatever you brought." He sat up and slumped forward. Jeneil put dinner together and joined him on the sofa, handing him a small bottle of imported ale. He took it, staring at the label. "What's the special occasion?"

Setting her plate on her lap, she smiled. "Life 'ten', nice guy 'zero,' I thought you deserved it."

He chuckled. "I think you're incredible." He looked from his plate to hers. "I wasn't serious about three portions. You don't have very much."

She cut an asparagus spear with her fork. "The heat has my appetite at low ebb. I'll take advantage of that today."

The telephone rang and Dennis got up with his plate and ale to answer it. It was a chairman so he ate while he handled the lengthy call. Jeneil watched, moved by sympathy for the current condition of his life. She could see he was relaxing though and she was glad she had chosen his favorites from the deli. Hanging up, he cleaned his fingers with a paper napkin and poured the rest of his ale into a plastic cup.

"I feel rejuvenated." He sat on the desk looking at her while he finished his ale. "You changed your clothes," he commented, noticing her long, loose dress and sandals.

She nodded, putting her plate on the table. "I wanted to be comfortable. The day had strangled me too and I didn't want to give tonight's session leftover energy." He smiled, appreciating her attitude and the way she looked. "Now that we're both rejuvenated, let's get to the script," she said, reaching behind her for her copy.

Dennis sat next to her with his copy and slouched into the cushions. "Thanks for having those reports right by the phone. The board is pleased with this season's numbers." He smiled and sighed. "I feel good right now. I really do." He turned his head slightly and kissed her shoulder, enjoying the light scent of her perfume.

Leaning forward to get a red pencil from the coffee table, she moved away from him as she sat back. The closeness concerned her, especially since Karen had mentioned it. Their special bond had returned in full force just as it had been the year before bringing awkward moments and long lingering looks that usually ended in warm smiles and most recently blushes to her cheeks. Jeneil opened to the paper-clipped page and looked over her list of notes from previous sessions with Line and Derek.

Dennis shook his copy of the script. "Oh, damn it! Don't tell me I've lost my notes." He sat forward and shook the pages again. "Shit, I have." He got up and went to his desk. "It's probably Freudian; I hate those limitations Derek and Line have imposed. That whole third scene of the first set got fragmented."

Jeneil watched as he flipped through the pages. "You didn't transfer your notes to your script then?"

"No," he moaned, "I didn't get to it last night." The telephone rang and he answered it quickly, embroiled in annoyance at his lack of organization. "Karen, what is it? No, well yes, I am mad. I'm mad at myself. I've lost my notes. Where? Oh shit, that's just great." He looked at Jeneil. "Karen found my notes by the bed, nice huh?"

Jeneil smiled. "Then take my script and I'll use yours. Having transferred the changes, I remember most of them and it'll bring your script up to the minute."

"Okay," he said, nodding. "No, Karen, I won't be coming home for them. No, don't worry, I've eaten. Get some rest; your ankles looked swollen today. I think you should lie in bed and incubate that porker of a kid for the next month. It wouldn't surprise me if it was born adult sized. Your stomach's the size of a base drum now. What are you getting at? Geez, I'm not blaming you, I'm blaming the kid for crying out loud. Everything I say lately aggravates you. Okay, you can't take diuretics. I'm not complaining about your thick ankles." He shook his head and paced. "Look Karen, if we continue talking your blood pressure will soar. Let's end it. Turn the air conditioner on high and eat an ice cream bar. No, Karen, I'm not counting the number of ice cream bars you're eating. I've got to go, get some rest." He hung up and slumped over his desk, shaking his head. He straightened. "I hate being pregnant." He slipped onto the sofa again.

"Do you?" Jeneil asked, grinning. "At least you can still bend over your desk. Karen can't see her feet and it took her minutes to get in and out of the car today. I can't believe how such a frail body can expand like that to accommodate another life. Standing next to her, I've always felt like a towering Amazon." Jeneil sighed. "She's amazing."

Dennis smiled gently. "You're quite a lady," he said, touching her cheek tenderly.

"Well Mr. Blair, what's it going to be?"

He watched her steadily for a second and then grinned. "Let's go over Scene Three and see if there's any way around those limitations." They worked quietly on their own and then compared interpretations. Dennis paced. "Am I being too protective because it's my creation? I can live with the irritation if it's ego but that scene still feels fragmented."

Jeneil sighed. "This one doesn't seem to adapt too easily."

Dennis stopped pacing. "Then you see it, too." Rolling his script in his hand, he paced again and hit the side of his leg with it as if it might whip his mind into line. "It's tough putting my own work through; I have to be careful to maintain my position as director and not playwright."

Jeneil understood. "But you still have an obligation to the piece of work. You protect the creative level on other productions, why not yours?" He stopped pacing and smiled at her. She smiled broadly. "This one has magic too, Dennis."

"Keep talking, beautiful, I love it. So what do we do with Scene Three?"

"I say let it be for now and let's skim over the rest of the play using Line and Derek's approach. Maybe there's something we can use to trade and compromise." She sighed. "It irritates me to apply those words to a work of art." She stood up and paced, too. "Can you trade or compromise part of a painting or a piece of music? I love this in its entirety. There are sublimities that will be lost in the delivery on stage. I think it's in the wrong media. It might be a better screenplay than a stage play, but it's too late now. We're knee deep in commitment."

He smiled and walked to her, loving her loyalty. "You have trouble directing all my plays. The fan club is appreciated." He put his arms around her and she melted to him, lost in the discouragement of mutilating his work.

"Oh, Dennis, I hate how money guides everything, even art. It's another conveyor belt."

"I'm used to it, honey. I can live with compromise. Responsible limitations sharpen your skills and thinking."

"I love your attitude," she said, lifting her head to look at him. She smiled gently and the closeness between them erupted. He kissed her lips lightly and the kiss lingered as he held her closely. "Dennis," she cautioned, going to the desk to regain control.

He watched her and then went to her side. "What do you want from me?"

"Nothing, I don't know what you mean," she answered, struggling to avoid further discussion.

"I want a definition of what's between us."

"We're friends, Dennis. Is that what you mean?" Jeneil had been concerned their closeness would lose its delicate balance forcing a confrontation like the one the year before.

"Like hell we are. It's beyond that and you know it," he answered emphatically.

She closed her eyes. "Dennis, don't. Please don't give it words. We shouldn't even give it thought."

He touched her arm. "Jeneil, that's Victorian, straight from the era. I'm tired of pretending. I want to talk about it." He slipped his arm gently around her waist.

She moved away. "Dennis, you're married."

He took her wrists. "Define it, Jeneil. I want to hear your definition because if you don't have one then what you are is a tease."

She looked up quickly. "I'm not teasing."

"Then what are we, Jeneil? Me, Robert, Steve, where are we with you?"

She felt insecure. "Dennis, you're all my friends, good friends. Why are you even risking that friendship by doing this?"

He looked at her steadily and she avoided his stare by looking away. Touching her chin, he forced her to look at him. "Words, Jeneil. Give it words."

"Dennis!" she pleaded.

"No, honey. Peter kept you as a little girl, dependent on him. It's time to grow up. You're a woman, I'm a man, and there's electricity between us. Why?"

"Dennis, look at our circumstances. I'm lonely and your marriage is under enormous stress from the pregnancy."

He held her chin. "You mean it's just harmless physical desire on my part?" he asked, and then he smiled. "Honey, I'm involved with someone."

Jeneil was shocked by the admission. "Oh, Dennis! What about Karen? That's not fair." She felt tears sting her eyes.

"You really are only a kid," he said, equally shocked by her lack of experience and sophistication. "Honey, Karen and I have an agreement. She doesn't mind."

Jeneil stared, even more shocked. "I can't believe that. I know she's worried about us."

"She's afraid of you because she knows how strongly I feel about you. I'm even a little afraid of you myself and seeing that you're really a kid scares the hell out of me because I know I'd give all of it away if you asked me to. And with your lack of experience, do you know what you want?"

Jeneil no longer felt insecure or threatened; she was curious. "Dennis, what have I done to have gotten you to this?"

"Don't take all the blame. You're right, our circumstances haven't helped but it's more. You need me for some reason. I can feel it. I sense it. What do you want from me? I want it defined."

"I don't have words, Dennis. It doesn't fit a phrase or a category like love or hero worship. My attraction to you is your talent, your dedication. The magic electrifies me."

"I can't believe that, it's too lofty, Jeneil. What I'm sensing is far more basic, more primitive."

"What do you want me to say, that it's physical? What you teach me satisfies a hunger, a desire in me as strong as a physical desire. The feeling overwhelms me and I think our circumstances cloud our ability to see. You're married and I belong to Peter so any physical desire is out of the question."

"That's an essay, I asked for a definition of your feelings."

"I gave you one," she answered. "It satisfies my mind."

"There's your mind again," Dennis said, sighing.

Jeneil studied him closely. "Dennis, I'm in awe of your talent. It's an incredible attraction, it's intense and passionate. If you weren't married and I didn't belong to Peter, I'd want you to make love to me in order to experience more between us."

Dennis smiled. "Jeneil, was it so tough to say that you want my body? Grow up."

Jeneil sighed and shook her head. "Dennis, I'd make love to your body to be near your brain. Is that primitive enough? I can't make it more basic. The physical wouldn't last between us."

"How do you know?" he asked, amused by her whole defense.

"We are cerebrally passionate, Dennis. I fall in love in a physical relationship and that would destroy our cerebral passion putting us at zero. Karen is ideal for you. To her, you're a man. She accepts that and that's what a good solid relationship should be in order to last. My hero worship or whatever we call it puts you at a superman level. It's unreasonable. You'd be unhappy there and I'd be disillusioned when I saw you as a man in other areas a life together requires. So why take a perfectly good demigod and force him to be a man. You have the best of two worlds; Karen's love and my worship. Why rock the balance of that?"

Dennis stared in disbelief. "Well, I'll be damned. You're a brainy wench; a clever, maneuvering, brainy wench." He took her wrist firmly. "Let's go."

"Where?" Jeneil asked, surprised.

"Back to work or would you call it raping my mind? Come and worship me, you brainy bitch." He laughed. "I have good instincts and I was right to be afraid of you. Your mind is incredible." He hugged her to him, laughing with enjoyment.

"Then you're not mad at me?" She smiled, holding him. "Are we still friends?" she asked, wanting reassurance.

"Honey, we're anything you want us to be. Anytime your feelings change, let me know, I'm flexible," he said, throwing his head back and laughing.

"I'm confused."

He kissed her lips lightly. "No, honey, you're fine. The rest of us run in and out of the cuckoo's nest." He went back to the sofa still laughing.

*****

Jeneil unlocked the door to her house and walked in feeling very discouraged. She put her briefcase and purse away and hung her office clothes up in the bedroom. Pacing before a poster of Chang, tears rolled down her cheeks.

"Oh, Chang, this all has to end soon. Where am I headed? If we had been together and I came home and confessed I told Dennis that I'd sleep with him, you'd be destroyed. It's a strange world out here and I don't like it. Husbands sleeping with other women with their wives consent. Chang would rage and Irish along with him, but Jeneil is getting churned by the madness trying to make sense and get along. Life was easier when we were together. They considered you primitive, a Neanderthal who kept his woman on a chain. It was easy for me that way. Nobody expected anything from me physically. Now it seems my every feeling translates into physical because I'm alone. No one seems to understand cerebral the way you did. No one seems to understand me the way you did."

Jeneil caught herself using the past tense. "Do!" she corrected. "It's all madness and only slows down progress." She leaned against the poster for comfort. "Progress," she said, sighing, "I thought I was making progress but I'm finding that the theatre isn't my niche either." Tears fell again. "Now I'm back to drifting and I don't know what it all means. Right now I think I'd trade places with Karen and enjoy nobly shuffling around with a new life inside me, created by us. Why do I struggle with life when others seem to understand it so easily?" She smiled. "I know, Chang, I hear you; I'm into helium, right angle thinking, tilt and crazy kid. It looks like we're going to miss my birthday, too. You've almost finished your residency." She sighed again. "And now the Dragons. What are we facing, Peter? Are you safe? I can't bear to even think about what you're facing."

She shivered. "I want it over. When will life settle down again? When will you finally call and be a part of my life?" She studied the face of the serious young man in the poster and touched it lovingly.

Four

Peter was on days exclusively now and in surgery for most of it. That pleased him; it made life bearable. He and Steve avoided each other except briefly on Monday mornings in the scrub room when Steve nodded to indicate that Jeneil was okay.

"Dr. Chang, telephone." He looked up and made a notation in a medical chart before going to the viewing room.

"Pete, it's me."

"Lin Chi!"

"I'll call you at the fourth booth," she said quickly, hanging up.

Peter reported to the desk and headed to the line of telephone booths. Opening the door of the fourth one, he sat anxiously waiting for her call. He hoped it was good news. Uette's baby was due in October and if something wasn't discovered soon her baby would be born carrying his name. His first born child and that was a special place he had reserved for a child he and Jeneil would have together. Uette had ruined Jeneil being the only Mrs. Peter Chang; the thought that she would also ruin the patriarchal order of their children infuriated him. He smiled wondering when he'd gotten so Chinese.

"The Songbird," he said, and the telephone rang and he answered quickly. "Lin Chi, are you okay?"

"Shit, Pete, so far but I don't know for how long."

"Why?" he asked, his stomach tensing. "A problem?"

"Problem has not begun to cover it." She sounded overwrought and nervous. "That bitch, Pete. That bitch was the private number for Mark Chun! Mark Chun, Pete! Dude, the guy's sick. There ain't nobody higher except for the old man. Oh, Pete, have what's left of me cremated and blow my ashes in her face."

"Shit!" Pete gasped. "What now?"

"We wait, Pete. We wait. She was his favorite, man. That girl could teach you some tricks. Mark Chun, my kidneys collapsed when I heard. Word is he's strangling mad that she split. It's being said that Old Man Chun is holding him buttoned because she's married to you. He doesn't want any crossover into the community and nobody has forgotten Ki and you bleeding on the street. They can't risk the noise, but he'd love to teach her a lesson. You were her cover, Pete. Once she married you, Mark was tied in a knot and couldn't reach her. Damn smart bitch."

"That's why she panics when I say I'm leaving," Peter said. "Then she doesn't have any muscle?"

"It doesn't look like it, Pete, but lay low. Mark Chun's a short circuit. His idea of teaching her a lesson would be to kill her and get even with you by erasing the White Princess. And Pete, count on it. When he gets wind that somebody's asking questions, he's going to send muscle to find out why. Bo and I bought brass knuckles."

Peter closed his eyes. "Oh shit, Lin Chi. I told you to sidestep any walls."

"Pete, walls I would've seen. I never dreamed the bitch would be connected to Mark Chun. Nobody leaves his coop. She's either desperate or crazy."

"Can I go see him, Lin Chi?"

"Not smart, Pete, not smart at all. The dude is sitting in the coop raging. What do you think he'd do to the man who took his favorite lady?"

"But how can I be sure it's his baby?"

"Pete, if it isn't yours then it's his because nobody else would touch his hens, nobody."

"So now what, we wait, that's it?" Peter asked, discouraged.

"So we wait some more and hope Mark hears about me nosing around on a good day and maybe he'll leave me enough strength to use crutches for the rest of my life."

"Lin Chi, I never wanted it like this. I didn't."

"Pete, let's see if Bo is right. He was careful not to leak out the reason we were nosing around, hoping the question mark would be our ace. They'd need us in order to know why all the questions."

"And then?"

"Depends on how interesting they find the news."

Peter sighed. "Lots of ifs, Lin Chi."

"I'm counting them too, believe me. I hope Bo is as smart as I think he is. I've got to hang up, Pete. Bo and I stay together now as much as we can."

"If Mark's interested, will he move soon?"

"I don't know. He loves letting time pass so you begin to sleep with both eyes shut and then zap," Lin Chi said, and Peter's stomach sickened. "I've got to get back, Pete. It's getting dark out."

"Lin Chi, I'm really sorry."

"Pete, I owed you. That's the odds in Russian roulette. Ain't nothing against you, but I'd like to even the score with that bitch. I really would. But like Bo said, 'worry about not bleeding, not getting even.' I've got to run. Bye, honey."

"Bye, Lin Chi," Peter answered, somewhat dazed.

*****

Peter drove home slowly, trying hard to calm down. The thought that Lin Chi and Bo were in danger ate at him and not being able to do anything about it stirred his anger. He fought against it remembering his Dragon training that anger clouded one's thinking. He wondered what his next move should be. If he confronted Uette with all his information, what would that do? A red flag went up in his mind; she was a slimy, conniving bitch and could easily react with another lie. He couldn't tip his hand with her. She was used to shit and could easily hire muscle to get at Jeneil even if it meant lying to her father for the money. He would have to wait it out silently; she had him completely tied in a knot.

Peter gripped the steering wheel tightly as he realized the position he was in, caught in a crossfire between Uette and Mark Chun. That was why anything he uncovered through Lin Chi hadn't helped him at all. The whole mess was tied to Mark Chun now and his reaction to the news that Uette was carrying his baby.

Peter tried hard to remember Mark Chun. He remembered Ki being concerned about some of the guys who had applied to the Dragons, feeling they were a different breed of street kid, too professional. Ki turned down applications and the Dragons became an elite group and impenetrable as a result. Ki had told Peter he felt another Chinese gang would form and he dreaded it saying they didn't have time to fight one another. Ki had been worried about the new guys on his streets and felt trouble in his blood. He had told Reid and Peter about one in particular, a guy who called himself TAO, who circled the streets like a predator, staying in shadows and slithering out only to cause trouble. Ki didn't trust it; he smelled a fake and armed himself against a Chinese invasion by stepping up security and training within the Dragons. The men loved Ki and were impenetrable or so Ki and Peter had thought. Neither expected the weak link to be Reid. Ki had told Peter just before his assassination that he'd found out who the predator was.

"Mark Chun," Ki had said. "We have to be careful now. Peter, these guys aren't human. They don't care about our streets or our men. They want our name. The Dragons have power, our name is strong. They can't start their own gang. They need us to push their filth." Peter remembered Ki being under pressure after that. Peter had tried to spot Mark on the streets but he was illusive, and whenever Peter would ask who TAO was, the guy blended into a group so well that Peter was never sure who was being fingered. Shortly after that, the assassination ripped the Dragons wide open. Peter again grasped the steering wheel tightly realizing the one guy who had probably put the blood money in Reid's hand was now the one person he needed to get him out of his marriage to Uette.

The thought sickened him and he hated Uette for making him swallow his pride by having to wait for Mark to make his move.

"Mark Chun," Peter said through gritted teeth, remembering holding Ki's lifeless body in his arms as he slipped into blackness himself. Peter put his hand to his stomach and felt the network of scars. "Mark Chun," he growled. "Uette, you'll pay for this. No skirt shits on a Dragon. I'm going to feed you to him. He deserves you."

Going into the lobby, he called Bo's diner and left a coded message for Lin Chi to call him the next day. He rode the elevator smiling as the plan that had surfaced in his mind calmed him. If it worked even Lin Chi and Bo would be spared. He thought of Jeneil telling him that it was somebody at the very top. She had good instincts and would have made a great Dragon. Chang was at the surface and in control when Peter stepped off the elevator. He unlocked the door to the apartment, his throat dry from the anger he was swallowing, and he went to the kitchen. Dinner was out of the question; food would never stay down. He grabbed a diet soda and tore open the flip top ring.

Uette walked in and stopped when she saw him. "What's wrong with you?" she asked, and walked closer as she stared at him. "You look like a whole different person. Are you angry at something?"

Peter let the cold drink soothe his throat. "No," he answered, "I don't like the heat."

Uette continued to stare. "I could have sworn that was anger." She then smiled. "I made dinner, a chef's salad. It was pretty good."

Peter looked at her, trying to still his anger. "No thanks, I'm not hungry. You're cooking now? What happened? Are you feeling better?"

She looked embarrassed. "Dr. Vandiver was going to hospitalize me if I didn't take better care of myself."

"You look better already," Peter commented, noticing her coloring.

She smiled, pleased by his remark. "I do feel better. It's amazing how a person's attitude can make a big difference."

"You're right," Peter said, nodding. "Attitude counts a lot in medicine. Well, I'm tired and hot. I need to rest." He took another diet soda and headed to his room. Yeah, attitude meant a lot, he thought, and he grinned as he felt the change within himself since deciding to take control of the situation.

*****

Lin Chi called Peter at work the next day. He was in surgery but after working through the coded messages and guarded places to call, they finally connected.

"What's up, dude?" she asked.

"Lin Chi, I've given this whole situation some thought. I'm going to call Mark."

Lin Chi gasped. "Shit, man, don't you listen?"

"Lin Chi, it takes the attention off you and Bo. You've paid me. You don't owe me big enough to risk your life."

"It'll cost you yours," she answered sadly.

"I can live with that more than yours and Bo's."

Lin Chi sighed. "How the hell are you going to call him?"

"I have the name of the modeling agency in New York."

"Oh, Pete, this is sick."

"No, Lin Chi, just listen. Once I get through to Mark, I'll ask for a meeting. He'll probably head for you and Bo to back up my story so you're not off free yet, but after talking to me, I hope he'll be angrier at Uette than the rest of us."

"What are you peddling to him?" she asked, sensing a difference in his attitude.

"The truth, Lin Chi. It's part of saving face."

"Oh, Pete, saving face, Mark Chun doesn't know honor and dignity. Saving face to him is muscling someone who insults him."

"That's exactly the point. We don't belong in the crossfire. I want the gun pointed at the right person. It's time for the shittin' bitch to face up to her lies."

Lin Chi sighed heavily. "Pete, I can hear it in your voice. You're serious about this. Well dude, get ready to see some familiar faces pass through the ER and make sure your hospital insurance is paid up, too. This roller coaster is about to speed downhill."

"Lin Chi, I can't promise you won't get hurt and that bothers me, but I can promise that you'll survive."

Lin Chi laughed. "Some damn tough Dragon kid, all guts and steel, aren't you? How the hell did you attract the gentle White Princess?"

"Luck," Peter replied, smiling, "pure luck."

"Well dude, let's hope your luck holds out."

"It will," Peter answered confidently, "because once I realized that Mark Chun was tied to a conveyor belt I knew we had a chance."

"Conveyor belt? Pete, make sense."

"I am. You and Bo just keep watching for shadows and when they show up tell them the truth, the whole truth, naming me behind it all. Okay? I can't control his muscle and that sickens me, but I can make sure we're not hurt badly. Mark's conveyor belt is the image he has to protect. He can't get his hands dirty. His father won't let him. I'll use that."

"That's it? Pete, that's flimsy shit!"

"It's my only ace, Lin Chi. I've got to go." Peter hung up and took out some coins. Dialing the operator, he asked how much a call to New York would cost. Inserting the coins, he dialed the agency he remembered from Uette's letter. His throat was tight and he put himself back to the streets mentally where attitude counted for a lot of strength. A receptionist answered. "Mark Chun, please."

The receptionist hesitated, obviously surprised by the direct request. "I'm sorry, Mr. Chun isn't available. Can someone else help you?"

Peter decided to open fire in order to attract attention. "This is Peter Chang and I want to talk to Mark Chun," he said, getting the distinct feeling from the silence on the other end of the line that his name was familiar.

"Hold on, Dr. Chang. I'll have your call processed."

Peter grinned while he waited, knowing his name was familiar since he hadn't said that he was a doctor. "This is Mr. Chun's assistant, I'll handle your call," a man said coming on the line, his voice deep and tough.

"I'm sorry, but I'll only deal with Mark Chun. I have some information he'd be interested in and remind him that we're not kids anymore. Muscle will be useless to him. My lawyer has been alerted and Mark's father will be too shortly. If he's interested in the information then he has to collect it himself. This is Dr. Peter Chang. I'm on staff at Cleveland General in Upton. I'm in surgery all morning but he can contact me just before noon any day on the fifth floor. And remind him that we're both professionals now; this needs to be dignified." Peter hung up and leaned against the phone booth, holding his breath before exhaling deeply as the tension eased. "Okay, shit head, it's your move now." He stood up and walked back to the floor wiping the moisture from his forehead.

*****

Steve called Jeneil on Wednesday. His week had been filled with meetings and dinners and TV nightly news at home alone, and he needed a weekend with her. She hadn't been home earlier when he called and his mind zeroed in on Robert Danzieg. He waited and tried again. "You're a busy person," he said when she answered. "I called earlier."

"Dennis and the assistant director were working on the new play. I stayed, too."

"Are you okay?" he asked, hearing a tone in her voice that hadn't been there before.

"I'm tired," she answered quietly, "and discouraged."

"Something other than Peter and you?"

She sighed. "I feel a restlessness stirring. I hate being unsettled and I feel unsettled from the restlessness."

"Is Wonderland losing its charm for you?" he teased.

"No, this annoying restlessness has been playing tricks on me for months now. It's like catching a cold. I develop symptoms and then it passes, but this siege is lasting longer. Nothing seems to appease it; reading, painting, yard work, the *Sea Urchin*, nothing works."

Steve listened carefully. "What worked the last time?"

Jeneil thought for a second. "Going through a box of family history."

"Then that's what I prescribe."

"Maybe," she answered, smiling. "How's life treating you?"

"The usual," he answered simply. "What are you doing this weekend?"

"I'm going to New York."

Steve sat up, jolted by the news. "Why New York?" he asked, trying to hide his shock.

"Robert's been working there and he's asked me to spend the weekend in New York. I need the break so I said yes."

"Jeneil!" Steve was losing his grip on control. "Jeneil, you're going to spend a weekend in New York with Robert?"

Jeneil furrowed her brow. "Steve, somehow the way you say it makes it sound different. Robert has been different lately, less overwhelming."

He wasn't comforted by her words. "Well, I guess it's between you and Peter, but that certainly doesn't sit well with me."

Jeneil looked at the receiver, shocked by his pronouncement of judgment on her. "Now wait a minute, Steve. Robert is a friend, just a friend. He knows New York like it's his backyard. He wants me to see some of it with him. There's nothing…nothing…wrong," she stammered, struggling for a defense. "You're not being fair."

Steve was annoyed. "You're Pete's, what the hell is Robert up to?"

Jeneil sighed. "He thinks I'm free, but that's not the point. This isn't anything but a trip to New York with a friend."

"Right," Steve answered sarcastically.

Jeneil clenched her fist. "I don't like your attitude."

Steve paced and rubbed the back of his neck, realizing he sounded like a jealous boyfriend. "I'm sorry, Jeneil. Like I said, it's not my business."

"How come I still feel dirty?" she asked. "You don't believe me, do you?"

"I don't trust Robert Danzieg!" Steve answered hotly, and then caught himself again. "I'm sorry. It's none of my business."

Jeneil sighed. "This summer is a total nuisance. It's nothing but negative vibrations."

Steve was out of patience and losing control. "Well, have a nice weekend," he said, hoping his sarcasm wasn't obvious.

"Steve, don't do this. I don't deserve the guilt you're forcing on me."

"I'm shocked, that's all. You're more sophisticated than I am and that's a real surprise."

Jeneil tried to be cheerful. "You can use Wonderland if you want."

"Thanks," he replied. "I'll see you."

"Steve, will you call me next week?"

"Sure," he heard himself answer, wondering how she had gotten him to as angry as he was.

"Want to come to New York with us?"

"Oh, Robert would love that," Steve sneered.

"He wouldn't mind."

"I'll bet he wouldn't."

"Would you go if Robert wasn't?"

"Yes," Steve answered.

Jeneil smiled. "Well how come it would be fine for me to go with you but not Robert?"

He saw her baited trap too late. "Smart mouthed bitch, aren't you? Well I'll answer that, wise guy. Because I keep my clothes on around you and I trust me. I don't trust Robert."

Jeneil laughed. "Ooo, you sound just like Peter. You've got a strong street kid strain in you. Are you going to keep your wife on a short leash? That's Neanderthal, Steve."

"I'm glad you think it's so funny, bitch."

She laughed again. "Peter called me names when he lost an argument, too."

"Shut up," Steve answered, trying to be angry but giving in to her teasing.

"I love you, Stevie," she said, laughing.

He smiled a half smile. "Don't wait for any blessing, honey. I still don't like it."

"Just don't be mad at me. Tell me you're my friend and you love me."

"I love you, Jeneil," he said sincerely.

She smiled. "Good, now I can have fun in New York."

"Yeah, and keep the ninja moves handy."

Jeneil laughed recognizing Peter's words. "Boy, you and Peter are so alike."

"I find that a compliment."

"It is," Jeneil answered sincerely. "I love you both, I really do. I'll miss you babysitting me. Go find yourself a wife this weekend. I want to win my bet. You're supposed to be married by the end of the year and you can't meet anyone babysitting me. I'm fine."

"Right," he answered. "I'll call you next week."

Steve laid on his bed thinking about her, wondering if he and Peter had her straight. Maybe they needed to be protected from her. Peter was welded into a suit of armor because of her and he, himself, had fallen off the mountain. It sounded like Robert was on his way up the mountain now and Dennis would lay across a puddle for her. "I love you, Stevie," he mimicked, shaking his head. She was either very smart or very stupid and he didn't want to find out which because then he'd have to face what that made him. She was changing. It was subtle, but she was changing and she was restless. Steve sighed. He had a feeling summer was going to cost plenty.

*****

Jeneil hung up and went to the deck for a breath of air and a view of the expanse of twinkling sky over the water. Breathing deeply, she paced aware of her restlessness. The scenery didn't work for her. Opening the door, she went back inside and turned out the lights. Settling under the sheets, she found herself trying to force sleep. Her mind reviewed her life and she didn't enjoy it. The restlessness energized her and she snapped on the lamp beside her bed. Remembering Steve's prescription, she went to the closet and dragged out the box of family history.

She sighed and shook her head. She wanted to tell Peter her middle name was Serena but why was that so important to her? She looked at the poster of him. Because she belonged to him and he should know everything about her. She shuffled through the papers and pulled out the family tree. The idea of ancestors fascinated her. She thought of Peter's grandfather and the enormous book of history he had accumulated and that had tripled in size from his trip to China. Looking at her mother's half of the tree, she frowned. Seeing it incomplete unraveled her sense of order. She put it aside. The box wasn't holding her interest. Going to the living room and her stack of books, she browsed and settled on something light. Taking the pictorial tour of European sights, she settled onto the cot and browsed through it enjoying the photography. It was fun to relive some of her travels with Mandra. Turning the last page, she closed the book realizing she wasn't anywhere near ready to sleep. She sighed heavily, tired of the restlessness in her mood and in her summer as well.

Turning onto her back, she stared at the ceiling and studied the familiar defects in the plaster then sat up as a feeling stirred within her. Going to the closet again, she pulled out the box of family items. Okay restlessness, what was it, some mystical connection to another dimension? What would appease it? Name it and give a girl some peace. She believed in stirrings as some interesting turns in her life had resulted from listening to them, the most incredible being Peter. He was a gift from the wind. That was why she had wanted them married with the wind as a witness.

Looking at the box, she shook her head not knowing what to select. Closing her eyes, she smiled. "Okay restlessness, I'm turning myself over to you. Make your choice free from my consciousness and then maybe you'll rest." She felt the box with her hand; no stirrings within her surfaced. Even stirrings were clouded by her restlessness. She sighed. Maybe she needed a more direct message. She chuckled, amused with the game until something tore the skin on her forehand causing her to open her eyes. Her hand was bleeding slightly. Checking the box, she wondered what caused it. Looking over the manuscripts, she noticed a staple protruding from some of the pages.

"Well, I asked for a direct message," she said, lifting the culprit manuscript to look at it. "A study of Great Britain during the era of the Druids!" she said, surprised. "Druids, eighteenth century magicians or was it more religious?" she asked herself, pulling the dictionary to her lap and reading what was listed. "Well look at that, the word was in a lot of European languages; Latin, French, and Celtic. A society? They weren't just magicians, but poets and prophets, priests and judges. Originally it meant much, very strong and knowing, coming from two root words." She laughed. "Jeneil, why are you looking in the dictionary when your father provided a whole manuscript of research?" Returning the dictionary, she settled in with her father's manuscript, more curious about his interest in it rather than reading about Druids. After reading a page, she lifted her eyes and smiled realizing her restlessness was gone. She returned to reading, enjoying the peace that now filled her.

Five

After leaving the playhouse at four the next afternoon, Jeneil headed for Wonderland. The thought of an evening alone didn't appeal to her so she headed north toward a small restaurant where she occasionally enjoyed a quiet meal. Thoughts of her family tree passed through her mind and she wondered about her mother's side being incomplete. The idea that her mother had been ostracized by her own family made her curious. Passing by the small restaurant, she continued on telling herself that a drive would help her relax and unwind, but she knew there was a house in Devon that held answers.

"They must be gone by now," she told herself, and then argued that maybe neighbors could give her some information. She knew her mother was the oldest of three girls and that she had an older brother. It all seemed ridiculous as she continued driving, but it was one of the silly things a person did to settle the unsettled recesses of the mind.

The drive seemed shorter than the hour it had taken and she stopped at a service station for gas and directions. The town was small and all its main businesses were presented on two streets. She turned left at a small white church on the corner of Spruce and drove down Maple. Looking at the scenery, she smiled to herself filled with excitement of her mother's childhood. She told herself what she was doing was silly but, having seen the streets, she wanted to see the house where her mother grew up. Maple was a long street and she continued on. The station attendant had known the Alden place and described the house. He had said it was once part of three large farms on Maple Street, but the fields had since been turned into real estate developments.

The white house came into view and Jeneil felt a twinge in her stomach as she saw a swing on a large tree, remembering her mother telling her about it. There was also a place by the garage where three lilac trees grew clustered around a flat rock. It had been her mother's place to recover from childhood struggles and to mediate. Her mother had said a wisteria grew with the three lilacs and had reminded her of herself; never seeming to quite fit in despite trying so hard to. The wisteria was the same color as the lilacs and was part of the cluster but never quite made the group.

Looking at the house and yard from where she parked by the curb, she wondered if the new owners would mind if she wandered in back to see the lilacs and wisteria. Her mother had painted the rock white one day pretending it was a throne and she wanted to see it. Noticing a car in the driveway and having summoned enough courage, she headed to the door. The lawn needed to be cut and the flowerbeds needed some work. As she started to climb the wooden stairs to the front porch, the door opened and a woman who looked to be in her late thirties spoke sharply to someone behind her about watching her money. The woman turned and frowned when she saw Jeneil.

"And what are you selling? Whatever it is, she doesn't need any and she can't afford it."

"I'm not selling anything," Jeneil answered, staying on the bottom step, unsure about the situation.

The woman looked her over curiously. "Do I know you?"

Jeneil shook her head. "I don't think so. I'm not from this area."

The woman shrugged. "Oh well, I just thought you looked familiar." The woman continued down the stairs. "Listen, my mother's an old woman on a fixed income. Don't sell her anything, please. I can't afford it."

"I'm not selling anything, really," Jeneil reassured her, and the woman nodded and continued down the sidewalk to the car in the driveway.

"Nedra, who are you talking to?" a voice called from the house.

Jeneil climbed the stairs slowly; the voice struck her as sounding very familiar. She heard footsteps through the house heading her way and she waited on the porch. A woman with whitish-grey hair appeared at the screened door and Jeneil's heart stopped momentarily. The woman looked so much like her mother it took her breath away. Jeneil's mind whirled as she remembered the name on the mailbox was Baxter and she wondered if this woman might be one of her mother's sisters. She stared at the woman not quite believing that what might be before her was family, real honest-to-goodness family. The car backed out of the driveway and honked. The older woman waved and her smile faded as she stared at the girl on her porch who looked so shocked. The woman put on eyeglasses that hung from a chain around her neck and looked Jeneil over carefully.

"Do I know you?" the woman asked.

Jeneil struggled with her words, wondering what her reception would be if her mother had been so unwelcome. "No, we've never met but I think you might have known my mother. I'm Jeneil. My mother's name was Jennifer."

The woman looked stunned and covered her mouth. "Oh my goodness!" she gasped, opening the screened door to look at Jeneil more closely. Tears filled the woman's eyes and rolled down her cheeks. "Jeneil! Oh my goodness, you do resemble Jennifer; her nose and chin, the eyes. You have the same eyes!" The woman put her hand to her throat and Jeneil recognized it as a gesture her mother had, too. She smiled glad the woman didn't seem angry. The woman looked around as if shocked that she was standing there. "Come in, please come in, Jeneil."

The living room was cooled by an oscillating fan and was neat and pleasant, furnished in a colonial style. "Please sit down," the woman said, taking a winged chair herself. "You'll have to forgive me; I'm just so stunned that you're here. Where is Jennifer? I tried to locate her a while back but got nowhere and now you turn up on my doorstep. How incredible!"

Jeneil sat on the sofa. "My mother passed away six years ago."

The woman's shoulders drooped and tears filled her eyes again. Taking a handkerchief from a pocket, she dried her tears and shook her head sadly. "I had really hoped," she stopped. "We lost touch with her," the woman said sighing, staring at her hands.

Jeneil fidgeted. "Are you her sister, Rebelah or Rachel?"

The woman looked up quickly. "Oh, I'm Rachel. I'm sorry; you seem as shocked to be sitting here as I am that you are."

Jeneil nodded. "I recently came across a letter to this address. I live in Upton and I wanted to see the house my mother grew up in. I was coming to ask permission to see the lilacs and wisteria near the garage. You resemble my mother; it was a shock for me."

Rachel smiled. "Except for your hair and your smile, which are definitely Neil Connors, you are an Alden. You look just like she did the last time I saw her. She was just about your age too, a junior in college."

Jeneil took a breath, desperately wanting to ask questions. "I was going through some family papers and I found a letter my mother had written to her father at this address." She hesitated. "It was returned unopened." Rachel looked down at her hands and sighed, but remained silent. Jeneil was disappointed having hoped for an explanation. "I guess her father had already passed away."

"No," Rachel answered sadly. "I wish I had known. I would love to have had her address. My father is still alive."

"He is?" Jeneil responded, shocked.

Rachel smiled at Jeneil's reaction. "Yes, he is. He's ninety-eight years old and living in the VA hospital. Mother is gone, Rebelah passed on in childbirth with her third, and James is in Alaska. It's just father and me here now. My husband and I bought this house when Father got too old to afford it or look after it. The farm was his pride. That's all he had was the farm and his pride. Most of the acreage has been sold."

"I opened the letter my mother sent to him. She mentioned a…," Jeneil struggled for a gentle word, "…a disagreement she had with him but I don't have any details. Do you know what happened?"

Rachel nodded, wiping away tears. "Oh, yes, I know. We all knew. Father wouldn't let us forget. Rebelah and I were almost under lock and key after Father and Jennifer exploded."

Jeneil assumed it was serious and drew some courage. "Grandmother Serena Randolph kept in touch with my mother. I've been wondering why my mother's mother didn't."

Rachel held her throat. "Mother died early in life over the battle between Father and Jennifer. He forbade my mother to contact Jennifer in any way. It broke her heart. He was and still is a very strong willed man. We couldn't even whisper her name for fear that he'd hear it. Every picture of her was supposed to have been burned. We hid them."

Jeneil was taken back with surprise wondering what her mother had done. She couldn't stand it any longer. "What did my mother do that caused this problem?"

Rachel shook her head. "Looking back and thinking about it over the years I came to realize that she was only being Jennifer. She was as strong willed as he was. Even as a young girl, she would oppose him. Not him really, but his heavy hand. The lilacs were a refuge from the battles in the summer and the hayloft in the winter. She was different from us. She always was. Father wanted us to be teachers but Jennifer wanted to study art and to go to France to study her sophomore year."

"That was what caused the problem?" Jeneil asked, very surprised.

"Oh no," Rachel said, sighing. "Everything fell apart when Jennifer came home her junior year and Neil Connors began writing to her from France. Then, he showed up in Boston and took a teaching position in Crestfield, a private school there. Father forbade Jennifer to see him but she didn't listen. They were so much in love. Rebehah and I were green with envy. He was so good looking and his Irish brogue was so European. Jennifer was very different after France, more self-confident, extremely independent and cosmopolitan. She and Father could barely stay in the same room together for more than a few minutes without arguing. Then, Neil showed up." She smiled. "He was so gallant. He came to the house and asked Father for her hand in marriage. Can you believe that? Rebehah and I were so impressed. Father threw him out of the house."

Jeneil raised her eyebrows. "You mean he refused?"

Rachel shook her head. "No, I mean Father actually chased Neil out of the house, calling him names and shouting obscenities."

Jeneil was puzzled. "Why?"

Rachel smiled gently. "Father was an odd man and life was different back then. The land around here was being bought by people coming from Europe. Father felt threatened and called them foreigners. But Neil was…," she stopped, and looked embarrassed. "Well, he was Irish with an Irish brogue and he was Catholic, which was worse. Father wouldn't hear of an Alden connected to that." Jeneil stared in disbelief, outraged. Rachel shrugged and rubbed her temple. "She and Father had an ugly row. I'll never forget Jennifer standing right there." She nodded toward the bottom of the staircase. "She was red with anger and trying to control it. She called Father an ignorant peasant and told him that she would be moving out. He told her that she would either stop seeing Neil or give up the family. She ran upstairs and came down with her bags packed when a taxi showed up and went to Boston with your father. Grandma Serena told us they were married a few months later. Father forbade Grandma to visit Jennifer, but Grandma wasn't intimidated by Father. She visited anyway and spoke openly about Jennifer and Neil, who made his name in education and became a professor." Rachel chuckled. "Grandma Serena talked about Jennifer at Sunday dinner. Father would be nearly blue with rage and then shout at her to shut up. Grandma would touch the corners of her mouth with her napkin and tell Mother how grateful she should be that Jennifer married so well. She'd look at Father and scowl, 'At least Neil wasn't an ignorant peasant.' Father would storm out of the room."

Jeneil wrinkled her eyebrows. "That's what the problem was all about? My father was Irish and Catholic? He was an atheist!"

"That was worse," Rachel added.

"I guess your father was a very religious person?" Jeneil asked, trying hard to understand.

"No, he went to church on holidays. He just had some very strong opinions and a lot of pride."

"His opinions meant more to him than his daughter?" Jeneil asked, completely shocked.

Rachel watched Jeneil. "You have to understand. I think it started out as anger and then grew to bitterness. Would you like to meet him? The VA hospital is thirty-five minutes from here by car, an hour by bus."

Jeneil was having trouble dealing with the new information. "I'm not sure I should. He returned her letter and my father's telling him she had passed on. I don't know why he'd accept me."

Rachel looked sad. "Jeneil, he's an old man. His family is gone and his grandchildren never visit. He sits in the hospital and sometimes tears roll down his cheeks. Maybe seeing you would settle his heart and give him a chance to die peacefully."

Jeneil sighed. She didn't like the man and she hadn't even met him. "It seems like a small enough thing to do so a person can be at peace."

Rachel smiled warmly. "Jennifer and Neil did a wonderful job with you. You're closer in age to my grandchildren but I understand you. They have purple hair they glue into points. I could be at peace knowing the future had young people like you handling it."

Jeneil shrugged. "I'm finding that people with purple spiked hair are complaining about the present and concerned about the future, too. You probably have more in common with your grandchildren than you think."

"Your mother saw things differently, too. I haven't had my dinner. Will you share it if you haven't eaten and then we'll visit Father?"

Jeneil stood up. "Let me take you to dinner. I'd like that."

Rachel smiled. "That would be a nice treat. I'd like that, too."

*****

Jeneil liked her aunt and dinner had been pleasant. As they rode the hospital elevator to her grandfather's floor, she struggled with mixed emotions. She had a grandfather just as Peter did, but a pall overshadowed her excitement. He had disowned her mother for marrying her father for a reason no clearer than deeply rooted prejudice. Jeneil had a prejudice of her own against people who were prejudiced. She pulled herself together and hoped for the best. Rachel nodded to several of the staff in the corridor then stopped at a room.

"Thank you for doing this," she said, touching Jeneil's shoulder lightly.

Jeneil nodded. "I hope this has positive results. At his age, anger can't be healthy."

Rachel patted Jeneil's shoulder then walked into the room. Jeneil followed and counted four beds. Two elderly patients were bedridden and one was sitting on the edge of his bed. Another sat in a chair in the corner staring out the window. His chest looked shallow and his clothes too big as his body grew backward from the deterioration of age. Jeneil took a deep breath where she stood at the foot of the empty bed while Rachel went to him. The elderly man looked up at Rachel like he was expecting her but void of emotion. Jeneil had a strong desire to take him into the sun and fresh air hoping some spark of vitality would show itself from the change in his routine alone. He looked beaten, like he'd given up the entanglements of life and was now waiting on the sidelines like a death row prisoner might. Jeneil felt pained by the image and was moved with compassion.

"Father, this is Jeneil," Rachel said, pointing to Jeneil. Jeneil stepped closer, watching the elderly man carefully. His cloudy blue eyes stared back and she felt he recognized her, not as a granddaughter but as her mother must have looked years ago. She held her breath as she waited for a reaction and was surprised when a tear rolled down each of his cheeks. "Jeneil is Jennifer's daughter, Father," Rachel explained close to his ear. "She wanted to visit you and meet her grandfather."

Jeneil watched as anger filled his cloudy eyes and a scowl distorted his deeply lined face. He turned his head away and again stared out the window. Rachel sighed and shook her head. Anger began to fill Jeneil as she witnessed the obvious snub he was giving her because her parents had made him angry. She decided he was an ignorant peasant as she thought about the letters he had returned unopened.

"I'll wait in the solarium while you visit with him," Jeneil said to Rachel.

"No, Jeneil. He'll wallow in his anger and avoid me, too. We might just as well leave."

They drove home in silence. The visit had ruffled Jeneil's nerves as she dealt with the anger that still dotted her thinking. She felt defensive of her father and the wonderful husband and father he had been and was hurt by her grandfather's disapproval because he had been Irish. What an unyielding, unforgiving, decaying human being her grandfather was, she thought, as she pictured his look of anger and the reaction he had to her visit.

Driving up to the house, Jeneil pulled to the curb. "This has been quite a night for me," she said, sighing.

"It's been a delightful one for me," Rachel said, smiling. "I found a niece. Rebehah's husband remarried a year or so after her death and the children don't know me as their aunt. James is in Alaska and I haven't seen his children in years so I've never had nieces and nephews in my life until today. I'd like it if you would call me Aunt Rachel."

Jeneil smiled liking this cheerful woman who reminded her of her mother. "I'm very glad that I've met you, Aunt Rachel, I really am." She hesitated for a moment. "I'd like to speak frankly if I may."

Rachel looked somewhat puzzled. "Of course."

"Well, my parents provided for me very well. It would please me if I could help you."

"Help me?"

"This is a big house and yard, keeping up with all the work must be quite a task. Would it help to have someone do the yard work and maybe someone to help in the house even once a month? Your arthritis must make certain jobs tough. My mother's did. I didn't have the joy of giving presents over the years, let me catch up now. I know my mother would be pleased."

Rachel was touched. "This place is beyond me. My children keep after me to sell it, but it's always been my home. I couldn't live in an apartment."

Jeneil nodded, understanding completely. "Then it's settled, Happy Birthday and Merry Christmas for the past years."

"You are really very sweet," Rachel said, smiling.

"Not really," Jeneil replied. "It's just inspired. It isn't every day I find an aunt."

"Will you keep in touch?" Rachel asked hopefully.

"Yes, I will," Jeneil answered, opening her purse and taking out a pen to write her home telephone number on the back of her business card.

"You're president of a business?" Rachel asked, surprised.

Jeneil laughed. "It runs me really."

"You hyphenated your parents' names for the business?"

"No, my parents legalized it when I was a baby."

Rachel sighed. "Jennifer was always different; she frightened Rebehah and me with her plans sometimes. She wanted to travel the world and paint. We were frightened for her."

Jeneil smiled. "She did travel the world and her paintings were sold in two galleries."

"Well, that's wonderful," Rachel said, smiling. "I'm glad her life pleased her and I'm glad she was wise enough to have children. You must have pleased her, too."

"I remember having fun with them. I hope they did, too."

Rachel sighed. "I wish Father had looked at his life less narrowly; he might be more peaceful today." Jeneil couldn't disagree but she felt no compassion, her hurt for her parents filled her more at the moment.

*****

Jeneil arrived home tired and weary. Life and all its changes rushing at her made her weary but the idea that her parents lived separated from family because of the ignorant prejudice of one narrow-minded man made her the weariest. Two sisters had missed knowing each other because their father refused to grow up. What would his reaction be to her life? Peter was Chinese; her grandfather would probably make her leave the country. She shook her head. She was worn out. Sometimes people wore her out. She sighed, going to change her clothes.

Her telephone rang. "Hi, honey."

"Robert," she answered, smiling. "Please don't tell me the weekend is cancelled. I couldn't take that."

He laughed. "Bad day?"

"I'm just weary," she replied. "I need a fun change. I need to be in a cosmopolitan atmosphere where people homogenize more than they do in a small town."

"Then New York it is for you, beautiful. I called to make sure you're still coming."

"I'll be there, Robert. I'll be there with bells on and ready to experience the magic."

"What brought this on?"

"I think I'm ready for a larger life," she said. "This one feels a little cramped right now."

"Well, lucky me," Robert laughed, enjoying her words, "lucky, lucky me."

Taking luggage from the bedroom closet, Jeneil began to pack while she thought about her grandfather. She wished he was more like Peter's and marveled that deep in her heart Mr. Chang felt more like family and was equally surprised that Mr. Alden didn't. Rachel was beginning to feel somewhat like a relative and she smiled knowing that her mother would be pleased. The image of her grandfather's angry expression pressed on her mind. Fresh air and sunshine wouldn't help him at all; he was too wrapped up in anger and hatred. She got out a garment bag and some outfits to take on her trip to New York wanting desperately to leave all the negative vibrations of her summer behind. Thinking about Uette and Mr. Alden, she decided they had a lot in common as she secured the lock on the garment bag. Because of their selfishness, they had changed the course of people's lives and had denied them certain freedoms. Anger filled her and she went to get her music hoping to change her mood. "New York, I hope you're my miracle cure."

*****

On Monday morning, Jeneil found that she had more positive energy in reserve. That pleased her since lately she had found herself struggling with discouragement over her separation from Peter. Life felt too temporary and she had a hunger for roots, a hunger to build a permanent life. Very little gave her satisfaction and even the hopes of Adrienne and Charlie buying Wonderland had been shattered. Local citizens had stormed the bank threatening to pull accounts if the property was sold to blacks. Jeneil sat at her desk and thought about the situation. The thought of allowing all her work in Wonderland to be reclaimed by the wild growth of nature disturbed her. The banker had told her that the locals didn't mind her buying the property since she had made so many improvements to it that it was an asset already. She leaned back in her leather chair. And one-half of my name is Alden, she sighed again, thinking how well her grandfather would fit in at Weeden. Adrienne and Charlie were less annoyed than she was about the bigotry. She got up and paced. She had to let the banker know her decision and a smile crossed her lips as a thought materialized. Why not buy the land and rent it to Charlie and Adrienne? The farm would be in her name and Charlie would run it. Actually Charlie had triggered the idea, laughing when he heard the news and said they should tell the bank, *'We is yo' slaves, Miss Jeneil, jus' lookin' afta' yo' land fo' yo.''*

Adrienne was skeptical when Jeneil approached her. "I don't know, Jeneil. What about our children? They'd grow up around that kind of hatred. I can feel the hatred out there but at least I'm not dealing with it every day. Our children would every time we ran into townspeople. I think Charlie and I had better realize that a farm is out of the question."

Jeneil sighed and paced. "Where will you and Charlie settle?"

Adrienne shrugged. "I don't know. Sometimes I think we shouldn't have children either. The struggle of having to test the water every time we look at property." She shook her head. "It's like I'm tied to a thick rope that some faceless person yanks if I step somewhere unapproved."

"That's illegal."

Adrienne laughed. "You can't legislate the human heart and its prejudices. And you'd better get used to that, my dear friend, because Peter will run into the same problem."

"No, he won't," Jeneil replied quickly. "He wants to live at the beach house and that's under Maitlin School District. People in that area are used to all kinds of ethnicities because of the State University."

"Lucky you," Adrienne said, sighing.

Jeneil smiled as a thought came to her. "Adrienne, why don't I buy Wonderland and more of the surrounding acreage? The house can be summer rental property and Charlie can still plant the fields. You can live in Maitlin; it's not that far from Wonderland."

Adrienne frowned. "Jeneil, we've looked there. Property costs are way beyond us."

"Not if I hold the mortgage."

Adrienne stared at her. "You're crazy."

Jeneil was getting fired up over the idea. "No, I'm not! I'll build a barn for farm equipment with a small apartment above it for you and Charlie to stay in on weekends until you're ready for Maitlin. When you're pregnant, you'll have to stop working. I'll hire Charlie as caretaker. It'll be a good part-time job for him and it'll help me. Our children can go to school together. The ethnics in the area are professors and doctors. Their children go to Hubbard School. State maintains it for its teacher's college."

Adrienne smiled. "You've checked this all out, haven't you?"

Jeneil nodded. "As soon as Peter said he'd like to live at the beach house. I'd love to have you and Charlie close by."

Adrienne sighed. "Well, I know Charlie has really enjoyed this summer working the fields. He'd love to spend summers there even if it was in an apartment over a barn as a caretaker."

"Then it's done," Jeneil replied, heading out of Adrienne's office. "I'll buy Wonderland. There's more than one way to skin a bigot."

Adrienne laughed. "I love hearing your plans for you and Peter. It makes me come alive."

Jeneil nodded as she got to the door. "I know. Even more than my trip to New York and that was real fun. I'm ready to settle down. This summer has created a hunger for permanency. I can't wait until Peter has the situation resolved."

*****

The good spirits of the day followed Jeneil home and she changed to her swimsuit, got into the *Sea Urchin* and bobbed on the water under a sky full of stars and a three-quarter moon. She had packed her father's manuscript in plastic and had taken it along with a flashlight. It was a more pleasant reading place than the skimpy cot in her bedroom. Her telephone was ringing as she entered the house from her floating library and she answered quickly.

"I was about to give up."

"Steve!" Jeneil smiled broadly.

"You keep late hours at the playhouse."

"I was in the *Sea Urchin*. It's so pleasant bobbing under the sky. The ancient Japanese listened to crickets chirping while gazing at a full moon as a way of soothing the spirit. It works and the moon wasn't even full."

"How was New York?"

"Great, really great. Robert is using a loft that belongs to a dancer he knows. It was an offbeat place. What a city! I loved the whole weekend!" she said, reliving the vibrant feeling as she talked.

"How was Robert?" Steve asked boldly.

"Fine," Jeneil answered, puzzled by the question.

"Did you need ninja?" Steve asked more boldly. Jeneil didn't answer. "Where did you go, sweetheart? Why the silence?"

"Oh, Steve, you're a pain," she answered quietly, embarrassed.

"So you found out Robert was looking for more fun than New York was offering."

"It was my own fault," she defended. "I told him that I was ready to experience a larger world and he misunderstood. I wasn't ready to change as much as he thought, that's all. He was very nice. He understood after I explained the misunderstanding."

Steve grinned. "Too bad, I was hoping you had broken his kneecap."

"You're awful," she said. "Has Peter uncovered anything?"

"I don't know, honey. He avoids me like the plague. He said it's best if we aren't seen as friends."

"I wonder why?" Jeneil questioned, surprised to hear that.

"He doesn't want the Dragons connecting you to him for your own protection."

She sighed. "I feel bad about my summer until I think about his. Poor Peter."

"He looks tired. This hasn't been easy. I can't believe the tension he can live with. His motivation must be strong. You've cast a spell on him, kid."

Jeneil smiled. "I hope so, Steve. I tried hard enough." They both laughed and Steve listened to her laughter knowing it wasn't a joke to Peter or to him since he was bewitched himself and she hadn't tried hard to do that. She didn't even know about it.

"Where are you off to next weekend?" he asked, holding his breath.

"Let's see, Nebraska? No. Oh, I remember, I'm going to spend most of the weekend with a friend I haven't seen in a while. It'll be fun I'm sure, it's been a long time."

"Oh," Steve replied, trying to hide his disappointment.

"Are you free?"

"Yes, but I'd rather not intrude on your reunion with your friend," he responded quickly.

"It's you, silly."

Steve held the receiver tightly. "Cute, Jeneil."

She chuckled. "Would you like to choose the fun? Are you free all weekend?"

"Yes."

Jeneil wrinkled her eyebrows and thought. "Steve, you are the quietest person I know right now. I can't believe you're the same Dr. Steve Bradley I heard rumors about in the hospital. Your life is so sane."

Steve laughed lightly. "I told you it was gossip hype."

"Oh, really?" she teased. "Why aren't you dating?" she questioned seriously.

"I am," he assured her.

"But you give your weekends up for me. Your dates must get annoyed."

"Are you complaining?"

"Not at all, I love spending weekends with you," she answered, and electricity raced through him. "I feel close to Peter when I'm with you. I remember the triad."

Steve frowned. "The Spragues invited me to a barbeque at their house on Sunday. They asked me to bring you."

"Do you think we should allow that kind of couple thinking about us?" Jeneil asked seriously. "What if Peter hears about it and your dates, too? I don't want any trouble."

Steve closed his eyes. "Pete asked me to keep an eye on you and I don't mind. I'm not dating anyone in particular." Jeneil was surprised considering how Peter had been suspicious of Steve's feelings and she was once again impressed with Steve's loyalty.

"Steve, you're really a special guy. I can't believe how blind I was to your nicer qualities. I was actually afraid of you."

"Why?" he asked, surprised and curious.

Jeneil shrugged. "I'm not sure anymore really. I guess mostly the gossip was a bit much and you didn't seem to mind it."

Steve smiled. "I like my life now. It's mine and I don't like people trampling on it. The probation was good for me. My life was out of control."

Jeneil smiled. "You have learned to like quality."

"Once I met you, yes," he answered, meaning her. "I'll tell Dr. Sprague I can't make it."

"No," she responded. "No, let's go. We'll tell them the truth, we're just friends."

"Better be sure, Jeneil, people from the hospital will be there."

"I don't hide anymore, Steve, and we are friends, so let's go. As long as Peter doesn't mind, there's no real problem."

"Right," Steve answered quietly.

*****

Jeneil thought about Steve as the days passed, thinking how much of a real friend he actually was. Of all the men in her life at the moment, she trusted him the most. The summer had changed her other relationships, some for the better as in Robert's case and others had become more cautious as in Dennis's case. But Steve was unchanging. He was steady and loyal to Peter and to her. He really was Sir Steven the Loyal and she loved him for it. She loved him deeply because of the trust she had in him. It made her realize how trust was so important to her in a relationship with a man. It was the same quality that first drew her to Peter. She trusted him emotionally and physically. It was odd how much Steve and Peter were alike. Imagine finding two men like that in a lifetime. Luck of the Leprechaun it was.

A deeply rooted feeling of trust was missing in her relationship with Robert. She enjoyed his zest for life and his magnetism fascinated her. He wasn't superbly good looking like Steve but had a quality about him that was best described as animal magnetism. Women planted themselves in his path just as they did with Steve. She guessed it had to be his passion shining through for all he did. In that sense, they were compatible. He was a study for her because he walked through some very heady situations and never seemed to lose his balance. Now that he had stopped being so overwhelming around her, she enjoyed being with him. A certain amount of trust had evolved as a result but he was still too avant-garde, too bohemian for her. She needed to be in the background. She knew that but their friendship gave her some much needed confidence around men and she loved him for that.

She smiled and added pearls as she finished dressing for a charity dinner dance Robert had asked her to attend with him. The cause was a worthy one, the food would be Tiel's, special evening clothes were required and she intended to have some fun. Steve's dance lessons had come in very handy since Robert had been inviting her to so many parties.

Six

Steve got through surgery and began his morning rounds. He was ready for the weekend and was glad it was Friday. Stopping at the charts to check on the results of some tests, he became aware of three nurses watching him closely. "Is something wrong?"

Jane got up and walked to him with a newspaper in her hand. The two other nurses followed. "Have you seen last night's paper?"

"No, why?"

Jane handed him the newspaper opened to the Society Section and pointed to a photograph. "Are you and Jeneil over?" she asked sadly.

Steve took the newspaper and saw Robert with his arm around Jeneil. He read the article that described the charity event and the attendance of Robert L. Danzieg, Chairman of the fund-raising committee, and his escort for the evening, Jeneil Alden-Connors, Entrepreneur and President of Alden-Connors Corporation. Steve noticed how dreamily Robert looked at Jeneil in the photo. It created the right effect; they looked like a couple.

Morgan Rand replaced a medical chart. "Well Bradley, looks like you've been bumped."

"What happened?" Jane asked. "You looked so right together at the restaurant."

Morgan folded his arms, enjoying the moment. "Jeneil found her true level, that's all. The President of Alden-Connors Corporation and an entrepreneur belong at a charity gala."

Steve held back the remark he had on the tip of his tongue. "We're just friends, Jane."

"Is she serious about this Danzieg person?" Jane asked.

"Jane, really, what do you think?" Morgan asked, looking at Steve. "The guy is drinking her in with his eyes and she looks comfortable with him. I've heard of him. He's one of the most eligible bachelors. His family is California society. Our quiet, shy girl in Records is now a swan and she'll be looking for swans to socialize with. I say good for her, that's where she belongs."

"Well Rand, she'll be at Sprague's barbecue on Sunday," Steve said, pausing, "with me." Steve grinned at Morgan's look of shock. "Does that mean she considers me a swan?"

"Oh, good!" Jane smiled, accompanied by beaming smiles from the other two nurses. "She is a complete surprise."

"She's quite a person," Steve said. "She walks her own route."

"I saw her at the playhouse a couple of weeks ago. She said she's working there. Is the newspaper wrong?" one of the nurses asked.

Steve shook his head. "No, she has her own business. She's also an entrepreneur and a full-time volunteer at the playhouse for the summer."

Morgan watched Steve steadily surprised he was obviously close to Jeneil. "Wow, doesn't she take time to breathe?" the nurse asked with raised eyebrows.

"Yeah, this weekend at Dr. Sprague's barbeque with me," Steve said, and he smiled at Morgan. He turned to leave and saw Peter watching the group. He met Peter's stare and Peter walked away rubbing his forehead and frowning.

*****

Peter answered his page and took the call in the viewing room. "Grandfather, Robert Danzieg is a friend of hers," he answered confidently.

"Are you sure of that?" his grandfather asked, studying the newspaper photo closely.

"She buys his work. She's a fan," Peter explained.

His grandfather sighed. "Things are feeling very confused to me, Peter, too confused. Uette told us about the newspaper article."

"She would," Peter sneered.

"The women think Jeneil has tossed Steve aside. They're having fun with the new twist."

"They would," Peter replied dryly.

"Peter, are you sure you haven't lost control? The situation's a mess right now. Uette said you're very distant toward her. She can't believe you're still mourning over Jeneil. She feels you're blaming her for losing Jeneil. She's upset. You don't keep in touch. Saving face has been set aside. I'm very concerned, Peter."

"Grandfather, I'm following the rules. I'm trying to get at the truth by telling the truth."

"Where?" his grandfather asked. "I haven't heard from you."

"It's better that you don't get involved right now."

"Why?" the old man asked, more concerned.

Peter sighed wearily. "Grandfather, this stays between us, is that clear?"

"Of course, Peter. It's been that way all along."

Peter rubbed his forehead. "If Uette even suspects what's happening, I could lose big."

"What's happened, Peter?"

"I know who the baby's father is. It's Mark Chun."

The old man gasped. "Oh my goodness, how did she ever get involved with…how could she? Oh, Peter, this is terrible. What happens now?"

"That depends on Mark. I can only continue to follow the rules and tell the truth."

"To Mark Chun?" his grandfather gasped.

"It's his baby, he should know." Peter heard his grandfather sigh heavily. "Grandfather, I have to get back on duty. Don't worry, I feel very calm about this. It feels right to me."

"Peter, this is beyond all of us now and you can be sure that if the Chuns are involved disaster will follow. Please watch yourself."

"I will, Grandfather."

Peter looked at his watch as he returned to the medical charts; it was eleven-thirty and he was scheduled for surgery after lunch. Taking an envelope delivered by an x-ray tech, he went to the viewing room and clipped the x-ray into place. He turned to pick up the report and caught sight of someone vaguely familiar standing at the nurse's desk. He felt a tingle on the back of his neck as instinct told him that Mark Chun was there to collect his information. The telephone rang and Peter's heart pounded in his chest as he picked it up.

"Dr. Chang, a Mr. Mark Chun would like to see you," the nurse announced.

"Send him in," Peter answered, and he hung up. He went to the viewer to steady himself. It had been so long he had almost lost hope that Mark would stop in. He heard the door open behind him and he concentrated on saving face in order to forget Mark, Ki, and the Dragons. He wasn't playing games; he was dealing with the truth. Peter turned to face Mark. They looked each other over quickly. Peter recognized him from his shadowed positions on the streets in New York where he had stood behind others and watched. He still looked like a predator, Peter thought, as he noticed the look in his eyes.

"I'm Dr. Peter Chang." Peter stood up straight, aware that he was taller than Mark and had a larger frame.

"I know," Mark answered, unsmiling. "You've got a lot of nerve. I don't need to be reminded to be dignified. I'm good at what I do, Dr. Chang."

Peter stood tall and unshaken. "I guess you're here for the information."

"Maybe," Mark answered guardedly. "What are you looking for?"

"Nothing, this isn't a business deal. I have information that you have a right to know." Peter saw Mark's eyebrows move slightly in surprise and he decided to hit him straight and hard to see his reaction. "Uette is pregnant and it's your baby." It worked; Peter saw Mark almost lose his grip. Mark straightened up and pulled himself tight.

"What are you, a comedian?" Mark scowled. "You're married to her."

Peter kept his eyes on Mark. "She's seven months pregnant and I've never touched her. So if the baby isn't yours then I'll keep looking because the father has a right to know. I'd want to know."

"Then why'd you marry her?" Mark asked, trying to hold back his complete shock.

Peter began his campaign. "Because she's a conniving bitch," he said, spitting out the accusation. Mark's eyebrows moved slightly again. "She nailed me for it. I didn't know she was a snake and I turned my back on her. I've been too busy these past years to listen to the noise in the street. It cost me big."

Mark grinned slightly. "What, are you tired of her so you're looking to bail out?"

Peter shrugged. "Check out my story. I married her to save face; the bitch nailed me pretty good. I had no choice. I married her with plans to divorce her after the baby's born. I'll be rid of her either way. I just thought you should know that she used you to nail me. The baby's yours. It happened in January and I can't believe you're not man enough to know who you get pregnant."

"Don't push me," Mark said, his face filling with anger.

Peter leaned against the table. "Let's cut the shit, Chun. Don't waste time threatening me. You can't get your hands dirty and you know it. I have witnesses that you've been to see me. My lawyer knows I'm approaching you with the news and he'll be telling your father. Besides, all I want from this meeting is to let you know that Uette shit on us both. Two big men and she shit on us. Telling you she did it makes my gut feel good, if you can understand that. Once the baby's born I walk, but now I can sleep because I've exposed the bitch's lie. Why wouldn't she marry you?" Peter asked, staring right into Mark's eyes. He could see Mark holding himself together by sheer will.

"Are you finished?" Mark asked, in a voice that sounded tense and strained.

Peter nodded. "That's my information. It's yours for free. You can check the court records for our nuptial agreement. I'm not hiding anything. I never could stand a bitch shittin' on me. The marriage is a hellhole, she'll probably be as glad to be rid of me as I am to dump her. I just wish I knew why she didn't marry you. I don't know why it's so important to her that the baby be named Chang and not Chun. Do you?" he asked, hoping the question felt like thumbscrews.

"I have other business to handle today. I just thought I'd stop by and see the great Peter Chang and hear his big information. Some doctor," Mark said, grinning venomously, "gets nailed by a skirt for getting her pregnant and tries to blame me. You're soft, Chang, and pathetic. You're not a comedian and I don't think you're funny. I wonder what Uette would say if she knew how her husband talks about her."

Peter stared Mark down. "Ask her, Chun, I dare you." He grinned. "Thanks for stopping in. I can rest now. I just wanted the truth made known. And remember something; I'm not so far from the streets that I'd bring you here to make an ass of myself. You've been given the truth and I'm even with the bitch, that's all I wanted."

Mark glared at him for a second and left closing the door behind him. Peter watched him walk away as he listened to the steady pounding of his own heart. He sighed, wondering where it would all go now. He had attacked Mark's ego hoping Lin Chi's information was accurate and he couldn't ignore his wounded pride. He would have his lawyer notify Mark's father of the news and of the meeting as protection for himself and Uette as well. He didn't want anyone hurt or even worse, he just wanted the truth known. That was saving face to him and it felt clean even though the situation stunk.

Peter faced the x-ray and took a deep breath. "What now, Doctor?" he asked himself. "We wait." He sighed and rubbed his forehead trying to avoid thinking about the one way it could all go wrong; if Mark asked Uette and she told him that he'd made up a story because of Jeneil. Peter closed his eyes knowing that would be the end for him and quite possibly Jeneil as a way for Uette to retaliate and get even with him. He wiped the moisture from his forehead with the back of his hand. "Truth has to cure this mess. It has to." He took a deep breath realizing the point of no return had been reached. It was up to Mark now and all he could do was wait. He had to stay away from Steve and Jeneil in order to convince Mark and Uette that it was all over. At the moment, he even felt kindly toward Robert for the picture in the newspaper. He swallowed, choking on the frustration he felt for the helplessness of the situation.

*****

Peter left for home that evening exhausted from the physical drain of the afternoon's scoliosis surgery. He had been the primary surgeon and assisted by Dr. Maxwell. Dr. Sprague had also scrubbed and observed. Peter unlocked the apartment door enjoying how it felt to be a surgeon. It was the only thing that offset the tension of Mark Chun's visit. He was a prisoner and he knew it, but he savored the feeling of having exposed Uette's lie. It was a small victory, but its taste was sweet and satisfying.

He walked into the kitchen where Uette was putting a plate together. She turned and smiled warmly. "Hi," she said, "I've prepared your favorites." He didn't answer. "Sit down; I'll get you some iced coffee."

"I'll handle my own dinner."

"Oh, now really, we can ignore the agreement now and then. Sit down," she insisted, grinning. He sat at the kitchen table and noticed the newspaper opened to Jeneil's picture. Uette sat near him, placing the coffee before him. "The jungle cat with the great body finally got to her," she said, pointing toward the newspaper. Peter didn't answer. "Why can't you let go of her?" she pouted. He remained silent and took a bite of potato salad.

"Peter, she's not being loyal to you. She's not. How does she explain this picture? I can't wait to hear how she squirms out of this."

"I don't know."

Uette sat up, surprised. "You haven't talked to her?" He shook his head. "How come? You mean she didn't call to even explain that photo?"

Peter cut a slice of ham. "We haven't talked in weeks."

Uette studied his face wanting to trust his words. "No message with Steve either?"

Peter chuckled. "Steve! He's so much in love with her that picture caused him the most trouble. I knew it. They were close before this news hit. I wondered if Steve would survive her." Peter sighed.

Uette was wide-eyed from shock. "Well, this is a complete surprise. What caused your change of mind? You sound disenchanted."

Peter took a drink. "I'm not disenchanted with her. I'm in love with her but I'm facing reality now." He sat back in his chair. "Her uncle couldn't stand me before this mess and now he wants me out of her life completely. I can't blame him. I'm not her speed. She's money and refinement. I could never figure out what she saw in me. Danzieg's her speed; culture, family. He's been after her for over a year. Every time I turned around the guy was there waiting for me to mess up, and boy, did I ever. I wouldn't make it in her world anyway. I know that now. This marriage made me step back and see it."

He picked up his plate and Uette touched his arm. "Wait a minute, are you saying it's over with her?"

He nodded at the photo. "Doesn't it look like it? The words haven't been said but the message is pretty clear. She's gone to her own kind. There's no way her uncle will accept me and this baby in her life. Actually, I can't do that to her either."

Uette's throat began pulsating. "You blame me for losing Jeneil, don't you?"

He nodded slowly. "Yeah, I do. She meant everything to me and you ruined it with your lie. You and I are going to get divorced, but I lost Jeneil trying to save face. That eats at my gut."

Tears rolled down Uette's face. "But Peter, the baby is yours. That's not my fault, not entirely anyway."

He stared at her as she said the words so convincingly. The shock of her sincerity filled him. "You actually believe that, don't you?"

"It's true, Peter," she cried softly. "I'm sorry you lost Jeneil and that you're so hurt. I fell in love with you. I never meant to hurt you."

He shook his head. "I won't believe that until you tell the truth," he said, standing up.

"I am!" she insisted. He picked up his iced coffee and went to his room, leaving her crying from hearing the truth and at a loss not knowing how to deal with his attitude.

*****

Steve arrived at Jeneil's and found her talking on the telephone. "I'm furious, Robert. You did that deliberately. You asked the photographer to snap us. An entrepreneur! Really Robert, I don't care if I qualify as one. Because I don't like being a headline, that's why I'm annoyed. Well, my staff noticed and everyone at the playhouse, too. We're practically engaged. Oh, that got to you. I'll sue for alienation of affection." She laughed. "You'd marry me to get even. Sounds like a great marriage." She chuckled. "No, I'm calming down, but no more parties for me if that's what happens. Is that a promise? Why me, Robert? Alicia Arnel was clamoring for your arm all night. She would love to have seen her photo in the newspaper. She's last year's news? Nice answer. Do you think telling the truth makes you less of a cad? I don't care if the word is outdated. Man about town, you mean animal on the prowl. I don't know why I go to parties with you if I feel that way! Yes, I do." She laughed again. "To become immunized against men about town. After you, I can handle Don Juan. He's too ethnic for me? You're hopeless. Have I made myself clear about publicity? Good. When, next week? But the play is opening soon, I don't know, we'll discuss it next week. No, I'm not angry anymore. I know you didn't mean to thrust me into the spotlight."

Steve listened as Robert manipulated her and he felt irritated. That damn guy was a snake, he could squirm through anything.

Jeneil hung up and turned to Steve. "Sir Steven." She went to him with *The Evening Gazette.* "Did Peter see the photo?"

"I'm sure he did but he never mentioned it. He apparently knows Robert. I'm the one who wants to wring his neck."

"You!" She stepped back slightly. "Why you?"

"The guy irritates me. I'll take that hug now," he said, grinning as he slipped his arms around her waist.

She sighed. "I couldn't believe I was seeing myself in the newspaper when Charlene showed it to me. Entrepreneur! Can you imagine! I called the office at closing today. There were messages from five stockbrokers and several charity groups. I was going out on the *Sea Urchin* to unwind. Want to come with me?"

"Sure, let me get rid of these clothes." He went to the bedroom to change from his suit. Jeneil was spreading herbal insect repellant on her legs when he stepped into the hallway. He stopped breathing for a second seeing her in a bathing suit. "Holy shit!" he gasped, slipping back into the bedroom to breathe. "Holy hell, how do I get in a boat with that body and not react?" He brushed his hair for something to do. "Professional detachment, Doctor, she's a patient. She's a female patient with a body that would make Earth spin off its axis. Holy shit, Pete must be near crippled by now leaving that for all these months. I suspected she was something else but until actually seeing it all together in one visible package. Oh man, thank heavens it's not a bikini, I'd have to chloroform myself." He sighed. "Shit, I hope I can get past this racing electricity. Oh, baby, you're totally incredible. This isn't fair. It really isn't." He put his brush on the ledge of the mirror. "I find something like that and it belongs to somebody else."

Jeneil appeared at the door. "Don't you have a bathing suit?" she asked, looking at his khakis and sport shirt.

"Yes," he replied. "I, uh, this is okay for me. In fact, I think I'll wear the shirt hanging out," he said, pulling his shirt over his pants, grateful for long shirttails.

She shrugged. "Suit yourself. Want some repellent?"

"Yeah, how'd you change so fast?" he asked, trying to act calm.

"I had shorts and a blouse over this," she answered, smiling.

"You look terrific in a swimsuit."

"Thanks," she answered unemotionally, and left for the kitchen. He followed, smiling because she was completely unimpressed with his compliment. "I made sandwiches to eat on the boat. Is that okay with you?"

"No," he answered jokingly, "I'd like a cooked meal."

"There's the stove fella, call me when tea's ready," she said, grinning.

"Then why did you ask if I didn't have a choice?" he teased.

"Look Steve, don't be brainy tonight, I've had a rough day."

He laughed. "Okay, beautiful. Let's go look at the moon and listen to the crickets like the ancient Japanese...."

"Bullfrogs," she interrupted.

"What?"

"Those are bullfrogs screeching mating calls, not crickets." She picked up a plastic bag and headed out the door.

"Thanks," he said to himself, "I needed to know the whole marsh is swinging while I sit in a boat trying not to think about it. Celibate," he said, spelling it out and then he laughed and followed her to the *Sea Urchin*.

They pushed out to the marsh opening and anchored by jamming a pole into the shallow water, tying the tow line to it. "Mmm feel that gentle breeze against your skin," she said, resting against the side of the boat.

"Oh shit," he moaned to himself, "this is going to be torture, sheer torture."

Unpacking the food, she placed it on a clean towel. "Is your body scarred?" she asked, unwrapping her roast beef.

He almost dropped his sandwich. "Is my body scarred?"

"Yes, you're always so fully clothed down here except for your knee length safari shorts. Peter was like that and I found out later he had scars."

"Uh no, I don't have any scars," he answered, not believing how the evening was beginning with her gorgeous legs and torso on display in the well-fitted swimsuit.

"Air baths are good for you," she said, eating a cherry tomato. He looked at her wondering if she was real. If it was anyone else, he'd suspect a come-on immediately.

"Where are you going with this conversation?" he asked, amused.

"You look pale and unnaturally colored, flushed at the cheeks."

He took a bite of his sandwich to keep from laughing as he wondered how she'd handle the truth that it was a natural reaction to his fear that his body would react to her air bath. He decided against it. "And what do you make of that?" he asked, drinking some ale and controlling a grin.

"You're neglecting your health."

"Geez." He smiled. "I felt great when I left home. Maybe I'm seasick."

She chuckled. "Make fun but I know I'm right. All those overcooked vegetables and chicken in pasty white sauce you eat at seminars are taking their toll on you. And then when you get home, you have junk food, right? Chips and cookies?" He stared at her and she smiled. "I am right."

"What are you, a frustrated nurse?" he asked, laughing.

She shook her head. "No, I love health. It's something to be achieved and worked at. How's your stamina in OR?"

"Jeneil!"

"Say after a few hours? Drained by the end of the operation? Need a coffee boost to spring back?" She grinned as he stared at her. "All of the above, huh? Let's get you a blender tomorrow. I'll teach you to make power shakes."

He shook his head and smiled. "Man, you're bossy."

She shrugged. "Everyone's entitled to good health. You're being robbed. I can help."

He sipped his ale. "Well, this isn't the best of foods either," he said, tapping the bottle.

"It is for you. You're B-complex starved."

"You can tell that?" he asked, and she nodded. He smiled and finished his sandwich.

Keeping the grapes handy, Jeneil cleared everything else away. "We'll be serenaded soon. The bullfrogs start after sundown." She settled back against the boat and closed her eyes. Steve could see her relax, the tension draining from her face. She was gorgeous and not only physically. She was healthy and alive.

"Why are you holding your hands like that?" he asked.

"I'm doing a yoga position. Holding the fingers like this connects into Earth's energy."

"Lying back like that? I thought yoga was pretzel twisting your body."

"Some Asana require twisting but Savasana is the pose of rest. In fact, I should be lying flat and not propped up like this. Want to try it?"

"I'm a diehard," he said, making a face.

She laughed. "You can't make an intelligent criticism until you've tried it. Come on, we'll lie flat together side by side." She slid her body to the opposite side of the boat and spread out the large beach towel. She looked at the sky. "This is an ideal time for Savasana; the coolness of night is beginning. Stretch out," she said, fixing the towel and watching as he lay down. "Steve, you're too tight. Take off your shirt."

"Hey lady, I thought I was going to rest, not strip."

She laughed. "I promise nothing physical will happen to you. I know you're celibate."

He wrinkled his brow. "You're so subtle, woman."

"Please take your shirt off; you're wrapped so tightly it's affecting my breathing."

He paused on the remark he could have made realizing she was serious. Sitting up, he undid his shirt and slipped it off.

"Good. Close your eyes and concentrate on feeling the wind against your skin. Doesn't that feel pleasant?" She spoke softly and he began to chuckle. "What's so funny?"

"I once saw a porno movie that started like this."

She sighed. "Your aura is so twisted and knotted."

"Well, it was a good porno movie," he said, chuckling.

"You need a focus," she said. "Lay down."

"Hey Jeneil, are you going to focus me?" he asked, with a smirk.

"You're not going to undo me, Bradley, so give it up and cooperate. I'm completely cerebral."

He laughed. "Ooo, mother untouchable, untwist my aura and help me focus," he said, lying down.

"Now close your eyes and make your mind the strongest part of you. It is in control," she said soothingly. "Think of your body lying in the boat. Think of the boat lying on the water and the water lying on the earth. Move from each slowly and go back to the boat from the earth gently and slowly. The world is far away from you now. I can't touch you; you have separated from it in order to rest. You are connected to the water and the earth; you will now connect to the air. Breathe in slowly and gently, feel the air as it enters your nose and fills your lungs with oxygen. Now exhale slowly and gently as your mind transfers the air throughout your body. The air is food. Let the air feed you. You are part of all the energies now in a gentle soothing cycle. The air will cleanse and feed you, let the air into your body, feel the air bathe your skin. It holds you gently as you lay on the boat that is lying gently on the water, which is lying gently on the earth. Breathe in the air and let it work for you. It brings life from the energies around you; earth, wind, and water. Breathe in the air's energy, breathe out and transfer it to every cell, gently, slowly." She paused. "Very good, Steve. You did well. How do you feel?"

"Relaxed," he said, surprised, "very relaxed. That's really interesting."

"You focus well."

"How do you know?"

"Because I pressed my finger against your chest and you never reacted. You were onto Prana strongly."

"How long did this take?"

"About three minutes I guess, why?"

"I wouldn't mind trying this at work."

She slipped onto the beach towel and lay beside him. "It's frightening how much tension we accumulate. The mind is our greatest defense. A healthy mind and a healthy body are absolute necessities. No wonder the Greeks emphasized both." She giggled. "I wonder if the idea developed after the Olympics began."

"You think of such odd things."

She laughed. "You're being kind. I really think of zany, low key trivia. That's why Bill called me dipstick growing up."

He turned his head and smiled. "I think it makes you cute."

She grinned and they were silent a few seconds. "I've really had to concentrate on relaxing this summer. I'm glad I know how. My life is unsettled, I feel bolted to a conveyor belt at times."

"The playhouse isn't working for you?"

She shook her head. "And that makes me tense. I thought for sure I'd found my place. I've loved working with Dennis, Line and Derek, but especially Dennis." She sighed.

"You have a serious case of hero worship," Steve said seriously.

"No, not really, I have a passion for his talent."

Steve grinned. "You can direct your passion like that?"

"Yes, can't you?"

He laughed lightly. "No, passion seems to be a blend with me. I buy the package deal."

She laughed, enjoying his simplicity. "Must make life easier." She raised her arm and offered the back of her hand to a dragonfly. It lighted for a second before flitting away. He smiled as she settled back noting it had been a natural reaction to her. "I just found out my middle name is Serena." She exhaled and laughed. "Why do I feel better having told someone that? I guess it must seem weird that I didn't know I had a middle name."

Steve folded his arms. "No stranger than my question. I was left anonymously on the doorstep of the home. Where did my name come from?"

She turned her head quickly, causing the boat to bob. "You don't know?" she asked, and he shook his head. "You never asked?"

He laughed. "I was too busy using the name to find out where it came from. Now that's strange, Jeneil."

She stared at him for a few seconds then moved next to him, wanting to be close to him and comforting. "That somehow seems healthy to me. If you can't change the past then it's better to be living in the present and molding the future. You fascinate me," she said, noticing the sky had grown darker causing the brightest stars to appear.

He turned his head to look at her. "Do I?"

She nodded. "Yes, you do. You're like an onion. I had to get past the crusty outer skin to find that you are layered with fascinating qualities. You're a superlative."

He smiled. "You, I think, create superlatives by the way you look at everything. All the world, life, and people fascinate you." She smiled gently causing his heart to pound. He looked up at the sky. "Boy, I can't believe where life caused me to drift."

"What do you mean?"

"I used to be the White Stallion and now I'm an onion." He sighed dramatically and Jeneil began to chuckle silently, once again causing the boat to bob. He looked at her and grinned. "What's so funny?"

She looked at him and bit her lower lip, holding back a laugh. "Gee Steve, what's so wrong about being the White Scallion?" She tried to keep a straight face, but she broke into laughter and leaned against him.

"Jeneil, that's a terrible joke!" he chuckled, finding her cute.

"I know it is," she said, and laughed all the more. She began to get to him and he turned slightly and pushed at her to move. "Stay on your side before we capsize!" she screamed, as her side of the boat dipped from the sudden shift. The boat bobbed furiously, untying the slip knot on the tow line. Feeling the slight tug, she lifted her head. "I think we just weighed anchor, mate."

"Oh damn," he said, sighing. "I'll get it."

"No, don't," she replied. "Let's drift," she drawled, "them there bullfrogs is making me near plumb deaf. Passionate critters, ain't they?"

He grinned. What was wrong with that? He wouldn't mind a few mating rituals himself. Sounded natural to him, gorgeous critter, and he had his suspicions from watching her moves that she was a passionate critter, too.

They drifted to the mouth of the bay as the moon climbed higher in the sky. Drifting aimlessly under a night sky was a good gauge of how tethered they were to the world. Yoga had helped disengage Steve from the stampede and he totally enjoyed the sensation of moving about without effort on his part or a definite plan in mind. He broke the silence that surrounded them. "I think bobbing and drifting is therapeutic."

Jeneil smiled. "I agree. Where are we all rushing to and from?" There was silence again. "I found a grandfather and an aunt two weeks ago in Devon."

"You thought you were alone?" he asked, surprised.

She nodded. "I still am really. My aunt is a lovely person but I'm having trouble feeling a biological bond to her. Until I see her, that is. She looks so much like my mother. I don't like my grandfather." She sighed. "And I'm not proud of that. He's a pathetic, aging, lonely human being who's all snarled and tangled in bitterness."

"What's his problem?"

"I suspect several things but in my case, my father was Irish; that tied him to being Catholic even though he was an atheist and then agnostic. There wasn't too much about him that the old man approved of for his daughter. He chased my father from the house when he asked permission to marry my mother."

"Holy shit," Steve commented, "he's a hothead."

"He sure is." Jeneil sighed. "My mother wasn't allowed to contact the family because she left to be with my father."

Steve shook his head. "What the hell is wrong with people? Charlie and Adrienne can't buy a house in Weeden. Your mother isn't allowed to marry who she wants. I don't understand it. It doesn't make sense."

"It doesn't make sense to me either but the image of him sitting so forlornly in that hospital chair haunts my thoughts. I feel obligated to him. My parents insisted that you can't separate yourself from your family. I think I'm caught in an emotional crossfire between obligations because he's my grandfather and anger that he emotionally abandoned me. He's sick, I know that, but do I have a responsibility to help him?"

"Why are you even struggling with it?" Steve asked. "None of it is your doing."

"I know, but my parents, Mandra and I would sit and discuss responsibility to the human race, the haves and the have nots. They believed in the improvement of human society and civilization being brought about by acts of kindness and generosity, which would place the recipient in debt to do a sincere and unselfish deed for another."

"Are you kidding me?" Steve asked, finding the theory very idealistic.

"That's the truth, Steve. My parents and Mandra lived their lives by that ideal. That's why I can't understand my mother allowing her father to do this. Why didn't she camp on his doorstep until a truce had been met? She just sent a letter that he returned unopened. That was the end of it. I can't figure it out," she said, rubbing her temples.

He turned on his side and watched her. "Hey kid, it's history, why let it fill you with tension?"

She smiled. "Because I can't put it to rest, my conscience nudges me about it daily."

"Conscience?" Steve repeated, surprised. "Why conscience, honey? It isn't your battle."

"Isn't it? I'm alive, he's alive. We're here together. The situation has been put in my lap."

"What can you do?"

Jeneil shrugged. "It takes an hour for Aunt Rachel to visit him by bus and his grandchildren don't visit. Maybe I could move him to a nursing home closer to his family to solve that problem. Yes," she commented distractedly, "my conscience just settled back when I verbalized the idea. I'll call Aunt Rachel about it. Bobbing is therapeutic."

Steve chuckled. "Hell, this is cognitive therapy. Let's start on my life."

Jeneil laughed. "Fine, Herr Bradley, vhat seemsh to be der problem yah?"

"I'm doing more with my life and getting less out of it. And if you tell me its overcooked vegetables, I'll toss you out of the boat."

Jeneil frowned deliberately. "Ooo, lipshen to der hoshtility bees stron mit you. You ah sexually repressed maybe yah?"

Steve looked at her and chuckled. "Zee shrink is a shtupid lady to ask such a question mit her body packaged in dat swimsuit."

"What!" Jeneil replied, shocked. "Don't you dare blame me, you're celibate by choice!"

He laughed. "Then stay out of my sex life unless you're volunteering to be the cure."

She grinned. "Boy, are you feisty. Freud would say your libido is inhibited."

"So what did he know about cognitive therapy?"

"Dummkopf! I'm a Freud fan. You wouldn't even know about therapy at all without Herr Freud. He's the papa of mind cures and based on his findings I know exactly what's wrong with you."

Steve smiled and shook his head. "Oh geez, this should be really good. Go ahead shrink, lay it on me."

Jeneil lifted her chin arrogantly. "Your problem is definitely sexual. You're a passionate man who has chosen celibacy and because you are also discerning, your mind and body are in conflict now." She smiled, pleased with her diagnosis. "Pretty good, huh?"

He looked at her and grinned. "Okay, Dr. Smug, what's the cure?"

She clasped her hands before her meditatively. "Don't think this college dropout can find a cure? Well, watch me," she boasted, grinning mischievously. "The solution is a matter of forming a compromise that your mind and body can agree on."

"Double talk," he repudiated, "be more specific."

"Okay fella, you like your medicine straight, then you've got it. What you need is orgasmic substitution."

He choked, shocked by her directness, and he lay back laughing. "Jeneil, that sounds kinky as hell. You are a complete mind bend at times."

"Are you rejecting my theory?" she asked, being falsely aloof.

He sighed. "I have a question, Dr. Smug. What the hell is orgasmic substitution?"

"Cheap thrills, fast highs, quick kicks; skydiving, hang gliding, land sailing, surfing," she said, leaning on her elbow and Steve stopped laughing. "So where did you go?" she asked after a few seconds passed.

"You're pretty sharp, Dr. Smug, very sharp indeed. I've always wanted to try some of those things. I think I will."

"Are you crazy?" she asked, staring at him. "They're dangerous."

"So is sexual orgasm if you're not physically fit."

She lay back and sighed. "Gosh, we talk about anything lately, don't we? When and how did our relationship become so open?"

He treated the question rhetorically. "On our way to buy a blender tomorrow, let's stop by the municipal airport."

Jeneil didn't answer as she struggled with the question she had posed. She thought about her relationships with Dennis, Robert, and now Steve. Each relationship had changed during the summer. Or had she changed? A twinge of guilt flitted through her conscience as she asked herself if any of it could be considered a betrayal of Peter. She shivered slightly realizing she honestly didn't know anymore. The almost seven month separation seemed so long and her thoughts left her insecure.

Steve checked his watch with a penlight. "Hey, it's almost midnight. We'd better get back to land."

Jeneil nodded in agreement wanting to get to her room so she could lean against the poster of Chang for support and renewal. She belonged to him and nothing could change that. He was very close to her, very vivid in her mind, and she pushed at the guilt that brought unrest with it.

*****

Peter closed the novel, sorry he had finished it. He identified so strongly with the whole story. Well if his life ended like the book, he'd be happy. He smiled picturing the wolf dog lying lazily while puppies romped all over him. He picked up the glass unicorn and smiled; can't beat that baby, you, me, and a bunch of happy kids. Putting the unicorn to his lips, he could still feel the magic of her kiss. She had a real knack. He hadn't left her anything of him; he had no idea the fog in their life would last so long. What did she have to remember him by; a picture of Chang, the rebellious, smart-mouthed kid? He sighed. Could she hang onto that? Was it enough? Looking at the unicorn, he remembered her words, *'When the Prince returns the glass unicorn the Princess will keep her promise to marry him.'* He smiled, calmed by the thought. "She belongs to Chang," he said quietly. Turning off the lamp, he got under the covers feeling secure. "Everything will be fine. She likes happy endings. She demands happy endings even if she has to create them. Right, Songbird?"

Seven

Jeneil was a wreck on Saturday after stopping by the municipal airport where Steve signed up for skydiving lessons. "It's insane!" she said, walking to the car. "Completely and totally insane! Are you even listening to me?" she asked, grabbing him by the arm.

Steve stopped. "Jeneil, you heard the man. He's logged in hours of sky time and he's still here to talk about it. He looks like he thrives on orgasmic substitution." He grinned and began walking again.

Jeneil ran to keep up with him. "I made that up! I was joking!"

"I know. What are you so upset about?" he asked, stopping by the car door.

"You could get hurt," she answered, panicked by the thought. She put her arms around his waist and clung to him.

He held her close and kissed her temple. "Hey, it's okay. I know a great Chinese doctor."

"That's not funny!" she scowled, stepping away from him, and he smiled and opened the door for her.

"Get in before you completely freak on me," he said, and she sighed and shook her head as she slipped onto the seat. Walking to his side of the car, he noticed something deep within him was ecstatic over her concern. "Let's have lunch at The Creamery," he said, starting the engine.

"Lunch!" she shrieked. "Do you think I can eat or sleep ever again knowing that a maniac surgeon is in the sky somewhere making like a bird! What if you land on your hands?"

Her concern was getting to him and if she was his, he'd have kissed her passionately. He laughed to himself thinking if she was his, he wouldn't need an orgasmic substitution. "We're having lunch at The Creamery," he said quietly, pulling out of the parking spot.

She folded her arms in exasperation. "I hate it when you ignore me. I absolutely hate it."

"You're gorgeous when you're fuming."

"Soft soap won't work," she scowled. "I intend to fume from here to The Creamery and quite possibly through lunch."

What a waste of good passion, he thought, merging into the flow of traffic.

*****

All of Jeneil's efforts to convince Steve to give up the idea of skydiving failed. He had been deeply impressed by her concern when she burst into tears and he had pulled the car off the highway to comfort her. In all his life, he had never met anyone who had shown that much concern for him. It felt great and he had to resist the urge to kiss her. His love for her became more difficult to hide after that encounter although he was finally able to convince her that he'd be just fine while skydiving. He couldn't believe the fears she had of certain things. She had learned to deal fairly well with her fear of water, impressing him with her ability to come to grips with it on her terms which were, *'I'm here, they're there, and we'll compromise only if I understand each step that's before me.'* She held an immoveable position on anything she feared or mistrusted and only budged after investigating and testing her feelings and footings along the way.

Steve found her courage and determination impressive. She had accepted the fact that he was going to skydive and had stopped objecting to it, but she clung to him more and he loved her more for it. He knew when Peter returned to claim her he would feel a real loss, but he'd pay that price to be around her, to feel her love and concern, and to look after her. Something deep within him was convinced that she was his. The feeling puzzled him but to him it was truth. Something was thriving and growing on that feeling and her trust in him as a friend. He provided the friendship and was ready to offer more if ever she so much as hinted at a change in their relationship. They had grown closer over the summer and she was less hesitant about sharing her thoughts and feelings. They talked about things openly and he found he really cherished her friendship aside from the deep love he had for her as a woman. The combination was so heady that he knew the word that applied to his feelings for her was devotion. There was nothing he wouldn't do for her.

All his thoughts and feelings were sorted, assigned, and labeled as he sat in the director's box at the playhouse Saturday night. Although he spent most of the production alone, he felt quite secure by her side at the cabaret afterwards. She went out of her way to see that he fit in, explaining a piece of literature or an interpretation of a piece of art as it was being discussed. As he listened, the language and attitude of the group became put-on and elitist and he enjoyed when Jeneil leaned in to explain to him in simple dialogue what the hassle was about. She was unassuming and he was crazy about that. Her route was a crooked path that she wove into almost all areas of life simply because they fascinated her. He couldn't believe he once found himself with her interviewing female mud wrestlers about their view of the sport and why they were attracted to it. She had started by talking to two and before long had been invited to their favorite drinking place and sat surrounded by a bevy of mud wrestlers. Steve had watched her studying them, absorbing them, listening to and communicating with them freely. Their talk was earthy and some might think shallow and self-centered but Jeneil seemed to understand. She was unassuming and her sincerity was visible. To him, she was a total kick in the head, an absolute breath of fresh air and incredibly sexy because of it. With her, he was off the conveyor belt and walking at tilt, which he enjoyed thoroughly.

*****

Sunday mornings at Wonderland had come to mean early morning visitors. The theatre group stopped by at daybreak to renew their spirits and had renamed Wonderland, The Haven. In the quiet of the early hours, they seemed like churchgoers, reverent and seeking solitude. As the sun grew stronger and the group grew larger, it took on the appearance of a family gathering. Jeneil let it all happen. She locked the closet where she kept her good jewelry and her father's manuscripts and family records, but the rest of the house was completely open. She had never brought in more furniture than a cot in each bedroom and fabric covered boxes that were either used as end tables or bureau drawers if anyone ever unpacked. No one usually did. The Haven was a temporary summer place.

Labor Day was drawing near and the phrase, "the end of summer," was heard often in conversation. Jeneil had asked Steve to choose what she should wear to Dr. Sprague's barbeque. It was the first time he had been in her bedroom and he was stunned to see the huge poster of Peter on the wall. As it loomed before him, it sobered the feeling of headiness he had allowed to develop. Without seeing her complete wardrobe, he knew he wanted her to wear the backless, exotic red print sundress. She looked stunning in it, especially with a gold slave bracelet worn on her upper arm. Her tanned coloring seemed suited to it and her eyes were outstanding and penetrating. Men became giddy and school-boyish when she wore it and it was his hope that Morgan Rand would be reduced to a babbling idiot. Her thick, shiny, dark hair had grown over the summer and waved gently on its own creating an unrestricted look that made the total outfit sensuous.

Steve smiled as he held the car door for her and caught the light scent of her perfume, which alone made a person want to stop and talk to her. It was expensive and imported, and she seemed to know just how much to wear. He had to stand very close when talking to her in order to absorb a satisfying amount of its scent. Then, he'd become aware of her shoulders, tan, smooth and exposed, which forced him to concentrate on her eyes to avoid being rude but at that point he'd become lost in her eyes that changed color subtlety in the sunlight.

He grinned remembering the reaction men at an outdoor concert had to her in that outfit and her reaction to the men. As their behavior ranged from giddy to sultry and with flashing eyes toward her, her behavior became silent and watchful. She had studied them behind quiet eyes and a serene expression that made men do very strange things due to raging hormones. She hadn't known how to handle them and her silent serenity became a look of mystery. Men she barely knew or had just met would kiss her cheek as they said goodbye. Steve could tell it startled her and he knew why they did it; they couldn't stand to be around her and not make contact, even innocently. They had to touch her or go mad but the spell didn't stop there; once they kissed her cheek and felt her outstandingly smooth skin they wanted more, much more. Reactions varied from a gentle squeeze to her arm or a low, soft growl near her ear. When they left, Jeneil remained silent but stood closer to him, putting her arm through his or holding his hand. The encounters were innocent and complimentary but they left her wanting protection and Steve understood why Peter hovered over her. After witnessing the sparks and having Jeneil cling to him, he had to control himself but it felt so incredibly sensuous that it was worth it.

Judging from the number of cars at the Sprague's, they were the last to arrive. Steve found a parking spot and went to open her door. As Jeneil stepped out, he couldn't wait to see the reactions of people from the hospital. The quiet, shy girl from the record department was returning as a beautiful swan who was still quite shy but didn't look it anymore. They walked to the Sprague's house and Jeneil took Steve's hand. He smiled at her knowing she had the jitters.

"It'll be fine, honey," he said, squeezing her hand. She nodded and took a deep breath as they walked the length of the driveway to the backyard. There was a large crowd and heads turned as he and Jeneil came from the side of the garage. The transformation was electric, Steve had been right about the outfit, and the reaction she caused was staggering. She held Steve's hand tightly and he took her directly to Dr. and Mrs. Sprague, who were at a large half drum barrel barbeque under a bright blue canopy.

Mrs. Sprague smiled when she saw them, holding her hands out in welcome. She took one of Jeneil's hands, giving it a squeeze. "You look stunning."

"Thank you," Jeneil replied. "What a perfect day to barbeque. Is the hospital completely closed down? Everyone seems to be here." Steve noticed Dr. Sprague grin as he looked Jeneil over and then he looked at Steve and raised his eyebrows approvingly. Steve grinned as other guests came over to them, some not recognizing her.

"Steve, you devil. Where do you find these beautiful women?" Kirk Vance asked, looking Jeneil over, grinning lecherously.

"How are you, Dr. Vance?" Jeneil asked politely, knowing he was an anesthesiologist with a reputation for appreciating women.

"Have we met?" he asked, visibly shocked that she knew him.

"I used to work in Records at the hospital."

Mrs. Sprague chuckled. "Too bad, Kirk, your reputation has preceded you with this one." Dr. Sprague looked up quickly, shocked by his wife's remark. Dr. Vance was in his thirties and divorced, some thought because of his appreciation for the female species since Mr. divorced Mrs.

Dr. Vance accepted Mrs. Sprague's barbed remark good naturedly. "Carol, I've never hidden my hobby from anyone, I'm rather proud of the fact that I'm a peace negotiator in the battle between the sexes. I believe relationships should be treated like an art form." He grinned at Jeneil. "You're a single modern woman living in a free society. Wouldn't you like to see a new movement that elevated the battle of the sexes to an art form?"

Jeneil smiled, intrigued by his theory. "That's interesting and I do think the battle needs something. I'm surprised to hear you presenting an art form into the war. There are movements in every phase of life. I guess your battle once had a superlative art form called harem. It deteriorated into cheap thrills and polar opposites. In your war, I'd need to know if I was hearing the sounds of marching or a snake's tail rattling before I'd touch it." Everyone laughed and Dr. Vance looked at her closely, amazed that she was serious.

Mrs. Sprague put her head back and laughed while applauding. "Jeneil, I've never seen anyone communicate with Dr. Vance on his level and win." Steve looked at Jeneil and smiled broadly while Dr. Sprague grinned as he turned a piece of chicken.

Dr. Vance smiled and flashed his eyes at Jeneil. "But sweetheart, in all art forms it's the study and experimentation that create superlative, opposites at all levels. Don't you agree?"

Jeneil smiled to herself thinking Robert's friendship had prepared her well. "Dr. Vance, that's some theory. You're right, opposites. The Chinese call it Yin and Yang. War strategists have opposites, peace and war. In the battle of the sexes, there would be opposites too I guess. Isn't it called stalking? But again, I would need to carefully study whether I was being courted or stalked as prey." The group laughed again while Dr. Vance looked her over carefully.

Mrs. Sprague laughed with delight. "I love it; I love this modern era and its liberation. Women see it all clearly and call an ace an ace. There's no fooling them. We believed in fairytales back in my era and couldn't tell the forest from the trees because of it." Tears rolled down her cheeks. "My goodness, I'm laughing so hard I'm crying."

Jeneil saw pain in the woman's eyes and wondered why. "I believe in fairytales, Mrs. Sprague. I believe in their reality."

Mrs. Sprague looked surprised. "But they're not real, believe me, they all have happy endings. Life doesn't." Dr. Sprague frowned, basting the meat heavy handedly out of irritation.

Jeneil smiled winsomely. "But look at the message from Cinderella. She had courage and faced hard work, cruelty, and pain but never let it eat at her. She knew she was the only one who cared for herself. I think she would have gotten to the ball without the help of mice and a fairy godmother. Those things made her story fiction. She was clever; she wasn't a mealy-mouthed goody two shoes who smiled sweetly under duress. She knew physical abuse would be added to her list of woes if she back-talked, so she smiled sweetly until she could escape. After what she lived through with three emotional dregs, life in the palace would be a piece of cake. Do you actually think she just happened to notice that the prince was at her house checking feet or that she just happened to leave the glass slipper? She knew it was her chance at the brass ring and she took the risk. She reached for the sun knowing that even to land on the moon would be superlative by being at the ball in the first place. She called an ace an ace, too. She wasn't starry eyed; she knew if she wanted a chance at the stars then she'd have to walk in the atmosphere at heights where the air is thin and full of pelting meteors. My guess is she decided that even if the prince was a total frog, her place of power as his wife put her in a position to make a real change and she was content with that. She made her own happy ending."

"That's beautiful," Dr. Vance said, smiled broadly as he leaned forward and kissed Jeneil's cheek. Steve heard the low growl.

Mrs. Sprague stared wide-eyed at Jeneil. "Well, I'll be darned, where is that version written? That's terrific told straight."

Steve had listened to Jeneil with deep interest and wished a person could make his own happy endings. Dr. Sprague folded his arms as the meat sizzled and as he watched the quiet girl from Records he began to understand how two of his best doctors had clamored for her glass slipper.

Dr. Vance moved to Steve's side while Mrs. Sprague talked to Jeneil. "Get back to Friday parties, White Stallion. We need the superlative you've encountered in her. I'd like to see her there," he whispered, and then he walked on.

Steve and Jeneil each took a cool drink and stood under a small maple tree to take a break from the sun. "This is the start of the usual round of parties," he told her. "The associates are bringing in new people; they like to know you can hold your glass, your liquor, and your tongue properly in a social setting."

"Who's new?" Jeneil asked.

"George Taczks, Ken Folliet, and Morgan Rand."

"I thought I heard that Drexel Bernard was enlisted, too."

"He signed on with me," Steve said, smiling. "You're good at keeping this all straight."

Jeneil shrugged as she perused the group. "Well, it certainly helps to have worked at the hospital. I've noticed that doctors who are married to nurses on staff there seem to fit in better otherwise the wives have nothing to talk about. I guess every profession brings its work home. Dr. Taczks' wife looks completely lost."

"She's probably going through an identity crisis. This is the first time I've seen her when she wasn't pregnant."

Jeneil frowned. "That's not very nice of you. I hated all the remarks that got passed around about her at the hospital. I guess they have a lot of children."

"Four," Steve replied.

"Well, that's not really so many."

Steve raised his eyebrows. "Are you serious? You only get two kinds, a boy and a girl, after that you're only repeating yourself."

"Maybe I'm just used to my neighborhood. It's really their business anyway. Mrs. Rezendes has six, Mrs. Foukas has eight."

Steve swallowed his drink with a gasp. "Those aren't families, they're broods."

Jeneil laughed. "And they're the cutest study in genetics. You can group them into families just watching the children play. The Vargus children are a very interesting study. Mr. Vargus is Hispanic and Mrs. Vargus is Polish. They have five children; three dark-haired dark-eyed, one dark-haired blue-eyed, and one blonde-haired dark-eyed, but you can tell they're the Vargus kids. Makes me wonder what the Chang kids will look like."

"Well, if they're not all dark-haired dark-eyed Chinese then Peter should see a lawyer. A Chinese mother and a Chinese father won't create blonde." Jeneil and Steve turned at the sound of another voice.

"Rand," Steve said, smiling tolerantly.

"Are you two antisocial?" Morgan Rand asked, smiling.

"No, we stayed too long by the barbeque and we're cooling off before going into the sun again," Jeneil answered.

Morgan smiled, looking her over slowly. "You've become a beautiful swan, Jeneil."

"Was I an ugly duckling?" she asked, laughing.

Steve grinned. "Say something else, Rand, so you can change feet."

Morgan ignored Steve. "Certainly not, Jeneil, certainly not, just very reluctant to be a swan, that's all."

"Actually, Dr. Rand, if you look closely you'll see it's only a costume. Underneath I'm a hen wondering what all the fuss is in the barnyard."

Morgan smiled. "Not true, Jeneil. I know a real swan when I see one."

"Oh, really, Morgan, what a transparent line and you're not even blushing. You lack conscience, dear, as well as originality," Sondra Rand said as she joined them. "Well, introduce me, will you? I know the blonde, good looking one." She grinned and waved her fingers at Steve. "But I've never met a female entrepreneur before. I've been hearing about you, Jeneil. Your friend, Robert Danzieg, and I have mutual friends and acquaintances." She extended her hand to Jeneil. "I'm Sondra Billings-Rand, Trassade Class of last year."

Jeneil shook her hand briefly. "Jeneil Alden-Connors, State dropout, junior year." Morgan laughed and Steve smiled, enjoying her unassuming ways.

"A college dropout who is the president of her own company and an entrepreneur, fascinating," Sondra replied. "What is the secret of your success?"

Jeneil smiled. "A wise father, a brilliant corporate lawyer, and a responsible management team."

"You've inherited then?" Sondra asked, smiling. "Brilliant I say, only way to do it big anyway. Was your major in Business?"

"No, Literature, American and British."

"Really? You're all over creation, aren't you? How do you manage without a specialty?"

Jeneil shrugged. "I've learned to live lopsided, I guess," she replied jokingly.

"Well, applause to you," Sondra said. "We have a genuine self-made woman here, Morgan."

"Oh, I hope not," Jeneil said, laughing. "I heard the definition of a self-made man was someone who couldn't understand the blueprint so he designed it his way using guesswork." Steve and Morgan laughed.

Sondra smiled. "Don't kid yourself, Jeneil; women designed all the blueprints."

Morgan sighed. "Sondra is pro-women's movement in case you didn't notice."

"Smile when you say that, dear. Be brave even if you have to pretend." Sondra grinned falsely at Morgan as a triangle was rung indicating the food was ready. "Oh good," Sondra sighed, "I'm near collapse from hunger. These outdoor things are so primitive."

Morgan shook his head and sighed. "Sondra, say it louder so Sprague, Young, and Turner will hear."

"Oh goodness, that's right; we could end up having to move to a larger city and real civilization if they don't take you into the fold. Check your blood pressure, Morgan; the thought must have panicked you."

Steve looked at Jeneil as they headed toward the buffet. "The only time I feel sorry for Morgan Rand is when I see him with his wife," he whispered to her.

Jeneil was curious about their choice in each other as spouses. Morgan was from a long line of doctors. He was an outdoors person who liked gentlemen's sports; horseback riding, swimming, and sailing. Jeneil was surprised that he'd been attracted to Sondra who seemed so involved with intellectual interests. Her taste in clothing seemed stylishly erotic, if the two could be combined, and she combined them well. Trassade was an elite girl's college and while Downes was hardly second rate, girls from Trassade usually gravitated to men from the ultra-socially prestigious Payton. She smiled to herself. Individualists, she guessed. No one would put Peter and her together either.

Jeneil and Steve joined the main body of people clustered together in laughter and fun. She disliked large groups and found that she enjoyed the barbeque more when part of smaller groups. Large groups felt smothering to her after a while, especially party groups. To her, they had a pulse and a collective personality that always seemed to evolve from good natured kidding to cruelty and even a twinge of viciousness that eventually caused her skin to hurt from tension. Keeping to the periphery and as out of sight as possible, she was separated from Steve as he was drawn into the group. She went to look at a section of yard that was sprawling with flowers in wild and profuse bloom.

"Don't like parties?" Morgan asked, joining her.

She smiled. "I like parties but I'm a cousin of Fanny Dooley. I like people but I don't like groups. They're like sparklers you buy for a firework display. From a distance they're bright and exciting, but when you get too close you can feel the frenzy as the excitement burns and the individual sparks sting as they hit your skin."

He watched her, totally impressed. "What in the world were you doing at the hospital?"

She was surprised by the directness of his question and its bluntness made her withdraw as a precaution. She studied his face and realized there was nothing ulterior but rather a gentleness about him that calmed her. She shrugged. "Hiding, I guess. I didn't want to be an entrepreneur full-time but life doesn't like drifters either so I played at working. The compromise worked until life looked more closely and insisted I play by the rules. That's why I left the hospital, life caught up with me."

He laughed lightly. "You're a combination of opposites. Shy and bold, quiet and daring."

She nodded. "I guess so, maybe that's why I don't understand groups."

"Oh, I think you understand them very well, probably too well, but your sensitivity won't allow you to build up a tolerance to them."

She laughed. "Is there a cure for that, Doctor?" She paused. "What a question to ask a doctor. You're obligated to reply psychotherapy."

"Not me," he said, laughing heartily as he enjoyed her humor. "I'm standing here with a group of flowers and you remember." They both laughed and Jeneil decided she liked him. She felt an arm slip around her waist and she jumped, startled by the sensation that passed over her.

"Sorry," Steve said, "didn't mean to scare you."

"It's okay." She patted his hand and smiled.

Morgan watched Jeneil and Steve watched Morgan. "What do you think of leaving now?" Steve asked her.

She nodded. "Yes, it's a long drive for you and you have an early schedule." She smiled at Morgan. "Dr. Rand, you're a good group person."

He smiled broadly knowing it was a compliment. "Thanks, I feel the same about you. And please, call me Morgan." Steve was surprised that they seemed to like each other.

After a round of goodbyes, it was another half hour before they actually left. Steve held onto her as they talked their way to the exit, not wanting her to disappear again. "You're a puzzle," he said, as they walked to the car. "You open Wonderland to the world but you're not a party animal."

"The people of Wonderland aren't a group, they're clusters. There's a difference."

"What did you and Rand find so funny? You two looked like buddies when I got there."

Jeneil smiled. "He's always been nice to me. I like his manners and we discovered that we're not group people. We prefer a smaller number of people. You and Sondra are lucky; you both deal easily at parties."

"No, I don't," he disagreed, "but it's what's going on so I deal with it."

"You mean I run away?"

"You disappear," he said, smiling, "very cleverly, too."

She laughed. "Some date, huh? I run off and leave you. Except at the end, you had a death grip on me. Were you afraid I'd disappear again?" she asked, smiling.

"Yes," he answered honestly, and then he laughed. "You were fine talking to people as we were leaving."

She stopped at the car door. "I'm good at hello and goodbye. It's everything in between that ruins me at parties." He laughed, kissed her cheek, and opened her door. "I'm better at one on one," she said, getting into the car.

"I'll bet you are, beautiful. I'll just bet you are." He sighed and got behind the wheel.

*****

Peter yawned as he walked into the medical room. Jane Simpson brought him a cup of coffee. "Break time, Pete. It's a necessity on Monday mornings."

"Oh, thanks," he said. "Has the lab sent up any results on the Rotuno case?"

"It's Monday morning everywhere, it'll probably be another half hour."

Diane Lueger ran up to the nurse's desk. "Hey, you two," she said to Jane and an LPN.

"Oh boy," Jane said, laughing, "news from the Sprague barbeque. It's about time." She leaned against the counter with her coffee cup. "I could scream, I had duty yesterday and missed it. Start at the beginning. How far along is Mrs. Taczks?"

"She's not," Diane snickered, "and Dr. Lassiter brought his wife and she looked fine to me. She never had anything but Perrier, but the big headline is the girl from Records. She sure has changed! I think she turned Dr. Vance's head; he's been asking about her all morning. She looked absolutely stunning and had a gorgeous dress on. M-O-N-E-Y." Peter sat back with his coffee pretending to check a chart as Diane continued on. "She has a great look; even her hair looks stylish, windblown, and her sundress showed off her tan to perfection. Ooo, I wish I could get that all-together look but I don't have money or time for salon treatments and tanning spas. She has a lot of class. She doesn't talk too much but she's very pleasant when she does." Diane looked around and then smiled. "Dr. Rand was buzzing around her quite a bit, but with his mouth of a wife, she must have looked like heaven. I nearly died laughing when she went to Mrs. Sprague's flower garden and Dr. Rand beat out Dr. Vance by a minute. Dr. Vance looked so cheated."

"Where was Steve?" Jane asked.

"He was around. They came holding hands and were together most of the time, but like I said, she's got class and when he got talking with the group she mingled a bit then went to the flower garden. He went to find her and never let her out of his grip after that. Dr. Vance talked to her and she practically got into Steve's pocket. He's lucky Dr. Vance wasn't the one who joined her in the garden, he seemed to like the package."

Jane sighed. "I'm worried; do you think she's really interested in that social column guy, the artist?"

Diane shrugged. "She and Steve looked pretty tight. Do you think they're in…?" Peter sat up and rubbed his forehead.

"I hope so." Jane smiled. "He's crazy about her, I could see it the night I saw them at the restaurant. I hope it's serious."

Diane grinned. "Well, somebody woke her up to the facts of life because she's not the shy girl she was in the records department. She got her act together and she stayed right by Steve most of the night. I think they are because he gets lost in her words when she talks. You're right, he is crazy about her." Peter got up and threw his cup away, the pain in his stomach steady and intense.

*****

The parties continued and Peter heard more and more of Steve and Jeneil in attendance together. He turned a deaf ear but not before almost giving in and calling Jeneil at her office just to be assured. He hung up disgusted with himself before he even dialed. He had to trust her; she certainly trusted him, even after months of marriage to Uette. It was nearing the end of August and nothing had happened since Mark Chun stopped by. Peter hadn't counted on Mark not caring that the baby was his, discouragement all but dragging him down as his family made plans to celebrate the completion of his residency. Jeneil's birthday was getting closer and days in their lives were passing and they were missing them together. It seemed strange to him and he felt cheated, adding to his hatred for Uette. He clung to the note Jeneil had sent him, a photo of her from the passport machine, and the glass unicorn. He endured it all because the unicorn reminded him that Jeneil was his and the mess would end. Uette's baby was due in October and if nothing else happened to exonerate him then he would make plans for a divorce. He felt sick to his stomach at the thought that it would all end up on him despite putting everything on the line to clear his name. He hated Uette for that, too. He put his thoughts aside and hoped the next month would change things for him and Jeneil.

Eight

Dennis's play was scheduled to open in a week and Jeneil was working long hours at the theatre, grateful for the distraction so she wouldn't think of Peter completing his residency and beginning a new life she wouldn't be a part of. She dreaded her upcoming birthday and it was hard to be cheerful knowing she would spend it without him. A hatred for Uette was developing and she was finding out firsthand how hatred could eat at a person like a disease. She struggled against it telling herself it would only be a matter of time before the marriage ended, even if nothing else was uncovered. Those were the terms of the prenuptial agreement. She didn't understand how Uette could be so sneaky and still win, and she felt bad for Peter knowing he'd have to swallow his pride and dignity if nothing was uncovered. Her thoughts stirred her anger towards Uette and she tried to avoid them by throwing herself into the frenzy of the playhouse.

She rested for a minute and she leaned against the filing cabinet in the office before doing some breathing exercises and dance steps to rejuvenate her body. She sighed, the metal of the cabinet felt cool against her face. Her head was aching from working around fumes in the scenery department. Robert walked in and he rubbed her back soothingly and then, standing behind her, massaged her neck and shoulders gently.

"You looked pretty green in there, honey. Are you okay?"

She nodded. "I have a headache. I came in here to do some yoga. I'll be fine."

"I can cure headaches," he said, closing the office door. Taking her hand, he led her to the sofa and tossed the cushions aside. Jeneil watched, surprised that the sofa was a bed and that Robert was opening it.

"Robert, what are you doing?"

"You need to lie down so I have enough room to work beside you. I give great back rubs that cure headaches."

"No, Robert, that isn't necessary. Yoga will take care of it." He took her hand but she resisted. "I don't want to."

"Jeneil, don't tell me you still don't trust me. I've been the epitome of good behavior lately."

She smiled, knowing he was right. "And I enjoy being with you much more now."

He grinned. "Good, now lie down." He took her arms and sat her on the bed.

She sighed. "Oh, why not, prissy women give headaches and get them too or so I'm told." She turned on her stomach.

"This might take longer," he said. "It should be done skin against skin."

"Uh-oh," she said, "I'll pass on that."

He laughed. "I thought you might. It's okay. I'm confident about my massages."

Jeneil decided that she'd enjoy the break even if his massage didn't work. He began by gently feeling her spine and then massaging from the small of her back outward. She smiled; it felt good but Peter was far better, his specialty was the spine after all. And Robert was right; skin against skin was really the best way. She settled for the moment and let her mind relax as yoga had taught her in order for Robert's massage to be effective. He really had been different lately. He still hugged and squeezed and kissed, but he didn't rush at her anymore. She enjoyed his friendship much more as a result and they had actually become closer since the tension had been eliminated. She was glad because she really liked Robert. Their souls were communicating again.

"How's your head?" he asked, after a few minutes.

"Much better," she answered, "a lot better, thanks."

He leaned forward near her ear. "You have a terrific body."

"Thank you for that objective and professional opinion, Mr. Masseuse," she said, turning onto her side as she felt his hands glide gently toward her waist.

He leaned on his elbow and touched her cheek with his hand. "You're so beautiful."

"We'd better get back to work, Robert." She moved away from him quickly and stood up. He grinned and got off the sofa bed, and she replaced the cushions after he refolded the mattress and slid it into position. "Thank you. You're a nice person. Want some apple juice?" she asked, going to her desk.

He watched her. "You're tough, honey. I give you one of my better back rubs and you tell me I'm a nice person and offer me apple juice. I could end up in therapy because of you."

She chuckled. "It's not you, Robert. I'm cerebral."

"What's that?" he asked, taking the cup she offered him.

"Mentally conditioned to be physically celibate." She sipped her drink.

Mrs. Nordstrom, a volunteer, appeared at the door. "Mr. Danzieg, we've finished the panel of beige, should we start shading?"

"No," he said, putting his cup down, "no, I'll shade. The next panel should be ready from the workshop. I'll go get it." He looked at Jeneil with unanswered questions in his eyes. "Thanks for the break."

"Thank you," she said, smiling gently. He nodded and left with the new discovery about her filling his thoughts.

*****

Peter stayed at the hospital as long as he could without it looking strange and left reluctantly, hanging in the locker room before walking slowly to his car.

"You're later than I thought you'd be." Uette came from the kitchen smiling. "I fixed a special dinner."

"Why?" he asked unemotionally.

"Because I wanted to. With your hours so regular now and that awful second shift being a thing of the past, I'd like our life to be saner."

Peter wanted to laugh at the thought of their life being sane at all under the present conditions and felt their relationship would be considered off-center. "My mother said she'd send some lasagna. They were having it last night. She makes great lasagna."

"I threw it out," Uette replied.

"Why?" He was surprised and disappointed. His mother's lasagna had been the bright spot in his coming home.

"I didn't know that you had asked for it. She makes me crazy with her fussing. Make sure you rest, Uette. Don't overdo it, Uette. Would you like some help, Uette? I can hire someone if you'd prefer, Uette." Uette exhaled and shook her head.

He was annoyed. His mother was genuinely concerned for Uette to the point of lecturing him every chance she got about being a decent husband and Uette didn't appreciate her. She didn't even like her. He thought of his mother's treatment of Jeneil and the kindness Jeneil showed in return.

"Come on, dinner's ready. Sit," she said, pointing to the dining room. "I'll be right there." He sat at the table and looked at the flowers and candles, the good china and crystal, and wished he didn't have to. The closer it got to her due date, the more he resented her. The baby wasn't his and he didn't want it to have his name. Uette brought a bowl of chicken salad and another with a green tossed salad. "I'm starting to understand this cooking business now. It's not so bad once it makes sense."

Peter wondered what happened to the leftovers from the day before. His mother's lasagna would have been a free meal, too. He reminded himself not to be so critical, she was at least cooking. The chicken salad nearly blistered his tongue and he drank some water.

"It's too spicy," Uette said. "I think I'll leave out the curry powder next time." The telephone rang and she went to answer it as Peter recovered. "It's the hospital," she said, frowning, and Peter got up quickly.

"Pete, its Jerry Tollman."

"Yeah, Jerry, what is it?"

"I'm in ER and two people were just admitted. The woman asked to see you."

Peter froze. "What are their names?" he asked, holding his breath.

"Lin Chi Ding and Robert Calvers."

Peter's heart stopped. "Was it an accident?"

"Looks like a mugging."

"Thanks, Jerry. I'll be right in," Peter said, and hung up quickly.

"Aren't you going to finish dinner?" Uette asked, as Peter went to the door.

"No," he answered, and closed the door behind him.

Peter's heart beat furiously as he drove to the hospital wondering how severely Lin Chi and Bo had been beaten. Anger combined with fear and he had to concentrate on calming down. The ER was busy and he strained to look around for Jerry.

"Jerry, where are they?" Peter asked, catching sight of him in the second aisle.

"Cubicles 3 and 4, want their charts?"

"Yeah," Peter replied, trying to breathe normally. Looking at a chart, he saw broken ribs and lacerations. He reached cubicle 4 before he finished reading. Bo was lying on the Gurney as an intern stitched the skin over his left eyebrow.

"Hey, Pete," Bo said, trying to smile.

Peter sighed heavily as his chest tightened. "Shit, man. What'd they hit you with, a truck?"

"I freaked," Bo replied. "They started on Lin Chi because she did all the talking and I saw fire. Cool me, huh?"

Peter shook his head. "I'm sorry, Bo. I really am. I'll cover what the diner loses from being closed."

"Closed?" Bo asked. "When we started looking over our shoulders, I started looking for a grill. They came to the diner just as we closed, made it look like a robbery, even busted up some booths. They were bad anyway so I can replace them now, insurance will cover it. You can help me by putting Lin Chi in a strait jacket or else I won't live too long."

"Damn right, you stupid ass," Lin Chi said from the next cubicle. "You're lucky they beat you on your head. Wait until I get my hands on you for that kamikaze stunt you pulled."

"See," Bo said, "straight jacket or Valium, either one's okay with me, Pete."

Peter looked at Bo's chart. "You're going to be hurting really bad tomorrow." He sighed and shook his head.

"Nah," Bo said. "It takes more than four gooks to cream a brotha', Doc."

"They sent four?"

Bo nodded. "Go look at Lin Chi, you won't believe it. I almost expected it. There have been some new faces in the diner lately, black faces I've never seen before, so I figured I was being set up for something. It's in the eyes, Pete. I thought maybe a heist. I never linked blacks with the other group. Lin Chi did though. She was ready."

Peter drew the curtains to Lin Chi's cubicle and walked in closing the curtains behind him. His stomach knotted at the sight of her left eye nearly swollen shut. The corner of her mouth was swollen and her lip was cut. "Oh, baby," he said, taking her hand and holding her head to get a better look at her eye. Nearly the whole left side of her face was purple. "The lousy bastard," he choked up. "Shit," he said, gritting his teeth.

"Hey, dude," she said, looking at him with concern. "I don't think you got it all straight. We're home free, Pete. Don't you get it? Look at me." She pointed to her face. "No broken nose, only a bruised eye, and they didn't touch my body. Not one broken bone. Not one, Pete. The muscle was Mark's personal special forces. They knew exactly what they were doing, man. This was a thank you. They couldn't let us get off completely free after we snooped so far into their ranks but it could've been a helluva lot worse." Peter couldn't believe how well she and Bo were taking it. "You got to him, dude. You did it." She squeezed his hand gratefully. "We're like this because of you. If they came after us on a fishing trip, we'd have really bled. Your talk with Mark eased it, even the diner. It was so well planned. Only the booths that needed work got smashed up and they ripped off the register to make it look official. Bo can collect insurance so we're coming out of this ahead of the game. There would be no broken bones if that fathead Bo hadn't gone after them like some hero. He pushed them so they had to knot him. He was outta control."

Peter kissed her unbruised cheek. "You're one helluva woman, Lin Chi. I mean that."

"Well, look at you," she said, touching his face affectionately. "The White Princess has turned you into Prince Charming. I like it. It goes with your new life here and it looks good on you, don't lose it." She patted his face. "Pete, I gotta tell ya something. I expected a hit when I saw new faces in and out lately. While I was waitin' for the other shoe to drop, I got real mad at the bitch. I did, Pete. I expected to bleed bad for her...." She paused and took a breath. "When I told them the truth like you said to do, I added a little more. I told them she was telling only a certain few that she wanted you because

Mark was scum. It's probably true anyway, she just ain't said it to nobody. I figured she deserved to have her ass kicked for lying so I kicked it good. I hope you ain't mad."

He stared and then shrugged. "What the hell, my guess is he won't hurt her because of the baby anyway." He sighed. "I just wish I knew what he was going to do about it."

She patted his hand. "Don't wait for a call from him to talk it over. We just wait some more, Pete. We wait and see what he does."

"Do you think he might not want anybody to know the baby is his?"

She shrugged. "I can't read it anymore. Nobody I know has ever pulled what that bitch did. So the odds are up for grabs. What's your panic?"

"The baby's due in October and I don't want it to carry my name." He paced and shook his head. "Everything I do gets me closer to nothing faster." He ran his fingers through his hair. "You and Bo get mugged and for what? The ball never falls in my court."

She looked at him compassionately. "Don't hit bottom yet, Pete. At least you know who the father is."

"Yeah," he said quietly, "but what good has it done me?"

Jerry Tollman walked in with x-rays. "Want to read them, Pete?"

"Yes, I do, Jerry. Thanks a lot for calling me, too."

Jerry smiled. "You bet. The viewer's free now."

Peter involved himself in their care and stayed with them until they were released, making sure Lin Chi's kidney wouldn't trauma as a precaution and that they had enough painkillers for three days. Lin Chi had driven in because Bo had been bleeding, but Bo drove home. As Peter drove home, he thought of the two of them being so cheerful about how easy the attack had been. Lin Chi was a very thin woman who wasn't very tall and Peter felt mean and ugly when he got to the apartment thinking of the pain her injuries must have caused her.

"Hi," Uette said, smiling as he walked in. It took every ounce of determination in him to stay silent. He thought of Jeneil and headed toward his room without talking. "What happened? You were fine when you left here."

"Nothing," he answered sullenly, "an emergency, okay. I'm tired."

"Can't you stay and talk to me for a while?"

He turned sharply as anger choked him; anger that her lie had caused two decent people to be beaten for trying to get to the truth. He thought of Jeneil and stayed calm. "No, I have early rounds."

"Well then, just have dessert. I killed myself making a Baked Alaska. It wasn't easy for me," she pouted. "It's bad enough the hospital ruined dinner."

He was out of patience. "Uette, shove it." He turned and walked to his room, slamming the door behind him.

"Good grief!" She shook her head, stunned by his outburst. "What a pill! Doctors are no fun. The Chinese Stud, humph, he's more the Chinese Dud." She felt her stomach as the baby moved. "Stupid baby anyway, why would he think I'm sexy?" Tears rolled down her cheeks. "This isn't fair," she cried softly, feeling sorry for herself and for the life she had been convinced so many months ago would be perfect. She didn't have much time before the baby was born and then he would walk out. It just wasn't fair. Why couldn't he see the truth? She'd have to raise the baby by herself and who would want her with a kid trotting behind screaming mommy? She had ruined her life because of Peter Chang. He owed her. She paced angrily. Jeneil didn't even want him anymore. Why would she? She had a life most girls would kill for; money, freedom to have fun, and men at each elbow every time she turned around. The joke was on Uette; the memory of Jeneil was so entrenched in Peter that he couldn't see straight. Jeneil could teach her some tricks, the way she breezed through life and men's hearts without any effort. "Wake up, Uette, a mouse isn't a jungle animal and that woman knows her way around the jungle. It's in her blood."

*****

Peter kept in close touch with Lin Chi and Bo, going to the diner after work for a week to help clean and set up for business. Business had picked up after the attack, people coming to see the damage and to buy at least a cup of coffee. He took Lin Chi's favorite Chinese food from the China Bay one night and they had dinner in one of the new booths. Lin Chi and Bo were both smiling now that they could, and Peter left for home reluctantly after having dinner with them. It was the first enjoyable meal he'd had since marrying Uette. It wasn't the food, it was the company. The relaxation he felt was like a short vacation.

He missed Jeneil and there were things happening in his life that he wanted to discuss with her and felt that he should. Dr. Sprague and Dr. Maxwell had each approached him about joining their practices. Each had a different style; Dr. Sprague's was large and corporate while Dr. Maxwell's was smaller and had a less business atmosphere. He was tempted to call Jeneil since his choice would affect her too, but he couldn't risk jeopardizing her so close to the end of their situation. He couldn't be sure he wasn't being watched and he realized how paranoid that seemed, so he assumed that she would tell him the choice was his to make. Feeling that he wasn't corporate material, he thanked Dr. Sprague and began the legalities of a partnership with Dr. Maxwell. In saving face, he had come to realize that he was not civilized and probably never would be. He liked Dr. Maxwell's practice; it was Medical/Surgical which was where he felt comfortable. He wouldn't be making the kind of money a larger practice would command, but Dr. Maxwell was one of the best and he felt satisfied with that. Dr. Sprague had understood and surprised Peter by asking to continue their weekly meetings, stating he wanted to see the situation through to the end. Peter had been impressed when Dr. Sprague changed them to dinner meetings acknowledging his official status as a doctor and allowing him the dignity of that position. He liked Dr. Sprague and was glad it had been a professional decision, not a personal one, between him and Dr. Maxwell. It would have been a difficult choice.

Dr. Sprague had been a strong supporter over the past months which Peter hadn't realized until Dr. Sprague told him that in his case the medical group had broken protocol. They hadn't invited him to parties to be observed because they were impressed with the stamina, performance, and dignity he had shown in his personal life over so long a period without so much as a flicker of it interfering with his professional life. His personal life was kept so quiet that the only murmurs passed through the corridors were about marriage not seeming to agree with him because he'd lost weight and looked tired. Knowing that marriage and medical training were two different careers to juggle at the same time, gossips never looked more closely and Peter's silence was accepted as part of who he was. The medical group assessed all of those qualities and decided he had proven himself without the usual screening.

Dr. Sprague had told the group he knew Peter's personal life well and that his choice in a wife would meet with their approval. He then hoped he was right not knowing how Steve and Peter intended to explain Jeneil. The situation was getting tight but he trusted the three since they had juggled it so well and Steve had told him that Jeneil was Peter's. He admired Steve for that because having seen the two of them together he knew Steve's feelings were genuine. It saddened him in a way to watch Steve pay the price and he hoped Steve would find someone like her. Dr. Sprague liked Jeneil and decided she was the ingredient that made the trio work so well. She was a combination of opposites with an offbeat view of life that allowed her to accept the trio and both maverick surgeons as normal. She was different but she didn't advertise it like Morgan Rand's wife whom the group accepted readily because she was a Trassade alumna and her family was socially connected and on the cusp of what was deemed being elite. At least her biting tongue was usually reserved for her husband. Jeneil seemed to fit in better than Sondra Rand or Mary-Elizabeth Taczks, who seemed reluctant to fit in at all but who was at least quiet, pleasant, and very supportive of her husband's career and its demands.

Everyone was different in their own way and what the medical group hoped to achieve by screening was to eliminate extreme elements and absurdities. The group was too large and worked too closely to have difficult personalities restricting the camaraderie the senior doctors hoped to achieve. Fitting in was important and the senior doctors had found that socializing regularly was good for the group as it grew over the years so they continued the tradition. A subtle division had emerged over the years as the original doctors became the senior members of which Dr. Sprague was the youngest with the newer or intermediate members being the majority. With the older members lay the diehard prestige and power, with the newer lay the energy with a subtle power.

*****

Dennis's play opened and since it was the last production of the summer season, the pace began to slow at the playhouse. The critics were very generous and the audiences were very large, Dennis now having a following of faithful fans. The baby cooperated and didn't make its debut until a week after the opening, forcing Karen and Dennis into the role of parents to a nine pound son whom both basked in with great pride. Jeneil stopped by the hospital to see Karen taking with her Crab Monique from Tiel's, which was Karen's all-time favorite restaurant fare. Karen ate without conscience for having worked so hard to produce Matthew Blair whom his father called "Bruiser, the Sumo Wrestler." He teased Karen that the baby's swaddling clothes were twin-sized sheets and he was going to return the baby carriage her parents sent for a garden cart instead. While nine pounds sounded huge, the baby seemed quite small to Jeneil. She had never seen a baby so newly arrived. Hollis's were born while she was away at college and Mrs. Rezendes's last one had been two-months-old when she had stopped to talk to her during a walk. Jeneil looked at the babies in the nursery with awe as they accomplished some of the first achievements required of them; breathing and crying. They looked so beautiful and new and absolutely amazing. Her eye caught sight of a slightly darker skinned baby and she smiled seeing its dark straight hair. Checking the tag on its bed, she saw that it was two-days-old. She thought of Peter and missed him and then, thinking about Uette, she felt anger stir. Wanting to avoid negative vibes, she went back to Karen's room to visit with someone who was cheerful and happy.

"Hey!" Robert said, walking into Karen's room, seeming surprised to see Jeneil. "I was just at Wonderland. You told me earlier that you'd be home so I went to surprise you with dinner from Tiel's. I wanted to go out on the *Sea Urchin* before summer was over."

"You didn't mention it to me," Jeneil defended herself.

"You don't announce a surprise, honey," he said, chucking her chin. He kissed her lips lightly then visited with Karen, fawning over her and praising the wonderful job she had done in producing a baby. Jeneil understood Robert's magnetism as she watched. He truly appreciated women and fully believed that Karen was more deserving of praise than Dennis, feeling her contribution was greater. Karen absorbed his words through every pore and beamed her gratitude for the praise. Dennis walked in carrying a colorfully wrapped gift and Robert kissed Karen's cheek before taking Jeneil's hand and tugging her to her feet. "Come on, beautiful, let's leave the parents to discuss Matthew's college fund. I'd like to drift on the *Sea Urchin*." Slipping one arm around her shoulder, he headed quickly toward the door saying his goodbyes. Jeneil turned abruptly, leaving his grasp and returning to pick up her purse, taking a moment to say a decent goodbye. Robert leaned against the doorframe watching her steadily. "Love your spunk, beautiful," he said, taking her hand as she joined him at the door. Dennis watched closely as they left. Looking down at the floor, he rubbed his chin and sighed before going to the door.

"Robert," Dennis called softly.

Robert and Jeneil turned. "What?"

Dennis faltered. "Uh…nothing really, it'll keep."

"Okay," Robert said, turning to leave. Jeneil looked at Dennis curious about his behavior. Dennis gave her a half smile and held up his hand in a wave goodbye.

"Be careful on the boat," Dennis said quietly.

Jeneil smiled gently and nodded. "We will be." She waved briefly and Dennis watched Robert put his arm around her waist and squeeze her to him as they left. Dennis rubbed his chin and sighed, staring at their backs as they got on the elevator.

Nine

The air was still and warm reminding everyone that summer was not over even though Labor Day had passed. Daylight was clinging to the last hour allotted to it giving people a chance to extend summertime fun before fall officially arrived. Jeneil changed to a swimsuit and waited on the dock for Robert to bring food from the car. Having also changed, Robert left the food with Jeneil and waded to the boat. Holding it for her, she climbed in after it had settled. Dunking under the water, he then climbed in.

Jeneil shivered. "How can you do that? There are all kinds of sea life racing about in that water and you just wade through it all."

He grinned, drying his hair with a towel. "I've had assertiveness training."

She laughed. "I believe it. I think you could out stare a shark." He smiled then opened the picnic basket and handed her a food container and silverware. "Ooo, the butterfly shrimp with Tiel's cold herb lemon sauce. Robert, you're sweet. This is a great choice and I love picnics in the *Sea Urchin*."

"I do, too," he said, buttering a roll. Turning on music from a small cassette player, he settled next to her as she sat sideways across the boat. He poured some mineral water.

"No wine for you?" she asked, surprised since he always had wine with dinner.

"No," he answered simply, holding his glass up in a toast, "to a very special woman."

"Who?" she asked teasing, and he gave her an enchanting half smile. "May she learn to accept a compliment graciously one day."

"I think she's terrific," he said, cutting into a shrimp.

"Let's not talk about me, Robert. Who's sponsoring the collection at TAI's museum? I slipped in to see it on my way back from a meeting today. There wasn't any literature so I was lost but some of the workmanship reminded me of one of the Faberge' collection."

"The silver one with the chained stopper?"

"Yes."

He nodded. "It struck me the same way, but I don't know who's sponsoring it. I do think it's poorly presented. There wasn't any literature when I was there either."

Jeneil thought for a minute. "I find it irritating when I come across a display of something I find interesting and there's nothing to help me understand it. There's a gemstone collection at the Natural History Museum that's so pretty, but you need to know gemstones in order to identify them. If people took the time to study all the subjects on display, they wouldn't have the time or the admission to visit the museum. We fall so far short in self-education in some museums. They cater to the initiated." He smiled and kissed her cheek gently. "I'm glad you agree," she said jokingly. He chuckled and closed his food container. She handed hers to him and he took the cloth napkins and replaced everything in the picnic basket. Settling back against the side of the boat, he leaned closer to her and was silent. Jeneil watched him. "Is something wrong?"

"Life isn't perfect, sweetheart. There's always something wrong somewhere for somebody."

She smiled. "That would make a good chorus for a song. There's always something wrong somewhere for somebody," she sang quietly. "Too bad," she giggled, "its tempo fits a happy Jamaican beat but the words are too sad. Maybe a country western song. Or maybe it's a Shakespearian melodrama. Alas! Anon life doth always scattereth rain clouds that washeth human tears that earth might live."

He smiled, amused, and turned his body slightly, resting his arm on the edge of the boat. "Has anyone discovered that you've escaped yet?" he asked, teasing.

She nodded. "Yes, but I'm so cute and harmless they usually keep my secret," she replied, and then snickered. He chuckled and shook his head.

"You're a study," he said, twisting a lock of her hair around his index finger.

"Please, let's not talk about me," she said, frowning.

He watched her steadily. "Okay, let's talk about prissy women."

She wrinkled her eyebrows. "As gossip or a dissertation?"

He grinned. "Is there ever any gossip about prissy women?"

"Of course," she replied, raising her knees and resting her arms on them. "Gossips will talk about why she's prissy. Gossips talk about everybody."

"Why are women prissy?" he asked, watching her.

She shrugged her shoulders. "Ain't none of my business, fella. The constitution allows life, liberty, and the right to be prissy."

"Do you think they're prissy by choice?"

She looked at him. "Is it any of our business? And I want to know why this isn't a dissertation. It sounds like an interview. You ask questions and I answer them." She grinned and raised an eyebrow. "Oh, I get it, you're calling me prissy." She laughed lightly. "I'm not prissy. Prissy is tied to religious beliefs, isn't it?"

He grinned. "Then what's cerebral, an atheistic word for it?"

She smiled as she watched him. "Robert, I'm eccentric, not stupid. Don't you think I've noticed that we're talking about me and the subject is sex or rather my attitude about it? Is our relationship slipping back to physical?"

He shook his head. "You are the slickest woman I've ever met. How the hell can you look like that in a swimsuit, have a head full of brains, and be so backward about sex?"

"I'm not backward about sex. I know all about it."

"Prove it." He smiled slyly, figuring he had her in verbal checkmate.

"Okay." She grinned. "We'll start with the birds and the bees or maybe rabbits are more your speed. There are female rabbits and male rabbits…."

He chuckled. "You're a bitch, my beauty, but I can play your game of mental football, too."

She raised her eyebrows. "Is that what I'm doing? I thought I was playing Scheherazade."

He smiled and watched her steadily. "Let's dissertate, beautiful. You wanted to. I get to choose the subject."

She looked at him, surprised. "Maybe to be fair something should be tossed, like you out of the boat."

He laughed. "No, I choose the subject. Now this is a serious question, after all cerebral is intellectual." She waited cautiously and watched as he put his head gently on her shoulder. Then, he leaned toward her and kissed her cheek, staying close to her. "I would like our relationship to be sexual. Why can't it be?"

"Oh, Robert, you're going to ruin this evening."

"Answer my question," he whispered.

She sighed. "Because I don't want our relationship to be sexual."

"Is it me?"

She closed her eyes and sighed again, hearing the sincerity in his words. "Robert, we've talked about all this before," she replied, bringing her knees closer to her and wrapping her arms around them.

He shook his head. "No, we've talked about Peter before. You still care for him. Its nine months later, honey."

"Robert, I more than care for him, I'm in love with him."

He studied her profile as she stared ahead and he put his arm around her shoulder. "Jeneil, it's over. The guy's married. He's gone. Shit, even he wouldn't want you to stop living. Honey, you have to move on." He kissed her temple gently.

She bit her lower lip hoping she wouldn't become emotional. "I'm sorry, Robert; I'm not made that way. When I'm over loving Peter then I'll think about another relationship."

He touched her hair, following a wave as it flowed to her neck and then he kissed it. "Jeneil, you'll get over Peter by getting involved with someone else. Maybe a physical attraction first and then the emotional will follow." He kissed her shoulder.

"I don't believe that," she said flatly. "It's impossible to give yourself to someone if you're in love with someone else. Peter is special to me." She swallowed as she felt her throat tighten with emotion.

"Let me prove something to you," he said sincerely.

"What?" she asked, and turned her head to look at him. Loosening the tight grip she had on her knees, he took her hand. "Robert, don't," she said, beginning to resist.

He held her hand tightly. "Jeneil, honey, trust me. This will be physical, not sexual."

"There's a difference?" she asked, raising an eyebrow.

He stared in disbelief. "Honey, didn't you ever make out when you were dating as a kid?"

"No," she said, "I never dated as a kid. Oh, wait a minute. Yes, I guess I did make out once with a good friend who taught me how to kiss."

"You never dated?" he asked, still in disbelief. She shook her head. "Where'd you grow up, in a convent?" He kissed her cheek. "Holy shit, what are you, a nun who left the order or something?"

She became annoyed. "No, I wasn't a nun and I'm not a freak, Robert. Okay, so I didn't date but I'm a woman, a woman capable of passionately loving a man and I have done just that, in fact so well that I still love him and probably always will. I have no problem with my sexual identity. I just didn't follow the usual path on my way to achieving it."

He rubbed her forearm gently. "I didn't mean you were a freak. You just shock me. I thought naïve was a gimmick with you and to learn it isn't, well, it's…it's…a shock."

"I'm not naïve," she insisted.

He smiled. "Honey, you are. You understand love but not dating. You understand marriage but not courtship."

"Does anyone understand dating? Is there courtship at all anymore? There seem to be degrees of urges; coming on to someone, putting a move on someone, and now something called making out which isn't sexual, it's only physical. Personally, I think the rules of the whole game are governed by what one's conscience will tolerate."

"That's about it, honey." He squeezed her hand gently, totally overwhelmed by his latest discovery about her. He slipped his arm behind her and stroked the back of her neck lightly. Kissing her hand, he smiled at her. "Jeneil, you and I are going to make out."

"Robert, you don't understand," she said, pulling her hand away quickly.

"Relax, honey. It'll happen when the moment's right and this isn't the moment."

She sighed with relief. "Then the craziness is over?"

He lay back against the side of the boat and smiled. "I want to drift on the *Sea Urchin* before the season is over. The moon is full, bullfrogs are croaking, crickets are chirping, and I'd like to absorb it all and fix it as a memory to brighten my winter days."

Jeneil smiled broadly. "Now that's the Robert I know and love." She relaxed and slipped beside him and rested her head on the boat's inflated side.

He turned his head and looked at her. "You're quite a woman."

"Oh, Robert, let's stop talking about me. That's how things went wrong before. We recovered, so let's not push our luck."

As the boat bobbed and drifted, Jeneil understood how Robert had wandered away from friendship. The full moon was spinning magic, using its romantic silver light to soften everything it touched. The sensation of the boat's movement combined with their bodies wearing just the plus side of naked made the effect electrical. Jeneil became aware of the sensuousness of the atmosphere. There was an ambiance and she made a mental note to do it with Peter. It felt too good to not be enjoyed with him and she knew he'd like it a lot. She smiled to herself, wishing she could call him and have him meet her at Wonderland. She allowed herself to think about him physically; his strength, his gentleness, and his incredible passion.

Robert watched her closely. He leaned closer to her and kissed her lips gently. She didn't resist and he kissed her more strongly. She still didn't resist. Slipping his arms around her, he drew closer to her. The kiss became electric and he was surprised and pleased when she responded to him. She responded to his kisses fully and he felt passion growing between them. He had always thought she must be passionate but experiencing her responsiveness convinced him. He had made another discovery about her; she didn't know what it was, she had no idea how far was too far, and she didn't play games. It was all or nothing with her and he didn't want to stop.

Jeneil hadn't realized how much she missed being physical. She missed being kissed and being wanted, and the feeling of passion within her felt familiar and enjoyable. It wasn't until Robert moved her swimsuit strap and she actually saw him that she brought herself to the reality of the moment. She was married! She belonged to Chang! She grabbed Robert's wrist with both hands. "No, Robert. No, please. I'm so sorry." She pulled away quickly and sat up, using his immobility from shock as the second to act. She adjusted her swimsuit and covered her face with both hands, trying to calm down.

He moved to her side and put his arms around her. "Jeneil, baby, don't back away," he said, kissing her neck.

"Robert, please, you have to listen to me." She moved away from him and the boat tilted and bobbed.

He sighed. "Honey, you're going to ruin the moment. Listen to your body."

"Robert, it's not over between me and Peter."

"What!" Robert stared. "But he's married."

She rubbed her temples as she wondered what to tell him. She sighed and shook her head. "This is all my fault. I should have been honest and open. Robert, Peter got married to save face. He's trying to prove that the baby isn't his. Either way, he plans to get a divorce and we're going to be married."

"His wife's pregnant and you're waiting for him?" Robert asked, shocked by the news.

"The baby isn't his, Robert," Jeneil reminded him.

Robert scooped up a handful of water and rubbed his face. He scooped up another handful and drizzled it over his chest. Running his fingers through his hair, he shook his head. He began pulling the tow rope into the boat to bring them to shore. Jeneil watched, wondering what he was thinking. He docked and secured the line. After getting out of the boat, he held his hand to her and she stepped out.

"Jeneil, it's the end for me, honey. You and Peter are beyond normal." He touched her cheek lovingly. "I love you, really. I think you're something special, my feelings were getting desperate and deeper, but I'm gone. I do have to thank you though. I never thought I'd know what to look for in a serious relationship, but after you, I know I want a woman who'll react to my work the way you did the first day I saw you in Mike Phillip's gallery. I've been crazy about you since then. I thought we'd be terrific together sexually and after tonight I know we would've been." He looked at the ground for a second and then back up at her. "But you're never going to be free of Peter. I accept that now and I can't handle it. What you expressed as you looked at the sculptures, I want you to express to me as a man. You feel that for Peter. I couldn't live with the jealousy; I'm not made of the right stuff. It's beyond me." He kissed her lips softly. "I wish you and Peter the best. I hope it works out for you." Touching her cheek, he smiled. "You're beautiful, kid, don't change. Above all, set you free. The drums I've been hearing are yours, honey. They're deep inside of you. Let them beat out the rhythm and listen to it. Don't be afraid to dance." He picked up the picnic basket and walked away.

Jeneil stood on the dock watching him leave as tears streamed down her cheeks. She tried to deal with all she was feeling but she had no idea what Robert's goodbye meant and she wondered if she had lost him as a friend as well. His words had taken her by surprise. She saw the headlights of his car through the shrubbery and watched as they backed away and drove off. She experienced a feeling of loss. Walking to the house, she wiped the tears that fell. She showered and felt better. Turning off the lights, she went into her bedroom and stood before the poster of Chang.

"You and I need to talk, Peter. The summer is ending just in time, for me anyway. I've wondered throughout the past days and months if my life had tinges of betrayal laced through it, but tonight I learned something about myself. I'm capable of betraying you." Tears filled her eyes and spilled down her cheeks, her throat sore from holding back sobs. "I can try to justify it and say cerebral had been set aside, that I was thinking about you when it happened, but they would just be excuses. The truth is I slipped from superlative. I lost sight of it momentarily and that's all betrayal takes. I need you to achieve superlative. Lesser than that is confusing and doesn't make sense to me. Your black and white approach to life seems so clean and simple after a summer of grey. Grey is like a mist, like the fog that has penetrated our lives. I told Chang that I would never betray him. Can he accept an almost? In his black and white philosophy is almost in the shaded grey area between? Is it forgivable?"

She wiped the tears that fell. "I had gotten smug in my attitude about Uette and her connection to the Dragons, even judging her harshly, but now I can identify with the confusion it must have taken to get herself so entangled. I've been angry at her for the lie she used to trap you. It's almost totally understandable now because if Chang doesn't understand my near betrayal I know I'd use both excuses without conscience to argue my defense just to have him forgive me. I understand Uette now." She sighed. "I'm grateful for that, I guess, because the hatred I was feeling for her fed my confusion in the grey area. Superlative isn't grey, it's white. Nothing can be seen clearly looking through anger and hatred. I hope the Prince returns the glass unicorn soon because the Princess is having a real struggle getting through the quest unscathed." She leaned against the poster and cried softly.

*****

Jeneil threw herself into the corporation and the playhouse's final days to keep from thinking about her loneliness. The bright spot and sense of contentment came from her father's manuscripts which she found interesting. Once the temporary life of summer was over, she planned to work on his writings. She was relieved that Robert wasn't angry and that he wanted to remain friends as much as she did. After witnessing how smoothly he handled the situation, she decided there was a definite advantage to experiencing relationships for finesse alone. Her own lack of sophistication in that area seemed at best comical and at the very least pathetic, considering her age. Without too much analyzing, she could see that single life was not for her. A steady, solid relationship felt secure and allowed her far more freedom in her life than being single. The confinement of being alone, eligible, and part of the game was too mentally and emotionally taxing.

Looking back at her relationship with Peter, she could see that the effort and progress they had made as a couple to be committed to each other was interesting and at times exciting. There was also a sense of satisfaction at having been able to communicate so well with at least one other human being. Their relationship made her feel complete and fulfilled. She decided that she was definitely monogamous and could easily spend the rest of her life belonging to one man and working on that relationship to a superlative level. It's what she wanted and she couldn't wait for Uette to have her baby so Peter would be free. Each day became easier as she reminded herself that Peter loved her and would understand what happened between her and Robert. Each day that passed meant another day closer to her reunion with Peter and life became exciting as she began mentally planning the details of that celebration.

The end of September was around the corner and the air was becoming cooler during the day and chillier at night. Summer's light and airy atmosphere was replaced by fall's more somber personality made visible by sweaters and jackets worn as people adjusted to life and its evolution to yet another season. The playhouse was almost completely unwound and packed away, and a harvest party was decided upon as a congratulations and farewell to officially end the season. During the planning, Wonderland was suggested as the ideal location. Jeneil didn't mind since the details weren't left up to her and the party was a 'bring your own' kind of event. She didn't like large parties that she had to prepare for and hostess.

*****

Peter stood before the mirror and fixed his tie. He was having trouble getting used to dressing in suits every day. He had to order more and had gone to the tailor Jeneil and Steve had used. As he put his new life together, he missed Jeneil. He felt cheated thinking about her fussing over Steve as he began private practice. Calling Uette an obscenity under his breath, he picked up his suit jacket and left the bedroom. Uette was in the kitchen sitting at the table with a cup of coffee. His mother had had a party for him and Uette had made life a living hell the weeks before insisting that it was her place as his wife to have the party. Uette and his mother had an argument which left his mother very hurt. She no longer called or brought food by since Uette had called her an overpowering, overprotective, intrusive person and a royal pain. There had been an icy silence from his mother since the argument three days before the party. Peter had let the two of them battle it out, not interfering figuring they deserved each other. He simply walked out of the room anytime Uette tried to explain her position. She had finally stopped trying and had become silent for the past two days. Peter sighed with relief that he hadn't contacted Jeneil or Steve either. At least he could be sure she wasn't stewing over that.

"Peter, I'm going away this weekend," Uette said, fidgeting with her coffee cup.

"Okay," he replied, not caring.

"I need a break before the baby is born. The argument with your mother has left me tense and my family is furious that I was even part of it, my grandfather especially. The turmoil is draining me. My grandmother gave me money for a baby layette but Phyllis is having a baby shower for me in another week, so I'm going to take money and spend it on me and a weekend in Boston. I'd like a fur jacket." Peter choked on his juice wondering how much she'd been given. She sighed. "With you making a better salary now, we can afford to buy baby furniture ourselves." He noticed she had been doing that a lot lately, talking like they were a normal couple. "Any objections to that?" she asked, without looking up.

"Nope," he answered. "I'll have a new budget for you next month. Trust me, it won't give you too much more than you have right now. I want to approve the amount of money that's spent on anything."

"Of course," she said, still fidgeting. "My parents told me they'd buy the baby furniture, but things are so icy there toward me that I can't be sure anymore."

"Whatever," Peter said, rinsing his glass and putting it in the dishwasher.

Uette called out to him as he reached the kitchen door. "I appreciate you not taking sides in this war with your mother. Your silence is so pleasant compared to the lecturing from my family about dignity, honor, and her being your mother and how that's a place of respect. I love your strength and steadiness. I'm glad you're not old-fashioned Chinese."

Peter sighed. "Uette, don't mistake my silence for more than it is. She's my mother. You and I are going to get a divorce. That's the tune to that song." He walked out.

Uette grinned as she listened to the apartment door close. "Don't be too sure of that my darling husband. I like having a gorgeous hunk of a husband who's a doctor and looks after himself so well that he's no trouble at all. I can teach you to have fun. That's all you need to be perfect. I like getting what I want and you're it. I put myself through a lot of trouble to become Mrs. Peter Chang. I deserve the name. It's owed to me. I've worked hard to achieve it. It's my name and you belong to me."

Ten

Jeneil was in the mood for a party by Friday night. She and Steve had collected wood and debris the week before for a bonfire, and she had everyone collect glass jars so she could make candles with melted crayons and wax to put along the beach. She bought potatoes to bake over the fire and several pounds of butter and assorted toppings, and had scoured the nearby wooded areas for green sticks for roasting hot dogs and marshmallows. As she stood in the kitchen reviewing her list, the only things missing were Peter and Steve and she wished they could be there. Steve was taking skydiving lessons and missing class would set him back. Jeneil understood even though she bit her tongue on the issue of skydiving. She sighed noticing how her circle of people was becoming smaller and smaller. Gone with summer, she thought, and then smiled. Maybe it was for the best because she really should have her life free of entanglements and commitments for when Peter returned. She wanted to give him her full concentration for a while, just a century or two. She chuckled and checked her supply of matches and other items, having gotten extra in case things had been forgotten. For someone who didn't like to plan large parties she sure had a long list. She shook her head and, looking around, declared herself ready to party and have some fun. There was a positive flow of energy and she felt sensitive and receptive, just the right party mood. A door slammed in the driveway and she looked out the kitchen window. Robert had arrived in his pickup truck with a load of lumber and just plain junk.

What's all this?" she asked, going outside."

"I cleaned out my studio. A bonfire's the only way to get rid of it all."

She smiled. "You're a party animal, Robert. They're your natural element."

He smiled as he looked her over. "A long dress is hardly an outfit for an outdoor party, especially one as delicate looking as that."

"Pioneer women never complained."

He laughed and tossed a broken wooden chair to the ground. "It's a nice dress, soft and gentle, like you." She curtsied and he watched her for a second. "It looks handmade."

"It is. I got it in Marrakech."

"Is that a boutique?"

She chuckled. "No, a city in Morocco."

He stopped tossing wood. "You've been to Morocco?"

She nodded. "I was a traveling companion for a close family friend."

He grinned. "You'll never stop surprising me."

A car rumbled down the gravel lane announcing Dennis and Karen's arrival. "Where's my nephew?" Jeneil asked, looking in the backseat for the baby she enjoyed holding.

"Night out for mommy," Dennis answered, and he hugged Jeneil. "You look costumed," he said, smiling approvingly.

"I am. I felt very blithe in spirit and the inner me selected this."

Dennis laughed lightly. "Your inner you has good taste. You look huggable," he said, and he hugged her again.

"Like he needs an excuse," Karen said, giving Jeneil a hug, too.

They joined Robert and helped carry wood to the bonfire area. People started to arrive in large groups by the time they finished and Robert began the ceremony of the bonfire where everyone contributed something to be burned that they wanted to forget. A picture of a soured summer romance, a page from a script an actress had ruined, whatever the memento the bonfire was the place to cauterize the memory. If there was no memento then the problem was scribbled on a piece of paper and added to the grain sack, which Robert called the sack of woes, to be burned and blotted from reality. Jeneil added the summer's separation from Peter although she didn't need the sack of woes; she was ready to put it all behind her and be about a permanent life as Mrs. Peter Chang.

The ceremony was a good party starter and cheerfulness permeated the group as woes were collected. Robert tied the sack then climbed a stepladder where he chanted something in Latin and tossed the sack into the blazing fire. A cheer went up from the crowd as it caught fire destroying the bad memories leaving them free to have fun. Music played and the once sedate group transformed into a party. Jeneil walked through the crowd and mingled, stopping to talk or sample something someone brought. There were faces she didn't know, husbands or wives of playhouse staff or volunteers she hadn't met, but as she learned who was who there was one person she couldn't pair up with anyone. Like her, he seemed to be an observer. She had seen him watching her several times while she talked to a group or a couple but he never seemed to be with anyone. He looked gaunt, almost emaciated, and he stayed near the bonfire and spoke to people from time to time. She couldn't remember who he had arrived with and he didn't appear to have brought any food. Curious, she walked over to him near the edge of the bonfire where a group was cooking wieners.

"Hi," she said, smiling as she stood next to him, "I don't think I got your name. I'm Jeneil." She extended her hand.

"John Stanton Milcroft." He smiled personably and took her hand. His hand felt bony which caused Jeneil to look at it.

"My goodness, what incredibly long fingers," she blurted, his hand wrapping around hers, almost skeletal in appearance.

"Are you into hands and reading palms?"

"No." Jeneil laughed lightly, somewhat embarrassed about her outburst. "No, I'm just impressed by your fingers. Are you a musician?"

"Yes!" John smiled. "I'm a guitarist. You're pretty good," he said, studying her face.

"What kind of guitar?"

"Both acoustic and electric."

"What's your style?"

"Everything with a love for rock and a passion for classical," he answered sincerely.

Jeneil's mind awoke. "Oh really, we have an acoustic guitar just waiting for talent to bring it alive. Can I talk you into performing?"

"Sure can."

"Great!" She laughed, pleased she'd found some entertainment. "After everyone finishes eating we'll drag it out for you." She looked around. "Where's your dinner?"

He shrugged. "I'm just lucky to be here. I had to make connections for a ride and didn't have time to pick anything up."

"You don't have a car?"

"No, I'm from New York and here for the summer cape scene. After the summer gigs, I'm going back."

"That's soon then."

"Yeah, just about. I came up here to see some friends and then down to Marble Point to complete the summer. The crowds are really thin now. I shouldn't have stayed so long but I was having fun and there was a group limping because their guitarist took a week to get married. When he gets back I'll go to New York to see what's starting up."

Jeneil studied him. "Who are you here with?"

"I came in with Elyse and Raylin."

Jeneil relaxed recognizing the names of two actresses from the playhouse. "Aren't you at all hungry?" she asked, noticing how very thin he was. "There's more than enough of everything. I baked some potatoes and there's cold cider in the fridge. Why don't I put a plate together for you?" She smiled. "You did bring something after all, you brought your talent. I can at least provide the food."

He smiled warmly. "That's very nice of you, Jeneil. I am hungry."

"Then why don't you come to the deck and get acquainted with the inexpensive acoustic we have while I get your plate together."

*****

Browning a beef patty in a skillet and adding barbeque sauce to it, Jeneil thought how even John's blue eyes looked hungry. She went to take him a tall glass of cider while his dinner simmered and he tuned the guitar, but Robert met her at the door and backed her up into the kitchen.

"Who are you playing house with?" Robert asked, and she raised an eyebrow. He smiled and kissed her cheek. "Who is he?"

Jeneil shrugged. "A friend of Elyse and Raylin. He plays guitar and didn't have time to bring anything."

"So Florence Nightingale found another wounded bird to feed."

"Oh stop!" she whispered. "He looks so thin. I thought he could use a meal." She went to the stove to check the burger.

"Can I have some cider even though I'm not consumptive?" he teased.

"Of course," she said, and he got a glass and stood beside her as he drank.

"He sounds like he knows what he's doing."

She nodded. "He said he was working on the cape for the summer. He's leaving for New York in a week."

He listened and nodded. "Well, at least we'll get to sing along tonight."

"I don't think so, Robert. I think he plays back-up and he said his passion is classical. Looks like you're the only strum-around-the-campfire-and-sing type of guitarist here."

"Twist my arm," he said, smiling. She laughed and kissed his cheek gently then took the skillet to the table and arranged the food on a plate, adding some cold vegetables along with a baked potato. "Honey, you shouldn't be so open with people. You've really put yourself out doing this for the guy."

"Why?" she asked, looking puzzled. "What's the harm with helping people out?"

He leaned toward her ear, "Because you look too good in your outfit."

She smiled. "Don't ever stop flirting, I'll miss it."

He grinned. "Speak up if you want to take me up on it anytime."

"I thought we had demarcation lines?"

He laughed. "Hell, I'm not normal either so why worry. Old habits are hard to break, especially ones that look and smell like you." He kissed her shoulder.

She laughed. "I love you, Robert. You are so forgiving."

John opened the screen door. "Hey, something smells terrific in here. Holy…look at that feast! You shouldn't have done all that. A wiener would have been fine."

"It was no problem," Jeneil said. "Here, take the plate. Your cider's on the counter."

Robert watched John. "What New York clubs have you played in?"

John sipped his cider. "Club Luminos, Electric Apple, and Valspar. A couple of small spots out of Manhattan, too."

Robert nodded his approval. "Nice places. I'm glad some talent showed up."

"Whose place is this?" John asked.

"The worlds," Jeneil answered, laughing lightly.

Robert smiled. "It's Jeneil's, but it's been a pit stop for the playhouse staff all summer."

"Sit somewhere," Jeneil said, realizing John's food must be getting cold.

"The deck was pleasant. I'll get back to the guitar. Thanks for the food. You're a class act, Jeneil," John said, and went outside.

"Guess he's okay," Robert said. "He has good taste; he called you a class act."

Jeneil smiled. "Let me refill your cider and let's rejoin the party. This is a good crowd, they came to have fun."

Jeneil visited with the group again leaving John to eat his meal in peace. She clapped her hands to the music in the double garage where Robert had organized a square dance and was playing caller.

"He has an electric personality," John said, near her shoulder.

Jeneil turned, surprised he was there. "Yes, he does and he loves parties. His life is a party really."

"Is he your man?"

"No, we're very special friends."

"You look close."

"I love him. He's a wonderful guy," she said, and John smiled as he watched her. Robert started another dance and Jeneil looked at John. "Want to dance?"

He held his shoulders in a shrug. "Man, I don't know how to square dance."

"Neither do I. Let's go make fools of ourselves," she said, laughing as she took his hand.

They fumbled their way through with the others who didn't know the steps and finished laughing hysterically at the mess the square was in. Robert laughed declaring them all hopeless city slickers then announced that John would be playing guitar. Jeneil got John another glass of cider and waited with him on the deck while he warmed up. He was skilled with the guitar and his fingers moved effortlessly over the strings.

He looked up at her and smiled. "Ready as I'll ever be. Let's get to the stage so I can pay for that great dinner you made for me."

Everybody loved him. He played a few songs from almost every style but became vibrant when he got to his repertoire of classical pieces. Jeneil was spellbound and the group applauded and cheered. John took it in stride and just nodded his thanks as he finished. Several people went over to him and he was swallowed up by the crowd who all felt camaraderie for entertainers. It was a large brotherhood; whether you were an actor, musician, playwright or poet, you were a member of the family. Jeneil went to the house and got her tape recorder. John had impressed her and she wanted to see if her intuition was right by having her advisor for The James Gang hear him play. Waiting anxiously for the crowd to release him, he looked around after the crowd thinned as they went on to the next planned activity. Seeing Jeneil on the screened deck, he went to join her.

"John, you play so fantastically! I'm almost speechless," she beamed, and he smiled and sat on the bench. She sat on a lawn chair opposite him. "Would you play some pieces so I can record them? I'd like an agent I know to hear them."

"Are you serious?" John asked, and then laughed. "Boy, this place really is Wonderland. Would you like to record one that I composed?"

"Yes!" Jeneil smiled broadly. "That would be really great."

"Let me run through it once before you tape, okay?"

Jeneil sat back and became almost mesmerized by the piece he played and had a lump in her throat when he finished. "John, that was incredibly beautiful," she said, holding back her emotions. His gentleness and sensitivity permeated the piece leaving it penetratingly haunting. "Let's record inside. The acoustics will be better but still far from perfect."

They sat on the cushions in the living room and taped some of his work. Jeneil was awed by the number of pieces he had completed. Robert and Dennis walked in as John was rehearsing his fifth composition to be recorded.

"Private concert?" Dennis asked.

"No," Jeneil replied, "I'm taping. I have a business associate who's an agent. I love John's work."

Dennis watched as John absorbed Jeneil with his whole being, smiling and studying her face. Robert and Dennis stayed for the recording and were just as impressed with his work as Jeneil was.

"Have you ever tried recording your stuff?" Dennis asked.

John shook his head. "Been too busy staying alive."

Jeneil looked surprised. "You mean you composed all of these pieces and never did anything with them?"

John smiled. "It wasn't the road I was on. I try to get work, at least that's how my drummer beats the tune."

Jeneil was aghast at the discovery. "That's a shame." She sighed. "John Stanton Milcroft has a natural feel for an album cover."

"An album!" John laughed and shook his head. "You don't dream small, sweet lady."

"Yes, an album," she said excitedly. "I feel the jazz spark. Picture the title, *John Stanton Milcroft, Moods from a Classic Guitar.*" She clapped her hands. "It's perfect! I can smell success. It's the same feeling I got when I heard The James Gang and I wasn't wrong about them," she beamed with delight. Robert, Dennis, and John stared at her in disbelief.

Robert gave a laughing kind of cough. "You know The James Gang?"

"Since when?" Dennis asked, smiling broadly, completely impressed.

"I was their first groupie," she said proudly.

John was near shock. "They're moving through Motown like lightening! You really know them?"

She nodded. "I know their agent, music arranger, manager, and I know all the boys."

Robert joined her on the floor. "Honey, without understating it, how do you know these people? They're shaking down trees as the New England Cowboys. It's unheard of. They're a fast rising new group."

She smiled proudly. "I met them in a small club here in the state and we became friends."

Robert stared at her, completely bewildered. "Wait a minute! I saw them do a TV interview. They claim they owe their big break to a fairy godmother that turned pumpkins into concert tours and records. They all waved at the camera and smiled, 'Thanks Jackie, we love you.' Do you know Jackie?" he asked, almost guessing the answer.

"They meant JAC-EE Records," Jeneil replied.

"Jeneil, spell Jackie Records," Robert persisted.

"J-A-C hyphen E-E," she answered simply.

"J-A-C, huh? Maybe Jeneil Alden-Connors?" Robert asked, staring at her, demanding honesty. "Remember, Wonderland is truth."

She nodded gently in answer to his question. Dennis dropped to the floor beside her. "Holy shit, my gopher is a Motown mogul?"

John stared wide-eyed and Jeneil raised her hands indicating the tumult was uncalled for. "Wait, before everybody gets the wrong idea I am not JAC-EE Records. I only own it." All three men fell back against their cushions. She sighed and shook her head. "You see, I knew you wouldn't understand. That's exactly why I don't tell people. I don't own JAC-EE Records, Charlie Bowdine does, and Tony Pinzano is the executive. He's the brain power behind it. His and Charlie's, not mine. My involvement is through reports and advisors. The fact that the three of you have heard of The James Gang is a result of Charlie and Tony's work, not mine." She sighed. "Does everyone have that straight?" They stared at her and smiled. "Please guys, that part of my life is stampeding as it is, I don't need my personal life run down by it." She turned to Dennis. "Your gopher is the real me. JAC-EE Records is part of how I make a living, is that clear?"

Dennis nodded and grinned. "You're something else."

"No." She held up a cautioning finger. "No, I'm not. I'm just Jeneil. Now then," she said, looking at John, "this is unfortunate for you. You could get the wrong impression. Please don't think I can open magic doors. I pay these experts good money to make money for me, so it's not financially smart for me to go in and tell them their jobs. If they say no to any of this, I have to listen to them. The James Gang calls me a fairy godmother but it's their talent and drive that are moving them, not me. I'm only behind them."

John smiled. "You're a class act, Jeneil."

"That's true if it means I like life simple and real. So now, let's record that song." She settled back on her cushion. Dennis and Robert watched her, then looking at each other, they smiled broadly and shook their heads still not believing what they had uncovered about the real life of their quiet gopher. Once the recording ended, the four of them went outside. It was getting later and people were beginning to leave. As the group got smaller and smaller, singing around the campfire ignited and talk began about plans for the following season at the playhouse. As it got later and later and the last of the coffee was gone, it was decided by all that it was time to leave. There was the hustle and bustle of gathering belongings and heading to cars, and Robert and Dennis performed the goodbyes while Jeneil gave John her business card so he could contact her since he wouldn't have a permanent address and she wouldn't be at Wonderland much longer. He stared at her as if he had something he'd like to say but was hesitant.

"I'm going to push this cassette, I can promise that. I really love your work. Please make sure you call me," Jeneil said, giving him a quick hug.

John nodded and smiled. "You really are a class act."

"Someday tell me what that means."

As John walked off toward the driveway to catch his ride, Dennis and Karen came to Jeneil carrying their baskets and blankets. "I'm sad to see Wonderland come to an end," Dennis said, looking around. "It's been a great summer. We came up with some of our best ideas floating on that raft. Thanks again for all your help. You're badly underpaid."

Jeneil smiled. "It's been an education for me, Dennis. I owe you for the experience."

He kissed her cheek and hugged her. "You're something else, honey. Stay in touch over the winter. Let me know if you'd like to hang around the kid."

She nodded. "My immediate plan is to get my life ready for Peter. I'm not thinking past that."

Dennis smiled, noting her enthusiasm as Karen hugged her. "Invite us to the wedding, okay? And keep in touch."

"I will," Jeneil said. "I want to watch my nephew grow."

Karen smiled appreciatively. "Thank you for this summer, Jeneil."

Dennis took Karen's arm and headed toward their car. Karen turned. "Jeneil, I meant to ask, where did you meet the guy who played the guitar?"

"Here at the party," Jeneil answered. "He's a friend of Elyse and Raylin."

Karen looked puzzled. "That's odd, I asked how they knew him and they said they just gave him a ride. They said he's a friend of yours."

Jeneil was surprised. "Well, that is odd. Maybe I misunderstood what he said. I've never met him before. Oh well, I didn't misunderstand his music. I'm glad he came."

Karen smiled. "He was good, wasn't he? That's why I asked about him. I saw him get out of Elyse's car."

Dennis interrupted. "Honey, I'll meet you at the car. I'm going to go to the garage and see if Robert needs any help."

"Okay." Karen nodded. "Bye, Jeneil. Let us know where your next nest will be, maybe in Bermuda, and I'll visit in January while it blizzards here." They both laughed and Jeneil waved as she went to check the bonfire embers.

"There doesn't appear to be too much damage," Robert said, slipping on his jacket as he joined her. He was the last to leave.

"None at all," Jeneil agreed, "and it was a lot of fun."

"Want some company tonight?" he asked, watching her.

His question surprised her. "Do I look lonely? Besides, you're due in Boston tomorrow."

"I can stay and leave in the morning."

"I'm just fine, Robert. Why are you concerned?"

"No reason, just a question."

She slipped her arm through his as they walked to the driveway. "You make parties fun. I think it's a talent."

They stopped at his truck door. "Lock up, okay?" he said, doing up his jacket.

"Are you worried about something?"

He shook his head. "Not really, it's just you're alone out here. Sometimes it gets to me."

She smiled. "It's a very peaceful town. I've felt safe here all summer."

He nodded. "Okay then, I guess I'll head for home." He kissed her lightly and held her to him, feeling the warmth of her shawl.

Jeneil laughed. "Robert, you'll give me the jitters if you keep worrying like you are."

He held her shoulders. "Honey, go inside and signal that you're locked up and safe by blinking the porch light."

"Robert!"

"Please, sweetheart," he pleaded. "It's late. When I drive off, I want to know you're safe."

She laughed again. "This isn't New York."

"Please, Jeneil."

"Okay," she said, shrugging, and kissed his cheek before walking back to the house.

Robert started the engine and waited. Seeing the lights by the front door blink, he tapped his horn and drove away slowly watching as Jeneil waved from the front window. He had given himself a case of the jitters and the lane seemed darker than normal. Jeneil seemed vulnerable to him on so many nights but especially that night. He continued to drive still debating whether to stay.

The town highway was a two-lane road with narrow shoulders. There were no street lights and clouds obscured the moon and stars. He shivered and turned the heater on low. What a deserted area, he thought, and dangerous; he could barely see ahead of him. Feeling with his foot, he stepped on the switch for high beams then reached for the radio. Looking up, he thought he saw someone walking on the road in the distance. He slowed down but didn't see anybody. Damn, he had spooked himself and would be glad to be on the state highway where he could see. That girl was a marvel; she thought his warehouse was spooky but the only thing the town needed was fog and it would be the ideal setting for a horror movie. He sighed thinking he should have stayed with her. He passed the intersection for Route 24 but the highway entrance was only a mile or so ahead. There was more traffic on Route 24 but he preferred the highway because it was well lit. Seeing something flashing on the side of the road ahead, he slowed down as he approached. Recognizing Dennis's hatchback sedan, Robert pulled over and jumped out of his truck.

"Problem?" Robert asked, meeting Dennis between their vehicles.

Dennis shrugged. "I don't know. I guess I'm spooked. Just before Route 24 I passed Elyse Lydeck's car stopped on the side of the road. I looked in the rear view mirror and that guitarist was getting out. I slowed to a crawl and she passed me. Did you see him walking on the road?"

"No," Robert answered, "I didn't see anybody."

Dennis sighed. "He'd be on 24 if he's hitching. I guess I'm being silly."

Robert smirked. "I'm spooked, too."

Dennis shrugged. "Karen thinks I'm crazy. We're supposed to get home for the babysitter but I told her I just wanted to be sure you made it. The guy made me nervous."

Robert nodded. "Me, too, but he was okay with Jeneil. Too okay if you know what I mean. I would have passed him if he was heading back there. Is that your concern?"

Dennis nodded. "Who the hell is he? Where'd he come from?"

"Damned if I know," Robert said, "but I didn't pass him so he must have hitched on 24."

Dennis smiled. "Thanks for stopping, I feel better."

"Sure, it's getting to be October and Halloween time, spooky is in the air."

Dennis laughed. "Make fun," he said, heading back to his car. "I'll follow you onto the interstate." Robert nodded and ran back to his truck.

*****

Jeneil sat at the kitchen table with a small glass of cider. She was too wound up to sleep. Seeing the aluminum foil wrapped potatoes on the counter, she got up and unwrapped them, being careful not to shake off any ashes. Packing the potatoes into a plastic bag, she took them to the refrigerator. They had been good and there were only six left. She stopped suddenly as a tingle went down her spine. Was that a noise on the deck? She waited but didn't hear anything. She heaved a sigh. Robert had her spooked. She opened the refrigerator door and put the bag on the bottom shelf when she heard the screen door open slowly and someone knock. Her heart stopped and she closed the refrigerator door as silently as she could.

"Who's there?" she called, going to the door slowly.

"It's John."

Jeneil parted the white cotton curtains and flipped on the back porch light. John stood there smiling. Jeneil smiled and undid the lock, opening the door. "What's wrong?"

"I missed my ride to the cape on 24."

"Uh-oh," she said, stepping aside to let him in. "Would you like to use the phone?"

He shrugged. "That's a start."

She pointed to the wall. "Right, the phone's there."

He went to the telephone and dialed. Waiting a few seconds, he replaced the receiver. "No answer."

"Great," she said. "Where are your things? Can I drive you to your friend's place? How can I help you?"

He watched her and smiled. "You have got to be the nicest person I've ever met."

For no reason Jeneil could understand, her spine tingled again and she wondered why. John seemed nice enough. He was a passive sort of person and quite easy to be around. She tried to put aside her unreasonable fear. "John, how are you going to handle this situation?"

He shrugged again. "I'm at a disadvantage because of the late hour. It's so dark that walking is difficult."

"Of course," she said, agreeing. "And dangerous, especially on the town roads, I'm impressed that you walked back from Route 24. I'm surprised you and Robert didn't pass each other. He'd have given you a lift into Upton, he was going that way. You could have had your choice of options from there."

He nodded. "My night for lousy luck, I guess. But the biggest problem is a place to spend the night. Hitching is impossible at this hour."

Jeneil became concerned. She remembered what Karen had told her about John and that nobody at the party had known him. It was a fact that made her nervous and one she knew she couldn't ignore. If it was earlier in the summer she could have let him sleep in the garage, but the night was damp and chilly and the garage was unheated. The situation was uncomfortable for her since the obvious solution was to allow him to stay in the house. She felt the pressure of that choice.

John smiled as he came closer to her. "I understand your problem. You don't know me and letting me stay here is a risk. You can't be too careful these days."

"I'm sorry, John," Jeneil replied, embarrassed. "I don't really know you and it isn't my way to allow strangers into my life so easily." She realized a solution and smiled, pleased that she had an answer. "John, there's a motel on Route 24. I'll drive you there and in the morning I'll pick you up and help you make your connection."

"I don't have money for a room," he said quietly.

"I'll take care of it," she said, still smiling.

John kept his eyes on her as he moved closer. "I can't allow that, Jeneil. I can't pay you back. Every dime of my summer money is accounted for."

Jeneil was getting very uncomfortable. "John, I don't want you to repay me. Consider it New England hospitality." She forced a smile, wondering what his next move would be.

He continued watching her and smiled warmly. "Jeneil, don't be afraid of me, I won't hurt you. I think you're the most beautiful person I've ever met."

Jeneil had to force herself not to panic and run when he raised his hand and touched her cheek. She now understood her instincts about the situation. He was coming on to her and again she forced herself not to panic as the touch of his hand on her skin frightened her. Judging by the glassiness of his eyes and his slowness to respond, she suspected he was on something and she knew he could become a different person if she became hysterical. She reviewed her options in her head. She had never knocked anyone unconscious before and she wondered how much time she'd have to go to the bedroom to get her car keys. That was crazy yet she knew the only escape was the car and she knew she had to buy some time in order to get out of the house and she had to do it quickly. She took his hand from her cheek and smiled cheerfully.

"Then it's settled, John. You'll stay here tonight." She went to the cupboard and got a glass. "I'll get you some cider. I have extra pajamas that you can wear." She moved quickly to the refrigerator hoping quick moves would be a distraction to him. She remembered to stay positive and cheerful. "Why don't you freshen up, John? The walk from Route 24 must have done you in. You'll feel better after a nice shower."

Jeneil poured cider into the glass and saw how badly her hands were shaking. She heard footsteps on the deck stairs and her heart stopped wondering if John had returned with the friend or friends he had met on Route 24. Suddenly she realized how vulnerable she really was and her throat hurt as she held back panic. She turned to look at the door as it burst open. Robert stood there wide-eyed and slightly out of breath, not believing that John was standing in her kitchen. Tears almost spilled down Jeneil's cheeks as she realized that she had been rescued, her mind grasping the moment while John frowned with annoyance at Robert's intrusion.

"Robert," she said, smiling cheerfully, putting the cider bottle back. "Don't tell me your truck broke down and you walked back, too. John missed his ride on 24 and walked in. He's going to spend the night here." Robert stared at her in shock. John smiled and took the glass of cider she held out to him. "Why did you come back?"

Robert was caught off guard. "I…uh…my jacket, I left my jacket somewhere around here. I'll go and look for it," he said, looking from Jeneil to John and back again.

Jeneil held her breath. "It's really dark out there. I'll get the fluorescent lantern for you." She looked at John. "Were you going to take that shower now?"

John smiled broadly. "Yes, that's a good idea."

Jeneil patted his arm gently and smiled. "Good, there are plenty of towels in one of the vanity drawers. Robert, the lantern is on the cellar wall, I'll be right back. John, follow me." She took his arm and walked out of the kitchen while Robert stared in disbelief. Jeneil waited for the bathroom door to close and then rushed to her bedroom, returning with her purse. The water from the shower was running and Jeneil ran to Robert, pushing him out the door and onto the deck. "Let's get out of here," she said, in a harsh whisper.

"Honey…," Robert said, as Jeneil ran down the deck stairs.

"Robert, now! Please, right now," she pleaded, trying to stay calm. He took her hand and realized she was shaking.

"We'll take my truck," he said, putting his arm around her as they walked quickly to the driveway. He backed out and headed down the lane. Jeneil burst into tears as she sat next to him, her body shaking uncontrollably. Forcing herself to gain control, she dried her cheeks. Feeling a bulk of material beside her, she reached for it. It was Robert's jacket.

She stared at him. "You didn't forget your jacket."

He stopped at the intersection of the lane and the town road and shifted into park. He put his head back and sighed with relief. "No, I didn't forget my jacket. I met Dennis on the highway; he saw John get out of Elyse's car at 24. He wondered if I had seen John walking back to your place. I hadn't and Dennis and I drove away, but I kept thinking that I'd seen someone walking on the road. He must have ducked out of sight as I passed." He covered his eyes with one hand. "Honey, that guy isn't all he's claiming to be. You shouldn't leave him there. He'll probably rip you off. He crashed the party somehow."

"It's okay, Robert. There isn't much of great value in there. He's on something. I'm almost certain of it. If I call the police, he could be arrested for possession of drugs."

Robert ran his hands over the steering wheel. "Maybe he should be arrested. Who is he? He came back for more than a night's sleep, sweetheart."

Jeneil lowered her head. "I know but it's my fault. My attention to him at the party caused this." Tears rolled down her cheeks. "I'll never learn. I look at the world asexually and I think everyone else does, too. This time I was in big trouble." She cried softly and Robert put his arm around her, holding her close and understanding why Peter hovered over her.

"Are you sure you want to just leave him in the house?"

She nodded and dried her eyes. "He has talent, Robert. It's a beautiful gift. I don't want him arrested. I'll deal with it tomorrow. Steve usually comes in around seven-thirty."

"Honey, everything in me says forget him. Dennis and I can't understand why that kind of talent isn't blossoming somewhere. He's a drifter. None of it makes sense."

"That's because you and Dennis know your places in life. It's easy for you to make sense out of everything. Drifting isn't dangerous; it's a symptom, that's all. I'm drifting and I'm not dangerous, am I? I'm just unfinished. Maybe John is, too. I can't forget that music. Robert, he's gifted."

Robert sighed. "Okay, we'll leave him in the house. Do you want to come home with me and drive back with Steve tomorrow?"

She looked at her watch. "No, it's late. I own the Quiet Pines Motel on Route 24. We can stay there tonight. It's close by and you can at least rest for your meeting in Boston."

"You own a motel, too?" He shook his head. "The things I'm learning about you."

She smiled. "It's just north of the intersection about a mile."

"I know where it is. I've stayed there." He kissed her cheek. "I could tell money was being put into it. It's become a very nice place. It used to be called Twin Pines. So do we stay in one room?" he teased.

She grinned. "If all the others are filled and if I can tie you to the bed."

He laughed. "Jeneil, you kinky devil."

She hugged him. "Robert, thank you for coming back tonight, I…," the words refused to pass through her lips.

He held her tightly. "Don't say it, honey, and don't even think about it. It's over. It's a nightmare that never happened."

Eleven

Jeneil awoke early and showered, then went next door to Robert's room. He was on the telephone. "Okay Elyse, thanks. No, I just wondered. Yeah, I'll see you." He replaced the receiver and sighed. "Honey, Elyse and Raylin met John at a diner farther up on 24. They were lost and stopped in for directions. John began talking to them and said he was going to the party too, but had missed his ride and was hitching. He said he was at the diner to get warm and see if anyone was going that way. He talked like he really knew you, but when I asked her to think about what he said, she couldn't be specific. She just found him in the car with them heading for your party. She was shocked because he sounded so convincing." Robert raised his eyebrows. "I don't know about him, honey."

Jeneil sighed. "This doesn't sound good."

They drove back to Wonderland hoping they'd arrive before Steve in order to explain John's presence. As they rounded the turn in the lane, they could see flashing lights and they looked at each other with concern. Jeneil saw Steve's car and her heart pounded as she recognized a local police cruiser and a State Highway Patrol car.

"Something's very wrong," Jeneil gasped, and wrung her hands as a state trooper walked onto the lane signaling them to stop.

"You folks have business here?" the trooper asked, going to Robert's side.

"She lives here," Robert answered.

The trooper looked surprised. "Are you Jeneil?"

"Yes, I am. What's happened?"

The trooper didn't answer. "Rand, tell Al she just drove up."

"Oh damn, that's good," the Weeden officer said, and ran into the yard.

"Come with me, Miss." The trooper went around to Jeneil's side and opened her car door.

"What's this all about?" Robert asked, jumping out and putting his arm around her.

"We're trying to find out," the trooper said, walking quickly toward the yard. Robert and Jeneil followed him to the driveway. They both stopped suddenly at the sight of Jeneil's car. The front windshield was fragmented and smashed, and the driver side window was completely broken out. The door was dented badly.

"Holy shit," Robert said.

"What happened?" Jeneil gasped.

"Jeneil!" Steve yelled, and ran to her followed by another state trooper. Steve grabbed her and held onto her. "Jeneil," he whispered, his voice cracking. "Honey…." He held her so tightly he was hurting her.

"Steve," she said, trying to look at him, "what happened to my car? What is all this?"

Steve stepped back covering his eyes and taking a deep breath, obviously very upset. The state trooper who was with him patted his shoulder. "He got here this morning and found that your house had been vandalized. There was no trace of you; we've been thinking the worst. He's reacting to good news, that's all. He'll be okay. Do you have any idea who did this? I guess you didn't spend the night here?"

Jeneil could not believe how much Steve was shaking and she put her arms around his waist. He held onto her, kissing her cheek several times. "Jeneil, baby, this was worse than the boat." He kissed her lips, surprising her.

Robert answered the trooper's question. "We had a party last night and a guy cracked it. He got a ride to 24 then doubled back. I came back to check on Jeneil and found him in the kitchen with her. He expected to stay the night. She talked him into taking a shower and we left while he was in the bathroom. We stayed at the Quiet Pines Motel expecting to come here this morning and deal with him."

"But John couldn't have done this," Jeneil said.

"John?" the trooper asked. "Did you know him?"

"Only from the party, I thought he was a friend of some guests. He must have left and then the vandals broke in."

The trooper studied her face. "What's John's full name, do you know?"

Jeneil nodded. "John Stanton Milcroft."

The trooper turned to the officers behind him. "You were right, Chuck; they were connected." He looked back at Jeneil. "Did you leave on friendly terms?"

Jeneil looked at Robert. "No, I ran out on him. I couldn't get rid of him so I left figuring he could sleep here."

The trooper nodded. "Why don't you think he could've done this?"

Jeneil looked at her car. "Because John was gentle, this is...this is violent. I wonder where he went. Did he leave a note?"

The trooper looked at Steve and then at Jeneil. "Miss, John Milcroft was hit by a car out on the town road last night. He's in pretty bad shape at Maitland General."

"Oh no!" Jeneil covered her mouth, completely overwhelmed by the news. Tears poured down her cheeks. "Oh, Robert, we should have driven him somewhere."

Robert closed his eyes and took a deep breath. "No, honey," he said, taking her from Steve and holding her shoulders. "No, honey, listen to me, the guy was looking for trouble." He held her shoulders tightly as she continued to cry. "Honey, remember last night for gosh sakes."

"I know, I know," Jeneil said, nodding as she cried.

The trooper sighed. "It's pretty certain Milcroft did this. Forensics is on the way but it's all tying together. We need to know if he took anything. You'll need to check through your things."

"Oh shit, does she have to?" Steve asked, running his fingers through his hair.

"I'm afraid so," the trooper answered compassionately.

"I don't have much," Jeneil said, regaining her composure. "This was my summer home."

The trooper nodded. "Let's just check inside." He turned and headed for the house.

"Damn," Steve groaned, and put his arm around Jeneil as they climbed the deck stairs. The screen door was hanging on one hinge and the screen was shredded. The glass on the inside door was broken, splintered, and bloodstained. Jeneil stopped and stared. Steve held her tighter. "Honey, hang tough and then we're out of here."

"Oh my gosh," Jeneil whispered, and continued toward the door. Robert was by her side looking just as shocked.

"Try not to touch anything," the trooper said, as he walked into the house. Jeneil looked around the kitchen. A drawer had been pulled out and spilled onto the floor. Several cupboards were open, but nothing seemed to be missing. "Looking at the contents of the drawer, can you tell if anything is missing?"

Looking at the spilled gadgets, Jeneil struggled to remember what she had in the drawer. She wrinkled her eyebrows. "A knife is missing," she answered, catching her breath. Steve held her closer to him. The trooper made a note before going to the living room. "Nothing is missing," Jeneil said quietly, looking around. "I didn't have much in here."

The trooper nodded. "Did you keep any jewelry here?"

Jeneil nodded. "In an envelope in my bedroom closet."

The trooper looked at Steve and sighed. "Then we'll have to check in there."

"Shit," Steve mumbled.

The trooper sighed again. "Jeneil, your bedroom seems to be where most of the damage is so you should expect to be shocked."

Jeneil felt Steve tighten his hold on her. He leaned toward her and kissed her temple. The trooper headed for the bedroom and Jeneil saw him grimace as he walked in.

"Baby...," Steve said, stopping. He sighed and shook his head. "I...well, the guy," he stopped and swallowed hard then kissed her lips lightly, surprising her again. He held her and walked to the bedroom door.

The room smelled terrible and she wondered what it was. Everything was thrown around, clothes and boxes of papers and white fluffy material she couldn't identify. The odor was stifling. It was unmistakably human waste and she was confused about it being in the bedroom. Her poster of Chang was torn to pieces. She felt dizzy.

The trooper pointed to a door. "Is that the closet where you kept your jewelry?"

Jeneil nodded, gasping at the sight of the damage that had been done to it. It was splintered. She waved her hand before her face and grimaced. "Where is that awful smell coming from?"

"Can you check to see if the envelope is missing?" the trooper asked.

Holding her hand to her nose, Jeneil went to the closet concerned about the box of manuscripts. It was still there and untouched. She looked on the shelf. The envelope was missing. "It's gone," she said, backing away from the closet. The trooper and an officer were standing side by side. She thought it seemed deliberate and odd. The odor penetrated her senses again and she noticed flies in the room. "Is there human waste in here?" she asked, looking around.

"Yes ma'am," the officer answered, "it's usually meant as an insult."

Jeneil shook her head. "John didn't do this then. He couldn't have. This isn't him."

The officer sighed. "Ma'am, a manila envelope containing a few pieces of jewelry was found on John Milcroft's person when he entered the hospital. He did do this. Learn from this, ma'am."

Jeneil noticed brown printing on the wall obscured by the officer standing before her. "What's that?" she asked, stepping around him, gasping as she got closer to her bed. The mattress was shredded and there was an irregular circle of yellow staining the stuffing. There was a pile of human feces inside the circle and it was smeared at one side. Her heart pounded and she could barely breathe as she saw the missing kitchen knife stabbed into her pillow. She covered her mouth with both hands and read the brown printing on the wall; *'Fuck you bitch.'* Her heart pounded in her ears and she couldn't move; she couldn't seem to take another breath.

Robert walked into the bedroom and gasped seeing the mattress and the sick message. He turned and ran out to the deck where he could be heard being sick.

Steve held Jeneil from behind. "Come on, honey." He pulled her away and headed out of the bedroom, continuing down the small hallway and out the door. He took her to the screen house, sitting her on a lawn chair. She obeyed willingly to whatever he did, barely noticing what he was doing. He rubbed her hands briskly. "Come on, baby. Let it go. Come on, get rid of it."

She couldn't remember how to breathe and she felt panic seize her as she struggled to remember how. She heard a scream and then felt herself gasping for air as tears streamed down her face. She felt nauseous and weak, and she began to dry heave. Her body shook out of her control. She screamed again and burst into sobs. Giving into it, she began to relax and pull it together. Steve rubbed the back of her neck gently and kissed her temple several times as she worked through it.

"It's okay, baby. It's over. It's gone. You're right here, honey, and you're fine. None of it touched you. You were smart to leave and now you're just fine." Jeneil clung to Steve's arm and sobbed, grateful that he was there with her as the madness spun her emotions.

They stayed only a few minutes more, leaving Jeneil's business card with the police. The forensic team arrived and the scene was a hive of activity. Steve took her to his car and Robert held her before she got in. Steve understood Robert's loss for words and his clenched grip around her. It satisfied and calmed a panic, a fear deep inside to feel her close and alive and breathing. Her warmth was a reality, the complete opposite of the other reality that had resulted from a mind confused by drugs and rage; a reality that had spilled into fury, catapulting itself into oblivion. An officer had called the hospital to see if John Stanton Milcroft was conscious and could be questioned. He was told that Milcroft had died an hour earlier, a victim of his own anger and destructive fury.

Steve put his arm around Jeneil as they climbed the stairs to Camelot. It had been weeks since Jeneil had been there, but she felt so shaken that she needed to be around what was familiar and secure to her. The apartment was stuffy from having been closed during the hot summer. Jeneil and Steve opened windows and sat on the sofa feeling stale air being exchanged for cool fresh air from outdoors.

"Camelot looks different," Steve said.

Jeneil nodded. "All the plants are at the office where I knew they could survive. This place feels vacant, doesn't it?"

Steve smiled. "It just needs you and your touch to bring it back to the real Camelot."

"And Peter," Jeneil added, watching absently as the breeze moved the white curtain away from the wall rhythmically. She sighed. "I hope we can regain Camelot."

Steve was surprised to hear her say that. "You have doubts?"

She looked at him and smiled weakly. "I have reality. Peter and I have been separated since February. For whatever the reason, the situation isn't budging. I'm changed, Peter must be changed. We'll have something else but I'm almost certain it won't be Camelot."

Steve patted her shoulder. "You're still traumatized, honey. Give it some time."

"I hope so." She rested her head on the back of the sofa. "If Peter can't prove the baby isn't his, he'll be a very different Peter."

Steve watched her. "When will they get a divorce?"

"A month after the baby's born according to the agreement."

"Shit," Steve mumbled, "that long?"

"Why?" she asked, turning her head to look at him when he didn't answer. "Why, Steve?"

He shrugged and sighed, uncomfortable with his answer. "Because I haven't felt comfortable all summer with you alone at Wonderland. I want you married and settled so I can breathe again."

She smiled and touched his face lovingly, appreciating his concern. "I found out this summer that I'm not meant to be single. The security and stability of a good marriage are essential for me. Marriage is soul food. There's more freedom in marriage. Society leaves you alone when you're married. You're free to be who you really are or who you're becoming instead of spending time explaining your singleness or defending it and even justifying it to yourself."

"Well put," Steve replied, "I agree completely. I'm going to get married."

"You've found someone?"

He watched her face closely for a moment and then shook his head. "No, but I'm going to. I've heard that it happens to some men. They reach a point where they want to be married. I'm there now for all the reasons you just described."

Jeneil grinned. "Then you'd better stop babysitting me and start falling in love, fella. Do you realize that you've given up your summer for me and Peter?" She mournfully sighed. "Uette, how many lives have been affected by you?" She patted Steve's hand. "Sir Steven, I release you from your sworn duty to protect me so you may go about the countryside to find the one fair damsel who will claim your heart and share your hearth."

Steve paused, tempted to be completely honest. "That's not in the cards for me. I'll settle for a woman who can handle a sensible and dull life because that's what's on my hearth."

Jeneil looked at him with concern. "But love makes it exciting, Steve. You should marry for love. How can you be happy otherwise? It will always feel like something's missing."

Steve smiled at her simplistic view. "Jeneil, love in marriage hasn't been dealt to me in this card game."

"Marcia hurt you so deeply that you can't forgive her? You don't trust women?"

Steve could see the compassion in her eyes and he wanted so much to be honest with her. He and Peter were nearly strangers now, they barely spoke, but it was for Jeneil that he held back. She belonged to Peter and it wouldn't do any good to tell her. "The explanation isn't that simple."

She watched him for a second and then she took his hand. "Marry for love, Steve. You deserve that and so does the woman you'll marry."

He patted her hand. "I'll try. That would be a nice twist in this whole mess."

"What mess?" she asked, not understanding how his love was connected with a mess since the only mess she knew about at the moment was hers.

He squeezed her hand. "Stop being so serious. You must have driven your parents crazy with questions as a kid."

She laughed. "Actually, they drove me crazy. I looked up answers in books but they would ask, Jeneil, what do you think about this? Or how do you feel about that? What would the result be? What are the possibilities? Is it probable? Is there another point of view?" She shook her head and smiled, remembering them fondly. Steve watched her, enjoying the sound of her voice and the feel of her hand in his. He agreed that being in love was exciting and decided that requited love must be quite a trip judging from the electricity of a one-sided love.

They spent a quiet weekend together taking a ride to the country and walking the back roads where she gathered fall flowers and dried grasses. Steve could tell she was still unnerved because she stayed close by his side and hugged him without reason. He loved it all; her gentleness, her sensitivity, and her need for him. The only thing lacking was marriage and a physical relationship, but he didn't allow himself to think about either one. He limited the fantasy knowing all too well that in another month or so she would be gone from his life and married to Peter, but he didn't allow himself to think about that either. He enjoyed the moments that were handed to him, satisfying himself with the idea that he would at least know what love felt like if he were lucky to find it again with someone else. He watched as she picked green ferns and yellow flowers with brown centers, and he watched as she walked to him obviously pleased with her collection. He put his arms around her and she melted into them. Her cheek felt soft against his face and his heart pounded at the thought that if he moved his head ever so slightly he could kiss her lips. He wanted to but she turned her head and kissed his cheek softly.

"I love you, Steve," she said quietly, hugging him.

His heart felt like it exploded in his chest sending electricity all through him. Would life allow him to find someone of his own who would say those words to him and cause the same reaction? She smiled at him causing his ribcage to feel like it was melting and he knew it would be impossible to find anyone who would reach him as deeply as Jeneil had or to feel as much his as she did. He didn't dare kiss her lips; truth was too close to the surface as it was and it was so near the end of their special relationship that he didn't dare risk it. She needed him; she needed his friendship now more than ever, especially as she recovered from the horror of Saturday and struggled with the loneliness of separation from Peter. He knew that she didn't need more shock and turmoil in her life. She needed a friend and he intended to be there for her as one.

*****

The weekend was too long for Peter. It was getting more and more difficult to avoid Uette and the tension increased as October began. He headed to the hospital feeling low as he realized it was very likely that Mark Chun had decided to leave the situation alone. Peter had wondered about Mark's options and it was becoming obvious that Mark's baby would be born Peter Chang's and there was no way for him to clear his name. The thought made him sick to his stomach and left him very discouraged.

The day had been long but Peter wished it could be longer since going home to Uette was a nightmare he'd like very much to avoid. Making rounds was a pleasure; it's when he got to see patients and find out how they were doing. The human side of medicine worked for him and made the technical side less gruesome. All his patients had been seen and the hour for going home was upon him. A feeling of dread surfaced because Uette was pushing him to go shopping for baby furniture. He wondered why they couldn't borrow some from her cousins. Once he moved out she could use his bedroom, but how could they fit more than a crib at the moment? He sighed knowing his attitude stemmed from not wanting to accept Mark's baby as his own and that made him feel bad for the baby.

Steve watched Peter walk toward the elevators and he wrestled with the idea of telling him about the horror at Wonderland even though Jeneil had pleaded with him not to say anything. She did say that she wished Peter would call since it was getting so near the end and she didn't see the harm in just talking to each other. He thought it would be great for Jeneil's morale if Peter called so he rushed to the elevator to catch him.

"Hey, Pete, are you getting used to the regular hours or do you still wake up panicked that you should be in the emergency room?"

Peter smiled. "The hours feel strange."

Steve sensed something but he didn't know how to read Peter anymore; their close bond was gone. "How's it all going, Pete? What's happening? Any news?"

Peter sighed. "Yeah, it looks like this baby is mine. I'm just waking up to it, I guess."

Steve stared in shock, not believing what he was hearing. "What now?" he asked, forcing the words out as they rang in his ears.

Peter shook his head. "I don't know how to tell Jeneil. I don't want to face her right now."

Steve was speechless and totally stunned. "I'm sorry, Pete. Man, that's tough."

"How is she?"

Steve struggled whether or not to tell him. "Pete, she...well...I. Jeneil needs a sane lifestyle. She needs a normal situation. What's happening is taking its toll on everyone." He struggled to find the words to soften what happened at Wonderland.

"Is something wrong?" Peter asked, watching Steve struggle.

"No," Steve replied, deciding not to mention anything since Peter was already dealing with his own problem. "No, it's been a strange summer, that's all. So much has happened. We really should talk sometime."

"Are you going down?" Peter asked, as the elevator doors opened.

Steve shook his head. "No, I still have patients to see. Get yourself straightened out and we'll talk."

"Is there a problem? Is Jeneil okay?"

"No. Yes, yes, Jeneil's okay," Steve insisted. "There's no problem. I just thought I'd bring you up to date, but your news is bigger. Mine, it'll keep."

"Okay," Peter said, and as the doors closed he wondered why Steve seemed so on edge.

Peter drove home thinking that maybe he should call Jeneil. It was time to prepare her to accept the fact that Mark Chun's baby would be named Chang. He sighed and gripped the steering wheel angrily not wanting to accept it himself. Pulling into the apartment parking lot, he saw Uette's car. Well, she was back from Boston. Peter sighed as he walked into the building. Uette looked tired when he entered the apartment.

"Peter, I didn't make any dinner. I'm too tired."

"Are you okay?"

She nodded. "Yes, I think I just walked too much over the weekend. I had a really severe pain Sunday morning but it passed and I'm okay, just tired and discouraged. I look so awful in fur jackets with this stomach and they didn't have what I wanted."

Peter studied her face; she looked exhausted. "Maybe you should call your doctor."

"No, I have an appointment on Friday. He'll only tell me to rest anyway so why bother."

"Be careful you don't miss any symptoms," Peter cautioned.

"I don't have any symptoms, even the bleeding has stopped."

Peter wrinkled his brow. "Bleeding? When? For how long?"

Uette smiled, appreciating his concern. "Sunday after the pain. It was only slight and I'm okay now. The reading material said that bleeding sometimes happens towards the end of the pregnancy."

Peter shook his head. "Well, all I know is there are degrees of bleeding. Maybe you should tell the doctor and let him decide."

Uette laughed. "Peter, if I fuss now, he won't pay attention when I really need him. That's what I hear, don't cry wolf."

"Where have you heard that?"

"Women," she replied, lying down on the sofa.

"Well, I'd like to know if my patient had severe pain followed by bleeding."

"Then you're lucky you didn't go into obstetrics because you'd never be off the telephone. There are false labor pains and all kinds of fun things that'll begin happening this month. If you'll just take care of dinner that would help."

"No problem," he said, "I'll make myself a cheeseburger. Would you like one or a frozen dinner?"

"I'm not hungry," she said, "but I'll take a diet soda with a lot of ice if you don't mind."

"Uette, you really should be careful. Have you eaten at all today?"

She smiled appreciatively. "Yes, I had a slice of toast for breakfast and an orange for lunch. I'm just not hungry, but I can't get enough liquids for some reason."

"Then drink juice, it's more nutritious."

"Peter, I love your concern but I need to rest more than argue. Please, a diet soda."

"Okay," he answered, and headed to the kitchen.

Peter had gotten off the elevator thinking he might approach Uette about starting a divorce action before the baby was born. Steve's behavior had unnerved him, but seeing her like she was made him decide against it. Maybe she would deliver early. It didn't seem right to approach her about divorce as she began the final month. He'd wait a week and see what happened and then he'd call Jeneil. He shook his head as he poured diet soda over several ice cubes in a tall glass. The baby must be ninety percent cola and ten percent snow. What a crazy bitch. She thought she had him fooled but he knew she was still on the stuff. Well, he hoped she wasn't going to be sorry. A habit was a habit and the baby would pay for it, too. So would he when he had to walk the floor with a baby crying from withdrawal. He sighed, taking the drink to her.

She took the glass from him. "You really are a sweet guy."

"Yell if you change your mind about dinner," he said, leaving quickly before she began one of her long, flowery, 'you're so terrific' speeches that she had been pulling lately. They irritated him.

"I love you, Peter," she called, as he headed away. He clenched his jaw and continued to the kitchen insulted by the words. She was using him, the bitch. Peddle that to Mark Chun, it was his baby.

*****

Steve arrived at Jeneil's apartment still done in by Peter's news and feeling sorry for Jeneil. With all she'd been through recently, how the hell was she supposed to swallow the fact that the baby was really Peter's after telling herself it wasn't for all those months. He sighed. Life had its finger stuck on that shit button. He couldn't believe it. If anyone deserved a happy ending it was her. How the hell was she going to make lemonade out of that lemon? He sat on the sofa silent and solemn as he waited for Jeneil to change, wondering how Peter would tell her. He felt sorry for Peter too, knowing the news would make it hard for him to face her. Taking his glass and joining Jeneil at the table, he watched her as she chattered. Ordinarily her chatter was amusing but he was so distracted by Peter's news that he missed a lot of what she said.

"Steve, you've been quiet tonight. Are you feeling well?" she asked, as they did dishes together.

"I'm fine," he answered, and she studied him for a second before putting away the dishes he was drying. "How was your day? Full-time at the corporation must feel different."

She shrugged. "It was mostly odds and ends."

"What are you going to do now?"

"I don't know, Steve. Finding out that the theatre isn't for me has left me in a lurch. My life is so upside down right now. This is the most unsettled I've ever felt. Even my junior year in college wasn't this bad because I thought that once I left school I'd simply slip into whoever Jeneil really was and here I am still drifting."

"You seem to know yourself pretty well."

She sighed. "I know how to stay healthy and what my favorite color is, but I know I don't belong in the theatre. I know I don't want to be in the corporation full-time, but what do I want to do? I'd like to have a positive feel to my life. I want to do something with my life, but what? Everything I've done so far has been temporary and I know that isn't me. It feels negative. I'm waiting for a positive turn. I'm Jeneil, I'm a…." She looked at Steve and shrugged. "What am I?"

"Well, keep looking."

"I'm running out of things to poke into and now that there's a void in my life the corporation could swallow me whole without my consent," she said, almost dropping a goblet.

"Why is that so bad?" he asked, wondering about her fear.

She leaned her head against the open cupboard door. "It's stampeding, Steve. My enterprises have grown and they just keep growing. I backed The James Gang hoping for a loss and now I own a record company. I couldn't tell them to drift in order to cost me money, so I turned them over to experts and now the whole thing is even bigger. I bought a small farm and lots of acreage thinking it would be a financial drain, but the guy in charge is a whiz on a large scale. If he gets any better I'm just going to make him a full partner to reduce my tax burden. He's incredible. The place is bulging with poultry, eggs, and vegetables. And my shopping plaza," she sighed, shaking her head, "I bought it because there were always one or two stores empty and it needed work. Nice little tax drain I thought. The Alden Corporation put up its new office building across the street and suddenly my shopping plaza is a prime target for businesses who want to cash in on the traffic to the building."

"You own Lakeland Plaza?" he asked, shocked.

"Yes, have you heard of it?"

He laughed. "Every doctor in the office wants that piece of real estate. Why don't you sell it?"

"Because its value has tripled, that's why. It's financially better for me to spend money developing it and the land around it. I'm putting up an office building of my own next door and moving out of the Fairview office and into the Lakeland building. Adrienne will run the buildings and my real estate, and Tony is going to need a larger staff to run the other businesses. I don't know some of the people who work for me anymore. It's lost its small business feel. It isn't fun anymore." Steve began to laugh, trying hard not to, and Jeneil shook her head. "That's what Hollis and Bill do."

"Honey, is it so hard for you to sit in an office and do business?"

"I'd go crazy, Steve. I really would. Tony and Adrienne go to business lunches and meetings to negotiate. I couldn't live like that. I can take research reports, financial reports, and statistical analysis sheets and they make sense to me. If I have questions, I go and talk to people but not at long lunches or meetings over drinks. My kind of work doesn't need me behind a desk for eight hours. The only thing that will probably save me is marriage."

Steve smiled. "Jeneil, I think you and I will be successful in marriage because we appreciate all its unromantic benefits. We both see it as freedom."

"I agree with you," she said, smiling and then she sighed. "Where is Peter? Why hasn't he called? It's the beginning of October, hasn't he heard anything? I don't understand why he doesn't at least call now." She frowned and Steve watched her sadly. "Have you seen him at all?" she asked, and Steve nodded and remained silent. "What does he have to say?"

Steve swallowed nervously. "Honey, call and talk to him, it's allowed in this era of liberation."

"What have you heard?" she asked, looking in his eyes and noticing something.

"Jeneil, honey, call Pete."

"Did you talk to him?" she asked cautiously.

"Yes," he replied, feeling uncomfortable.

"Why do you keep insisting that I should call him? Steve, what do you know?"

"Honey," he said, giving into her pleading, "he didn't know how he was going to face you. So why don't you call him."

Jeneil's heart stopped as she heard his words. "Why would he have trouble facing me? I want you to tell me, Steve. Stop telling me to call him," she insisted, leaning against the counter for support while he stared at the floor. "Steve, what is it?" She felt herself getting emotional sensing she was about to hear something horrible. Tears rolled down her cheeks. "Steve," she said, her voice cracking and her courage faltering, "what is it?"

He couldn't stand her tears; he knew she must be imagining the worst. He took a deep breath and exhaled. "Honey, he said that the baby is his."

Jeneil bolted upright, knocking a goblet to the floor. It shattered and the broken stem hit the side of her sandaled foot, breaking the skin. She ran to the bathroom as her tears turned to sobs. Her hands shook as she daubed peroxide on the cut and she could barely see straight to do the bandage as tears filled her eyes and streamed down her face. When she finished, she ran to her bedroom slamming the door.

Steve had finished cleaning up the broken glass when he heard the door slam. Going to the bedroom door, he heard her sobs. "Oh damn," he groaned, "why did I tell her? Honey," he called, "I'm coming in." He opened the door slowly and saw her lying across the bed sobbing into the quilt. His heart ached for her and he wished he hadn't been the one to tell her and to cause her that kind of pain. Lying behind her, he rubbed her arm gently not knowing what to say that would ease the pain and shock. He kissed her shoulder. "Honey, I'm sorry."

"He made love to her," she sobbed, hitting the quilt with her hand. Steve understood her pain and feeling of betrayal.

"No, honey, love had nothing to do with it, nothing. It was a crazy set of circumstances. He was away from you, he wasn't fully conscious, he must have had more than he thought he had to drink or it would never have happened. Jeneil, you have to remember that. You have to understand, honey."

She continued sobbing as Steve's words mingled with her anger and hurt, and then she remembered the night with Robert on the *Sea Urchin*. Her sobbing eased and Steve was encouraged. He had begun to feel panicked and really wished he hadn't told her. Her crying became silence for a few minutes and then she began crying again softly.

"Honey, aren't you understanding it yet?" he asked, confused by the relapse of tears.

"Yes, I understand fully," she said, continuing to cry. "He's going to stay with Uette."

"What?" Steve replied. "How the hell did you arrive at that? The baby's his but he doesn't love her. Jeneil, come on, geez. Get a hold on all of it."

"I have," she said, through her tears. "He told me if he found out the baby was his, he'd stay with Uette. That's probably why he can't face me. He doesn't know how to tell me."

"That's crazy, Jeneil. Really, it's outrageous. This is way out of hand. The baby is his, nothing else has changed."

Jeneil shook her head. "You're wrong, Steve. Everything has changed. I'm beginning to think Dennis was right. Uette is crazy about Peter. Maybe all of it is what he wants now."

Steve felt sick. "Jeneil, listen, I wouldn't have told you anything if I had known you'd overreact like this."

"I'm not overreacting. He isn't calling me, Steve. I haven't heard from him in weeks and neither have you. It's happened again, I'll just bet," she said, crying harder.

"What's happened again?" he asked, confused.

"Nothing," she replied, evading his question.

He sighed. "I wish I had kept my big mouth shut but you looked so hurt I thought you were imagining the wrong thing, now this...this is worse," he said, sighing again. She sat up and grabbed more tissues. Steve sat on the edge of the bed next to her as she cried softly. "Honey, let's call Pete and settle this."

"No!" She looked up quickly, drying her eyes. "No," she said emphatically, "let's just wait to see what he does. I don't want to pressure him if he's interested in Uette."

"Oh shit!" Steve stood up and paced. "The guy hates her guts. He can't stand being around her. This is crazy."

"Steve, promise me you won't say a word. We'll just wait to see what happens. Certainly you can understand my pride and his dignity in this." She stopped crying abruptly, surprising him. "Promise me, Steve."

"Okay," he replied reluctantly, "I promise. I think you're wrong but I promise."

Jeneil pulled herself together and asked what Peter's exact words were and was quiet after Steve told her. He left her reluctantly that night. She was calmed but quite shaken by the news and he was worried about her. He called her at the office the next day and was told that she wasn't expected in for a couple of days. There was no answer at her apartment even after he kept calling later and later. He tried calling her apartment the following morning but there was still no answer.

*****

Jeneil walked on the beach listening to the screeching of the gulls. The cleaning crew was working inside scrubbing everything so the beach house could be locked for the winter. She had taken a garbage bag and was clearing the beach of debris. Officially, the beach closed on Labor Day so city work crews didn't clean it after that even though the good weather continued bringing sunbathers and picnickers to the cove. Having finished tossing the last of the beer cans into the bag, she removed her work gloves and sat on the sand near Salter's Point and watched the waves roll in. A whitecap broke against the rocks she had once climbed over to get jellyfish and shark eggs to show Peter. She allowed tears to fall hoping she'd more quickly come to terms with her feelings.

Given the situation, stability wasn't something she could easily grasp. She kept struggling with feelings that she belonged to Peter and everything would be fine, then she'd remember what Peter had told Steve about the baby being his and both her heart and hope would sink. She knew it was vital to remain as positive as she could and that she had responsibilities to take care of or else Hollis would step in. She put her work gloves back on, picked up the bag of trash, and headed back to the inlet.

"You're acting like you're the only one who has ever lost at love before. They have all survived and have even gone on to find happiness." She heard the words as she said them aloud but her heart wasn't comforted. Her head was sane and philosophical, but Irish was in a low anger.

Later, there was a deep emptiness inside of her as she faced the wind. Nothing was working. Nothing seemed to bring the positive attitude she had hoped to achieve and she interpreted that as having to grin and bear it because nothing would change it. The thought became more entrenched every time she thought of Peter's words to Steve. Well, it looked like his mother was right. Actually, the only thin hope she had had come from Steve and that was Peter couldn't stand Uette or stand being around her.

Staying at the beach house until the following afternoon, she headed back to her apartment clinging to Steve's words because she desperately wanted to. As hard as she had tried to prepare herself for the worst, Steve's words helped her to remember the ceremony on the patio and she knew she belonged to Chang and always would. She also knew Peter would never forget that night either.

Twelve

Jeneil's apartment was bare after being away all summer and she needed to buy food and provisions to get life back in order. Keep purpose in your life, she lectured herself, showering and putting on an outfit she liked to mentally prepare herself for a much needed shopping trip. She marched down the stairs determined to regain as much of her old Camelot as she could. At least there she was peaceful within herself even though she was unfinished. She opened the front door as Steve approached the front steps.

Seeing her, Steve smiled and left his look of concern on the bottom stair as he ran the rest, closing the front door behind him. "Jeneil, baby," he said, taking her in his arms, "no more disappearing, honey, please. We're more to each other, aren't we? I deserve more than that, don't I?" He kissed her lips lightly. "You scared me."

"I'm sorry. Sometimes I need to be with my inner-self."

"Then let a guy know, sweetheart," he said, still holding her. Adrienne and Charlie watched from the top landing and looked at each other with raised eyebrows. Adrienne began talking to Charlie to announce their presence as they walked down the stairs.

"Hey, you two," Adrienne said, smiling, "we can say our goodbyes right here."

"Where are you going?" Steve asked.

"Two week vacation," Charlie answered.

Jeneil laughed. "And after moving the office, Adrienne deserves one."

"Take care of yourself," Adrienne said, hugging Jeneil, and after hearing about the incident at Wonderland she hugged Steve, too. "Make sure she's okay for me."

"You bet." Steve smiled, putting his arm around Jeneil. "There's a long list of people with a vested interest in her."

Adrienne smiled at him. Over the summer she had seen that Steve cared quite a lot for Jeneil and she was comforted by that because she had come to like Steve. It surprised her now how right they looked together and she hoped the best would turn out for her soul sister who, it seemed to her, was getting some lousy breaks. Neither she nor Charlie could believe the baby was really Peter's and Charlie was upset enough to want to deck him. Saying their final goodbyes, they left.

Steve smiled at Jeneil. "Come on, honey; we'll go to dinner and then do some shopping for both of our apartments." He hugged her again. "I'm glad you're back." She took his hand, glad he had shown up.

*****

Peter got home to find Uette dressed for going out.

"We're going shopping," she said. "The baby could be born anytime this month and I want to be ready. So you either go with me to get the things we need or I'll charge whatever I decide to spend. I'm tired of waiting."

Peter sighed, having expected it sooner or later. "Okay, just let me get something to eat."

"No," she pouted, "we're eating out."

"No," he insisted.

"Yes," she persisted, "or I'll leave while you eat here and I mean it."

He knew she meant it and was afraid of what she'd spend. "Okay, but nothing fancy, someplace where we go in and out."

She smiled, delighted to have gotten her way. Laughing, she hugged him. "Thanks you sweet guy."

He pushed her gently away. "Don't do that," he scowled. "The closer we get to the end, the more rules you seem to break."

She went to the door laughing. "Come on, my sweet husband; let's get our baby something to sleep on."

He frowned at the phrase, 'our baby,' and he walked to the door.

*****

Steve and Jeneil waited by the checkout counter of the market when they heard somebody call his name. They turned and Steve smiled. "Dan Moretti, how are you?" he asked, extending his hand.

Dan looked at Jeneil. "I know you. I'm sure I know you."

"This is Jeneil," Steve said, "she used to work in the records department."

"Yes! You've cut your hair," Dan said, and Jeneil nodded and smiled. "Well, this feels like old home week. I just ran into Peter and his wife at the Parkway Restaurant. I didn't know she was expecting. They were out shopping for baby furniture. Man, how life changes. Steve shopping for his apartment and Peter shopping for a baby with his wife wrapped around his arm. She sure looked happy." He smiled and Jeneil felt her stomach twist. "Well, great seeing the two of you. Take care."

"You, too," Steve said, smiling as Dan walked away. He put his arm around Jeneil's shoulder having noticed her reaction to Dan's news.

Returning home, Jeneil unpacked her items and put them away. Steve watched her from the kitchen doorway. She hadn't said a word since hearing about Peter and Uette out to dinner and shopping. It totally shocked him so he knew Jeneil must be hurting. She closed the freezer door and then turned away. He noticed her shoulders slump and he heard her sniffle.

"I'm sorry, honey," he said, going to her, feeling sorry for the mess life had dumped on her. She turned quickly and put her arms around him. He held her closely, kissing her temple.

She sobbed. "He's gone, Steve. It's all over. Now I know why he can't face me."

"I'm going to kill him tomorrow," he said, kissing her cheek.

"No," she cried, "no, leave him his dignity. Having to admit he was wrong about the baby must be embarrassing. He probably told you hoping you'd tell me. Let's leave it at that."

Steve couldn't believe how gentle she was being toward Peter or that he could feel more love for her, but he was and it was mixed with a generous amount of respect. He held her, letting her cry, wanting to destroy the guy who only a year ago was his best friend. He choked up as she sobbed. Her pain was very deep and very real, and there was no way he could lessen it for her.

"I'm right here, sweetheart, right here," he said, and he felt her cling tightly to him. "You'll get through this, baby. I promise you will and I'll be right here. You can count on that." She melted into his arms and stayed there.

*****

Peter tried to catch Steve several times at the hospital but he seemed illusive. After almost a week, he began to wonder if Steve was avoiding him. He sighed as he went back to his office. His marriage to the bitch had him paranoid and imagining all kinds of things, but the gnawing feeling within continued and he seriously wondered if he should call Jeneil. Uette seemed too caught up in buying things for the baby to be spying anymore and his only concern was for Jeneil, but he knew he still needed to be cautious.

At dinner that night, he wondered if he should approach Uette openly. The pregnancy seemed to be going along fine; she had lost seven pounds but her doctor had said some women lost a little at the end of the pregnancy and had ordered her to force herself to eat. She was trying hard to do that but just didn't seem to have an appetite.

He watched as she picked at her food. "Uette, I think we should talk about the divorce."

She looked up, surprised. "What about it?"

"Our agreement states that you will get the divorce. I think you should see a lawyer and get the whole thing started," he said calmly.

"I'm not getting a divorce," she said, sitting back in her chair.

"You signed an agreement."

"I don't care!" she answered. "I'm not unhappily married. I don't want a divorce."

Peter was shocked. "Uette, we're not really married. I can't believe you're accepting this situation as a marriage and you want it to continue. Now, before you're confined with the baby, see a lawyer."

"No," she replied.

Peter looked at her. "Then I will. Any violation of the prenuptial agreement constitutes grounds for a divorce."

She stared at him steadily. "Any violation of our marriage as it stands now and I'll have Jeneil killed."

"You're crazy," he replied, stunned by her plain language.

"We're not getting divorced. I want a chance to be a wife to you without this baby in the way. The pregnancy has been the problem all along, that and Jeneil."

He couldn't believe what he was hearing. "Uette, make sense. This isn't a marriage and I want out."

She shrugged. "It's your choice, but you won't be able to have Jeneil because I'll put a contract out on her."

"Why?" he asked incredulously.

Uette leaned forward and glared at him. "Because she ruined this marriage. Between her and being pregnant, I haven't had a chance to be your wife. I want the chance to make this marriage work."

"By forcing me to stay married to you? Listen to yourself. You're talking crazy."

Uette smiled sweetly. "I am crazy...crazy about you."

Peter felt sick. Uette was obviously not thinking rationally and he decided to drop the subject. He got up and cleared his dishes, rinsing them and putting them in the dishwasher. He couldn't believe her attitude and he hadn't counted on her wanting to stay married. Feeling quite certain that she was sick, he knew he had to get some help. He went back to the dining room to clear her dishes and was surprised to hear her in the bathroom being sick. Clearing the table and filling the dishwasher, he started it on the wash cycle. She was still in the bathroom when he returned so he called her doctor.

"Dr. Chang, what's the problem?" Dr. Vandiver asked.

"Uette's in the bathroom throwing up. Is her pregnancy progressing normally?"

"She hasn't been a model patient, but I haven't seen anything to indicate trouble."

"Did she tell you about the sharp pain and bleeding?"

"No, when did that happen?"

"Weekend before last," Peter replied.

"I saw her last Friday and the exam didn't indicate anything unusual. She said the baby's not moving as much but that happens toward the end. It's in birth position already."

"Then why is she vomiting now?"

Dr. Vandiver chuckled. "Dr. Chang, you know I can only guess why but it could be that she's catching a cold. Damn nuisance for her, too, if she is. I see her next Friday and I'll give her a thorough screening, how's that?"

"I think that might be wise," Peter agreed.

"If her symptoms seem to get worse, bring her in before Friday. She really hasn't taken this pregnancy as seriously as she should have, you know. Until a month or two ago she was a nightmare and then she straightened out, but I had to threaten to hospitalize her. She has the worst health habits I've ever seen for a woman these days. She doesn't know her own body at all and she doesn't want to. Was this pregnancy an accident?"

"Why?" Peter asked, caught off guard.

"Because I get the feeling she's just living through it, tolerating it."

Peter nodded. "Have you asked her?"

"Yes," Dr. Vandiver replied, "but Dr. Chang, I'm going to be honest, I'm never sure who she is. She said the pregnancy was planned but she isn't acting like a woman who wanted to be pregnant. She says the marriage is happy and stable, so I don't know what I'm up against. I'm just glad she didn't decide on natural birth because she just isn't committed enough. I have to admit that I'm worried about her as a person, but I haven't seen signs with the pregnancy. I think though she's unstable emotionally, but then I just found out last Friday that she was a drama major in college so maybe that's what it is. Some personalities are not measured as quite normal, but fall within the legal framework of the definition. They're on the fringe so to speak. I have a patient who's an artist and she's spacey, too. Artistic temperaments sometimes create eccentric personalities, so maybe her love for acting is what I'm up against. Psyche's not my field, so she has been a headache case for me."

"Thanks Dr. Vandiver." Peter replied.

"Thank you for calling Dr. Chang. I'll put her through an intensive exam on Friday."

"A blood test too." Peter suggested.

Dr. Vandiver was silent. "What are you looking for?"

"Drugs." Peter replied.

"Oh shit!" Dr. Vandiver groaned. "Why the hell didn't you tell me this before?"

"I could be wrong." Peter answered. "She has been trying hard to look after herself. I thought she was open with you."

"No." Dr. Vandiver sighed. "Damn that woman. She's not even straight with herself then. That's it for me then Dr. Chang. When she comes in Friday and I find anything even slightly out of the way, she's being admitted. It's me and this baby who will be affected by her abuse and neither one of us can succeed in labor and delivery without her help. I should pull her in right now to really cover my ass." He sighed. "Now I'm wondering what the hell she's missed in symptoms. Watch her closely."

"I'll try, but my field isn't obstetrics"

"What is your field?"

"Orthopedic surgery."

Dr. Vandiver shook his head in frustration. "You surgeons are the only smart ones in the whole group of us. It's all in your hands. You're in control of the situation. You do it your way."

"I'm sorry, I didn't step in earlier." Peter sighed. "I've hidden my head in this mess for too long."

"Marriage is in trouble isn't it?" Dr. Vandiver asked.

"It's not even a marriage."

"Well, don't wake Uette up. Her fantasy life might get her through this. Don't rock the boat until after the baby's born. The baby and I don't deserve complications. We're innocent."

"I know." Peter sighed. "I'll watch her."

"Thanks." Dr. Vandiver replied. "I do wish you had called me earlier, but my field of medicine is full of surprises so we'll take it as it comes. Call me anytime about anything Dr. Chang, no matter how seemingly minor."

Peter hung up and paced knowing that he'd better not call Jeneil. His mind panicked that Uette could even say the words about having Jeneil killed. Peter rubbed his forehead wondering how he would get out of the marriage peacefully. There seemed to be no end to the nightmare that saving face had brought him. Yet, he couldn't help but feel that the idea of saving face was good, it was just necessary for each person involved to understand honor and dignity in order for the principals to work right. He sighed. "Songbird, how long will you wait? How long will I be tied into this mess?" He worried about Steve's edginess. "What's happening with Jeneil?" He wondered. Uette came from the bathroom. Peter watched her. "You don't look too well."

Uette held her hand against her stomach. "I'll be okay."

"Are you getting sick like that often?"

"No." She snapped. "That was the first time; it's probably a result of my husband asking for a divorce." She cried.

"Forget I asked." Peter answered and went to his room.

Uette dried her eyes and smiled as she heard the door close.

Peter sat on his bed looking at the unicorn. "That's it Songbird. I'm locked into this prison until the baby's born and then I'll see how to ease myself out. I have to keep you safe, Honey. I can't risk having you hurt." He envied Steve. It was Friday night and he knew that Steve went to Wonderland on Fridays for the weekend. He sighed and reached for a medical journal hoping to avoid a bout with discouragement.

Thirteen

Uette and Peter's mother were still not speaking. Peter went to his Grandfather's birthday dinner and Uette to visit her family. He was glad for this separation from her. She was acting like they were really married, and he couldn't stand being around her for long periods of time. He sighed when Sunday was over and he could get back to work. He watched for Steve in the scrub room on Monday determined to make an appointment with him and catch up on what was happening like Steve had suggested. Peter caught him as he headed to OR 4. "Steve can you spare some time today?"

"Yeh Pete." Steve said, quietly. "We need to talk. How about 5th floor after late rounds today?"

"Good." Peter agreed. "I'll be there." Steve nodded and went into the operating room. Peter didn't like the way he looked. Something was wrong, he could feel it. He put all of it aside and went to scrub.

*****

The street before Peter was barely visible as he drove to his mother's after work. His whole body was in pain after having talked to Steve. He parked the car and was at the door to the house, but he couldn't remember walking to it. Knocking, he walked in. They were finishing dinner. His mother was surprised to see him. "Pete, can I get you something?"

He rubbed his forehead trying to think and then he went to the cupboard for a glass. "Yeh, I could use a stiff drink." He went to the cabinet in the living room and poured an inch of bourbon into the glass he held. He drank it down and felt the burning through his chest. He coughed and was tempted to pour another.

"Peter?" He turned. His Grandfather was watching him.

"I came to talk to you Grandfather. I need to talk."

"Okay." His Grandfather took the bottle from him and replaced the cover. "Let's go to the green house." Peter nodded and followed him to the kitchen.

His mother looked concerned. "Would you like some dinner? Don't let that witch of a wife drive you to drink, Peter. In another month or two you'll be back with Jeneil, I can understand why you were lying to Uette about you and Jeneil being over. You were at least healthy with Jeneil." She sighed.

Peter stopped and stared, struck by her words. "Oh Hell, just look at the progress we've made here. Now she's Jeneil. Now she has a name." He was getting angry. "What happened, did my honorable Chinese wife show you what real scum is, and now Jeneil is decent? She's not trash anymore? She's no longer filth to you?" He shouted, angrily. His mother looked shocked by his outburst as well as everyone around the table.

Tom stood up. "Peter calm down."

His Grandfather touched his arm. "Peter let's talk." Peter rubbed his eyes. "I'm sorry." He said and headed to the greenhouse leaving everyone puzzled.

Peter paced frantically as his Grandfather watched, becoming more concerned.

"Peter, what is it? Something has you very upset."

Peter swallowed hard. "I can't say it." He ran his fingers through his hair. "The words won't come out."

"I'll get some tea." His Grandfather suggested.

"No." Peter sighed. "I'll only choke on it."

"Tell me what's happened."

Peter stopped pacing and held his hand against his stomach and drew in a deep breath.

"I talked to Steve after work today." Peter held onto his stomach and sat down on the bench, heavily.

His Grandfather felt a feeling of dread pass through him. "What happened to Jeneil?" He asked.

Peter sighed, heavily. "Jeneil and Steve were married on Friday."

Peter bolted from the bench as if the words had stung him, and he went to the green house window.

His Grandfather stared as the words hit his chest with force too. Looking around for his chair, he went to it quickly and sat.

"Married?" The Grandfather gasped. "But I don't understand."

"What's to understand?" Peter replied. "It's hard to misunderstand the word, married?"

"But none of this seems like Jeneil. She never told you, there was no notice, no hint?" His Grandfather said.

Peter continued staring out the window. "They tried I think. Steve was trying to tell me something a couple of weeks ago. There wasn't time then. This is probably what it was.

He said he wanted to tell me before the news went through the hospital. Nice of him wasn't it?"

The Grandfather was still confused. "Peter, call Jeneil. Call her and ask her about this."

Peter spun around totally shocked. "Are you serious?! She's been married for three days and you want me to call her." He laughed and held his hand to his ear like a telephone. "Hi Steve, It's Pete, can I talk to your wife, I'd like to know why she isn't my wife. I hope I'm not intruding." Peter laughed again. "Grandfather, are you sure you understand honor and dignity?" He sat on the bench and covered his face with his hands. "Oh damn, what a shock." He said, clearing his throat.

The Grandfather shook his head. "This isn't like Jeneil. She understands honor and dignity. She's honorable, she keeps her word. She would allow you her dignity."

Peter rubbed his eyes and sighed. "She does understand honor and dignity, Grandfather. That's why she married Steve. Think about it. My mother insulted her with filth every chance she got and slaps her face probably the first time anyone ever did. Nice mother-in-law. Then I have to marry Uette. Steve told me a while ago that Jeneil was having trouble explaining the marriage to her friends. They think she's crazy and I don't blame them. Steve had started by saying that he thinks she needs a normal life. He was trying to explain it then. My life isn't her style, Grandfather. I've known it all along, I guess. I'm a street kid. She doesn't need me and all the shit in my life. And last but not least by far is Uette." He stood up and paced. "Uette, that lying piece of sewer filth. This is her fault." He stopped pacing and grinned. "And that shittin bitch has lost her ace. It's over scum. You're axe has been blown out of your hand and the ball in my court now and I'm going to shove it down your lying throat."

The Grandfather was confused. "Peter, you're not making any sense.

Peter looked at him. "Grandfather, my Chinese wife told me last Friday that if I try to get a divorce she's have Jeneil killed."

His Grandfather stood up, completely aghast. "And you didn't report that?"

Peter shook his head, amused. "Grandfather this mess has been beyond saving face for months now. She'd deny she said it. But it's over for her. She cost me Jeneil and it's going to cost her the war. I'm going home and blow that prison of hers into small bits." Peter headed to the door.

"Peter." His Grandfather called. "If you play the game her way, you have to get down to her level."

Peter snapped on his top coat, angrily. "Well that suits me just fine."

The Grandfather shook his head. "Peter, think about it. Her level is the sewer. You've worked hard to change your life from that."

Peter stopped. "Grandfather, I've been held prisoner in her sewer for the past eight months. Now's my chance to walk out of it. I've taken her shit to protect Jeneil. Well, Jeneil's gone now, thanks to that shittin bitch. I owe her for this. I owe her big." He walked out, slamming the door after him.

The old man sat in the chair, sadly. "His language, his behavior. What has this cost him? Certainly more than the Songbird. Much, much more." He thought about Jeneil and his eyes became moist. "And how will you survive all this? None of it sounds like the Songbird. None of it. The Songbird is caught in something because she was unprotected. Oh Peter, real pain is watching your children make mistakes when you knew you had the answers to help them and they wouldn't listen. They don't understand. Honor and dignity would be to call Jeneil and discuss the situation honestly. It's never the easy road Peter, but it's less trouble in the end." He thought to himself.

"Father?" The old man was startled by his daughter's voice Tom and Lien stood by the chair.

"Why is Peter so angry?" Lien asked.

The old man sighed. "For the same reasons he was angry as a boy, life continues to play tricks on him." He sighed and shook his head wearily.

*****

Peter drove home as the fury of the news ate at him. He cautioned himself to calm down as his fury became channeled in one direction, Uette. His mind was in agony that Jeneil was gone. "She's married." He thought and pain shot all through him. He walked up the three flights of stairs to the apartment hoping to subside his rage. He unlocked the door and walked in. Uette came from her bedroom and stopped when she saw Peter's face and decided not to heckle him about missing dinner and not calling.

"Dr. Maxwell called you."

Peter went to the phone. "Wayne, it's Pete."

"Natalie has come down with some kind of a bug. Do you think you could cover the seminar in Boston for us? Dr. Slovik said he'd be available to take over some of our cases. I hate like hell to miss the seminar. The Germans are sending in three marrow experts and I wanted to catch that. Dr. Vlahoff is flying in from the west coast. All that talent and I have to miss it.

Peter couldn't believe his luck. The seminar would give him time to settle down. He was wondering how he'd be in surgery and he knew that with his anger, he'd better get away from Uette. "I'll cover it, Wayne."

"Could you leave tonight? The morning traffic to Boston could kill you. You'd have to leave so early you might as well stay over and rest up."

"No problem. I'll be there."

"Will your wife mind you being gone three days?"

"It'll be fine." Peter assured him.

"Pete thanks for being so agreeable. I was hoping to save seminars for you till next year. The wife hates them. Not many wives love them. They interrupt life too much. She's thrilled that I finally have someone to share the load."

Peter smiled. "I'll handle it."

"Keep track of expenses and we'll have Jean reimburse you."

"Fine." Peter answered. "I'm on my way."

"Thanks, Pete. I mean that." Peter walked past Uette to his bedroom.

She followed and watched as he got out his luggage. "Where are you going?" She asked.

"Three day seminar in Boston."

"But what about me?" She asked, frowning.

"What about you?" He glowered at her.

"I'll be here alone, what if I have the baby?"

"I hope you do." He said, closing his suitcase and putting his suits in the garment bag. "That way I can get a divorce and be out of this shit."

Uette was stunned by his attitude. She hadn't seen him like this since they were first married. She folded her arms. "I thought I made myself clear about us and divorce."

He went to the bathroom and returned with his shaving items and toothbrush. He looked at her and grinned. "Oh, I guess you don't know that we have new rules around here, bitch."

The name surprised her; she hadn't been called that in weeks. "You think I'm kidding?" She asked, raising her eyebrows.

Peter snapped the carryall bag closed. "No." He said, facing her squarely. "I believe a piece of scum like you would buy a contract, but screw you, shithead. Jeneil's gone." Peter picked up his bags.

"Gone? Gone where? What are you talking about?" She asked.

"She married Steve last Friday."

Uette's eyes widened in shock. "Married! You're lying! She didn't!"

Peter smiled. "What's the matter, bitch, notice a hole in your parachute? Is the ground rushing up to meet you? I'm out of here, scum for a three day seminar and then a divorce after that."

"No!" She shouted, following him to the livingroom. "How will I reach you if I need to." She asked, nervously.

"You won't need me. Call your father. You're his headache again. Not mine."

She grabbed his arm. "Peter calm down and think. My friends could hurt you."

Peter laughed. "Go ahead, do me that favor, you shittin' bitch.. I told you my life would be worthless without Jeneil. Your ammunition blew up in your face when Jeneil married Steve. Trust me, your friends would be putting me out of my misery because then I'd be free of you completely." He walked out leaving her staring at the door.

She paced, frantically. "That stupid, stupid witch. She never stops messing up my life! Married to Steve! That's exactly what Karen said she would do. So why is he blaming me!?" She cried. "I didn't count on this. I need to have his mother's help. Oh damn!" She stomped her foot. "Why is his life so surrounded by witches? Doesn't he know anybody who's sane?"

*****

Steve went to the Doctor's parking area. He sat in his car and closed his eyes just to rest. He couldn't get Peter's expression out of his mind. "Why was he so stunned?" He asked himself. He left her. What did he expect? Sheez, what a mess!" He sighed and started the engine. "Peter didn't even tell me what he wanted. He just looked like his stomach had been kicked and thanked me for telling him, then he bolted out of there. Shit, I didn't want him to hear it from anyone else. Damn it! Why the hell am I feeling guilty? He never even offered Jeneil the same dignity. And Jeneil...." He sighed, remembering Friday night. He was such a nervous wreck through the short ceremony before the judge and he couldn't believe that Jeneil was really Mrs. Steven Bradley after it. She had been calm through the whole thing, while he shook like a schoolboy. It was an absolute marvel to Steve how calm she was. He had expected her to back out. The marriage idea had started as a joke to lighten a sad moment for her. He never expected her to say yes. All he had said was: "Jeneil, I think you and I should get married to each other. We understand each other and we understand marriage. No romantic delusions, we could just take each other out of the singles game and continue a great friendship."

He had even laughed, but she looked at him seriously and said. "That's a good idea, when?" After the blood tests, he asked if she was sure. After the license application he asked if she was sure. After her business trip to Nebraska, he thought she'd come back and change her mind. But they continued through the whole procedure and she said "I do" as calmly as if she never doubted it to be right. He opened the car window for air as he remembered what happened after the ceremony and the quiet drive to his apartment. She had walked in to the apartment calmly and stayed standing near the door. He had taken his coat off and went to help her take hers off. She jumped a foot as he touched her shoulder, shocking him. She burst into tears and said she couldn't deal with it, then she opened the door and left. He remembered how sick he felt. He had let her go and spent the night dozing and pacing wondering if she'd come back. She never did. He went to her apartment the next morning feeling that he understood what had happened and was ready to face whatever was waiting for him. She had answered the door looking very embarrassed and they walked up the stairs together in silence. He paced while she made coffee and then they sat on the sofa. He remembered how uncomfortable she looked and he smiled understanding what was wrong. He assured her that he knew that she loved Peter and he heard himself tell her that he didn't expect a physical relationship in the marriage. She had looked surprised and relieved, apologizing for her behavior and for not realizing all the details that should have been worked out before the ceremony took place. Like where they would live. She said she just hadn't thought about it and it wasn't until she was standing in the apartment that she thought of all the details involved in a marriage. She apologized for being so hysterical. They spent Saturday working out the details of their marriage and wondered where to find a two bedroom apartment. He went to his apartment to sleep and she stayed at hers. They went to breakfast Sunday and looked at an apartment in Fairview 1900 that the lessees wanted to sell the four months left on their lease because of a transfer out of state. The apartment was completely furnished and they wanted to sell all the furniture with it. Steve and Jeneil talked in the hallway deciding to take it and Jeneil wrote out a check for the four months plus the cost of the furniture. The tenant, had no idea the woman who was subletting their apartment was the landlady. Jeneil had explained that she and Steve were newly married since Friday and hadn't had a chance to combine accounts yet. Steve was speechless. Jeneil told the shocked tenants to verify her name at the building management office on Monday as a credit reference for the large check. They had each gone to there individual apartment to pack their things and they hadn't seen each other since. Steve had received a message at his office from Jeneil on Monday morning telling him that the apartment was vacated and that she sent a cleaning crew in and would he like to have them move him from his apartment? He called her; she was at her lawyer's office so he left word to have his things moved. He went back to work completely shocked at how take charge she was. He had been married for three days and had seen and talked to his wife more on a weekend when they were just friends, then since marrying her on Friday. He drove into the indoor security parking area and found his assigned spot. Apt. 1412 A&B slots. Jeneil's car was parked in the B slot. Steve felt stupid parking his old lynx in slot A while her late model Torrence was in the B slot looking assembly line new and subtlety money. The corporation had replaced the car that was damaged at Wonderland. A car was part of her salary.

He closed his eyes. "Bradley are you crazy?" He thought "You're in Fairview 1900 married to the owner of the building. It's a marriage in name only and you're so in love with her you can't see straight let alone hide it much longer. This is real life you ass! You'll sit across the table at breakfast and share the same bathroom. Do you think you're superman?" He sighed and rested his head back. "No problem." He said, half aloud. "Just the thought of her jumping like she did at my apartment and bolting out on me will keep me straight. Well, this is it Dr. Steven Bradley. This is home and it's complete with a Mrs. Steven Bradley also known as your good friend. Go up the stairs and begin married life. He locked his car door. "Boy, you've never believed in fairy tales and now you are in one up to your ass." He rode up the elevator wondering what life was going to be like. By the time he got to the 14th floor, he was as nervous as he was on Friday at the judge's chamber. He took the keys that had been delivered to his office and unlocked the door to the spacious livingroom done in beige and shades of green with splashes of orange and rust and brown. The drapes were open to a view of sparkling stars and city lights. It took his breath away as he stood there. Jeneil came from the kitchen in a long black dress and pearls wearing a white apron with a ruffle around it.

"Hi." She said, quietly. "Isn't that view spectacular at night."

"I'll say." He answered, feeling strange there with her and not knowing what to do.

"I moved a small table to the window. The view is so beautiful; I thought we could have dinner there."

"Okay." He said, wondering what to do with himself.

"All your things are in your room in boxes along with your luggage. Would you like some help? Dinner can be put on hold for a short time." She smiled. "I made pot roast."

He smiled at her. It was his favorite and he knew that she was trying to make the best of the situation. He appreciated that and it calmed him slightly.

"I'll change." And then looking at her outfit, he decided that he'd better not. "Uh, I'll stay in my suit. I'm really hungry, could we eat now?" She nodded and returned to the kitchen. He went to freshen up and to check out his room. His medical books were in boxes the end of the hall and he wondered where he would put them. Everything he needed immediately seemed to be there. It was a very nice bedroom. She had given him the master bedroom and had taken the smaller one. He remembered that she had taken the second slot in the parking area leaving him the first. He smiled. "She doesn't pull rank."

"Pretty upside down isn't it?" She said from the doorway.

He turned. "It won't take long to sort it out, except for my books."

"There's a shortage of book shelves in the whole place." She replied. "I'll have that taken care of. There's room for your desk in here too."

He grinned. "You move fast."

She smiled. "Dinner's on the table, getting cold." He nodded and followed her to the livingroom. The view was very impressive, but dinner was awkward and by the end of it, he found himself missing easy going Camelot and his good friend Jeneil. She had done her best to make dinner special, crystal and china, candles, wine, but they were strangers to each other and there were awkward silences between them.

"I think I'll get my room straightened." He said as he finished dessert. He couldn't take anymore of the awkwardness. He helped clear the table and fill the dishwasher. The kitchen never seemed to be a mess from her cooking; she kept everything to a minimum of effort. "Dinner was delicious." He said, sounding stupid to himself, but it was true. "I'll get to my room." He added and left. Closing the door to his room, he sighed as discouragement over came him. "This is awful, I miss Jeneil." He said, rubbing the back of his neck. He concentrated on putting his room in order. He was thirsty by the time he finished and wondered what cold drinks were around. As he walked past her bedroom, he heard her sniff. He could tell that she was crying. He stopped before the door wanting to go in and talk to her. He shook his head. "I'd better not." And he continued to the kitchen and then back to his room and to bed. There was no sound when he stopped by at 5:00 in next morning. He headed to early surgery.

*****

News of Steve's marriage tore through the hospital. Jerry Tollman and three other first year residents were scrubbing. "Man that was fast." One intern commented. "One week you hear they're dating and just friends and the next they're married."

"Maybe he got her pregnant." Another snickered.

Jerry glared at him. "Grow up Burton."

Morgan Rand had arrived. "Exactly Burton, grow up. This isn't a high school locker room. Dr. Bradley married a lady remember that.

Burton grinned. "Oh yeh? If everything is so new to them, then how come no honeymoon?" Burton has missed all the warning looks he was getting from the other residents.

Steve stood by his elbow. "Burton it seems to me you could use more time studying procedure. You still need too much coaching on basics. Spend more time with the books and less time thinking about hormones, yours and mine or become an urologist." He continued to another sink leaving the upstart resident embarrassed.

"Was that the White Stallion who just called the kettle black?" Burton mumbled.

Jerry Tollman looked up. "Yeh, Burton, it was, but he, unlike you excelled in both. He's right your procedure shits. If you want to study the guy so much watch his hands in OR and protect the public from a surgical menace."

"Sheez, what a bunch of deadheads." Burton replied and scrubbed in silence.

Steve looked for Peter and saw only Dr. Maxwell. "Where's Dr. Chang?" He asked, stopping by his sink, briefly.

"Three day seminar in Boston." Dr. Maxwell answered.

Steve nodded. "You miss faces when they're not here."

Dr. Maxwell smiled. "Medical brotherhood."

"Yeh." Steve said, and continued to OR #3 relieved that Peter was okay and into business as usual. Steve thought about calling Jeneil at her office during the day, but not having a good enough reason, he didn't and he arrived home to find an empty apartment. He reheated the pot roast and ate at the kitchen table alone. A bookcase had been put in his room along with her desk from the old apartment. He unpacked his books wondering where she was. By 8:30 he was getting concerned. He called Camelot wondering is she was there. The line rang a busy signal. "Maybe she's moving things." He tried again fifteen minutes later. As he replaced the receiver, he noticed the number on his telephone. He was dialing the same number. "That's why it's busy. She must have had the service transferred to here and kept her old number." He thought. "Where is she?"

The apartment door opened and in walked Jeneil. He watched her take off her coat and hang it in the closet. She looked great. He liked the fact that her business clothes were soft looking and not suits with lapels and shirts. She wore jackets and blouses.

"Hi." She said, moving her neck from side to side and massaging it.

"Tired?" He asked.

She nodded. "Did you manage any dinner?"

"Yes, did you?" He asked.

She nodded again. "I've been at a dinner meeting with my accountant and lawyer." She sighed. "Two and a half hours. I think I need my own staff of accountants. The firm I use is having trouble keeping up with the changes which affects information to my lawyer. What a drain, we're all trying to eat and read statistics and reports. I hate dinner meetings. Do one or the other, dine or meet. With Adrienne away, the office is limping. I'm going to soak in bubbles." She opened her purse. "I'm having an answering gismo put on this phone tomorrow. Here's the message it'll carry if you approve." She handed him a type written card. "There's a recording at your old number giving this new number. I hope you don't mind that I kept my telephone number here and not yours. I've had mine for so long." She stopped and took a deep breath. "Oh dear, I didn't think. I could have had two separate phones installed and you could keep your old number too. That's what Peter...." She stopped herself and rubbed her temple. "I'm going to soak in bubbles. Between moving the office recently and moving from Wonderland to Camelot and then here, I'm losing my grip. I'll be glad when Adrienne gets back from vacation." She turned and left.

Steve watched her and worried that she was wound too tightly. She ran the bath water and must have filled it with scented bubble bath because the smell of her perfume traveled on the stream as it swirled from the bathroom. He went to check the water which he thought was running a long time. It was steamy and smelled like her perfume. He turned off the water since the thick bubbles had reached the top of the tub. Her bedroom door opened and she stood at the bathroom door looking anxious. "Did it overflow?" She asked. "I forgot I had run the bath." He could tell that she had been crying.

"Nothing's damaged." He assured her. "The tub has an overflow drain. We all forget things. See the tub's just getting filled."

She laughed lightly seeing the steam. "What do you think doctor? First, second or third degree burns from this?"

He smiled. "I'd add cold water that's for sure." He felt awkward standing in the bathroom with her at the door in her robe and slippers. "I'm in your way." He said. "So if you'll step in here or out there, I'll leave."

"Oh." She said, realizing she was in the doorway, and she walked in. He passed her and left feeling like a klutz. Pouring a cup of coffee in the kitchen, he took it to the livingroom and sat. He took the card she had given him for the telephone answering machine. It read *"Dr. Steven Bradley and Mrs. Jeneil Bradley Alden-Connors would appreciate your message being left so they can return your call as soon as possible."* He smiled. "Mrs. Jeneil Bradley." He liked the sound of it and then he sighed. "Mrs. Steven Bradley is trying very hard to be brave, but Dr. Steven Bradley isn't being fooled." He sat drinking his coffee and thinking. She finished her bath, went to the kitchen and returned with a tall drink of water and ice. She asked if he'd like to change the telephone message. "No." He answered. She passed pleasant small talk and then said goodnight and left. He had passed her door on the way to his room and then went back to listen. There was silence from her. He went to bed. The next few days passed pretty much the same with Steve becoming more concerned about how tense she was and listening to the crying she was doing in her room. He decided to wait. Adrienne was due back at the office on Monday. He hoped that would help.

*****

Peter unlocked the apartment door wondering what he'd find waiting for him. He had stayed in Boston until after the rush hour and treated himself to a cheeseburger at a diner he'd found on a narrow side street near the hotel that had the taste of cheeseburger down to a science. The seminar was more pleasant than he had heard described by some doctors and it was a three day cheeseburger heaven for him once he found that diner. He had them at each meal even bringing one in for a bedtime snack each night. He skipped the luncheon food that was provided and slipped into the diner returning early to socialize with the other doctors after lunch. The trip had been fun and he found that it had helped him to relax quite a bit. The surroundings were different and everything was a distraction. It was only at night that he would remember that Jeneil was married to Steve and the pain would almost paralyze him. So he tried to avoid remembering it, but he wasn't succeeding to well. What surprised him was his hatred toward Steve. He blamed Steve and Uette completely. His third surprise was Chang's silence. It was like he had been anesthetized. Peter was grateful, because he knew he would have to deal with Uette for the divorce and he was glad to have Chang out of the whole situation. His level of raging frightened Peter because it had become so intense during the marriage to Uette. The apartment was quiet, actually silent. Normally her TV would be on in her bedroom. Her car was in the lot. He smiled. "Maybe she had the baby? Relax Doctor, the seminar was the limit of your good luck, I'm sure." He went to the kitchen for a cold drink. There was a note on the table. *"Peter. I've gone away for the weekend."* Her handwriting looked totally different, the note was scrawled. "Shittin bitch." He mumbled. "Probably popped. At least you left the car here so you won't hurt anyone." He went to his room. The telephone rang. "Grandfather, how are you?"

"Worried, Peter. Where's Uette?"

"I just got in." Peter replied. "She left a note that she went away for the weekend."

"Away? Is that smart at this stage of the pregnancy?"

Peter chuckled. "I hope she's on another planet and loses the directions how to get back."

His Grandfather was silent. "Peter, Mr. Wong called me. Uette was near hysteria after you left on Monday."

Peter was irritated. "I told her to go home so her father could watch her. Why was she hysterical?"

"Because you blame her for Jeneil marrying Steve." Peter felt the pain hit his stomach at the words. The Grandfather continued. "She said you called her obscenities and verbally abused her."

"Abuse." Peter sneered. "What the hell does she call this mess we have been in for eight months?"

"Peter I believe her because you were angry when you left here."

"Grandfather, I was mean and ugly, but I was no where near abuse level."

"Peter she's pregnant and due any time, finish this with honor and dignity."

"Is anybody telling that bitch to use honor and dignity? The Wongs should have given her lessons in how to spell them. The lying bitch won't ever quit will she? And this will be the ex Mrs. Peter Chang. What fun!" He snapped. "I never covered visitation rights in the agreement. I didn't think it would be necessary. My mistake."

The Grandfather was surprised. "Will you want visitation rights?"

Peter was silent for a moment. "The baby will carry my name. It'll think I'm the father. I know what it's like to not have one. Divorce isn't shameful. I'll stand by the kid if it thinks I'm the father. Kids are entitled to that and this kid's got a real problem with her for a mother."

"Peter I'm surprised and very pleased."

"It's no big deal, Grandfather. This whole thing is such a lousy break for an innocent kid. The mother doesn't want it, the father doesn't want it. I can relate to the kid's handicap. I was a kid who had a rapist for a father and they called my mother names like it was her fault. That was rough to take. No kid who carries my name will go through it. I couldn't take it all over again."

The Grandfather listened and swallowed past the lump in his throat. Life had not dealt easily with this grandson. He was a victim and the grandfather felt the pain too, but he also felt the pride as he watched the man try to correct injustice in life, even if it meant that he swallowed his own pride. He was capable of great love. Malien was right; he did have a good heart. His grandfather smiled. "Peter, let that attitude show through on this. Be careful with Uette, she is in a delicate condition."

"I know that. I'm under control, now. Getting away was good for me. Don't worry Grandfather, the Chang name will shine."

The old man felt reassured after he hung up. He sat in his chair thinking about the oldest of his Grandsons. "He is capable of great love and his good heart makes him susceptible to great hurt, too." He thought. "It was hurt that made him such an angry boy." He was impressed with Peter for caring about justice for the baby when life had only given him injustice. "He was always an exceptional energy." He thought. "He'll need it now to face the newest injustice that's been handed to him. How will he handle the loss of the great love he's had. The hurt that is sure to replace it will be as equal to the deep love he had for the songbird. That's going to be great pain, Peter. I hope you're wise enough to deal with it so Yin and Yang are balanced." He thought of Jeneil and wondered how she would deal with her loss too. He missed the girl who seemed so much like a natural Granddaughter to him. Life seemed to have dealt harshly with all three of the people involved. All of them were strong energies, but his concern was for Jeneil who had been asked to handle two others besides herself. Life was requiring the most delicate and gentle of the three to be the strongest. "Life creates opportunities to make heroes of us all." He sighed. "It's up to us when the ring drops before us to become heroes or tragic victims." He looked into the cage as his songbird chirped, happily. "Learn from nature, Jeneil. It's life's instruction book. Listen carefully and you'll understand why the caged bird sings."

Fourteen

Jeneil groaned inwardly all day Friday, wishing it to be over. Finishing a list of business items for Adrienne, she sighed and sat back. "I need to malfunction, but I can't." She closed her eyes. "There's no time to slip off the conveyor belt." She felt herself choke up and she deliberately sat forward at attention to distract herself. Getting emotional was happening to her quite a bit lately, and at the oddest moments. The feeling of wanting to burst into tears would well up in her even during meetings with no reason for it. She was becoming concerned about it. She had the feeling that if she gave in to it, she would cry for days without stopping and that would be embarrassing to say the least. She knew she wasn't fooling Steve even though he just watched her and stayed silent. "Poor Steve." She sighed. "His wife's a maniac. She rushes off on him. She has cooked one decent meal for him since Monday and she's rarely been home all week. He's such a good friend." She choked again. "Or at least he was until we got married. Now we're awkward strangers. I know it's because of me. He watches me like a ninth floor patient now." She felt tears sting her eyes. "Oh no, not here. My staff will think I'm bankrupt or something!" The telephone rang and she answered quickly, grateful for the distraction.

"Mrs. Bradley, there's a Mr. Danzieg here to see you. He doesn't have an appointment." Jeneil has tried hard to get Rachel to call her Jeneil and to relax about doing business but she was fresh out of business school and concerned about making a bad impression.

"He's a good friend, Rachel. Send him right in and Rachel?"

"Yes, Mrs. Bradley?"

"Please call me Jeneil."

The girl laughed. "I will pretty soon, I'm sure."

Robert knocked and opened the door looking very puzzled.

"Come in." Jeneil smiled. "Tell me about Boston."

Robert looked around her new office. "I take an assignment in Boston for a few weeks and you move away? Holy Shit! You own the damn Lakeland Plaza too?"

She smiled. "We're not talking about Boston yet, how did it go?"

"I'm not finished there. I came home to breath."

Jeneil intercom buzzed. She hit the Conference Call button. "What is it Rachel?"

"Mrs. Bradley, Jeneil. The engineer from the plaza wants to know if you authorized overtime."

"Yes, I okayed it when Domenic called before lunch. The weather's been good, we can afford the time now before winter arrives. I have tenants screaming to get into those stores."

"Thanks." Rachel answered and buzzed out.

Jeneil sighed. "Robert, I want you to do the lobby in this building. You know the sculpture you did for the National Bank building? I want a similar one for the center foyer here. It'll be roped off so you can use natural materials. I'll give you a free hand on the display. What do you think of something dripping in mineral deposits?"

Robert was staring at her. "What did she call you?"

Jeneil stopped, realizing that Robert hadn't heard about her marriage. "Steve and I were married last Friday."

"Married!?" He said, in a half whisper, half gasp. He stood up. "What the hell happened?"

Jeneil was frightened; tears were so close to the surface. She swallowed hard. "A lot I guess. The baby was actually Peter's after all and he decided to stay married to Uette." She shrugged. "The end."

Robert covered his mouth and shook his head. "So you turned around and married his best friend?!" Jeneil was stricken hearing it that way. Robert caught his breath. "What are you doing, getting even with Peter?"

Jeneil was shocked. "No!" She replied, strongly.

"You married the guy's best friend on the rebound. Jeneil, that's a nasty left hook you swing."

"You don't understand." She stammered.

"No, and I'll bet Peter's shocked too."

"That's enough, Robert." She said, feeling her throat beginning to hurt. "It wasn't like that."

"Well, there goes my weekend. I came here to see how much free time you have, but I don't think Dr. Bradley would allow his new wife to date?" He sighed.

"How come that son of a bitch married you? What's his game plan?" He snapped, angrily

"Robert please don't." She said, standing up slowly, beginning to feel sick to her stomach.

"Why didn't you call me? Or even Dennis. What did you do, slip into an emotional time warp?"

Her stomach began to hurt. She walked to the louvered doors and opened them to a small closet kitchenette. She ran a drink of water for herself bolting it down. The pain in her throat stopped.

Robert was standing beside her. "Hey, you're pretty strung out." He said, quietly.

She nodded. "I've been short-staffed for two weeks. I've moved the office to here and moved my personal life three times within the last month. Yes, I'm feeling very strung out and I never realized that marrying Steve would look the way you just described it." She drew another drink of water and sipped it. "It wasn't like that at all. He's a nice guy."

"Hell, I'm a nice guy too, you didn't marry me." He pouted.

She shook her head and smiled. "Robert, sometimes life overwhelms me. I don't need a husband who overwhelms me too. You're a wonderful friend. I'd ruin that if I married you."

He smiled warmly. "I doubt it, beautiful." He sighed and touched her check, lovingly.

"Are we still friends?" She asked.

"I put up with a lot from you." He grinned. "Yes, we are."

She smiled and he looked serious. "I've been waiting for the right moment to tell you something, this might be the right time or never, I guess. I'm in love with you, Jeneil." He said, and he kissed her lips.

Steve cleared his throat startling Jeneil and Robert. Jeneil looked embarrassed and Robert slipped his arm around her. "Ooops, Dr. Bradley. I'm going to mold a bell for your neck. Will you accept that I was congratulating the new bride as a reason for kissing her?"

"Is that what you're using as the reason for telling her you're in love with her, too?"

Robert smiled. "Dr. Bradley, you eavesdropped. "Okay, we're all adults here and you deserve it anyway for stealing her when my back was turned."

"Robert!" Jeneil said, sternly.

"Relax, beautiful." Robert kissed her cheek, lightly. "What's he got to complain about? You go home with him, don't you? I'm the disgruntled party in all this. I should challenge him to a duel." Her telephone rang. He squeezed Jeneil. "I'll call you about the lobby." She went to answer it. He stopped at the door, and looked at Steve. "Don't slip up with her blade man, not even a fraction of an inch. I have more patience about her than you and your buddy Asian."

"Is that a threat?" Steve asked, staring at him steadily.

"No, a promise." Robert smiled. "Congratulations, new groom." Steve didn't answer. Robert threw a kiss to Jeneil and left, who was watching them closely as she talked on the telephone.

Jeneil signaled to Steve to take a seat. He closed the door and went to see the view from her windows. Jeneil hung up and watched him as he leaned against the window frame and she choked up again. Taking a deep breath she went to him. "Not a very peaceful view." Steve said, as she joined him.

"A good business view though. A busy street with people going about their business."

He nodded. "Makes sense." He said quietly, watching the traffic.

Jeneil scrutinized his face, he looked so tired. She hated the awkwardness. Their friendship was damaged and she missed it. She choked up.

"I'm sorry about Robert, Steve. He really doesn't mean some of what he says as strongly as he says it."

Steve looked at her. "How can you tell what he means and what he doesn't?"

She wrung her hands, embarrassed at Steve having seen Robert kiss her and tell her he loved her. She didn't know how to answer him.

"I'm sorry." She said, staring at her clenched hands and her explanation for the apology wouldn't form.

Steve let the situation pass. "Are you finishing here soon?"

Jeneil looked up and smiled grateful that Steve was going to overlook the silly episode. She felt little stamina for a scene, and Steve was entitled to one. "Yes, I can leave now. My appointments are completed. How are you out so early?"

"Dr. Sprague took my afternoon rounds."

He didn't add that Dr. Sprague had said. "You're looking tired, Steve. Honeymoons have a practical purpose to them too. Try one. Get a good start on the weekend and rest."

"How about dinner at Danoli's Garden?" He asked.

She smiled. "I'd like that." She wanted to hug him, but for some reason the thought made her choke up.

"I'll get my coat." She turned and went to her closet. He reached for her coat and held it for her. She wanted to say thank you, but holding back had caused a lump in her throat and she was sure that any show of sentiment would cause her to sob. "I'll let Tony know

I'm leaving." She dialed and talked to him a minute. "Ready now." She smiled picking up her purse.

They walked the short corridor together and then stopped as Charlene called her.

"Four offices left in this building, Jeneil and I had a call from a finance company interested in an eight room suite."

Jeneil raised her eyebrows. "Do a thorough check on them. That's a lot of remodeling. I'd like a longer term lease and a company with a mature history. Check it carefully. The officers too and how long they've been with the company, and what happened with the woman in Fairview 200 who complained about the water tasting strange?"

Charlene shrugged. "Roy said she's a hypochondriac."

"No!" Jeneil said, sternly. "Have Roy take a water sample and have it tested. Send the woman a copy of it and I want one too. If it's fine then change the filter or washer in her tap as a placebo. Leave a note for Adrienne to watch Roy. I want him reminded that the tenants are paying top dollar in there for pampering. The pampering doesn't stop because the office has moved out. He's a maintenance man, not a psychiatrist. He's being paid to pamper those people."

Charlene smiled. "Could you talk to my landlord?"

Jeneil smiled. "If she's a chronic then her lease won't be renewed, but she's to be pampered until her lease is finished. Keep track of her complaints. Tell Roy she's to sign a work order for everything she requests of him. Make a form up if we don't have any. Specific and legible. That should keep everybody honest and gives us evidence for dealing with either side."

"Okay." Charlene said. "That makes my job easier, thanks. I like that better than Roy's suggestion."

"What did he say?" Jeneil asked.

Charlene looked hesitant. "He said to have Adrienne call the old bat and tell her to drink the water from the tap, not the toilet."

Jeneil stiffened. "That's uncalled for. Underline the note to Adrienne to watch Roy and drop by unannounced to inspect Fairview 1200 regularly." Jeneil shook her head. "I was worried about moving the offices from there."

Charlene smiled. "Thanks and have a nice weekend."

"Charlene, have you met Steve?"

"No." Charlene smiled and extended her hand to Steve.

"Dr. Bradley, congratulations and best wishes to both of you."

"Thank you, Charlene." Steve shook her hand. Jeniel and Steve got on the elevator. "I had Charlene all picked out for you, Steve."

"She's not my type." Steve replied.

Jeneil raised an eyebrow, jokingly. "Oh really? Why? Are you afraid she'd steal your thunder, you'd have to struggle for sunlight because of her beauty when you're with her?" She grinned. Steve smiled at her tease. It was the first sign of normal between them in a week and he loved it.

"Hell, that's not so tough. I'm married to you aren't I?" He grinned.

Tears filled her eyes surprising Steve. "Jeneil...." He said reaching for her arm. The elevator slowed for a stop and he backed away as Jeneil dabbed her eyes quickly with her leather gloves. They rode in silence as the car filled with people.

"My car." He said as they walked from the building.

"Why?" She asked.

He shrugged. "Because it's mine." She looked at him surprised by the answer. He held the car door for her and then got behind the wheel and turned the key. The motor didn't make a sound. "Shit." He sighed. "I just had this damn car fixed for this same problem."

"I don't trust electrical problems." Jeneil said. "Maybe it's time for a new car."

"When I get a decent down payment together." He responded.

"We have enough." She replied.

"I don't." He said.

"Steve, that's silly."

"Jeneil, it has taken me years to have a decent income. I'm making good money now and I feel great about that. I don't want to be swallowed up by your money. I like being me."

She nodded. "Okay. That's pretty clear."

He sat back. "I'm sorry, that just spilled out."

She watched him. "I understand, yell anytime I block your sunlight."

He looked at her wondering if he'd hurt her. She smiled warmly. "I really do understand. My life stampedes, you're smart to protect yourself. Let's take the Torrence. It doesn't belong to me or you. It's leased. That's pretty neutral."

He smiled, they were reaching normal again. "Then I'll need to get something." He reached behind the seat and picked up a thin long box and handed it to her. She took it looking quite surprised and opened it. Inside was long stemmed yellow rose with fern and baby's breath, wrapped in green tissue paper. She read the card. "*Happy First week's Anniversary of our greater friendship.*" It was signed. "*Love Steve.*" She didn't lift her head and Steve noticed the tears falling on the tissue paper. "Jeneil." He sighed. "I think we'd better talk."

Taking a tissue from her purse, she dried her tears and took a deep breath. "No Steve, I'm not capable of talking right now. I'd be babbling and incoherent within ten minutes if I tried. Let's go to Danoli's Garden, the beauty of the place is what I really need. It'll be restful and pleasant."

He was worried. She was too tense, too strung out and unable to deal with her emotions. Deciding that the parking lot of her office building wasn't a practical choice for a heart to heart talk anyway, he chose to take her to dinner so she could at least relax before he sat her down and tried to uncover what was happening to her.

*****

Jeneil strolled through the garden even touching different rock clutters that were nestled amongst the foliage. He watched her as she sat on a park bench nearby. She was enjoying the garden; it was absorbing her and healing her. She said it was what she needed. He smiled and sipped his wine hopeful that she would pull together. He was beginning to formulate opinions and theories about her emotional decline and most of them we're tried to having gotten married. After having toured the whole garden, she returned to him and sat on the bench. "This is nice." She smiled and he even thought she looked better.

"You must be starved." She said. "Let's see if they can fix us into the crowd I hear in there."

"We can leave. We don't have to face a crowd. There are other places." He offered, not wanting to ruin the peace he saw in her.

She smiled. "This is fine. I'm rested and relaxed. The garden was a great choice for me." He stood up and placed his wine glass on a nearby tray stand. She watched him, feeling very grateful that she had met a Steve Bradley in life. Standing too, she took his hand surprising him. He smiled encouraged by at the sign of normalcy and they walked to the restaurant. The food was so good and the atmosphere so above average that the restaurant attracted crowds especially on Friday night. Friday's crowd was the party crowd and so the garden was almost empty as everyone went to the bar to begin relaxing for their weekend. There was talking and laughing and a feeling of people wanting to party. Steve requested a table in the Tuscany Room which was a continuation of the garden, quiet, small and intimate which pleased Jeneil. She smiled and squeezed his hand as the Maitre'de told them that there table was ready. He was amazed at how improved she had become. He would have kissed her cheek, which he usually did as a friend, but since being married the friendship was so strained, that he held back, not wanting to disturb the gentle bond he felt between them at the moment.

"Hey! Dr. and Mrs. Steve Bradley." They heard someone say from the bar called "Travoli Garden." It really was a street scene in the bar area, it was where some people loosened up and prepared for good food, in short it was controlled bedlam. "At least it better be Mrs. Steven Bradley with him." The voice said coming into the hallway. The Maitre'de stopped and waited as Steve and Jeneil turned.

Steve smiled. "Drex."

Drexel Bernard smiled. "Do I get to kiss the new bride or isn't that allowed? You two are into a different form of life. I can see that. Individualists."

Steve looked at Jeneil. "This is Drexel Barnard, one of the associates with the group." Jeneil extended her hand as Steve introduced her to Drexel. She had heard of him. He wasn't a doctor from Downes; He had been practicing for two years and had joined Sprague's team. He was a graduate of Payton and his family was the elite society in the state. He was divorced and had recently married Barbara Towers, a nurse from Radiology. Jeneil didn't know her too well; Radiology had been Sarah's responsibility in the office.

Drexel smiled at Jeneil personably. "I've been hearing your name a lot lately. It's nice to finally get to met you."

"Should I worry?" Jeneil asked.

Drexel grinned, amused by her remark. "No, not at all. You seem to be surfacing as a minor miracle amongst the people I know."

"I think I should worry." Jeneil replied.

Drexel laughed, heartily. "Hey you two have to join us. We've got a group here from the hospital and we're waiting for two large tables to be freed. Steve was disappointed, he and Jeneil needed to be alone to repair their friendship. "Well actually Drex, Jeneil and I are celebrating our anniversary."

"Anniversary?" Drexel questioned. "You just got married."

Steve nodded. "A week ago and...."

"Oh damn, that's terrific...wait here." Drexel went back to the bar and returned followed by his wife and several others from the hospital all smiling and gathering around Steve and Jeneil insisting they join the crowd.

Steve shook his head. "No really, I have a table in the Tuscany room for us."

"Oooo hooch and smooch room." Barbara smiled at Steve and looked Jeneil over.

Larry Gaines laughed. "We'll save it for home, Steve, we've been looking for a reason to party here and a belated wedding reception was voted on." He signaled the Maitre'de." "Add them to our group and cancel their table." The Maitre'de nodded and left.

"We're in the Roman Garden room it falls short of a Bacchanalian festival, but what the hell it's too public here anyway." He laughed enjoying his own joke. Jeneil watched

Larry Gaines and decided that she didn't like him. More people from the group came from the bar announcing that their tables were ready.

Steve felt Jeneil hold his hand tighter and he turned to apologize, but the crowd surrounded and separated them moving in swarming fashion to the Roman Garden Room. It wasn't until the group surrounded the table that Steve had clear access to Jeneil again and he was by her side in a flash.

"Are you okay?" He asked, concerned. She nodded and smiled benignly.

"I'm sorry." He said, as he held her chair and took the next one to her.

"It's okay, Steve." She said, quietly and looked around the two large tables at the people who had gathered for a party and had declared the theme to be a wedding reception for her and Steve. They qualified as a group by her definition, boisterous, unthinking and bordering frenzy. She sighed to herself and hoped for the best because most of the people here was the ones she avoided at the hospital. This was Cleveland General's grape vine. If you were part of it, you did nothing right by their judgment and narrow view of life and people. She felt queasy for an instant as she realized that her whole working career at the hospital was spent trying to be invisible because they reminded her of the gossip from Loma and her first horrible impression of Steve was a result of his camaraderie with this group. He had been the epitome of what the group was and he had progressed to being their mascot and onto the legend of the White Stallion which forced him to his probation. She looked around and had trouble believing that she was now Mrs. Steven Bradley and celebrating the week's anniversary of her marriage with the people she couldn't stand. People who, when she heard them gossip about someone, she would rage in her mind and think they were filthy dregs of society. She swallowed hard as a feeling of being displaced filled her and she reached for her water glass as the air began to feel stifling. She struggled to bring herself and her thinking into a positive flow in order to survive this dinner by changing her attitude. Steve listened to the chatter and smiled to himself, proud of who he had become. He remembered this group and their crazy parties. He had met Rita through this group and he also remembered that it was this very group that he used to laugh at as they laughed at others and he'd feed them false gossip to make them look foolish. It was that crazy game he played with them that tripped him up and put him on probation which almost cost him his career with the Sprague group. He became acutely aware of Jeneil by his side. He looked at her and smiled to himself as he remembered the crazy gossip she spread that cleaned up his image and cemented his future. He loved her for that and much more. He knew she couldn't stand this gossip and him because he had been tied to it.

He put his arm on the back of her chair and leaned to her kissing her temple gently. "We can leave." He whispered into her ear. "Get a headache and I'll fake a cerebral hemorrhage." She turned her head quickly to look at him and laughed surprised and amused by his words. "I'm serious." He said, softly and grinned.

She swallowed a laugh and bit her lower lip to stop another. "It's okay." She whispered. "They just want to celebrate and we walked in with the reason. They mean well, they want to celebrate the happiness of two people who just got married. It has a touch of humanness about it."

He stared into her eyes. "But with this group, I could never be sure it was a celebration or an execution." He whispered, softly.

She got caught up in his silliness. "We can keep our knives handy for when they start raking us over the coals. Let's order the round ravioli and wing them like Frisbees at any big mouth gossips across the table."

He smiled broadly and broke into a slight laugh. "Hell this party has some great possibilities."

She grinned. "It's all a matter of attitude."

"I can see that." He smiled at her lovingly for her attitude and for being so good natured.

"Oh well, you look at those two." Larry Gaines said in mocked disgust looking at Steve and Jeneil. "Ignore them for a minute and they begin to snuggle and coo. With each other no less!"

Jeneil was positive that she could never like Larry Gaines. Steward Greene began to sing Raging Hormones to a Bach piece until Jeneil wanted to splash him with her iced water to see if he was hysterical. She was sure that if she was dying she'd never go to him as a doctor.

"I think it's nice." Lynette Wagner dreamingly smiled and wiggled in her chair. Jeneil tried to remember what she'd heard about Lynette, the nurse in obstetrics and gyn. "It certainly looks damn sexy." Lynette added, reminding Jeneil of what she had heard about her.

Trina Calderone from the 3rd floor desk smiled. "Let's quiet down before we embarrass poor Jeneil and make her blush." Jeneil wondered what Trina was doing in this group especially with the man next to her. Dr. Kirk Vance. He had been staring at her with his dark eyes for what seemed minutes. She was avoiding even looking at him.

He laughed a deep throaty laugh. Jeneil thought it seemed to be rehearsed or studied. Its deepness almost vibrated through you. He reminded her of a synthesizer because he made sounds that seemed human, but deep within his eyes lay a look that wasn't like any human she had known. He made her uncomfortable because he seemed too synthetic. He raised his drink to his lips. "Well I'm fascinated." He said, in his deep throat voice. "I would expect this Mona Lisa to blush until I remember that she has roped, tied and branded the White Stallion."

Steve put his arm around Jeneil. "The White Stallion's gone, Kirk." Steve laughed. "He was fiction anyway." Jeneil turned and smiled at him, proudly for his abandonment of this gossip. The table broke into laughter.

"Fiction!" Larry Gaines wiped the drink he spilled down his chin laughing at Steve's remark. "Sheez, I'm still trying to perfect the one technique you showed me." Jeneil looked at Steve.

"Maybe we should order now." He said, fidgeting in his seat. The table broke out in laughter again except Kirk who grinned and watched Steve and Jeneil together.

Dinner had gone pretty well for Jeneil as the table turned to others and the group left her and Steve alone. She was even feeling hopeful about getting out of there unscathed.

"How come you two didn't take a honeymoon?" Steward Greene asked. "Or invite anybody to your wedding?" Jeneil's hope vanished and reached for her glass of water.

Steve fidgeted. "Well Jeneil has executives away on vacation, it wasn't a good time to get away from the office and we both decided that we didn't want to fuss about a ceremony. How could we decide where to draw the line, when we combined her business associates, the hospital and medical associates' people? The groups having their round of parties. It got too complicated." Jeneil stared at her glass of water wondering how Steve has made up such a reasonable explanation, none of it was true.

Steward Green laughed. "Yeh, I thought so, raging hormones."

Steve shrugged. "Believe what you want."

"Are you going to get away?" Drexel asked. Jeneil stayed silent counting on Steve to maneuver them through the rocky course.

"I'm not sure." Steve answered.

Lynette grinned. "I think you should Stevie, you look awfully tired." Jeneil fidgeted and drank some water.

Drexel laughed. "Sprague thinks so too. He took rounds for Steve today and told him that honeymoons had a practical purpose to them and he suggested they try one." There was laughter and hooting from the group. Except from Kirk who Jeneil could feel staring at her from his seat directly opposite her. Jeneil wished she could join the ice cubes in her water glass, she felt small enough to fit.

Steve sat back in his chair. "What's this fascination with my sex life?" Jeneil was impressed with Steve's questions; it seemed like a good offensive move. She continued watching the ice cubes melt in her glass.

Kirk drank some wine. "Jeneil." He said, seeming to drop his voice an octave and whisper the name. "Didn't I see your picture in the paper not too long ago in the social column somewhere?"

Drexel smiled. "Yes, the summer cotillion. We were there too."

Kirk watched her steadily. "Weren't you with someone else?"

"Robert Danzieg." Barbara Barnard smiled.

"We're good friends." Jeneil answered, wondering if they were hinting at a rebound marriage to Steve.

Drexel laughed. "Jeneil, you're too modest."

"Well that's what the newspaper said." She answered, dryly.

The table laughed. Kirk grinned. "What's the real story?"

Jeneil couldn't believe this vulturous group. They had a taste for jugular. "That's the truth." Jeneil answered and took a drink of water. Kirk looked at Drexel. "The Mona Lisa's last name is Sphinx. What's the real story Drex?" Jeneil looked up at Kirk resenting the insinuation that she was covering up the truth.

Drexel looked at Jeneil and smiled. "Maybe it's not the time, considering she's celebrating her wedding anniversary."

Jeneil was uncomfortable. "I don't understand this fascination with Steve's sex life." She blurted out. The table broke up, Steve along with them; he put his arm around her and kissed her cheek.

Kirk watched her and then looked at Drexel. "What were you going to say before Mona Lisa sent up the smoke screen, Drex?"

Jeneil watched Kirk wishing she had ordered round ravioli since it seemed like a good time to fling one and yell "food fight".

Drexel smiled. "Robert Danzieg said Jeneil's the most fascinating woman he's ever met." Steve changed positions as annoyance filled him.

Jeneil stared right at Kirk. "Was that shocking enough for you?" She asked, bordering sarcasm. Steve looked at her, wondering if she was nearing the edge. The group looked at each other and raised their eyebrows, surprised by Jeneil's spunk.

Kirk smiled at her. "What's so fascinating about you, Mona Lisa?"

Jeneil was reaching her limit. "Why are you asking me? Robert made the statement." Steve watched her surprised by her show of fangs.

Barbara smiled. "She also got his vote for being a truly sexy woman."

Kirk grinned. "Oooo, tell us how you got that title, Mona Lisa?"

Jeneil stared straight into his eyes. "What do you want me to say, that I wrote Kama Sutra when I was twelve after years of experimenting and research." There were hoots around the table. Steve watched her shocked that she even knew the Kuma Sutra existed.

Trina Calderone laughed. "Is she really the girl from records?"

Kirk smiled. "Fascinating Mona Lisa, very fascinating."

Jeneil watched him annoyed by his hammering. "Have I passed any test you have been giving here?" She asked. Steve was stunned. The others smiled.

Kirk grinned. "Very nicely." He said and held up his wine glass to her in a toast. Jeneil resisted the urge to say choke on it and her anger surprised her. She drank some water to make sure she wouldn't say it and wished she could leave. The talked turned to the waitress who returned for dessert and drink orders.

Steve put his arm around Jeneil and kissed her temple lightly. "Ready for that headache, now?" He asked, quietly.

She nodded. "It would be very close to the truth." She replied, wearily.

The waitress stopped for Steve's order. "Nothing for us except our check, please. We have to be leaving."

"What?" Larry Gaines replied. "You're not having dessert?"

Steward Green laughed. "Not here anyway."

"We're moving the group to my place, later." Kirk said. "You're both welcomed to join us."

"Thanks Kirk, but I think we'll pass, Jeneil's had a difficult schedule this week." And then realizing he had left himself open to a remark, he looked at Larry Gaines and smiled. "Don't say it, Gaines. Don't say it." Everyone laughed.

Trina Calderone smiled. "Steve, do you see much of Pete Chang, lately?"

Steve felt awkward. "No, not really." He answered.

Jeneil looked down at her purse as the name caused pain to race through her. "Too bad, I was hoping for a scoop on his life. "His wife's expecting." She added.

"So I heard." Steve replied.

Trina shook his head. "He should have married the other girl. The one who was sending the two of you all that good food. He looked at lot better when he was going with her."

Jeneil clutched her purse lightly, as her throat tightened.

Barbara Barnard turned to Trina to make some comment and Steve took the opportunity to say goodnight to everyone so they could leave before more was said, he was hoping to spare Jeneil any pain. Kirk held his glass up in a toast. "Best wishes and much happiness to the both of you." He smiled.

Larry Gaines laughed. "And to each other, too."

Drexel smiled and joined the toast. "Yes, Happy Anniversary."

"Thanks." Steve said. Jeneil smiled. "Ready?" Steve asked her.

She nodded. He put his arm around her and they left.

*****

Jeneil was silent during the drive home and went straight to her room when they got to the apartment.

Steve answered the ringing telephone. "Adrienne. I'm glad you're back." He said. "Jeneil's been a wreck without you at the office."

"Steve what the hell is this note Jeneil left for me?" *Married Steve, now live in 1492 Fairview 1900."*

Steve was surprised by Adrienne's tone. "The note says it all, Adrienne."

"Not by a long shot, Steve. What the hell are you pulling?"

"What?!" Steve was shocked by the words. "Wait a minute, Adrienne. I not pulling anything."

"Steve, I'm warning you, that girl has been kicked real good, lately, if you're messing with her and she gets hurt again, I'll turn Charlie loose and that's a promise. He's still itching to muscle Peter."

Steve was deeply shocked. "Adrienne, wait a minute. I thought we knew each other. Why would you think I'm pulling anything with Jeneil? I wouldn't hurt her for the world."

"Yeh, you're a good friend. Peter said the same thing." She snapped.

"Oh shit, Adrienne, he didn't hurt her deliberately, I'm sure of that."

Adrienne sighed. "I don't trust this whole thing."

Steve was hurt; he had gotten to know Adrienne and Charlie over the summer and really respected them. "Adrienne, it's me Steve. The one you thanked for being there for Jeneil. What's this sudden threat?"

"Steve being a friend relationship is one thing and a husband is something else. How the hell did you go from one to the other in less than two weeks?"

"Maybe Jeneil had better explain. I'll get her." He knocked on Jeneil's door. "Adrienne's on the phone." Jeneil opened the door and Steve could see that she had been crying. He sighed and followed her to the livingroom.

Jeneil cleared her throat. "Adrienne, you had great weather the whole two weeks. That's terrific. How did everything go?" Jeneil asked twisting the tie to her robe around her finger.

"Jeneil, baby, what is this all about. You got married to Steve? Why?"

"It's a good move."

"Honey, you make it sound like a business deal. Where are words like romantic love and passion?"

Jeneil's eyes filled with tears. "Those are unstable commodities, Adrienne. They're too risky."

"Is he good to you? Can you deal with the physical of it and all so soon."

"That was an unnecessary complication that isn't involved in this." Jeneil answered.

Adrienne gasped. "Jeneil, you sound like you're talking to your stock brokers. What the hell are you telling me, that you and Steve don't sleep together?"

"Exactly."

"Oh my gosh." Adrienne groaned. "And that hulk of a man agreed to that?"

"Yes."

"Oh my gosh." Adrienne sighed. "Jeneil, when can I see you? I've got to see you and talk to you. This is scary, Honey."

Jeneil sighed. "Adrienne it's okay. It's a good move, believe me."

"Oh sweetie, a good move was buying Lakeland Plaza and having it triple in value. Those aren't words you use to describe a husband and a marriage. What has your Uncle Hollis said about this?"

"He doesn't know yet."

"Oh my gosh! How long have you been married?"

"One week tonight." Jeneil answered.

"Tell him Jeneil, please."

"I was going to this weekend."

"Can I come over in the morning to see you?" Adrienne asked.

Jeneil shrugged. "All right, if you want to."

"I'll be there around eight, Honey. Call Hollis, Jeneil."

Jeneil frowned and shook her head. "Okay, I will." Jeneil sighed and rubbed her temples after hanging up. Steve watched her. She was back to tense and strung out. She paced and twisted the tie to her robe and then went to the telephone and dialed. "Hi, Crissy, its Aunt Jeneil, is your daddy home?" She waited and paced. "Uncle Hollis, no nothings wrong. I just wanted to let you know that I got married last Friday."

"What!" Steve heard him yell the word. Jeneil closed her eyes and took a deep breath. "But…" He said and sputtered. "But how….? Where did he get…? How did Peter get a divorce so fast?"

Jeneil's heart almost burst at the sound of his name. "I married Steve Bradley, Uncle Hollis."

"Steve Bradley?" Hollis tried to place the name. "Steve Bradley!" He nearly shouted. "He's Peter's best friend."

"Oh Sheez." He groaned. "Oh damn, how did that happen?"

Steve watched Jeneil wrap both ties around her hand and pull at them strongly. She looked angry. He watched her take a deep breath. "Uncle Hollis, It's been a difficult week for me, I've moved the office, and I've had people on vacation. I've moved my apartment. I just called to let you know that I got married. I'm very, very tired, and I don't want to discuss this."

Hollis sighed. "Jeneil, you have to. From the business aspects, if nothing else."

"Fine." She replied. "Just give me some time to rest."

Hollis was quiet. "This is such a shock, Jeneil. I always thought that I'd see you get married. Maybe even give the bride away at the altar." Jeneil felt bad and was deeply touched by Hollis's caring.

Tears rolled down her cheeks. "Thank you for caring that much, Uncle Hollis. But I'm not a religious person. I wouldn't have been married in a church anyway. You know me, I'm not normal. You can do all that for Crissy." She smiled and wiped her tears

"Is he good to you, Honey?"

"Yes he is."

"Are you happy?" He asked.

"I'm fine." She replied wiping the tears that were falling.

Hollis knew she was crying. "Jeneil , then why are you crying?" He asked sadly.

"Because, I'm very tired, Uncle Hollis."

"Jeneil…."

"I'm going to hang up now." She said.

"When can I meet him?" Hollis asked.

"I haven't thought about it, but soon." She answered.

"Jeneil…?"

"Hollis, I'm very tired. I'll call you again. Love to Marlene, bye." She replaced the receiver and wiped her tears.

Steve went to her. "Jeneil, I think we should talk."

She shook her head. "I can't Steve, I'm too tired. My head is swimming from people talking. That ridiculous group at dinner tonight and now this. My life is run by a committee. I have to pass every thought by a staff of professional people. I'm tired and I'm going to rest." She headed to her room.

"Can I get you anything?" He asked. She shook her head and continued to her room and closed the door. He sighed heavily. "Happy anniversary Mrs. Bradley, maybe what I should have brought you was a case of tissues." He picked up the yellow rose that she had put on the table in the livingroom and forgotten. He took it to the kitchen to put it in a glass of water. "I heard of people crying through weddings, but I think I've got the only wife who's going to cry through the marriage." He paced. "But this won't continue. It can't continue. I won't let it, Honey, and I'm not speaking as an emotional husband. I'm speaking as a doctor."

On Saturday morning Steve left for a sky diving lesson and to pick up his car. Jeneil was in her room and had never come out. He had knocked on her door and waited. He opened it. She was sleeping. He had his breakfast alone wondering if he should wake her. It was late morning when he returned. He heard talking from Jeneil's bedroom which surprised him. Going to the kitchen, he poured some juice and wondered if the visitor was Adrienne. He became aware of how confusing the marriage was to him. His rights as a husband didn't seem as clear since the marriage was only an arrangement. Her bedroom door opened and closed and Adrienne passed by the kitchen door. Steve called to her. She came into the kitchen wiping her eyes. He felt uncomfortable. "Adrienne. You're Jeneil's good friend. I'd like it if we could be civil. I don't want trouble with us." Adrienne nodded and her eyes filled up. "I can see that Jeneil's is contagious." He said, watching her. Adrienne tried to laugh, but cried instead, confusing Steve. "Want to talk about it?"

"I always cry at weddings." She said, trying to smile. "I've got to go." And she turned and left.

Steve sighed as he heard the door close. "Shit. I've had enough." He said and went to Jeneil's room. He knocked and waited, there was no answer. He opened the door. The room was darkened from the drawn shades and Jeneil was sleeping. He left quietly, surprised that she was staying in bed so late.

Fifteen

Peter sat at the kitchen table finishing his coffee. He wondered if he should get the baby items that were still on the list and then thinking that Uette might not have crossed off what was received at the baby shower, he decided to wait until Uette returned from her weekend trip.

The telephone rang and he went to get it almost hoping for an emergency so he could leave the apartment before she got back. Life had been pleasant having been in Boston and having her away when he returned. He hadn't seen her in days. He lifted the receiver and answered. "Peter can you come over here now?" His Grandfather asked. "We need to talk. It's very important."

"What is it?" He asked.

"The Wongs are here. They want to see you." The Grandfather sounded too formal.

"I'll be right there." Peter hung up.

*****

Peter parked the car and headed for the house wondering what had happened and he thought maybe Uette had her baby while she was away. He knocked and walked into the kitchen. Tom appeared at the door to the diningroom. "In here Pete." He said, looking solemn and he turned to the diningroom. Peter undid his jacket and took it off as he walked in. No one looked up except Uette who was sitting at the head of the table. Peter froze in his steps as he saw her. Both of her eyes were bruised and swollen and almost shut and her lips had stitches and were badly swollen. There were bruises all over her face. He walked to the empty chair across the table from her staring in disbelief.

 "What happened to you?" He asked.

Tears rolled down her cheeks. "I told you he'd say he didn't do it." She cried. Tom patted her arm.

Peter's mouth opened in shock. "What?" He gasped. "You told them I did that to you? I haven't seen you since Monday. What is all this?"

"Oh sit down." Uette father said, angrily.

"Roland, please." His father cautioned.

"No father." He snapped. "I'm tired of this saving face business. Look at her. That's not even fair. Look at the size of him."

Peter looked around the table and then back to Uette's father. "Mr. Wong, I swear, I never touched her."

Mr. Wong was out of patience. "I don't want to hear it." He said, glaring at Peter.

"We're only here to talk about getting a divorce action started. Uette has had it with you and this kind of life. She wants out and considering this latest event, I want her out too."

Peter stared at her and she lowered her eyes avoiding looking at him. His mind was thrown into confusion by the sight of her and the blame being thrown on him. He was at a loss for words and his medical training surfaced as he studied the bruises on her face. They looked familiar; he had seen the same type on Lin Chi. He sat up straight as he pieced the situation together. Mark Chun had stepped into the picture. Peter was sure of it. But why was she blaming him? His mind raced through all possibilities and he realized that Uette was trying to save face her way. She didn't want her family to know about her connection to organized crime. His heart sank realizing that she was setting him up a second time to take the fall. His heart pounded in his chest and anger filled him. He ignored it trying to think clearly about how to deal with this. All he had was the truth. He sighed inwardly realizing that the truth hadn't helped him at all through the whole nightmare, but it was the only thing he had. This was the final battle of the war between him and Uette. He heard his name called.

"Peter." His Grandfather said. "Uette has asked for a quick divorce."

Peter thought about it. "Mark Chun must want the baby as his! But where does her protection come in? She'd have to explain him being in the picture." Peter was confused. "This Shittin bitch is a Pro. I can't follow her moves." The truth is all he had. He sat back in his chair. "The prenuptial agreement says that the divorce will take place after the baby's born. She can live with her family until then." He wondered if he could flush her out of her sniping spot.

"No!" She said, almost panicked. "No. I want to be rid of you before the baby's born!" She had handed Peter an ace. Her panic said it all. Mark Chun was leaning on her.

"Well, I'll set aside the legal agreement if she tells us who the baby's father is."

She watched him. "I'm not going through that again. You know who the father is Peter, you just won't accept it." She snapped.

Peter rubbed his eyes; he was hoping he wouldn't have to fight her with heavy swings. She was so beaten and bruised as it was. He shook his head and decided the situation was survival. It was saving face. It was truth and that was all he had. He stood up and ran his fingers through his hair. "Uette, I do know who the baby's father is." He watched her eyes become cautious like an animal wondering if it's being cornered.

The men looked up at him surprised. His Grandfather nodded at him. Peter nodded in return. The Wongs watched them.

Mr. Chang sighed. "Lu, this isn't easy for me. It's been a difficult eight months for all of us especially Uette and Peter. We knew this wouldn't be a pleasant ending for whichever lie was uncovered. Peter would like to tell you something. I'm asking that you allow him the respect of listening to him without becoming offended. I'm asking forgiveness now for having to cause this hurt to you." Uette eyes were becoming panicked.

The Wongs mellowed to Mr. Chang's approach for formal honor and dignity and they became curious.

"Have him speak, Liam." The senior Mr. Wong nodded. Mr. Chang nodded to Peter.

Peter bowed to the Wongs. "Accept my apology for any offense and hurt I might cause."

"It's accepted, Peter." Mr. Wong replied. "Tell us what you have to and we'll share the burden." Peter stood up straight and looked at Uette. She was staring wide-eyed at him.

He turned from her and looked at her Grandfather. "I know who the baby's father is. I've spent months looking for him."

"He's Crazy." Uette answered.

Mr. Wong watched his granddaughter. "Have her allow Peter to speak." He said to his son.

"He'll lie." She said, getting animated. "He's a snake; he'll wiggle out of this."

Her father touched her arm, gently. "You'll have your turn."

"He's a liar father. Don't even listen to him." She said near panic. "You watch yourself Peter, I mean it." She threatened. "This baby's yours, now shut up!" She yelled. "Shut up!"

"Uette!" He father stood up. "Maybe you should leave the room."

"No!" She replied, pleadingly. "No, He's going to be vicious, he's mad at me because Jeneil got married. That's what this is all about. He's getting even with me by making up stories."

Her Grandfather watched her and then he looked at his son. "She'll be quiet or I'll take her from the room myself."

Uette's father was surprised. He nodded. "Uette, you heard your Grandfather." She began to cry, softly.

Mr. Wong turned to Peter. "Continue." He said.

Peter sighed. "The baby's father is Mark Chun." Both men stood up looking aghast at the name. Uette was in open shock at Peter's words. She stared at him. Peter continued. "I didn't beat her up. He did or he had somebody do it. When I found out it was his baby, I met with him and told him. She had run out on him and used me to protect herself from Mark Chun." Uette's Grandfather was standing rigid and ashen colored.

"That's impossible!" Uette's father gasped. "You're wrong!"

Uette was staring at Peter and anger began to surface. She stood up slowly. "You lousy bastard!" She spat out the words. "You filthy son-of-a-bitch!" The men looked at her as she vented her pent up emotions using words that shocked them. "You're the one who told him! Look at me." She shouted. "I could have been killed. I've been trying to make this shitting marriage work and you were betraying me." Tears rolled down her cheeks. "I learned to cook for you." She shouted. "And you're the one who told Mark." She glared.

Her Grandfather steadied himself. "Shut up before you prove yourself to be even a lower piece of filthy trash. You're at an unspeakable level already. Shut up and sit down."

She looked at her Grandfather. "Don't you call me names? I'm sick of this Wong family name having to be fairytale so shining bright in order to protect your fantasy of ancestors."

Her father grabbed her arm. "Uette watch you mouth! He's your Grandfather." He held back rage and was shaking visibly from it.

She pulled her arm from his grasp. "Keep your hands off of me, you sanctimonious fake."

Her father raised his arm to hit her and his father grabbed his arm. "Don't Roland. She is executing herself. She's her own punishment. Don't get down to her level or she'll spread her disease through the family. That's not a Chinese custom, that's the violence in this country."

Uette raised her eyebrows and laughed. "He'll catch my disease?" She sneered. "Have your honorable son confess his sins! I'd like to see him whitewash that."

"What are you talking about?"

She sneered at him. "Don't stonewall me." She glared at him. "I'll confess for you. Grandfather, your wonderful son here takes money from the Chuns. That's right, those awful Chuns who the Wongs are too good to even say the name. Your son and a bunch of the other good moral men in our Chinese community are on a dole list in the Chun organization, probably for fencing stolen goods. I saw the list myself and my father's receiving some good sized bucks."

Her father shook his head in disbelief. "Is that what the Chuns told you?" He asked.

"Get real." She laughed. "The less they thought I knew, the better off I was. I tripped over the book by mistake in Mark's office, but I saw your name right there plainly written every month."

"Oh Uette!" He said, with deep pity. "Uette that list isn't for money they give to us; it's for money they take from us. It's extortion money. They call it a tariff for using the docks." He sat down and lowered his head. "Uette, you know so very little. The brightest of all the girls and the most ignorant. I can't bear to see my failure in you. I'm embarrassed for what it's done to my father's name."

Uette's Grandfather lowered his head. "Roland the embarrassment isn't for what's been done to our name. The greatest embarrassment is what the Wongs have done to the Changs, most especially to Peter. The Wong's can't repay him for what he's suffered. If this was old China, there would be an execution and I would offer myself along with her, believe me." His voice cracked with emotion and he cleared his throat. "I have to apologize and ask forgiveness and I can't bring myself to even bow to them in humility. My shame makes me feel that unworthy." Tears rolled down his cheeks. He turned away from them to collect himself.

The Changs were silent. Uette paced. "Happy now, you shithead? What's this going to prove?" She glared at Peter. "Big deal, you won, tough guy."

Her grandfather spun around angrily and her father stood up quickly. "Shut up!" He said. "Shut up or so help me, I'll finish what Mark Chun started on you and feel justified doing it. Believe me; I'll go to prison a proud man. I'm sorry I inflected you on this life, so shut up! I can't stand your attitude. You have no conscience, no morals, you are diseased. You don't seem to understand that you owe Peter Chang a debt you can never repay! But you're going to try. I will personally see to it that the complete truth of what you've done is told accurately in the Chinese community. You will carry the shame for what you've done and Peter will be sung as a hero from the lips of your father, and that's not even a beginning to repayment of the debt. That's just to set truth itself right. I intend to cover the cost of a law suit against you in Peter's name charging you with everything the law will allow and it'll cost you everything you hold valuable. That should be easy to assess because everything you value has a price tag on it, but when all your valuables are totaled they won't begin to equal the value of his name because of the honor dignity and pride he's attached to it. That's what doesn't have a price tag on it.

Uette's father looked at Peter. "And Peter, I'm in your debt, too. I would consider it a great favor and a matter of personal dignity and pride if you'll come to me for help in anything. I'm begging you to allow me that so I can begin to wash some of the shame off me." Peter watched and listened, overwhelmed by the success he had in clearing his name and embarrassed that he had caused the Wongs to expose their honor and dignity before outsiders. It hadn't been pleasant to witness.

"Mr. Wong, what I think I'd really like is to have my mother brought in here and told the whole truth. She believed Uette's lie. I'd like my name cleared with her."

Uette laughed. "Oh brother, get a load of this pile of garbage. Peter you are definitely crazy, totally soft in the head. You can't tell black hats from white ones." Her father turned, glaring at her. She backed away. "All right, I'll shut up, but you people are really sick, I swear it. At least with the Chuns, you can tell who the bad guys are, even they didn't lie about it."

"I'll get Lien." Tom said and left the room.

Peter's mother walked into the kitchen with eyes reddened from crying. She looked worried and confused about being there. Her husband put his arm around her shoulder. "We have something to tell you, Lien." He said.

Roland Wong bowed to her. "Mrs. Lee. We've have brought you in here to correct an injustice. We owe you an apology."

Peter's mother was surprised; she looked at all the people in the room. "You mean my son didn't do that to Uette?" She asked, as tears spilled down her cheeks.

"I never touched her." Peter replied and enjoying how it felt to have witnesses behind him.

She glared at Uette. "Then why did you blame him?" She asked, angrily.

Roland Wong sighed. "We have another injustice to correct." He said, sadly.

His father touched his shoulder. "Let Uette confess it. She should ask Mrs. Lee's forgiveness."

Uette got off her chair, quickly. "Oh, now wait just a minute here. I can understand your fantasy about honor and dignity and bowing to each other, that's like stupid rules for a sport game or something and if you want to run your life like that, fine, but don't anybody here make me bow down to the likes of her."

"Uette!" Her Grandfather snapped.

"No, Grandfather, No. You talk about honor and Dignity and pride. Why should it cost me my pride to bow to her and ask forgiveness. She's not white and I don't mean the race."

Tom was annoyed. "That's enough."

Peter was completely shocked by Uette's attitude toward his mother. He was getting angry. "Watch your step." He said. Her father fumed at her.

Uette looked around the room. "Now wait just a darn minute here. Then why am I getting called diseased for what I did…"

Peter's mother looked at everyone. "What did she do?" She asked confused by the conversation.

All the men lowered their heads from embarrassment except Peter. "Mom, the baby isn't mine. Mark Chun is the father and she knew it. She set me up."

His mother covered her mouth as it opened to a gasp.

Uette rolled her eyes and sneered at her. "Oh really what's so shocking Mrs. Lee. Tell me you've never heard that story before."

"Uette!" Her Grandfather gasped.

Peter's grandfather stood up. "Lee, she's going too far."

Uette's father went to her. Peter watched becoming confused about what was happening.

She backed away. "I'm sick of all this. You tell me I'm no good, I'm diseased. How's she so different?"

"Uette, shut up!" Her father took her arm. Peter was watching in shock.

"No!" Uette said. "You want me to ask her forgiveness. When's her turn?!" She yelled.

Her father grabbed her by both arms. "Uette, for gosh sakes, have you no decency?"

"Why do I have to pay and not her? She's still living the lie. Her grown son thinks his father's a rapist. That's pathetic, but she doesn't have to apologize? Tell me that you honorable and wise Grandfather? How is that justice?"

"We're leaving." Her father said and pulled her.

She pushed him away. "No, I'm tired of all of you getting on my case." She looked a Peter. "Are you smartened up yet, tough guy. Where is the black hats and where are the white hats, huh?" Peter stared as the words attacked his mind." Uette was bordering raving. "This family shit they pull on us is a whipping stick, Peter. You worry about exonerating your name with her." She turned and sneered at his mother. "You sneaky liar, he's more free from sin than you are, you hypocrite."

Her father gasped. "She's out of control! I can't hit her, the baby, the stitches, the bruises." Uette glared at Peter's mother. "I'll apologize to her when she apologizes to Peter and tells him the truth. I want to hear the words from her lips." Uette was raving and getting worse.

Peter's mother was pale and shaking from anger and shock and hurt. "Uette." She said, trying to steady her voice. "There's a difference between what I did and what you did. I didn't trick Peter's father, the baby was really his." Peter stared at his mother in shock"

"I knew it." Uette waved her hands frantically in the air. "Can you see it, Peter?" She shrieked. "Aren't they good at whitewashing it, huh? They whitewash what they do wrong and beat on us for our mistakes. Hypocrites Peter, that's what they are!" She was shouting. She turned to his mother. "You're not getting off so easily. Justify the lie to Peter, huh. Explain that." She looked at Peter. "Watch this one Peter, it'll be a dandy but don't let her fool you tough guy. She lied damn good to you. You're father wasn't a rapist. He was a white man and she got pregnant to trap him but he wouldn't marry her.

Buy that. This bitch who preaches to me for my lack of morals."   She laughed hysterically. Peter's mother cried softly.

Peter watched Uette realizing that she was nearing hysteria. "But to them, I'm trash, Peter." Uette laughed. "Her generation" made mistakes." She made quotation marks with her fingers in the air. "But our generation. I'm just filth. I'm not allowed no explanations, no excuses." Her father came at her out of concern. She backed away laughing. "Scare me, Father. Go ahead and threaten me." She laughed hysterically as tears rolled down her cheeks. "But make it a good threat, because I've been threatened by experts. Mark Chun's going to amputate pieces of me an inch at a time if I don't get a divorce before this baby's born and give it his name."

She turned to Peter and bowed. "Thank you for that and all because I fell in love with you." She laughed. "Miss Mouse!" Uette screamed. "It's all your fault! I hate you! I hate you!" She continued screaming and crying.

"Oh my gosh." Her father said, watching his daughter lose control. "What can we do for her?"

Peter went to her and put his arms around her tenderly, she clung to him sobbing like a drowning person would to a life preserver that had been thrown to him. He held her and remembered Jeneil's father's words. Facing the wind wasn't easy. The light hearted and the light headed could be blown aside. It was the mature kernels that would land safely after facing truth. "Uette, you've been spinning so fast because of your lies that you're dizzy. Look around you, the carousel has stopped. All you have to do now is step off and take the brass ring that's waiting for you, kid. No more lies, no more being used. The white hats are right here with you. You can tell the white hats, they're the ones who are there for you when you land in shit. They'll help you make it right and clean it off. Mark Chun's not going to hurt you. His father won't allow him to harm his first grandchild. The baby's that's been such a nuisance to you is your ace now. Stop spinning Uette, so life will make sense. I know, because I had to jump off a spinning carousel too." He could feel her calming down. Pulling the chair closer, he had her sit. He took her pulse. "Try counting to a hundred slowly." He said, as she continued to cry and shake, slightly. He turned to her father. "Have her sip some water. She missed a doctor's appointment Friday. Call Dr. Vandiver and tell him it's an emergency. She should be checked. He's expecting her for tests anyway."

Mr. Wong nodded. Peter felt drained. "I'll have to get the quick divorce. I don't think she can cope with the details of flying somewhere for me. Your lawyer can work it out with mine. I'll be available Monday at the office. I need to stop my own carousel this weekend."

Mr. Wong nodded again. "Peter, thank you." Peter shook his head. "Don't thank me; this marriage has contributed to what's happening to her now. It was a battle for survival. She needs professional help."

"I know." Her father replied. "She'll get it."

Peter nodded and walked to the chair for his jacket. He looked at his Grandfather who was standing near the table. "Somebody should have told me." He said, quietly. He turned, his mother was watching him. He stared at her steadily and she lowered her eyes. He put on his jacket and left.

There was an odd feeling of mixed emotions racing through him including shock and embarrassment that he had missed the truth about his father. Looking back he remembered snickers and outright decisive laughter when he defended his mother by saying she had been raped, but he always assumed it was guys trying to be creeps. Even Lin Chi looked surprised when she heard him say rapist, but she never said anything. It was part of the Chinese network of saving face. The affront would be more serious to the person exposing the hurt. Until Uette used the truth as part of her own defense, he never doubted that his father was a rapist. All of it had taken its toll on him and he packed the weekender from his luggage set having decided to get away to a motel room and think. He felt tired and drained and he wanted to rest. The apartment was Uette's and a prison to him. His room at his mother's house was out of the question at the moment. He had no place that was his. Heading to his car, he thought of how life played tricks. For months he had lived with the idea of exonerating himself and he had always imagined racing from his prison to Jeneil's freedom and Camelot, but that was even gone. He could feel Chang's anger inside of him and he was disappointed that he wouldn't get the chance to prove his innocence to Jeneil. He knew that was Chang's anger that wanted to tell Jeneil that he was innocent and that his father wasn't a rapist. Chang was raging for that chance. He had won the war and the triumph felt empty. He felt beaten, bruised and amputated, a victim and casualty of his own struggle in the war that life dropped on him.

*****

Steve watched the sky darken from the large window in the livingroom. He had fallen asleep on the sofa and was surprised that it was so late. The apartment was quiet. Jeneil had been sleeping soundly when he went to check her at lunch time. He had let her sleep. Considering how tense she had been, he thought the natural medicine for her was rest. He found that his nap had helped him to relax, too. The tension of the week and adjusting to new surroundings had made him tired. He shook his head as he thought of how people found it normal that he and Jeneil were tired. They were assuming that the reason was physical passion. "Jeneil you're right, Honey. There are Plexiglas walls between people, and because they're transparent, we think we can see clearly. It makes me wonder what I'm missing, too." Hunger reminded him that it was late and he went to Jeneil's door and knocked. There was silence. He opened it and walked in. Standing by her bed, he watched her sleep. Thinking that it was odd how she was sleeping for so many hours, and as far as he knew, she hadn't eaten all day. He wondered if she might have been pretending to be sleeping to avoid him and then he realized the paranoia in that thought, but he couldn't just put it aside either. Becoming concerned for her health, he touched her shoulder lightly. She never even stirred. He shook her gently, she startled awake, and he was reassured that she wasn't pretending. She was disoriented for a minute and then grasped the moment. He sat on the edge of the bed. "You've been sleeping a long time, are you all right?"

"I'm just very tired." She answered.

"Did you take something?"

"No." She replied, yawning. "I'm just very tired."

"You haven't eaten." Steve said.

"I'm not hungry."

What about some liquid?

"I don't want anything." She answered.

He sighed. "Jeneil, we really need to talk."

She looked around the room. "Do we have to talk in the middle of the night? Can't we wait for daylight? I'm still very tired."

"It's early evening, Jeneil."

"Of what day?" She asked.

"Saturday." He said. "Can you remember the month and year?"

"Yes, 212BC and this is Rome isn't it? You're Caesar Augustus and I'm Perfidia. Did I pass the sanity test?" She chuckled.

He smiled. "You're a real bitch when you're tired."

She laughed lightly. "Thanks for waking me to say that."

He laughed and began to relax, seeing that she was all right except for being very tired. "Okay." He said, standing up. "I'll let you get back to sleep."

"Thanks." She said. "I'm really feeling very tired, that's all." He closed the door quietly and went to fix something for his dinner. He was encouraged by the brief conversation with her, but her inordinate tiredness had stirred a thought and he wondered if she was dealing with depression. Having thought that, his next question was could the marriage be the cause. At the moment all he could do was wait and see.

*****

Sunday morning was a beautiful and sunny. The morning air was crisp and Steve thought it was perfect for a walk. Tucking the Sunday newspaper he'd had gone to buy under his arm, he unlocked the door to the apartment. "She'll be ready for some fresh air after more than twenty-four hours in bed." He knocked on her door. There was no answer. "It's almost nine. She must be fully rested by now." He thought. Opening the door, he stuck his head in. She was lying in bed awake. He walked in. "Did you hear me knock?"

"Yes."

He was surprised. "Well, why didn't you answer?"

"I didn't feel like it." She answered, simply and without emotion.

The answer stunned him. "Why didn't you want to?"

"Because I've been pretending for weeks now and I'm tired of pretending. I didn't feel like answering so I didn't. I just wanted to be honest."

"You're not on anything are you?" He asked.

She shook her head. "Am I incoherent?" She asked.

"No." He replied and swallowed past the lump in his throat. "Are you getting up today?"

"No, I don't feel like doing that either, I'm tired."

"I see." He answered. "Okay." He turned and left the room.

"Oh shit, she's slipping." He said, anxiously, as he went to the kitchen. Putting some ice in a glass, he filled it with grapefruit juice and returned to the room. He knocked. There was no answer and he wasn't surprised. He announced that he was going in and he opened the door. He went to her bed and sat down. "I brought you some grapefruit juice. You have to drink it whether you feel like it or not." He said, calmly. She looked at him and took the glass, sipping slowly. He watched her. "Jeneil, you don't like answering to knocks at the door and getting out of bed, is there anything you do feel like doing?"

"Lying here and resting." She answered, setting the glass on the night table.

"That's not doing something, Honey. That's the opposite, not doing anything."

"No, it isn't. I'm breathing and thinking and taking inventory of Jeneil. That's doing something. At least, it's wearing me out."

The answer surprised him. He reached for the glass of juice. "Drink the juice, Honey."

"I did." She replied, looking puzzled.

"All of it Sweetheart, you've only sipped a mouthful."

"Is it necessary to gulp? Why are you rushing me?" She sat up and concentrated on drinking. She was almost at tilt and he wasn't sure of her answers.

"Honey, we have to talk."

"Finishing half the glass, she placed it on the night table, and sighed, wearily. "You keep saying that. Is there something specific, because I'm not up to chit chat? I'm too tired." Her directness was a slight surprise.

He decided to plow right in. "I'm worried about you, your tiredness and your withdrawal. It would calm me if I knew the cause."

"Oh." She replied. "I'm going to malfunction."

"What?"

"Malfunction." She repeated. "It's when I pop off the conveyor belt before I get thrown off. Normally, I plan some kind of trick, but this is going to be a mental malfunction. You shouldn't worry."

He was. "Honey it's not good to just lie here, not moving and not drinking or eating. It's been over 24 hours and yet I'm forcing you to drink juice."

She smiled. "Steve, I've been up. I guess you went out. I thought you were sleeping. I drank a large glass of water with ice, had a really quick shower and came back to bed exhausted. That's why I'm not very thirsty, right now. Mental malfunction is very tiring. At least it is for me, so I use as little physical energy as possible to allow for it."

He watched her, she was at tilt and then he wondered if it was her normal level. A question surfaced in his mind. He braced himself.

"Do you know why you're into this mental malfunction?"

Tears filled her eyes and spilled down her cheeks, but she didn't answer.

His heart sank. "Jeneil, what's making you cry?"

She bit her lower lip and reached for a tissue. "I don't want to talk about it. I'm dealing with it in my mental malfunction.'

He wasn't comfortable with the tilt level. "I need to know." He said.

"Why?" She asked, drying her eyes.

He sighed. "Look at it from my side, Sweetheart, you're withdrawing and incommunicative. You're showing some serious signs here."

"I'm only eccentric." She said, quietly.

"Spill it, Honey. You'll have to spill it." Steve pushed.

"Doesn't life ever rush at you?" She asked.

He shrugged. "Life doesn't know any other pace."

She shook her head, marveling at him. "It's the music at the prom. You understand it. You never land on the cracks, that's incredible."

He smiled. "What happened have you lost the beat?"

She sighed. "I've not only lost the beat to the prom music, but I can't even hear the music. I think life moved the prom to a new location."

He smiled. He always did like the offbeat way she looked at things and then he remembered that it was important that he examine offbeat.

"How are you going to find the prom then?" He asked.

"I have to travel through my mind and look for it. That takes time and energy and life wouldn't let me rest, so I'll have to declare a malfunction and just take the time to search. Adrienne's back now, I can steal some time."

The answer's too abstract. "What's making you cry?" He asked. Tears rolled down her cheeks. "Answer the question, Honey."

"There are monsters in the malfunction." She replied.

He saw the smoke screen. "Answer the question, Honey." He repeated. "So I can hear you spell eccentric. Can you understand that? I need to hear you spell your kind of eccentric." She nodded. "What's making you cry?"

She twisted the tissue in her hand tightly. "There are a few things, but my real concern is that I hate Uette and I'm angry at Peter." She cried, softly. "And my anger is heading for hatred and scaring me. I've got to head it off before it devours me." The clarity of her answer almost stunned him.

He took her hand. "You're a good speller, Honey. How long does the malfunction last?"

She shrugged. "Until I understand me and can hear the music at the prom again. I'll never understand it but I need to hear it at least."

He nodded, I can accept your malfunction if it's got food and water in it."

She smiled and squeezed his hand. "You're okay for a science guy who understands prom night."

He smiled and kissed her cheek. "Finish your juice." She drank it down quickly and he took the glass. "I'll let you rest." He said, standing.

"Thanks." She sighed. "I'm worn out from talking." He smiled and left the room to prepare a breakfast for her of scrambled eggs and toast. The fact that she talked so openly encouraged him. Their friendship was still strong. Putting the food on a tray, he returned and there was no answer when he knocked. He went in and found her sleeping soundly. He watched her and grinned. "There's nothing wrong with you kid, except you don't travel at normal, you cruise at superlative. That's pretty thin air at that altitude and you burned out in your reentry into normal." He smiled. "Hatred and anger are normal down here. Rest Beautiful, you're not normal unless you're at hyper-speed in superlative so rest and struggle back there to where Jeneil lives." He was filled with love for this girl who thought it was important to resist hatred. Putting the tray on the bureau, he went to the bed, bent down and kissed her cheek lightly. He touched a wave in her hair and smiled. "I love you, Jeneil. I always will." He thought, sighing with relief that she wasn't crying because she was Mrs. Steven Bradley.

Sixteen

The talk at the hospital Monday morning was the spontaneous reception with Steve and Jeneil. Peter was reviewing a chart for a patient in recovery and listened as two nurses talked. Jane Simpson has been beside herself with joy when she heard that Steve had married Jeneil, and she listened with delight at the news of them at the restaurant celebrating a week's anniversary. Peter felt his stomach cringe at the thought of them being married a week already and Jeneil was even celebrating the event. "They're something together." Hilda smiled "It was so romantic. Steve put his arm around her now and then and would kiss her temple or her cheek. Oooo, it's so cute and sexy." She whispered.

Connie grinned. "Yes but she is a real shocker. When she worked here, she was so quiet, you wondered if she had an IQ that even registered on the charts, but she's got definite spunk to her. Kirk always ties me in knots, because his eyes nearly melt through you. I hate clashing with him, but Jeneil met him straight on and even sliced through his remarks now and then. I was impressed, very impressed. It felt good having Steve back in the crowd again, but he's not the same guy. He's tied to her and he's holding the reign and keys. She doesn't move too far away from him. He's happily married and holding the leash tightly."

Peter was surprised as he listened to the grapevine talk about Jeneil. They were the people she avoided. They were the reason she wanted their relationship to be a secret. She had said that she didn't want them tracking it and yet she was now part of it and they loved her. "Has she changed?" He asked himself. "Things can't have gotten so different."

Hilda laughed. "It was cute teasing them about being tired and they really look tired, too." She raised her eyebrows. "Things must be good, Steve all but melts when he's looking at her."

"Mmm, mmm, mmm." They all said and laughed.

Peter felt the pain pass through him, he'd had never thought about physical. The pain was excruciating. He replaced the chart and turned to leave. He was dealing with tension of his own lately. Taking an envelope with x-rays, he went to the elevators. His office was a haven and he enjoyed being there. The hospital was a place to tolerate. Between hearing about Steve and Jeneil there, he had to run into him from time to time. It was awkward and always left him rattled. He was working hard at putting everything behind him, but it wasn't easy and he was grateful that he was now in private practice where he had his own life free from theirs. More than once, he sighed with relief that he hadn't taken Sprague's offer to join the Surgical Group where he'd have to work in close association with Steve. Being in the same state was bad enough to handle.

*****

He buried himself in his work and began to make a life of his own. He had gotten an apartment. And was beginning to feel steady except for the bouts with tension and the dream about the street fight which had returned as a regular part of his life. His professional life was moving, but personally, he knew he was a wreck. He knew he was having trouble bringing both worlds into one. It all seemed easier with Jeneil. She knew how to handle life at all levels and she even helped it make sense to him. He avoided an apartment at the Tiverton Arms where all the up and coming doctors were and had taken one in a building where upper management executives were. He didn't know anyone and that suited him just fine. He avoided his family and kept to himself. Life was easier that way. As each day passed, he learned to avoid thinking about Jeneil. The only reminder was the feeling of emptiness that was left, but at least it wasn't pain until he heard her name, thought about her, or saw Steve.

He sat at the bar of the Tannan Restaurant and waited for Dr. Sprague with a glass of mineral water. It was there usual weekly meeting. He felt a hand on his shoulder. "Hey Pete, am I late?"

"I hadn't noticed." Peter answered as Dr. Sprague stood beside him. He ordered a scotch on the rocks and sat down next to him.

"How has the past week been?" Dr. Sprague asked, watching his face closely.

Peter shrugged. "A little easier than the week before."

Dr. Sprague saw the tension. "What are you drinking?" He asked.

"Mineral water and a slice of lemon, why?"

"It looked healthy, I just wondered."

Peter smiled. "Jeneil liked…." He stopped himself and wrinkled his eyebrows and ribbed his forehead. "It's a nice compromise between liquors and sweet soft drinks." Dr. Sprague saw the hurt. The hostess notified them that their table was waiting. They brought their drinks and sat down ordering they're usual no frill meal of steak and salad. Peter sighed. "Well, we have cause to celebrate tonight." Dr. Sprague listened, wondering what good news finally had filtered into Peter's much needed life. "Uette finally admitted that she lied." He smiled.

Dr. Sprague smiled, broadly. "Oh damn Pete, that's great! Really, really great. I was beginning to think you were going to be locked in as the father." He held up his glass. "To freedom, then."

Peter smiled slightly. "I'll drink to that." He sipped his drink. "I want to thank you for staying with me through all this and for these weekly dinners. I'll miss them in a way."

Dr. Sprague watched him. "Pete, can I suggest something?"

Peter looked up. "Sure." He said, becoming curious.

"Why not try psychotherapy?"

Peter grinned. "Have I gone over the edge?"

"It's better to not wait until you do, Pete. You've been through one hell of a strange experience these past months and you've lived with threats that would topple a normal life. These things leave their marks. Add to that your loss of…." Dr. Sprague took a drink. "Pete, Dr. Nefida, is considered quite good. He's known for his work with ethnic and cultural adjustment."

Peter smiled. "This gets better and better. Is my prejudice showing?"

Dr. Sprague sighed. "In a way, yes. I get the feeling that sometimes you look up and ask yourself what the hell Peter Chang's doing here."

Peter nodded. "You're right, I do."

"Peter, cognitive therapy is only a chance to talk to someone who has seen others go through life on similar paths with similar encounters and who have found solutions. He rubbed his chin. "I'll be honest with you. I'm thinking of going for some sessions myself." Peter was surprised. Dr. Sprague took another swallow. "I'll tell you I was looking forward to the kids growing and leaving so the house would be quiet and life routine and normal." He shook his head. "But not in this lifetime, I guess. My wife is going through something, she'll drive us both to drink. I thought it might be menopausal, but it's got other symptoms too." He shrugged. Maybe I'll send her for sessions too if I can suggest it in a telegram when I'm away." He raised his eyebrows. "Oh wow, what she'd make of that suggestion. Try therapy, Pete. I've seen it work for some every sane men." The waitress brought their dinners and Peter thought about the idea as their conversation was interrupted. It did appeal to him, especially the ethnic part. "In any event, Pete, don't be offended. I have the highest regard for you and your stamina, but the very quality that makes you a damn great surgeon, could kill you in life. You're terrific at blotting out what's around you so it won't touch you or your career. That's fantastic, but brought too far and life could be too rigid."

Peter nodded. "You're hitting very close, Dr. Sprague."

The older doctor smiled. "Life is one crock of liquid shit. If you feel too deeply and you're too caring, you'll get swallowed up and the crock spills on you and if you try not to feel, the crock spills too. Where's the happy medium, Pete? It isn't easy to feel deeply and care strongly. It must hurt a lot."

Peter nodded. "You idea is more reasonable than mine."

Dr. Sprague watched him. "What's yours?"

"I'd like to leave. Maybe go to New York, take a job at a inner city hospital."

Dr. Sprague understood. "That's not really unreasonable as long as you're going to something and not just running away from something."

"A bunch of something's." Peter answered.

The older doctor watched him. "Wayne Maxwell would be devastated."

Peter shrugged. "That's why I'm still here. The signed contract and I'm learning so much from him. The guy's incredible."

Dr. Sprague smiled. "So blot all the nonsense out, Pete and concentrate on medicine, then take all the rest at your own pace. Dr. Nefida will show you how."

"Yeh." Peter replied, sighing. "That's reasonable too and it sounds great."

Dr. Sprague finished his salad. "Apply that incredible stamina you have to everything else and you'll succeed like you have in medicine, I'm sure."

"I hope so." Peter said. "Because not too much makes complete sense right now except medicine."

Dr. Sprague watched the young surgeon before him with pride. He had achieved miracles in his professional life where his entire concentration had been for the past years, and now that he was free to also be human and have a private life, there wasn't one. He had wondered how his two maverick doctors would handle life in the real world and of the two; he felt that Steve needed Jeneil more. He had already been showing signs of unrest and dissatisfaction. The guy was insatiable about life. And secretly Dr. Sprague was relieved to have him married. He hoped that Jeneil was up to coping with the very complex man who was now her husband.

*****

Steve walked into the apartment carrying two brown paper bags and a long thin white box. Sitting then on the counter in the kitchen, he then removed his top coat and went to the closet. After hanging it, he reached into his left pocket and removed another package. Unwrapping it as he returned to the kitchen. Tossing the paper in the trash container, he put the clear vase on the counter.

"Now for some vegetables." He said, half aloud as he removed his suit jacket and went to the refrigerator for a cucumber and a tomato and then to the sink.

He had listened at Jeneil's door before returning to the kitchen and there was no noise. Her car was in the parking area, it had been there all weekend untouched. She had been staying in her room living through the malfunction. It was Friday and two weeks since they'd been married and nearly a week since she dropped out of the game called normal life into malfunction. He'd been watching her closely and was now wishing he was seeing more positive signs of improvement in her. She wasn't dealing with business at all. The telephone rang and the recorder snapped on. "This is Hollis, Jeneil and this is my seventh call today unanswered. If someone doesn't answer soon, I'll be stopping by uninvited by noon tomorrow."

Steve raced to the telephone and clicked off the recorder. As he lifted the receiver. "This is Steve Bradley. I'm sorry sir. I only know you as Hollis and Jeneil's Uncle. I just got in and I haven't checked for messages."

There was silence. "Well, finally I made contact with human life there. The name is Hollis Wells. Where is Jeneil?"

"Probably in her room. Mr. Wells. She's resting."

"From what? The story I'm getting is that she's not doing anything to rest from and I know that marriage wouldn't send her into hibernation."

"Who told you that?" Steve asked.

"Adrienne. She's quite a friend to Jeneil, defends her in everything, even if she shouldn't."

Steve could see the handwriting on the wall. "I'll get Jeneil." He answered.

"You took the words right out of my mouth." Hollis replied.

Steve knocked on her door. "I'm coming in, Jeneil." The room was in darkness. "Jeneil, Hollis is on the phone." He talked in to the blackness.

He heard her sigh. "I'm not taking calls."

"You better take this one Jeneil. He said he'd be here by noon tomorrow."

She sighed again. "I'll be right there."

He closed the door and returned to the living room wanting to see how she'd handle it. Jeneil walked in holding her robe closed. "Uncle Hollis, I'm not taking calls so whatever it is will have to wait. Is the family okay?"

"Yes." Hollis answered, set back by her remark.

"And Bill?"

"Yes."

"Then it can wait. Goodbye."

"Jeneil!" Hollis said strongly. "What the hell is this? What do you think are you doing? What do you mean it can wait. You own a business that needs its owner."

"What would you do if I died? Just do that." She said. Hollis sputtered in shock from her answer.

"Jeneil!" He shouted.

"Okay pretend I'm unconscious and can't respond." She replaced the receiver and headed to her room. "If he calls again, I'm unconscious and I'll bolt the door if he shows up tomorrow."

Steve was aghast. "Honey, don't put me in the middle."

"Then you can be unconscious too." She closed her door. The telephone rang. He closed his eyes; quite sure he knew who it was. He wondered how he could make a good impression with a beginning like this. He answered.

"This is Hollis Wells and I want somebody to explain what the hell or who the hell I just talked to, because that couldn't have been Jeneil! I don't believe it!"

Steve took a breath. "It was Mr. Wells. To use her words, she's malfunctioning."

"Is she on something?" Hollis asked, sounding shaken.

"No she isn't." Steve assured him.

"Oh my gosh, she's slipping out on us isn't she?"

Steve saw the tight spot he was in. "Mr. Wells, I've been watching her physical health and she's holding on."

"But mentally?" Hollis asked.

"She hasn't lost touch with reality." Steve replied.

Hollis was upset. "Not today you mean. What the hell are you waiting for? Is she getting help?"

"Mr. Wells, she's only asking for a breath from the tension. The fact that she knows it's necessary is a positive and healthy sign."

Hollis sighed. "It's her personal life not her business life. I knew all this was too fast. She's just not a girl who does things impulsively and it's tripped her up. The tension's probably from you." Hollis shouted.

"Wait a minute." Steve said, not having expected to be blamed for her condition. "I haven't done anything; I'm not making demands on her." He groped for a defense. "Mr. Wells, she's in love with Peter. She expected to be his wife and her whole future was pulled from her hands. She's shocked, she's hurt, she's angry and she can't pretend. She's just trying to deal with the emotional turmoil inside of her."

"How interesting, Dr. Bradley." Hollis said, caustically. "How interesting that you know she's in love with Peter, but you married her anyway. You don't sound too much more steady than she is."

Steve sighed. "It's not like that."

"Oh, how is it like? I really want to know, because try to see it from my side. She's been badly hurt and the guy's best friend marries her knowing she's not in love with him. I'm very suspicious of your motives Doctor."

Steve hadn't seen this. He had only wanted to marry Jeneil and take care of her. He hadn't thought how it would look to anyone. "Mr. Wells, I don't know what to say. I understand your concern."

"Oh good." Hollis replied. "I'm glad you do, then you won't mind helping me out with a solution so my blood pressure will return to normal."

"What can I do?" Steve asked, wondering what he meant.

"Sign a legal document releasing any and all claims to Jeneil's financial interests."

Steve felt like he'd been kicked. "Holy shit, you really think…. Send the damn paper and I'll sign it." Steve answered quickly, trying to regain control. "Anything else?"

Hollis was silent. "Yes, considering how I just found her, there should be a clause in case of incompetence that you still have no claim, but will turn over her interests to someone else and that person will be endowed with legal power to act in her behalf in her business life and her personal well being."

Steve was shocked. "Mr. Wells are you afraid that I'll commit her or that I won't."

"Let's just say I'd like two heads making the decision." Steve was struggling with anger, but tried to see Hollis's side. "Mr. Wells, let's go one better and make you the other person. How's that? Need any more assurances?"

Hollis was calmer. "Just let me add this. If you mess up with her and she suffers more, then you'd better be prepared to practice medicine on another planet because I can be mean as hell when pushed." Hollis sighed. "We seem to understand each other Dr. Bradley and I appreciate your seeing my concerns so clearly, thanks. I'm telling you that girl gets more difficult as she gets older. When she was living with Peter, I wanted her married, and now that she's married, I wish she wasn't because I don't trust it."

"Then maybe you should trust Jeneil." Steve answered.

Hollis sounded wearily. "I will when she sounds more like the Jeneil I know and she's functioning normally in her life again."

"That's understandable." Steve said.

"You're very agreeable, I'll give you that." Hollis replied.

"Mr. Wells, we're on the same team, we have the same interest and concern for Jeneil. I wouldn't hurt her for anything."

Hollis laughed. "Oh shit, I heard those very words from Dr. Chang."

"What can I say, Mr. Wells." Steve was out of words and a defense.

"Yeh." Hollis moaned. "Life doesn't come with a guarantee does it?" He sighed.

"Mr. Wells, if I could sign one, I would. I don't know how to prove to you that my motives are honorable."

Hollis was silent. "Its okay Dr. Bradley my blood pressure's slipping back to normal. I'll get back to you about the papers."

"I'd rather be called Steve."

"You've got it. Can I call tomorrow and check on her?"

"Of course."

"Okay, Steve, then tell her to regain consciousness." He laughed. "She's really a kick in the head. I like her spunk."

Steve smiled. "Sometimes she sounds more normal than the rest of us."

"I know it. Her parents were pretty outstanding people. I can't help but think they'll be very pleased with her. They were different too. But I'm the one who's left trying to help her balance the life they left her. She's been given a tough path in some ways."

Steve didn't know what he meant, but he was just relieved that the tension between them had eased. He went back to the kitchen feeling calmer and was surprised that he liked Hollis in spite of the insults he had to swallow from him. "He likes the kid, that makes him okay." Steve said, washing the tomato. His anger cooled and he chuckled. "He thinks I'm after her money. Sheez, I'm not exactly a pauper and my earning potential is very impressive too. Boy he acts like she's very wealthy, instead of well off, but he cares. That's understandable."

Having set out the dishes for dinner, he went to her room. He knocked and waited. He heard a quiet. "Come in."

"Jeneil, I brought in some dinner, let's eat at the table."

"What happened with Hollis?" She asked.

"I thought you were unconscious?"

"But you weren't and I left you in the middle."

"He's giving you some time to be unconscious."

Jeneil sighed. "Thanks Steve, I'm sure it was something you said. I can't believe I was so rude. If he doesn't quit as my lawyer, I'll be lucky."

Steve had made his way through the blackness and sat on her bed. "Honey, maybe it's time for some help."

"What kind?" She asked.

"Somebody to talk through what you're feeling."

"If you mean psychotherapy. No." She answered, flatly.

"Don't attach any stigma to it. It works." Steve said, quietly.

"I'm not attaching anything to it, but I'm me. I'll work this out myself. I'm not normal; I've come to accept that, I don't want to be given any normalcy tests. I know I wouldn't pass one."

Steve sighed. "You might regain consciousness faster with help."

"No I won't." She said, quickly.

"How do you figure that?"

"It'll take a month to get an hourly appointment for once a week. By the time he sorts through my name and shoe size, another month is gone and we haven't even started to talk about my thoughts. You're talking two months before he even begins. I don't have that kind of time. Malfunction is a condensed version of psychotherapy."

Steve wanted to laugh at her evaluation, because it was true.   "But Honey, in psychotherapy, one person is objective."

"I'm objective Steve. You don't understand malfunction. If I stayed in my normal routine, I'd be distracted by life's demands. By withdrawing, I can give some quality time to my thoughts."

"But I'm not seeing any improvement. You're only lying here."

She snapped on the small lamp beside the bed.

The sudden light blinded Steve and he waited to focus. She looked rough. Her eyes were puffy from crying and her nose was reddened from stopping. She shook her head. "You're quite a man of science." She said. "You look into blackness and think you see the light. Behold my medicine." She pointed to her night table where several books were stacked. He looked them over. They ranged from poetry to philosophy right through books on theories of social interaction and there was one on literature.

"Honey, you're using theories and fiction to improve?"

She stared at him.   "What would a psychotherapist use?   He can only use what information I feed him and that would be fiction wouldn't it if it's colored by my anger and hatred? I'd be working my way to the truth and how would he know that it is true if his source is unsure."

Steve smiled. "You're one of a kind."

"Everybody is an individual so how do you decide what's normal? That's why I don't trust psychotherapy for me. Offer me what normal is and allow me to accept it or not. I'm me and you're you and that's our gift from life. Half the problems in society happen because somebody wants to determine what else everybody should be and do. People are only alike for a small portion of who they are in a group. The rest is malleable material and a sacred possession of the individual."

He took her hand and smiled. "Let's have dinner or your malfunction will give me a headache. Now I understand how you get tired from it."

She smiled. "Why can't I eat in here?"

"No." He answered with directness. "Give me one night. You've eaten in here alone all week."

She was surprised by his attitude. "Okay, then give me a few minutes to get there."

He squeezed her hand and smiled. "You've got it." He stood up and left.

Steve put the dinner in the microwave and he heard her go into the bathroom. A few minutes later she came into the kitchen tied if not pulled together and she was even dressed. "What smells so good?" She asked.

"BBQ ribs from Joli's Rib Rack." Steve said.

Jeneil smiled, appreciating his caring. "You're one of a kind, too." He smiled.

She helped him carry dinner to the diningroom and saw the long white box by one plate.

"That's your seat." Steve said and went to hold her chair.

She sat down recognizing the box. It was the same kind that held the last yellow rose he gave her. She could feel the tears begin as she unwrapped it and saw another yellow rose. Embarrassment filled her as she wondered what happened to the last one. She couldn't even remember putting it in water. Drying her tears she looked up at him. "You're better at this marriage business than I am." She said, and opened the card. *"Happy Anniversary to the second week of a great friendship. It's really nice having a special reason to give you a flower, Love Steve."* His kindness overwhelmed her and she just gave in to crying. "You're such a liar." She laughed and dried her eyes. "I'm a groundhog lately and it must be irritating."

He smiled. "It's nice to have somebody here to come home to." He said. "Even a groundhog."

She choked on his words and concentrated on not crying, fearing that she would sob uncontrollably. She agreed it was comforting to hear him unlock the door at night and be about his routine. It made her feel less alone. "I really appreciate my roomie." She smiled. "He's a great cook. I get power shakes for breakfast and some very decent dinners." She reached over and touched his hand. "I owe you for all this."

"No Jeneil, I'm not breaking even yet returning favors that I owe you."

She laughed. "Goodness, all mutually admired, we even sound newly married."

He laughed and squeezed her hand. "Thanks for having dinner with me. I miss my friend even though I don't mind the groundhog being here."

His words touched her and became medicinal, they added to the healing process that she was struggling to achieve. After dinner, Jeneil stayed and helped in the kitchen and then went to the livingroom to sit. Steve smiled as he watched her, encouraged that she was staying and he was even hopeful that the malfunction was turning to positive as he went to change from his suit. She was standing before the large window overlooking the city. He joined her. It's a nicer view at night." He said.

She nodded, agreeing with him. "Yes it is. All the ugly details of reality are blotted out. You don't see exhaust fumes or the litter, just yellow, red and white lights, moving and blinking through the darkness." He smiled, enjoying her observations.

She turned to him. "I've learned something this past week and standing at this window has given to a vivid definition. "I've never liked apartment buildings, I prefer houses, and standing at this window, I understand why. I'm in a tower here, removed from life around me. In a house, I make a home. A home is near the earth. I need roots. Do you realize that I'm in several places? Some of my things are in Wonderland, some at Camelot and others are in Nebraska. This place isn't a nest. It doesn't feel like one to me."

He was surprised. "Won't moving be strenuous? Where would we go?"

She shrugged. "I really like the town where Dr. Sprague, Turner and Young, live. It's charming and picturesque."

Steve sighed. "Honey, I can't live there."

She raised her eyebrows. "But Why? You said it was soothing there."

"I like the town. It's soothing, but I can't live with the old guard from the Surgical Group. I have to make sure I stay connected to the future. The younger doctors are buying in Glenview. Can't you see the political mistake that would be to join Sprague? He was my sponsor, but I have to play my hand with an eye on the future."

She was staring. "Steve, your life isn't your own. Why do you have to let your decision be connected to the surgical group at all?"

Steve shrugged. "Because that's the way the game is played. Do you think it's an accident that Sprague Turner and Young all live in Marshfield? That was probably the political future back then. Now it's Glenview."

"Are you in trouble because you live here in this building?" She asked.

"No, Fairview 1900 is elite in the apartment circuit, although only the single doctors live in them. An apartment building isn't real estate"

She smiled. "You mean, it's apolitical?"

He grinned. "I can see the stupidity of it all, too, but I didn't make up the game. It's what's happening. It's the price I pay for being in a large surgical group. Fitting in is important."

She chuckled. "Boy did you make a mistake in choosing a wife then. I never fit in. I can hide pretty good, but I never fit in."

He laughed. "What I really like about you is that you're different. It's refreshing that you don't fit in."

"Am I politically safe though?" She asked.

He was embarrassed. "You make me sound calculating."

"No, Steve I understand. That's why I don't like groups. The collective thinking scares me."

Steve smiled. "The pressure isn't that rigid."

"I guess not, you can choose the color of your car and what flowers will grow in your yard."

Steve laughed. "Are we having our first fight?"

Jeneil smiled. "No, but we are facing our first problem."

He put his arms around her shoulder. "Well, we don't have to solve it right know do we?"

She looked at him and grinned. "Nice move, Dr. Bradley. I can tell you understand that solving the problem means that one of us will have to give in so you think tenderness might work in your favor."

Steve shook his head. "Now that's what I mean, why even think about it when we haven't even looked at our options yet?"

Jeneil chuckled. "You're political Steve, very, very political. What a sneak!" She laughed.

Steve smiled. "Just concentrate on your malfunction."

Jeneil laughed even harder and went to sit on the sofa. "Mr. Husband, you are clever."

"I can't be, I'm not fooling Mrs. Wife."

Jeneil watched him and then smiled. "Have you smuggled any junk food in here yet?"

"Some. What are you after? Crackers and Cheese or just a confession." He asked.

She shook her head. "Too healthy. Don't you have anything artificially flavored, colored, and sweetened?"

He smiled. "Oooo, hard core attack. There are some chocolate things without chocolate in it with cream that isn't cream."

"Perfect!" She smiled, getting up. "Point the way. I think I'm getting better, my eating habits are now atrocious and my nesting instinct is activated. I'm making progress." She turned and smiled as she walked to the kitchen. "Do I have to leave any for you?" She grinned, mischievously.

"I'm joining you." He said. "I love a binge, too." He smiled watching her. His good friend was there with him and he wanted to enjoy her. He knew she may be a groundhog tomorrow, but it was all right because today she was Jeneil. He went to the kitchen decidedly an anniversary convert. He now believed in them strongly.

Through the weekend she disappeared into her room again and he wondered and worried. She stayed puffy eyed and red nosed. By Tuesday, he decided that he should really be trying to draw her out since she had done so well at the anniversary dinner. Even kissing his cheek when she said goodnight and taking her yellow rose to the bedroom with her. He had been very encouraged. They were being included in invitations to dinners and parties and he begged off saying that Jeneil had to get settled in the office and the apartment, but now in their third week of marriage, the excuse was becoming suspicious so he excused her with a serious cold and knew that was only good for a week. As a hope for improving the situation, he called her from work after leaving the answering machine off. Dialing several times and hanging up, then dialing again until she answered out of curiosity. She had laughed when he told her he was lonely.

"I need a wife, Jeneil. There are invitations being extended to us and I don't think they understand malfunction."

She smiled. "Then tell them I'm out of town."

He chuckled. "Okay, right after you're over your bad cold, but I'm still lonely. I miss my friend." She choked up. "Can't you leave a few problems unsolved and fake it like the rest of us?" He asked. She laughed as tears rolled down her cheeks.

He smiled. "I really am glad I'm married to you. Friday's dinner was fun for me. Let's get away, Jeneil, just for the weekend. A no-fuss place. How about the cape? It's off season and deserted. We can live in jeans and just walk or rent bikes."

She sighed as she thought of the work involved in getting away.

He seemed to sense her thoughts. "It's really no fuss Honey, two jeans, two tops, please. I'm going crazy. I'm not as good as you are at having fun. I'm bored out of my mind."

She laughed. "Okay, let's get away." She agreed.

"All right Honey! I owe you for this, I really do."

*****

She began to get cold feet as the weekend drew closer to reality. But he wouldn't let her back out and he even helped her by getting her luggage out Thursday night and forcing her to get jeans and tops and a change of clothing together. They were finished in no time and he had their winter jackets set aside with the luggage, so he'd just have to leave the office early and pick her up on Friday. Hollis was happy to hear the news and Steve got a thank you. Steve had felt resentment when Hollis had told him that Bill Reynolds would be returning from the Orient soon and that he'd send him to see Jeneil telling Steve that Bill and Jeneil are very close and that he's good for her. He had hoped that Bill would pull her out of this. Steve swallowed his resentment, but he secretly promised himself to have her smiling and normal before Hollis's miracle worker arrived. Jeneil was feeling very much like his wife to him and he felt responsible for her welfare. He resented the way Hollis seemed to claim ownership to her. Steve felt that it was only a matter of time before he told Hollis that her name was now Mrs. Steven Bradley. He was proud of himself for thinking that because it was such a class improvement from "Back your ass out of my business or I'll kick it out." which is how he felt when he was told that Bill was being sent in.

His Friday afternoon rounds were finished and he marked several charts, then taking his top coat he smiled a Connie, Hilda, and Jane. "Have a great weekend." He said, turning to leave.

"Hey Dr. Bradley." He turned. Jane held up his medical case which he had forgotten on the desk. He laughed and shook his head as he returned to get it. "Where are you tearing off to?"

He beamed. "My wife and I are going away for the weekend."

"I thought she had a cold?"

He smiled. "It's very improved and her doctor suggested sea air." They all looked puzzled.

"So where are you going?" Jane asked.

"To the Cape."

Connie laughed. "The Cape! There's nobody there."

"I know." Steve grinned and took his case.

Connie raised an eyebrow. "Won't that be dull Doctor, with no one around?"

He smiled at her. "Best way to avoid spreading her cold, don't you think?"

She winked. "Have you had your flu shot yet?"

"I'm immune." He said turning to leave.

"Sorry, you'll miss the party at the Barnards." Hilda called.

"Me too." He said, heading for the elevator.

The nurse's all smiled at each other. "Lisa, is that too much or what?" Hilda said. "Oooo to make a man flip out like that over me. I'm going to corner her at a party someday and pick her brain."

Connie smiled. "He's a different guy."

Jane grinned watching him get on the elevator. "I'm really glad he's happy. I felt as bad when he lost his last girl, but he was never this excited when he was with her."

Connie nodded. "Drex said he was disappointed in that redhead. He thought Steve liked less contrived women. Who would have guessed that he'd end up with the little librarian, but she has him walking on air. How interesting. Kirk calls her "Mona Lisa" and wonders what's behind the gentle smile."

Jane tried to recall the name. "Kirk? Kirk Vance, the Anesthesiologist?" Connie nodded. Jean looked around to see who might hear her. "I heard that his eyes and voice alone could put you under." She whispered.

"They usually do." Connie chuckled.

Hilda choked on a laugh. "Connie, that's filthy."

Connie shrugged. "Never mention Kirk Vance on Friday." They all laughed.

*****

Peter finished his rounds and stopped to check medical charts. He hated Fridays. Finishing his notations, he returned them to the racks. He sighed and rubbed his forehead.

"Have a nice weekend, Dr. Chang." Jean smiled.

"Oh thanks. You too." He said, and walked away.

"He looks rough." Hilda commented

"I know he does. That is not a happy man." Jane added, sighing.

Connie watched him. "He and Steve don't speak, have you noticed? I think Peter avoids him."

"No." Hilda answered. "How come?"

Connie shrugged. "It probably has something to do with that blow up in the scrub room. They were never right after that. I heard they fought over Peter leaving his girl for the shark. I'll bet he's sorry he married her, he has never looked happy since he did."

Jane shook her head. "What a shame. He and Steve were really good friends."

"The best." Hilda said, sadly.

"Maybe he should take Steve's advice and go back to his old girl." Connie replied.

"His wife is pregnant, though." Hilda told her.

Jean sighed. "I wish he'd get a divorce. He looks so sad. He's such a nice guy."

Connie laughed. They were hell raisers and a ton of fun, at least until Pete settled down and then Steve caught Pete's quietness too. They became so tight lipped; I'll just bet there's one good story behind all this."

Hilda looked around. "I heard a rumor, well really more like a remark that the two of them had the same girlfriend."

"What?!" Jane replied. "Who the redhead?"

Hilda shrugged. "There were never any details, just the remark."

Jane shook her head. "That's crazy. Pete only dated Chinese. You can't trust gossip around here. I swear, I don't know how most of these outrageous stories get started."

Seventeen

Peter headed back to his office. He was scheduled to move into his new apartment. He knew he had to let his family know where he was, but really didn't want to. While moving his belongings from the apartment, Uette's father had stopped in for some of Uette's things. Dr. Vandiver had hospitalized her the Saturday of the explosion. The sharp pain had been a medical problem that had left the baby in distress. The beating, which she reported as a mugging while she was in New York and the resulting tension coupled by her own neglect of her health was too much and the baby had died in the womb. It had been a boy and Peter was listed on the record as being the father of a still born male child. It didn't matter to him. Nothing much seemed to anymore.

Mr. Wong had suggested that Peter take the apartment furnishings, since Uette was moving back home, but Peter didn't want any of it. He took the cleaning supplies and buckets along with the trash containers having remembered how much they had totaled when he bought them. He had bought furniture that was being sold by a tenant who was getting married and moving out. That was fine since the movers never had to leave the building, the moving cost was minimal. Life was settling into a routine, it was orderly and very empty. Peter appreciated it, the tension began to ease. He unwrapped a bar of soap and placed it on a sponge which reminded him of Jeneil. He pushed her name from his mind and went to the kitchen. He had brought the diet sodas from the apartment, but there wasn't much of anything else on hand. The thought of having to go to a market tired him. His doorbell rang surprising him, since the entrance signal never buzzed. He opened it. His Grandfather stood there holding a tan paper grocery bag. He smiled. Peter was surprised that he knew how to find him.

"Am I allowed inside?" His Grandfather asked. Peter nodded and stepped aside. "Your mother sent some food." He handed Peter the bag. "You'd better put it away, most of it is frozen." Peter went to the small kitchenette and began unpacking the wrapped packages. They were labeled. His mother had sent portions of lasagna.

"She didn't need to do this." Peter said, closing the freezer compartment.

"I'll tell her you said thank you." His Grandfather replied.

"How did you find me?"

His Grandfather looked sad. "My Grandson should have told me, but Mr. Wong mentioned that he saw you at the apartment when I visited Uette." Peter nodded. "She's doing fine, mostly sleeping and resting from all she's been through." Peter stayed silent. "She asked to be remembered to you." Peter walked past him quickly and went to the livingroom.

His Grandfather followed. "I expected that reaction but I told her I would tell you." Can we sit down, Peter?'

"I'm not really up to having company." He replied.

His Grandfather watched him, steadily. "I'm not company, I'm your Grandfather."

Peter grimaced. "Explain the responsibilities of that job someday. You and I seem to have different ideas of right and wrong."

"Well I'm here. Why not now?" Peter fidgeted. The Old Man was determined. "I want to talk to you."

"Grandfather…." Peter began.

"Now, Peter."

Peter sighed and sat down. "Why not. Let's get this over with."

The Grandfather sat. "Well I'm sure you want to know why I didn't tell you about your father. Peter it took me awhile to accept it myself. Your mother had told us that she'd been raped. We accepted that. It was Malien who came to me months later with gossip she'd heard about Lien and a white boy. She said she believed it the gossip because putting some of your mother's laundry away, she saw a picture of her with him. Your mother was suffering so much at the time that I didn't want to add to her burdens and I really didn't accept that she had lied to us. I believed her. It really wasn't until her worries with you and Jeneil that I could see it. It wasn't something your mother talked about with anybody. There were things that made me wonder, like her behavior with you when you were born. She really lived for you. There was never any anger or resentment. We were surprised and pleased." He shrugged. "Since that was the story she was insisting to be truth even to you as you got older, it never made sense to tell you about gossip being talked about by a handful. It was only a possibility, so why hurt your mother. Does it really matter if he was a rapist or a man who used your mother and wouldn't own up to his responsibility? They're both dishonorable types."

Peter looked at him. "It makes a difference to me, Grandfather. One's a diseased human being with no conscience at all, the other may not be very responsible or mature but at least in my mind he was more of a decent person who was capable of loving my mother. She must have loved him so he had to have some decent qualities. You seem to forget that whatever my father was, I was a part of him. He's in me, in my mind. It was always there, especially with Jeneil caring about family and wanting her children to be proud of their ancestors. She accepted it, Grandfather which shocked me, but for me there was that dread of how we'd tell our children. It affected me more than Jeneil. I never felt good enough for her. It affected my attitude about our relationship. I struggled to stay with her especially when she had guys with the right backgrounds interested in her. I wondered, why me?" He swallowed hard.

His Grandfather sighed. "I've never seen that side to the mistake. To me you were always an innocent victim no matter what story I believed. You were you and part of me and the Chang name." Peter was silent. "You mother is waiting to see if I bring the food back. She's suffering again for her mistake. It was embarrassing to have it confessed before men. She hasn't told me this, Tom has. Your mother was foolish and headstrong, but she was a moral woman. She never lied to him. She intended to never marry. It was only the street fight that made her consider Tom's offer of marriage. He knew that, she didn't lie then either." He sighed. "She'll be glad to hear that you are keeping the food."

"Well she lied to me." Peter said, matter-of-factly.

His Grandfather nodded. "Yes and you should settle it with her."

"Not yet." Peter said. "I'm too angry at her right now, she's included in the group of people who cost me Jeneil." The Grandfather could understand that. Peter felt his stomach pain. "Have you eaten?" He asked the Old Man.

He shook his head. "I was too worried about coming here."

Peter got up. "That container of stew looks pretty big and it wasn't frozen. I can heat that."

His Grandfather smiled. "I took it out this morning hoping that we would have dinner together."

Peter smiled. "There are some people I can't stay mad at, you're one of them. I knew you'd have a reasonable explanation about the mess."

His Grandfather smiled. "Peter everyone usually does if you ask for it."

"No Grandfather, not everybody. Steve will never be able to explain his betrayal."

"Has he tried?"

"He tries to talk to me, but I can't pretend. I'm not civilized enough to accept what he did."

The Old Man sighed. "Peter, if you don't listen, you can't learn."

Peter shook his head. "Grandfather, I'm worn out. It's always me giving in. I know I'll end up accepting whatever is my mother's explanation. She's my mother. Uette is a bitch and yet I can accept her selfish reasons as her explanation. I've had to accept a baby being stillborn and carrying my Chang name, but there's no way in hell that I'll accept Steve's explanation after telling me that he knew Jeneil belonged to me so his selfishness I can't accept."

*****

Jeneil smiled as Steve opened the apartment door. He stopped, shocked to see her ready to begin the trip. She looked better then he'd seen her look in two weeks. He went to her. "Honey, you look great!"

She laughed. "Steve I can see the exclamation point on that sentence."

He was embarrassed. "I'm sorry; I just expected to pull you out of bed." He put his arm around her. "Is this just surface, or are you feeling great clear through." She let him hold her. "I have a clear perspective on some things and others will need some time. My feelings aren't so negative and extreme now and that's what I wanted. I feel calmer inside."

He kissed her cheek. "Honey, you're something else, you handled it yourself."

She smiled at him, lovingly. "No, you said something that made sense. Everyone is walking around with a problem." She shrugged. "So I'll fake it like everyone else." She didn't add that he had reached her by saying that he needed a wife. They had an arrangement and she intended to keep her part of the bargain. She did like being married. The security and freedom it allowed her was already being felt. Life would settle down and make sense. There wouldn't be anymore pressure about being in a physical relationship. With the loss of Peter, she had lost her interest in a traditional life. She could settle for peace and security. Steve understood that. She hugged him enjoying all those thoughts and her feeling of gratitude besides. She wasn't alone, and she knew she had made a good move in getting married to Steve, something deep inside of her sensed it. The decision was right. She hugged him again. He looked at her surprised, beginning to be overwhelmed by her display of emotion.

He smiled and handed the long white box to her. "Happy Anniversary."

She smiled broadly and opened it looking forward to the yellow rose and green fern with baby breathe. "Thank you. I knew you would make a great husband for somebody."

He laughed. "I know you really did want to win your bet, that's why you married me before the end of the year." She laughed and he studied her face. She was faking the cheerfulness, but there was strength in her now that had been missing. Her eyes were still a bit swollen, but not red and puffy. Her coloring was still weak, but he was encouraged. He felt strongly that Jeneil was back now. She smelled the rose and thanked him as she hugged him again. He held her glad that her good friend was with him for the first time since they had been married three weeks ago. The closeness was between them again and he accepted that gratefully, knowing that you make your own miracles when life allows you the chance and he had been given the chance. He held her tenderly knowing that her display of emotion was probably only gratitude as well but it was a chance. "I love you, Jeneil." He said, quietly as his heart beat rapidly from the idea that he was free to say that to her and eventually tell her the truth. She was now his wife.

She pulled away slightly and looked at him. "I love you too, Steve." She smiled.

*****

The drive to the cape was even pleasant. He would draw into conversation when she lapsed into silence and because she was bravely trying to fake it like the rest of humanity; she made an effort to resist her desire for silence, solitude and withdrawal with her thoughts and her memories. As they walked into the small inn, Jeneil suddenly wondered how they would handle the sleeping arrangements and she became a bit shaken that she hadn't thought about that before. She realized that she seemed to be overlooking many details about an arranged marriage. Moments that the arrangement made awkward. She waited while Steve dealt with the desk clerk. He turned to her and handed her a key to her own room. She relaxed inside and became filled with a feeling of love for Steve's sensitivity toward her. He seemed to anticipate her needs and that felt so secure and calming. Her trust in him had grown more quickly since they had been married. She knew he could be trusted and that added to the reasons she loved him. He unlocked her door and turned on the lights. "It was adequate." He said, looking around. "Considering it's off season." He put her luggage on the stand at the foot of the bed.

"Did you register as Dr. and Mrs. Steve Bradley?" She asked.

"No, just Steve and Jeneil Bradley. Why?"

"I just wondered what the clerk is thinking."

Steve smiled, "I couldn't care less. He's rented two rooms. He's happy. We could be cousins or brother and sister for all he knows."

She chuckled. "Of course with such a strong family resemblance between us. What else would he think?"

He laughed lightly and kissed her cheek. "It's about midnight; I'll see you in the morning." She nodded and watched him as he left.

*****

Steve turned over in bed opening his eyes to a room filling with daylight. He looked at his watch and was surprised that he'd slept so long. The drive had tired him adding to the strain of a early surgery schedule. He could hear the seagulls and he looked around the room. It was simply furnished. The double bed was comfortable and he had slept undisturbed.

"I like life simple and uncluttered." He thought, turning onto his side as he stretched. His arm rested on the pillow beside him and he thought of Jeneil. "It's okay Honey. I've been given a chance and that's more than I had two months ago. Life's never given me chances in a normal style anyway. Why would love and marriage be any different? He smiled as he remembered that they had a future together at least and the thought was exhilarating. He threw back the covers and stepped onto the floor to head for the bathroom. Tying his shoes, he then stood up and reached for his jacket. He noticed that a note had been slipped under his door. It said. *"This was a great idea. Decided to walk on the beach. Hope you slept as well as I did. "* He smiled. "And it might even be nicer together someday, Mrs. Bradley." He liked the sound of that name and the face that went with it. "And the body too." He added, and then cautioned himself to slow down or run the risk of messing up the chance he'd been given. "It's okay Honey, I understand and it's okay." He walked down the stairs of the Inn and crossed the narrow street to get to the beach. The day was sunny with a strong breeze coming in from the ocean and he could hear the surf before seeing it. Standing on a knoll he scanned the beach, then he caught sight of Jeneil in the distance. Jumping off the knoll, he walked quickly toward her delighted that she was out on her own and not lying in bed withdrawing.

"This was a good move." He thought as he got closer. She had taken her coat off which concerned him because the wind was strong and chilled. He picked it up from the sand as he approached, thinking to lecture her, but he became distracted by her behavior. She was moving into the wind as it swirled at her, actually seeming to dance with it. He stopped and watched becoming fascinated with her ability to dance with the wind. He had heard of dancing in the wind, but this was different, she was dancing with it like she believed it had form and was a partner. She could tilt her head back and the wind would brush her hair back seeming to caress her cheek and neck.

"Holy Shit!" He thought, catching his breath as the electricity pulsed through him. "She's incredibly sensuous." She stopped suddenly and opened her eyes. She looked around quickly and saw Steve standing near her. "Why did you stop?" He asked.

"The energy was interrupted." She answered simply, almost like she was awaking from a sleep.

"What energy?"

She smiled gently at him. "Poor Steve, you don't know the full scope of your wife's eccentricity do you?" The sound of the word "wife" coming from her shot all through him and he went to her wanting to kiss her. He stopped and took her coat, holding it for her to put on instead. She stared at him intently and then touched his hand. He was shocked by the warmth of her skin. "Please don't leave me." She said, choking with emotion.

Her words choked him. He dropped her coat and put his arms around her. "Leave you?" He said, holding her closer as she put her arms around him. "Not me, Honey. We've made a bargain. Why would I leave you?" He asked, feeling oddly disconnected. The moment itself felt strange to him like he'd drifted into a dream. He held her shocked by how warm she felt even though she had been standing in the chilly wind. "Honey, this isn't making sense to me."

"I know." She answered, kissing his cheek. "I'm feeling cosmic."

"What's cosmic?"

She smiled and moved from his arms. She touched his cheek tenderly. "Poor Steve."
She smiled. "It's the line that crosses the "T" and dots the "I" in eccentric. You have no
idea who Mrs. Steven Bradley really is."

He looked puzzled and then he smiled. "Jeneil, sometimes I really have to count the six
pack carefully with you to make sure two aren't missing or empty." She smiled and then
studied his face seriously. "Are you okay?" He asked, becoming concerned about the
way she was looking at him.

She smiled. "I'm okay. Cosmic disconnects me, but I'm stronger after it's over." She put
her arms around his waist and clung to him. The suddenness surprised him and he held
her wondering what all of it meant. Jeneil you're not dull, that's for sure." He laughed.
She looked up at him and smiled. "I'm really glad I'm your wife. It feels right."

He felt his heart pound and he wanted to kiss her as a man would kiss his wife, but he
resisted knowing that he couldn't handle it since the moment was so explosive and he was
sure she couldn't handle it either. He knew she was wandering between two paths, one
leading away from Peter and the other toward him. The ingredients were there. She
trusted him and she loved him deeply as a friend in her style. He could see that. He
smiled and leaned toward her, kissing her lips lightly, then he hugged her enjoying the
electricity that raced through him. The feeling that she was his filled him and it felt so
good to not have to struggle against it, anymore. There had been a special closeness
develop between them even when she was with Peter. It had grown to friendship and
beyond which had confused him, but he knew now that if he just waited, the special
closeness could make her his. He held her wondering why the brass ring had been handed
to him in this chance that life had so miraculously given to him. He kissed her cheek. "I
love you, Jeneil" He said.

"I know." She replied, not moving from his arms. "You've always been such a great
friend that this feels right. It's what keeping me steady right now and I love you for it. I
love your sensitivity and caring."

He smiled to himself. "I can wait Honey, because one day you're going to be hear it the
way I'm saying it. I've been given a chance, that's enough for now."

*****

They looked through the brochure at the inn and Jeneil decided that she'd like to eat at a
restaurant in a nearby mall because the glass of juice pictured in the ad looked so good.
Steve had laughed accepting it as logical considering her behavior that morning. The
food had been good and in a good portion. He had been hungry and was prepared to order
two for himself. Jeneil had watched him eat all of his breakfast and finish hers. She
could have eaten more, but her diet portions wouldn't allow it and she marveled that he
and Peter were alike and she struggled to brush it all aside not wanting to cry in a
crowded restaurant. She struggled in order to survive as well, because if, she thought
about Peter then being Mrs. Steve Bradley didn't make sense to her and there were times

when that name felt right to her too. She sighed to herself wondering why life never came to her as normally as it seemed to others. As they walked past a gift shop, Steve stopped. "Be right back." He said, going inside. Jeneil wondered what he had seen that sent him inside and she looked at the window display as she waited. In the corner was a glass unicorn. She felt tears stinging the corners of her eyes as she remembered the glass unicorn that Peter had given her. "You promised to return it, Peter." She said half aloud, surprised by the anger she felt. She turned away and took a deep breath and then exhaled as Steve left the shop with a white box in his hand.

"Oh please, not a glass unicorn." Jeneil pleaded in her mind. "Or I'll come unglued. I really will."

"For you." He smiled, handing the box to her.

Jeneil took it hoping for the strength to deal with a glass unicorn and she imagined herself sobbing in front of all the shoppers walking past them. Lifting the lid, she separated the tissue paper and sighed. "Seagulls!" She said, laughing with relief. As she held the small piece of driftwood with the two seagulls perched on it. "I love it!" She said.

Steve smiled. "It's a reminder of our first trip together."

"You are a romantic Dr. Bradley, definitely a 12th Century man." Jeneil laughed feeling much calmer inside.

"Hey, that's an achievement." Steve said.

"Sure is." Jeneil smiled as she replaced the gift in the box. You rank right up there with Francis of Assisi."

"Who?" Steve asked.

Jeneil slipped her arm through his and squeezed it. "He's a 12th Century saint."

Steve smiled. "Knights in shining armor, 12th Century saints. I think I'd rather be a ordinary man."

"That's impossible." Jeneil laughed. "Or you wouldn't have been born so extraordinary." He smiled as he put his arm around her shoulder and squeezed her to him as they continued through the mall corridor. She stopped at the wide entrance of a darkened video arcade. "These places are a phenomenon. Look at the kids in there already at this hour." She smiled at Steve. "Let's go find what the stampede's all about."

He laughed. "What another interview, like the mud wrestlers?"

She laughed. "No, let's play some games, too." She pulled him inside.

"Jeneil are you serious?" He asked, laughing. Taking some quarters from her purse, she looked at the available games.

"Here's one." She said, stopping at a computerized game of wizards and inserted a coin. The game buzzed and bleeped beginning its display of obstacles as Jeneil watched trying to understand it.

Steve laughed. "Honey, take the control stick, the machines beating you."

"How can it? I haven't begun yet. I'm only studying it."

Steve shook his head and laughed. "Sweetheart technology doesn't wait for you to study."

She smiled. "I thought that only time and tide didn't wait for man." The buzzer signaled the game over flasher. "Well that's hardly fair." She said. "It ate my quarter while I'm trying to understand the game."

Steve laughed. "Make that time, tide, and technology not waiting."

"I guess so." She chuckled inserting another quarter and holding the control knob quickly in readiness. The screen moved and Jeneil watched. "I still don't understand what's expected of me."

Steve reached over and moved the control stick. "There you are." He said, pointing to the maze on the screen. "You have to maneuver through the maze." He pushed some buttons on the control panel. "These help destroy invaders and whatever obstacles come at you."

"How do you do that?" She asked.

"They're labeled as weapons." He answered, becoming fascinated. "Honey, you have an invader in a corridor. Right there! Move ahead fast!"

"But the maze keeps changing." She said, immobilized by the movement on the screen. There was a flash and the computer notified her that she had been vaporized by a troll. "The machine is a thief." She stared at it bewildered. "It's not working right."

Steve laughed. "Don't you see the pattern?"

"No, I only see the screen changing and it distracts me."

"The maze moves down as you continue through the corridors." Steve explained.

She looked at him. "Have you played this before?"

"I've never seen it before." He said.

She frowned. "Then you play, and I'll watch so I can see the pattern you're talking about." Handing Steve her quarters, she moved away and stayed by his side watching with amazement as he maneuvered through the changing grid on the screen and the points began to total, but she never saw the pattern he was talking about. He got liquidated by something called a "tork" after his score was in the thousands. "You've never played this before?" She asked, surprised.

He shook his head. "Never had the time or quarters for the games, but I know what the attraction is, it's a great tension soother."

She laughed. "Are you serious? It gave me a slight headache! It rushes at you with bleeps and buzzers in order to get you tense and distracted."

"Blot it out." He said.

"You can blot out all the sounds and movements?" She asked, surprised.

He nodded. "It's a great game. Think you can manage to stay awake while I play one more game?"

"Sure." She replied and watched him instead of the game as he played against the machine and she became impressed with his power of concentration and his eye-hand coordination. He scored higher in the second game even knowing he'd get zapped because he was losing stamina. Jeneil was very impressed. "Try another game." She suggested.

He smiled. "No. I want to spend the day with you, but that's a fun machine. It's really therapeutic." He put his arm around her shoulder as they walked out and Jeneil realized that she didn't know this man who was her husband as well as she thought she did. She smiled to herself thinking. "He's still the White Stallion." Then she realized that the marriage would give her the chance to know him better and that fascinated her because this confusing man was not what she had thought he was at all. He was proving himself to be much more than her first impression of him. She watched him as he unlocked the car door.

"What are you staring at?" He asked, wondering about her silence.

She shrugged, slightly embarrassed for staring. "I was just thinking that marriage gives people a chance to get to know each other better. I like the closeness marriage offers. I believe in marriage." He smiled as he closed the car door and went to get behind the wheel aware that her words had started electricity pulsing through his chest, but he cautioned himself to slow down realizing that they were hardly close in this marriage. He understood that he was completely ready to have her as a wife in every sense of the word, but she was only at the beginning in seeing him even as a man, let alone a husband in a traditional way. Excitement filled him as he got in the car wondering if she had at least gotten closer and that's what had prompted her to stare and remark about marriage. He pulled out of the parking area feeling very encouraged that the brass ring was close.

*****

Steve found it difficult to sleep. The day and evening had gone so well as the sensitivity between them continued. They had found a club with a jazz group and had stopped in after dinner. The club was small and intimate, the tables were very small and people had to sit close to each other. Between their quiet pleasant conversation and having to sit with his arm around her, he was very aware of her and energized by the end of the evening. He held his breath as she kissed his cheek goodnight wanting so much to hold her and wishing they were settled into a real marriage. He sat in his room reading a magazine about New England life until he felt calmed and relaxed and then he finally went to bed.

The next morning, he opened his eyes realizing that it was late morning, he rushed through his shower and dressing. Jeneil had left another note that she was at the ocean. He raced across the street expecting to see her in the distance, but she was sitting nearby on a bench watching the waves roll in. Walking to her, he was anxious to see how things between them would be. He watched as she dabbed at her eyes with a tissue and hope drained from him as he saw the tears. He sighed. "Oh shit, Pete, let her go. I'll handle it. I want to. Let her go on with her life." He thought as he stopped at the end of the bench. Jeneil looked up. "Hey, you're finally awake." She smiled. "The sea air must relax you."

"He sat next to her, looking concerned. "What's the matter, Honey, tough morning?"

She sighed. "No, a tough moment."

"Want to talk about it?" He asked, hoping to know where she was putting Peter in the past.

She shrugged. "It's probably best to not talk about it. I have to get on with my life whatever that is going to be." She sighed, again. "The Corporation, I suppose."

"Dennis wants you at the Rep. He's called a few times."

She shook her head. "I don't think so. It's too big. I just don't have the stamina right now to deal with the politics of a professional troupe. No, I think I need my life settled first and bring all of Jeneil's nests into one by closing down Wonderland and emptying out Camelot to a new nest."

He stayed silent not wanting to face the issue of where they would live. Jeneil broke the silence as she looked at her watch. "Let's leave for home now and stop by Glenview."

"Glenview?!" Steve asked, surprised.

She nodded. "Let's see what their homes are like. They must have a brochure. The development is very professional. It's a good real estate investment."

He was touched that she was giving in. "Jeneil we don't have to live there."

She smiled. "Yes we do. Corporate politics is important. You have a career, I don't. We'll build our lives with your career in mind."

He smiled and kissed her cheek. "You're pretty easy to live with, Mrs. Bradley."

"So far." She sighed. "So far, but a month is hardly conclusive. So let's do something positive and get our life into a home. The positive energy from the work it'll require will be good for me." She stood up. "Come on. I'm anxious to start a new nest." She smiled.

He watched her. "Can we eat first?" He asked. "I'm starved."

"Oh." She said, surprised. "That's right, we haven't eaten yet." She sighed. "I guess I'm not quite well yet, I forget to eat when I'm unraveled. It's another gauge I use to know when I've left eccentric. Eating and nesting let me know when I'm normal. My style anyway." She smiled, gently. They stood up and put his arms around her. "Mrs. Bradley, I love you and your style of normal." She snuggled to him. "You say that so easily. You're such a great husband." She sighed; enjoying being held and having him care. He touched his lips to her temple and kissed it tenderly not daring to kiss her lips knowing that he'd prove to her why it was so easy for him to tell her he loves her.

After leaving the real estate office, they stopped for a light dinner and returned home talking positive about living in Glenview. Steve was deeply impressed that she made the decision for his career move. He had seen some of the homes there having been to a few parties at the Barnards and dinner at the Capras. Jeneil had wanted to study all the written material with house and lot plans before seeing any.

*****

A visitor was waiting in the lobby at Fairview 1900 when they arrived. The handsome dark haired mustached man smiled at them as they entered. Jeneil smiled and ran to him putting her arms around him in a hug. The man held her tight. Steve wondered who it was as Jeneil stepped back and then kissed him. He waited.

"Steve." She said, smiling and holding the man's hand. "This is Bill Reynolds, a very close friend from Nebraska." She squeezed Bill's arm to her. "Bill, this is Steve Bradley, my husband and a good friend too." She laughed.

Each man extended hands to be shaken. Steve recognized the name of Hollis's miracle worker and he was glad that Jeneil was looking so improved. Jeneil leaned against Bill's arm lovingly. "What are you doing here?" She smiled, broadly and Steve could tell that they were close. Bill hugged her again.

"I stopped by to kiss the bride and meet the groom you little sneak. You shocked the stilts off Hollis. I've been in China."

Jeneil smiled. "Have you been waiting long, can you visit for a while." She asked in the elevator.

"Actually I was hoping to bunk here for the night and leave in the morning. Will that be any trouble?" Bill asked.

"No." Jeneil assured him and Steve wondered how they were going to explain two bedrooms as he unlocked the apartment door. "If you'll just put the bag on my bed, Steve. I'll handle it later." Jeneil said, letting him take her coat. Steve was aware that Bill had caught the remark about her bed and he could tell that he was being looked over carefully.

"I'll make some coffee." Jeneil said, going to the kitchen. Bill watched her. "She's a lot better than Hollis described." He said to Steve, sounding relieved.

Steve nodded. "She has improved a lot this past week."

"Good." Bill replied. "She's special to Hollis and me." He sighed. "I'd like to get my hands on Peter." Steve was going to defend him but decided to stay silent, realizing that his position wasn't too secure either.

Jeneil returned to the hallway and picked up both luggage pieces. "I'm going that way Steve; I'll put yours in your bedroom." Steve noticed the remark hit Bill with real force. Jeneil walked down the hallway.

Bill was staring at Steve intently. Jeneil disappeared into the bathroom and Bill opened fire. "I want to talk to you, privately." He insisted, strongly. Steve nodded almost expecting it and he walked to the kitchen and pointed to a chair for Bill to sit. Steve sat across from him and braced himself. He could tell Bill was upset.

Bill watched him steadily. "Look." He began. "When I get upset I'm not diplomatic, so I hope this goes well. Hollis told me you're Peter's best friend so I'm already concerned about you being her husband for that alone. But now to find that the two of you are in separate bedrooms." Bill took a deep breath. "Shit, this isn't my business, but what the hell's going on here?! Hollis never mentioned this weird shit. Are you gay? Is that why Jeneil married? I couldn't believe she could hop from one bed to another so fast and with Peter's best friend. That's not Jeneil."

Steve stayed calm even though the words had stirred fire in him. He could tell that Bill was concerned for Jeneil and Steve knew how the situation must look. Steve sighed. "Bill I'm going to level with you because I know you're concerned about Jeneil. When she found out that Peter was staying married, I jokingly proposed to her. She shocked me by seriously accepting my offer."

"Is this some sort of a joke?!" Bill asked, getting angry.

"No." Steve answered, quickly. "No, we both decided to get married, but she's still in love with Pete. You said it yourself she can't move from one bed to another, so quickly."

Bill leaned forward and rested his arms on the table. "Talk to me straight. If you're not gay, then how the hell is a two bedroom marriage acceptable to you? Hollis told me that you signed a release to any financial claims so what the hell are you after? This looks damn sick to me."

Steve sighed and decided on full honesty. "I'm in love with her. She doesn't know it. I've been in love with her for months, even while she was with Pete." He shrugged. "I know that sounds dishonorable, since he's was my best friend, but she never knew about my feelings. She still thinks I'm a good friend." Bill sat back in his chair, shocked by Steve's admission. "Then you really want this marriage and Jeneil so you played the long shot?"

Steve nodded. "I hope you won't tell her, she's not ready to hear it. She doesn't even suspect anything. It's better that way for now and I can live with it."

Bill shook his head. "Man, you are playing one closely called game here. How the hell can you be sure she'll feel when she's over Peter, if she ever gets over him? Damn, she was totally his."

"I know that." Steve answered. "But being in a marriage with her puts all the aces in my hand and she did accept my proposal. That indicates some kind of bond with me, some kind of trust."

Bill stared and then sighed. "I can't argue with that." He shook his head. "She's always been different. She scared her father with her piety. He thought she would become a nun."

"A nun?" Steve asked, surprised.

Bill laughed. "She took what she learned in Sunday school very seriously. She takes life seriously. He was actually grateful when the gossip broke out and she became disenchanted with Christians. Then the family's friend, Mandra took her under her wing as a traveling companion and she was into global peace and racial equality on a full scale. Jeneil's parents were bohemian and pacifists." Bill smiled. "The kid's life was unusual. She had parents old enough to be her grandparents. She grew up out of her era. My parents wondered how all of it would affect her."

Steve shrugged. "She terrific, I like the finished product."

Bill nodded in agreement. "I think so too and my parents are impressed with her as well. They loved her parents, but I agree with them that Jeneil has a tough row to hoe because she's different and life seems to know that and it gives her odd situations to live through." He sighed. "But not this, not a two bedroom marriage." Bill looked at Steve as he rubbed his chin, nervously. "How well do you know her?"

Steve wrinkled his brow. "Why, what do you mean?"

Bill searched for words. "She's capable of being a nun, you know."

Steve smiled. "Yeh and I saw her take my cynical Chinese friend and completely knock him off a mountain, when they lived together."

Bill smiled. "Good, do you plan doing the same?"

Steve was taken back by his directness.

"Don't wait too long, Steve or Jeneil will become a nun in her attitude. She's been trained well. Her parents taught her cerebral in order to survive the cruel gossip and then Mandra taught her survival skills to survive people for humanity. The kid's not in this dimension. My father thinks that if Jeneil became a nun she'd achieve sainthood and he's a protestant minister. She naturally drifts into realms where ordinary people can't breathe. It's her way. After the gossip, she withdraw from people and the experience unearthed some qualities in her that can best be described as ethereal. She can get into realms that most people think are odd or mystical."

Steve remembered her in the wind. "Well I know she plays with helium." He said.

Bill shook his head. "No, it's not playing and it's not helium. It's a natural quality with her and left to her own devices, she gravitates to it. She needs a connection to earth. Her father knew it. Jeneil and I were good friends growing up and the gossip affected both of us differently. I ran wild and Jeneil withdraw. The stupid guys in the town came to her like a pack of hungry wolves." Bill took a breath. "I'm going to tell you something." Bill fidgeted. "Her father asked me to… well he was concerned about this ethereal quality and asked me to teach her about sex." Steve was startled. Bill noticed. "I know it sounds weird, but you'd have to know and live through those long years of gossip and whispering. Jeneil became withdrawn into her own world and more and more innocent and ethereal from it. Her father was worried that looking like she did somebody would misuse her. Like he said, "Innocent and purity will attract evil." And boy Jeneil was pure. So he was worried. He knew I was crazy about Jeneil and he was only trying to introduce her to a part of life that she was so far removed from and getting farther. So far that it actually worried him."

"So he gave you permission to make love to her?" Steve asked, wanting to clarify the words in his mind as he struggled to believe such a liberal father insisted.

Bill nodded. "I knew what he meant. He hoped the physical experience would wake her out of her convent lifestyle and he knew I wouldn't hurt her. He wanted her to be introduced to the pleasant side of sex to offset what the boys and the gossip was doing to her." Steve wanted to ask, but he could barely believe the conversation.

"Well, did you?" He blurted out the question, shocking himself.

Bill shook his head and then chuckled. "I tried even before I had his approval. She was something else in jeans and shorts, even in braces, but her mind never worked that way and she was dedicated to living Sunday School rules to the letter. Her father teasingly called her St. Jeneil of the Perfected. After the gossip, I ran wild and learned what Sunday school never taught. And when her father gave me permission, I tried, but she ended up driving me crazy. I finally told her straight that she looked too innocent for her own good and that she should learn to kiss properly at least. That reached her mind. She hadn't realized there was something she didn't know about sex. Because she had taught me the difference between boys and girls when we were little kids. She read books and prided herself on knowing about sex. Her parents were very open with her so she was surprised that she didn't know something. And she wanted to learn so I taught her to kiss and she would have learned more except a nearby farmer was wandering in the woods calling to a stray cow. After that she just couldn't make the gossip about us true. I understood, she was surviving the ugliness because she knew she was innocent and she can't pretend. I still don't know how the hell she went from her ivory tower convent to living with Peter, but I watched her get real, living with him and I began to relax about her. When I was in Wonderland, I saw the look return. Ethereal is back in her life." He rubbed his forehead. "Steve, make this marriage normal fast." Steve looked at him, questioningly. "Let her know how you feel about her. She looks too innocent. She'll become a nun and you won't reach her at all. It can be deadly, Steve, I know. She puts herself trustingly in your path looking terrific and innocent and when you get closer, you know she'll freak out if you try anything."

Steve's mind flashed the memory of Jeneil on the night they were married as she bolted from his apartment in a panic. "Is this a problem?" Steve asked. "Do you think she needs professional help?"

Bill shrugged. "She's always been odd, full of extremes and contradictions. She's wild in a way because she doesn't fit in. She's a wild flower. She's hard to gauge against normal. She seemed okay with Peter. In fact she shocked the hell out of me with how naturally she marched into a sex life."

Steve smiled. "But she looked innocent while she was with him too."

Bill smiled. "You're odd too; maybe you are good for her, because you can sit here and easily talk about her being with Peter even while you're waiting for her to become your wife." He shook his head. "All three of you seemed normal together. Who knows what's normal really." Bill said, resting against the table. "I just want her to be happy and you really sound like you're in love with her and she trusts you, I can see that. So we'll play your game." He pointed at Steve. "But take my advice and play the game fast, don't let her climb the ivory tower." A door in the hallway closed and they heard Jeneil in the hallway. She came into the kitchen. Steve was stunned by the long blue dress she was wearing. Bill smiled at her. Jeneil kissed his cheek.

"The chair in the den turns into a bed. I've made it up for you." She looked at the two men who were watching her. "Have I missed something?" She asked. "Why haven't you poured coffee?" She went to the cupboard for cups and saucers. "Are you hungry, Bill?"

Steve and Bill looked at each other and smiled. Jeneil noticed. "Hey, I did miss something; you two have had a good talk. I can see that." She smiled, pleased that they were getting along. Putting the dishes on the table, she kissed Steve's cheek. "Did you find that you both have something in common?" She asked.

"Yeh." Steve answered. "You and friendship."

Jeneil smiled and put her hands on their shoulders. "You really are good friends, the best." Giving them both a squeeze, she then went to the refrigerator for cream. Bill grinned at Steve, who smiled and was very glad to have been given a new understanding of the woman he was in love with, married to and who he hoped someday to be his wife.

Eighteen

Steve was surprised that Jeneil was up before he was the next morning. She had fixed him a power shake and was making eggs for Bill. He left for early surgery leaving her and Bill to visit. At a break in surgical cases mid-morning, he called her and got the recording. At lunch, he went home to turn off the machine so he could call her periodically. He was determined to keep her functioning like she had over the weekend. The apartment was empty which surprised him and her car was gone. Going to the telephone, he dialed her office and reached her secretary, Charlene. "I expect her back any minute now, Dr. Bradley; she went to her lawyer's office and then lunch." He was shocked to hear that she'd been working all morning. "Here she comes; she's just walked in the office. Can you hold?" Steve waited, not believing she'd jumped back onto the conveyor belt. They hadn't had a chance to talk with Bill staying over.

"Hi." Jeneil answered.

"Honey, when did you decide to go back to work?" He asked, noticing that her voice sounded strong.

"This morning after you and Bill left. I know I need to be doing things and after two weeks away from here, the things piled up on my desk."

"How are you holding up?" He asked.

"My energy ebbs and flows. I'm not stable yet, but I am determined. I thought I could work just the morning and then leave, but too much has piled up, I'll have to stay."

Steve was pleasantly shocked by her attitude. "Honey, I swear you're not dull. You're like a fire, near embers one day and burning down trees the next."

Jeneil laughed. "I've looked over the lot and house plans in Glenview. I like the sound of the Tecumseh area. It has 1½-2 acre lots. That's pretty close to secluded in a development the size of Glenview." Steve was silent. "Where are you?" Jeneil asked.

"Right here." Steve answered, quietly. "Jeneil, that part of Glenview is beyond me. I don't have that kind of money. The Sayard section would be my limit. The Capras and Tyachz live there. I don't have a down payment large enough for Tecumseh. You're talking about people like Theodore Sloan and Martin Drummond. Those guys have gotten stocks and bonds as birthday gifts all their lives. Tecumseh is beautiful, but over my head. You married a working class surgeon Jeneil. I don't even have a family, let alone one with money."

 Jeneil got serious. "But Steve, the Sayard section has only 1/4 and 1/2 acre lots or less. It can't be private, the areas too newly developed to have full grown trees."

"Tecumseh's wide open too, Honey." He reminded her.

"Yes, but your neighbors are two acres away and there's an undeveloped stretch of land that runs behind Tecumseh with a stream along it if I'm reading the topographical map right. There's one house available in that section. According to the map the backyard rambles to the stream. I can live with that. I won't feel so confined with nature's backyard as a neighbor on one side of us. It sounds ideal."

Steve pinched his lip. "Who's around us? Does the layout list owners?"

"Let me check it." Jeneil replied. Steve heard papers rustling.

"Here it is. It's not an updated map. There are houses red "X'd" which means they're sold but there are no names of the owners. Oh this area of Tecumseh is adjacent to the end of Sayard. The Tyachz are only six houses in from the stream."

Steve wondered. "How many zero in the price, Jeneil?"

"Five." She replied, quietly.

Steve caught his breath. "And the single digit over five?"

"Yes." Having noticed his reaction to five zeros.

"Honey, I'm two years away from affording that. My car itself would be an eyesore there and I'm just ready for a new car having scrimped every dollar since being in private practice. If I put that money into a house, I can't get a car and I'm left stripped besides. That's not practical."

Jeneil was silent as she thought. "Well my salary here includes a car and a place to live, I can afford it. I have a buyer for our lease in Fairview."

Steve closed his eyes. "Jeneil, I can't afford it and you told me to let you know when you're standing in my sun."

Jeneil was silent again. "Steve, I can't live in an apartment building for two more years and I like privacy. It has to be Tecumseh."

Steve felt his back stiffen. "Well I can't live in a house that's owned by your corporation, and where's the agreeable wife I had over the weekend?"

Jeneil sensed his irritation. "She's right here, Mr. Husband, wondering why you don't have to take a turn at compromising in this marriage. Mrs. Wife has compromised by living in Glenview." Jeneil replied, sternly.

Her answer jolted and loosened Steve. He sighed. "Look you haven't even seen the house and grounds. You might not even like it and you're tough to negotiate with." He chuckled. "Let's talk about this at dinner."

"I'm not budging." She laughed.

He smiled. "We'll discuss it at dinner. I have to get back to work."

"Chicken." She chuckled, teasing him. "Cute excuse, Mr. Husband."

"I'll treat you to dinner. Your choice of restaurants." He said, enjoying her teasing.

"Count on it." She answered, sounding threatening.

He laughed as he hung up and took a deep breath.. "Sheez, she's getting to me over the telephone now." He picked up his top coat and went to the door. "Chicken?" He laughed at her remark about him. "I'd make you eat those words if we were really playing house you sexy wench." He closed the door shaking his head as he realized that he had come home to check on a fragile and ailing wife and had met a woman called Jeneil the Amazon. He took a deep breath to slow down the electricity racing through him. "She sounds alive again! She's got her fire back." He smiled at the thought as he pressed the signal button for the elevator. "Mrs. Steven Bradley, how many woman are you?" He laughed to himself.

*****

Steve inserted the coins into the public telephone and dialed the apartment. "The day went too well." He thought, as he tried to calm down. Jeneil answered. "Honey, the car frizzed out again." He sighed. "Can you stop by the hospital for me? We can continue on to dinner, but don't ask me about Tecumseh with my junk heap of a car acting up."

Jeneil chuckled. "We'll discuss it at dinner."

She surprised him by driving directly back to the apartment and disappearing into her room when they got in. He wondered if she was slipping back, but the dining table was set with candles and crystal and the kitchen smelled great. Jeneil returned wearing a long hostess gown. "Wow!" Steve smiled, looking her over. Jeneil modeled the outfit executing a graceful turn, regally after his remark. "I give up." He said. "We'll buy the whole damn development of Glenview. You use heavy artillery when you negotiate."

She laughed and touched his cheek, tenderly. "Mr. Husband, you're a very nice guy." She hugged him. "I'm bringing dinner to the table." She said and disappeared toward the kitchen. He decided to keep his suit jacket on and he went to the diningroom after washing his hands. Jeneil was waiting at the candle-lite table for him.

"What's all this?" He grinned. "Just for a house?!"

She smiled and poured his wine. "No, I came across something today that I thought required a special dinner." She looked at him, lovingly. "And an apology, Steve." She said, swallowing hard to hold back emotion.

"An apology?" He asked, puzzled.

She nodded and lowered her head in embarrassment. "When I went through the papers on my desk today, I came across a copy of the legal agreement you signed forfeiting any claim on my financial interests." She sighed and then frowned. "I'm really very sorry, Steve. That must have been humiliating. I apologize for having that happened to you. I had no idea Uncle Hollis was planning that. It never would have happened if I had known." He smiled as she fumbled through the apology, obviously deeply embarrassed. Her sincere reaction made up for the hurt the document caused.

"It's okay Honey, Hollis is concerned about you. I don't think he realizes how much surgeons can earn. I'm not exactly poor right now and my earning potential is impressive, but he was worried so let it pass."

Jeneil watched Steve realizing that he really had no idea what her financial worth totaled. She squeezed his hand and smiled. "I love you, Steve. Thank you for understanding Hollis." She went to the serving table and arranged the food on their plates. Setting Steve's before him, she sat down with hers and enjoyed being at dinner with the husband who was still impressing her. She had never wanted to be married for her money and she now had a husband who had never asked about her money and didn't seem to care. She was truly impressed. She felt that special feeling of love for him that was becoming so much vivid since becoming his wife. She watched him cut his braised chops and could understand why he was so deadly to women. "He is actually incredibly handsome." She thought, noticing his well-styled hair and even features and his blue eyes were not lecherous. When she first started working at the hospital she thought he had lecherous blue eyes. She looked away concentrating on her plate as she wondered why he married her. She hadn't thought about it before. He had asked and she had said yes. It seemed right at the time. It still seemed right. "Well it isn't for money." She assured herself. "Then why?" Her mind asked. "Who cares?!" She replied to herself, not wanting to think about it. "It's an odd marriage that defies reasonable thought. He wanted a wife, I wanted a husband. We were very good friends. We are good friends. I'm enjoying the marriage. He's a wonderful husband. He isn't my husband." She said, surprised by the thought. "We're good friends who are married to each other." She looked at him again. "Why did he agree to that?" She asked, realizing she had not looked into an arranged marriage closely. He looked up and saw her watching him. Jeneil blushed and reached for her water dropping her fork clumsily and blushing more deeply as it cracked against the plate noisily. "I'm sorry." She apologized and drank some water.

"Are you okay?" He asked, surprised by her behavior.

"Yes." She coughed as the water nearly choked her. She cleared her throat. "Yes, I'm okay. I am." She smiled, nervously. "I'm really okay."

"Good." He said, watching her as she tried to decide which hand to hold the fork in. He smiled as he watched her thinking that the fragile girl was back as his wife. "Why is she blushing?" He wondered and then he remembered she had once told him that she had three selves. He smiled, thinking. "I've seen her shy and fragile and I've seen her self-confident. What's the third?" He wondered, fascinated by the combination. "Well, she's not dull." He chuckled to himself. "You never know who you're with around her."

They spent the evening examining the material on Glenview. He agreed that the location she was looking at in Tecumseh seemed nice and they decided to make an appointment to see the house. He got her to agree to look at Sayard too. Steve backed off from arguing about the cost understanding that what it would take would be to sit her down to talk dollars and cents. But she seemed immoveable about Tecumseh and his last hope was that she'd hate the house and lot and find something she liked in the less expensive Sayard area. He could tell this whole house issue could be a big problem if it wasn't handled right and he didn't want trouble. His main concentration was on the two of them getting closer. He remembered Bill's advice about making the marriage normal as quickly as possible. He looked her over slowly as she sat next to him reading the contractual brochure. "She's incredibly beautiful." He thought. "What I wouldn't do for the chance to kiss that damn earlobe of hers." She stretched her legs out slipping her leather scuffs off as she became deeply engrossed in the Glenview contract. Her movement was slow and sensuous. He turned away knowing that he was going too far and he picked up the plot map wondering who the neighbors were in the Tecumseh area. He felt encouraged that she was sitting right next to him and feeling very comfortable being there. Leaning forward, she picked up a pen from the low table and circled something on the contract, then bringing her feet onto the sofa under her long skirt she leaned against his arm.

"Oh man, she's a snuggler." He breathed in quickly and he wondered how Peter had gotten her from the ivory tower that Bill mentioned. He wondered even more how Peter could have walked away from her. "It doesn't make sense if you think about it." He thought. "Peter was crazy about her." He thought of Jeneil's struggle now to survive the separation from Peter and he saw her bravely trying to make a new life for herself. He smiled, watching her curled up against him and he liked her as his wife and he marveled that life for some unexplainable reason had given her to him. Leaning his head toward her, he kissed her temple gently.

She looked up at him and smiled. "What was that for?" She asked.

"I like being married to you." He answered.

She nodded. "I'm enjoying the marriage too. It was a good move. I'm glad you're not disappointed." He smiled as she turned the page of the contract and continued reading and he began to understand Bill's advice and the ivory tower a little better. Normally on any date, the moment would have ignited some magic. He could tell that she was even aware of the ambiance between them and yet she wasn't affected.

"I've never dated a nun before." He thought. "Much less tried to get one interested in sex. How the hell did Pete do it?" He asked himself, knowing that Peter never chased women, they usually approached him. It was a trait in women that each appreciated. They both liked women who weren't afraid of sex and they were usually honest. He and Pete agreed that there was a difference in approaches. There was flattering and flirting, which neither one liked and then there was the woman who knew what she wanted and where she was going with it and those rare breed were what he and Pete always watched for because they were women who usually want a man in the traditional sense. She usually had no illusions; she usually knew that great sex took two people to make it magical, not a super stud which was fiction, not an unequal role playing encounter, but a real man and a real woman together honestly. He looked at Jeneil as she read the contract and he couldn't believe this quiet fragile girl had turned Peter inside out and had even had him, a good friend, in love with her without even having seriously kissed him. He knew that some of her attraction was her honesty. She could let him know that she needed him, that she needed holding and caring for. He had seen her at times with Peter. She gave herself honestly. "So where is the door to the ivory tower?" He asked himself.

She stretched and yawned. "I'm done in. These sentences are only words now. I'm going to bed." She said, sitting up. Gathering all the material on Glenview together in a neat stack, she looked at him and smiled. "Mr. Husband somewhere in this bunch of literature is the house of our future and I'm going to find it. It's time for our lives to settle down and get real." She stood up and slipped into her scuffs. "I have a feeling that Jeneil will evolve as a natural process, so I'll just keep floating until she surfaces with whatever she's supposed to do."

Steve smiled enjoying the relaxed and positive tone in her attitude. "That's the secret, Honey, just keep listening to the prom music until it makes sense."

She smiled as she studied his face. "The prom music almost makes sense with you around." She said, seriously. "You're good for me, Steve, I'm glad we're married." The sentiment seemed to embarrass her and she fidgeted. "I'll see you in the morning." She said and left quickly.

He raised his eyebrows and smiled. "Is that the answer? Was that how it happened, Pete? Is the third person in Jeneil's self the one that knows she's a woman and knows what she wants? Did she approach you?"

*****

His schedule at the office has eased up after he got married since the senior partners thought he and his wife should have time to adjust to married life. His choice in a wife was very well received and they were delighted to have someone so well connected with their group.   Now that the marriage was a month old, Steve could tell that he was expected to bring business back to normal in his rounds of medical association meetings and seminars which were held at night.   He was disappointed, but he knew it couldn't be helped.   It was the corporate structure, and except for the dinners which were usually terrible, he enjoyed learning and exchanging medical information.   Jeneil understood.   Steve was concerned, he hoped she wouldn't slip back and he was sure his absences wouldn't help them become closer.   The week flew by when two medical meetings were required on separate nights and he had gotten in after Jeneil had gone to bed.   By the second night he missed seeing her and he wished they were really married.   His life felt lopsided, but there wasn't anything that could be done about it and so he accepted it.   By the latter part of the week, he was surprised to hear music coming from her room at 5:00 in the morning as he got up to shower and get ready for early surgery.   The second morning of the music, he couldn't stand it and knocked on the door to find out what she was doing.   He never quite recovered from seeing her in leotards when she opened the door which she wore to dance in and do yoga.   After that the music would bring the image of her in the electric blue skin outfit to his mind.   He wished he hadn't knocked.   They made their appointment to see Glenview and they came away at a impasse about their future home.   The Tecumseh house was very nice, but the backyard was defected.   It sloped in the backyard which was mostly mud when they stopped to see it. Jeneil walked on the street to the wooden bridge and viewed the yard from the stream.   She loved it, which shocked the real estate agent who couldn't sell the house because of the bad slope. Steve liked the house but he couldn't accept the price.   Jeneil couldn't accept Sayard and they left Glenview without speaking to each other leaving an anxious real estate broker hoping they'd return.   Steve stopped at a deli and brought lunch determined to drag his silent pouting wife home and show her in black and white why Tecumseh was out of the question.   He was ready for her with his budget all neatly laid out on paper.   He watched her get glasses from the cupboard.   She hadn't spoken to him since Glenview and he was getting tired of it.   He hated the tension between them.   It was the weekend and he had hoped to make the most of their time together.

"Jeneil."   He said, as she put a glass of milk on the table for him and sat down with her lunch.   "This is silly, Honey.   Angry silence won't help."   She picked at the cold chicken with her fork.   "I'm not angry.   I'm hurt."   She answered.

"Hurt?"   The word shocked him.

"Yes, you refuse to be reasonable.   You refuse to see my side in this."

He went to his room and returned with the papers listing his finances and he placed before her on the table.   "This is reality, Honey.   I can't afford Tecumseh.   Check it out.   You'll understand what I'm saying."   She picked up the papers.

"Look at the squeeze the rent on this place has put on me this past month.   I've paid two rents; I still have a lease on my old apartment.   You can see that I need a car."   He watched her face as she studied the papers hoping for signs of understanding and acceptance. He wanted the problem over.

"Well I can see one glaring error already. This has only one income listed. Where's mine?" She asked.

He smiled. "You don't have one from what I can see. You get paid in cars and rent or something. And let's not talk about the business buying the house. I can't live in a house owned by your corporation."

"Well, that's unreasonable." She pouted.

He sighed. "No, it isn't, Honey. It's ego. It's pride. It's self respect. But it's not unreasonable."

She looked confused. "I don't understand."

He was silent and then he sighed and stood up to pace. "Jeneil, until seven months ago I never even had a place that was all my own. I've lived in a dorm my whole life in the home, in college, and med school. Seven months ago Steve Bradley finally got a place all his own and it feels damn good. I like the feeling, Jeneil. I want my name on the deed. Maybe it's ego, but it gives me an identity. I want my own home." Jeneil felt her throat tighten and tears spilled down her cheeks. She bit her lower lip hoping she wouldn't sob.

Getting up quickly, she went to him, putting her arms around him and nestling against him. "That's reasonable." She said, not controlling her voice at all well.

He held her enjoying how she felt to him. He kissed her cheek. "Honey, I wish I could give you Tecumseh."

"I understand." She said, sniffing and clearing her throat.

'Then what now? Shall we try for Sayard?"

She sighed. "You can't afford Sayard, either or you won't get a car." She left his arms and paced. "By the way you put your money in the wrong kind of bonds."

He looked at her. "The bank account executive suggested those bonds." He replied, defensively.

She shook her head. "He's wrong. There are some corporate bonds with a high yield return. If you had bought them seven months ago you would have your car by now. You don't need turtle bonds yet. You're young and upwardly mobile and with the assets you have already you could have gotten a car loan easily. Why are you waiting for such a large down payment?"

Steve grinned as Jeneil marched across his finances making him look foolish. "It's my old pickpocket days as a kid, Honey. I like the cash in my hands, plastic never got me anything."

She went to him putting her arms around his neck. "Well you've all grown up in to a man now and the plastic will say Dr. Steven Bradley. Remember the diner, your cold feet, and all the plastic cards and the little amount of cash you netted the day you decided to become a doctor? That wasn't a coincidence. Those doctors knew investments. Cash was nothing." He watched her, amazed that she remembered.

"You have quite a memory." He smiled.

She grinned. "Get on the ski lift and head for the slopes, Dr. Bradley. Walking up the icy mountain is too slow." He loved the color in her eyes.

"I have a broker I'd like you to meet." She smiled.

"You're beautiful." He said, noticing the way her eyebrows arched and tapered.

She looked at him, suspiciously. "I still want Tecumseh." She whispered, staring into his eyes the way he was staring into hers.

"You got it." He said. "Help me rob a bank."

She smiled and left his arms to get his financial papers. "May I help with this statement?"

"Why?" He asked.

"I'll get us into Tecumseh."

He groaned. "Jeneil, turtle bonds or corporate bonds I'm two years away from affording Tecumseh. How the hell did we get back to square one?"

"We're not." She said.

"You're stubborn." He said, sitting next to her with a sigh.

She smiled at him. "You made an investment that you haven't listed."

"What's that?" He asked.

"Your wife. Mr. Husband, your wife."

"No." He said, quickly. "I don't want your money. I want to buy the house."

She frowned. "Now that's unreasonable and bad financial planning besides. Even if you buy the house using only your money, the community property law states that it's half mine, bless those little suffragettes, so why not let me pay for half? Why are you standing in my sun?"

He shook his head knowing he was in trouble on this issue. "Jeneil, no."

"But Peter." She said, and the name blasted between them like a siren. She heard it and he heard it. She stood up. "Excuse me." She said and she ran from the room.

He sighed and rested his head on his arms, then sitting up straight, he shook his head. "No." He said, standing up. "She's mine."

He knocked on her bedroom door and heard the quiet. "Come in." She was sitting on the edge of her bed.

He sat beside her. "Why did you run off?" He asked.

"I thought I was going to break down. His name races through me." She closed her eyes and took a deep breath. "It hurts." She bit her lower lip and struggled to hold back tears. Standing quickly, she went to the bookcase and chose a book on philosophy, then she paced while reading a particular page. Inserting a cassette in to the player she continued reading and pacing while music swirled about her. Steve watched as she brought herself under control without crying. Sitting next to him, she put her arm through his. "Now about Tecumseh." She said.

"Incredible!" He sighed deliberately and smiled.

"Do you really mind if my name is on the deed too?" She asked.

"No, of course not." He squeezed her arm. "It's for you and you can pay the other half. I'll cover the down payment and closing costs. You're my wife."

"Then let's divide the expense. I'll have my salary structure changed to include payment of half the monthly mortgage payment to you and you can pay the other half. I'll cover the down payment and closing costs"

He sighed. "That sounds like a complicated mess my money. Your money."

"Steve." She pleaded. "If I had an ordinary job with an ordinary income, you would accept a two income marriage. I know I'm all entangled in the corporation, but don't hold my odd life against me. I'm trying to compromise."

"I don't want to be house poor, Honey. I want to travel. I want an expensive sports car. That sounds flagrant I'm sure, but I want it."

"Travel?" She asked. "You want to travel?"

He nodded. "There's a whole world out there that I haven't seen because I've been tied to poverty. Well I'm free now and I want to stay that way. He sighed. "Oh hell, we both have our wants."

"You want a private home and roots, don't you?" She asked, surprised by the information she was uncovering about her new husband.

"Not the same way you want one. You nest." He smiled.

"You don't like that?" She asked, listening closely.

"I think it's cute, but I can't get excited about crab grass and real estate."

"What does excite you? What do you really want?" She asked. "What makes life light up for you, anything?"

He thought for a minute. "Yes, OR and learning surgical techniques and…" He stopped.

"And what?" She asked, becoming curious. He looked away from her and down at the floor. "What?" She asked, nudging him.

"Marriage." He answered quietly, knowing he couldn't say her.

She was surprised. "Marriage!? Marriage is magical for you?" She smiled. "Why? Do you know why?"

He nodded. "Yes, I know why. You said it once. The closeness. Having someone care that you're alive. I mean really care. Sharing your life with someone. Man that's gut level. Someone you can trust, who really understands you."

His answer surprised her. "Then why did you settle for this arranged marriage?" She asked, feeling bad that he hadn't waited for love if he felt so deeply about unity.

He looked at her. "Jeneil, you really care, you really understand me. I feel closer to you than I have to anyone else, ever. I like being married to you. I like the way you nest even if making one isn't exciting to me. It's exciting watching you make one." He shrugged. "That's as clear as I can get."

She was deeply moved by his words. "Put your arms around me, Mr. Terrific." She said, as she snuggled closer too him. He slipped his arm around her shoulder and squeezed her to him. "You're really odd." She smiled and kissed his cheek.

He laughed, slightly. "We'll you're not exactly ordinary either, you know." And he made the mistake of looking at her as she smiled the gentle smile that made him crazy. Electricity raced through him. The moment had weakened him and he kissed her lips. The high voltage shocked him and he made the kiss brief leaving his heart pounding in his chest.

She studied his face as if puzzled and then she hugged him. "You're a great guy." She said, softly. "I love you. You're always there to push me up."

He smiled at her. "Mrs. Steven Bradley, you're quite a woman. I love you, too."

*****

Tecumseh and the house was never mentioned during the following week. Jeneil was preoccupied with papers that she was bringing home every night. They seemed to routinely go to the den after dinner. He would read and she would bury herself in an arm full of papers. He had asked her what all the work was, but she had smiled gently and replied. "Just a little business." The routine was very enjoyable for him and he would rush in from sometime in front of association meetings in order to spend some time in front of the fire in the den with her and a cup of Ovaltine before bed. He was very encouraged about the marriage. She had begun to kiss him on his cheek before going to bed every night and even clinging to him or giving him a lingering hug. He wondered what it all meant and he was still at a loss about how to move the relationship from just friends to a real marriage. While she had become demonstrative about her feelings for him, she never passed the line to anything more intimate. After giving it days of thought, he knew that he would never approach her for several good reasons starting with the memory of the sick feeling in the pit of his stomach when she bolted out of his apartment, the night they were married. He had also told her that he wasn't interested in a physical relationship. He had lied deliberately knowing she would have backed out of the marriage if she had to face being physical. Having thought the matter through, he felt certain that Peter hadn't approached her about a relationship. It had to have been her idea since he knew that Peter never dated whites. Steve decided that he would wait for the third person of Jeneil's self to surface. Until that time, he bided his time contenting himself with showing her glimpses of the love he felt for her in as many ways as he could think up. He hadn't missed a yellow rose for their anniversary every Friday since they had gotten married. He smiled as he rode up in the elevator from the parking garage with the yellow rose in the long slender box tucked under his arm. He had invited her to dinner, but she had told him that she wanted to cook and spend the evening at home. He unlocked the apartment, anxious to see her wondering what the evening would be like after a whole week of her extra attention to him. Surprise is what he felt as he entered the apartment to dim lights and the drapes opened to the beautiful street and sky scene outside. A tall slender man got up from the sofa as he walked in, carefully looking Steve over. A second man got up from the armchair turning to look at Steve. Jeneil walked in from the kitchen after hearing the key in the lock.

"Hi." She smiled and went to him, kissing his cheek.

"What's happening?' He asked looking her over. The long red dress looked special he liked her in red. Her dark eyes and hair seemed more intensified surrounded by the color. He noticed the diamond earrings and small diamond necklace. "You never told me we were having company." He said, looking at the two men.

"I'm not company." The shorter of the two men smiled. "I'm Ron Chatfield, Jeneil's lawyer, were good friends." He extended his hand to Steve as he and Jeneil walked toward them. The tall slender man was still watching Steve closely.

Jeneil went to him and took his hand. "This one's not company either." Jeneil said, cuddling to his arm.

The man smiled at her warmly. "Hell no, I'm family sort of. Hollis Wells." The man said, extending his hand to Steve. The man didn't fit the image Steve had of him. He was younger and dressed money. Solid, confident, money. From his hair style to his expensive shoes. He was far from the small town hayseed lawyer Steve had expected.

"Nice to meet you, Mr. Wells." Steve answered, aware that his voice lacked assertiveness and he wanted to be assertive around Hollis in order to claim his position as Jeneil's husband since Hollis always sounded like he outranked him in Jeneil's life.

"The name's Hollis, Steve. Call me Hollis."

Jeneil smiled. "Steve would you mind if you went right into dinner? These two have been here a while already and they really should be doing some eating now."

Steve shrugged. "Fine, Honey, if I had known I'd have left the office earlier."

"You're fine." She said, reaching for the box under his arm. "Is this mine?" She asked smiling.

"Oh yeh." Steve replied, feeling awkward.

"Happy Anniversary." Jeneil said, hugging him with one arm gently to his neck. She kissed his cheek and lingered in the hug, surprising Steve. He put his arms around her waist gently aware that Hollis and Ron were watching them closely. Steve wondered what was happening.

"Can I do anything?" He asked as Jeneil slipped away from the hug. He was aware that she seemed emotional and again wondered what was happening.

"Yes." She said. "Would you get some wine and let it breathe while I put some dinner on the table?"

Steve nodded and followed her to the kitchen as Hollis and Ron went into the diningroom.

"What's happening?" Steve asked her, quietly.

"Just a little business." Jeneil smiled gently.

Business wasn't discussed at dinner which surprised Steve, but he got a chance to get to know Hollis better. Steve decided that he liked him. Hollis was definitely a Jeneil fan. He could easily be her blood relative for the kind of caring evidenced by him. Ron Chatfield was a study to Steve. The warm smiles and lingering looks he gave Jeneil caused Steve to think that if Ron wasn't dealing with smitten, he was at least definitely overwhelmed and Steve couldn't blame him. Jeneil had made a real dish that she said was one of her mother's unfussy recipes and she brought in pears halves in some pleasant tasting sauce for dessert. Her skills as a cook couldn't help but impress the people eating the meal.

Steve watched her and became more impressed with her beauty and the total package that was Jeneil. "She's my wife." He marveled to himself completely in awe of that fact as she poured coffee for the men. He became aware of Hollis watching him as he watched Jeneil. Hollis grinned pleasantly at Steve and stirred his coffee slowly. Ron Chatfield got up and went to the livingroom returning with his briefcase. The table had been cleared except for small dishes of nuts and mints and the coffee butler. The atmosphere was changing to one of a definite business tone. "Why don't I take my coffee to the den?" Steve said, taking his cup and preparing to leave.

"We need you here." Jeneil smiled. Steve looked surprised and sat down again.

Ron Chatfield watched and then smiled slightly as he removed his suit jacket. "Dr. Bradley, we need your signature in a few documents."

"Mine?" Steve asked, not even sure he heard right.

Ron nodded. "You know I have to tell you that I think you have one hell of a fantastic wife."

Steve smiled. "I'll sign that document, I agree completely." Hollis smiled and sipped his coffee. Jeneil grinned as she watched Steve from across the table. Ron shuffled through a few papers and taking one he handed to it to Steve and another to Jeneil. Hollis reached inside a slim leather case beside him and removed some papers. Steve looked his papers over as everyone got settled. Skipping past the heretofore and whereas parts, he noticed one line that indicated a company called Bradley Investments naming him as president and Secretary and Jeneil as Vice President and Treasurer. "What's this?" He asked, completely puzzled.

Ron smiled. "That document allows you to do business legally."

"Business?" Steve questioned, "Since when is all the red tape necessary to buy a house?"

Ron grinned. "Like I said you have one helluva fantastic wife."

Steve looked at Jeneil. "What's happening here, Honey?"

Jeneil smiled. "This is a birthday present, Steve." Steve sat up straight in his chair. "Don't you tell me that you set up a company in order to buy the house in Tecumseh? That's not even funny." He said, watching her steadily. "You know I wanted to buy that place on my own. You said you would help. You never said anything about forming a corporation to buy it. My name, Honey, remember?"

Hollis and Ron watched him and then smiled at each other. Hollis sat forward. "Steve, Jeneil told me that your income alone wouldn't cover the house in Tecumseh, but she didn't want her salary structure changed because of the tax problems it would cause her, so she came up with the idea of forming a real estate company in both your names." Steve was still puzzled. "So what does that mean? Is the house in Tecumseh owned by our Real Estate Company?"

Ron smiled. "No, Dr. Bradley, your beautiful and brainy wife just simply tripled your income so you can afford to buy the house yourself which is what you wanted."

Steve wrinkled his brow deeply. "How the hell can she triple my income?" He asked.

Ron held up the papers in his hand. "With these." He smiled. "With these and your approval which would be foolish to withhold. She used your bond and savings holdings as the bases for Bradley investments."

Steve shook his head. "Hell, I'm no financial wizard, but even I know that won't triple my income."

Ron smiled. "No, but Jeneil is transforming some holdings to Bradley Investments to which will make the investment very active."

"What holdings?" He asked. "I've signed a paper. I can't touch her money. I don't want to. I'm not exactly poor. I just can't afford Tecumseh right now."

Jeneil watched his confusion. "Steve, everything is just as it was except you and I own a company together using your bonds and savings and I transferred ownership of Lakewood Plaza to our real estate company, Bradley Enterprises will give us a joint income like normal couples."

Ron chuckled. "Normal? Jeneil my income is normal; Lakeland Plaza is the leprechaun's pot of gold."

"Lakeland Plaza?!" Steve gasped.

Ron laughed. "Congratulations Dr. Bradley, you now own the hottest piece of real estate of this decade. Not bad for just coming home to a beautiful wife and a great meal. Here use my pen, maybe some of your luck will rub off on it." He placed his silver pen before Steve who looked at it blankly and then at Jeneil.

"Please sign, Steve." Jeneil said, quietly. "I'd like us to have "our money" so our lives will be more normal."

"Honey, I'm a surgeon. I don't understand real estate. I don't want to know real estate." Hollis watched, listened, and relaxed

Jeneil clasped her hands before her on the table. "My staff and I can handle it. Steve, my point is that it'll be "our money." Normally that will be put into a joint account like other married couples. That's not so hard to take is it? Please, Steve. Then you can go ahead and make the deal for the Tecumseh house yourself. I'll stay out of it. My accountants will give you a financial statement on Lakewood Plaza so you will know exactly how much your income has increased."

Ron Chatfield sighed. "Financial Statement? Jeneil the title, "Owner of Lakeland Plaza." will open doors by itself."

Jeneil got up and went to Steve's side. "Would you like some time to think about it?" She asked, stopping by his chair. "Maybe you're overwhelmed right now."

Steve absorbed her excitement. Her smile, her beauty, her generosity, the feel of her hand on his arm. Looking into her eyes steadily, he took a deep breath. "I'll sign." He said, quietly becoming lost in the softness that was deadly about her to him.

Jeneil smiled broadly and then hugged him. "Oh thank you, Steve. All I want is a normal life for us and our marriage."

The next hour became a marathon of signatures and shuffling papers under the direction of Ron Chatfield. Hollis had flown in to witness all the legalities and to meet Steve. As the men gathered their belongings to leave, Steve clearly felt that he had Hollis approval as Jeneil's husband. The genuine and caring warmth that Hollis showed to Jeneil was now extended to Steve also. It was a huge change from the parental authoritative image Hollis had been showing Steve during telephone calls. Ron lived past the airport and was driving Hollis to catch his flight. Jeneil had arranged a private plane for him since Hollis had insisted on witnessing the deal. Jeneil hugged Hollis who held her in a loving parental way, smiling and placing a kiss on her forehead reminding her to take care of herself. Ron had kissed her cheek lightly and told her he'd be in touch soon. The two men left leaving Steve and Jeneil standing at the hallway door together. Steve folded his arms and grinned at her. "That was definitely the most complicated birthday present I've ever been given. There's something to be said for the simple tie and cufflinks as a gift."

Jeneil smiled, pleased by the whole evening. "Yes, but now I'm free, completely." She sighed as if she had actually been released from bondage.

Steve noticed and was puzzled by her words. "How are you now free?" he asked.

Jeneil stood before him resting her hands on his folded arms.

"My whole life is tied into the corporation. Paper shuffling has become a matter of routine to me in my life. All I am, everything I have, everything I do has to be passed through a system of legal entanglements to determine the ramifications. Bradley Enterprises represents a simple real estate investment that separates me from the layer corporation and allows me an uncomplicated corner of my life as Mrs. Steven Bradley, who has a joint income with her husband like any normal marriage. I was going to have Hollis rescind the legal document you signed relinquishing rights to my other investments, but as I thought about it, I could see the freedom the situation offered us. No matter what happens, the stampede won't touch us and we can be free to move on our own through Bradley Enterprises." She put her head back and sighed. "I love the freedom of marriage." He watched her bask in the feeling of freedom and he slipped his arms around her waist. She moved into his arms and rested against him.

"No regrets about getting married then?" He asked, lovingly holding her.

"None at all." She sighed. "The minute you mentioned marriage, an inner prompting nudged at me and it sounded completely right. It's proven to be a good decision. All that's normal and steady in my life right now is packaged in this marriage. It's Jeneil's life line for some reason. I want that protected. I'll guard it like freedom and fresh air to me. I just want us to be happy and normal." She said and then she became silent.

Steve held her and wrestled with the thought that this moment was the perfect opportunity to approach the idea of a real marriage relationship in order to be completely normal. The words marched up his throat and he clenched his jaw to hold them back from being said. The pit in his stomach reminded him of the night she bolted out of the apartment because she couldn't face the idea of a physical relationship. "She's not ready!" His mind lectured. "She's only discovering normal; she hasn't clearly defined it in her mind as it applies to this marriage. She's still Pete's. Don't rush her. If she's gravitating to normal then the question if a physical relationship will surface naturally when she is ready to deal with it?" He closed his eyes and continued holding her. He was ready for a normal marriage to her. So ready that it was difficult to be patient. At times the love he felt for her would really strangle him. He kissed her temple tenderly. "I love you, Jeneil." He whispered. "I'm glad we're married." She nodded her head gently, agreeing with him, but she stayed silent.

He smiled knowing it was wise to not have mentioned what he had been thinking. His mind relaxed in thought. "When you respond to those words the way I mean them, Jeneil, then you really will be Mrs. Steven Bradley. I'll wait, Honey. I'll wait."

Nineteen

Early the next morning, Steve tied his robe around him after his shower and opened the bathroom door. He could hear Jeneil in the kitchen. He stopped wondering why she was awake so early on a Saturday. Going to his room to dress, he realized the tension of their arranged marriage. He wouldn't allow himself to be around her even in a robe. Not for her, but for him. He was afraid to get too comfortable around her. She took no notice of it one way or another. She was completely unaffected by any sexual attitude about their relationship. She would wear a robe after she had a shower and seem to feel comfortable sitting and talking to him. She had said once that she looked at life asexually and now he believed her. Never had he met a woman who was asexual until Jeneil and the idea that she didn't live her life tied to physical urges completely fascinated him. He laughed at himself realizing that he had been involved with women who he wished would be less physical and be more mental. He had often missed being human with some of them. When the relationship was only physical, he felt like a body and he understood the term "sex object." But Jeneil was the reverse, a total and complete person. The awareness had begun when he became celibate and he had found that he liked being out of the sex game. He enjoyed being an individual. That had been his first serious fascination with Jeneil. She looked at him as a person. To her each person was an individual. Her fascination with people was their individuality. He clumped people together like one big category, but she sorted them out. He smiled as he thought of this quality in her as he finished brushing his hair. Taking his jacket from the closet he continued to the kitchen where something smelled good. She was wearing a black cashmere sweater and black wool slacks and a apron. Her cheeks were flushed from being near the hot stove. Two loaf shaped mounds were cooling on the counter and she was taking a square pan from the oven.

He looked at his watch. "Honey, its 7:00 am. What are you doing?"

She emptied the hot contents of the square pan onto a wire rack to cool. "Getting back on track." She smiled and ate a crumb from the steaming golden square. "I've lost control of my health diet over the crazy summer. I'm climbing onto the wagon again."

Steve smiled. "Oh sheez, are you really a health nut?"

"Shouldn't we all be?" She said, washing the baking pan and drying it. "I don't suppose you put anything in your stomach before you throw yourself out of that airplane do you?"

Steve chuckled at her low key jab at his hobby. "It's called sky diving, Jeneil."

She shrugged and sliced one of the dark loaves. "It's still throwing yourself out of a plane which is defying natural laws making it a bizarre thing to do if not an insane one." She took a container from the refrigerator.

"It's organism substitution, Jeneil and it was your cure for my boredom in life, remember?" He teased.

She spread some white concoction on the dark slice she had cut. "Steve, sometimes I have offered you intelligent advice even brilliant advice. I think it's curious that you chose to follow my absurd joke as advice." She bit into the slice and stared at him with feigned aloofness.

He watched her. "Hey, don't I get some of that?" He asked, nodding at the slice in her hand.

She wrinkled her brow. "Do you really eat before skydiving?"

"Yes, I've learned to land on my feet not my stomach." He replied.

"I've got to see this." She said, slicing some for him and putting it on a plate. She pushed the white concoction to him.

He picked up the spreading knife. "Are you coming with me?" He asked, completely surprised.

She grinned. "Well, I was hoping to get you to the Tecumseh house and maybe put a deposit on it."

"What is this?" He asked, curious about the texture.

"A health bread." She answered, watching him.

"It's nut bread, gone crazy." She added with a smile.

"It's good. What's the white stuff?"

"Yogurt fruit spread."

"Your mother's recipe again?"

"No, my mother was a gourmet cook. I'm into basic food mostly, but I sprinkle life with gourmet and meat and potatoes cooking too. I'm not a purist."

"You are a health food nut." He said, swallowing the last of the slice.

"Are you afraid I'll serve you sea weed?" She asked. He grinned.

"Not me." He smiled. "One of the things I like about you is your health. You know what you're doing. I've seen you in action with your herbs and witches brew. I've felt better after you taught me about power shakes." Steve said, honestly.

Jeneil raised her eyebrows. "Well goodness gracious a doctor with an open mind about diet and vitamins and their curative powers."

He poured some juice. "Coming with me?" He asked.

"Tecumseh too?" She grinned.

"Tecumseh too." He nodded and smiled.

She gave a slight screech and hugged him. "Oooo thank you." She beamed. He enjoyed her gratitude appreciating the fact that she was allowing him to play the husband role since he knew that she could march into Glenview and but the Tecumseh house on the spot in her name alone. It was then that he understood how much she really did understand marriage and how committed she was to making theirs a success. He liked the feeling of security that fact gave him and he appreciated the birthday gift she had given him even more as he understood the freedom it allowed him to buy the house in Tecumseh for her. She was nesting and making the nest big enough for him. He liked that, it sounded like progress and a step closer to completely normal. As he held the wool plaid shirt jacket for her to put on, he leaned forward and kissed her cheek. She smiled, "You know Steve, we could drive to Boston so I can do some Christmas shopping and on the way you could order the 5X7 Sports car at Lamphear Ltd."

Steve laughed. "Sports car?! Jeneil I'm saving up for a car, but I'm two years away from the 5X7."

She turned and smiled. "Steve, I don't think you understand what Bradley Enterprises means. Ron was right. Your income has tripled."

He grinned. "Let's see what the house will do to our budget first."

She chuckled. "Steve, I had a feeling you'd have trouble grasping the numbers on all this, so I saved this paper for us to study privately." She opened her purse and took out a long business sized manila envelope. "I took your budget figures and my budget figures and combined them into the Bradley Enterprises income. I've shopped around at banks on the mortgage payments in Tecumseh and car payments for a 5X7. Dr. Bradley we need to talk about what to do with the rest of our combined incomes after the house and car are brought or taxes drain us."

Steve looked shocked. "There's money left after buying the house and the car?" He took the envelope, quickly.

She smiled. "Lakeland Plaza is a gold mine Steve. I paid almost nothing for it and the rents from both the new office building and the circuit of stores have tripled. You're now in an income bracket where people learn to spell tax shelter in capital letters. No pun intended." She laughed.

Opening the envelope, he zeroed in on the new income figure and nearly dropped the paper. "Oh my gosh!" He said, covering his mouth as he saw the amount of his total amount. "Oh Jeneil, I don't know about this."

She shook her head. "There's no discussion about it, Steve. It's my contribution to the marriage as wages. Please remember the freedom I have now. Let me enjoy." She pleaded. He gave a low whistle as he followed the statistics of their estimated house and car expenses leaving a sizable net income. She looked over his arm at the paper. "It would be smart to double up on mortgage payments just in case the market declines. But we don't have to decide now. There's no rush. I've found buyers for the Fairview lease and the lease on your old apartment. Except for furnishing the Tecumseh house, our personal expenses are really very modest." She explained. Steve stared at the paper hardly believing it was real. Jeneil watched him and smiled. "Do you realize that you are the landlord for the Alden-Connors Corporation? Of course I expect Bradley Enterprises to hire J/A/C Management Co. to look after the rents and upkeep on Lakeland Plaza and we're good so we're not inexpensive."

Steve smiled and shook his head slowly at her, completely overwhelmed but the reality of the figures. "You crazy kid." He said and grabbed her shoulders. "You wonderful, crazy kid." He held her as the excitement of it all penetrated his understanding. Putting his arms around her waist, he hugged her lifting her completely off the floor. She smiled, hanging onto his neck as he spun her around enjoying the excitement he was showing over the birthday gift. Lowering to the floor gently, he laughed and kissed both cheeks several times and then her chin and nose. She let it all happen enjoying his enthusiasm. Giving her a hug he then turned away and slapped the counter lightly. "I don't believe it!" He said. "I can't believe this I just can't believe it. Steve Bradley in that income bracket. I can't be." He spun around quickly to face her. "Oooo, you are something else, sweetheart. Something beyond belief." He hugged her again and looked down at her. "Jeneil…. Honey" He faltered. "I don't know how to thank you." He said, getting lost in the sparkle of her eyes. He touched her cheek, tenderly. "You are so incredible." He said, in almost a whisper, completely in awe of her. She smiled gently and his heart turned over. Pulling her to him, he kissed her lips fully, warmly and with more feeling than he had ever allowed himself before. Jeneil was surprised and then shocked by his kiss and its feeling. She struggled gently and he released her afraid that she would panic. "I'm sorry, Honey." He said a bit breathless, as the electricity from the kiss and the excitement of the moment raced all through his body. He held her shoulders gently. "I'm sorry Honey; all of this has made me a little crazy." He touched her face, lovingly. "I didn't mean to scare you." He said.

She stared at him, somewhat confounded. "It's okay, Steve." She said hoarsely, and cleared her throat. "I understand." She said, slightly breathless and not understanding at all what was happening to her with Steve. Tearing a piece of paper toweling, she handed it to him. "That's not your shade of lipstick." She said, laughing nervously. He laughed and took the toweling from her. She picked up her purse and left the kitchen quickly saying that she was going to fix her makeup. He watched her leave as he wiped his mouth becoming concerned that she was upset with him.

Jeneil closed the bathroom door and tossed her purse onto the vanity counter. Covering her face with her hands, she took a deep breath and then exhaled. She turned and looked at herself in the mirror. Her face was flushed. She touched her cheek feeling the warmth, not believing what Steve's kiss had caused her to feel. Pulling a tissue from its box she cleared the lipstick quickly. She sighed and then splashed her face gently with water. She was still shocked by the kiss. She had kissed Dennis, She had kissed Robert and Franklin, but the kisses hadn't caused what just happened to her. It was electrical mildly like Peter's. She stared into the Mirror. "The night with Robert on the boat, I was thinking about Peter." She thought as she stared at her reflection and felt the usual pain from the thought of his name. "This was different." She whispered to the mirrored image. "I wasn't thinking about him this time." And a sense of guilt and betrayal filled her. Cupping her hand she ran the tap water and filled her palm and sipped to wet her dry lips and mouth. "Peter's not yours anymore. There is no betrayal except on his part." Her mind screamed strongly angered, causing Jeneil to stand quickly realizing the truth in the words. "What is this?" She asked herself half aloud, becoming annoyed by the turmoil. Taking her cosmetic case from her purse, she reached for the liquid makeup undid the cap and dabbed her cheeks blending the makeup over her skin. She remembered Robert's words that a physical relationship was possible first and then an emotional one would follow. Replacing the cap on the makeup, she dropped it into the case. "There will be no physical. I can't." Then her mind reminded her of what her body had felt from Steve's kiss. "I won't." She spoke to the mirror, defiantly. "This marriage is perfect right now as it is. Physical will change it. I don't want this ruined. We're peaceful and contented. We're even happy together. I'm still in love with Peter whether he wants me or not. I'm not like a radio that can be turned off and switched to another channel and I'm not Steve's type anyway. We agreed to an arranged marriage because it isn't complicated. I'd get confused in physical. I understand the marriage the way it is. Just the way it is. The marriage works well without physical. We don't love each other; we would only be using each other if we were physical." She thought about how Steve kissed her, realizing that it had warmth. "It was the moment." She justified the thought. "We got caught up in the moment. Both of us." She nodded at her image feeling very comfortable with the explanation. Applying her lipstick, she blotted it gently and gave her hair a quick brushing, putting everything back in her purse. She brushed her hand lightly over her shoulders for stray hairs. Picking up her purse, she looked into the mirror. "Get a grip on cerebral, Irish. Peter's gone. Nebraska and Jeneil understand that. Don't you dare mess up this marriage for me! I'm comfortable with Steve. Life is settled. I'm happier than I thought I ever could possibly be. The pain from Peter's loss is bearable because of this marriage. I don't want things to change. I've had a whole sunrise of changes. Mrs. Steven Bradley seems to be an in-control person, let her find Jeneil's place."

Steve put his jacket on and began to pace slowly, wondering why Jeneil was taking so long. He was beginning to regret having kissed her so honestly and he wondered if any damage had been done to their relationship. He heard the door open and Jeneil's steps in the hallway. She walked into the kitchen putting on her coat. "Ready to throw yourself from a plane?" She asked, smiling.

He relaxed and breathed more easily, everything seemed fine. "All set." He said, joining her in the hallway.

They walked to the elevators and Jeneil caught herself as she went to hold Steve's hand. "Maybe we're getting too comfortable with each other." She thought as she put her hand in her coat pocket instead.

*****

The airfield was quiet. The sky was a clear blue and the air was cold and crisp. Jeneil waited in the lounge for Steve to suit up. She had never seen him jump before and she wasn't particularly anxious to watch it now. His interest in sky diving unnerved her. She was learning what opposites they were in some ways as he seemed to rush in where she feared to tread. There were three others going up with Steve besides the instructor. Steve was the rookie of the group. Jeneil would hear the short briefing the instructor was giving. He and Steve would jump together on the last circle which would give Steve an opportunity to watch the others. One couple was jumping together. They were experts and into free falling choreography. The woman sitting in the lounge with Jeneil stood up and hobbled over to the counter. Jeneil noticed that her foot was in a cast. Balancing herself against the side, she called to one of the men as they were about to leave. "Hey Richie, make it a real knockout for me." She laughed and gave him a thumbs up signal.

The young man laughed. "I'm out first Honey, so start walking out to the field now. You should be their by the time I land." He joked, and returned her thumbs up sign.

Jeneil was standing and watched the instructor check each person's gear. Steve was straightening the belt around his waist to his parachute. Jeneil thought he looked good in the green jumpsuit. He looked up and saw her watching. He smiled. She smiled at him and waved slightly. He shook his head "No." and gave her a thumbs up sign. She nodded realizing the mistake and she made a thumbs up sign too. He smiled and watched her for a minute, then left to catch up with the group. She watched them board the small engine plane and she went to another window to watch it taxi and take off. Her stomach felt queasy. "Are you going to the field?" The young woman in the foot cast asked, as she positioned her crutches under her arms.

"Well, yes. I guess so." Jeneil answered, hoping she hadn't just agreed to do something equally as bizarre as skydiving.

"The shuttle leaves in a few minutes from behind this building if you want a ride over."
"Oh thanks." Jeneil smiled. "I guess you're going to ride over since you're on crutches."

The girl nodded and joined Jeneil. "This foot's a nuisance. Normally I'd jog to the field if I'm not jumping with Richie."

Jeneil held the exit door for the girl and they sat together on the shuttle.

"Did you break your foot diving." Jeneil asked.

"Gosh no." The girl said. "Jumping's a piece of cake. I broke my foot hiking the White Mountains up north. I didn't watch where I was going and stepped into a hole, turned my foot at just the right angle and landed on it too. Lucky me." The girl sighed.

Jeneil smiled, compassionately. "You must be going crazy. You don't seem to be a sit still person with hiking, jogging and sky diving as hobbies."

"I'm not." The girl replied sadly, "and I'll probably miss ice staking too."

Jeneil smiled impressed with the girl's boundless energy.

"Are you into sports and exercise?" The girl asked. Jeneil hesitated. "We'll I'm into yoga and interpretational dancing." She answered, embarrassed how tame they sounded by comparison. The girl grinned. "You're Steve's wife aren't you?" Jeneil nodded.

The girl laughed, good naturedly.

"What's so funny?" Jeneil asked, curious about the joke.

The girl laughed warmly again. "Steve mentioned in class one night that that he wouldn't be in one Friday because he was getting married. We kidded him and asked him to bring his girl in for a crash course in diving so you could hold the ceremony as a group free fall." The girl laughed. "Now that I've met you, I understand why Steve laughed so hard."

Jeneil didn't get the joke. "Well I know that Yoga and interpretational dancing sound nothing compared to diving, but I'm not a crème puff either. It's still exercise." She insisted.

The girl smiled. "I'm not being insulting. In fact it was really cute the way Steve described you."

"How did he describe me?" Jeneil asked, wondering how she could be described, cutely.

The girl grinned. "Steve said you were not the diver type. He said that you're feminine, soft and sexy and that was okay with him." The girl giggled. "Renee Curtis and I hit him with our folded parachutes screaming that we were feminine, too." The girl laughed. Jeneil laughed, too.

"He deserved to be hit for that remark. Good for you and Renee." She said. She was surprised with Steve's description of her. She hadn't really thought of herself as traditionally feminine, soft, or sexy, or that Steve did either.

The shuttle driver got aboard. "Well ladies, let's go pick up the pieces." He said, getting behind the wheel.

"Oh my goodness." Jeneil mumbled.

The girl chuckled, finding Jeneil's fear amusing. "He means the parachutes." She laughed.

"Oh." Jeneil replied, quietly.

The plane could be seen approaching the wide field. "This will be Richie." The girl said, getting out of the shuttle as quickly as her crutches allowed. Jeneil watched the small plane and her stomach tensed as a body fell from it. "Yeh Richie!" The girl yelled, happily pounding one crutch on the ground and hooting. Jeneil watched her intrigued by the way she was sharing her boyfriend's jump. "Oooo beautiful, Baby." She yelled. Jeneil looked up to see the body spread out and floating. She held her throat and winced only relaxing when the tethers appeared behind him and the misshapen blob opened to a sturdy umbrella shape causing the diver to ease toward the ground. Jeneil was surprised that the impact of the landing was hard, since the floating seemed so slow and feather like. The parachute drifted behind the man settling to the ground. The girl waved excitedly to the diver who unhitched his parachute and helped the shuttle driver gather it together. The plane was approaching again. "Watch the Curtis's." The girl said. "They're fantastic." Jeneil watched as two bodies separated from the plane and her stomach tensed again. The bodies connected hands and rotated slowly in the air. The girl applauded. "Oh magnificent!" She smiled broadly.

He boyfriend joined her. "Come on Jill. Get that foot healed. I'd like to learn to do that."

"Oh yeh, Richie. Me too." She applauded again as the two bodies drifted apart and opened chutes. Richie ran onto the field to help the divers gather the chutes.

Jeneil's stomach felt sick realizing that Steve would be next. The plane approached and she felt her body tensing up.

One body fell from the plane and then another seconds after. Jeneil wondered why and which was Steve. She couldn't determine color at that distance. One body made a frantic movement and then the other began dropping rapidly. "What's happened?!" Jeneil asked, choking up. "Somebody's falling fast what's wrong?" She asked, frantically.

"Steve practices dead drops." Jill explained.

"Oh my gosh! That's Steve!" Jeneil covered her mouth as her stomach became sick.

"It's okay." Jill reassured her. "Steve knows what he's doing."

"Open that chute!" Jeneil yelled and then coughed from her tight dry throat. The others watched her panicking. The shuttle driver took her arm, gently.

"Mrs. Bradley, he's fine. He's just fine. The dive is perfect."

Jeneil's eyes filled with tears and she began to shake. The driver put his arm around her shoulder. "See the chute's opened. He's fine, Mrs. Bradley." Jeneil watched through tears as two parachutes drifted to earth. "Are you okay?" The driver asked. Jeneil nodded and wiped the tears from her cheeks.

"Thank you." She said. "I think I'll walk around to pull myself together." She turned and walked toward the shuttle to sit. Her legs felt too weak. She breathed carefully hoping to be fine before Steve landed. She sat and watched the two bodies land. She saw the green suit fall over as it hit the ground. She jumped off the shuttle and headed toward the group wondering if Steve was hurt. The others hadn't fallen. The driver and the other two male divers went to help gather the parachutes.

Steve stood up. "Damn that left foot of mine. I always screw up landing with it first."

The instructor smiled. "You rolled into the tumble though. That's good. It was a good dive, Steve."

The shuttle driver laughed. "But you nearly killed your wife. You should have explained your jump to her. She thought something was wrong when you dead dropped. She turned the color of your suit."

"Oh great!" Steve said, looking for Jeneil as she ran from the shuttle toward him. He walked toward her as the others followed. "Jeneil." He said, holding his helmet in one arm and extending his other to her wanting to console her when he saw the anxious expression.

"You maniac!" She growled and swung at his helmet, knocking it to the ground, shocking Steve. "You're suicidal! Totally insane!" She shouted at him and burst into tears.

He took hold of her shoulders, firmly. "Calm down." He said, firmly. She covered her face and sobbed. Putting his arms around her gently, he pulled her to him. She slipped her arms around him clinging to him desperately and crying.

"It's okay, Honey. Look at me. I'm fine. Sheez sweetheart, you're being a little ridiculous, don't you think? Sky diving is safe." He said, rubbing her back gently.

The instructor picked up Steve's helmet and went to him grinning. "Don't be too hard on her, Steve. If my ex-wife had cared that much, I'd have stayed married to her." He patted Jeneil's shoulder. "Mrs. Bradley, he's good. He knows what he's doing." The instructor smiled as Jeneil clung to Steve. "Steve, why don't you skip the second jump?" He said. Steve nodded in agreement.

"No." Jeneil said, lifting her head and sniffing. "No, do the jump, Steve. I am being ridiculous. I'll just run to the pharmacy for some chloroform. I'll be fine." Everyone laughed.

Steve hugged her to him and she clung to him sighing, as her heart beat began to beat normally again.. Everyone headed to the shuttle allowing Steve and Jeneil to walk together alone. As she boarded the shuttle Jeneil stopped. "I'd like to apologize for my behavior." She said. "You people told me he was fine, but I panicked anyway. I'm sorry; I'll be okay the next time." Everyone smiled.

Richie laughed. "Go up in the plane this time, Mrs. Bradley."

Jeneil raised her eyebrows. "There isn't enough Valium in the world to get me through that." She took a seat and Steve sat beside her, slipping his arm around her shoulders, firmly. She nestled against him enjoying the feeling of having him with her and forgetting her concern that they might be getting too comfortable with each other. Jeneil struggled through the next dive too only managing to stay calm as she watched Steve floating in the air by using deep concentration at almost yoga level. He had told her that he really likes having her along, but she wondered about the stamina it would take to witness him in such danger every week. As she waited for Steve to change into street clothes, she remembered her mother's concern every time her father took Mandra's Austin Healey on the back roads. She saw her mother's concerned looks and her frequent stops at the window facing the carriage house where the cars were kept. The look of relief on her mother's face when she'd heard the red sports car on the long driveway was very noticeable. Jeneil has asked about her concern and her mother had told her that her father had a heavy foot. The Austin Healey runs off with him, it has an exhilarating fascination for him. Jeneil had asked why she didn't ask him to stop driving or to drive slower. Her mother had smiled wisely and told her that what she loved about her father was that he was a man, his own man and to put him in a cage or in tethers and chains would make him a domesticated animal which neither one would appreciate. Jeneil had understood as she understood the similarity now in her own marriage with Steve's interest in Skydiving. "If I had married a quiet librarian." She thought. "He could have a wall of books fall on him I suppose. Life itself is a risk." She tried to reason with herself, but she fought hard against the thought that bizarre is like playing Russian Roulette and she had to keep telling herself that she had no right to confine Steve. She sighed thinking that marriage wasn't really very easy even an uncomplicated arranged marriage like hers.

*****

The stop at Tecumseh was more to her liking. She felt comfortable in the house and ideas for decorating would come to her as she moved through all the rooms. She liked the house even though it wasn't the same feeling she had for the house at the ocean. She and the ocean house had an affinity for each other. It was "her" house. Her soul had always felt at rest in it, but knew it held too much of her and Peter in it as well and she knew that she couldn't be at peace in it any longer. The pain was too great. So the Tecumseh house was a good alternate, a good compromise in her uncomplicated, arranged marriage. She felt an infinity in Tecumseh too oddly enough, not for the house, but for the land. She felt an "oneness" with the earth when she stood on the sloped backyard which was a horror scene of mud and partially unearthed rocks exposed but erosion as the weather worked against the development company who had tried to do basic landscaping. It wasn't even a normal slope that steadily eased into a backyard; instead it looked like several mounds of earth had attached themselves to a normal slope causing a mutation in the terrain. A slope itself was an unpopular feature, but a mutilated slope was a "dog" to sell the agent had said. Jeneil loved it and the stream with its rambling unsettled patch of uncluttered nature land beyond it. All the other surrounding properties dropped into a gully at the stream, but the Tecumseh house eased into it as a result of the odd slope. Jeneil liked having access to the stream without dropping into a ditch as she called the gullies. She liked being able to see "Her" Stream. Steve smiled watching her in the yard and he knew that an apartment was not for her. There was something about the expression in her eyes when she was in the backyard that vibrated fire. She'd have to be turned free out there or wither. He knew it. He saw it in her as she stood on the slope facing the stream. They went inside with the agent who was into wringing his hands knowing that Jeneil has been the only woman so far who had accepted the yard. All three leaned against the kitchen counters.

The real estate agent undid the buttons on his coat. "You know I've mentioned you two at the corporate office, making it sound like a great favor to them personally and the developer wants you in the house." Jeneil smiled.

Steve looked puzzled. "Why?" He asked.

"Well, this house needs special people in it. People who will appreciate its special features and we think we have found the special people of discernment." Jeneil bit her lower lip.

Steve shrugged. "Fine let's talk black and white."

The agent rubbed his chin. "What will it take to get you in here?" He asked.

"What's the price?" Steve questioned. Jeneil watched.

"Well now, this house is comparable to the others in this area. It's the same design as the Barnard's"

"Dr. Drexel Barnard?" Steve asked.

"Yes." The agent smiled. "You know them?"

"Yes." Steve answered.

"Good." The agent smiled. "Then, you already know your neighbors."

"Who else is here?" Steve asked.

"The Barnards are to this side of you, the Rands are diagonally in the house across the street. The Tufton's are directly opposite on that street. Are they all familiar?" Steve nodded. The agent smiled. "Well this really is your house."

"We haven't bought it yet." Jeneil answered, quietly.

The agent looked at her. "I thought you liked the place?'

"I love the yard and the stream"

The agent shook his head. "Selling real estate is a real study in human nature." He chuckled. "Those features have been my worst obstacle with this place." He shrugged. "Okay, how can we make you love the house, too?"

"Is there any movement in the corporate office?" She asked.

He studied her face, "Some, but this is Glenview, Mrs. Bradley, we can't discount severely a house of this caliber. The Barnards would be outraged. I'm sure you can understand that." Steve watched Jeneil, wondering what she was doing.

"Yes I can." Jeneil answered, just as quietly.

"Then what are you looking for?" The agent asked.

Jeneil put her hands in her coat pockets. "Well I can understand that the neighbors must be complaining about the house being empty for so long because of the enticement to vandals and the eyesore of a slope in the backyard must irritate them."

The agent silently watched her. "You've been giving this some thought, Mrs. Bradley. I can see that."

Jeneil nodded. "Would the corporate office be agreeable to adding a large double door off the dining room and a bi-level deck across the back of the house built to a simple design?"

The agent smiled. "I know they would be. That's it?" He asked, grinning. "That's really easy."

"Well, that's not quite all of it." Jeneil said. Your contractual brochure states that landscaping is included."

"It is." The agent said.

"Well don't you agree that the slope requires more than basic landscaping? Actually it is what's keeping the house from selling. The slope is going to be very costly for just the right people who buy the house. Do you think the corporate office would be agreeable to additional landscaping if the right people paid what the Barnard's paid for their house?"

The agent watched her and smiled. "No problem. We're not taking pine forest here are we?" He asked.

Jeneil laughed lightly. "No, we're talking terracing."

"Oh!" The agent said, brightening. "That would work. See that, you really need to have a feel for the place to find the solution. Mrs. Bradley, you are my ray of hope for this place. Are you agreeable to a set amount for additional landscaping?" He asked, encouraged.

Jeneil nodded. "Yes, just about what you would have severely discounted the house if we were stubborn people. Terracing is expensive, but it's about all that will work back there."

Steve thought he saw the agent stop breathing. The agent coughed slightly. "Well your offer is going beyond my authority, Mrs. Bradley, but let me call corporate office on the cellular phone in my car. This is an unusual offer and an unusual yard."

Jeneil nodded. "Yes and it's been empty a very long time with winter just around the corner, too."

"Yes, you're right." The agent said, watching Jeneil closely. "Let me make that call. I'll be right back." He said, going to the door quickly. Jeneil poked into the cupboards while she waited.

Steve watched her unconcerned attitude. "Aren't you afraid you'll kill the deal? He asked, grinning.

"No." She said. "It would be crazy for us to invest so much in landscaping here. We would never get our money back in resale. The place will still be only comparable to the Barnards. The developer knows that. He'll be happy to break even on this place just to have it sold. Landscaping is a good investment here for him. All he'll be doing is discounting the house severely without it showing up on paper. They'll sell the house and the Barnards are not insulted because they will have paid the same price for their place. The house is sold, the muddy backyard eyesore is patched up, and everybody's happy especially the very wealthy neighbors whom corporate office cares most about. After all, Dr. Bradley, "this is Glenview" and the "Tecumseh sector", you heard the man." She smiled.

Steve grinned. "Honey, you're a bitch."

"I love you, too." She grinned.

The agent burst through the back door, smiling broadly. "Mrs. Bradley, corporate office loves your idea. They're pleased that you're interested. I've been authorized to list up your requests on the sales agreement."

"Wonderful." She smiled. "That's great news."

"It sure is." The agent smiled talking out papers from his briefcase, quickly.

"Now, can we settle on a deposit?"

"We've come prepared." Steve said.

Jeneil opened her purse. "I'll write the check from my account. It's my maiden name, Dr. Bradley and I are transferring holdings so we still don't have a joint account. You know legalities, but I assure you the check is good." She said, filling out the check which she handed to him.

The agent's face muscles dropped as he looked at the check. "Is something wrong?" Steve asked.

The agent looked at Jeneil and grinned. "You know I had a feeling I was being slicked by a pro. Alden-Connors, that's Lakeland Plaza. I know Sam Bolger, the agent who sold you Lakeland Plaza. Your legend to real estate agents. When we lunch at "The Buckle", Sam loves to tell the story of how this wide-eyed innocent young girl walked into his office one day and offered to buy Lakeland Plaza. He said he almost didn't have the heart to sell her the dump because she looked like a beginner until she pulled out estimates and research papers that knotted his socks. After she sliced some fat off the price and the sales agreement was all legally signed, Fat-cat Chatfield shows up along with a tall thin money lawyer from Nebraska. He couldn't figure what such slick money wants with a run down group of stores. He passed it off until Adelphi put up the corporate building across the street from Lakeland Plaza and the rest is history. Now Sam figures you for the slickest scout this side of Geronimo. What did you have, an inside scoop that Adelphi was building there?"

Jeneil smiled. "No, actually I was looking for a tax loss."

"A tax loss?" The agent broke into laughter. "I love it. Wait until I add that to Sam's story the next time I'm at the Buckle. What a business. It's a million laughs." The agent said.

Jeneil smiled. "Would you mind if I tour the house again?"

"Not at all." He said. "Stay as long as you'd like. I've enjoyed meeting you both." He said, extending his hand to Steve and then Jeneil. "Just secure the door when you leave."

Jeneil turned from the doorway, "Oh by the way, I heard a chain saw buzzing deep into the woods across the stream. I hope it's not being developed."

"No it isn't." The agent smiled. "Believe it or not, a small piece of that land was bought by a privacy freak. He's got just certain trees being taken down and the house is at the back of the property. That's why you hear the noise. They should be finished soon. Your property back there should stay just as natural as it is now; the guy has a thing about being alone. I guess."

"Who is it?" Jeneil asked.

The agent opened his book. "A Dr. Vance." He said.

"Kirk Vance?" Steve asked, surprised.

"That's him." The agent nodded. "Well enjoy the house." He said and he closed the back door as he left.

Steve wondered about their choice as he realized who their neighbors would be. "Jeneil, I hope you'll like living here." He said.

She turned to look at him. "Why wouldn't I?"

"Honey, you're just moved yourself smack into the middle of "The Group" from the hospital."

"Well we knew that didn't we? Wasn't that the reason for buying here, to be part of the political group? Besides one of them is a privacy freak. That's my kind of neighbor. Isn't this the best group? The big money, the good families, well educated and elite. The fun crowd, the "in" group." She said, as she went to the hallway.

He followed and sighed again as he thought to himself. "Not this group, sweetheart. Not this group. Be grateful, you're surrounded by two and a half acres and a wooded stream between you and Kirk Vance. You'll never fit in here, Sweetheart, never. I hope you can be happy with this house." He thought and he moved to catch up. The sound of the chain saw buzzed through the silence and Steve put his arm around her shoulder wanting to keep her near him as he thought about their neighbors.

*****

The rest of the day was as much fun as most of the beginning. They stopped at the sports car dealership where Steve has been visiting for years to dream over the cars on their floor. Jeneil enjoyed watching Steve gather all the salesmen together to announce that he was there to really buy an SX7. All the salesmen applauded and congratulated him. The sales manager broke open a bottle of Champagne. Jeneil became choked with emotion as she watched Steve realize a longstanding dream of buying the sports car and swimming in the delight of buying it. The only disappointment was that the platinum colored model they had didn't have red leather seats and Steve insisted that the car had to have deep red leather seats because his wife looked fantastic in deep red. Jeneil couldn't believe that he actually chose to wait for a factory ordered model in order to have red leather seats because of her. He had smiled at her warmly as he said. "What good is the car without my fantastic wife, too?" The sentence had left overwhelmed and the gentle hug and his whispered thank you had her choked up and speechless. There were moments in her life when her money had brought her genuine pleasure. Watching Steve now ranked very high as one of those times. The moment left a closeness between them. Their emotional bond was stronger.

As they drove on to Boston more warm smiles were exchanged then usual. Steve squeezed her hand more often. Jeneil felt a sense of oneness which outright surprised her since she always felt that she would never achieve that except with Chang. Peter was still a strong part of her and her heart would feel deadened when she thought of him and her inner self would feel a deep sense of loss and even pain, but there was now this feeling of being a part of Steve. Jeneil smiled wondering if the feeling was a natural result of passing the usual milestones in a marriage, even an arranged marriage. The milestones of buying the first home, the first car and the first child. Her heart stopped as the word child passed through her mind. "Children." She thought and she suddenly realized that she had overlooked yet another facet of an arranged marriage. "Steve is an orphan. He should have children so he can begin a lineage, his future." She fidgeted. "What have I done to him?" She thought.

Steve touched her hand, gently. "Honey is something wrong? You look so concerned." Steve said. She looked at him steadily, seeing him differently and she was unprepared for the interruption of her thoughts at that point. Steve wrinkled his brow. "Jeneil, you're flushed. Your cheeks are red. Are you okay?" He touched the back of his hand to her face, looking concerned.

"I'm fine." She replied, through a dry throat taking his hand from her face as the awareness of his touch seized her. "Maybe something allergic." She added quietly and she opened the car window. "Oh gosh." Her heart sank. "What else have I overlooked in an arranged marriage? The idea seemed so right and it's such a good relationship. Were we crazy? Are we crazy? It will work right won't it? Why not? It can work; we're doing great so far." Her mind openly debated until she felt a sick headache begin. Opening the car window wider, she breathed the cool air deeply. Steve touched the directional indicator and turned into a Service Travel Center off the highway and stopped the car.

Putting his arm behind her on the seat, he took her hand in his.

"Hey, you look sick." He said, concerned. She rubbed her temples. "It's so crazy; I've just started a headache. I'll take an aspirin." She undid her coat feeling overheated.

He watched her. "Let's go inside and get some juice or water. Walking might help, too." He suggested. She nodded, struggling with a confused thought process and a slight headache. He kissed her cheek, gently. "You're looking very fragile, Honey." He smiled, as he thought of something. "Who are your three selves?"

"My three selves?" She asked puzzled.

"You told me once that you had three selves. I've seen two. One is shy and fragile."

She grinned surprised that he had noticed. "Nebraska." She smiled. "That's Nebraska, afraid of everything." She laughed with a gentle laugh.

"One is confident." He grinned.

She nodded slightly. "Jeneil."

"Who's the third?" He asked, watching her steadily, anxious to know anything about the third self.

"How did we get into this?' She asked.

"What do you call the third self?"

"Your question sounds like I'm qualifying for therapy."

She laughed uneasily and fidgeted. "I've seen the movie, The Three Faces of Eve."

Steve smiled. "Those were three separate personalities. Yours are selves. I think there's a difference."

"Whew." She sighed. "That's good to hear, I thought I had fallen off eccentric."

He laughed and then returned to his question. "How is the third self, Honey?"

Jeneil realized that she was resisting revealing Irish to him and the realization surprised her. She couldn't imagine why. Having realized that, she stopped resisting and searched her feelings, curious to find that she felt vulnerable. "Jeneil?" Steve asked, wondering about her silence. She looked at him for a second and then bridged the gap between vulnerable to trust.

"Irish." She answered, quietly. "I call her Irish."

"What's she like?" He asked, completely fascinated.

Jeneil shrugged slightly. "Crazy." She answered, and then she laughed briefly.

"Why is Irish, crazy?" Steve continued, feeling oddly drawn to her at the moment.

Jeneil studied his face concerned about his interest in Irish. Again she felt vulnerable. There was a softness in his blue eyes. Her gentleness felt reassuring. She trusted him.

"Irish is primal." She said, in almost a whisper.

"Primal? You mean basic?" He asked.

Jeneil grinned. "Oh Irish is basic alright. She's uncivilized." She shook her head. "And she's getting worse." She added.

Steve sensed an odd feeling between them at the moment. He had been feeling a closeness toward her all day, but now watching her, he felt that she was past fragile and into something more. "Vulnerable!" The thought struck him suddenly. "She's vulnerable." His heart pounded as he grasped the fact that she had been resisting him and then she opened up. He felt really close to her at that precise moment so close it was almost an oneness. Never had he ever experienced such a delicate moment with a woman or another person in his whole life. His mind absorbed her. He watched her sitting quietly almost hushed somewhere in her thoughts.

"Jeneil you're beautiful." The thought came from the center of him as he blended into his love for her.

"Thank you." She whispered shocking him back into the moment.

"For what?" He asked shaken by her remark. He wondered if... "No." he thought. "That's crazy." "Jeneil." He said, hesitantly. "Why did you say thank you?"

She looked at him. "You said something nice about me." She looked puzzled. "Didn't you?" He watched her not daring to ask what he had said. She grinned. "Oh, oh." She raised her eyebrows. "You have just passed through the portals of the twilight zone. I'd better get some water and take that aspirin."

Steve couldn't stand it now, he had to know. "Honey, what did you think I had said to you?"

She shrugged. "Something nice. Something about how I look."

Steve held his breath.

"No." She corrected herself. "No, I thought you said I was pretty, but you didn't, you had said something about who I am." She wrinkled her eyebrows. "Well, that doesn't make sense does it?" She rubbed her temples. "I don't know, it sounded pretty close until I try to make sense of it. Boy do I need an aspirin. Do you feel odd?" She shook her head. "Irish is strange, Steve. She dabbles in cosmic." She sighed. "But I like her, she's honest and very impulsive and..." Jeneil stopped. Steve listened carefully.

"And what?" He asked.

"Nothing." Jeneil replied, not wanting to say that Irish was passionate.

Steve watched her and he realized that Irish was fiery. She's the one who knocks men off mountains. That's who Pete encountered. "Irish is passionate." He thought. "That's Jeneil's superlative. Holy shit, if I'm this crazy about her already, how the hell will I survive Irish?"

"Are you okay?" Jeneil asked.

"Yeh." Steve smiled. "I'm okay. Jeneil, you're not ever dull." He touched her cheek, lovingly. "Let's get some juice." He went to her side and opened the door. He locked the car and turned to her, putting his arm around her shoulder.

She looked up at him. "Steve, do you think an arranged marriage can really work?"

"Where did that come from?" He asked mildly stunned by the question.

She sighed. "The idea defiles normal. We live in a dimension that requires normal. I just wondered."

He stopped becoming concerned. He looked at her. "Do you want it to work?" He asked.

"Yes. Yes, I do." She said satisfying and calming him by her sincerity.

"Then it will work." He smiled.

"I guess it had better work." She said. "We are so completely entangled now. We own a house, a car, combined incomes, a real estate company." She snuggled closer to him for comfort and reassurance that she hadn't made a decision about the marriage that was wrong for Steve. "Irish." She thought. This is your doing. You're impulsive. You've entangled Steve in our strangeness now you had better make this work. He's not like Peter. Peter understood Irish."

Steve held her tighter as they walked into the service restaurant. He became aware of her next to him, aware of her as being his totally. "Honey." He thought. "I'm entangled in this in more dimensions than just normal." "Irish." He smiled to himself. "Irish." He thought becoming more fascinated.

Twenty

The topsy-turvy summer had Jeneil's schedule warped. Christmas shopping was usually finished earlier, but the strange summer had changed that and Jeneil found herself having to be in crowds which she never enjoyed, shopping for Christmas gifts as well as furnishings for the Tecumseh house. What she did enjoy was the pressure, the demand on her and her time. It made the thoughts and feelings of Peter stay buried as her concentration centered on putting order in her life and controlling the details of the new house which she was determined to be settled into by Thanksgiving. She took on the high pressure deliberately. They arrived home from Boston pretty well spent and eager to rest. Steve liked being with her, even though he hated shopping. He had discovered shopping with her was an adventure because she became distracted at times and could end up in second-hand stores or old book shops. But mostly he liked being with her as she poked around in the routine of her life. He found it fascinatingly odd watching her in a second hand store where she found a necklace that actually excited her. She was crazy about the necklace. The dealer has looked her over noticing the cashmere and wool and seemed puzzled that a piece of junk jewelry has caught her attention. He had even asked if she had some particular outfit it seemed right for. "I'm going to make an outfit to match the necklace." She had answered him.

"Don't you want real pearls or diamonds?" He asked, pointing to the fakes at the base of the metal work.

She smiled. "I can have a small pearl and two small diamonds put in this."

"You'd do that to a piece of…" He stopped himself.

Jeneil looked at the man. "This isn't junk. It has real character." She said, feeling the white petal filigree between her finger and thumb and rubbing the black stone with her index finger. She bought the necklace for $2.00 and left the shop treating it like a priceless treasure securing it in the deepest recess of her purse so she wouldn't lose it.

Sitting by the fire in the den with a mug of Ovaltine, she draped the necklace over a sketch pad and began drawing outfits becoming totally absorbed in the project. Steve smiled watching her drift into the world of design wondering about his wife who had recently tripled his income, bought a new house in an exclusive development, and helped him get an expensive sports car and now sat designing an outfit she was planning to sew herself for a $2.00 necklace. He shook his head, knowing that was all part of why he was crazy about her. "She lives at tilt."

*****

Early Sunday morning Sienna had called to invite Jeneil to a Sunday lunch. She and Franklin were living together. Steve had watched Jeneil take the call and she had asked if he could go along. "Yes, we are becoming a real twosome Sienna." Jeneil smiled. "That usually happens when two people get married." Steve swore he heard the shock wave across the room as he sat at the kitchen table with a newspaper, coffee and the remains of breakfast. Jeneil laughed. "We got married very quietly, privately and with no frills or fuss. Well thank you, yes I will accept your best wishes for much happiness. Goose liver pate'? Oh my mother made that for our New Year's Eve buffets. Yes it is good." Steve grimaced and drunk some coffee trying to wash away the feeling left on his tongue at the thought of goose liver. "Are you sure you're up to this before the concert?" Jeneil asked. "Yes, thanks for thinking to ask me. See you then, bye."

"Oh boy." Jeneil smiled joining Steve at the table. "Sienna's practicing some recipes for holiday parties and she's put together a lunch for sampling and opinions. Sort of a dress rehearsal. She really has style."

"Why goose liver?" Steve's tongue felt funny again and he sipped some coffee. "That sounds so awful. Poor Franklin. He probably just wants cheese and crackers or simple pot roast." Steve shook his head.

Jeneil sighed. "She has offered to teach me to cook, but I just can't get into gourmet that deeply. It's so delicious but I saw my mother take hours with details. Her pressed duck was outstanding, but the work it took. Maybe I should learn, since I'm going to live in Glenview."

Steve stared at her. "Honey." He said.

Jeneil looked up at him from the Home Furnishings section of the newspaper. "What?"

He shook his head. "Uh, uh. Don't take lessons. Sienna's gourmet cooking shits. I'm bringing a ham and cheese sandwich for lunch."

"You're no fun." She said, smiling. "And eat it in the car before and after. Don't hurt her feelings."

He smiled. "At last you're allowing me the sandwich."

She shrugged and turned the page. "There's room for all types in life we just need to leave wing space for everybody. "Let's stop at Mike Phillips Gallery on the way over. There's a painting Robert did that would look great displayed on that brickwork in the den of the new house. It's bold and the colors would be enhanced by the earth tones in the brick. The paintings been sitting in the gallery for months. It's such an odd painting, but it has a special meaning for me."

"Why." He asked, not really liking Robert in her life.

"I sat for it."

"He painted you?"

She nodded. "Surrealistically. He claims it's really me. Really what he saw in me. You won't believe what he saw. It's bold, intense, dramatic and chaotic. We had just met and we struggled with each other. The painting must be a result of that struggle because I can't understand or see me in it. It's intense turmoil, a deep struggle, with an odd center of tranquility. The painting's not moving because of the content. It demands its own wall. Not many people have the space or desire to enshrine a painting. I think it's into group them now that people are into collecting as a hobby."

"You don't?" Steve asked.

She shrugged. "Depends on the paintings, I think. And I should remember to bring one of my mother's paintings from Nebraska on my next trip. My Aunt Rachel will love it as a Christmas gift I'm sure." She sighed. "I should visit soon and my Grandfather too, I guess. Rachel said he seems happier in the nursing home. I know she's thrilled to not have to travel so far."

"Still wrestling with guilt?" Steve asked.

Jeneil thought for a second. "Not guilt so much as feeling that something with my Grandfather is unfinished between us. Peace maybe. I'd love to bring him the painting my mother did of the farm, but I'm afraid he'd hurt himself destroying it."

She stood up. "Well enough of that. I'm going to get dressed."

*****

Mike Phillips smiled broadly as Steve and Jeneil entered the gallery. "Jeneil you look great!" He kissed her cheek, briefly. Robert's bringing me up to date on you. Is this the spouse?" Jeneil nodded. "Dr. Bradley, Mike Phillips." Steve extended his hand. "Dr. Bradley, welcome to my gallery. It's a pleasure to meet you. We'll probably see you here often too." He smiled, personally. "And so Jeneil is this just a tour?"

"No Mike, I'd like to buy Robert's surrealism."

"Oh no! Jeneil it went a week ago. I'm sorry. I would have saved it if I had known you were interested."

Jeneil was surprised. "You sold it! I am really shocked."

"Me too." Mike agreed. "But I had a crowded opening here last week and when the dust had settled Robert's surrealism had been moved."

"I wonder who bought it. The painting is so odd that I'd like to know what the owner saw in it."

Mike nodded. "Robert wondered too, but it was a cash transaction. I have no idea what the owner even looked like. Sandy said she can only remember that it was a man. We had wall to wall bodies here for that opening. Robert was very curious. He thought the painting's content was something that a woman would identify with. He was surprised that a man bought it. Of course he might have bought it for his wife who liked it. I don't know. It's out of my grasp now." Jeneil looked around. "Well then, I'll take a quick tour. I'm Christmas shopping and filling a new home."

Mike smiled. "Oooo, I'm glad you stopped in. Let me know if I can help. For you, I'll unlock storage."

"Thank you, Mike." Jeneil smiled.

"Any time." Mike said. "I have to meet with a new artist, but have Sandy call me when you're ready."

"I will. You've enlarged the Colonnade area."

"Yes, Robert's been sculpting up a storm. They move at Christmas time." Mike answered as he walked away. "Buzz me, okay?"

Jeneil nodded and took Steve's arm. "Can we do some shopping for you while we're here?"

Steve laughed. "Me buy art as gifts? Who'd believe it?"

Jeneil smiled. "What about the Sprague's."

"I guess you're right, Honey. This Christmas I have a job and money. A basket of fruit won't quite make it anymore as a gift."

Jeneil laughed. "Money complicates everything."

He smiled. "But I can live with the tension, believe me." She laughed and squeezed his arm as she walked to the photography area with him.

*****

Peter unlocked his apartment door and placed the plastic garment bag on the chair. Switching the grocery bag to his other arm he closed the door and went to the small kitchenette to put the food away dropping the mail on the small table in the livingroom. He felt tired shopping and errands always wore him out and he had been called to the hospital on Saturday for a patient in crises, which put him a day behind on his personal errands. He had gone to the mall to buy a sport jacket and a tie not expecting the crowd of Christmas shopping he found there. Putting the last can of soup away; he sighed and then went back to the livingroom. Picking up the mail, he sorted through it setting aside the junk to be thrown out. He stopped as he saw the familiar handwriting on the light blue envelope. A month had passed and he had still not gone to see his family. His Grandfather called him regularly to stay in touch, but otherwise he hadn't seen or spoken to anyone else. His cousin Ron had called once, but he was on his way out to a seminar and he had cut Ron off abruptly. Ron never called back and Peter never called him either. He wondered abut the letter he was holding from his mother, knowing that he didn't want to read it. Dr. Nefida had told him to take life at his pace and deal with what he could. The sessions with Dr. Nefida were something he was having trouble dealing with, but he took them anyway thinking sometimes shit won't go away so you wade through it. He hoped it would be easier to open up in therapy once he became accustomed to talking about himself to a stranger. Throwing the junk mail out, he took the rest of it along with the garment bag to the bedroom. He hung the jacket in the closet and opened the bureau drawer slipping all the mail into it. He turned and looked at the wall where the painting hung. He smiled and sat on the foot of his bed to look at it closely. He had brought it over a week ago and he was really enjoying it. The idea to buy it came to him when he was driving home as the sun was setting. The sunset reminded him of Jeneil. The wind reminded him of Jeneil. Full moons reminded him of Jeneil. Life reminded him of Jeneil, and so he had stopped struggling to forget her. He remembered the painting Robert had done of her and he went to the gallery and bought it, glad that he did. The painting was a source of comfort to him. He had gotten more peace from discussing problems with the painting than he had from his few visits with Dr. Nefida. The painting reminded him of the balcony in Vermont where Jeneil blended into the sunset. And he had felt the incredible oneness with her. The painting wasn't as peaceful as the experience in Vermont and he wondered why Robert had painted Jeneil in such strong turbulence, struggling with something, but the colors were right and so he liked the painting. He looked at it now and then laid back on the bed. It was easy to think about her now after he began feeling her presence in the wind and full moons and sunsets. He didn't miss her as much painfully. They brought pleasant memories of her and smiled remembering that she had given them to him as wedding gifts. "Crazy Kid." He smiled. He had settled her in his mind like he had done with Ki. She was no longer a part of his life. Like death, he couldn't change it, but he still had her reality through memories. Instead of resisting thoughts about her, he resisted thinking about her with Steve. Steve didn't exist to him anymore. Everything was easy after that. No tension, no anger. Steve married someone Peter didn't know, because his Jeneil wouldn't marry Steve. It was that simple and now life was easier. Dr. Bradley worked at the hospital and Peter heard people talk about him and his wife Jeneil, but they were both strangers to Peter. They weren't the people Peter knew because friends didn't betray you and your wife didn't marry your best friend and so Dr. Bradley and his wife were strangers. Life was very easy now. His medical career was everything in his life. His patients provided all the deep human contact he needed. He even enjoyed the notes they would send him when they went home. Dr. Maxwell was openly surprised at the closeness Peter's patients achieved with him. The thank you notes stunned him. His career filled all the gaps and emptiness. Wayne Maxwell was becoming a good friend as well as a surgical partner, but Peter had learned a lesson. If you keep friends at a distance then life isn't complicated. No deep feelings, no deep hurt. He remembered an official looking letter amongst the mail. Getting up, he went to the drawer and took it out. Opening it quickly, he smiled. "Divorce Decree." He read. "Wonderful." He thought. "Get that shit buried too. Taking out the important paper file, he tucked the Decree inside. "You cost me plenty, you shittin' bitch." He said, angrily. "I'm talking to a painting now instead of to her because of you." He secured the file pouch and replaced it back in the drawer and he noticed the light blue envelope with his mother's handwriting. He wondered if she was writing about his decision in the divorce. The Wongs were good to there word and had wanted to file divorce against Uette for Peter. He had refused and asked only that she give up the Mrs. Peter Chang. The Wongs complied. They had wanted to keep their word about setting the truth in the Chinese community. Peter had refused. He couldn't see what value it would have since the truth would only dirty Uette who was trying to straighten her life out and it would make him look like a fool for getting so trapped by her in the first place. The Wongs complied reluctantly and Uette had sent him a note thanking him for his consideration. Which he tore into bits and set on fire in the kitchen sink. He hadn't wanted anything from her and the Wongs which disappointed them and both Mr. Wongs had sent legal documents to him from their lawyer giving Peter official authority to collect on an open indebtedness from the Wong family. "What I want, you can't give me." He had said after opering it, and he tossed the documents in the drawer. The Wongs had put word out in the Chinese Community that the failure of the marriage was caused by Uette entirely who was too and completely unprepared to be a wife. Peter's name became golden amongst the Chinese families who couldn't believe the glowing praise the Wongs had for him and his tolerance and patience with a poorly prepared wife. His name soared to the top ranks of eligible bachelors, even divorced. The Wongs were so deliberate and thorough with their praise of him that his birth was ignored if not forgotten since the Wongs were exacting about Peter's honor and dignity and compliance with Old Chinese ways. They made it known that they considered the divorce a great loss to the Wong family. His Grandfather told him that John had started a family joke that every Chinese father who had marrying age daughters were now twisting their arms hoping they would break so they could meet Dr. Peter Chang., the great orthopedic surgeon and bachelor. Peter picked up his mother's letter and then put it back in the drawer. Sitting on the bed he looked at the painting. "She cost me you, Baby. She's part of it." And remembered the unhappiness and cruelty his mother had brought to Jeneil's life, the names, and the car accident. He remembered the letter his mother sent to Jeneil and how he had wanted to throw it out, but Jeneil had said that it was important to open letters because problems can't get settled if you avoid them. He smiled at the painting and then went to the drawer and opened the letter. Taking it to the bed, he sat down to read it.

"Dear Peter

This letter won't be easy for me, but I know that it's necessary. Before anything else gets said, I want you to know how proud of you I am for the way you handled that awful marriage and the dignity you showed handling the divorce."

Peter shook his head. "Proud of me. I was gutter dirt to you until Uette showed her snake tactics and fought with you. What trash."

He sneered and continued reading. *"I must seem like a hypocrite because I didn't believe your side of the story and I regret that now, but we have never been able to talk openly and I can't blame you there. You have certainly shown more strength of character than I have and I wish I could take the credit for having taught it to you, but I know I can't."*

"The Dragons taught me." He said. "Those other pieces of street filth you screamed about for years." He sighed and returned to the letter.

"What I like to have you know." The letter continued. *"Is the reason I lied about your father, but maybe I should explain your father first. I was just out of school and his family owned the business where I worked. It was my idea to keep our dating a secret because I needed a job, and I was afraid I'd be fired. Races stayed with their own much more in those days. Your father and I were good friends and our feeling became deeper very quickly. He was going to be leaving for college in the fall and we were planning to married after he graduated. He said he could face his family's fury about the marriage if he was prepared to provide for us on his own. They were well known manufacturers. I was disappointed. I had hoped he'd marry me when he went to college and then I got scared that we would lose each other if we became separated, so I got pregnant assuming that he would marry me. I was wrong. He felt that I had betrayed him; he knew that I had gotten pregnant deliberately. We argued and without all the details, we just didn't get married. I dealt with that quickly and turned my thoughts to the child I was going to have. Having children out of wedlock was a greater shame when I was a girl and the shame was not only on the mother, but on the child too. I felt bad that because of my selfishness, my baby would be called names that it didn't deserve and so I came up with the idea of rape in order to protect the baby. By the time you were born I had told the story so often, I almost believed it myself. The story seemed to work at the time, but hearing Uette tell my truth, I really wonder if you and I were the only ones who believed the lie. Your Grandfather has told me how much inner suffering a rapist father has caused you. I never knew that. I'd like to think that if you had told me your feelings about your father, I would have told you the truth, but I don't know that either. The lie made life easy to face myself, I guess. I can only say that I'm sorry for any hurt my mistake and my lie shame caused you. I would like to have your forgiveness, but I'm not asking for it. I asked too much from you already over these years with just my lie, but I wanted to explain and tell you that I'm sorry, Peter."*

Peter sighed and refolded the letter, returning it to the drawer. It was the most honest and straightforward he heard his mother be. He stretched out on the bed and looked at the painting. "Baby, sometimes life can be a real bitch." He said and he sighed deeply.

*****

Steve and Jeneil had returned home weary from their round of Sunday stops. Shopping at the Gallery, lunch at Sienna's and Franklin's, the afternoon concert where they had met Dr. Young and Dr. Fisher with their wives and joined them for cocktails. They arrived home happy to rest and relax. Each dropped onto the sofa in the den and sighed vowing to not move for a week. Jeneil inserted a cassette into the stereo unit and waited for the sounds of Dvorak. "I'm hungry." She said, snuggling a sofa pillow to her.

"Want to eat out?" Steve asked, hoping she would say no.

Jeneil groaned. "No, please, no more social. Let's raid the fridge." They settled on Friday's leftover veal dish and cold sliced vegetables. Steve built the fire in the den and Jeneil warmed dinner and Ovaltine in the microwave. They met at the fireplace and ate stretched out on the rug, lazily. The fire crackled and danced rhythmically, warming the room with soothing heat and light creating a comfortable atmosphere that relaxed them both causing each to drift to sleep.

They startled awake by the telephone ringing and each was shocked to find that they had drifted together while asleep. Jeneil snuggled to Steve's chest with his arm around her. They sat up quickly looking surprised and embarrassed and Steve got up to check the answering machine. Jeneil gathered the debris from dinner going to the kitchen quickly shaken that she had snuggled to Steve while asleep. The call was for him and she went to shower, and then to her room without saying goodnight.

He turned off the apartment lights and headed to his room concerned about her silence. He knocked on her door. "Jeneil." He called, and he heard a quiet,

"What."

"Goodnight."

"Goodnight, Steve." She answered. He was disappointed that she didn't come to the door. He had begun to look forward to her kiss and quick hug. He went to his room, concerned.

*****

Jeneil put her full effort into the Tecumseh house. She felt confined and unsettled with her possessiveness in several spots. Most of her time was taken with handling details of the house and she had started sewing the outfit she designed. Steve rarely saw her in the evenings which concerned him. He missed that, too. But Jeneil was getting herself into line by trying to offset the closeness that was developing between them. He missed her and was annoyed with himself for having drifted too close to her while asleep on the rug, feeling that the incident was causing her to withdraw, now. He took his cue from her and he stayed away from her too, continuing their routine of sitting in the den with Ovaltine before bed, but alone. He missed her, but he knew the relationship was in a delicate balance right now and that she must be feeling threatened. The situation reminded him of a kid at the home who had bought a parakeet with the fiercest temper imaginable. Steve had suggested live dissection of the beast but Anthony insisted that the bird was only scared and everyday Anthony routinely followed a set plan until the bird trusted him. Steve had been impressed as the bird finally approached Anthony slowly one night and was about to eat seeds from his hand when two of the younger boys burst into the room screaming which scared the bird into regression. Anthony started again keeping a log of each day's progress, noting that it took fewer days the second time to bridge the damage until finally the bird ate from Anthony's hand and eventually sat on his finger. Steve sighed. "Yeh, but Anthony had total control. He had withheld food and hunger was a strong motivation. I'm not in total control and Jeneil's not hungry." Steve sighed remembering that Anthony had gotten a top award in the science fair for his efforts with that bird. Both he and Anthony learned a lesson on patience with that bird.

*****

It was Wednesday and nearly the end of the week and except for dinner, Jeneil stayed by herself in her room all evening. Steve was discouraged. He heard her in the kitchen and was tempted to just go and get more Ovaltine, talk to her briefly, than leave, but he decided against that feeling sure that his best card would be to keep his distance. Hearing her footsteps in the hall, he picked up the medical journal and began reading as he waited for her to pass by the door. The footsteps stopped. Steve wondered why, but he didn't look up. He sipped the warm Ovaltine and was aware that she had come into the living room. She sat on the sofa quietly. He looked up. "You're up late." He said. "Heavy workload this week?" He asked, making conversation.

"Sort of." She replied, quietly watching him.

"You have a lot going on, be careful. It's easy to overdue around this season. Stress cases increase this time of the year."

She nodded and smiled blandly. Looking at his watch, he put the journal aside and stood up. "I have early surgery. I'd better get some rest." And he said goodnight quietly as he went to the door.

She answered his goodnight and watched him leave. Sitting on his bed, he sighed. "I hate this, damn it. I hate this so much. Pretending, watching, waiting. Shit games. I hate playing games."

*****

Steve walked into the scrub room the next morning feeling low. He had overslept, Jeneil had called him, gave him a power shake for breakfast and he left. Nothing between them had changed. He joined Dr. Sprague at a sink. "Heard you were at a concert yesterday." Dr. Sprague smiled. Steve nodded resenting his life being so visible. The thought made him realize he was out of sorts. He caught sight of Peter scrubbing at the corner sink. He glared in his direction and then went back to scrubbing noticing that Dr. Sprague was watching him steadily.

Dr. Winslow and Dr. Sloane stopped at the sink. "Steve what's this I read in the paper about the Lakeland Plaza transferring to a Bradley Enterprises. How the hell did you ever pull that deal off? What a plum of a package. That's the hottest piece of property around. My broker couldn't even get anyone to take my offer seriously." Dr. Sloane asked, totally impressed.

"It's a birthday gift from my wife." Steve answered, simply not elaborating.

Dr. Winslow whistled. "A birthday gift. Bradley, man are you aware of what your gift is worth? You've got yourself quite a woman for a wife, then. She must care a lot. She gave you the very best." He chuckled.

Steve glanced at Peter in the corner. "Yeh, I guess she cares quite a bit." He answered, scrubbing harder. Dr. Sprague watched him.

"Well, glad to have you aboard the investment train. Let's do lunch sometime. I'd like your input about a well rounded portfolio. The topic seems to be as individual as fingerprints." Dr. Winslow patted his shoulder. "Yes Bradley, let me know when, I'd like in on that, too."

"Sure." Steve replied. The two doctors walked away. Drexel Barnard took a sink opposite Dr. Sprague and Steve.

"Hey Steve, word around Tecumseh is that the mutation plantation was sold to you and Jeneil. Have they got it wrong? Are you moving to Tecumseh?

"Yes." Steve answered.

"Well I'll be. Did you know that Kirk's is building "Walden" in the woods?"

"Yeh, I heard."

"Well, son of a gun." Drexel laughed. "Hail, hail, the gangs all here. But why did you choose that place? The back yard's a killer to maintain. You'll never get a yardman to do that slope."

"I don't know, Drex. Jeneil's got some plan for it."

Drexel smiled. "Well, wait till the gang hears who's coming to town. Was that your Torrence parked there on Saturday?" Steve nodded. "Oooo, Steve be careful you don't make the rest of us look like paupers. Is that your main car or second?"

"That's Jeneil's car." Steve answered.

"Are you still pushing the Lynx around?" Drexel laughed.

"For a while." Steve replied. "At least until my SX7 gets here from the factory."

Drexel Barnard stopped scrubbing. "Ah come on Steve, we don't want you in Tecumseh if you're going to show off. Be reasonable man. My wife will chew my ass for months now. An SX7, sheez."

"Were not showing off, Drex. Jeneil knew I always wanted one."

Drexel grinned. "Tell me you're hired help for Jeneil directly from London and I'll put my place up for sale tomorrow."

Steve smiled, weakly. "I don't think Jeneil is planning on help."

Drexel sighed. "Steve, teach her the rules of fitting in. Okay? Maverick isn't funny when you can buy SX7's like lollipops."

"Don't worry Drex, that's it for showstoppers. We're quiet people."

"I hope so man. I hope so. A wife nagging about status symbols is no way to live. Ask the man who knows."

"I'll probably cut my own grass. How's that?" Steve said.

Drexel smiled. "Now you've got the beat."

Dr. Sprague waited as Steve was gloved, and then walked into OR with him. "Well I was going to ask a favor, but it looks like your life is spinning right now."

"What favor?" Steve asked.

"Boyce Bolger got sick at the New York Seminar."

"I'll take it." Steve replied quickly, shocking Dr. Sprague.

"But it goes all next week." Dr. Sprague cautioned, "You've got a lot going on."

"No problem, When do I leave?"

Dr. Sprague watched him. "Well I don't want to push. I know its short notice."

"When's the next flight?" Steve asked.

Dr. Sprague looked puzzled. "Is everything okay with you?"

"Fine." Steve replied. "Is Tollman assisting?"

Dr. Sprague nodded. "Let him do some network."

"Sure." Steve said and went to check the chart. Dr. Sprague watched him and wondered.

Steve's cases and appointments were rescheduled and reassigned and he left mid-morning to pack. His flight was leaving at noon. Putting his luggage by the apartment door, he went to the telephone to call Jeneil and let her know about the seminar. After dialing two digits, he hung up. Taking a piece of paper from a drawer, he left a note for her explaining the trip and where he could be reached, then he left it on the kitchen table. "My wife cares, Dr. Winslow." He said. "She just doesn't care if I'm here." He snapped his top coat from the chair, picked up his luggage and left.

*****

Jeneil arrived home and went to the kitchen quickly. A meeting with Ron Chatfield had run late and she was hoping to have dinner ready by the time Steve got in. There were plans about the house to be discussed. She was leaning at every level to close quickly on the property. Turning on the kitchen light, she noticed Steve's note. She also noticed that it was signed Steve, not Love Steve. She sighed slightly wondering how to deal with the situation realizing they were too distant. Maybe it was for the best, better too distant than too close. She ate dinner alone in the kitchen and then worked on the outfit she was sewing. Weary of sewing a while later, she took her sketch pad and began designing the terraced slope and deck for the house. She was surprised that it was eleven. She wondered why Steve hadn't called. She wandered into the kitchen after her shower at 11:30. "Why hasn't he called?" She asked herself. Emptying the dishwasher, she sighed. "I hate Games. Why am I waiting for him to call?" She picked up the telephone and dialed the hotel. "What room is Dr. Bradley in?" She asked the operator.

"I'll check that for you." The operator replied. "That's Room 918. Shall I ring for you?"

"Yes, thank you." Jeneil said. She let it ring several times and then hung up. She looked at the clock. It was 11:45. "Well, medical seminars keep strange hours." She thought, twisting the tie to her robe around her finger. Turning off the kitchen lights, she went to bed.

She was edgy Friday, knowing that she had caused the divide in the compatibility of the marriage, but she didn't know how to change it. She called the hotel from her office after lunch. "How late are the medical seminar meetings held?" She asked some manager she had been given.

"That varies. The one today ends at 7:00pm. Can I help you with something?"

"No, no thanks." Jeneil answered. "I'll place the call after that. Thank you."

At 4:00 Rachel bought a long slender white box to her office. Jeneil looked up and recognized it. She smiled. "Where did that come from?"

"The florist just delivered it. How romantic." Rachel smiled and left.

Jeneil took the yellow rose from the box. It was just what she needed to receive. The card was inside. She opened it quickly. It said *Happy Anniversary* and was signed Steve. It wasn't his handwriting Someone knocked, Jeneil looked up.

Adrienne walked in. "I thought I'd duck out early tonight. Do you need me?"

"No." Jeneil smiled. "Enjoy the weekend."

"Thanks. Is Steve coming back this weekend?"

Jeneil shook her head. "He's away for another week."

"Then how can you close on the house?"

Jeneil shrugged. "I'll work that out whenever I make connections with Steve, I guess."

Adrienne watched her and then closed the office door. Sitting across from Jeneil's desk, she folded her arms.

"Trouble?" Adrienne asked.

"Complications maybe." Jeneil said. "I'll probably need a courier to take papers to Steve. The hotel must have a notary on staff."

"I mean at home." Adrienne shook her head. "Why am I asking? The whole marriage spells trouble."

"We're okay." Jeneil said.

"Uh huh, except my husband's missing." Adrienne said, finishing Jeneil's sentence.

Jeneil rearranged her pencils. "He's not missing. He's been gone a day. We're settling into the next phase of marriage. We're separate people with separate careers and demands. See, he even sent the yellow rose."

Adrienne nodded. "Yeah and I can see how happy it's made you."

Jeneil smiled. "Go home Adrienne. There's nothing wrong. Are you and Charlie on track every day of your lives?"

Adrienne watched her. "No, but we have a cure that you don't."

"Platonic can work." Jeneil insisted. "We've done okay so far."

Adrienne sighed. "Is that how it's handled. He takes a run in the paddock from time to time?" Jeneil felt it was too personal to say that Steve was celibate. Adrienne watched her. "You don't even discuss it, do you?" She asked.

Jeneil fidgeted. Adrienne stood up. "Oh Jeneil Honey, where's your brain, girl. You cannot interfere with natural without trouble. Even the Catholic Church doesn't house nuns and priests together and they study celibacy." Jeneil watched and listened as. Adrienne walked around the chair rubbing her neck. "The guy is healthy and normal. You're asking too much of him."

"I'm not his type, Adrienne." Jeneil said. "I've known love. I can't settle for sex. Steve was hurt once…"

"That's a crock!" Adrienne snapped. "You're a woman, he's a man!"

"Adrienne, I known love, I can't settle for sex. Steve was badly hurt once, he can't love." She shook her head, sighing. "We're a good blend. We understand each other."

"Okay girl." Adrienne sighed. "Don't check for faults in the nuclear reactor. But Jeneil, I'm telling you, you are postponing an explosion of major proportions. You're not stupid by any means so you're either ignoring it or trying to reason it through, but I refuse to believe that you don't see it. Ugh!" Adrienne screamed. "Your marriage will drive me crazy." She said, going to the door. "See you Monday."

Jeneil smiled. "Adrienne, I love you."

Adrienne smiled, too. "Damn girl, even my own blood sister don't reach me like you do."

Jeneil laughed. "I'm watching things carefully, Adrienne. I'm not stupid."

Adrienne chuckled. "Jeneil have you ever read the sex advice columns in woman's magazines. No two columns can agree on one solution to the same problem. But you're watching this carefully. You're a beginner. Your problem is that you define them. Take some advice from Dear Adrienne, Go home pack a nightgown and go to New York with your husband. Forget going home leave from here and wear a smile when you get there. Turn the damn mare loose in the paddock with the Stallion. Jeneil let natural work for you."

Jeneil smiled. "I love you, Adrienne."

Adrienne shook her head. "I hear you, girl. I hear you. I'm going home. See you Monday." She waved and closed the door. Jeneil smiled and then looking at the card again, she frowned and then sighed.

*****

The apartment began to feel empty to Jeneil as she sat at the kitchen table eating dinner. She touched the yellow rose gently in the vase. "Oh Steve, I'm so inept at relationships and our lovely, peaceful, arranged marriage is getting confusing. How do I find a balance? I miss our friendship and yet when we're good friends now we drift too close to each other. But I miss you. I belong to you. I want this marriage to work. But I don't want just sex, and I couldn't please the White Stallion anyway. Even if what I heard about the White Stallion was 80% hype gossip. The 20% that isn't sounds like it's beyond me. I'm too simple, too plain." She sighed. "You told me yourself that you're not interested in a physical relationship. But how far is too far? Tears came to Jeneil's eyes. I'd rather not be married to you if it will cost us our friendship. I love how we are together. I need our closeness. You're so much like Peter. He was more Neanderthal, but you both let me breathe. You allow me my own life." She cleared the dishes and took them to the dishwasher. The telephone rang. Wiping her tears, she went to answer it, smiling.

"Jeneil? Ron Chatfield. I pulled some strings and got a closing for Tuesday at 3:00. You owe me a case of bourbon so I can marinate some executive palms." He laughed.

"Oh." Jeneil said, grasping the conversation slowly, having expected it to be Steve calling. "You'll have it Monday morning and thanks Ron. I really appreciate the muscle."

"It's okay." Ron replied. "You don't usually push so it must be important."

"It is." Jeneil said. "It is. Thanks again." Replacing the receiver, she looked at the clock, 8:15. Maybe he's in his room now. She dialed and let it ring several times and then replaced the receiver feeling very discouraged. She redialed leaving word with the hotel operator to have Steve call her. The rest of the evening was spent hand hemming the outfit she'd made and making the hook loop with silk thread. She yawned and checked her watch. "11:36!" She said, shocked. "Where is he?" She called the Hotel. "This is Mrs. Bradley, was my message delivered to Dr. Bradley?"

"Mrs. Bradley, he hasn't called in for messages. If he does we'll give him your number."

"Called in? Isn't he in the Hotel?"

"No ma'm, he's listed as being away."

Jeneil was confused. "Away? Doesn't the seminar hold sessions on weekends?"

"Yes, away means not expected in his room tonight. He has a forwarding number. It looks like a Staten Island exchange. Perhaps you'd like to call him there."

Jeneil was stunned. "Uh no, no thank you. He'll get his messages when he returns Thank you." Thoughts began filtering through her mind. Thoughts that made her uneasy. She made some Ovaltine and then went to her room and packed some books wanting to stay with her plan of moving to Tecumseh, and gathering all of Jeneil into one place. That represented order and progress and she found comfort in packing. She went to bed at 1:00 exhausted hoping she'd sleep quickly to avoid any more thoughts.

*****

Saturday she went to Wonderland and closed down the house bringing her belongings to Camelot from where she planned to have the movers take everything to Tecumseh and storage. She was tired and hungry. She went upstairs to Adrienne's and invited herself to dinner, not wanting to face the empty apartment and her thoughts.

It was 9:00pm when she got in. Checking the answering machine, she found a call from Steve saying only that he had returned her call. It sounded abrupt and cold. "Why is he angry?" She thought. Continuing to check all the messages, she found another call from Steve placed at 7:15. He had explained that he called her between sessions earlier and didn't have much time since everybody wanted to use the telephones. He assumed there was no emergency since he hadn't heard and he suggested she leave the full message on his voice mail or they could spend the whole weekend trying to connect. He had said be careful you don't overdue it and the call ended. It didn't leave her comforted. She called his room, there was no answer. She left the full message about the closing on Tuesday with the hotel operator feeling like a haunt of a wife and wondering what these strangers must think of the odd relationship between Dr. and Mrs. Bradley. She decided to treat herself to a special bath. Filling the tub with warm water and bubbles, she brought in the cassette player, some classical music and a tall glass of apple juice and ice. It helped, but the apartment felt like a museum after hours. She felt alone. Opening the door to Steve's room, she went inside and sat on the bed. "Gosh, he's neat." She thought looking around. The desk with the cleared top, except for a notebook, remembering Peter's clutter. She shook her head and smiled. Her father was a different person, too. Out of curiosity, she went to his bookcase. One section of it held medical magazines. She grinned and checked the dates. They were stacked chronologically. Each in order. She chuckled. "He's a neat freak." She smiled as she looked at the closet door. "Jeneil, you're invading privacy." She lectured. "Yeah!" She grinned wickedly and opened the doors. His casual shirts were all hanging neatly facing in one direction and buttoned at the neck. His dress shirts were in a garment bag and just as neatly arranged. His ties were sorted on the tie rack according to color. Jeneil smiled and covered her mouth. "My gosh." He's a neat fanatic. He's worse than I am. She liked order, but her desk had a catch all notebook where she tossed things to be sorted, and filed at a later time. She had a junk drawer where things went until she found a place for it in the order. "You have military blood, Steve." She smiled loving the tour of his room. Feeling a twinge of guilt, she looked at the bureau and its drawers. "Why not, I've snooped this far." There were no drawers out of order. "Oh my gosh, He's cemented on to the conveyor belt. No wonder he hears the music at the prom. "Not even a junk drawer?" She said as she opened the last drawer. "Aha!" She chuckled as she saw the "catchall" drawer, but it was neat too. She smiled. "I thought it was a cultural or something, but he must be into super grooming." The withering yellow rose in the corner caught her eye, the card was under it. It was the first anniversary rose he'd given her. The one she had misplaced somewhere as she began to malfunction. Emotion filled her and she felt a lump in her throat. "I'm a terrible wife." She thought, reading the card. As she went to replace them, she saw the framed marriage certificate. She thought that was odd. She had never seen a marriage certificate framed before. "They get filed somewhere, don't they? You frame diplomas and awards. For showing off pride and boasting things." She thought. She sighed as guilt filled her. She had never even thought to file their marriage certificate and he had thought to frame it. "It's too bad Marcia hurt you, Steve because if you were capable of loving a woman, she would be absorbed by your quality of romantic attention to details. Replacing the frame, card and flower to the drawer, she closed it and then returned to his bed, not wanting to leave. She felt less alone surrounded by his belongings. Stretching out on the bed, she lay there quietly and eventually drifted to sleep. Waking in the middle of the night feeling chilled, she reached for the spread and blanket rolling them around her and stayed curled up across his bed where she slept snugly until morning, when she awoke completely refreshed.

Twenty-One

Jeneil dawdled over breakfast Sunday morning not wanting to go to Camelot and pack away that part of her life. She was hoping Steve would have helped her. He seemed to know how to distract her so the pain was tolerable. She concentrated in a philosophical attitude as she drove to Camelot, hoping that a "Well that's life" point of view would help. She touched the familiar door sign with its gnomes, elves and fairies painted on it and remembered that she had painted it shortly after she had quit college and moved in. The name of Camelot had come to her because she felt it appropriate. She was beginning a new life; one that she felt sure would be perfect. "It was for a while." She thought, going inside.

By noon the walls were bare and her art work and African collection were boxed in crates that the mover had provided. All that was left was the bedroom. Stripping the walls of artwork and condensing the items from her sewing corner, she secured the crate. Standing, she turned to face the bureau. It was the last thing that had small items to be packed. Items that she really didn't want to face. Going to it, she stopped and looked at the frame lying face down where she had put it weeks ago when her world crashed around her. She felt the pain begin at her stomach. "Where do I pack it?" She asked herself. "I suppose I should throw it away." Her throat tightened at the thought. "Maybe I should return it to Mr. Chang." Tears filled her eyes. "No, it might seem melodramatic. The second woman showing her contempt." Tears spilled down her cheeks. The wooden treasure box that Peter had given her for her birthday was at the other end of the bureau. Taking her pieces of Jewelry from it, she put every item that Peter had given her inside it. She picked up the frame and felt her hands tremble. Without turning it face up, she placed it inside the treasure box. The two enameled bracelet's he had given her were with the jewelry. She picked them up and placed them in the box. "Well that's it. I wish it was that easy to pack the memories and the pain away, too." She swallowed past the lump in her throat. As she went to close the treasure box, she remembered one more item. Opening the small bureau drawer, she rummaged through the contents looking for it. She had angrily thrown it in the drawer weeks ago. Seeing the small filigree circle, she picked it up and held it in her hand. "Well I guess the Princess's magic didn't work after all." She said. "Our wedding ceremony didn't last the summer, let alone forever." Giving in to tears, "Oh Peter." she cried. The words poured from her in utter anguish as she sank slowly to her knees releasing vocally the tears she had tried so hard to control for so many weeks. How long the room was filled with her pain, she didn't know. She became aware she was kneeling there in the silence of the room. The ache in her throat had eased. She opened her fist and looked again upon the scalloped ring from the wedding ceremony on the balcony of the ocean house. She placed the ring into the treasure box with the framed picture of Chang and closed the lid. There was a trunk in the corner of her closet. She put the treasure box in it and refastened the bolt on the trunk

Returning to the bureau, she picked up the pieces of jewelry and went to put them in her jewelry box. The jewel case that Steve had given her for Christmas was beside it. She picked it up and opened it. The dried yellow baby rose was inside. She smiled. "You're always there, Steve. You and your comforting friendship." She felt a peace. Closing the case, she touched her lips to it gently. "I'm going to be a good wife. This marriage will work." She smiled again and returned the jewel case to the drawer. Jeneil finished packing. The job seemed easier as she concentrated on her marriage and the future ahead of her. There was something very comforting about placing roots. Finishing the odds and ends of packing, she gathered her purse and coat. Looking around the apartment with its boxes and crates, the place hardly resembled the Camelot she remembered. "Change can make things unrecognizable." She sighed. "Well the best that was in Camelot will stay in my memory unchanged." That passing thought caught her attention. "I'll remember that when anger and self pity remind me of the hurt and betrayal. What was good in that relationship can stay in my memory unchanged, too. She opened the door, the Camelot sign swung gently on its hinge. Taking it down, she put it in a box near the door and locked the apartment. She was anxious to get back to the Fairview apartment. Her new life seemed to spread before her with hope. It was positive. "I need positive right now." She said and closed the heavy front door behind her. "Let's go and face tomorrow." She said, confidently. Nebraska leaned on Jeneil for hope and Irish was strangely silent.

*****

Steve read the message the hotel clerk had given him. His jaw tensed and he headed to the elevators. The seminar had given him an opportunity to stand back and look at himself, Jeneil and their marriage. He had worked his way through a lot of feelings in the few hours that he'd been away from her. Some of them refused to be worked through. One was anger. He was angry at Peter for the whole warped situation. He was angry at Jeneil for refusing to deal with reality and he was angry at himself for allowing the fantasy of Jeneil to get the better of him. Jeneil belonged to Chang, he deluded himself into thinking that life would follow a normal course and Jeneil eventually be his. Her reaction to just waking in his arms changed that. The blinders were off now and he was living in reality. She would probably always belong to Peter. Accepting that fact now, he had to ask himself what has to be done. "What now?" Most of his free time had been spent walking the streets and thinking about "What now?" He was glad to have been invited home by a college buddy he ran into, just to get away from thinking. His ex-roommate had recently married and they were getting settled into a new home. The visit helped Steve deal with his dilemma. Truth surfaced and his choices seemed clearer. It felt good to be able to tell his college friend that he had just bought a house and Steve had realized that he really wanted that. He wanted marriage, he wanted a home and he wanted a wife. The marriage would work even better now since he was giving up his fantasy of Jeneil being a real wife. "We're good friends." He thought. As he rode up to the ninth floor in the elevator. She wanted a husband, I wanted a wife. We both wanted marriage. We have it. It was an arranged marriage from the beginning; she had never lied to him. He was the one suffering from delusions, not her. "The kid plays with Helium and stays closer to normal than most people I know." He said to himself. At the moment, the only problem he could see was reminding her that he is her husband and the job came with certain rights.

He closed the door to his room and went to the telephone. There was no answer. He left a message on the answering machine. He went to take a shower and get settled for bed early. He had been keeping late hours and celebrating reunions with different classmates he was meeting at the seminars. It was catching up to him. He turned down the bed and lifted the receiver again.

*****

Jeneil had gotten in and checked for messages. Steve had called. She looked at her watch. He had called recently. She dialed his room, anxious to be able to finally talk to him. There was no answer. "This is incredible." She said as she hung up. She got a glass of juice and the telephone rang.

"Jeneil its Steve."

"I just called you." She smiled relieved to be listening to his voice unrecorded.

"I was in the shower."

"You have been keeping some late hours." She said, teasingly.

"I know. I've met some old school friends here and we've been holding reunions. I stayed with a roommate of mine Saturday night." Jeneil noticed something in his voice, an edge, coolness. "You've been on the go, too."

"Yes, I packed Wonderland and Camelot. I'm all set for the closing Tuesday."

"That's why I'm calling, Jeneil. What about me? I can't be there. Isn't this house in my name too? I know I haven't sunk as much money in it as you have, but I'm going to pay the mortgage."

Jeneil was surprised by his biting tone.

"Of course the house is in your name too. I was going to courier the papers to you."

"Well, how great." Steve replied. "Is it so hard for you to wait until I get back? I'd like to sit in the banker's office and do this the right way. I don't plan to buy too many houses in my lifetime. Do you mind if I do it traditionally?"

Jeneil was stricken by his words. She hadn't realized he would feel slighted.

"Yes, of course." She said. "I mean no, no I don't mind. I didn't think clearly. I'm sorry."

"I have rights in this marriage Jeneil."

She looked at the receiver shocked by his biting words. "Yes you do, Steve. I've apologized for not thinking. It wasn't deliberate."

"Well, you stampede sometimes, Jeneil."

She rubbed her temple. "I can see how you feel that way especially in this. I'll work on that. I told you to let me know when I was standing in your sun." She said, trying to be more cheerful in her approach to offset the annoyance in his.

"Well consider yourself told." He said, flatly.

She wrinkled her brow. "I'm sorry I upset you."

"Forget it. The seminars finished by Saturday noon. My flight is at 3:30 Saturday, so expect me sometime Saturday, I guess. Trying to catch you in is too tough."

"Okay." She said, quietly.

"Is everything okay there?" He asked.

"Yes." She answered wanting to add "Well I seem to have a communication problem with my husband." But she didn't say it.

"Then I'll see you Saturday."

"Fine." She replied. "Steve, thank you…" She heard the dial-tone. He had hung up. She replaced the receiver. "…for the yellow rose." She finished the sentence and took a deep breath hoping to recover quickly from his abrasive tone.

*****

Steve sighed as he paced. The telephone call had left him rattled. He knew he hadn't handled it well. There was another feeling besides anger that he was having trouble working through and that was hurt. He knew that he was feeling hurt. As much as he could accept the reality and truth of the arranged marriage, her resistance of him hurt. "I'm not a monster. I could make her happy. The marriage could be better." He sighed and went to his bed. "Forget it, Steve." He lectured. "You are married a nun and there's no door to the ivory tower. Irish was amputated when Pete dumped her. Don't expect anything. Life will be easier that way."

The telephone call left Jeneil rattled. She skipped dinner and went to change for bed. Going to his room, she sat on his bed, hoping for her positive mood to return. She had enjoyed being surrounded by him the night before. She had leaned on the thought of their marriage as hope. His telephone call had damaged the feeling. She sat there feeling like an intruder. She left the room and went to hers and paced. "What's happening?" She asked. "What am I doing wrong? He told you, you're stampeding. I don't know Jeneil, you're father teased you about being a nun, sometimes I wonder if that's where you belong. Nobody would wonder why you're single. No dating, no marriage." She sighed. "No, I don't belong as a nun either. They're dedicated people who know what they want. They're not searching. What a mess. You'll never get a relationship right. You lived with Peter, that didn't last a year. You've been married a month and that sounds like it's in trouble. You're playing at working. You're wandering in life aimlessly." She stopped by the closet door. Her new outfit was hanging on the rack. She looked at it. "Jeneil take a look at your life. You've invested hours making an outfit to match a $2.00 necklace. That's been the highlight, the lift in your life, recently." She sighed. "You'd better make sure you never get sick. "If ever you have to be hospitalized, it's all over. You'll be making bracelets the day after you're admitted. If you're lucky enough to avoid a strait jacket. No wonder Steve's uptight. He's probably tired of eccentric."

*****

Jeneil was at work early Monday morning and checking with everyone involved with the home. She had asked permission to move in before the closing. Permission was granted, given who she was and the developer being very anxious to have the place occupied. Jeneil thought to call Steve and leave the message, but she decided against it, remembering the last call and its negative affect on her.   After thinking about the encounter, she had decided to show Steve that his wife had a normal side. She could be less eccentric and she was determined to show him how expert she could be at order. He likes things neat. She had thought and then decided that she'd have their lives settled into the Tecumseh house by the time he returned. He would be away for his birthday. The smooth move would be his birthday gift. The excitement of the idea felt delicious and it injected a positive energy flow into her that lasted the whole week, as she pushed herself at a frantic pace to prepare the house. By Friday, the house was ready to be lived in and Jeneil was completely done in by overseeing the numerous details of such a quick move. She had closed Steve's apartment and moved its furniture. She had Camelot moved to Tecumseh and everything had been moved out of their Fairview apartment except the beds. She had taken her full maintenance crew and gone to Tecumseh to unpack on Friday. The house had been a frantic place all day with the drapery company and the service people making deliveries or working. The builders were finishing the deck on the back of the house and she had spent the day directing people, approving jobs, or answering question after question of: "Where does this go? Where do you want this?" The tedium and tension had her worn through by late afternoon when everyone began to leave. She closed the door to the last worker and sighed. Going through the house, she checked doors and windows, going to the attached garage last. She smiled with delight looking at the contours of the car through the blue protective material fitted to it. She had the SX7 delivered and parked in the garage. It was her special birthday gift for Steve. She had bought volumes of red material and fashioned a huge global shaped bow that she secured to the car cover on the roof. Setting the alarm system, she left for the Fairview apartment pleased but definitely tense.

Buying fast food through a drive-thru window, she went home and ate standing at the kitchen counter. The apartment was bare, except for the beds and small odds and ends which she would handle before the cleaning crew came in. Cleaning the counter, she decided that she to take a warm bubble bath. "Make it special." She said aloud. "You deserve it." She hoped she would rejuvenate her body and spirit. A mini spa. The idea appealed to her and she left to set up the bathroom. Putting the cassette player on the bathroom vanity, she ran the water in the tub and left to turn down Steve's bed. She had been sleeping in it for the past two nights since the movers had been there. The echo of the apartment irritated her and she had found that sleeping in his room helped her to maintain her sense of "High" for the whole project of settling Tecumseh as she came home each night exhausted. She put her nightgown on his bed and tied her robe around her. The bathroom looked like a rainforest when she opened the door. The stream swirled into the hallway. She left the door open not wanting to wait for the steam to drift. She needed a hot bath to relax her muscles immediately. Putting the Rossini tape into the cassette, she got into the tub feeling her muscles respond to the heat. The perfume scented bubble bath floated on the steam surrounding her. "Wildflowers." She said, closing her eyes. "I'm lying in a field of wild flowers growing on a mountain." She laughed and looked at all the white bubbles she had tripled her usual amount and the tub was filled with volumes of suds. "It looks like I'm on the snowcapped top of the mountains. She laughed and settled against the porcelain tub that had been heated by the hot water. The music, the bubbles, the scent and the warm water were working their magic and she could feel energy being restored throughout her. She smiled. "It'll take a week to rinse out these suds. They were the thick kind with small bubbles that had body to them. She used to love those kinds of suds as a young girl; they could stay in shape longer than wet large bubble suds. She could make snowmen and animal shapes with them. She sculpted a snowman quickly and stuck it to the wall. It clung fast. "Oooo, these are great suds." She smiled and decided on a duck next. She remembered the soap suds hairdos she used to make and she made a mound that covered her head completely. She checked her image in the chrome circle surrounding the tap. "You look ridiculous!" She laughed. "It's the hairdo." She defended herself. "Eeet is not right for madam." She said, pretending to be in a French styling salon. "No, no, no, the lady she eez more exotic. That pouf is for Cinderella. No Madam Bradley is more like Cleopatra." Using the chrome circle as a mirror she styled the angled Egyptian look for herself. "Better." She giggled at the distorted image. "A big improvement. Thank you Fife. You know my inner-self, definitely she's exotic, a real man-killer. "Knock 'em dead Jeneil, that's me alright." She settled back in the tub and made a snowball. Her mother used to help her with some sculpture and they sometimes had a contest to see how many sudsy snowballs they could balance on her head in one stack. She had found that the trick was to make the first snowball bigger and get gradually smaller. She tried to remember their record. She thought it was sixteen. Making the snowball in her hand larger she placed it on her head.

"One." She said and began making another. "Oooo, what a great malfunction this is." She said. "A trip back in time. I love it." And she added the second snowball.

*****

Steve sighed and rested against the elevator, exhausted from the day's pace. He had forgotten what Friday night's could be in Manhattan. For all the traffic and crowds, he wondered if it was worth leaving Friday instead of Saturday. It had been elbow to elbow through the whole airport. It felt great to have finally parked his car in the lot at Fairview and he was riding in an empty elevator for the first time all week. He unlocked the apartment door and slipped his luggage inside. The empty living room stunned him. The bare walls were a shock. He walked in slowly and heard the classical music playing loudly in the bathroom. "What's going on?" He asked, looking around at the empty apartment.

Jeneil splashed the water making more suds. She was ready for her 18th snowball. He arms weren't long enough since the 12th number and she was now using the back of her long handled bath brush which she found that wet slightly and working quickly, the snowball would slip off onto the next. She had gotten her large hand mirror to help direct the project. Steve stopped at the bathroom door, shocked as he watched Jeneil reach with the brush and added a glop of suds to her already covered head. Jeneil screamed as she saw the figure in the doorway, not knowing someone else was in the apartment.

"Steve!" She smiled, surprised and delighted that he was home. The look of shock on his face reminded her of what he was seeing. She was in the bathtub dressed appropriately for being there and playing a stupid kids game. She pulled the shower curtain forward and covered her suds covered body.

"Jeneil, are you okay?" Steve asked and Jeneil heard the shock and concern in his voice.

She smiled, nervously. "Uh yes, this is a kid's game. You try to see how many snowballs you can balance on your head." She pulled at the suds realizing how bizarre she must look.

"Where's all the furniture?" He asked, still very stunned. She wiped the suds from her brow and cheeks.

"If you'll close the door." She said. "I'll get out of here and explain."

"Okay." He said. "I'll get my luggage." He closed the door and Jeneil sighed, making a grab for the spray shower attachment.

"So much for showing him he has a normal wife." She said, working quickly to rinse the suds from her and then his last words struck her. "I'll get my luggage. Oh my gosh! My nightgown's on his bed!"

Turning the taps off quickly, she stepped onto the mat and wrapped the terrycloth robe around her. Wrapping a towel around her hair, she put her feet into her slippers. "I hope his luggage is in the car." She opened the bathroom door frantically and went to his bedroom.

Steve was standing by his bed looking very puzzled about the turned down covers and her nightgown.

Her heart sank as she rushed in and then she slowly walked to the bed. He stared at her questioningly. She picked up her nightgown and rolled it up in her hands backing away slowly toward the door. "I uh, well, I'm sure this must look very weird." She said, feeling her mouth getting dry. "It's really quite reasonable. You see I... well... The apartment felt very empty. Like a museum, very vacant and so well, it seemed less cold if I slept here. I felt less alone. I didn't touch anything. Uh well, that's not quite true, but I didn't move anything." She held her hand up swearing truth to her words. "Everything is just where you had them. You're very neat and orderly." She said, aghast that she said it, and she was glad to feel the doorway behind her. "You see it's all quite reasonably explained." She smiled, nervously. "Well excuse me, I'm still dripping." She said, closing the door and leaving.

He stared at the closed door and began to grin as everything began to filter into his mind. "Jeneil, you are never boring." He laughed lightly, and went to his closet reviewing his whole entrance in the apartment. He smiled. "Well, things have improved on the home front. My wife has been sleeping in my bed. Maybe I should buy her a marriage manual so she can learn that she's allowed to sleep there even when I'm home." He laughed and shook his hand remembering her total embarrassment trying to explain it. "She a comic Goldilocks." He laughed again, as he unpacked his suits from the garment bag.

He went to the hallway. Jeneil was still in her room. He went to the bathroom anxious to shower after the pace of the day. There were globs of suds here and there and her mirror and bath brush sat on the bottom of the tub. He chuckled remembering her adding a glob of suds to an enormous column of white dripping suds balanced on her head. The door opened and she appeared at the bathroom door looking sheepish.

He tried to be serious. "Is it okay if I take your toys from the tub?" He asked, trying not to laugh, but not succeeding.

She smiled, relieved that he was taking everything so well. She laughed and went to him with a hug. "I'm glad you're home." He pushed her from him, gently.

"It's good to be home." He said. "Where's the furniture?"

"In Tecumseh." She smiled. "It's a birthday surprise. We're closing Monday, but they let us move in. We can go there tomorrow." She smiled, excitedly. "I'll let you take your shower." She was going to hug him again, but then remembered that he had pushed her away before. She backed away. "I'm exhausted. I'll see you in the morning." He nodded and watched her leave. Closing the door, he smiled and then turned on the shower.

Lying in bed, he could smell her perfume faintly on the pillow from where she had been sleeping. He smiled into the darkness as he reviewed what was happening. "Anthony." He said. "You and your parakeet have been a great help to me. I've got a difficult bird, too and I realize now what her food is. Love. She likes hugging and snuggling and being held. She thrives on it. So like you Anthony, I'll withhold the food until the bird comes to me, and I'll wait because she will have to make the move. That's the rule Anthony, just like your bird. The big move, Jeneil. It's too hard to hold onto celibacy when I get too close to you. So we don't hug, hold hands, or snuggle until Irish wakes up and decides to be a real wife." He was pleasantly surprised and very encouraged by his homecoming.

*****

Jeneil let him sleep until 10:00 and then knocked on his bedroom door. "Come in." He called.
It's moving day." She was excited about showing him the house and the car. She was anxious to begin her new life in Tecumseh. Like Camelot, she had the strongest feeling that Jeneil would taste life. She was ready for the change.

Steve acknowledged being awake and then smiled, still encouraged about their future. He had braced himself in New York to accept the arranged marriage, but he was deeply relieved that he might have a normal one yet. He knew that he loved her. He learned that in New York too. As annoyed and as hurt as he was, having Jeneil as his wife excited him.

Stopping for a quick breakfast they continued on to Tecumseh. "Welcome home, Dr. Bradley." Jeneil smiled as they entered the beautifully cultivated entrance with the understated sign saying Glenview. She kissed his cheek. He had made sure that he kept away from displaying affection, but it was difficult. Her excitement was infectious. Pulling into the driveway and parking, he sat back. "Well, this is it." He said. "Life in suburbia."

She handed him a set of keys and they took their few pieces of luggage from the Torrence.

"Let's go in through the breezeway." Jeneil smiled. Steve unlocked the door and they entered their new life there. "Will you put the Torrence in the garage?" She asked. "I think the remotes are in there."

"Well be using it later to go out." He said.

"I think I'd like it inside." Steve shrugged and went to the garage door entrance. Opening it he stopped then looked at her quickly breaking into a smile as he recognized the shape under the car protector. "Happy Birthday." She said giving him a kiss on the cheek and snuggling to him. It was difficult for him to remember to move away from her, the moment was electrical and he wanted to hold her close, very close. He moved away gently and went into the garage.

Jeneil followed and helped him uncover the beautiful, shiny, platinum colored SX7. "What a beauty!" He said in a hushed tone of reverence. He opened the door and looked inside examining every inch of the interior. Getting behind the wheel, he ran his hands over the dashboard and the leather seat. "Incredible." He said, still overwhelmed. "Steve Bradley owns a SX7."

Jeneil was standing by the front fender on the rider's side. She waved and held her thumb out like a hitchhiker. He laughed and unlocked the door. She got inside quickly and looked around. He watched her. She looked great in the car. He was right to get the deep red leather. "It is gorgeous." She smiled. "Congratulations, Dr. Bradley."

He smiled and couldn't stand it anymore. He put his arm around her and hugged her. "All of this is because of you, Jeneil. Thank you for all of it. I mean that sincerely." She clung to him aware that this was the first real affection he'd had shown her since being home. It felt so good. "No." She said. "You would have gotten it eventually. I just made it happen faster."

"Thank you for that then." He said. She smiled and enjoyed being held.

They wandered through the rooms on the first floor. Steve liked how she had done the decorating. Her trademark was there. Living green plants of all sizes. Long reedy trees and broad leafy rubber plants or clusters of basketed smaller pots throughout. It felt warm and comfortable. It was a big house and the plants filled areas of rooms or hallways, softening the bigness of them.

The doorbell rang. Steve and Jeneil looked at each other. "Already?" Steve said as they went to the door.

Barbara and Drexel Barnard smiled broadly as they opened it. "Are you officially here?" Barbara asked. "I saw all the workman yesterday."

"It's official." Steve smiled.

"Steve you devil. You disappear to a seminar on moving week."

Jeneil laughed. "Moving was my birthday surprise."

"Shock." Steve corrected.

"Oooo. Happy Birthday Steve." Barbara hugged him and kissed his lips, lightly. Jeneil watched and thought it had been awfully sensuous the way she brushed against Steve. Barbara smiled at Jeneil. "Careful dear, don't spoil him by making life easy, or the rest of the husbands get disgruntled and the wives get annoyed at you." A horn blew at the end of the driveway. All four turned.

The dark tinted windows to the black Brandon eased up and Kirk Vance waved. "Hey Barnard's, you're not home. Company's looking for you."

"We're welcoming the Bradley's and you're not company." Barbara called.

"It's official?" He asked, smiling.

"We've brought the first bottle of wine." Drexel said. "It's official."

Kirk Vance got out of his car and joined them at the door. "Well great. Welcome to Tecumseh."

Drexel laughed. "Get him, he's lived in his tree house for a week now and he's out playing Mayor."

Kirk shook Steve's hand. "Good to hear you're one of us."

Steve wanted to say he wasn't. "Thanks." Steve answered.

Kirk looked at Jeneil and grinned. "Hey Mona Lisa." His voice deepened and he concentrated on her eyes from under his thick lashes. "What a nice addition to the neighborhood." He leaned toward her placing his hands on her shoulders and kissing her cheek, gently. Steve watched him and then Jeneil. Kirk looking at her, stepped back. "Fun is always happening here."

Steve felt Jeneil move closer to him and slip her hand in his and he could tell that Kirk had done something. Jeneil was moving closer for protection. His jaw tensed. Jeneil knew she didn't like Kirk Vance. She couldn't believe how slick he was. The slight massaging of her clavicle as he held her by her shoulders and the way he ever so softly rubbed his chin across her cheek and breathed warmly on her skin before his light kiss had unnerved her. She didn't like him at all. "Hey Barb." Kirk smiled. "Is there room at your lunch table for one more?" He asked, slipping his arm around Barbara Barnard's waist.

"Always." Drexel smiled pleasantly.

Barbara looked at her husband and slipped her arm around Kirk's waist. "I'll do the inviting, thank you darling." She smiled broadly at her husband and winked, and then looking at Kirk she grinned. Just one more." She said. Jeneil watched all three, thinking that they were very odd people.

Drexel handed the bottle of wine he was carrying to Steve. "Welcome to Tecumseh, you two, here's a hello gift from the Barnard's."

"Thanks." Steve said, quietly.

"Yes, thank you." Jeneil smiled. "That's very nice of you." Barbara took a small envelope from her pocket and handed it to Jeneil smiling warmly. "We're having our usual Christmas party, please come. Excuse the invitation delivered this way. I knew you were moving soon and I didn't want it lost somewhere or catching up to you at New Years." She touched her cheek to Jeneil's briefly and smiled again. "I'll give you the numbers of my yard man and Hilda, my helper. Don't pass Hilda's number on, please. I know you must have the appreciation and understanding capable of dealing with domestic help. Good ones well trained and responsible are so hard to come by. I guard them like gold. She's wonderful and discreet."

"Thank you." Jeneil said and smiled, feeling guilty that she didn't like Barbara since she was trying hard to be so pleasant. Steve closed the door as they left and sighed deeply.

"Lets look at the rest of the house. The designer and I have worked out the terracing. I'm very pleased with the sketch."

Steve watched her and smiled appreciating the way she either ignored it all or never saw her neighbors clearly. "Oh this marriage will work. You can bet your ass I'm not letting go of this woman. Nobody ever called Steve Bradley stupid." He thought as they climbed the stairs and he hoped the marriage could be normal. "Everything is much safer that way." He thought.

"This is your bedroom. I bought the bedroom set from your old apartment. It's very fine quality furniture. We'll put the one at Fairview in one of the other bedrooms." And then realizing she was stampeding, she looked sheepish. "If that's okay with you, that is. It's your room after all."

Steve smiled, noticing the change in her approach. "Actually the bed is more comfortable. I like things this way."

"Fine." Jeneil said, relaxing

"You've had everything unpacked for me. This is great. This has been a lot of work for you Jeneil, I can see that. Thank you for this too." He smiled at her genuinely pleased with all she had done. She smiled at him and the warmth of their friendship was between them again as their eyes spoke the emotions that words wouldn't. Steve cleared his throat. "Where's your bedroom?" He asked.

"Just across the hall." She said. "I'll unpack my luggage and then can I go for a nice drive in the SX7?"

He smiled broadly. "Great idea." He picked up her luggage by the door. "I'll put it in your room."

"Thanks." Jeneil smiled and went to fix the drape that was unhooked.

Steve opened the door and stepped into her bedroom almost losing control of his breathing completely as he did. Jeneil came in behind him. "You can put the luggage on the bed." She said.

Steve threw both pieces hard to the floor, startling Jeneil by the sound. She turned to look at him. "Jeneil!" He said, loudly as the pain knotted his stomach. Discouragement and hurt flooded him as he saw her bedroom exactly as it was in Camelot. There was the bed she and Peter shared. Everything exactly as it had been in Camelot.

Anger raced through him. "When the hell will you wake up?" He shouted. Jeneil stared, completely frozen by confusion. Never had she seen Steve so angry. Never had he spoken to her so cruelly. Steve walked furiously to the bed and back again. "You're hopeless. Completely hopeless." He shouted at her.

"Steve." She said questionly, struggling to stay calm not knowing what was happening or what to say.

Steve stopped before her, still filled with anger. "What is this, Jeneil, a shrine maybe? You and your memories of Peter, all entombed up here?" His words shock her deeply. The scorn was unmistakable. No words came from her throat. He looked around. "Well I can see that your bedroom isn't finished. Where's the poster of Peter? Or are you going for a full wall picture of him this time? How about a life sized statue of him on a pedestal?" He walked past her to the door and then turned. "Go ahead, bury yourself up here with your memories, because that's all you've got. He's gone Jeneil. Gone." Steve shouted. "None of this will bring him back. Oh shit." He sighed and left the room.

Jeneil felt herself choking and tears spilled down her cheeks as Steve's words stung her. She heard the front door slam. She was deeply hurt by his words and his anger toward her. "What's happening to us?" She sobbed, sitting on the stuffed chair to gather strength. She thought about leaving, but didn't know where to go. This was home. There were no other nests for either of them. She looked around the room. "Why is he so angry? If he's so concerned about my memories, why be so hurtful, so cruel?" She cried softly, feeling totally foreign in her marriage and the husband who was a stranger to her. "He's been different since he came back from New York." She said, reaching for a tissue.

She sat on the chair for a half hour completely worn out from crying. Getting up, she went to the bed to lie down. She and her mother had planned the bedroom together working out the colors on paper sketches to see how they combined. She and her parents had worked together painting the room as a birthday gift for her 13th birthday. She always loved the design of the room. The colors felt right to her. "It had nothing to do with Peter." She said into the dimming light of the room. She cried softly and turned onto her side facing the pillow where he used to sleep and memories of him flooded her bringing deep pain. She got off the bed quickly, understanding what Steve was trying to tell her, only he thought it was deliberate and it was only lack of thought on her part. "I'll sleep in one of the guest rooms until I get my new bedroom set delivered. That's all that needs changing. Steve's right, it's not healthy, I can see that. But that doesn't explain his anger." She said, thinking everything through. "Well Tecumseh, I thought I would taste life here, but I never thought the taste would be bitter. She sat on the sofa chair again, thinking as the room became dimmer. Feeling chilled, she went down stairs to the kitchen to make some Ovaltine. Putting wood in the fireplace, she ignited the match and had a fire burning quickly sitting close by for warmth. Her strength returned as the warmth of the fire and the warm drink combined and the chill disappeared. She had had a chance to think trying to see things from Steve's point of view. Most of it seemed clear to her. He was concerned about her becoming entrenched in memories of Peter. That was understandable to her, but the anger had her puzzled. As near as she could come to a reasonable explanation was that he was over tired through something about the New York trip. When she asked herself what it might be, her mind suggested the possibly that the classmate he went home with wasn't a man. Women become doctors too. What had Adrienne called it, a "run in the paddock?" The feeling that thought uncovered in her was a surprise. She felt hurt as if she had been betrayed and yet she knew it might happen. She had told herself that he could tire of celibacy. It was a possibility she had considered in an arranged marriage. What left her shaken was the thought that he might want out of the marriage. Maybe he renewed a previous college affair and discovered that each felt more deeply now. She sighed. "Well he'll have to tell me wouldn't he? And I haven't given him the opportunity since he's been back from New York with all the twittering I'm doing about moving here. He's been very distant toward me since returning." Her stomach tensed realizing that she might lose him and yet her mind knew that he deserved love if he found it. She had expected that as a danger in an arranged marriage. She braced herself vowing to make it easier for Steve to talk to her. One thing she knew for certain was that the kind of anger she had seen in him was being caused by a deep feeling and she assumed it was over a struggle between finding love and not wanting to hurt her. "Poor Steve." She sighed. She looked up as she heard footsteps outside. The front door opened. She braced herself, determined to settle things. Steve headed upstairs. Jeneil went into the hallway. "Steve can we talk?"

He stopped. "Sure." He said, having expected to. He had prepared himself to hear her tell him to get his ass out of the house and the marriage after the way he had spoken to her.

Noticing that he had left the house in just a shirt and crew neck sweater, she thought he must be very cold. "I made Ovaltine. It's in the coffee butler still warm and I made a fire. You must be freezing." Her kindness surprised him. He thought she was too calm and he was surprised by that, too. She went to the kitchen for a mug and returned to the den where Steve was sitting on the hearth by the fire. Pouring some Ovaltine, she handed it to him and she felt how cold his hand was as he took it. She sat on a chair opposite him. He sipped; keeping his head lowered avoiding looking at her. Compassion filled her for him in his struggle. "I think I understand what happened Steve." Her words shocked him, he looked up surprised. "You're concerned that I'd lock myself into old memories, unhealthy memories. You're a good friend." She smiled. "I can understand that concern." He was staring at her completely shocked. She fidgeted in her seat. "What I don't understand is the deep anger. If something's wrong, we should talk about it." Her whole attitude was a total shock to him. He wondered what to tell her. He wondered if she was ready to hear it all. He looked down at the floor struggling with the thought of total honesty for a change. He wanted truth. He was tired of games and pretending. She watched him steadily and could tell he was struggling with something. "Steve, do you want out of the marriage?" She asked, and gripped the arm of the chair. He looked up quickly; completely surprised that she had even thought that. She noticed his reaction and assumed that she had gotten close to something. The question stunned him. "I'd rather have honesty." She said. The truth was in his chest and ready to surface. She felt for his struggle and wanted to help. She decided to reach out to him. "We've never talked about sex, Steve. Just that it wasn't necessary to our marriage." That comment jolted him too and he encountered the darkness surrounding the scene outside.

He sighed as his mind assessed everything. He remembered that she had said she'd rather have honesty. "You're not ready for my truth, Jeneil." He thought and I doubt that you ever will be. To you, I'm a good friend. I don't know why I have to keep having my head kicked in to learn it, but I know it now, Jeneil. I've learned my lesson." He thought. He turned to her. "Was there anything else?"

"No." She signed wearily. "I think I've said more than enough."

"Then I think I'll unpack." He went to the door and then turned. "I owe you an apology for the way I talked to you earlier. I'm sorry. It won't happen again. He left. "You can bet on that." He said to himself as he walked up the stairs. "She can sleep with a mannequin that looks like him and I'll stay mute. I'm finished with all this shit."

Jeneil sat watching the fire. "Robert, I wish I had your finesse in relationships. Life would be so much easier." She worried about Steve. He seemed different, more so.

She made dinner and called Steve who hadn't left his room since their talk. He wasn't hungry and planned to take a hot shower and go to bed early. He said he hadn't gotten warm yet from having gone out without a jacket. Jeneil sat in the diningroom picking at her food. "I never knew marriage could be so lonely." She thought.

She looked around the empty table. "What a delightful group of people you are." She smiled. "Cybil you're so sweet to come in from Nantucket just for my dinner. Oh you're too lavish with your praise dear, anyone can make chicken stew. Rutger, what a charmer, this old outfit, stylish. I love your diplomacy. What do you imagine is happening with the "Big Board"? Is it bearish or bullish this year? A "Red Herring"". She laughed. "That's a good one, Rutger. Your wit's as sharp as ever. "The Money Zoo." She laughed again.

Steve leaned against the door frame behind her listening to her entertain imaginary guests. He laughed silently and shook his head. "How the hell did I ever get hung up on her? She's totally off the wall. She's not at tilt, she's into complete tumble." He thought, going to her side. She looked up startled to see him. He smiled. "Is there room in this crowd for one more?"

She seemed very glad to see him. "Are you feeling better?" She asked.

He chuckled. "Well I heard that Cybil was coming in from Nantucket for the chicken stew and I figure that I must be missing something good."

She bit her lower lip. "You never seem to see me when I'm being normal."

"Anything's possible." He shrugged. "Maybe someday soon." She laughed and watched him as he sat down. "I'm not sitting near Rutger am I?" He teased. "He sounds like an ass."

She got serious. "I'm really glad you're feeling better." She said.

He smiled at her. "I couldn't miss this first meal in our new home. They only come once." She got up and went to him hugging him strongly and kissing his cheek several times.

"Oooo, you are so terrific. I love you." She said, squeezing him. He held her gently, not even fighting the electricity racing through him and wondering why this excitement of hers couldn't translate into physical. He sighed. "Jeneil, you are never boring."

*****

Sunday morning there was a brunch at Tiel's being held by Jeneil's Soho group. Steve eased the SX7 out of the garage and they pulled out of their circular drive and onto the streets of Tecumseh. The SX7 turned heads as it drove past. It was a money car and it looked it. The SX7 turned heads as they drove into the security protected parking area at Tiel's too. It turned the heads of Dr. Sprague, Turner and Young. The car was a show stopper and everyone dawdled to see who would get out of the platinum colored sports car with tinted windows. Steve was aware of the watchers as he opened the door and stepped out to heads stretching and turning discreetly to see who the owner's were. Opening the door for Jeneil, he thought how she matched the car. She looked beautiful and chic money.

"We seem to have an audience." Jeneil said in a whisper through tight lips to be discreet.

"Seems that way." Steve replied just as discreetly.

Taking his arm, Jeneil smiled as they walked toward the building. "Hey Steve, this ain't too bad for an ex-pickpocket and a hick from the mid-west, huh."

Steve held back the laugh, he wanted to bellow. "You know how to stay humble, Jeneil. You're good for me."

She smiled. "Mandra always told me that the trappings mean nothing, Steve. Everyone bleeds the same color blood, and you'll find some wealthy who was scum and some poor who are noble, so it has to be more than money that makes a difference."

Steve smiled. "Took her truth straight didn't she?"

Jeneil laughed. "She was quite a person."

Several doctors were at the brunch and word of the Lakeland plaza ownership being transferred to Bradley Enterprises was commonly known. By the time the food was served, the news that Dr. and Mrs. Steve Bradley had arrived in an SX7 was commonly known too.

Dr. Sprague joined them. He had been concerned about what he'd seen before the seminar in Steve. Of all his protégée's, he felt that Steve would always feel like his natural son and he wanted Steve's personal life to work well too.

"Dr. Sprague." Jeneil smiled, warmly.

"Jeneil." He returned the smile. "I appreciate your understanding about us sending Steve to New York on such short notice."

She shrugged. "I hear it's the nature of the business."

Steve grinned. "It didn't faze her Dr. Sprague; she just packed up everything and moved out of the apartment before I got back."

Dr. Sprague looked concerned, he had been wondering about trouble in the marriage. The glaring looks Steve had for Peter hadn't gone unnoticed by the older doctor and knowing that Peter was now divorced, he wondered.

Steve saw the concerned look. "It was a joke, Dr. Sprague. She moved us into the house in Tecumseh."

"Oh." Dr. Sprague said, relaxing. "Your lives are really settling in well then. Your becoming entangled, a new home, an SX7." He couldn't be sure, but there seemed to be a difference between them, a more formal relationship like you'd see after years of just being together in a marriage. He remembered his wife's observation about electricity between them and he couldn't see it now. In fact he thought the change was in Steve. They weren't holding hands and Steve never got too close to her. Dr. Sprague hoped it was due to being at a social gathering, but his instincts were indicating warning signals. He smiled at Jeneil. "Can I be really rude and wrangle an invitation to dinner at your place sometime? We senior doctors seem to get by passed in the parties. The Glenview bunch are really social. I guess they think we old guys nod off at nine. I've been known to stay up and watch the late news occasionally."

Jeneil laughed. "I don't think you're being rude. You're very special to Steve; we'd love to have you come to dinner. Wouldn't we Steve?" She said, touching Steve's back, gently. Dr. Sprague noticed Steve move away, slightly. "Of course." Steve smiled. "I'm still sitting at your knee." He said.

"Dinner soon, okay?" He said, surprising Jeneil by his pushing.

"Is next weekend open?" Jeneil asked.

"Let me get Carol so we can work this out. I'll be right back.

Jeneil watched him walk away. "Am I wrong or did he seem anxious to have dinner at our house." She asked.

Steve smiled. "Cybil probably told him about your chicken stew on her way back to Nantucket."

Jeneil chuckled. "You're not going to let me live that down are you?" She said, slipping her arm through his and leaning toward him.

He turned from her, moving away from her and caught Dr. Tufton as he walked by. "Glenn, I have a report on a procedure I think you'll enjoy. I heard that you have been talking about it to Read. John Blackford from Estes Clinic has applied some of your theories." Glenn Tufton stopped becoming interested in what Steve was saying.

Jeneil had noticed the way Steve seemed to avoid touching her or having her touch him. She wondered about it since he seemed fine otherwise. They talked easily, but she noticed that she was just Jeneil now too. He didn't call her, honey or sweetheart anymore. Dr. and Mrs. Sprague joined her and she became involved in the details of the dinner. As the Sprague's walked away Mrs. Sprague looked at her husband with annoyance. "Warren are you getting senile? You were pushing that poor girl for a dinner invitation. It was almost outrageous."

"I know." Dr. Sprague sighed, "Carol did you notice anything wrong between them?"

"Wrong? No. What are you talking about?"

He shrugged, "I don't know a coolness maybe. The electricity you noticed once, is it still there?"

"I don't know," She snapped, "I was too busy dying from embarrassment over your pushiness!" Her eyes got moist, "Warren, for gosh sakes, worry about your own stable." She walked away in a huff.

"Oh sheez!" He sighed, "We're off and running again. I'm rude, I'm pushy, I'm nosy, I'm old, I'm boring." He walked away to join Dr. Young and Turner.

*****

The house closing was held at three and Jeneil was so glad that Steve had spoken up about wanting to be present. He was really taking the whole thing very seriously. It was a special moment for him. She was touched and thought that it was curious for him to not like nesting, yet be deep into buying a home and then she realized the difference. Nesting to him meant the fussing over the house that's usually done. The details of landscaping, pest control and weeds were never going to be "his thing". She smiled to herself. She found that she was enjoying discovering things about him. His neatness, his lack of interest in anything except medicine, an anger that surfaced from hurt and enormous patience which impressed her quite a bit. He was becoming a fascination to her. Pocketing the closing papers inside his suit jacket, they left the bank and went to Danoli's garden for dinner to celebrate. The atmosphere was festive and Jeneil wanted to continue the evening by going to their Venetian Room where dancing was held. She loved dancing with Steve, she found him easy to follow and she was enjoying being held. His coolness and distance lately were a strain on her. The difference in his behavior toward her was becoming unnerving. By the end of the evening the deep closeness between them had returned he had even kissed her cheek and she hated driving home in two cars not wanting to interrupt the feeling. She hoped they could sit by the den fire and just talk, the relationship felt like a happy normal marriage. Steve had locked the SX7, closed the garage door and said he was tired. He went directly to his room leaving Jeneil alone and disappointed. She climbed the stairs to her room and discovered that she really didn't like the house. It's bigness was more of an emptiness. She and Steve seemed swallowed up in it. The Fairview apartment being smaller made it easier for their lives to interact. The Tecumseh house separated them. Each bedroom had its own bath and Jeneil began to look at Tecumseh like an apartment house where Steve had his living quarters and she had hers. She felt displaced and alone going down stairs to make Ovaltine she made a vow that she would get up early every morning to be with him for breakfast just to have a chance to talk to him. She missed their close friendship. She was concerned that they'd slip into becoming pleasant strangers because the house swallowed each into their separate lives. She became discouraged that life would feel empty. Steve seemed to spend a lot of time in his room. The telephone rang and the deep resonant voice was unmistakable. "Mona Lisa, Kirk Vance here. This Saturday night my house Christening Party. I'd like you to come."

Jeneil squirmed, "I'll see if Steve is free." She said. "I'll have him call you back."

"I'll hold, Mona Lisa, I'll wait for you."

Jeneil went to Steve's room wondering why she felt that everything Kirk Vance said to her had a double meaning. She knocked and Steve came to the door. "Dr. Vance is having a house christening party can I tell him I expect to come down with the smallpox that night?"

Steve smiled, "Not one of your favorites is he?"

She wrinkled her nose, "I'd rather have surgery unanesthetized if he'd have to touch me."

Steve smiled and then looked serious, "What night?"

"This Saturday." Jeneil answered and wondered why Steve seemed to relax. "We're not free are we?" She pleaded.

"Jeneil, house christenings are serious business around here. The only excuse is death or seminars which some doctors consider to be the same thing."

"Why are they so important?" Jeneil asked.

"It's a show of friendship. Suburban traditions become ritualistic. Not going is a slight."

She sighed, "That sounds like we're going."

"Sorry, Jeneil. We'll be expected to have one in about a week too."

Jeneil looked panicked, "I hate hostessing large parties. I hate putting them together!"

Steve smiled, "It's an informal thing, tiny food on trays and booze." He said.

Jeneil frowned, "I think I'll eat a can of horsemeat dog food. Maybe I'll get anthrax and be unconscious until new Years day."

Steve laughed.

"Oh my gosh, he's waiting for our answer." Jeneil said and ran back to the telephone. "Dr. Vance." She said breathless from running and having forgotten leaving him waiting.

"Easy Mona Lisa, why the heavy breathing? It sounds erotic." Jeneil made an angry face at the receiver.

"I'm used to living in small apartments, so when I headed back to the telephone I lost my way with all the extra home here and had to check the map I had the developer post on each floor for me. After searching all the closets downstairs, I finally found it and located the telephone, but I slammed the door on my finger from worry that I was keeping you so long and now my nail is blue and smashed and I'm out of breath from holding back a scream because I'm in pain. See Dr. Vance there's nothing erotic about it. My nail looks ugly something's oozing out from under it. I'd better get Steve to give me first aid."

Kirk Vance laughed, "You are one weird lady."

"Very," She said, "Quite odd. I'm going for testing soon."

He laughed again, "Are you coming to my party?"

"Steve said we're free so unless my finger gets gangrenous Dr. Vance we'll be there."

Kirk Vance chuckled, "You're going to be one hell of a kick around here." He laughed, "I'm glad you're coming Saturday and the name's Kirk."

"Yes Dr. Vance, I know that. I heard Barbara Barnard say it the other day."

He snickered, "You're something else, I wish I didn't have more calls to make, I'd come over and help Steve with the first aid."

"Well first things first." She said. "I understand. I'd better go too. I'm bleeding on the rug and I'll be up late now cleaning it. Thanks for invitingness. Bye." She heard him laughing as she hung up. "Ugh!" She said out loud, "I feel like I should be deloused." She shivered. She heard Steve laugh. She turned and frowned. "I'm not a very nice person when I don't like someone."

He smiled, "Hell makes me wonder what you said behind my back when you first met me."

She looked sheepish. "Well I misjudged you." She said apologetically.

He chuckled, "Hey just for your information, I checked the maps in the closets upstairs and I found a phone in my bedroom. Why did you run all the way down here?"

She moaned. "Did you hear that bizarre story? He irritated me. This house distracts me. It's too big. A phone in your room," She sighed. "Someday promise you'll come to the office and watch me be normal."

He smiled, "I came down for Ovaltine. Want some?"

"Yes," she said brightening, glad for his company. She wasn't ready for bed or sleeping and it felt like she had hardly seen him all day. They sat in the den with their drinks and she chattered. He watched her. Finishing her drink she yawned and leaned against his arm.

He got up. "I've had it. The ovaltine is working. It's time for bed for me."

"Me too." She yawned. "I'm glad you came back downstairs, I wasn't ready for sleeping."

They walked upstairs together she hugged him in the hallway by his door and kissed his cheek. "You're my favorite person and house owning partner." She smiled, "I like being with you." She kissed his cheek again and went to his bedroom.

Steve watched her close the door and he sighed, "You sexy spitfire, all that energy you wasted chattering. I wanted so much to shut you up." He put his head back and moaned, "This is serious. I'm in trouble. Now I'll be up for another hour doing sit ups." He sighed and went to his room.

Twenty-Two

Peter sat fingering the edge of the certificate that Jeneil had given him. Just what to do with it had played on his mind. He had not needed it when he had finished his residency to set up practice. Joining Dr. Maxwell as a partner has required very little money outlay. Dr. Maxwell's office was small. His staff included his wife, who ran the office, an assistant nurse, and a receptionist to answer the telephone, take appointments and an office assistant to do the filing and help out wherever necessary . The smallness of the office suited Dr. Maxwell and his lifestyle. Dr. Maxwell loved being a doctor which showed in his talent, but to him his family time was also important and he was determined to keep his practice personal and low-key.

Personal and low-key suited Peter just fine and that played a part in his decision to join Dr. Maxwell in his practice. To use the certificate to finance his partnership with Dr. Maxwell wasn't necessary since both men were on the same page as far as "smallness" was desired. His Stepfather Tom and his mother and her sisters had all gone together and insisted that Peter accept a financial gift that was more than sufficient to cover any additional expansion that was necessary to move him into Maxwell's office along with hiring his own assistant nurse. What to do with the certificate had been praying on his mind. His first thought had been to give it back to Jeneil. He really didn't need it and with all that had happened; he really didn't want it and the problem of having to deal with Jeneil loomed large, something he didn't want to do. Besides it was oblivious to him that she really didn't need it. Whenever he thought about the money the one thing his mind kept bringing up was the car. That $300.00 car has been a blessing and had come at just the right time. Jeneil had said "If you want to pay the full price for the car then turn around and do something for someone else when you are the 'have' and they're the 'have not' by being able to return the gift 'forward' and help someone else. The prospect of doing just that appealed to him as something he had always wanted to do, especially since he had been around Jeneil and had seen what she had been able to do accomplish in the lives of other people. He felt sure his decision to use the certificate and the money it would generate to help others would meet with her approval. He looked at the certificate and his mind gave acceptance to the decision that had been formulating. He would follow Jeneil's method. 'Surround yourself with good people and let them do their job.' She had said. Peter smiled at the thought. "And I know just who to get."

Peter went to the phone and dialed the number. "Peter!" Ron recognized Peter's voice, which surprised him because Peter had been conspicuously absent around the family since the Uette debacle and he had not talked to him. "What do you need?"

"Is it possible we could get together tomorrow morning about 8:30 at my apartment.. I'd like to discuss something that might be of interest to you."

"Sure, am I in trouble?"

Peter smiled. "Not as far as I know." Both men laughed.

Okay Pete, I'll see you then." Peter pushed down the button to disconnect the phone, listened to the returning dial tone then dialed again.

"Mr. Thomson, I'd like to meet with you tomorrow morning. 11:00am would be fine. I'll have an offer for you on the property. Good, I'll see you then. Thank you for your assistance in this matter. Your welcome, goodbye." Peter replaced the receiver on the telephone and smiled. "Okay Jeneil, lets see if I can get this to work for me."

*****

Ron stepped off the elevator and headed for Peter's apartment He was curious about being there wondering just what it was his cousin wanted. "While I'll soon find out" He thought as he rang the doorbell. Peter answered the door almost immediately and stepped aside as Ron entered and walked to the center of the room, looking around at the decor and furnishings. "Pete, this is a nice place you've got here." Ron was surprised at how well the apartment was put together and he was impressed with this former gang kid cousin of his.

I've made some coffee." Peter motioned for Ron to sit down at the dining room table as he brought a tray with the fresh pot of coffee, a couple of mugs, some cream and sugar and joined him. After a few minutes of catch up, Peter opened a folder and took out the certificate Jeneil had given him and handed it to Ron. Ron studied it for a few minutes and gave out a slow whistle when he realized the enormity of the face value. "I want to invest in some real estate and was going to use this as a down payment. My lawyer has suggested that I sit down with my accountant on how best to use this certificate. Since you are the only accountant I know, you're it. Advise me." Peter smiled.

"Pete, this is worth a lot of money. Just what were you going to use it as a down payment on?"

"This apartment building." Ron choked on his coffee at the response and he grabbed a napkin and wiped his chin. He looked a Peter long and hard before speaking.

"Why?" Ron asked.

"It's a high-end building with mostly executives and professional people as tenants. It recently came up for sale so I thought 'Why not.' At some point I'm going to have to get involved with investments if only to protect my income. Jeneil taught me that much. What do you think of it"

Pete, I agree, it could be a very good investment if the terms are right, but I wouldn't use this certificate as a down payment. It isn't necessary, The value of the certificate is such that you can hold on to it and use it as collateral. Other than that I would not want to give you anymore advice without first doing a thorough search for you which I would be glad to do."

"For us."

"Uh, what are you talking about."

"Us. You and I. Partners."

"Pete...I can't..."

"Yes, you can. I'm a doctor, a good one and I'm certainly not a financial genius. You once told me that you would be very successful and in demand if you were in China but because of racial bigotry you thought you would never be given the opportunity, so we'll bring the Chinese community to you. I need someone I can trust. I'm offering you a 50/50 partnership. We use this certificate and we see where it takes us."

"Pete..."

"My earning potential as a doctor is more than I'll ever need. I want to be able to help others in need. Someone who is struggling and just needs a three hundred car." Ron looked at Peter, his eyes starting to water. He didn't quite understand Peter's remark about the $300.00 car, but he understood the opportunity before him. "You're the expert, go do your stuff and make me some money I can give away." Ron was too emotional to say anything. He just extended his hand to Peter. "I'll reheat the coffee. We have a eleven o'clock meeting about the building with the realtor and I need to bring you up to date with what I have done so far." Peter got up and walked to the kitchen to reheat make some fresh coffee and with his back to Ron he broke out in a big smile. "Jeniel I just sold my first $300.00 car.

*****

Steve walked into Dr. Sprague's' consultation room to give him some reports. Bill Reid was standing by the desk. "Dr. Sprague I wouldn't be asking if it wasn't serious. My wife is livid about me leaving for the seminar. She wouldn't mind it so much if my parents weren't coming in for Thanksgiving."

"You'll be back Friday. Thanksgiving's next week." Dr. Sprague replied.

"I know, but my parents called last night and my mother wants to come in tomorrow to avoid the traffic on the roads. We just bought the house, Jenny's not settled in yet and my mother can be a heckler. Jenny's afraid she'll put the house together when she gets here."

Dr. Sprague sighed, "I'd go myself, but I'm tied at the hospital for the rest of the week."

"I'll go." Steve offered.

Dr. Sprague looked at him. "You just got back from a seminar over the weekend."

Steve shrugged, "I don't mind. Where is it?"

"Stonehaven." Reid answered.

"Oh that's not that far away." Steve said putting the report on Sprague's desk.

Reid laughed, "Not in the SX7. You can fly there in a half hour."

Steve laughed, "No you can't the State Patrol watch especially for sport scars."

Dr. Sprague was concerned, "Steve it's not even your field of study."

"Yeah but I'm finding that everything relates to me. The body's nerve network and I enjoy learning how other areas interact around it, and the advancements being developed. The terminology isn't so different and they always have reports to be taken home for study. I can pass it along."

Reid was excited, "Dr. Sprague I'd consider it the greatest of favors."

Dr. Sprague sighed and rubbed his face, "Okay." He answered reluctantly.

Reid smiled and patted Steve's shoulder, "Thanks Steve. You just saved my marriage."

Steve smiled and followed Reid to the door.

Dr. Sprague called him. "Steve, close the door. I want to talk to you."

Steve sat down.

"First off." Dr. Sprague began. "Assigning seminars is part of my job description around here. You took that out of my hands with Reid. Next time offer to go privately and let me decide."

"I'm sorry." Steve said, "It wasn't intentional."

Dr. Sprague watched him. "I could see that, you sounded anxious to get away as Reid was to not."

"Just trying to help." Steve replied.

"Ok Reid's wife is happy. Now what will yours say? You were away for over a week only three days ago. She'd have a right to chew my ass off."

"Jeneil won't mind." Steve assured him.

Dr. Sprague watched him closely. "Don't you think she should? You're still newly married."

Steve realized what Dr. Sprague meant he fidgeted. "Uh well," He stammered, "Jeneil understands business. She has to travel out of town a few days a month herself. She understands."

Dr. Sprague was dogging, "That's fine, but why are you volunteering? Is she away too?"

"Sheez." Steve said fidgeting in his seat, "If I had known I'd get this hassle, I wouldn't have volunteered." He laughed good naturedly. "What's the problem?" He asked.

Dr. Sprague grinned, "You're still the slipperiest son-of-a-bitch to sit across from me."

Steve laughed, "I'm not being slippery. I just can't figure the interrogation about my marriage. I said the seminar is okay. That should be it."

Dr. Sprague sighed, "Okay but Sunday when I have dinner at your house, you're tasting all my food for me first. I have only your word that Jeneil is a saint and won't mind this seminar."

Steve laughed and stood up, "She's okay about this, trust me. I know my wife. I have a patient waiting."

Dr. Sprague watched him leave and close the door. "Yes, you know your wife do you?" He laughed, "He's an expert in little over a month. Trust me Steve if your wife doesn't mind you being gone so much, the marriage is in trouble. Mine would like to have separate houses."

Jeneil sat at her desk feeling low. Steve had called to say that he'd be late because of emergency surgery and asked if she would pick up his suits at the cleaners so they'd be ready to pack for the seminar. He was due in OR so they hadn't talked long.

She sighed, "Another seminar."

Robert Danzieg knocked quickly and walked into the office sneaking through the opened crack. Jeneil's intercom buzzed quickly several times.

Robert ran to her desk. Jeneil chuckled, "Oh-oh you've annoyed Rachel." She pressed conference call. "Yes Rachel?"

"Jeneil, Mr. Danzieg walked right past me. Could you explain to him why appointments are so necessary."

Robert sat on Jeneil's desk, "Why are they, Rachel?" He asked.

Rachel stammered. "Mr. Danzieg there are two other people waiting to see Mrs. Bradley. They have appointments. How do you think they liked seeing you walk in ahead of them?"

"I don't know? Did you ask them?" He said.

Jeneil covered her mouth to keep from laughing.

"Mr. Danzieg, it really isn't funny."

"Rachel if I had asked for an appointment would you give me one?"

"Not today, Jeneil is booked solid."

"Well then I'm glad I just walked in. I won't take long."

Rachel sighed, "I'm turning the next appointment loose in two minutes Mr. Danzieg, two minutes."

"Love ya, Rachel." Robert said. Rachel hung up. "Hi." He smiled warmly at Jeneil.

"Hi." She grinned.

"How do you stand being such a puppet?"

Jeneil shrugged, "It's life. And Rachel is good at keeping me in order."

He took her hand, "Are you pregnant?"

"No!" Jeneil answered shocked, "Why?"

"Dennis and I wondered why you got married instead of just living with Steve. We thought you might be ready for breast feeding or something and Blondie would make pretty babies."

Jeneil shook her head, "You are crazy, invariant too." She smiled. "Also I'll ignore that insult."

He kissed her lips lightly. "When do we see the new house or is Tecumseh too exclusive for your old show biz buddies. Are you choking on all the stethoscopes yet? Why aren't you at the Rep? I miss you."

She smiled, getting dizzy from the barrage of questions. "Robert you are so refreshing. You put a knot in the conveyor belt."

He smiled. "Come sweetheart. This isn't your swing."

"Where is my swing, Robert?" She asked.

"Anyplace but here, Honey. Add some extra help if you have to and crawl out of this tomb. Your muse needs freedom."

She smiled, "Today that sounds tempting."

He watched her eyes and saw the sadness. "Why?" He asked.

"I'm weary of the conveyor belt. Tomorrow Steve starts a three day seminar. I've killed myself moving to Tecumseh. "

"I have a charity dinner tomorrow night. Come with me."

"Robert I'm married." She said standing and pacing.

"But he's away for three days. I've been out with married women to these dinners before. I'm between women right now, so I always take a married friend when that happens."

"Between women? Robert Danzieg you poor man what happened?"

"My true love married a surgeon when I wasn't looking."

She smiled and pointed at him. "You are such a liar, but I love you." She hugged him.

He smiled. "Hey you're different now that you're married. Free hugs and everything." He said holding her.

Rachel knocked, "Mr. Danzieg."

"I'm leaving Rachel, I'm leaving." He got off Jeneil's desk. "I'll call you tonight about the time. I have to check the invitation. Thanks Honey, you're good at these bleeding heart things. They make sense to you." Robert said walking backwards.

Jeneil smiled and nodded.

He smiled broadly and threw her a kiss. "Love ya Rachel." He said chucking her chin as he passed by.

Rachel rolled her eyes at Jeneil and shook her head, "If the world had more like him society would be in chaos."

Jeneil laughed. "Society needs his sensitive eyes, Rachel and his chaotic energy."

*****

Jeneil waited dinner for Steve, nibbling celery sticks to keep her stomach happy. He came home tired and care worn. "Why are there so many seminars for you?" She asked as they sat at dinner.

He didn't know how to tell her that he had volunteered or that the reason he volunteered was to have a break from tension of being home because celibacy was difficult for them since like every normal husband, he was in love with his wife and appreciated all her attributes, physical included. "I'm helping Bill Reid, Jeneil. They just bought a house and his parents are coming for Thanksgiving. His wife needs him." She nodded and stayed silent. "You don't mind do you?" He asked.

"Well I can understand the Reids needing help..."

He watched her, "But what? I hear a but."

She shrugged. "Well the apartment seemed so empty; I can imagine what this house will be like here all alone."

He smiled, "Jeneil are you saying that you miss me?"

She looked up, "Well of course, I miss you. I've told you that."

The telephone rang. "I'll get it. It might be the hospital. The patient's in ICU."

"Is Jeneil home?" The deep voice asked.

Steve was set back by the voice, he couldn't place it. "Can I tell her who's calling?" Steve asked, himself wondering.

"No thanks, I can do that." The voice replied.

"Okay." Steve said raising his eyebrows. Holding the phone close enough to be heard by the caller he turned to Jeneil. "A comic for you Mrs. Bradley." He said a little piqued.

Jeneil got up from the table and took the phone. "Robert." Jeneil laughed, "What have you done to your voice? What do you mean you don't want my husband to recognize it? Why?" she asked puzzled. Jeneil was quiet as Robert explained and then she broke into laughter.

"Smart ass." Steve mumbled and poured himself more coffee. "You're not going to get me Danzieg. That's just what you want. I'm wise to your game."

"What should I wear? Is it formal or semi? Oh that's easy enough, okay."

"Wonderful I get to go to a Danzieg party." Steve scoffed in a mumble.

"Fine then I'll see you at 6:30 tomorrow. Bye."

Steve put his coffee cup down having heard the day and time and realizing that he won't going. Jeneil returned to the table. "Robert having a party?" He asked.

Jeneil straightened her napkin. "No we're going to a charity dinner." Jeneil replied.

"We?" Steve asked not believing how casually she was saying it.

She nodded, "Robert and I." She cut into her fish.

Steve a stared at her. "You're my wife!" He said.

She looked up having heard his tone. Taking her napkin from her lap slowly, she swallowed the food in her mouth, "I'll call him back." She said quietly and went to stand up.

Steve took her wrist. She watched him silently, not moving. "Shit Jeneil, stop looking at me like that. I'm not going to beat on you. I lost my temper once. You're acting like it's a behavior pattern. I've never touched you."

"I'm sorry." She stammered, "I'm just…well you're holding my wrist tightly."

He let go quickly and sighed, "I'm sorry. Is that a rule of our arranged marriage? You get to go out with other men?"

"It's not going out. We're going to a charity dinner together."

"I thought we were going to be discreet?"

"Steve!?" Jeneil said completely shocked by the obvious insinuation. She stared at him and shook her head slowly. "Sometimes, I don't know you at all."

"Yeh well this marriage is getting confusing for me too." He said.

She studied his face for a second. "Do you want out?" She asked.

"You keep asking me that, Jeneil. Are you the one who wants out?"

"No." She replied. "What's happening to us lately? We don't seem to be doing too well. We're becoming strangers." She said, straining to not cry.

Steve pushed at the leftover food in his plate absentmindedly trying to calm down, he wanted desperately to tell her that he'd like to have as much fun with his wife as Robert Danzieg does, but he can't afford the freedom. He got up and went to the door.

"I'll cancel tomorrow." Jeneil said.

"No." Steve answered not turning around, "No. I don't want you to do that. I was out of line again, I'm sorry." He left the dining room and went upstairs. Jeneil sat back in her chair and sighed.

*****

The early morning sky looked bleak to Jeneil as she looked out the kitchen window. Steve put his luggage near the breeze-way door. She hadn't seen him since dinner the previous night. He seemed distant. "Your breakfast is ready."

"That wasn't necessary." He said.

"I wanted to." She smiled, determined that they wouldn't face a separation in anger. One thing she learned from the previous night was that they both wanted the marriage. They both said that much. She remembered the struggles with Peter too. She sat with Steve and drank juice. Going to the door with him she cautioned him about driving carefully and to watch the weather.

He nodded. "I'll be back late, late Friday, unless the weather messes up then I'll stay over. The information on where you can reach me is on my bureau."

She nodded. He went to pick up his luggage. "Can I have a hug?" She asked quietly.

He smiled and slipped his arms around her gently. She hugged him tightly and he pulled her to him holding her close and kissing her cheek. "Jeneil I don't want to hurt you. I really don't."

"I know." She smiled, "We're still adjusting to marriage and getting to know each other better." She said still clinging to him. "We'll work it out." She pulled away gently. "I'll miss you." She said.

"Me too, Honey, me too." He said touching her cheek softly. He kissed her lips quickly and picked up his luggage. He got into the SX7 and opened the window. He just watched her standing there letting electricity happen.

She smiled, "Don't let the car's power run off with you."

He smiled, "Never, I've been driving an SX7 in my mind for years. It's like breathing to me."

She nodded and waved, feeling very glad that she had made the effort to get out of bed early this morning. Things seemed so much better between them now. She noticed that he had called her Honey. She watched him drive off and she returned to the kitchen to clean up and began her day too.

She watched the sky throughout the day. The blackness stayed. Weather was going to happen. It was only a matter of time. She rushed home to get ready for the charity dinner, leaving a note on the unlocked front door for Robert to ring and walk in so she wouldn't have to run downstairs to answer. Hearing the doorbell, she went to her bedroom door. "Robert?" She called, "I'm up here. I'm almost ready." She said adjusting the pearls. "I think you're early."

"I am." He said heading upstairs. "What a place." He whistled.

"It's too big." She said, closing the door and while securing the hook on her dress she went into the bathroom to brush her hair. Robert knocked at the bedroom door on the right and walked in, startled that the room was dark.

"Hey," He laughed, "What's the game? Is this a case of rape, I hope?" He reached for the light switch and snapped it. Looking around, he saw the medical books and the desk. "Sheez. Did you have any say in this room? It's filled with Steve's stuff and nothing else. What a tyrant." He joked.

Jeneil watched him from across the hall. "Who are you talking to?" She chuckled.

Robert turned quickly, "I thought you were..." He stopped and then walked across the hall into the other bedroom confused.

"Let me get my bracelet. I left it on the sink." She went into the bathroom as Robert looked around. The room was obviously Jeneil's. He looked across the hall puzzled. "I've seen things marked his and hers before, but never on bedrooms for newlyweds. What's the game going on here?" He thought. Something felt very wrong and Robert wondered how to ask her.

"Ready." Jeneil smiled holding up her fake fur jacket, "I'm wearing my jacket so they can see that I'm doing my part. Do they serve meat at this dinner?"

Robert laughed, "Yep and don't ask them to explain it either. They can't."

Jeneil laughed. "Paradoxes are nice."

Robert smiled and wondered how to ask her. The surprise of two bedrooms had his thought lopsided. Then thinking it might be big trouble, he didn't want to upset her when she had to face an evening of smiling. He decided to let it pass and just wondered. He helped her put on her jacket and watched her putting on her leather gloves.

"Oh honey, now what?" He thought sadly, "One guy takes all you have and returns nothing but lies and now this one likes to sleep alone. What lousy luck have you tripped on now?" He remembered the sadness in her eyes the other day at her office. He went to her with a hug, surprising her.

She smiled, "Let's get there while the food's warm."

He smiled and took her hand as they walked down the stairs.

Barbara Barnard fluffed the drapes at her bay window and watched the front door open to the house across the way. "Dex." She said, "Didn't you say that Steve took the seminar in Stockhaven for Bill Reid?"

Her husband looked up from the paper, "Uh huh. Why?"

"Who owns a red Porsche?"

Drexel got up quickly turning off the lights. "What are you seeing?" He asked, joining her at the window. "Oooeee, she's dressed for fun. Well, well, well Robert Danzieg. Hey,

Mona Lisa still lets Robert play huggy, squeezy. Arm around the shoulder, a kiss on the cheek." The Barnards looked at each other and grinned.

Barbara chuckled, "And I thought she was too straight. Maybe Kirk's right, he said he gets vibrations from her that feel like sizzling jungle heat."

"What fun." Drexel smiled, "She has great legs and a touch that makes you forget that you're civilized. And if that's not just extra material up front, oh boy."

Barbara smiled at her husband, "Are you becoming hormonal."

He grinned, "Whenever the lights go out, you gorgeous creature."

*****

The black skies and overcast weather continued with snow predicted on Friday. Robert invited himself to dinner hoping to talk to Jeneil about her marriage. He and Dennis were both concerned that she wasn't running free in life like she should. And Robert hadn't mentioned the new oddity of a two bedroom marriage in her life. A light dusting of snow covered the ground when he got to the house. Putting a chartreuse colored paper bag on the kitchen table he then hugged her. "First snow." He said. "Let's go caroling."

"What?!" She laughed. "Robert this is Glenview. Madcap just isn't done."

"Well it should be; especially here. These science types have their vision distorted from looking at life through a test tube."

"I don't know Robert. I'm new here. We're not even christened yet. It's important to fit in."

"In what a straitjacket?" He grimaced, "That's it, I was kidding but hearing you talk about fitting in and madcap not done. Get your heavy coat on. I'm cutting your strings puppet. We're going out and be madcap."

"Where?" Jeneil asked smiling knowing that Robert had a real flare for kooky things that cut stress.

"Caroling." He said, "Up and down that Kilimanjaro slope you have out back. First one to slip and fall has to rinse the dishes and fill the dishwasher."

Jeneil wickedly grinned loving the idea. The snow was the kind with big fluffy swirling flakes that make you dizzy when you walk through it. Caroling up and down the snow covered slope wouldn't be easy. You could be out of breath from singing and climbing and dizzy from being surrounded by falling snow. "It beats getting drunk." She laughed, "You're on." She went to the closet for her heavy boots and toggle coat.

He smiled watching her warm to the idea. "Here's a hat for you." She said tossing him a neon orange knitted one that would cover his ears.

"Do you have one any brighter?" He laughed.

She put one on in neon green. "That's so I can find you in the snow when you slip and fall. I'll carry you home."

He smiled, "Show me."

She put on her gloves, "What's in the bag. Should I refrigerate it?"

He laughed, "It's not dessert, and you said you'd handle that." He went to the bag and opened it taking out a thin cardboard box. "It's one of my old cameras." He said, "I'm giving it to you."

"Why?" She asked watching him unbox it.

"Because I'm worried about you working all day in a tomb and living in a mausoleum."

She laughed, "They do feel like that sometimes."

"There you see," Robert smiled, "your muse is yelling for help. Look through new eyes Jeneil, please. Walk into the world of art using this to see through."

She looked at him and the camera and became fascinated. "Okay." She nodded and smiled, "I like that idea too."

Robert was pleased. "I'll help you set up a darkroom."

"A darkroom? Robert we don't even know if I'll take to it."

"Honey, you will and some of the "high" comes from watching what you saw emerge through the lens like magic on the print doing it yourself."

His description fascinated her. "Okay." She smiled. "Okay." She hugged him becoming ignited by the thought. "Let's hit the slope." She said laughing. "Dinner will be ready in an hour."

They began their trek down the slope singing jingle bells and each one slipped falling to the bottom. The game had to be played from then on with whoever could walk up the slope and get back home winning. They began the climb up the slope amidst the swirling snowflakes that made your face itch if they landed on it. They stayed with Jingle Bells since they didn't get through it on the slide down. The climb up wasn't helping. Jingle Bells became laced with giggles, chuckles and laughter as they struggled to climb the slope steadily. Robert began making progress and Jeneil cheated by crawling on her hands and knees to catch up. Robert had turned to protest as Jeneil went to hold onto him to stand up. They both slipped and laughed hysterically as they slid back to the base.

*****

Morgan Rand walked into the kitchen of his house as his wife was making dinner. "Do you hear singing, screaming and laughing?"

She nodded, "Yes, it just started a few minutes ago. Maybe some kids are playing in the snow."

"There aren't any kids in this area." He said taking a piece of lettuce.

"That's right then who is it?" She went to the back door and listened. "It's coming from the Bradley's. The flood lights are on." Morgan Rand joined her and watched the two figures tumbling down the slope. Sondra Rand smiled, "Well they'd better have their fun on that slope now because it'll be mud in the spring. She's offbeat isn't she?" Sondra said watching the two figures.

"She is different." Morgan smiled.

"I never would imagine Steve going for her type."

Morgan grinned. "She's very extraordinary. Jerry Tolman still talks about her."

"Oooo a little heartthrob, is she?" Sondra said.

"I think so. Would you like to know who I think her last boyfriend was?"

"Robert Danzieg?" Sondra said still watching the two figures struggle up the slope.

"No, Peter Chang."

Sondra turned around quickly, "You're kidding!" She said raising her eyebrows, "But…" She stammered. "Oh my." She said, "She is misleading. She looks so quiet and shy but the Chinese Stud, the White Stallion and Robert Danzieg." She grinned. "Well what do you know! And Steve and Pete are good friends aren't they?"

"Used to be." Morgan answered. "That's another clue."

Sondra rested her chin on her folded fingers. "Oooo Mrs. Bradley are you going to spice up Tecumseh." She laughed as she saw Jeneil grab hold and both tumbled. "Look at that." She laughed again, "She has Steve acting like a kid."

"They're newlyweds." Morgan reminded her.

"We didn't act like that when we were newly married." Sondra replied.

"Maybe we should have." Morgan said, putting his hand on her shoulder.

Sondra looked at him. "I'm leaving if you're going to whine. My carrots are calling me anyway." She returned to the stove. Morgan watched the two figures enjoying the silly fun they were having and then his face got serious as he remembered that Steve was at a seminar. Going to the front hall closet, he got his binoculars and returned to the back door and focused them on the two figurines. "Robert Danzieg." He mumbled to himself. "Oh, oh."

His wife looked up. "Oh gracious, Morgan, have you slipped to a new level of tasteless. That's voyeurism. Ooo you're such an oaf!" She slammed the cutting knife down.

"It's not voyeurism. I'm only checking something."

Sondra shook her head, "I'll just bet you are. I've noticed how much you like her legs."

"She's a spitfire." Morgan smiled, "She's struggling like a she cat to keep up." He laughed.

Sondra smiled too, "Good, this place could use a spitfire or we'll all die from boredom. Mrs. Bradley welcome to Tecumseh." She grinned. "Leave them alone, Morgan. You've heckled him for years."

*****

Jeneil and Robert laughed as they lay sprawled out one-third of the way up the slope breathless from laughing and struggling. Robert rolled onto his side laughing, "I think we need to change the rules again, and make it whoever can crawl up the slope and to the house is winner."

Jeneil faced him, "I think you're right." She laughed, "We're turning this into ice."

Her face was wet with snow and red from the cold air. Robert thought she looked beautiful. Moving closer to her, he put his arms around her and leaned to her for a kiss.

Steve stood at the top of the slope watching. He had heard the laughing and had gone to the backyard to investigate when he got in. Anger filled him as he saw Robert move toward Jeneil. He was going to leave and then he stopped, curious about Jeneil. He stayed. Jeneil sat up quickly, "Robert no kissing, I'm married."

He took her hand, "Jeneil." He began wanting to ask about her marriage.

She stood up, "Robert dinner will burn. Let's get back." Steve smiled and moved away returning to the house. Jeneil smiled at Robert. "I'm going to walk up this slope. It's positive thinking Robert and assertiveness." And she began to walk steadily up the slope.

"Hey that's great!" Robert said and got up to try. "This is a lot easier." He said copying her pattern of walking sideways. He soon caught up and began to pass her. He nudged her slightly and she screamed, "No, no I'm almost there. Don't push me." She said concentrating very hard to stay steady. Robert kept climbing and got to the top. Jeneil begun slowly inching her way. "I feel some slipping." She said. "I'm too tired. I can't climb up again. I have to make it this time." She banged her foot into the snow more solidly and moved slowly to the top. "Oh, oh," She began to scream. "Robert catch me, please!"

Robert extended his hand as Jeneil threw her gloves to the top so she could hold on to him. He locked one hand around her wrist and she finished the climb. Steve watched from the kitchen window as Jeneil picked up her gloves and Robert picked up Jeneil tossing her screaming over his shoulder. "Woman, I'm hungry. Let's move this show indoors." Jeneil laughed as Robert headed for the house.

Steve moved away from the window fighting resentment. He and Jeneil used to act that way before they were married. He missed the fun. He missed her and he resented Robert for providing the fun that he had to withhold from her in their relationship.

The kitchen door swung open and Robert walked in with a laughing and struggling Jeneil over his shoulder. "Hi Steve." Robert smiled broadly seeing him standing by the table.

Jeneil struggled to lift up straight and look behind her. "What? Steve? Where?"

"There." Robert said turning around to face her the other way. "There's Steve." Robert said.

"Hey!" She smiled broadly balancing herself against Robert's back. "You got home. I thought you'd be snowbound, I heard that the northern states got a heavier snow. I'm glad you're home safely."

"That's enough." Robert said turning again and facing Steve with Jeneil facing away.

"Robert!" She laughed, "Put me down."

"I can't," He said, "You're frozen to my shoulder."

"I am not." She laughed.

Steve watched unsmiling as Robert teased him using Jeneil.

"Robert enough now put me down." Jeneil insisted, hitting him good naturedly.

"Can you cook if I move closer to the stove? Like this?" He said facing Jeneil to the oven while he faced Steve.

Jeneil opened the oven door and checked the meatloaf and baked potatoes. "Dinner's ready." She said.

"Great." Robert smiled, "Let's take our clothes off." He walked toward the small anteroom with the closets.

Jeneil smiled at Steve as they passed by, "I'm glad you're home." She said balancing against Robert's back. "You can't argue with him when he gets like this. You just let him finish at his own speed." She threw Steve a kiss and smiled, "I love you." She said disappearing into the anteroom on Robert's back. Steve shook his head and smiled. Her hair was in wet spikes and ringlets around her face which was bright red with cold. The lime green knitted hat was half off her head.

"I can't believe this marriage." He laughed to himself. "I'm away for three days and when I get home I find my wife making like a snow bunny with another man. She passes by on his shoulder and says I love you and my heart flips over with appreciation. Tilt is outrageous." He chuckled.

Jeneil and Robert came from the anteroom still looking wet. Jeneil put her arms around Steve's waist and he held her to him kissing her cheek. Robert watched them closely. "Was the driving rough?" She asked looking up at him.

"I left early when I heard the weather report."

"Oh good." She squeezed him and his heart flipped over again. She moved away kissing his cheek as she did. "I'll put dinner on the table." She said going to the stove and he knew why he had to get away for a few days now and then or go crazy. She was wearing a pair of old jeans that were worn in just the right places and a black turtle neck sweater. She had a great body and really showed it. She usually wore flowing or draping clothes or layers of them. Seeing her body as uncovered as jeans was a pleasant sight. Robert watched her taking her all in too and Steve was surprised that he wasn't angry. She looked too good and you expected men to look and appreciate her. He couldn't get angry about how she looked. She busied herself setting the kitchen table with a place setting for Steve and noticed them watching. "What?" She asked stopping.

"We're watching your body." Robert answered and Steve wondered where he got the nerve.

"Oh." She said and went to the stove to get the food.

Robert laughed and shook his head, "Oh." He repeated her words mimicking her. "Somebody made a mistake with her." He said going to the table. "She should have been a bimbo, but everything with her arrived well developed including the brain. Total waste," He sighed. "She could have been God's gift to men." Jeneil went to the anteroom. Steve sat at the table and they waited for Jeneil to return. She walked in firing the sleeves of a long baggy light blue sweater she had gone to put on over her black one.

Jeneil smiled, "Now you can watch my brain." She said, passing the platter of meat.

"Aw." Robert pouted.

"Big mouth." Steve said softly. Only Jeneil heard him since she was sitting between the two men at the table. She stared at him. Steve looked at her steadily and then grinned. She smiled, passed the green beans to him and wondered.

*****

The weather warmed and the snow disappeared the next afternoon. Visibility had been poor earlier in the morning and skydiving had been cancelled, leaving Steve with pent up energy and restlessness. Having looked for her through all the downstairs rooms, he climbed the stairs and knocked at her bedroom door and she called to him to enter.

"Hey," He smiled, stretching his head inside, "What are you doing for fun today? I'm going crazy. I even went out and picked up bits and pieces of stuff outside that the workmen left." Two corrugated boxes were near her bed. It was covered with papers. "What are you doing?" He asked coming inside and sitting on a corner of her bed.

"I moved so quickly that I didn't have time to get rid of excess baggage." She grinned, "We're not all like you. This is called junk Steve it accumulates when people don't watch carefully. You wouldn't know about that."

He smiled, "Just how thoroughly did you tour my room while I was away?" He teased and she chuckled. "Jeneil I think we need an intercom system in this place. I was looking all over for you."

She smiled and nodded, "We get lost in this house. It swallows us up."

"You're going to need help." Steve said, "This place is too big for you to clean alone."

She nodded, "I've taken care of it."

"Who; Barbara's woman?"

"No, I noticed a need at Fairview 1900. Busy people need maid service, so I started one. One of the women in my building cleaning crew was outstanding. Orderly responsible and cared about her work. I had her choose four good people and I put her in charge. Adrienne oversees it for me. They're like an army of pest control people. In and out in no time. They take my salary from Alden-Connors since my rent is no longer concerned. They don't have to be discreet they're too fast to be around long enough to see what's happening in the people's lives. You're so neat we don't mess up a house. I just need furniture polishing and vacuuming done and general cleaning."

"What about the yard?"

She shrugged, "It's dormant right now, but I think I'd like to do it."

"You!" Steve raised his eyebrows. "That's worse than the house."

She smiled, "I love the yard. I'll try until I'm sure I can't."

Steve smiled, "Well you've got things under control. What about the open house here?"

Jeneil looked up from sorting papers. "Once my blood pressure returned to normal I approached Millie, the manager of my Domestic Engineers Co. She used to work for a caterer. If I provide the recipes, she said she'd see that they get prepared. I've got my mother's own cookbook. She and Dottie will be here that night to look after the food and the buffet table." She smiled like she'd just eaten a delicious morsel. "I trust her. It's keeping me sane. She knows a bartender, are you interested? She said he shows up in a van complete with portable bar that he insists on bringing."

"Hell yes." Steve answered quickly. "A Tiel person is usually around at parties heating Tiel's catered food for these things, but that's been it for help." He smiled at her, "I know that all this horror is in your life because of my career. I think you're terrific for faking it."

She smiled, "Maybe I'll get even some day."

He laughed and then noticed a box of small square papers before him. They were grades for courses she had taken. "Why are they all separate and not in a transcript?"

"Because I wasn't matriculating, Steve, just studying."

Steve was shocked, he went through the papers quickly. "Jeneil, you took all these courses separately?"

She nodded.

"You must have enough here to have earned a degree!"

"I don't know, I never looked into it." She said.

"But you should!" He insisted, "This is crazy. You're probably graduated and don't know it!" He looked at her, "Jeneil you're going to check into it."

She smiled, "Hey, stop stampeding." She laughed, enjoying getting even with the weakness in him too.

Steve was undaunted, "How can you do all this studying and not apply for a degree?"

"Because I care about studying, I don't care about degrees."

Steve sighed looking at the papers. "Look at the grades you got. Holy..." He looked at her, "You will take these to the University and apply for a degree."

She was surprised by his attitude, "What's wrong, are you having trouble accepting a wife who's a college dropout without a degree?"

He was stunned, "That's shit." He said, "Don't do it then who cares." Each backed off from a confrontation and within a few minutes peace was between them again.

"Would you please choose my outfit for the Vance party? You've been to these things. You know what's worn."

He smiled, "Sure." and went to her closet. He returned with a steel grey wool suit.

Her brow wrinkled deeply, "That's militant. I only wear that to meetings where the men think I'm too young to know anything about business. It's a tough cold look. It's a costume."

Steve smiled, "Sounds, great."

"Stop clowning." She chuckled, "Tell me if the women wear short or long dresses and I'll choose for myself then."

"They wear slacks." He said knowing that she didn't.

"Fine. I have a plum colored wool pair."

"No." Steve said quickly, "No. Don't wear slacks."

She looked up concerned, "What's the problem." She asked. "Do they wear anything and everything is that why you can't decide?"

"No." Steve sighed, "Jeneil please don't wear slacks or designer jeans."

"I don't even own designer jeans." She said.

"Wear a layered outfit. They look great on you." Steve smiled, "Lots and lots of layers and loose so you'll be comfortable."

Jeneil stood up, "I'll choose something, thank you."

Steve followed her to the closet. "Not the neat dress with no back that you wear with the clave bracelet that's not good either."

"That's too summery, anyway." She said.

"I'll let my inner self decide how I feel when it's time to go. Boy you usually have no problem choosing something. Is this party that important politically?" She asked.

"No." He said realizing that she didn't understand. "Jeneil, let's go have some fun. Don't you know of a gallery opening or something? Is the world asleep today?" He asked.

She looked at him. "Wow, you're in a cage aren't you?"

"Yes!" He said, pleased that she understood and had given his mood a description. "I am. I need out. I don't care if it's just for a walk."

She looked at the papers on her bed. "Okay help me put these papers away and I'll get ready."

"Great!" He smiled going to her bed and picking up a neat cluster of papers. "How do you want this done?" He asked.

She grinned mischievously, "Just like this, exactly, like this." She said taking the papers from him. "You stand near the box, you hold the papers waist high and then drop them inside." She let the papers flutter and scatter into the box.

He raised his eyebrows, "But they were all sorted!" He said looking shocked.

Jeneil chuckled, "I'll survive Steve. Can you manager to create that kind of a mess or will the pain be too excruciating?"

"Shut up." He laughed good naturedly. He took a pile of papers and held them over the box. Steve began to laugh, "I can't." He said, "I really can't."

Jeneil laughed and kissed his cheek as she hugged him. "Poor Stevie you've been eaten up by the conveyor belt."

"Jeneil." He pleaded. "Don't make me do this." He laughed. "I'm bad, I admit it. It's phobic."

They both giggled as they held each other and then Steve became aware of her softness and warmth. Her perfume began to smell too good. He moved away gently. "Oh boy," He sighed, "You've shown me what a fanatic I am and I suspect it was deliberate."

"Stevie would I do that?" She teased looking innocent.

He grinned at her and nodded, "I'll make a deal with you," He laughed, "You get ready and I'll put the papers in the box according to your piles."

"Okay Stevie B." She said going to the closet, "Go neat yourself into a frenzy." She giggled. "Have fun." He smiled and began sorting the papers into the box for her.

*****

Jeneil packed a quick lunch and picked up the camera Robert had given to her. They went to the large central public library and toured their 2nd floor of displays on art to whaling. Jeneil went to business industry and science to check some statistics. Noticing a poster announcing a children's group appearing in the small theater in an hour, she took Steve's hand and wound her way through rows of books to the recesses of the library in the far corner where a row of shelves didn't quite go to the wall leaving a small nook. She got on the floor and backed herself inside. "Come on." She whispered to Steve.

"What are we doing?" He asked stooping to the floor.

"We'll have lunch here." She said quietly, "and then go to the theater. It's free and usually very good."

"We won't both fit in there." He said.

"Yes we will. Come on." She insisted.

Steve backed into the small nook chuckling to himself as he realized that he hadn't sneaked off into a cranny with a girl in ages. The home was full of them. He remembered learning some great things in nooks and crannies. Her idea became fun to him. Jeneil opened her purse and brought out lunch of nut bread and cream cheese sandwiches and oranges with shelled peanuts.

"How do you know about his place?" He asked.

She smiled, "It was one of my favorite reading spots." They talked and Steve actually liked being all snuggled up in the nook with her. She had gotten him out of the cage and he was relaxing. Jeneil separated the sections of orange to share with him.

"You are offbeat. Jeneil and I love it."

She smiled. Steve noticed the brown loafer first and wondered how to tell Jeneil. Two brown loafers stood in front of them before he had a chance to tell her. She looked up. "Stanley!" She smiled obviously happy to see a thin man who was wearing them.

"Jeneil?" The man questioned in quiet surprise and stooped down. "Jeneil!" He smiled just as pleased to see her. "You've cut your hair! You look so different. It's been a long time. I wondered what happened to you. I thought you might have gone back to Nebraska." The man joined them on the floor easily like he'd done that often and Steve wondered if that's how Jeneil knew two people would fit in the nook. Jeneil offered food to the man without words and the two kept talking. The man ate a nut bread sandwich not even taking notice of Steve.

"What are you doing here?" The man asked pushing his dark rimmed glasses onto his nose using one finger. He smiled warmly at her and Steve could tell that Stanley had experienced deadly.

"We're going to the theater and there wasn't any time to leave the building for lunch. Were we too noisy?" She asked.

"No." He smiled. "I smelled the orange. Nobody but you ever ate oranges in here. First I thought I was imagining it then I came right to the nook." He smiled warmly again.

"Did you get your degree in Library and Administration Science?" She asked.

He nodded, "I'm working on my masters now."

"Great." Jeneil smiled, "What happened to you and Heidi?"

"We're still going out."

Jeneil grinned. "Going out? Stanley do I have to propose for you too?"

Stanley laughed, "No I've proposed. We're waiting for me to finish my masters."

Jeneil smiled, "What's Heidi doing?"

"She's a nutritionist at the zoo."

Jeneil sighed with relief, "With her major I thought she was going to end up on the range in Africa or something and I worried how you'd get a library job out there in the brush."

Stanley laughed, "You're still crazy. Did you go back to college?"

"No I'm working on my masters in life."

Stanley liked that joke too and Steve smiled watching the two of them together. "You'd better get going or you'll miss the opening of the theater." He squeezed Jeneil's hand lovingly with two of his. "It was so good to see you again. Heidi and I wonder about you from time to time. It'll be good to tell her you're well." He looked at Steve and Jeneil realized she hadn't introduced them.

"Stanley Cole this is my husband Steve Bradley."

"Husband?!" Stanley beamed, "How nice. Heidi will love that too." He shook Steve's hand. "Mr. Bradley it's a pleasure to meet you. You look pretty normal. Heidi and I always thought Jeneil would marry someone unusual. She was very offbeat and artsy."

Jeneil laughed, "He is unusual Stanley, he's chained to the conveyor belt and he understands them."

Stanley laughed, "Conveyor belt. Gosh I haven't heard that term since I last saw you. We remember your advice though Jeneil."

Jeneil looked embarrassed, "Oh gosh did I preach too?"

"Sure did. You told us to slip off the conveyor belt now and then and we still do. It keeps us sane."

Jeneil laughed, "Me too."

Stanley got to his knee to stand up. "I'd better let you get to the theater, but gee it was great seeing you again. And meeting you too." He added as an afterthought to Steve. Stanley left and Jeneil gathered up the remains of lunch and shared the wash cloth with Steve. They headed to the theater.

"How did you meet Stanley?"

Jeneil chuckled, "Eating an orange in the nook. He caught me and read me the riot act. These books are his children and he yelled at how I was going to damage them by my carelessness. We got to know each other and I brought an orange for him after that. He was so shy. He'd blush more easily than I did. We'd go out for a sandwich now and then. One day I noticed that a very tall blonde girl kept watching Stanley. She was just like Stanley and me, shy and blushing. I was the most outgoing one. I became curious so I got to know her too. She liked Stanley a lot. I played cupid which wasn't easy because Stanley was pinned onto the conveyor belt. Heidi is taller than Stanley and was studying animal husbandry. Conveyor belt Stanley was looking for someone less tall and brunette and with feminine domestic shells, a home "ec" major." Steve smiled realizing that Jeneil fit Stanley's order. "Whenever Heidi was here I would ask them to go out for a sandwich with me. Heidi is very smart and she knew how to capture and how to train the animals. Stanley didn't have a chance once I invited them out for a sandwich and then pretended that I'd forgotten an appointment which left them alone. They're both smart and they knew that I had set them up. But Heidi knows animals. She just needed the opportunity and Stanley needed the attention. He looks great." Jeneil laughed with delight. "I love happy endings." Steve smiled and held the door for his artistic offbeat wife as they headed for a free performance at a children's theater. He laughed to himself realizing that his cage had been blown to bits. From the theater they went to an arboretum where Jeneil wanted to photograph late afternoon sun angles. Robert had offered to let her learn developing at his studio until she got her own darkroom which didn't sit too well with Steve, but he was curious about what she'd had photographed since he didn't see anything interesting in the arboretum.

Twenty-Three

Jeneil started to develop jitters about the Vance party after they had left the library for home. "I can tolerate parties with a purpose, but the ones with no purpose...ugh. A house christening doesn't seem to have a purpose. I can't imagine how a newspaper reporter would find anything there."

"What?" Steve asked confused. "What reporter?"

"I pretend to be a reporter at parties."

Steve laughed, "You really struggle with life don't you?"

"Are parties' life?" She asked.

Steve laughed. "I'm not saying. You'll begin a philosophical dialogue on me."

Jeneil smiled. Dinner was fixed quickly by both of them and then Jeneil faced the task of preparing to go to the party. She brightened as Nebraska took a seat and Jeneil became curious about why she hated going to this party. She imagined Dr. Vance's place would be like a huge evil castle of torture. Then she became curious wondering how accurate she was. She sat brushing her hair which was at a very difficult stage of growth. One section of the front hair would try to wave and would spill over her eye then flip back. She shook her head after trying different things. "Have it your way." She said to her hair getting up from the mirror to choose her dress. "Inner self what will it be?" She thought facing her closet. "I don't want to be there so something wallpaper so I'm not seen."

Steve put on his sweater and fixed his shirt collar wondering about the party. He was uneasy lately sensing that the group seemed to react to him like the White Stallion days. To him, those days were gone and he didn't miss them. He wondered who he was and where his life was going then. That wasn't the case any longer. He was dealing with boredom, but he liked Steve Bradley and knew him much better since his probation, celibacy and... He smiled. "Meeting Jeneil." Marriage to her wasn't easy, but being with her was still a kick. He wondered what she would wear and then he became concerned. Going across the hall quickly, he knocked. "Jeneil what are you going to wear?" Jeneil looked at the closed door surprised by Steve's question.

"Doesn't he trust my taste?" She asked going to the door as she tied her robe. She opened the door quickly, "Okay out with it." She said. "What's the problem with what I wear? No slacks, no jeans, no rust dress. What's wrong with my clothes?"

"Nothing." Steve said trying to make light of his question. "I just wondered."

"Oh." Jeneil said going to her closet. "My inner self chose a "nothing" dress." She held up a deep ivory colored dress with long loose sleeves gathered at the wrist. The neck was a slight scoop. "It looks apolitical to me." She said.

Steve smiled it was a nothing dress. It showed nothing. "It's great." He smiled again and relaxed. Even the shirt was gathered and loose. He really relaxed. "Just her legs." He sighed to himself and then he understood why Peter fussed so much about what she wore. He waited in the den for her to finish dressing. Jeneil walked down the stairs quietly. She could see him from the landing. "He looks so nice in whatever he wears." She thought noticing the way the sport jacket and pants looked on him. Steve turned hearing her at the door and caught his breath. She looked like something in the nothing dress. Mostly she looked fragile and innocent, and lately her hair would fall partially covering one eye looking soft and gently. Between the softness and thickness natural of her hair and the way the dress skimmed her body, she looked enticingly touchable. "Oh shit." He mumbled to himself. She noticed him watching. "I know. It looks very plain. It's a nothing dress. If the ladies are all sparkling, I'll slip away, pull out some jewelry and add it to the outfit." She held up her purse to indicate that she carried them.

"It's fine." He said surprised that his voice worked.

"After I put the dress on I realized that I had wanted to fix the hook on the back. The thread loop keeps slipping out. Will you fix it?" She asked tossing her purse to the sofa and turning her back to him.

"Fix it?" He asked, "How?" The hook was undone exposing some of her back. Her perfume lingered like a cloud close to her.

"Bite it." She said. Steve caught his breath. "But gently." Jeneil added. "It won't hold the thread loop. It just needs to be closed a bit. Look at the hook, you'll understand what I'm saying. If I do it, I'll have to take the dress off, that messes up my hair and I'll need to take my lipstick off too. It's less complicated if you do it."

"Right." He said reaching for the hook.

"Understand now?" Jeneil asked.

"Yes." Steve answered moaning inwardly about injustice he had to get close to her neck to put his teeth on the hook. It was her softness that always got to him the fastest and being that close to her the softness enveloped him. From the softness of her hair, to the skin and dress, he was getting dizzy from softness. He concentrated on the hook biting it quickly and moving away to breathe again. She hooked the thread loop smiling as she turned around.

"Its fine now, thanks."

"Sure." Steve smiled slightly.

"I'm ready." She shrugged.

"Sure you are." He said. "I'll get our coats." He went to the closet hoping the electricity could stop soon.

*****

Kirk Vance lived off the developed area of Tecumseh at the back of a lot full of trees. The long paved driveway was well lit by flood lights closer to the house. People were parking off the driveway on the cleared shoulders. Steve and Jeneil walked toward the house quickly. "He must have a lot of parties."

"How do you know that?" Steve asked.

"This is planned parking. He's fixed the shoulders to accommodate a lot of cars."

The house was vertical wood-stained, blending in with the tree trunks around it. The modern design seemed to fit in with the trees. The front was a wall of glass. The opaque drapes were closed and Jeneil could distinguish light of a chandelier in the distance behind. "Not an evil looking castle." She smiled to herself. "It's really interesting. It has warmth and charm so far." She thought. Steve rang the doorbell. Jeneil took his hand. "Nervous?" He asked.

She nodded slightly and her hair slipped to her temple close to her eye. Steve smiled and touched the wave gently pushing it back slightly. It felt soft. Leaning forward he touched his lips to hers. They felt soft too. Kirk Vance opened the door Jeneil and Steve were startled.

Kirk laughed, "Sorry I scared you, but you did ring my bell." They stepped inside. Kirk waited for them to remove their coats. "Hey you two are real fun." He said in his deepest voice. "Kissing games at the front door. I like your style Bradleys'."

Jeneil lowered her head embarrassed as Steve helped her off with her coat. Kirk put them in the closet as he watched Jeneil who still hadn't looked at him. She busied herself straightening and studying her cuffs.

"Interesting house." Steve smiled. "Very nice."

"I love it." Kirk answered watching Jeneil. "Mona Lisa." He said touching her chin to lift her head. Jeneil looked up and pulled away from his hand gently slipping her arm through Steve's. Kirk grinned and nodded slightly looking her over. "Nice look." He said. "Very nice."

Jeneil slipped into composure. "Your house seems to have oneness with the trees, like it's come to join them, not disturb them. It was an interesting study as we walked up the drive. I think it's amazing that you have mature trees growing so close to the house. I heard the chain saws working here and I thought of the damage but there's no evidence of building here. Like the house has grown from the ground like the trees. The architect must have had deep feeling for the design. It's sensitively placed on the land. Who was your architect?"

Kirk Vance studied her face with a serious expression on his for a second or two and then he smiled warmly. "I designed it." He said almost shyly. Jeneil was stunned. "Why are you surprised?" He asked.

"It's rare to see Art and Science combined. Have you studied design?"

He shook his head. "No. I've always wanted a house that nestled into the forest."

Jeneil smiled. "But you didn't build a log cabin."

Kirk Vance chuckled, "I like vertical lines. Not every house in the forest is a log cabin."

"I know," Jeneil grinned, "Hansel and Gretel found one made of gingerbread."

Kirk Vance leaned forward in a laugh raising his eyebrows at such a dumb remark being placed into a serious conversation. "Mona Lisa you're weird." He laughed. Steve looked at her and smiled.

"You've designed a beautiful house." Jeneil said sincerely.

"Thank you." Kirk Vance smiled. The doorbell rang. "Feel free to have a look around."

"I'd like to." Jeneil said as she walked away with Steve. Kirk watched her walk away as he reached for the front door knob. Jeneil was impressed feeling that he actually seemed very nice. She began to relax hoping she had misjudged these people. They were absorbed into the group at the party. Some were familiar others weren't. Introductions and small talk were done. Several of the men seemed delighted to meet the woman who had bought Lakeland Plaza and then transferred it for her husband's birthday. Others talked to her about investments and stocks. Steve could tell that his wife had impressed quite a few people who were anxious to meet the woman with the brain for business, yet this woman who could talk intelligently about stocks bonds and real estate stayed close by his side holding onto his hand like a child who was afraid she'd get lost. The men looked her over, the women looked her over and Jeneil faced them smiling pleasantly. Steve was impressed; she was great in groups when she had to be. Two of the doctors from the associates group stopped to talk to Steve and Jeneil slipped away hoping to get a drink. She was thirsty from talking so much.

A young woman came up to her as she made her way to the drinks table. "Mrs. Bradley," she said nervously, "I'm Jennifer Reid, Bill Reid's wife." Jeneil tried to place the name. "Your husband went to the Stonehaven seminar in Bill's place."

"Oh yes," Jeneil said, "You had just moved and your in-laws were coming in."

"Yes." The girl smiled surprised that Jeneil could remember so much. "I'd like to thank you for your husband doing that."

"Thank me?" Jeneil asked.

"Yes." The girl answered. "The men seem to pat each other on the backs, but I've been married to a doctor long enough to know that the women deserve some applause too. Thank you for understanding my needs."

"You're welcome." Jeneil smiled, "Were you able to get settled before your company got there?"

The girl rolled her eyes. "Just barely. You won't believe our attic."

Jeneil chuckled. "I know. I have a few boxes left to unpack. We've just moved too."

"I know Tecumseh in Glenview and your husband just bought an SX7. We're in Sayard."

"Oh we're neighbors." Jeneil smiled. "We'll be seeing each other a lot then, our open house, your open house."

The girl shrugged. "Oh I don't know. We're not ready for that expense. We have Bill's college loans and I'm still in school."

"What are you studying?" Jeneil asked, very curious.

"Chemical engineering."

Jeneil nodded. "Wow you have your hands full."

"I really do." The girl sighed, "I really didn't need the early in-law visit."

Jeneil patted her arm and smiled, "When are they leaving?"

"Tomorrow if my cooking doesn't improve."

Jeneil laughed, "Why isn't she cooking?"

"Because I don't want to seem like a failure. I'm trying to impress her. She's not impressed with women in engineering."

Jeneil shrugged, "Was she a great cook at your age?"

The girl stopped, "Probably not. Boy what an ass I am. I'm a wreck trying to be perfect."

"That's a nice trap we set for ourselves isn't it." Jeneil grinned.

"Yeh," the girl laughed, "I think I'll let her cook and tell her I'm taking notes. She loves praise." The girl smiled, "You are easy to talk to. I expected this dynamic overwhelming personality with all I've heard about you and your business smarts."

Jeneil smiled, "I've heard the praise about me, but really, I have expert advisors and professionals. I'm not a business whiz at all. I just own the company so I'm the one in the spotlight."

The girl smiled appreciating Jeneil's understated attitude. The girl's husband joined her, "Bill this is Mrs. Bradley."

"I know." Bill smiled.

Jeneil extended her hand, "Nice to meet you. If ever you and Jennifer find some free time or you're jogging past our house stop in and say Hi."

They both smiled.

"She's really a now person, Bill. Very together."

Jeneil grinned, "Did I tell you that? I'd better get something to drink, dehydration is causing delusions."

They both laughed and Jeneil excused herself walking away thinking. "I'm now and together? I'm constantly changing. I couldn't get through a semester of any kind of engineering curriculum including domestic. I don't even know where I belong in life. People talk to me expecting this wonder woman who speaks in stock quotes. I hate hype." She sighed.

She filled a glass with ice and poured club soda over it taking a section of lime; she squeezed it gently over the glass and took a swizzle stick to stir it. The first sip felt good. "Jeneil for people who don't like groups, we find each other in them often."

Jeneil turned and then smiled, "Dr. Rand. Don't we though?"

"You look done in already." He smiled, "And call me Morgan, please."

"I am done in. Fitting a hyped image isn't easy."

He smiled warmly. "What's wrong, people trying to have you teach them all you know in one paragraph?"

She grinned. "That I might handle. They want me to teach them what my advisors and professionals know but think it's me."

"Oh a reluctant eagle too, are you?"

"I'm a wren with a staff and committees that make me look like an eagle and when I explain that, people think I'm being modest." She held up her glass in a toast. "Here's to the small square of land where the real person in us can breathe freely and sit in the sun honestly."

Morgan Rand watched her wondering who that real person really was. She became more fascinating the closer he got.

"I guess I'll bring Steve a drink. He must be dry from talking too." She put her glass down and got one for him.

"How are you enjoying Tecumseh?" He asked.

"Just fine." She replied adding ice to the glass.

"I heard you and Steve having fun on that slope the other night." He said watching her steadily.

She smiled, "That wasn't Steve; that was a friend of mine. He has the greatest ideas for fun that are real stress beaters. We did get carried away. That slope was more challenging than we expected. I apologize for being loud enough to reach your house."

Morgan Rand liked her even more now, her honesty really pleased him. "It wasn't disturbingly loud," He assured her. "In fact it sounded like real fun."

She nodded and raised her eyebrows. "You know it was. It really was. A real dive off the conveyor belt. Join us next time."

Morgan smiled, "I just might do that."

"Good," She said. "Excuse me while I take this to Steve."

Morgan Rand shook his head as she walked away. "And she's unliberated enough to serve her husband a drink. You're a delighted mixture, Jeneil." He thought watching her wind her way through the party group. She joined Steve who was talking to Glenn Tufton. Steve smiled at her as she arrived.

Glenn Tufton stared at Jeneil as she handed Steve his drink. "Aw Steve, you bastard, an SX7, a brainy wife. Who's also a mistress and caters to you. You always did know how to live. Where did you find her?" He smiled.

"The American college of Stepford wives." Jeneil replied curtsying. Steve and Glenn laughed. "I'm going to tour the house." Jeneil told Steve.

"I'll go with you. Join us Glenn?"

"I saw it earlier." Glenn grinned and raised his eyebrows, "He's done some intriguing things." He raised his eyebrows and walked away. The house had different levels. Jeneil took her time passing over prints and paintings Kirk Vance had displayed in various rooms. Jeneil became more favorably impressed with him through his home. There was order and sensitivity and an interest in nature. She liked the house far better than her own. She smiled looking at a grouping of carved mahogany elk standing majestically on the corner of a mantle. If he's done the decorating, then he has a side to him that he doesn't share to easily.

"How well do you know him?" She asked.

"Just from parties." Steve answered quietly.

Jeneil nodded, "Well I guess we've seen all of this section. There's just the annex which is at the end of the hall to the left. Don't you find the idea of the annex interesting?"

Steve grinned. "I haven't thought about it. Why is it interesting?"

Jeneil shrugged as she looked around. He lives here. All the normal rooms are here and functional and then there's the annex. Rooms which he's chosen to separate from this life. I think that's curious."

Steve watched her impressed with her sensitivity and instinct. They went to the short hallway on the left where potted plants were placed near what would be a large windowed wall with drapes. Jeneil stopped and looked around, "Something's changing."

"What is?" Steve asked.

"The art is exotic. That carving on the wall is an African fertility goddess. Does Kirk Vance travel?" She asked going toward the draped wall.

"I don't know." Steve chuckled, amused by all her questions. He opened the wide sliding door for Jeneil and they stepped into a small room of glass giving a view of the earth and sky.   Lush green plants were scattered in groupings.

"Oooo" Jeneil sighed stopping, "This is really nice." She smiled. "The sky, the plants. It lets you escape. Oh this is beautiful. Even the sound of trickling water from the small pool and indirect muted lighting. What a delightful trip for the senses." She smiled turning slowly. Kirk Vance stood just outside the door listening to her description and watching her steadily. He stepped into the room. Steve turned. Jeneil smiled, "This room is magnificent. Is it your design?" She asked.

He nodded still watching her steadily.

"What was your intention?" She asked, feeling absorbed into the room.

"Exactly what you said Mona Lisa, an escape. The hallway where the senses are stimulated for fuller appreciation."

"Fuller appreciation?" Jeneil questioned not sure of his meaning. "Do you mean fuller appreciation of man's surroundings? Like Earth, growth, universe expanse freedom." Jeneil said looking around and turning slowly becoming part of the atmosphere of the room.

Steve watched her. What was happening between her and the room was intoxicating. She was actually adding what was missing in the room.   Human form that could achieve a oneness with the atmosphere.

"Ooo this is really nice." She said in a quiet whisper closing her eyes and letting herself fill the room. It was more intense than what he'd watched in her at DiNoli's garden. Electricity raced through him and he stopped himself by looking at the tiled floor as a distraction.

"Holy shit. She's incredible!"

Steve heard the slowly spoken hushed and barely audible words. He looked at Kirk Vance quickly. Kirk was riveted by her. Steve saw it. He became concerned and was about to go to her when she turned and opened her eyes.   "Wow." She said softly, "That was therapeutic."

"Therapeutic?" Kirk asked, quietly surprised by the word. "What did it cure, Mona Lisa?"

"Walls." She said, "Shackles, inhibitions."

Kirk raised his eyebrows with surprise, "You consider those things to be diseases?"

"Yes." She answered still looking around, "If they stand between man and his path to full appreciation of this energy. This is magnificent." She sighed. Kirk walked to her. Steve watched feeling very concerned about Jeneil and moved in closer.

"You are something else." Kirk said softly to her. Steve got even closer. Jeneil watched him. "You belong in this room." Kirk whispered, "I'm glad I saw you in it. I feel what you just described in this room. Having witnessed the experience through you gave my design and creation life outside my mind and my feeling. I saw it alive in you." He put his hand to her cheek and she moved away slightly. "No." He said softly, "No, don't. I just want to share the feeling. The room was designed for me. Its meaning is fuller knowing someone else feels it too." He smiled tenderly at her. Putting his hand to her chin gently he touched her lips lightly with his thumb. Steve was stunned and shaken that Jeneil wasn't moving. He went to her. Kirk smiled still staring into Jeneil's eyes. "Steve you have a very unusual and beautiful wife."

"I know that." Steve said putting his arm around her waist and he felt Jeneil lean against him. He relaxed slightly, but the moment had him unnerved.

Barbara Bernard came to the door. "Kirk some guests are arriving and some are leaving." She looked at all three. "Sorry." She grinned.

"Excuse me." Kirk said to both of them and joined Barbara.

Jeneil watched him leave. "He is unusual."

Steve put his lips to her temple. "Honey, he really is." He said, "Remember that."

Jeneil looked at Steve and then nodded. "Let's take a look at the last room."

The room had a double carved oak door and opened to a deep blue carpeted corridor with grey walls and indirect lighting at the ceiling. One large panel was carpeted in a deeper grey from floor to ceiling. "How odd." She said, "I feel like I'm in a theater." Steve sighed wondering if she was right. "Where do we go now?" She asked looking around and then she walked to the grey carpeted panel. "Oh here's the entrance." She said.

Steve was reaching his limit; he could see the other world of Dr. Vance unfolding. "Jeneil, let's go."

She didn't answer.

"Jeneil?" Steve called and he walked behind the grey panel.

The room shocked him, the floor was thickly carpeted in grey like the panel and the walls were pale blue. There were no windows a deeper shade of blue drapes were gathered and tied giving the walls design and softness. Dark blue chaise lounges were placed here and there and a small pool was at one end. Alcoves appeared along one wall where canopied platforms were sheltered. Steve went to Jeneil, "The money he must have put into this."

"Yes." She nodded sadly. "He's really captured the era."

"What era?" Steve asked.

"The era of decadence that precedes the fall of every great civilization, Greece, Rome. It doesn't matter what country. The symptom is unmistakable, man gone mad with infatuation of himself and his lusts."

"Jeneil you sound like you're going to pull out a bible and preach."

She smiled, "Why is it whenever someone speaks against the decline of man it's called religious fanaticism? Philosophers and politicians spoke up, poets and playwrights warned them too but nothing stopped the frenzy. Mankind fell in love with itself and began a narcissist dance toward the precipice."

"Saint Jeneil, ease up." Steve smiled, "He's just a man." Steve laughed, "With odd tastes in fun." He put his arms around her, "Don't be so serious, Honey." He held her.

"I feel cheated." She frowned. "I thought he understood cosmic. Back in the garden room, I thought he really understood. Instead he has discovered the Yen and Yang of lust." She sighed. "I'm being silly. Without the balance. I guess." She pulled away gently.

"Well maybe a little unfair." Steve said taking her hand. "It's his house and his money so it's his business."

"Sure." Jeneil answered quietly.

They left the room and Steve recurred the carved oak doors. Jeneil stood in the garden room and touched a shiny broad leaf. Steve stopped by her side. He saw the sadness. "Come on honey it's a room, only a room."

She sighed, "He tarnished this room with that other one." She shook her head. "And he calls this the hallway to fuller appreciation." She laughed lightly looking at the sky, "I'm so dumb, I thought he meant an expansion of appreciation for the universe or the cycloid and ecological harmony of the earth and man's place in it."

Steve rubbed her back gently and smiled, "Jeneil would you believe that some of us just see trees, flowers, stars and clouds, that's it?"

She looked at him, "But that was the beauty of this room Steve. It could be a place to contemplate man's surroundings using sensual stimulation, but instead it's a pit stop for a turn on. Why linger here and think when orgasm awaits only footsteps that way."

Steve caught the sentence and grasped the opportunity. "Jeneil, what's wrong with orgasm?"

She looked at him and then walked over to another plant. "Nothing. I didn't mean that orgasm should be eliminated, but." She shrugged, "I don't know; my idea won't translate well, I'll sound like I'm saying that the world should be celibate."

"You're not saying that?" Steve asked.

"No." Jeneil insisted, cleaning a leaf.

"Just you?" Steve asked pointedly.

Jeneil looked at him. "This room's sensuousness is effective; barriers seem to fall."

He walked to her, "You didn't answer my question."

"Why are you asking it?" She replied.

"Don't answer my question with a question."

She was silent.

Steve watched her slowly. "Ok. I'll answer yours. I want to know why you're celibate."

"Why are you?" Jeneil made a face realizing that was another question.

Steve smiled slightly, "Do you even know?"

"Yes." She said quietly, "I don't want just sex. I want love."

"Love?" He asked excited about the direction of the conversation.

She nodded.

His heart was pounding in his chest. "Jeneil are you even looking for it?"

The question struck her squarely, Steve could tell. She stared at him struggling for words. There was talking in the hallway. "We'd better leave." She said heading to the door. Steve put his head back and sighed. The door opened and four people entered the room. Steve went to look for Jeneil who was walking quickly back to the party. He found her talking to Sondra Rand who was looking at a painting in the living room. Steve stood by Jeneil's side for a few minutes and then a doctor from another hospital engaged Steve in conversation having heard about the new car. Jeneil moved on.

Steve looked for her having been through every room in the main house he headed for the closet to see if her coat was still there. It was. Kirk Vance was looking out the window that viewed the front yard. He noticed Steve at the closet. "Are you leaving?"

"I'm looking for my wife." Steve answered.

Kirk smiled, "She's out there." He nodded toward the window where he was standing.

"Without a coat?" Steve asked looking concerned as he headed for the window too.

"Morgan Rand has chivalrously given up his wool tweed for her." Kirk explained.

Jeneil and Morgan Rand were walking together and laughing about something. Morgan had the sleeves of his shirt and crew neck sweater pushed to his elbows. Jeneil was wrapped in his sport coat.

"She really is something, Steve. You're very lucky to have found her. Your wife is the only woman I've seen appreciate that garden room at that level. Most women want to rush on ahead. External stimulus is easier. She has worked at extending herself beyond usual limits." Steve noticed the slight shiver that passed through Kirk as he watched Jeneil. "Why don't you try to come to a Friday party sometime."

Steve decided that now was the time to set the White Stallion to rest. "Kirk those days are gone for me. I don't miss them."

Kirk smiled, "I can see why. But you can't hold her Steve, she's beyond a narrow realm. She belongs free. Like a beautiful butterfly or some rare bird. Did you see her in that room?"

Steve watched Kirk as he talked about Jeneil. "Kirk you're reading her all wrong. She is delicate and even rare, but she couldn't deal with a Friday party, believe me."

Kirk looked at him questioningly, "You mean that look is real? It's not a gimmick?" He grinned, "No wonder it looks so natural." He turned and watched Jeneil. "She's held; been private stock then? I can't blame them."

Steve didn't like the term being used to describe Jeneil. "Kirk she's mine. My wife."

Kirk looked at him steadily, "She's got you over the edge." He smiled, "I wasn't being insulting, the White Stallion would know that. I'm sorry if I've irritated you, really. I think she's beautiful. Enchantingly beautiful." Kirk watched Steve closely, "You can't hold her Steve. She's unfinished and she won't be confined there's a restlessness to her. What I saw in her in the garden room was only a glimpse of what she's all about. She doesn't belong as private stock, Steve, no more than the earth and wind. When she reaches her full potential, she will consume life, and swallow it."

Steve never flinched, "I don't know about earth or wind, but I do know that Jeneil is mine. That makes her untouchable." He warned.

Kirk was silent and then he nodded, "I understand how you feel, but Steve, you're missing what I'm seeing. Nobody will own Jeneil. Try and it will fail miserably. The girl is pure energy. you don't own energy, it's shared. I can tell that even Morgan Rand knows that and he's incredibly straight. "

"Well she married me." Steve said.

Kirk smiled, "Mona Lisa has you way over the edge. I envy you that. What a totally consuming experience that must be."

A couple came over to say their goodbyes and Kirk smothered them with his charm. Steve went to the drink table. Kirk had unnerved him with his talk about not holding her and sharing her and her restlessness. He covered the bottom of a glass with gin. "Restlessness." He thought, "It's this shittin celibacy. Well it's over. I don't know how the hell Pete put up with the sharks, but I won't. This marriage will be normal and soon." He put the glass to his lips and drank quickly. Filling the glass with club soda and ice, he drank a mouthful as he watched Jeneil and Morgan Rand walk in. Morgan helped her off with the sport jacket. She smiled at him. Steve put his glass down and went to them. "Jeneil, I'd like to leave now."

"Okay." She said.

"I'll get our coats."

She looked at Morgan, "I'd like to meet your horse."

Morgan smiled broadly, "Meet Raven? You say it like he's a person."

Jeneil laughed. "You talk about him like he is one. I used to ride. A family friend had horses and her groom talked about them like they were people too. Fiddler is sulking today Jeneil. Let her work it out herself. Take Pica instead."

"Then ride with me sometime." Morgan smiled.

"In what?" Steve asked holding her coat for her.

"Horses." Jeneil answered slipping her arms into the sleeves.

"You have horses?" Steve asked.

"At my father's place."

"Let's try it." Jeneil smiled, "When is a question mark though isn't it? With winter weather here and the holidays. Don't forget me, though please."

"I won't." Morgan answered, "I'd like the company. Sondra doesn't ride. She used to."

Steve watched the two of them making a date in front of him. He folded his arms and watched. "Well maybe we can talk her into it. And Steve here is from western New York he'll probably slip into a saddle like he's been born to it."

Morgan laughed, "Okay let's try it some time."

Steve unfolded his arms and relaxed hearing that he was being included.

Jeneil was silent during the drive home. She had waited until another couple had gone to Kirk Vance to say goodnight and she joined them, talking to him briefly and then withdrawing with Kirk watching her until she left the room. Steve had tried talking to her, but she was distant or not listening. He resented Morgan Rand having had more exchange with his wife than he did. . The marriage had definitely strained their friendship and he resented that too. Steve locked the car and watched Jeneil walk to the breeze-way door quickly. "Jeneil." He said going to her hoping they could talk. The conversation in the garden room had been important, he wanted it to continue. "Jeneil could we sit in the den and talk?"

"I'm tired, Steve." She didn't look at him. He could tell that she was avoiding him. She'd been doing that since their talk in the garden room. He watched her walk up the stairs. Discouragement began to filter in. Putting a sauce pan on the stove burner, he measured a mug of milk and poured it into the pan. He turned the button for the heat. He paced wondering about Jeneil's silence and withdrawal. "Not again." He said removing his sport jacket and tie. "The last time, she barricaded herself in her room every night after dinner," he thought undoing his cuffs. Slowly unbuttoning his shirt to the waist he pulled it from his pants. He felt keyed up and tense. He turned to check the milk. It was boiling. "Oh Shit!" He grumbled.

"What happened?" Jeneil asked coming into the kitchen.

Steve turned quickly, "The milk boiled, it'll take forever to cool." He watched her as she went to the fridge and poured cold milk into the pan and tested it. He stood next to her as closely as he dared. His chest was exposed and he found that he wanted it to be. He now understood Robert Danzieg's bare-chested outfit. It was language without words. "Look at me, I'm a man, notice me." He felt that way. Jeneil fixed the Ovaltine and poured two mugs, putting one on the counter for Steve.

"Goodnight." She said going to the door. Steve was anxious.

He went to her stepping in front of her, "Jeneil, I really want to talk to you."

She looked at the mug of ovaltine. "Steve, I'm tired, too tired to talk, too tired to even think. The Sprague's are coming to dinner tomorrow."

Steve sighed and stepped out of her way. She left quickly. He picked up his drink, "You're not tired, Jeneil, you're unconscious."

Jeneil's hands were trembling as she climbed the stairs. The questions Steve had posed to her in the garden room at the party had unraveled her. It shook the peaceful world she had imagined in her thoughts about the arranged marriage. "Are you looking for love?" She nearly missed a stair. "Why are you celibate?" She wondered if he was suggesting that they have...begin...She stopped at the door of her room to breathe. "Oh my gosh, what if he argues that we've been saying I love you to each other for a long time. Is the love in a friendship enough?" Opening the door, she went in and closed it quickly and leaned against it. What was shaking her the most was that her mind had begun to think that thought since the garden room. "I don't love him like I love Peter though. My body would respond to Peter immediately. The formula was complete. Formula," She argued. "A lot of good the formula did for you. You have a husband. But I'm not Steve's type for falling in love." Tears filled her eyes, "We would be just having sex." Tears spilled down her cheeks, "I don't know if I could handle that." She cried softly. "The White Stallion understands that decadent temple room. He called it an odd taste in fun. It's a room designed for orgies. Why can't people be honest? Call an ace an ace." She wiped her tears, "Maybe he was being honest. Orgies are fun to some people." She sighed and sipped her drink. "The White Stallion included I guess. I can't." She shook her head. "I can't."

*****

Dr. Sprague and his wife arrived at three the next day. Steve was glad to have someone to talk to. Jeneil had prepared dinner and he had joined her, but she was silent and distant.

"The house is lovely Jeneil, really lovely and you've added such charming touches." Mrs. Sprague smiled as they went into the living room after taking a tour.

"We're finding it too big." Jeneil said. Steve watched her thinking that it must have seemed too small to her today since she couldn't seem to get away from him completely but looked like she wanted to.

Mrs. Sprague nodded. "Warren and I thought that about our place too, but the children really filled it once they came along."

Jeneil fidgeted, "Can I get you something? The vegetable will be finished steaming in another few minutes. I have a pot of herb tea steeping."

"I wouldn't mind a scotch on the rocks." Mrs. Sprague replied.

Dr. Sprague looked at her.

"What about you Dr. Sprague?" Jeneil asked.

"Club soda and ice or the tea is okay too." He quietly answered.

"I'll get the drinks." Steve said getting up from his chair. "Scotch on the rocks sounds very good to me too, Mrs. Sprague."

Dr. Sprague watched Steve leave the room and then he went to help him. The two bedrooms hadn't escaped his notice during the tour. Something seemed very wrong to him. The coolness between Steve and Jeneil was too obvious. He hadn't known Steve to drink either. Jeneil excused herself to check the dinner. She approached the den where Steve was fixing the drinks on her way to the kitchen.

Dr. Sprague rubbed his chin. "Steve what's happening in your marriage?"

Steve was stunned. Jeneil was shocked and stopped by the door. "Happening?" Steve questioned. "Yes, the two bedrooms. Is everything okay between you and Jeneil?"

"We're fine." Steve smiled, lying boldly. "Separate rooms is fine?" Warren Sprague asked.

Steve shrugged. "We don't have the same sleep patterns. Sometimes Jeneil has work she brings home and I might have early surgery. Two bedrooms seem to work for us."

Dr. Sprague watched him. "When did you start drinking?"

"When your wife asked for one, it sounded good. What's the matter?"

Dr. Sprague sighed. "Nothing I guess. Steve my door is always open, not just to residents and interns. I don't like surprises you know that."

Steve handed him Mrs. Sprague's drink. "Everything's fine, but I'll come in if it changes. How's that." He smiled.

Jeneil was holding her throat as she listened to the situation Steve was handling. She closed her eyes and swallowed hard, then slipping past the door, she went to the kitchen quickly with the conversation still whirling through her mind. She added the fresh sliced mushrooms to the poached chicken and couldn't concentrate enough to remember what else she needed to put in it. She sighed. "Get hold of yourself, Jeneil." Taking a deep breath, she remembered pimiento and shred the green onions quickly. Turning the heat to low, she checked the broccoli spears, then took them from the steamer and put them into the herbed vegetable broth to steep. She poured herself some herbed tea and joined the others.

Steve looked up as she walked into the livingroom. "I'm sorry." He said. "You never told me what you wanted."

"It's okay. I was going to the kitchen to check dinner." She smiled and slipped her arm onto his back near his neck rubbing it gently to show affection so Dr. Sprague wouldn't worry about the marriage. "Dinner is nearly ready." She said and she went to her own chair feeling like a hypocrite for playing the game of normal marriage. She felt compassion for Steve having to handle the awkward question as he sat there listening to Dr. Sprague talk about the class of new interns. She thought he was heroic. Steve would comment from time to time. He saw her watching him. She smiled at him gently and confused him by her warmth. He grinned slightly and answered Dr. Sprague's comment. Mrs. Sprague was rubbing her forehead and becoming red in the face. Jeneil wondered if she was feeling sick and was about to ask when Mrs. Sprague sprang from her chair quickly taking her drink to the window. Jeneil wondered and went to her casually. "Are you alright?" She asked quietly.

Mrs. Sprague smiled. "Yes I am thank you. Old age is taking its toll. I don't have the patience for his hospital conversation anymore. Sometimes it makes me want to scream. He's one hundred and twenty-five percent surgeon, twenty-four hours a day." Jeneil was stunned by the admission and the criticism. She sipped her tea.

"Mrs. Sprague, could I impose on you while you're here." Mrs. Sprague looked at her. Jeneil plunged on in. "I'm planning to terrace the slope out back. If you saw the landscaping sketches, could you suggest some flowers or shrubs? You seem to have a flare for gardening."

"I wouldn't mind. Believe me it's new and different. The children have grownup to be as self-contained as Warren, including my daughter. I'm glad she's independent and self assured, but she thinks it blossomed in her magically. I fought for her rights to be as free and equal as the sons in our family." She took a mouthful of her drink. "Let's get to the sketch." Jeneil just nodded not knowing how to comment, on Mrs. Sprague's complaint or even that it was necessary. They went to the den and sat on the sofa with the sketch tacked to a piece of oak tag.

Jeneil found that Mrs. Sprague had a flair that stemmed from a deep interest in flowers and gardening. She never imposed her own ideas but asked Jeneil what her plans were and then suggested plants from her wealth of understanding about them. Jeneil was very impressed and very glad that she had asked her about the terracing. Dr. Sprague and Steve came into the kitchen as Jeneil was arranging the food in the serving dishes. "Where is Carol?" Dr. Sprague asked, looking very concerned.

"She's …." Jeneil began when the double doors to the diningroom opened and Mrs. Sprague whisked in from outdoors smiling and reddened from the cold. "Jeneil that deck is begging for greenery. Golden arborvitae could keep it from becoming monotonous." She stopped. "Oh excuse me, did I interrupt a conversation?" She asked, quickly.

"No." Jeneil smiled. "You husband had asked me where you were."

"Oh." Mrs. Sprague laughed. "Here I can help with that." She said, taking a serving dish from Jeneil.

"Soup's on, men." Mrs. Sprague smiled as she went to the diningroom. Jeneil followed her noticing the change. Dr. Sprague followed not believing in the change in her. Dinner was easy and she filled the time with chatter. Jeneil watched noticing that Dr. Sprague watched Mrs. Sprague closely, seeming to enjoy his wife. She cut her spear of broccoli and wondered if Thoreau was right about everyone living lives of quiet desperation. The thought discouraged her.

"Jeneil how did you get this chicken breast so tender?" Mrs. Sprague raised her eyebrows. "I've poached fish, but never chicken"

"I learned it by accident once, when I was making dinner and had a business call interrupt. I turned the heat very low and when I returned to rescue what I thought would be a mess, I found it was better done that way."

Mrs. Sprague smiled. "You're an interesting combination of new and old Jeneil. My daughter won't learn to cook beyond broiling and boiling. She's liberated, but not everything from our generation was useless, especially your training of the next generation."

Jeneil smiled. "We just need to mature so we can have a wider view of who we are and why. Then we can give you the credit."

Mrs. Sprague smiled. "Well, how come you know that at your age?"

"My parents told me." Jeneil replied. Mrs. Sprague laughed hysterically, finding that remark very funny and Dr. Sprague smiled as he watched his wife. Steve watched his wife and then smiled appreciating the warm and friendly atmosphere she had managed to create even though they were living through another struggle in their relationship.

He appreciated the display of affection she had shown him especially since Dr. Sprague was showing concern about the marriage. "Why am I pushing her?" He asked himself. "She's a damn good doctor's wife just like she is." But he loved her, he felt that as he watched the wave on her hair slip to her eye and she tilted her head slightly to replace it gently. "Then love her enough to back off." He lectured himself. "She never lied to you, Bradley remember that." Steve's mood improved after he reminded himself of the arranged marriage and their understanding. He wanted the closeness that the first few weeks of marriage had given them. He wanted their friendship restored. He vowed to ease up so she wouldn't feel threatened.

They had dessert and coffee in the den before the fieldstone fireplace because it was a less formal room. The Sprague's left with Mrs. Sprague hugging Jeneil and inviting them to Thanksgiving dinner with them. Dr. Sprague hugged Jeneil too, grateful that his wife had enjoyed the visit. Steve wanted to hug her, for making him look good in the marriage, but he realized that he had to withdraw again in order to show her that he accepted the arranged marriage. He knew her resistance was a result of her questions in the garden room at Kirk Vance's house. He was convinced of that seeing her mild surprise when he had kissed her cheek after helping her fill the dishwasher and then he said goodnight to go to his room. He saw the relaxed smile as he turned and added. "Will I see you for breakfast?" She had nodded and said goodnight, cheerfully.

"It's not worth it." He thought. "We get along too well to ruin it because of sex." He went upstairs to do sit-ups and read before going to bed.

Jeneil sat before the den fire alone reviewing what was happening. It was obvious that Steve had relaxed about wanting to continue their talk in the garden room. She sighed having found another facet of the arranged marriage that she hadn't considered. "Outside pressure." The marriage wasn't something people would understand. It was unusual and she thought about the possibility of twin beds for a second. "Are you crazy?!" She thought. "Share the same bedroom and stay celibate? You're crazy, Irish! Cerebral would never hold up to that, not the way he looked with just his shirt undone last night, let alone running into him wrapped in a towel after a shower. Sharing the same bedroom is outrageous. Put the mare in the paddock with the White Stallion is fairytales, Jeneil. You're right." She argued with herself and sighed wondering how much of a problem outside pressure might be. She had learned that every month a person in Tecumseh was expected to have a party. She had counted the number of people involved and realized that she'd be giving a party every six months. She sighed. "This is all going beyond the simple feeling of peace and security I felt when he suggested we get married. It felt so right, but it's becoming so complicated. She stared into the dying fire and missed Camelot. The memory of her life in her peaceful apartment brought a memory of Peter. "This is your fault Chang." She felt Irish rage. Jeneil got up quickly and paced. "It's not his fault. He just didn't marry you. He had nothing to do with you marrying Steve. He betrayed you." Irish screamed. Jeneil sighed. "That he did do, but I'm beginning to understand why, I think. He was probably more drunk the he thought, that coupled with feeling that Steve and I…" She stopped. "Why would he even think I'm Steve's type?" Jeneil rubbed her temples. "Gosh men are so difficult to understand? But he stayed married to Uette." Irish agonized, bringing pain to Nebraska and Jeneil too. "But he loved me." Jeneil defended him. "I know he did. That was real. What we had was beautiful, but the baby was his and the pressure if he divorced Uette would have been incredible. His mother would have raged." She stopped before the fire. "The presence of the mixed race was just too much. He stayed with his own kind. It was easier. I can understand that. Mandra had come to understand that in her own life. I understand, Peter." She said, into the glow of the embers and she felt healing begin. She smiled. "I knew it was important to avoid hatred or forgiveness can't be reached and without forgiveness there is no healing." She closed the glass fire doors tightly and headed upstairs feeling quiet and peaceful inside.

*****

One of the doctors in the group was scheduled to assist in a hospital in Ohio for two days while a visiting specialist from Austria performed what was considered only experimental surgery at Cleveland. The doctor had developed a bad cold with flu symptoms. Steve volunteered to cover it not wanting to miss what would be happening in that theater. Jeneil had decided that she'd stay in her room for the three days he was gone, She began taking her meals there as well. It felt cozier to her. She went to Robert's studio and learned to develop the pictures she had taken. Robert had been right. There was magic in seeing your subject emerge before you. She wondered what Robert's questions about her marriage meant. Barbara Barnard called to ask if she'd have her open house party the Saturday after Thanksgiving since the Barnard's Christmas Party was in early December. Barbara offered to call since the late notice was her fault. Jeneil welcomed the chance to get out of that part of the horror. Millie never even winced when Jeneil mentioned the short notice and had an estimated cost of the food. Handing Millie cash and free reign, Jeneil never thought anymore about the food. She called her friends to invite them and let Barbara handle the others. She began to feel comfortable about the whole party. Steve returned from Ohio the evening before thanksgiving catching an airport limo into Upton and there a taxi to Jeneil's office, since he didn't leave the SX7 at the airport, and he got a glimpse of how money can complicate life.

He walked into the office building feeling anxious to see her. Being part of the operation in Ohio had him overwhelmed. He had assisted in an operation that was only at a theory level in his training. He was excited and keyed up with energy. He needed to talk or he'd explode. Rachel signaled to him to go on in when she saw him. He left his luggage and top coat then headed to her office, knocking and walking in. Jeneil smiled warmly. "Hi."

"Hi." He grinned, going to a chair near her desk. "Are you leaving soon?"

She nodded. "Just leaving instructions. I'm taking Friday off. The housewarming party is Saturday."

He was shocked. "How come?"

She shrugged. "Tight social schedule. The Barnards asked as a favor."

"Sheez!" He sighed. "I'm sorry, Jeneil."

"It's handled." She said, going to the closet for her coat. "How did your trip go?"

"Don't ask." He said, standing and smiling. "Let's grab dinner. I'm dying to talk and if I start it won't end." He hugged her from feeling so good forgetting about his vow to keep his distance. She held him and studied his face.

"You're alive and on fire." She laughed.

"I feel good, Jeneil. I feel great." He hugged her to him. "I've missed you." He added

She smiled and liked hearing that. "I missed you, too. I've been living in my room. Steve I'd like to build a studio in the backyard. A place for me to clutter with messy paint and photo equipment. Do you mind?"

"No." He answered. "Why can't you find a room in the house?"

"It's the style of the house. None of the rooms have access to the right natural lighting. The studio will be small, maybe half a garage."

"Sure." He smiled. "Why not." He was impressed that she even consulted him. He looked at her and became thrilled that she was his wife. "I've missed you." He said. "I'm starved."

She grinned. "I made a pot roast for your homecoming."

He smiled. "You're beautiful!" He laughed, whirling her off the floor in his arms. She screamed and held on. Adrienne was standing at the door watching and smiling. Steve and Jeneil looked embarrassed.

"It's okay." Adrienne laughed. "I'm tired of decorum myself. I stopped to wish you a good holiday."

"Same to you." Jeneil smiled. "I'll call you on Friday."

Adrienne nodded. "And I'll be at your place early Saturday."

"I'll like that a lot." Jeneil hugged her. "It's been a while since I've talked to Charlie. We need to visit more."

Adrienne patted her back with a hug. "I know, seeing you every day isn't enough."

Jeneil laughed and pulled away. "Laugh at me, go ahead. I'm bemoaning the passing of my old life and you trash the sentiment."

Adrienne laughed and threw her a kiss. "Nice to see you, Steve. Welcome home." Steve nodded and smiled.

"I love the feeling of the holidays." Jeneil said, reaching for her coat.

"It's nice to have a wife for the holidays." Steve smiled. "This feels like a holiday to me because I'm with you." She smiled and hugged him, glad to have a husband for the same reason.

*****

Peter tossed his weekender and carryall in the backseat of his car and closed the door. Getting behind the wheel, he backed out of his parking spot of the apartments and joined the traffic flow. He decided to leave town for the holidays, much to the disappointment of his Grandfather and his mother. He hadn't visited since his marriage ended and they watched with concern as he withdrew from everyone and everything. He was going to take a motel room for the night and spend the holiday reading and thinking. He told them he was visiting friends. His psychotherapy sessions were beginning to unravel him and he needed time to absorb what he was uncovering about himself. He had called his mother after bringing up the situation in therapy and he discovered what he knew would happen all along. He would give in and forgive his mother, but at least he knew why now. Therapy had been doing that for him. He was uncovering the whys of his life with the help of Dr. Nefida and he remembered that Jeneil used to do the same thing. Facing the holiday with his family would only remind him of the disaster at the previous Thanksgiving when Karen announced that he was living with Jeneil. He missed Jeneil intensely. Her excitement for the holidays was infectious and she had the apartment full of things to munch on. He hated Karen. She and Uette were prime targets for his pent up anger. They had cost him Jeneil. It was difficult to forget. Peter also he needed some private time to absorb the news Ron had called him with earlier in the day about the Wongs. It seems that the Wongs had responded to an "invitation to invest" letter that Ron had sent out into the Chinese community and were very anxious to transfer their holdings to Peter and Ron and the new company. Peter was concerned about the obvious reason he thought they wanted to do this and he wanted to think it though thoroughly before committing to the decision. "Pick the right people and let them do their job" He smiled thinking about his new partner.

*****

Steve and Jeneil sat in front of the fire with their dinner plates to enjoy the cozy atmosphere. Jeneil chuckled. "We should have brought a four room house. We're only using the kitchen, the den, and the bedrooms." Steve smiled. "And I took a limo and taxi today because I hadn't wanted to leave the SX7 parked at the airport."

"Money can be a pain." Jeneil snickered and put her plate aside feeling full and comfortable resting her head against the sofa seat. Steve joined her. "Tell me about your trip." She said. "You keep interrupting yourself whenever you start."

Steve sighed; he had been waiting for this moment to talk. "Jeneil, you can't imagine what it was like being in that OR with Pfizer. Those of us assisting had been briefed on his procedure in a lecture and charts earlier in the day, and none of us quite believed it could even happen. That man knew our attitudes. No one said anything; but there was smugness to us. You know, like we thought we were pretty good. He showed us the new technique as effortlessly as an appendectomy. I honestly felt like a first year med student."

"But isn't the proof in recovery?"

He smiled at her pleased that she was listening. It was that about her that made him want to talk to her. "We had a lunch and slide presentation on previous cases and recovery. Pfizer is something to watch. His brain never quits. He opened the presentation to questions and we were all virtually at his knee and he never got puffed up in himself. He kept saying we have much to learn. Steve sighed. "If he has much to learn, sheez, I haven't even opened the book."

Jeneil smiled. "Do you think you can perform this procedure having assisted once?"

"I have a video of it." He smiled. "And I'm going to copy it for myself before I turn this copy in. I'm glad I had the chance to see it live. Pfizer is devoting some of his time to research. That must be fascinating."

Jeneil watched him. "I don't think I could watch the video, but I still know why Dr. Pfizer's way is so astonishing. Can you show me the procedure using that educational brain you have in your room? I can usually understand when you show me the procedure in terms of involvement. Then I grasp it."

He looked at her, keeping his head on the sofa seat. He smiled. "It's good to be home with you."

She smiled as she faced him. "This one touched you differently for some reason."

He nodded. "The other seminars were good, but this operation showed me how much I have to learn. It's a new door opened to me."

"I can understand that. Show me what went on." She asked. They went upstairs together and Steve pulled out his chart on the nervous system. Jeneil took the book he set aside and went to his bed to look at it. He got the procedural charts from the seminar and turned. She was lying on his bed absorbed in the book using the index for some reason. He smiled and joined her on the bed. He talked and she asked questions. She was lost in some areas, but it didn't matter. She seemed to understand what it all meant to him and she was pleased for him. He finished and they were lying side by side just talking until she yawned. He felt spent from having talked so much. Pulling herself up slowly, she yawned again. "I'd better get some sleep. I have to get up early." She leaned to him and kissed his cheek. "I'm glad you were there, but it's nice to have you home. The house felt empty." She said good night and left. He lay there enjoying having had her with him.

Twenty Four

He wandered downstairs very early Thanksgiving morning and found her scraping carrots. Several bags of carrots were beside her and a huge pot had been filled with carrots she had already scraped. It was the first he'd heard of her helping a church who feeds the needy and lonely on Thanksgiving Day. He picked up a vegetable peeler and began helping. The carrots got sliced and packed into bags. Taking several bags of frozen peas and putting them in a corrugated box, she added the bags of carrots and some cans of cranberry sauce. The food was delivered and Steve saw the respect Jeneil had earned from the people at the church. Four turkeys had been delivered fully cooked by a restaurant as she had done before. She left a box of clothes for the church's families who might need them and they returned home to her country eggs and biscuits. He got caught up on his newspaper reading and stretched. He hadn't even heard Jeneil for a while. It was getting to be time to be thinking of the Sprague's. Going upstairs to her room, he heard the guitar music. He knocked. She was lying across the bed and he could see the tears. He half expected the holidays to remind her of Peter more poignantly. He sat down beside her and rubbed her back. "Is it wise to listen to music that opens wounds, Honey?"

"This is a tough Thanksgiving." She sniffed. "It was traditional in my family to spend some time on Thanksgiving Day reviewing the year and seeing what needed mending or changing. It was an exercise in gratitude. I have a beaut this year, in John Stanton Milcroft."

Steve slipped onto the bed beside her. "Why are you even allowing yourself to remember him, Honey? That's a nightmare that's best buried." He kissed her shoulder and rubbed his arm gently remembering the horror of the scene at Wonderland.

"I owe him, Steve. Some of that night at Wonderland was my fault. I set him up. I let him believe that I wanted him to stay even allowing whatever fantasy he may have had to foster in his mind and then I ran out on him leaving him feeling like a joke probably" Tears rolled down her cheeks. "The night destroyed him."

"He destroyed himself." Steve corrected.

"But I was the catalyst. I know it was a matter of survival, but between us there's a bitter taste in my mouth. He was gifted misfit. The brilliance of a star that never understood how to shine." She shook her head. "That was his only real problem he didn't know how to belong here. He probably spent some strange years trying to make sense of the whole process called life. I promised him that professionals would listen to his music. He's found an audience for his greatness. I'm going to hire a detective to locate his family. Maybe in death he can provide what he probably struggled to offer in life but couldn't quite cope with his share of the burden of existence. At least I'll have set the record straight between John Stanton Milesoft and me and I can pay my debt to him by keeping my promise."

He watched her. "Do you set all your relationships to rest like that?"

She nodded. "It must sound ultra pious, but it's really a matter of conscience and gratitude. My family thought both were important. One without the other wouldn't work and both were connected to self-esteem."

"Jeneil, what about Peter then?"

She sighed heavily. "I wish Peter and I had ended normally with tears and a fitting goodbye. What was good about us was never said and laid to rest."

Steve was surprised by the healthy attitude about him. "Then you've begun to put him in the past?"

She shrugged. "I'm not sure. I suppose so. I can understand the baby and I can understand him not getting a divorce. With us, I think the racial thing was a difficult hurdle alone without the other burdens. He never even dated white before I came into his life adding to the strain of the racial issue too. He never lived with a woman before either. I really pushed him. I broke barriers in his life adding to the strain of racial issue too probably. We loved each other, but we couldn't make it work. Understanding makes it hurt less."

There was tightness in Steve's throat as he listened to her talk about Peter. She was healing he could tell and with that came hope that she could get on with her life. He smiled and touched her hand. "Your capacity to love and forgive is impressive."

"Is it?" She said. "To me, its survival. The opposites are self destructive, so selfishness seems to be my motivation. Survival a basic instinct."

He kissed her cheek. She smiled at him. "We have to be getting ready for the Sprague's dinner. Can I have a couple of those turkey shaped cookies?"

She smiled. "One of the small square carrot cakes is for Mrs. Sprague along with a small tray of seasoned nut-meats and dried fruits from the gourmet shop. All the other goodies are for us as leftovers. I love holiday leftovers." The feeling of love for her filled him and he kissed the back of her shoulder tenderly then rested his head on her back wanting to be close to her. She smiled feeling comforted by him.

*****

Dinner at the Sprague's was full of noise and people. Jeneil loved it. Even though it wasn't her family, it was a family. Dr. Sprague's eldest son has a three year old son himself who added to the fun of the holiday. All the children were married except the youngest of the three boys who was in college. Jeneil marveled at how Steve seemed like a part of the family. The Sprague family was obviously used to him being around. It became noticeable that Dr. Sprague was watching them, causing the same reaction in both Steve and Jeneil. They stayed close together and occasionally held hands or Steve put his arm around her. It actually felt great to be at a holiday dinner with his wife by his side. He felt complete and tied to normal. He felt her get comfortable with him as he sat with his arm around her on the sofa after dinner. He felt her lean against him and he kissed her cheek causing one of the Sprague sons to grin and ask how long they had been married. Jeneil sat up after that. But Steve wasn't being discouraged; he had been waiting for Jeneil to put Peter to rest feeling her natural path would be toward her husband after she did. She loved too easily for it not to happen he thought. Her food and air was love, she sought it out. He rubbed her shoulder gently feeling good about having a wife and that it was Jeneil.

*****

At noon Peter unfolded the napkin on the motel room desk and put the bread and mustard together with ham and cheese. The convenience store had been opened and he had decided to buy sandwich things instead of facing holiday people eating a holiday meal. He turned on the radio and ate as he thumbed through a magazine he'd bought too. Memories of Jeneil kept surfacing bringing deep pain. He had expected the holiday to be tough. But he had made up his mind to survive. His anger would erase the thoughts of Jeneil as they surfaced. Uette had called him. He had no idea what she wanted since he hung up on her before she said more than her name. "That screwball bitch will never learn to stay out of my life." He sighed, wondering what was happening since he had received a note or something in the mail from Karen too. He had marked it "Return to Sender' and put it in the mail slot at the office. It felt good to retaliate in such a harmless way. It fed the anger that was in him.

*****

Jeneil and Steve returned home ready for some peace and quiet. Their day had begun early and Steve faced a full schedule of surgery because of the holiday and his absence for the seminar. Jeneil put a cassette in the player and joined him on the sofa. He finished his coffee and moved closer to her. "You've got Mrs. Sprague all revved up about the terracing project. She's having real fun working on it and letting her family know she's doing it too."

Jeneil nodded and smiled. "She's good and I didn't realize that she needed some kind of project."

"What do you mean?" Steve asked putting his arm around her. Jeneil leaned against him. "I think she's going through one of life's passages right now. It isn't easy." Jeneil eased closer to him and put her head on his shoulder snuggling to him. He smiled knowing that she hadn't done that in a long time. He felt her relax and then fall asleep.

Smiling he looked at her and kissed her forehead. "Life's passages, huh?" He thought, watching her. "We'll you would know, Sweetheart, you're struggling with one yourself." He kissed her forehead again. "I'll wait." He thought. "I'll be right here when you wake up from both."

*****

The work crew arrived to clean the house on Friday morning and a locksmith as well to install a keyhole lock on the door to Jeneil's room. The telephone rang and Jeneil answered it in her bedroom when she had taken shelter. Millie was outdoing herself high polishing everything with her crew. Jeneil had rented three connection ovens for the extra baking that Millie decided she'd began Friday afternoon with two of her friends as helpers. They had each brought their own mixes and blenders and began working right after lunch. Jeneil sighed wondering if it might have been easier to call Tiel's, but realized that they wouldn't handle a party as such short notice especially so close to a holiday. She sighed feeling that none of this turmoil as evident at Kirk Vance's party and he was a bachelor. Mild jitters began. The telephone rang.

"Honey, I have some bad news."

Jeneil sat down as her heart thumped. "Steve, make it mild bad news, please."

"While I was away at the seminar, word of the open house was spread and I've had people we never expected asking about coming."

"What!" Jeneil gasped. "Many?"

"Most of the doctor's connected with the hospital, the medical school, and the administration."

Jeneil held her throat. "Numbers Steve, give me numbers."

"Thirty-five to forty-five"

Jeneil caught her breath. "That's the whole other party. Why?" She asked. "What happened? Is word out that we have gold door knobs or something? I don't understand."

"They want to meet you, Jeneil." Steve smiled.

"Me? But why?"

"Lakeland Plaza." He said. "I have my suspicions that your connection to the Mandra Foundation is being mentioned too, and nobody wants to slight you."

"Slight me?" She groaned. "Instead they'll kill me with these last minute plans. Oh my gosh!"

"What should we do?" Steve asked.

Jeneil sighed. "I'll check with Millie first and work from there."

"This is a mess, Honey. I'm sorry." Steve apologized.

"Oh Steve, this is a nightmare! I'd better get on this right away. Now I know why I hate parties. I saw my mother live through them.

"Will you be okay?" Steve asked, concerned.

"I don't know Steve, but I'm certainly grateful that you didn't wait until you got home to tell me this."

Millie and her helpers stared in disbelief when Jeneil broke the news. Millie sat down on a kitchen chair and covered her mouth. "Millie, don't panic." Jeneil said. "I'll panic, you think. Please!"

Millie laughed. "Jeneil's there's no way we can bake anything more in the time we have. I'd have to go shopping, too."

"Bake! That's it!" Jeneil said smiling. "Millie you're wonderful. We won't bake; we'll just add more food. My mother made cold marinated shrimp that was very good. I didn't plan it for this party to keep expenses down, but I don't have any choice now, and cheeses and spreads for crackers. How about cold vegetable trays?" Jeneil asked, gaining hope.

"That will work." Millie smiled. "But preparing that shrimp will take some time too."

Jeneil paced. "Well obviously I have to help in the kitchen. Don't panic Millie; I've been known to manage a kitchen from time to time." She got her mother's cookbook and looked under shrimp and then gasped. Forget it. That's too much work." Jeneil paced again as Millie continued at the mixer. "Call Tommy and order more liquor." Millie reminded her.

Jeneil stopped pacing. "Oh my gosh, liquor. Thank you, Millie." Jeneil dialed and conferred with Tommy, who suggested adding wine too, for the cheese. Jeneil told him to handle the amounts. Anything unopened could be Christmas gifts. She began calling restaurants to see if they would prepare plain cooked shrimp for her. After calling three restaurants, she had enough to cover the party along with stuffed tiny mushrooms by 8:00pm that evening giving her time to marinate them. All of which added to the volume of food. Jeneil leaned against the kitchen counter and sighed.

Millie smiled. "It sounds okay now Jeneil, with the vegetable trays, too."

"Millie can you add another person to help tomorrow?"

Millie looked at the other two. "Beatrice?" She asked, and they both nodded.

"Jeneil." Millie said. "Could we have uniforms?"

"Really?" Jeneil replied. All three women nodded.

"We were talking at lunch and none of us have clothes that would look good to be mingling in this party. My outfits are either too casual or too dressy."

Jeneil shrugged. "Okay, I need to rent more glasses and linen napkins anyway. What do you want, white blouses and black skirts?"

Millie smiled. "We were wondering about deep royal blue dresses with white organdy aprons."

Jeneil raised her eyebrows. "Do you really want to look that…that."

"Yes." Millie smiled. "We do."

"Millie you don't have to. This isn't Roden Drive."

"No, but it's Tecumseh and I want a picture of me in it."

Jeneil smiled. "Millie, Dottie, Terri, you people are wonderful. You're making me feel like I'm doing you a favor." She hugged all three. "Are you free on Sunday?" They all nodded.

"I'd like to treat you to a bonus because of the extra work tomorrow. How about reservations at La Fevre's Petit Chateau so you can be spoiled to death."

The women laughed. "Our husbands would never go there." Millie said. "How about the Brandon Steakhouse and tickets to the hockey game and we will stay and clean. Our husbands won't miss us."

"That's not the amount of the bonus. How do you want the rest?" Jeneil asked.

"Pickins, if there is any and you take our pictures."

The other women agreed liking that bargain, too.

Jeneil smiled. "Oh, you women are priceless. You've made yourself a deal. Now I'd better get to the cheese shop for cheese and to Mainelli's Produce Market for vegetables. I put the coffee on, help yourselves."

"We'll take the vegetables home Jeneil and bring them back sliced. We won't have time to stay here."

"I'll do the vegetables." Jeneil said. "If you'll make a list of how much I should buy while I call the rental place and get my coat, that will help."

Millie raised her eyebrows. "That's a lot of vegetables, Jeneil. That's a lot of work."

"I'm used to slicing a lot of vegetables. I helped St. Dunstan's Church with the Thanksgiving Dinner." All three looked at each other as she left.

"Ain't any airs about her. I wouldn't mind being a servant in this place."

Millie smiled. "Don't let her hear you use that word. She doesn't like the sound of it."

"Yeah, she treats you like she's your niece." Terri laughed.

Millie smiled. "I like her. She's honest and fair and I feel like my job's as important as hers. At least she thinks so. She said if she didn't come to work life would go on, if I didn't she wouldn't know where to begin. We actually sit and talk about cleaning, can you believe that? Her mother used to make housework a game. She pretended they were maids in a hotel."

"No wonder she ain't got any airs. She's been trained that way." Terri added. "Must be old money. It always shows." Dottie nodded in agreement.

Millie smiled. "I think she just cares about people. Really cares."

*****

Jeneil got control of the situation and picked up all that was needed. By the time she went to bed she was tired, but the only thing she worried about was how the two bedrooms would affect the people who wanted to tour the house. She insisted that Steve go to skydiving class and she made 100 small crabmeat appetizers and then she went upstairs to put herself through "the works", doing her nails and conditioning her hair with scented oil and taking an oil bath herself and getting between two old shower curtains on her bed while the oil did its work. She dozed off and awoke with Steve knocking at her bedroom door. She opened her eyes as he walked in concerned.

"Jeneil!" He stopped and stared at her wrapped in plastic. You must have fallen asleep." She saw him looking at the shower curtain sheet she had over her.

She laughed. "Just trying to make a silk purse, Steve."

He walked closer. "What have you done to yourself?" He asked, looking at her shining face and hair that was wrapped in plastic.

She chuckled. "I'm like your SX7. We both need oil."

He smiled. "Does this mean everything is under control?"

She nodded. Millie and her crew are due here at one. Tommy's is arriving an hour and a half before the party to set up. So I'm lying here playing SPA and I fell asleep."

He smiled. "You're something else, Honey. What shall I do?"

"Nothing right now. One of the crew is in charge of the door so we can greet and mingle and say goodnight. How does that sound as a fun evening? Want to rent a video and we'll pop corn up here instead." She smiled.

"Why not, you look like you have enough oil." He teased.

She laughed. "Sure, I'll bet you don't smart-mouth the SX7 like this. I know I'd come in second to the car."

"You look like a clean mud wrestler." Steve joked.

She made a face at him. "Go study brain surgery so I can get moving from here."

"Okay." He said, going to the door. He walked to his room, smiling. "Jeneil you've got a kinky side to you. All that shiny skin. Does she ever look ugly?"

*****

The women arrived and began there work in the kitchen. Jeneil and Steve joined them and helped set up. Both bathrooms were stocked with extra guest towels and Beatrice was assigned to keep them looking neat and unused through the party, as well as clearing glass and napkins that might accumulate. The idea was to party, but not have the room look like it. Of all types of parties, Jeneil disliked open houses because of the lack of control over the numbers or the atmosphere. She was wishing the evening was over.

Adrienne and Charlie arrived just as the bartender did and Charlie was glad to not get kitchen duty.

"Look at all this stuff." Adrienne smiled. "It looks very festive. You're under control."

"Magical Millie." Jeneil smiled.

Steve reached for a sample of the food. And Jeneil slapped his hand. "Every morsel is needed Steve."

"Jeneil, I'm starved. We never had lunch."

Adrienne laughed. "He wants normal too, with a hundred people expected."

Jeneil smiled and patted his arm. "I forgot to get it for you." She went to the refrigerator and returned with a plate.

"Oh thanks." Steve sighed.

Charlie walked in. "Tommy wants to know where your extra glasses are."

"The boxes near the door to that room." Millie pointed.

"Hey Steve. Where'd you get macho food?"

"My wife." Steve answered, and biting into a large sandwich.

"You had lunch." Adrienne laughed.

"Yeh, but there won't be any dinner, just sissy food."

"I'll fix a plate for you." Jeneil laughed. Charlie delivered the glasses and returned to claim his plate. Steve got him a beer and they disappeared to the den and football on TV. Adrienne arranged vegetables on a tray and Millie took her crew for a conference on the table design.

"Little over an hour to Showtime, girl." Adrienne commented. "You better make tracks to your closet."

Jeneil sighed. "Yes, I suppose I should. This can't be over unless it starts, can it." Adrienne chuckled. The back door bell rang and Barbara Barnard walked in all dressed for the party. Jeneil looked shocked. "Barbara tell me you're your clocks are wrong."

Barbara laughed. "You're fine, Jeneil. I came over early because I had the guilts for causing this mix up. Can I Help?" She looked Adrienne. "Oh Jeneil, what luck, you've found kitchen help who'll do food. Introduce me to this wonder, please and promise me you'll share her."

Adrienne looked up with growing annoyance. Jeneil was stunned that Barbara would simply assume that Adrienne was domestic help. Jeneil smiled warmly. "Barbara meet a very close friend of mine, Adrienne Wilson and one of the top executives in the office. She does food, but frankly she's better at real estate." Adrienne laughed and relaxed.

Barbara looked embarrassed. "Gosh, I really do apologize, Adrienne. It's just that we need a network of good help. I just…." She trailed off. She looked at Jeneil. "How can I help?" She asked, smiling.

"Barbara, I appreciate the offer, but I have people who are handling the evening for me." Millie and her crew walked in dressed in their uniforms.

Barbara stared and then looked at Jeneil. "Royal dark blue and white organdy uniforms. Isn't that just a tad too showy, dear?" Barbara asked, pointedly.

"Our dresses are too showy?" Terri asked, looking disappointed.

Millie looked Barbara over. "Pardon me ma'am, but this is what my crew and I wear. We think it looks very tasteful. It's worn in all the finer homes for large parties and one hundred and twenty guests would be considered a large party."

Barbara gasped. "One hundred and twenty? Where did you get that number?" She looked at Jeneil. "Those weren't my figures."

"Steve added some." Jeneil replied, trying to hide her annoyance with Barbara's rudeness.

Barbara looked at Millie. "What do you mean, crew?"

Jeneil stepped in. "Barbara, Millie is General Manager of Domestic Services Co. and she's very good and very specific about interference. I have the jitters about tonight and I'm staying calm because Millie has agreed to handle this on short notice. If she should decide to leave I'd be a complete wreck." Jeneil spoke very pointedly to Barbara.

Barbara got the message. "Oooo, yes of course." She patted Millie's shoulder. "You look very nice. You and your crew. Very tasteful for a large party, in fact I'm the one who needs to update the outfit. I thought this was going to be a small and informal. I'd better change. I'll see you at party time, Jeneil. Excuse me ladies, I'll take myself out of your arena. They look very professional." Barbara made her exit as everyone watched.

"Why didn't you tell her you owned the company?" Millie asked.

Adrienne smiled. "Because that is a tad too showy Millie, not the Royal Blue and white organdy uniforms."

"What a snip!" Terri scowled.

Jeneil rubbed her temples. "Could we please remember that attitude is vital? Our faces will show what we're thinking. There may be more like her here tonight, but please don't lower yourself to their levels. You are all dignified professionals who will make this party run smoothly. The ladies of the house count on that. Make them look good."

Terri looked embarrassed. "Excuse me, I was out of line."

Jeneil smiled. "She is a snip, Terri; we just can't let it show on our faces."

Terri nodded and grinned. Jeneil patted her shoulder. "Primpy neighborhood, Jeneil." Adrienne smiled. "And I'm a guest so I can be bitchy." Everyone laughed.

Jeneil looked at her watch. "Oh wow, I've got to be getting ready. Millie, Terri, Dottie, Beatrice, thank you very much. I'm calm because you're here. Adrienne, feel free to use the guest rooms to change." She left and raced upstairs and gathered clothes from her closet and took them to Steve's. She moved his bureau items to one side and brought some of hers. Taking the vase of flowers, she added them to Steve's room too and then went in for a quick shower to freshen up. Steve opened the door to his bedroom and noticed the changes. Taking off his shirt, he went to the closet for his robe. Seeing Jeneil's clothes hanging by his startled him. "What's happening?" He asked himself and turned to go across the hall to find out. Jeneil came from his bathroom wrapped in her robe. They were each surprised to see each other. Jeneil had hoped to be dressed and gone before he came upstairs.

"Jeneil, what's all this?" He asked.

She felt awkward. "Steve, I just think it would be wise to make it look like our marriage is normal so I put some of my things in here to make it convincing. We'll keep my bedroom locked and say that it's my studio and better kept untouched. Is that okay with you?"

Steve watched her closely. "Life is getting complicated."

"Only when one hundreds and twenty guests are expected to visit." She replied. "I just don't like my life being so scrutinized. Explaining a two bedroom arrangement defeats our original plan for the marriage. It robs us of our privacy and stop staring, I know it looks odd and hypocritical." She said, twisting the tie to her robe around her finger.

"Did I say that?" He smiled.

"You were thinking loudly." She grinned.

"Not me." He laughed. "It never entered my mind. You're the one struggling, not me." He said, very glad that he had taken his shirt off. It felt good standing before her that way.

"I'll let you get ready." She said, going to the door. He watched her and then taking his robe from the closet, he smiled. "Move in anytime, Honey. Anytime at all."

He was fixing his tie at the mirror when Jeneil knocked.

"Come in." He answered smiling before she opened the door. "Make it a habit." He mumbled.

She walked in. "I was wondering what suit you were wearing. Good a dark one." She smiled.

"Why?" He asked.

"Just silly. My red dress screams. I didn't want to overshadow you."

"You're red dress is a knockout." He said. It was softly draped and crisscrossed in front and back. "Now I know why you got greased up today."

"The dress isn't that low." She argued, holding her hand to her throat.

"Did I say that?" He smiled.

"Don't gaslight me." She laughed. "You know you meant that."

He smiled. "I like it. Any hooks to bit tonight?" He asked, brushing his hair.

"No." She answered, thinking the question strange.

"I'll see you downstairs." She said, going to the door.

"Jeneil." He called. She turned. "Your hair looks terrific. Shiny and dark. It's beautiful." He said, watching her in the mirror.

"Thank you." She replied, trying to understand what he was doing.

He smiled. "I just want you to know that I watch your brain, too."

She nodded and left the room. Standing in the hallway she turned and looked at his door. "Were those innuendos?" She asked herself. "He's in a very strange mood." The doorbell rang and she opened the door. "First arrivals are here."

"I'm ready." He said and joined her in the hallway.

"Is the room neat?" She asked.

"My half in our room is, dear. I'm phobic remember." He grinned.

"Have you been sampling the liquor?" She asked.

He laughed. "Mrs. Bradley, we have guests." She watched him for a second and then she took his hand to walk down the stairs. He looked at her and smiled then kissed her on the cheek.

*****

The party started to fill up fast and Jeneil became concerned, but they discovered that these were people with other commitments for the evening, but who wanted to stop in and be social. It was obvious that they were coming to meet Jeneil. Steve heard conversations about her as he mingled. "She's so young." "Not what I expected at all, but bright." "She knows her business." The words he was hearing quite a bit were "Mandra Foundation." He had thought that was the reason for the crowd.

Barbara and Drexel Barnard had been the first of the neighborhood to arrive. "My goodness, look at this crowd. Jeneil, red is a great color for you. I've got to see the food. They didn't use Tiel's." She made her way to the diningroom. The pace was hectic. And

Jeneil became immune to handshaking. Conversation was becoming a routine blur of pleasant short sentences and smiles.

Kirk Vance arrived and grinned slowly at Jeneil. "I thought deep ivory on you was stunning, but red is a real dazzler... You look sensational. You hair has such sheen. Mmm, you are a vision."

Jeneil smiled politely. "Dr. Vance, my ego is overwhelmed."

"Kirk, Jeneil Kirk." He replied in his deepest voice. "Hi Steve." He smiled and shook his hand. "Where'd the crowd come from? These things are supposed to be small and intimate so the neighbors get to know each other.

Steve smiled. "Cleveland hospital and Downes Medical school. Jeneil's connected to a foundation that's a contributor. Nobody wants to slight her."

Kirk nodded and grinned. "I don't want to either and she doesn't contribute money to me." He smiled and moved on as others arrived.

"Too late for him." Jeneil mumbled

Steve smiled at her having heard the remark. "Natural immunity." He thought, liking that about her.

Adrienne came to her side. "Two things." She whispered. "Everyone's complimenting the food, so you can relax. And Charlie wants to know if there's an escape room for him. I keep chasing him. He can't remember that he's a guest. I've had to chase him from behind the bar twice."

Jeneil laughed. "My bedroom or take the TV in the den to the basement, there are two roll-a-way beds down there. No place is safe otherwise. They're all over including the garage because of the SX7.

Adrienne nodded. "Basement it is then, thanks." She shook her head. "That man will never get civilized."

Jeneil smiled. "I like Neanderthal, personally."

Adrienne laughed lightly and blended into the people again. Beatrice opened the door to Robert, Dennis and Karen. Jeneil smiled and went to them quickly with hugs.

Dennis kissed her lips lightly. "You look incredible." He smiled.

Karen hugged her. "He's right. What did you do get a salon treatment or something?"

"No just an oil treatment."

"Sexy." Karen winked.

"Oil treatment?" Robert grinned. "Let me see." He said, touching her cheek and neck, moving his hand to the base of his throat. "Oooo soft." He said.

"Robert!" Jeneil whispered, hoarsely. "Don't do madcap here, please." She chuckled.

He smiled, broadly. "Madcap? I'll bet this place is filled with guys wanting to touch the hostess." Dennis and Karen laughed.

"Don't get me started." Jeneil giggled, holding back a laugh.

He kissed her cheek. "Trying to get you started is a full time job with me; you should know that by know." He kissed her lips firmly.

"Oh Robert. You have my lipstick on you now. Here take my handkerchief." She slipped one from her long sleeve.

"Hell no." He laughed. "Let the other guys eat their heart out. I got to touch and kiss the hostess."

Jeneil chuckled. "Robert you look silly."

Steve walked to them. "Robert, how's it going?' He asked

Robert grinned. "Can't tell from one kiss. Give me an hour or so with her."

"Robert!" Jeneil was shocked at how far he was going.

Steve ignored him. "Dennis." He said. "Nice to see you. Karen's how's Matthew?"

"Just fine." Karen smiled. "How about you?"

"Fine too." Steve smiled.

"I guess so. I heard you got an SX7." Karen replied. Dennis nudged her and she became quiet.

Robert watched Steve. "Can I show Dennis the SX7?" He asked. Steve nodded and reached into his pocket for the keys. "Look inside too." He said, handing them to him.

"I wish you'd turn your wife over that easily." Robert grinned.

"I can replace the car." Steve answered, unsmilingly.

"Oooo lucky you." Robert sneered. "Lots more where that came from, huh?"

Jeneil sighed. "Robert sometimes you show no mercy."

Robert grinned. "It's cool, Sweetheart." He chucked her chin, lightly. "Mmm, I love the oil treatment." He kissed her.

"How can you stand it, Steve?" He said, and then looked at Dennis and Karen. "Garage is this way." He walked away staring Steve down.

Steve took a deep breath and sighed, then smiled as four new arrivals came to them.

Kirk Vance sipped his drink and smiled at Barbara and Drexel Barnard. "So that's the renowned "Wolf Man" Robert Danzieg. He's awfully friendly with the host's wife."

Barbara chuckled. "He and Steve stand at twenty paces don't they? Subtle, but there's a duel going on." She whispered. "Looks it to me." Drexel commented.

Kirk chuckled. "And Mona Lisa stands in the middle trying to mediate. She has her hands full." He grinned.

Barbara watched Jeneil. "She can handle it in my opinion. And this is strictly hush news. We don't want to have it all through Tecumseh and the hospital. You know the gossip. Sondra Rand told me that she was Peter Chang's just before Steve or maybe while, who knows, they almost fought over something in OR once." Kirk and Drexel looked at each other, surprised.

"Both?" Drexel asked. Barbara nodded.

"Are you sure?" Kirk asked her, becoming very interested.

"I heard it said once, they were sharing a girlfriend, that's why the two of them got so tightlipped and private. She was sending dinners for the two of them. Is that sophisticated or what?"

"Both!" Kirk said, as he watched Jeneil. "Oh Steve, you're not playing fair. That treasure is private stock   The White Stallion has forgotten the rules."

Drexel chuckled. "Obviously something he doesn't want to share. She is very misleading. How does she keep the look of innocence?"

"She's different." Kirk replied. "Plays by her own rules. Very fascinating." He grinned. "The looks a killer though. Damn attractive, even in fiery red, there's the sense that she's somewhere in hiding protecting herself from the world around her. She looks more vulnerable then innocent. She makes you want to take her and lead her."

Drexel laughed. "That's a good piece of news, Barbara." Kirk smiled and watched Jeneil fascinated by the new information about her.

Robert joined Dennis at the buffet table. "Dennis do me a favor. Casually keep an eye on the guy near the fireplace in the livingroom and tell me what you think.

Dennis went to the other side of the table and glanced up casually. "The one with all the dark hair and the strong gaze from under the eyelids?"

"That's the one." Robert said, as he put a stuffed mushroom in his mouth.

Dennis filled his plate. "Something has him interested. He's watching something steadily."

"Not something Dennis, someone." Robert said. "Jeneil."

Dennis looked at him and smiled. "Jealous?"

"Worried." Robert answered, quietly. "That's Kirk Vance."

Dennis raised his eyebrows. "The Kirk Vance."

"There's only one Dennis and I just found out that he's a neighbor of hers." Robert sighed.

Dennis tasted some food, still eyeing Kirk Vance. "He looks like everything I've heard about him. Have you been to any of his orgy Friday parties?"

"Are you kidding?" Robert smiled. "I make my living from my imagination. I can't afford a chemistry major. We have friends in common. This shittin neighborhood isn't for Jeneil." Robert sighed.

Dennis chuckled. "You don't think Steve is, either."

"He's not." Robert said, going to Dennis's side. "It's a two bedroom marriage." He whispered softly.

Dennis looked up quickly. "Oh shit, what has she got herself into this time?" He sighed, too.

Jeneil joined them. "The crowd is thinning out and the food and drinks are lasting. I'll think I'll breathe." She smiled.

"You have quite a home." Dennis asked. "How many bedrooms?"

"Five." Jeneil answered, taking a cheery tomato from the tray.

Dennis watched her. "Are you going to fill them with kids?"

Jeneil was set back by the question. "Why would you like to rent one?" She asked, jokingly.

Robert laughed, softly. "Jeneil do the neighbors know you're renting bedrooms. "That's pretty modern and sophisticated."

"You don't quit." She smiled.

"What do you think of your neighbors?" Dennis asked.

Jeneil shrugged. "Don't know them too well."

"Best way to get along in neighborhoods like this." Robert sighed.

Jeneil sighed. "That's almost impossible around here, they are the partyinest people. One a month in the neighborhood, and I get the feeling there are private parties more often. Like Dr. Vance said, "There's always fun happening here.""

Dennis and Robert exchanged looks. Robert closed his eyes and shook his head.

"Come into the rep. Sweetheart." Dennis suggested, strongly.

"No thanks, Dennis. It's too big, but call me if you begin anything."

"What are we working on now?" Dennis asked.

"Absolutely nothing." Jeneil sighed. "I'm playing at photography with Robert's encouragement."

"Like it?" Dennis asked.

"I'm enjoying it. Robert called it new eyes." She smiled. "It is."

"She's not bad, either." Robert added.

"I've decided to build a studio in the back yard. Lately I've been thinking of things I'd like to do but it's messy like painting and working with wood. So I'm going to use the studio."

"Hey, that's good to hear." Robert laughed. "Your muse must be ecstatic."

Jeneil smiled. "I've decided to play at everything that interests me. And then maybe a specialty will surface."

Dennis finished his crab appetizer. "What's interesting to you so far?"

Jeneil smiled. "Promise you won't laugh?" Dennis and Robert smiled waiting to hear what she would say.

"Sewing, jewelry, wood art, photography and I'm starting a women's dancing session."

"What kind of dancing?" Robert asked.

"Exotic."

Robert laughed loudly and then gained control. "You, a belly dancer?" He whispered.

"I thought you promised not to laugh. It's really good exercise."

Dennis laughed, softly. "Jeneil, Honey zero in on something."

Jeneil shook her head. "No Dennis, I think it's time to burst upon life and turnover every rock that catches my eye. I used to feel guilty about dabbling, but I'm dealing in business. I'm earning a living, why shouldn't I have hobbies. I usually painted one or two canvases a year. I feel the need to express myself on canvas again. There's a restlessness in me for it, that and writing in my notebook. I'm uncovering a lot about myself by writing my thoughts down. My mother did too. It's like therapy. At least it quiets the restlessness when it becomes intense."

Robert smiled at her pleased with what he was hearing. "Go for it, Honey. Taste it all until the jungle drums are so loud you can't miss what they're saying. Try everything." He hugged her. "That's the best news, I've heard yet." He kissed her lips and put a crab appetizer in her mouth.

"What's the best news you've heard?" Steve asked.

Robert turned. "That she's building a studio out back so she can escape from this mausoleum you have her in."

Jeneil's shoulders drooped. "Robert, that's not nice."

Steve glared at him slightly and then turned to Jeneil. "Dr. Winslow and his wife are leaving."

"Oh." Jeneil smiled. "I'm neglecting the party. Nice chatting with you guys." She smiled and walked off with Steve holding her hand.

"He's affectionate toward her." Dennis observed. "And your interest in her irritates him, that's obvious." He sighed. "I don't understand what could be wrong."

Robert watched them walk away. "Well, I'm going to check blondie out. I run into doctors at parties. Let's see what turns up about the guy."

Dennis grinned. "You should think about giving her up, Robert. She has a thing for doctors, I guess."

"No, Dennis, my interest is more than just thinking she's terrific. She resists life. She has since I've known her.

"She's delicate, Robert." Dennis said. "She's gentle and vulnerable. She's only protecting herself from the crazy world. It's really part of her charm."

"But Dennis, there's a pulsebeat inside her and it's artistic. At first I thought it was just an appreciation, but it's more. It's a naturalness around the art sphere and a rhythm with it."

Dennis sighed. "Well she has a grasp for theater. All of it. She absorbs knowledge through her pores."

Robert smiled. "See you've noticed it too."

"Yeah, I have." Dennis said, quietly. "But where the hell does she belong. She's all over the place. She even looks natural hostessing this bash. She handles business well." He shrugged. "Where can she specialize with all this in her life?"

"The studio, Dennis. That studio will let her open up. She's got her ear to the jungle drum. If she just keeps walking toward it she'll be okay." Robert smiled. "The muse is waking in her and getting stronger."

The crowd began to thin as the hour got later and even the Tecumseh neighbors were leaving. Kirk Vance fixed his scarf inside his top coat and smiled at Jeneil. "This was a large party Mona Lisa, too large. I was hoping to get to know you better." He used his steadiest gaze and deepest voice.

"I'm sorry." She said. "This just stampeded. I hope the evening was pleasant in spite of the crowd."

"I enjoyed myself," He smiled, "and your food was a nice change. Everyone uses Tiel's so there's a sameness that's accepted, but your buffet was a refreshing change and delicious too."

"Thank you." Jeneil smiled.

"I hope to get to see you soon. Are you planning to be at any of the parties that are coming up?'

Steve watched him waiting to hear of a Friday Party and he was ready to step in.

"The Barnard's probably." She replied.

Kirk took her hand and smiled. "Good, that's just around the corner." He squeezed her hand in both of his. "You're so beautiful. I love your eyes." Jeneil smiled as benignly as she could. Kirk nodded to Steve and gave him a quick handshake. "You take the fussing your wife receives very well. I guess you expect it when she looks like she does. Her kind of beauty is a flame.

Steve watched silently feeling that Kirk Vance was coming on too strong with her. He was glad that Jeneil was immune to him. Steve felt the tension and resentment as Kirk kissed her cheek and said goodbye again to both of them. Jeneil was pleased that it was only a kiss and not one of his sneaky moves. Steve closed the door behind him and the Barnards, glad to have the party ended.

Jeneil went to the kitchen where Millie had things almost fully cleared away. Tommy had joined them as they sat with mugs of coffee. Jeneil got a glass of juice and joined them. "What was left? How closely did we estimate?" She asked.

Tommy took his list out. "Three bourbon and one gin left. Four bottle of Chablis."

"Oh Tommy, you did really well. They can be Christmas gifts." She smiled. "And a thank you for you. Which one would you like?" She asked.

"A Chablis?" He grinned.

Jeneil nodded at him and then she reached into a drawer for envelopes and handed each one. "This is my personal thanks to all of you. Steve and I appreciate how well everything went. Even the spills were handled subtly. You're a great team. People noticed." Millie smiled proudly.

Jeneil looked around. "Is everything all packed?"

Millie nodded. "We sent a small plate with Adrienne and we left a plate for you. Dr. Bradley liked the crabmeat appetizers and the mushrooms."

Jeneil smiled. "Thank you Millie, for your steadiness." She hugged the woman.

"Well, we'll be going so you and your husband can rest. It was a full night of steady visitors. You must be tired."

Nodding, Jeneil sighed. "I'm glad it's over." The crew packed up the last bit of evidence and were gone.

Steve smiled at Jeneil. "This was a nice open house. You pulled it off."

"With a lot of help from my friends." She grinned. She undid her bracelet and took off her earrings showing relief.

He watched her. "Is your husband allowed to fuss too? Kirk's right, you do get fussed over."

Jeneil smiled. "You know I've heard that every woman reaches a prime time when she looks her best. She's at her peak. The fussing surprises me. The word beautiful doesn't seem to fit my idea of myself."

"You can't possibly think you're ugly." Steve said. "No, just ordinary, bordering plain. I grew up in blonde blue-eyed country. Outstanding beauty was commonplace. I had to wear braces and so I became comfortable being wallpaper living around knockouts. I knew I couldn't compete. Then Bill and I had some gossip start about us that refused to die. Boys whistled at me, but I always felt it was because of the gossip. When I got older I noticed that I'd get whistled at when I wore jeans or shorts and sweaters, so I stopped wearing them. I felt sure someone somewhere would want to know me as a person."

Steve smiled watching her fidget with her bracelet knowing that even talking about herself physically made her uncomfortable. "You are beautiful, Jeneil."

She looked at him and hair slipped to her eye. She tilted her head to push it back. Whenever her hair fell across her eye he would develop the strongest urge to fix it for her just to touch her.

"You're far from plain." He said, sincerely. "The person you wanted someone to get to know first is beautifully developed and the package has grown to match the person. You've learned how to deal really well with some very striking features like your eyes and your hair and the braces must have worked, your smile is a charmer." She looked down at her bracelet opening and closing the clasp nervously. He walked closer to her. "And I've made you blush." He took her hand gently in his and lifted her chin to look at her. "I think you're beautiful and I'm glad you're my wife." He said, quietly. He put his arms around her slowly moving closer to her and he was surprised that she wasn't resisting. He just held her to him, not wanting to rush her; afraid she would resist or bolt from him. He felt her relax and he kissed her cheek softly feeling his heart pound in his chest. He rested his face next to hers, the softness and warmth of her skin had electricity pulsing in his chest as he wrestled with the idea of kissing her lips like he'd been wanting to long before they were married. He touched his lips to her cheek slowly and softly.

The telephone beside them rang and the sudden noise startled Jeneil, who moved from him quickly. She sighed realizing it was the telephone. "I'm sorry." She said. "It rang in my ear. It was so unexpected." She took a breath and Steve answered the call, deeply resenting the interruption.

"Steve, its Sheldon Taft. I apologize for calling so late. But I have a couple of favors to ask. My wife noticed an ear ring missing after we left your place and went to my brother's. It wasn't at his house and we've just finished searching the car with a flashlight. Is it possible that someone has found it there? We spent most of the time in the livingroom."

"No one reported finding an earring after cleaning up, Sheldon. What does it look like?"

"It's a gold clip-on with a pearl in the center surrounded by very small diamonds."

"Well, I'll look under things in the livingroom."

"I'd appreciate that, Steve. I'll hold on." Steve rested the receiver on the base of the wall phone.

"I'll help." Jeneil said, following him. They moved each sofa without finding the earring. Steve went to an armchair to check the cushions. Jeneil got on the floor near the long drapes remembering that someone had spilled a drink in that area. She wondered if in the commotion the earring had fallen. Lifting the drapes, she felt along the carpeting with her hand for a few feet. Her hand hit something. Picking it up, she held the earring up to show Steve.

He smiled. "Great work, detective." He went back to the telephone. "Sheldon, Jeneil just found it hidden under the drapes."

"Oh terrific." Sheldon sighed. "My wife will be relieved. They were an anniversary gift. She hasn't had them that long. I have another favor to ask and I wouldn't if it didn't mean so much, but my parents is visiting from Florida, we expected them at Christmas and Dad told us that he'll have to be in Switzerland on business during the holidays. My mother is really disappointed so we all decided to have Christmas this week. I'm scheduled to be at the Estes Clinic in Merriciote on Tuesday."

Steve closed his eyes knowing what was coming. "Sheldon any changes in seminars schedules have to be cleared with Sprague. He's nailed me for just jumping in."

"I've called him, Steve. He was annoyed. He said you've been to more than your share in the last few weeks, but he's leaving it up to you. I missed the holidays with my parents for two years for very flimsy reasons which I regret now and so have my brother and sister. We really should remember not to take them for granted." Jeneil listened and watched guessing what the conversation was about.

Steve hesitated, but he had heard about this invitation to attend Estes from associate staff meetings and had wished he could attend. He looked at Jeneil who was watching him. He didn't know how to let her know.

Jeneil saw the struggle and smiled. "It's okay with me. Will you be back for Christmas?"

"I'll be back this Saturday."

She relaxed. "There's no problem for me then."

Steve watched her and felt his chest fill with love for her and her gentle, quiet, attitude. He smiled and touched her cheek lovingly. She blushed, surprising him and then she left the room.

Steve finished the telephone conversation and stayed by the telephone for a few seconds after he hanging up. The encounter between him and Jeneil that had just happened had him encouraged. "Go Easy." He thought remembering how easily she had spooked from the telephone interruption, but he felt that he had made a bridge. He had reached out to her romantically and she hadn't bolted. She didn't respond like any other women he'd known in that situation either. He got the feeling that she felt awkward, like she really didn't know what to do. He smiled. "That's why I never liked dealing with virgins. I never knew what they expected me to do and how the hell do you ask? Besides the whole delicate situation that follows anyway." He sighed. "She's not a virgin, but she sure seems like one. Apparently virginity is more then a physical condition." He shook his head. "Jeneil, the White stallion would have given up on you. I know he would have, but Steve Bradley is a lot smarter than that ass. I'll wait and just make it easy for you to initiate more when you're ready." He went upstairs feeling very positive about the situation. Jeneil was taking her things from his room. "Need help?" He asked.

"This is the last of it, thanks." She said, holding some clothes on hangers over her arm. "Is the house locked up?" He nodded. "Then I'll just go to my room. Goodnight." She said and walked past him. She stopped and then walked back to him to kiss his cheek.

He smiled. "I'll take you to breakfast in the morning. Bring your camera and we'll chase some shadows. We deserve a break and thanks for understanding about another trip out of town."

She nodded and smiled. "I knew about that addiction of yours before we got married." She shrugged. "We all have them." Her hair slipped to her eye as she shrugged. He reached up and pushed the hair back in place. She smiled gently at him and he leaned toward her, kissing her lips lightly, but not as quickly as he would have before the encounter.

"Goodnight." He said, quietly. She nodded and backed away slowly, then she turned and left the room. Steve closed the door and smiled. "Hell that was worth sit-ups."

Jeneil stopped in the hallway. She turned and looked at his closed door. "Is he different?" She asked herself. "He is different." She shook her head. "What's happening? I wish life came with a script like a play. In fiction the dialogue meets the needs of the situation. In real life it's groping in the dark and awkward situations with unspoken thoughts. It's so infuriating." She opened the door to her room. "I'd even settle for a crystal ball. Anything that will help those of us with klutz tendencies."

*****

Steve's flight left late Sunday afternoon and he made the most of the time with Jeneil. Staying near her, holding her hand or holding her in his arms. He knew that she was going to miss him; he sensed that even before she said it. As he boarded the plane, he really wished he wasn't leaving. They were closer, the day had gone perfectly. He wondered what would become of their relationship.

*****

The empty house was filled with echoes when Jeneil arrived from work in Tuesday. Stepping onto the deck, she looked at the diggings at the base of one side of the slope. The workmen had begun the footings for the studio. The landscape architect had calculated its distance from the house so it would blend with the terracing when that work would be completed in the spring. The ground was too hard for gardening, but the studio was designed on stilts above the ground and an eventual blend with a deck that attached to the slope. She smiled, it was hard to imagine the awkward slope and the studio joining properly. One of the terracing features on the slope was to be small decks on stilts hidden by shrubs. She had designed it with children in mind. The area under the decks would make great hiding places, forts or small caves whichever the imaginations wanted. Some of the slope she planned to leave sloping for winter sledding fun. She had been thinking lately about adopting children so she and Steve could enjoy the benefits of family life and it would be a way for Steve to help someone who was getting as tough a break as he had been given. Uneasiness filled her as she thought about discussing it with him. An uneasiness that she couldn't understand. There was a lot lately that she wasn't understanding about her and Steve and she knew that it stemmed from his changed behavior. He was being romantic. She knew a discussion on the relationship would be necessary soon and she hoped sincerely that she'd have her thoughts and feelings clear enough to deal with it when it happened. Having to discuss the White Stallion made her the most uneasy and she was sure her feelings would probably be insulting to Steve. He wasn't as open as Peter was. Steve had a part of him that no person could reach. Jeneil accepted that in him, knowing that she had the same quality in her. It had to do with privacy. She felt that her acceptance of that quality in Steve was helping them to get along so well. She didn't require him to open up to her in a closeness that he wasn't able to handle. She understood and never asked him to. The closeness of his friendship was enough for her, more than enough since Peter was so much a part of who she was privately. She could tell that their love would always be part of who she is or would be part of who she would become privately. She didn't expect to achieve that special oneness or fulfillment with another man ever. Not expecting it or looking for it seemed to keep the wonderful memories of what they had in perspective and the pain of the loss wasn't so intense. Life became bearable for her. She had experienced a great love in her lifetime. It was an achievement that pleased her and left her confident within herself. It also left her lacking the need for a physical relationship. She had known love and sex alone seemed too false and cheap to settle for.

By Thursday, the skeleton of her studio was assembled. The building looked strange stuck in the backyard unattached to any visible aesthetic plan. It was an eyesore and Jeneil wondered what the neighbors must be thinking. No one had asked or commented, but then she hadn't been around much lately. There was still last minute Christmas shopping to be done in crowded stores filled with irritable and irritating temporary sales help. It all reminded her of why she usually shopped in September or October, but she was living with the results of an emotionally tumultuous summer. She looked at her studio from the upstairs back bedroom and laughed as she saw the pipes for the studio water and underground sprinkling systems leading to the strange building. The network of pipe added to the eyesore. The building looked like some storage embryonic offspring of the main house that wasn't completely developed like a new bird without feathers and attached by an umbilical cord of pipes. She noticed Amanda Tufton standing at a window studying the skeletal sculpture on Jeneil's yard. "Well, they've noticed it." She chuckled. "I'd love to hear what's been said at the dinner tables around her. "That oddball Bradley woman is at it again, dear. What is that thing?! It's weird, dear. Do we allow weird in Tecumseh?" She laughed and went to her bedroom, hoping the carpenter's would really work fast to close it in. With a snowstorm expected over the weekend, she was concerned that the work would stop. She thought about Steve and hoped she'd see him before spring since he would be trying to leave Minnesota where Jeneil imagined snowstorms were common and he'd be trying to arrive in New England where snowstorms were common, too. She missed him and she realized how very much she enjoyed being married. He was easy to live with, much easier than Peter was and she wondered if the difference was the physical relationship. "Two points in favor of celibacy.' She said, taking her shopping list to see what she had left to buy.

Twenty-Five

The weather forecast predicted snow due late Friday night. Jeneil looked at the sky as she left the office building. It had been a dismal heavy looking sky all day, and the air seemed too warm. She shook her head. "Ice storm, too. I'll just bet." She sighed. She hated ice storms more than snowstorms. They were the ones that snapped power lines and made moving about treacherous. Her stopping at a convenience store for candles and a minimum of provisions, she then headed for home as small snow flakes of very wet snow were beginning to fall sparsely. "Ice storms for sure." She said, glad to be heading home. She ate a light dinner quickly while listening to the weather report and heard the possibility of an ice storm predicted. "Uh huh!" She sighed, "I thought so." The flakes were coming down quickly now and sticking to trees. A lasting snow, too." She said, watching the stream began to be shrouded in white." "Get the camera, Jeneil. It'll be a beautiful sight tomorrow if you're able to get out of the house. Ice storms were wondrous sights to behold the day after, especially with snow as the icy coating on twigs of branches sparkled like diamonds if the sun was bright and it usually was. Icy snow storms usually emptied the sky and clear weather was enjoyed for at least a day which was good since some remote parts of the state would experience broken power lines which need repairing. She remembered one year when the ice was two to three inches thick and amidst the wondrous beauty the "morning after" was the damage to the trees., whose branches, some six to eight inches round were hanging broken by the weight of the wet snow and ice accumulation on top of that. She worried about Steve. The telephone rang; she hoped it would be him. He'd be calling every night which was different for him, but it made her feel less alone. She was disappointed as she heard the studied deepness of the voice on the other end of the receiver. "Dr. Vance, how are you?"

"Just fine Mona Lisa and call me Kirk will you? I'm sitting in my den and wondering about you. The Barnards told me that Steve's away and I'm calling you to invite you to have dinner with me. A few friends will be stopping in later; you're welcomed to help us celebrate the first lasting snowstorm. There's no sense in your being alone." Jeneil's brow furrowed deeply and she resented the invitation being extended because her husband was away. "Thank you Dr. Vance, but I've eaten dinner. Steve's due in tomorrow, so I won't be alone for long. There's really no need to wonder about me."

He chuckled. "Well yes there is really, what is that building under construction in your backyard?"

Jeneil grinned. "It's a studio, and you might tell the other residents that it will eventually tie in with the landscaping we'll be doing. I'm sorry it's such an eyesore now.

"It's mostly windows." Kirk Vance replied.

"I know." Jeneil answered. "I wanted to capture natural light."

"Are you an artist besides having business interests too?"

"Everyone has hobbies." Jeneil answered. "I dabble in things and some of them are messy."

"You're a curiosity to me, Jeneil. You don't follow one path. Why don't you stop by later anyway and be part of the crowd? I'd like to hear about this dabbling of yours."

Again irritation surfaced in Jeneil. "Dr. Vance. I don't like driving in icy snowstorms; I'm planning to stay right by my den fire to wait it out, but thank you for the invitation."

"You don't need to drive, the Barnards are coming and they're your neighbors.

"No thank you." Jeneil replied, more emphatically. "The way it's snowing, we could be caught in the worse part of the storm when it's time to come home."

"People usually stay over on Friday's anyway."

That sounded strange to Jeneil.

"I'd rather not, thanks anyway. I'm expecting to hear from Steve, he calls me every night. I'd like to be here."

"Well, okay, if you insist on being alone, but you're welcome to change your mind and I really wish you would. Don't concern yourself about the weather. I can come for you in my 4X4 Trailblazer. It gets through anything." Jeneil noticed that the deepness of his voice got deeper and more smooth as he offered his services.

She struggled to hide the irritation that surfaced in her. "Thank you, Dr. Vance. I'll remember that."

"Good, think about my offer seriously and Jeneil, the name is Kirk, remember that too."

Jeneil closed her eyes. "I'll try." She said, quietly

"See you soon then and I'm disappointed. I was hoping to get you here tonight. I don't give up too easily." The deepness of his voice felt like vibrations through the receiver.

Jeneil felt annoyance stir inside of her. "I'm really sorry. I feel safer here."

Kirk Vance chuckled, sensuously. "Do you now?" He laughed a throaty deep laugh. "Then I should change that shouldn't I?"

Jeneil looked at the receiver and gripped it firmly. "Thank you for calling, I'll let you get to your party preparations. "Thanks again." She hung up and stomped onto the den feeling very agitated for having been pressured so much. The telephone rang and her agitation was still in her throat as she went to answer. "I've had it with the man; I'll tell him off this time." She sighed and growled a hello as she answered.

"Wow, Honey what are you so angry about?" Robert Danzieg asked.

Jeneil laughed, relieved that it was him. "Nothing really." She answered.

"Tis the season to be jolly." He said, teasing her.

"So it seems." She replied. "Dr. Vance is having a party tonight. How this place can party so much is a wonder to me and in a snowstorm too."

Robert caught his breath. "This is Friday isn't it?"

"Yes, why?"

Robert held his breath. "Are you and Steve going to Vance's party?"

 "No. Steve's at a seminar." Jeneil explained, wondering why Robert sounded tense.

Robert relaxed. "I have those prints you wanted for the Fairview foyers. Can I bring them to you now?"

"In a snow storm, Robert? That isn't necessary."

"It isn't bad driving and I'm used to it anyway. I'll be in Fairhaven for a week so who knows when I'll get things to you."

"Well, if you're sure." She replied, reluctantly.

"I'm on my way and Jeneil do you have anything frozen that you can microwave for me? It would save me stopping at a restaurant."

"Of course." She answered. "I'll be glad to do that."

"Thanks Honey. I knew I could count on you. See you shortly."

Jeneil went to the kitchen quickly; it felt good to be getting dinner for somebody. She missed that routine with Steve away.

*****

Robert arrived later than Jeneil had expected. "The crazy city hasn't done anything about plowing city side streets yet. It was rough getting out of Upton." He stomped the snow off his shoes on the doormat. He kissed her lips lightly as he walked in. Barbara and Drexel Barnard looked at each other surprised as they saw Jeneil's guest. Kirk Vance had told them she was planning to spend the evening alone before a warm fire.

They drove out onto the street and made there way to the Friday night party, grinning. "Maybe alone means one at a time to her." Barbara snickered.

Her husband frowned. "Don't be catty dear. The group works best when everyone gets along well."

"I know, I hear." Barbara chuckled. "She's just such a damn surprise to me, that's all. And to think people at the hospital thought she was once studying to be a nun."

Jeneil joined Robert on the floor before the den fire after putting some music on. Robert sighed contentedly. "Honey, this taste so good. You fussed and you shouldn't have."

Jeneil smiled. "It's good to have someone fuss over. Steve's been gone all week. Having another voice in the house feels good. This place is large. I've decided to make the studio a little bigger so I can stay there when Steve's away. I hate the echoes and the emptiness in this place." She said, pouring more coffee in Robert's mug.

He watched her and then touched her cheek tenderly. "You're a natural companion, Honey. I'd find it tough to leave you. I'd miss your fussing. I don't know how Steve can be separated from you for so long. Is there something wrong with him physically?" Jeneil put the coffee butler down with a slight smack as the question stunned her.

"Robert what a question!" She laughed, nervously.

"Well, answer it." He said, watching her closely.

"No, there isn't." She replied. "Goodness nothing is sacred to you is it?"

"He put his plate aside. "Honey, are you happily married?"

She wrinkled her brow and looked at Robert. "Yes, I am enjoying being married. Why are you asking?"

He shrugged. "You two don't seem like newlyweds. You seem more like just good friends. Good buddies."

Jeneil fidgeted, uncomfortably. "Well that always the basis for a good marriage so I hear." She sipped some of her hot cider in order to look away from him.

"Yeah, but where's the fire and passion?"

Jeneil coughed as his question sent the cider down her throat in a gulp. "Steve doesn't show his emotions easily in public. It's just how he is." She said, avoiding looking at him. Robert frowned, not liking what he was hearing. He'd been doing some checking on Dr. Steven Bradley.

He kissed Jeneil's cheek and put his arm around her shoulder. "You're different with him you know. You're all bottled up in yourself in some ethereal sort of way. You look like a virgin." He sighed. Even the Taiwan Twit had you passionate and running free."

Jeneil held onto her warm cider mug to steady herself. She hadn't realized how uncomfortable it really was answering questions about an arranged marriage. Her admiration for Steve, grew stronger remembering how direct Dr. Sprague's questions to Steve were, at least Robert's didn't seem so bad. "Robert, lets not talk about me, okay?" She smiled at him.

He smiled and hugged her. "I care." He said. "I care a lot."

"I know you do." She patted his hand. "And I even love your caring, but I'm fine. I don't understand your concern."

He nodded and turned to watch the fire understanding her discomfort with the subject. He held his arm at her shoulder resting on the sofa seat and rubbed her arm gently.

They talked about other things which usually happened when they got together and the evening passed pleasantly for both of them. It was Jeneil who noticed the pinging sound on the window panes as Robert added a log to the fire. She got up and went to the window pushing the light curtains aside quickly.

She turned. "Robert it's icing over. The window ledge is already covered with a glaze. They went to the front door. A fine mist of icy rain was falling and the slickness of the ice could be seen covering the snow. Jeneil touched her foot to the ground and felt its slipperiness.

"Robert, don't drive in this, please. Stay here tonight."

"My car will be an ice cube by morning and your garage is full. It will take me all day to defrost it." He argued.

"No it won't. I have an invention that I made. Come on." She said, going to the garage. She opened a large cupboard and pulled out a bulky square folded plastic and wires. She handed it to Robert. "Put this over your car. I'll get the heavy duty safety extension cord and plug it in." She stopped. "Oh yes, put this patchwork quilt over it first. The wires can leave a mark on the paint finish once the ice melts. She handed him a bundle of folded cloth.

Robert looked at the invention and smiled. "You made this?"

"Yes and it works." She said. "I think I'll turn on the driveway defrosters, too. That way if the power goes, the driveway won't be so thickly coated. I have a barrel of sand here in the garage."

Robert laughed. "Where did you get so clever?"

"I think survival, Robert. It's like breathing to me. It burns in me. My car was once in an ice storm. All the tenants in our building made these blankets after mine worked. I had a special outdoor electrical outlet and we all ran these orange cords from the house to the cars. It looked weird, but it worked, Trust me. The ties at the bottom are attached to bottles of sand to keep the plastic from blowing away in a gale. Nobody in my building ever had to clean snow off their cars or scrap ice from the windshield. Put this rain poncho over your coat or you'll be glazed over too when you finish." She laughed.

Robert set about putting the defrosting invention over his already iced car, securing the last tie to the bottle of sand, he stood up and smiled. "She's clever." He laughed and headed back to the garage, closing the door behind him. "It's bad. Thanks for letting me stay here."

Jeneil smiled. "I feel better too; at least I know you're safe." They curled up before the fire again and talked until Steve called.

"You're having an ice storm." He said.

"You heard about it in Minnesota?" She asked, surprised.

He laughed. "No. Dr. Sprague called me earlier to check on the surgical schedule next week."

"What's the weather doing there?" She asked.

"A little snow every day. There are piles of the stuff all around, but the people seem used to it."

Jeneil smiled. "Then you'll be coming back tomorrow."

"Yes." He answered, liking the tone in her voice. "I can't wait." He said. "I'm tired of my hotel room. I want to be home with you. I've missed you."

"I have to." She answered, smiling. He felt the electricity in his chest faintly. "Are you okay? Do you still have power?"

"I'm fine and I brought in provisions. The generator will heat the house of the power fails, but the stove might not work, so I'll use the fireplace to cook if I have too. Or the camp stove in the garage."

"Okay." He laughed. "Sounds like you're managing, you really don't need me." He chuckled.

"That's not true." She said, gripping the receiver. "That's not true at all." She insisted.

He liked hearing that from her, too. He smiled. "Then, I'll see you tomorrow."

"Good." She said. "Very good."

Putting the warmed squares of gingerbread on two plates, she poured the light sauce over them and returned it to the refrigerator. Taking the plates, she went to the den listening to the house protecting them from the storm outside and she felt secure and warm and she wondered how people could just party through such a storm.   There had been cancellations on the TV and radio. "You're a stick in the mud, Jeneil." She laughed, to herself and joined Robert with the desserts. She liked having him there too. She stretched out her feet toward the fire, then turned her head and kissed his shoulder lightly.

"What's that for?" He asked.

"I'm glad I'm not out in the storm or in here alone." She answered, quietly. He smiled, liking her honesty.

*****

Steve turned the covers on his bed down and thought about Jeneil. He was encouraged about their marriage and anxious to get back to her. Things seem to be warming up a bit. He smiled as he got into bed. "But it will have to be her idea." He said. "That way, I'm sure that she wants me. I love you Jeneil and I want the chance to prove it to you, but I'll wait until you're ready. I don't need a dutiful wife looking after my needs. The honeymoon will never end once it begins. I promise you that."

*****

Peter paced restlessly in his bedroom. The evening had left him angered. Karen had called and he hung up on her without speaking. His mother called him shortly after that trying not to show her annoyance, but Peter could tell that she was very upset with him. Karen had been trying to apologize to him for her part in the mess with Uette. She had sent the note apologizing and was shocked that it had been returned unopened. He had listened to his mother's calm explanation and her lecture about being unforgiving. He was even softening until she said, "After all we didn't make Jeneil marry Steve. She did that herself." He had ended the call calmly, but her words kept racing through his mind, filling him with anger.

 He stared out the window into the pavement below. The wind was raging and Peter could identify with its anger. It reminded him of the day he married Uette. He left the window quickly and paced. "We didn't make her marry Steve, she did that herself." The words filled his chest and he sighed. Standing before Robert Danzieg's painting, he frowned. "You did make her marry Steve," he said aloud, "with your cruelty and anger and deceit. She's too gentle and caring to do that herself." He thought, choking up. "She loved me. You don't plan a wedding ceremony like the one on the balcony of the beach house unless you really loved the person. She loved me, but she's too fragile to put up with the shit I had in my life. You people caused the mess and she couldn't take it anymore." He sighed. "Songbird, I should never have married Uette. You were wrong about that." He stared at the picture and realized that the only thing in his life right now that had any meaning and value was his career as a doctor. He smiled, "Well maybe you were right about that. I don't know where my career would be now. But us, it cost me you, Baby." He paced again. "She did it herself." His mother's words intruded. "No." He said, emphatically. "She loved me enough to want my name cleared. I couldn't face myself if I hadn't cleared my name. She knew that. She wanted that for me. She was always being blamed by you. The only innocent one in the whole mess and no one could see it except my Grandfather. It was the damn race thing. If she had been Chinese nobody would have said a word against her. I didn't even keep my promise to her to stand by her even if it meant giving up the family. No, I put my career and myself ahead of her and now that's what I'm left with. It's what I deserve. I'd love to tell her that. I wish we had talked about all this. There so much I'd like to tell her if I had the chance." He went to the window and rested his head against the cold pane. "Rage." He said to the wind. "Rage for me too. I can't even do that either. Dr. Peter Chang has to be civilized. It's expected of him. It's what he chose and now he has to live with it."

*****

Jeneil opened her eyes and stretched under the warm covers. She listened to the quietness outside, and then pushed the covers from her to go to the window. "Oh wow, magnificent!" She gasped as she saw the glistening branches of the trees. The ground was sparkling with the handiwork of the ice storm.. She watched as some ice melted and dropped from a branch. "I'll lose the whole scene if I don't get out there fast."

She dressed, took her camera, left a note for Robert who was still sleeping and went out the back door. The steps were glossy and she stepped carefully with her thick soled shoes. Taking a piece of lumber from the covered pile, she sat on it and rode down the slope easily deciding to buy some sleds since the ride on the lumber seemed like such fun. Making her way to the stream, she focused her camera toward the trees and began shooting. "Gorgeous!" She smiled broadly, looking at the scene for her own appreciation. "Match that Hollywood, I dare you." Taking a deep breath. She laughed. "I love it. All of it!" And the sound of her voice scattered something through the thickets catching her eye. A rabbit had stopped to nibble some leftover blueberries and was now watching the visitor to his domain. "Perfect." Jeneil smiled and focused the camera. The rabbit moved away. "Stay still." She said, lowering the camera to look for the rabbit. She caught sight of it heading upstream. Looking at her choice of footings, she decided to climb the small slope onto the adjacent property and follow the stream. It was impossible to walk the gully. There were two many icy rocks, and she knew that the stream widened and narrowed all along the way. Crawling on her hands and knees she made her way to the top. The small climb would have been three or four steps ordinarily, but with the ice, climbing and walking were more difficult. She sighted the rabbit just ahead across the banks of the stream and she followed it. Standing near a tree growing on the edge of the gully, she looked for the rabbit that had scattered. It was hard to spot it against the soft brown and grey wood of the low thickets since it was the same color. "I need the eyes of a hawk or an owl to spot it." She sighed and then she smiled. "New eyes, Jeneil, new eyes." She said, holding her camera up to scan the thicket. She spotted it deep in the undergrowth. "Come out here and smile for me, Thumper." She whispered. The rabbit moved to a slight opening and Jeneil moved to the tree limb to balance herself closer to the edge of the gully. Another rabbit joined the first. Jeneil smiled. "Great, this is even better." She pulled the camera strap off her neck to get it to the other side of the tree branch for a better focus, being careful to watch her footing on the icy ground. She dropped her bag slowly from her shoulder too and leaned solely on the branch for balance.

"What have you sighted?"

Jeneil turned her head quickly as the voice startled her and her hand rested on the branch beside her. The camera slipped from her hand falling to the ground. She reached to grab it quickly as it slid over the ice closer to the edge. "No." She said. "Don't you dare go over the edge?" She reached out with her footing slipping over the edge along with the camera. Screaming and sliding toward the partially frozen stream, scaring the rabbits and some birds who were also feeding in the thicket. She grabbed hold of a sapling growing near the water's edge as she bounced to the bottom of the gully stopping herself, but the camera continued slipping over the ice splashing into the stream's cold water. Jeneil got onto her feet struggling with anger. She turned. "Dr. Vance you....Oooo." Stomped her foot angrily, breaking the ice covered snow into fragments. "You, you. Look what you've caused!" She shouted. "Look at my camera!"

Kirk Vance held onto the tree branch, looking shocked and concerned. "Jeneil, I'm sorry. I'm sorry really. Are you alright?"

"No!" She shouted. "I want to punch you. No, I'm not alright at all. I'm unreasonably angry at you and loving it. Oooo." She screamed and stomped her foot again almost slipping into the water. She grabbed the sapling and steadied herself. Closing her eyes, she breathed deeply to calm down so she could think straight.

"Jeneil, I'm very sorry. I'll get you out of there." He said. She looked up as he stood on the edge of the gully ledge.

"Don't stand too close." She cautioned and then watched as he slipped over the edge and down the side of the gully too, not landing as luckily, ending up with one foot in the icy stream before he stopped.

"Shit!" He shouted. "Damn it." He mumbled, moving out of the stream and shaking water from his drenched foot. "What a shittin mess!" He said as he stood up.

Jeneil watched him, he was hardly the super cool, super suave, he ordinarily portrayed. He had been tossed into silly and he looked like it was unfamiliar to him. She began to giggle. He looked at her. She covered her mouth and laughed hanging onto the sapling to keep from falling. "You think I deserve this don't you?"

"Yes." She said, laughing louder. "I was hoping you'd land head first in the stream." She held her stomach as she laughed. "You don't look a predator now, you look as dumb as I do, and I'm a klutz level." She hit her knee and laughed. "Mr. Cool fell into silly and can't deal with it." She stood up and laughed until she slipped and landed on her bottom. "Ouch!" She laughed, hysterically. "I landed on my pocketknife. It hurts." Tears rolled down her cheeks and she sighed as she calmed down and wiped her tears.

Kirk Vance watched her. "Mr. Cool fell into silly and can't deal with it?" He repeated her words. "You think I'm a stuffed shirt don't you?"

"The stuffiest." She laughed and nodded.

He grinned. "Watch me deal with silly. Just watch me." He turned and walked into the stream. Jeneil stood up looking shocked. "What are you doing!?" She gasped. "That's icy cold water. You'll get frostbite or something. Get out of there!"

"I'm getting your camera." He smiled as he headed for the black box wedged between two rocks.

Jeneil watched in disbelief as he slipped and fell into the stream. "Oh my gosh!" She yelled and covered her mouth trying not to laugh.

"Oh shit, not again!" He shouted. "Shit!" He slapped the water with his hand.

"Get out of there now!" She called. "We'll have a tough time getting out of here and you're soaking wet!" She watched struggling to be serious as he staggered out of the water carrying her camera dripping.

"That water is freezing." He chattered from the cold. Jeneil noticed that he had blood on his temple.

"You're cut." She said, concerned.

"I scraped my head on the slide down." He stomped his feet and shivered. "I'm freezing." He moaned.

"We have to get out of here fast." She said, blowing on her fingers

He looked along the water. "I'll walk the streambed along the gully and get out at the Barnard's place." He said, blowing on his fingers.

"You can't." She replied. "The rocks are icy and the stream widens as it goes that way."

"I'll risk it." He said. "I'm too cold to just wait for help. I'm already soaking wet so what the hell." He said, turning and walking off.

She sighed and looking around. Taking her pocket knife, she cut at the base of two small saplings until they fell over. Hurriedly fashioned points on them, she used them to jab into the icy snowy slope of the gully pulling herself to the top. Picking up her camera bag and a foil packet from the ground, she walked along the ledge until she saw Kirk Stumbling a few paces ahead.

"Dr. Vance!" She called.

He stopped and looked up. "How did you get out?"

"I'll explain later." She said, watching him shake. "Right now we need to get you out of there and warm." Opening her bag she took the narrow rope and tied one end to a group of saplings and tossed the other end over the ledge to Kirk. "Are you feeling strong enough to pull yourself up?" She asked. He nodded. "Then wait until I say okay. I'll hold the saplings from bending, I hope." She said, disappearing from his view. "Okay." She yelled. "Pull yourself up." Kirk Vance struggled and slipped and eventually groped his way to the top of the gully. Jeneil was worried about him, his hands were very deep red heading toward blue. "Start walking toward my house." She said. "I don't see any life at the Barnard's garage."

"They're at my place." He shook from being cold.

"Walk to my house then and I'll get the rope untied." Jeneil caught up to him since he couldn't walk quickly from shaking and the icy ground.

After what seemed to take an interminable length of time to her, they got through the backyard and into her kitchen. She went to the liquor cupboard and poured a shot of bourbon. He drank it quickly with a shaking hand. "Go take a shower." She said, looking worried. "And give me your clothes. I'll leave some dry clothes by the bathroom door for you." He nodded and headed to obey.

Jeneil opened a can of tomato soup and mixed some milk with it in a saucepan, then she put it on the heating burner. Taking his clothes to the laundry room, she put them through a wash cycle quickly, and then went to the guest room for the extra set of pajamas and robe. Leaving them folded by the bathroom door, she went to the kitchen to check the soup. She lowered the heat and went to the den to make a fire. She wondered if he was all right. She thought he should be finished. She knocked and could hear the water running. Opening the door a crack, she called to him. "Are you all right?"

"Yes, I'm okay." He answered. "The heat feels so good, I don't want to get out that's all."

"I've made a fire in the den and there's soup keeping warm on the stove. I've left dry clothes here by the door. Are you really alright? No toes or fingertips are black or something?'

Kirk Vance chuckled. "I'm really okay Mona Lisa."

"That's good to hear," She sighed, "take your time then." He smiled as he heard the door close.

The washer has finished its cycle and Jeneil put the clothes in the dryer. She began to relax. "He's a doctor." She thought. "He should know if he has frostbite."

She was surprised to see him sitting on the fireplace hearth when she returned to the den. "You're not quite a normal color yet." She said, studying his face. He smiled and tried to smooth back his tousled hair. "I'm feeling human." He grinned.

"That counts." She laughed. "I'll get your soup." He watched her leave. He had never seen her in jeans and a sweater before. Raising his eyebrows he whistled silently. "No wonder the White Stallion keeps her locked up and she's always hidden under layers of clothes. What a surprise."

Jeneil returned carrying two mugs and handing one to him, she sat in the arm chair.

"Why did you call me a predator?" He asked, sipping the warmed soup slowly. Jeneil tensed, embarrassed that her words were returning to haunt her.

She decided to be honest since the very worse; he'd never talk to her again which hardly seemed frightening. "You have this thing that you do with your voice and your eyes. It makes me feel its rehearsed behavior. Designed to… to… turn women on." She said bluntly, not having found a suitable polite way of saying it. "Is it rehearsed?" She asked, hoping to make him defensive.

"Is it a turn on?" He grinned.

She looked at him. "Quite frankly, no." She said.

"I find it insulting."

"Insulting?" He sat up. "Why insulting?"

She wished she hadn't started the mess. "It makes me feel like your laughing at me. Like I'm so you think, vulnerable to my hormones that a mere voice octave or eye contact leaves me susceptible."

He smiled, warmly. "Women's Lib?" He asked.

"No, not formally, just a woman who likes to be treated like one, a real one. Do you manipulate men that way, too?"

He grinned. "That sounds like Women's lib."

She shook her head. "No it isn't. The movement gave words and phrases for us to all coin. We already had the feelings and convictions."

"So I'm a predator because you think I try to lure women."

She nodded. "But you're actually very human; you even handled silly pretty well."

He smiled. "I really feel bad about your camera. I could tell you were stalking something, so I was trying to be quiet."

Jeneil felt the explanation didn't cover why he was so close to her ear or his hand near hers on the tree branch. "More studied turn-ons." She thought, and she wondered if she'd ever completely trust him. "Why were you out so early?" She asked.

He grinned. "I was bringing you some baked stuffed shrimp from DiNola's Garden. I remembered that you said you enjoyed it. I'm not sure where it is now." He laughed.

She smiled. "It's in my kitchen. I picked up the foil packet with my things."

"What were you shooting?" He asked.

"Two rabbits"

He nodded. "They're tough to get."

"Are you into photography?" She asked

"Yes. Wildlife."

"Really?" Jeneil replied. "That can't be easy."

"It's a study in patience. You'll have to see my pictures, some time."

Robert Danzieg had walked down the stairs quietly and had heard the two voices. He heard the last of the conversation and he couldn't believe that Kirk Vance was that friendly with Jeneil. His heart sank. Walking into the room wearing a robe and pajamas. He smiled. "Good morning." Jeneil turned and Kirk Vance looked up surprised to see Robert. Doubly surprised to see him in a robe. Robert noticed. "We must have the same designer." He grinned, looking at Kirk's robe. "I like your robe color on you." He said, going to Jeneil and kissing her lips lightly for Kirk Vance's benefit. "Where are my clothes, Honey?"

"Oh, they're in the laundry room."

Robert smiled. "What is this, you like playing elf."

She laughed. "No, it's a Japanese custom to launder the guest's clothes and have them ready in the morning."

"Yours should be nearly dry, Dr. Vance." She said, standing up.

Robert looked at him. "What happened to your clothes? I know you didn't spend the night here too."

"Fell into the stream." Vance replied.

Jeneil frowned. "My camera fell into the stream too, Robert. Do you think the film is okay? And the camera?"

"I'll check it out for you." He smiled.

A car pulled into the drive and Jeneil stood up to see who it was. She didn't recognize the car. Steve got out and closed the door, looking at the car and wires covering the one near the garage, curiously.

"Steve!" Jeneil smiled and went to the front door. She waited on the front step.

Steve smiled at her. "The driveway defrosters work very well. No shoveling is needed. I like that." He stood near her and put his arms around her. She hugged him. "You're earlier than I thought you'd be."

"I took the earliest flight I could get." He held her close.

Robert Danzieg came to the door and Steve was surprised to see him in a robe and pajamas. "How's the driving?" Robert asked.

Steve let go of Jeneil and stared. "The streets are tricky, but the trucks are sanding them now and the main highways are clear."

Steve followed Jeneil inside completely taken back by Robert's appearance, in the house and in a robe. He walked into the den and Kirk Vance stood up dressed just like Robert Danzieg. Steve looked from one to the other. Robert chuckled. "She's washing our clothes; it's an old Japanese custom." He hugged Jeneil and laughed. "You're cute Sweetheart; I want to hear you explain all this to your husband." He laughed again and kissed her. Kirk Vance smiled.

Steve looked at Jeneil. "Me too. I'd like to hear how you explain it to your husband." Robert and Vance laughed. Steve glared at the two of them.

"What's so funny?" Jeneil asked, looking at them and then at Steve. "Robert delivered some prints for Fairview last night. The ice storm began and I asked him to stay so he wouldn't drive in it. This morning I went out to photograph the storm's beauty and my camera fell into the stream. Dr. Vance went to get it for me and fell in. Robert was leaving for Fairhaven so I washed his clothes. Dr. Vance's clothes were wet so I washed his, too. It is an old Japanese custom." She shrugged. "I don't know why it's so funny."

Robert chuckled. "Jeneil it's not common for a husband to come home from a business trip and find two men in pajamas and robes with his wife."

"Well. I'm dressed." She said, causing Kirk Vance and Robert Danzieg to laugh again.

She shook her head and looked at Steve, "I have no idea why they're acting like twittering schoolboys. Where did you get the car?" She asked.

"It's a rental." He replied, resenting Robert's and Kirk's laughing.

Jeneil looked at all three. "Well I guess I should think about breakfast. I'll get your clothes, gentlemen."

"No breakfast for me, Jeneil." Kirk said. "My sleepover guests usually scrape one together. I'd better get back and play host though this is much more fun." He smiled.

"No breakfast for me either." Robert smiled. "I've got to get to Fairhaven. I'll just take a chunk of that gingerbread from last night if you still have some." He snickered. "And I think your husband just lost his appetite." He and Kirk, laughed.

"I don't find any of this that funny." She sighed as she left the room.

Steve looked at Robert and Kirk angrily and then went to get his luggage from the car.

No one was around when he returned. He put his luggage in the hall and paced in front of the fireplace in the den. The shock of the unexpected homecoming had him annoyed and he wanted desperately to calm down.

Kirk stopped at the door. "Where's Jeneil? I'd like to thank her for helping me this morning."

"I'll tell her for you." Steve said, stiff jawed. "You'd better get to your guests."

Robert came down the stairs. "Jeneil's outside uncovering my car."

"Tell her I said thanks." Kirk said to Steve and left.

Robert walked into the den, buttoning his shirt. Steve avoided him.

"I want to talk to you." Robert said, seriously.

"Send me a letter." Steve snapped.

"We're going to talk." Robert said, firmly.

Steve turned around quickly, looking angry. "Danzieg, don't give me orders! I have my gut full of you right now."

Robert glared at him. "Well that's really too bad, you jerk. I don't give a shit what you want. I'm concerned about Jeneil."

"Tell me something I don't already know." Steve growled.

"You don't care that Vance is here?" Robert tried not to yell. "He's interested in her."

Steve stared at him a second and then laughed. "Oh shit, that's a good one." He laughed again.

"Shut up." Robert insisted angrily going to him. Steve stopped laughing and glared. "I feel it funny I find your ass here more often than Vance. You're the one making moves on her. She's immune to him. She can't see through you." Steve replied through clenched teeth.

Robert studied Steve's face. "You don't give a damn about her do you? You're going to wipe your feet on her just like your buddy."

Steve fought real anger. "Danzieg, don't push me." Steve shouted.

"Don't push you!" Robert sneered. "She can't see through you and Vance. What are you setting up with him? I hear he likes sharing women. "She is not immune to him. She doesn't even know he's a chemistry major. She doesn't even know what that means." All your trips out of town. I've been checking on you White stallion and a two bedroom marriage doesn't quite compute. Your reputation is almost as bad as Vance's. The word is that you married her for her money and the trips are so you can still satisfy your taste for bimbos." Robert yelled.

Steve was shocked. "That's shit! Total shit!" Steve answered, deeply angered.

Jeneil went to replace the safety cord in the garage and heard the loud voices. Dropping the cord, she went into the house and headed to the den. She could tell an argument had started. She sighed as she approached the den recognizing Steve and Robert's voices and she could hear what they were saying more clearly as she got closer. "Shit my ass!" Robert yelled. "Then why two bedrooms, huh? Nice." Robert sneered. "A house in Tecumseh and an SX7. What the hell do you care what's happening. You're nesting fine." Jeneil stopped and covered her mouth in shock completely stunned by Robert's words.

Steve pointed at him bordering rage. "Back off, Danzieg, I'm warning you. One more word from you and I'll pull your shittin tongue out and shove it...."

Jeneil walked in quickly, surprising the two of them. Steve turned away. Robert ran his fingers through his hair. Both were red-faced from anger. "Robert your car is ready." She said, calmly. "The finish wasn't damaged at all." She said, trying to be cheerful.

"Thanks Honey." He smiled at her, warmly.

Steve turned around quickly, still angry. "Danzieg, stop calling her Honey. She's my wife, damn it! Get that clear or keep your ass out of here altogether. She's Jeneil to you from now on." Jeneil held her breath; she had hoped her presence would have calmed things down.

Robert clenched his fists. "Oh grow up and get civilized you Protozoan mutant or crawl back into your test tube."

Jeneil touched Robert's arm, gently. "Robert you should leave for Fairhaven so you won't have to speed." He rubbed his forehead and closed his eyes.

"Right. I'm sorry, Honey. This is my fault. I started it." He shook his head. "I started off badly and it got worse before I even knew it." He turned to Steve. "Look, I'm sorry about the way I said some things." Steve turned his back to Robert, angrily. Robert sighed and shook his head as he put on his jacket. He looked at Jeneil, seriously. "Honey." He said, putting his hands on her neck, gently. "Please be careful of Vance. The guy is way, way out of your league." He held her to him out of concern.

Jeneil smiled at him. "Robert I'm not fooled by him. He's honest in a sense. He's open about being a predator, that's being honest."

Robert sighed, and released her slowly. "He's more than that Jeneil, much more. He's a chemistry major. He has a lab and he makes some drinks that take you into outer space. He also has a taste for things that are weird by even my standards."

Jeneil looked puzzled. "You make him sound psychotic."

Robert smiled. "No Jeneil, a psychotic is identifiable. Kirk Vance can make bizarre sound sane. He's developed a taste for a level of sensious pleasure that makes even me blush."

She nodded, understanding. "I've seen his temple room."

Robert shook his head. "Make sure you don't see it in action on a Friday night. I heard that he slipped something into a girl's drink once and she saw herself on film doing some very odd things with men." Jeneil eyes widened

"That's shit." Steve said, interrupting. "Kirk Vance doesn't slip anything on anybody. You buy it and even makes sure he knows you well before he lets anyone trip out. He also monitors the first time which is always a very small dosage. If you know someone who was staked out at one of his parties, then blame the guy she was there with. Vance doesn't put anybody on film and he administers all the dosage himself. So there's no way anybody could freely drop something on anybody there. They film themselves. Sheez the guy's a respected Anesthesiologist. He knows controlled substances, he doesn't abuse them. He's got kinky tastes, that's all." Jeneil stared at Steve.

Robert's face showed real concern. "You are at his level, you piece of shit."

"Robert." Jeneil said, quietly. "Please don't."

He held her shoulders. "Jeneil do you know that your husband is called the White Stallion and that he was part of that crowd who tangos with Vance?"

Steve was annoyed. "The White Stallion is mostly fiction."

"Shit he is." Robert growled at Steve. "And shut up. I'm not talking to you."

"The White Stallion is history." Steve insisted, strongly.

Robert held Jeneil's shoulders, lightly. "Do you hear him, Honey? He's not denying it, Jeneil. Listen to him. Do you know what you've married?"

Jeneil took Robert's hands. "I know about the White Stallion, Robert. I also know that some of the stories about him were fiction. I worked at the hospital and I heard every story there ever was to be heard."

Robert looked shocked. "And you married him, anyway?"

Jeneil smiled. "I love the way you and Dennis worry about me. Steve worries about me, too." She added. "He's a good husband, Robert and he is my husband and this is his home. He's paying the mortgage and the taxes. I'd like you to respect him as my husband, if you can't as a man."

Robert studied Jeneil's face and then smiled. He put his arms around her. "Jeneil I'm crazy about you and I just fell in love with you for defending Steve that way. It shits that you belong to somebody else. Anybody else." He kissed her lips. Steve rubbed the back of his neck and tightened his jaw. Robert smiled at Jeneil. "You are a total kick, you know. He's your husband, I heard that clearly." He kissed her lips lightly and smiled at her.

"Still friends?" She asked.

"Yeh." He said, gently. "The best." He kissed her forehead, tenderly. "I'd better get to Fairhaven. She nodded and smiled. "Good luck and the gingerbread is in the front seat."

"Thanks." He said and left.

Steve had watched completely stunned by the closeness between Jeneil and Robert and he resented it deeply. He resented the fact that Robert held her and kissed her more than he could. He resented not having that freedom with her or that physical closeness.

The front door closed leaving Jeneil and Steve alone in the den in an awkward silence. Steve went to her. "That's a pretty speech you made to Robert about respecting me as your husband. Does that apply to you, too?" He asked, fighting his resentment. She looked at him steadily confused by his tone.

"Are you insulted by what I said?" She asked.

"Insulted? Hell no." He laughed, sarcastically. "I wish my wife would practice what she preaches. I find two men in robes in my house with my wife while I'm away. That's insulting." He said, showing his annoyance. "You shock me. You're pretty sophisticated."

Jeneil resented the tone in his voice and her whole attitude and implication. "Don't make my levels of sophistication sound like its so sordid, when you've been to parties with Dr. Vance. You shocked me with your defense of his lifestyle." She said, calmly.

"I wasn't defending his lifestyle." Steve answered. "I was defending him against a lie. The man respects drugs. He knows them well. He's offbeat, but then so are you."

Jeneil sighed. "I'm sorry, I'm not trying to argue, but your attitude about Robert is annoying me if you can accept Kirk Vance."

Steve stared as the words hurt him. "My attitude towards Robert!" He said. "The guy insults me everytime we're in the same room."

"I just talked to him about that." She said. "I know he's been insulting. He goes too far in his teasing. It's over now." She said, in defense

Steve shook his head. Her calm was irritating him and annoyance refused to settle. "Teasing, you call it teasing. You whitewash everything he does. Robert can't do anything wrong in your eyes, can he?" He snapped at her. "You're as crazy about him as he is about you." Jeneil watched, feeling helpless as Steve's anger grew. Steve headed for the door and then turned. "Why the hell didn't you marry him, Jeneil? Answer that for me." She stared at him and stayed silent unsure of what was happening. "We both know the answer to that one don't we, Jeneil. I make a better pretend husband for you. Robert would demand sex from you and you know that, so you took the path of least resistance." He picked up his luggage. "You should have married him Jeneil. At least he'd have you dealing in reality."

Jeneil felt numbed by his words. She went to the fire wanting to feel the warmth as the truth in Steve's words awakened her and reality felt so cold. She rubbed her temples as the tension in her grew. Reality rushed at her screaming that an arranged marriage is fiction. Pretending. That was the reality of her arranged marriage and she hated pretense. Another truth of reality loomed before her. Everything is physical. She never wanted to admit that, but it was truth, too. That truth was there, she heard it clearly in Steve's words. "Platonic is pretense too isn't it Steve? Were you just pretending when you said you weren't interested in a physical relationship in this marriage?" Anger stirred in her as she felt his lie become uncovered by Irish. Jeneil realized that Irish was the last holdout against Steve. Nebraska and Jeneil were crazy about him. His strength of character impressed Jeneil especially after hearing Robert's accusations in the argument and Steve took the slam in silence. The arranged marriage was causing him some real pressure and he took it. He never told Robert that the marriage was arranged. His silence protected her more than it protected him. She got married to be free from sexual pressures, to be free from the questions of why aren't you involved in sex. She needed Steve's silence about the pretend marriage and like a true Sir Steven the Loyal, he protected her with his silence. Nebraska guardian of the heart loved that about him and Jeneil, ruler of the head were committed to Steve, she knew why Irish wasn't. Irish was the most romantic of the three selves. And she belonged to Peter. Not even to Peter, but the mythical Chang. Jeneil had criticisms of Dr. Chang's character since the baby was really his and he had lied to himself. Nebraska had criticisms of Peter's loyalty since he didn't keep his word and divorce Uette, but Irish was in turmoil about Chang. She wavered between fierce loyalty and devotion to deep hurt and anger about Chang.

Jeneil paced before the fire. "That's the past, Irish." She sighed. "Reality is here and now, and the reality is that I'm into a pretend marriage that is under a lot of strain. The friendship I enjoyed so much with Steve is dying or changing because of the marriage. I'm not sure which, Adrienne, I think you were right. You can't put a celibate man and a celibate woman together in the same house and not end up with fireworks in bed or out of bed. One or the other. Positive or negative." Jeneil shook her head and paced. "Then what am I left with? Do I have two choices? Do I make the pretend marriage a real one or end the pretend marriage and be honest with everybody. Do you have a choice if it's honesty you're after?" She sighed. "If you make the marriage real won't you still be pretending? You'd have to pretend that you don't love Peter." She sighed. "Then ending the marriage is the most honest thing to do." Jeneil stared into the flame as she felt the emptiness in that choice.

"Jeneil." She turned quickly, surprised that Steve's voice was so close behind her. He looked uncomfortable and awkward. "I'm sorry." He stammered and rubbed the back of his neck. "Lately….I don't know." He shrugged. Between her thoughts about ending the marriage and Steve's sincere apology, emotion rushed at her and she put her arms around his neck clinging to him completely throwing him off guard. He slipped his arms around her slowly and pulled her to him even closer kissing her cheek tenderly. Jeneil noticed the difference in physical and closed her eyes. She knew she had to deal with truth and reality soon. The marriage wasn't good any longer the way it was. It wasn't good for Steve. It wasn't good for either of them, now that it was deteriorating their relationship. She had to deal with truth. He rubbed her back gently. "I've missed you, Jeneil." He said softly. She just nodded; afraid her voice would give her away if she spoke. She was strangling on truth and choking on reality. He kissed her cheek softly with a lingering kiss. "I was unpacking my things and I suddenly felt like such a jerk for what I had said to you. You've been honest with me Jeneil, completely honest about the marriage. I forgot that I'm a pretend husband and I acted like a jerk." She choked up and tears filled her eyes as the words "Pretend Husband" penetrated her reality. They sounded cheap and sordid. The marriage felt the same way now. She hated the pretend marriage and the disease it was causing between her and Steve. She had to face reality and fast. "We need to talk, Jeneil." He kissed her temple.

She caught her breath, she was afraid to talk. She wasn't ready to talk. She didn't know how she felt right now, let alone think and talk about it. She pulled away gently, trying to stay calm. "You're right, we do need to talk and soon." She said, avoiding looking at him.

"Now Jeneil. I think we'd better talk now." Steve said. "I think it's time for honesty."

She swallowed hard, and breathing became difficult for her. She wanted to run. She wasn't ready for honesty. She didn't want to hear it. Truth and reality hurt too much and she wasn't ready for the pain. She had to get away. Too much was changing and too fast. She felt trapped and caged and she knew that she had to get away. "Well talk when I get back, she said, trying to steady her voice.

Steve was puzzled. "Get back?" Get back from where?"

"Uh home." She said, feeling her stomach getting sick. "I'm going home."

Steve watched her, nervousness. "You are home, Jeneil."

"What!?" She said, stunned by his sentence. "Oh right, I am home. I meant Nebraska. I'm going to Nebraska."

He watched closely. "I thought you didn't have a meeting there this month."

She fidgeted uncomfortably. "It's for me. I want to get a painting for my Grandfather. My mother painted one of the farm. At least I didn't think he'd like it, but I think I was wrong. I want to give it to him for Christmas. So that's why I'm going home, I uh. mean to Nebraska. To get the painting."

Steve was getting suspicious "Can't you have them mail it to you?"

"No." She said. "I can't. It won't get here in time. The mail service is already over burdened and it's too near Christmas, now."

Steve folded his arms and nodded as he watched her. "I understand, Jeneil and if you wait to fly out any other weekend but this one, the booking will be difficult because people are traveling for Christmas."

"Yes." She said. "That's true, too." She backed toward the door. "I'll go pack." She said.

"What time is your flight?" He asked, knowing the answer.

She stopped. "Uh, I don't know. I have to call and make a reservation. I'd better get going. I have a lot to do."

Steve watched her turn and run up the stairs. He understood. She had just made the decision to leave while they were talking. He understood because he had seen this before on the night they were married. He dropped into the armchair. "Nice going Bradley, now she's bolting at a yen level. All the way to Nebraska." He felt sick. He felt sick when she bolted the night they were married. The pain was intense in his stomach. She didn't want him. It was that simple. "It's Peter." He sighed. "It's Pete, and it will always be Pete. She's that wonderful breed, a one man woman. But, he's gone, Sweetheart." He sighed, putting his head back on the chair. "I'd turn myself inside out trying to make you forget him. Just give me the chance. What the hell did you do to her, Pete? How did you get her to separate from you? She's welded to you and she acts like she'll die if she lets go. What are you two fused by some crazy mystical force? Are you suffering too. Pete? Are you regretting your decision? I hope so. I hope you're feeling the pain as much as she is." He choked up. "I'm in pain too, Pete. Just watching her go through this and knowing that she's my wife, but I'll probably never have her. She's entangled in the triad, Pete. All three of us are fused and jumbled in a crazy mess. How the hell does this puzzle work? Where's the key? How do we break the spell?" He sat, staring at the fire.

Jeneil appeared at the door with her luggage. "My plane leaves in an hour. I think I'll leave for the airport now to allow time for driving the icy streets."

Steve looked at his watch, surprised that so much time had passed. "I'll take you to the airport."

"You don't have to." She said. "Oh yes you do. You have a rented car."

"I'll get my jacket." He said, and he walked to the hallway, wearily.

Jeneil watched him and felt sick knowing that she was causing this mess they were in. She swallowed hard. "I just need to think." She assured herself. She watched Steve. "I don't want to hurt him." She sighed. He looked up and she looked away. He watched her and wondered.

Twenty-Six

They arrived at the airport twenty-five minutes before flight time. She went to the reservation clerk and he went to the rented car window. He waited by a cement column for her, while she waited in line. They had driven in separate cars so nothing was any clearer to him. She finished and walked toward him sorting through her purse. He noticed that she had trouble looking him in the eye. "They're boarding now." She said, shifting her Carry-on to the other shoulder.

He nodded. "Then you better get on."

She nodded. "I guess so. The freezer is full of food."

He shrugged. "I'll manage. Don't worry about me."

"But I do." She said and the sincerity touched him deeply.

He wanted to kiss her and insist that she go home with him, forget the damn trip. And get a real marriage started. "I'll be fine." He said.

She nodded. "Then I'll get on board." She turned and walked away. He sighed and swallowed hard as he watched her go. She stopped and then ran back to him hugging him tightly like she had in the den again catching him off guard and completely confusing him.

He held her. "Jeneil what is it? Can't we talk about it." He said, not wanting her to leave.

"I just need to think." She said.

"About what?" He said, holding her face in his hands so she'd look at him. "I'll give you some space. I won't push, I promise." He said.

"Don't make me cry, please." She said.

He kissed her lips, gently! "Honey, we're married. Married people work thing out together. They don't run away." She stared at him and remembered that she had said those words to Peter whenever he ran from a problem.

"I'm not running away." She said. "I'm not. I want to face reality and truth and I will."

"What reality? What truth? Why didn't you say this in the den?" He sighed. "We can't discuss anything while a plane waits for you."

The airlines announced boarding for her flight. "Don't go, Jeneil." He kissed her again. The call for boarding filled the terminal.

"I have to go." She said. "I have to." She turned and walked away quickly, not looking back.

"Shit." Steve sighed. "What the hell is happening? First she races off bolting from me, then she comes back and hugs me like she doesn't want to leave. Then she said she has to. She'll drive me crazy with this shit. What the hell is the answer?" He asked himself. The answer? What the hell is the problem? Damn it." He sighed. "I should have dragged her home." He stayed and watched the plane taxi down the runway and then leave the ground. He went to the car feeling like half of him had just flown off in the plane.

*****

Jeneil landed at the airport in Nebraska and called the estate to make arrangements to have the car pick her up at the bus terminal in Ridgeley. She had noticed that Mr. Parsons with a little stunned to be getting her at the bus terminal. She laughed, as she went to get her ticket. "I'll never have Mandra's style. Poor Parsons." Jeneil knew that she should have had him meet her at the airport, but he jabbered so much as he drove that she decided to bus into Ridgeley so the hour's ride would let her think. The plane had been full of talkative Holiday travelers aboard. She knew the bus to Ridgeley was usually pretty empty whenever she came home from college breaks. The bus was totally unoccupied except for the driver. And she rode uncomfortably having forgotten the tattered service the outer regions had on the bus line. Arriving in Ridgeley, she knew that she wanted to see Bill and she hoped that he was home. It was a forty minute ride to Loma and braced herself for Parson's update on current news. "Is Bill Reynolds in town?" She asked.

"Yes Ma'am. I saw his jet as I rode in for you. I thought you'd be bringing your husband this trip so we could meet him." Parsons smiled into the mirror. "It still takes getting used to thinking of you all grown up and married."

"Not quite." She said to herself. "Not quite Parsons." She thought. "I'm married, but far from grown up and I have to deal with that now." She sighed and settled back in the seat. Jeneil saw the sign indicating Loma town line. "Parsons take me to Mr. Reynolds's place, please."

"Will you be staying at the estate?" He asked.

"Yes, I've located my Grandfather. I think he might enjoy one of my mother's canvasses."

"Your Grandfather? Goodness, he must be getting on in years."

"He's going to be ninety-seven Parsons."

"Well bless his good life. The man must live right." Parsons chuckled.

Jeneil sighed to herself. "No, I think the power that created him is waiting for him to learn some truth, too. I must have more Alden blood in me than I think." The car turned into the long driveway to the Bill Reynolds place. "The back door, please, Parsons." Jeneil asked.

He chuckled. "I hope you never develop "airs" Jeneil. Oops, excuse me, ma'am"

Jeneil laughed. "What did Mandra say about "airs" Parsons?"

"They're only for the gauche who don't know any better."

Jeneil smiled. "You got all the lessons along with me as we traveled around, didn't you."

"Just about." He laughed.

Jeneil noticed the sedan parked next to Bill's sports car. "Oh no, he has company." She said, disappointed.

Parsons turned around. "Ma'am, if I could step out of line?"

Jeneil looked at him. "Go ahead."

"Go inside anyway. That's Mrs. Densley's car and she's not fittin' for Billie." Jeneil was surprised by Parsons strong tone.

"Who's Mrs. Densley?" Jeneil asked.

Parsons frowned. "Amy Farber. That's her third husband's name."

"What?!" Jeneil gasped.

"Oh huh. My feelings too, Ma'am. Get on in there."

"But." Jeneil stuttered. "Amy Farber?"

"She's houndin him, the shameless toots." Parsons guffawed. "Excuse me ma'am." Jeneil laughed. Parsons had been one of the town's people who sided with her and Bill when the gossip broke out. He never trusted Amy Farber and never said why.

Jeneil stepped out of the car as Parsons held the door. "You can put the car away and relax for the evening Parsons. I'll have Bill drive me home. I'd like to have a long talk with him. My old room will be fine.

"But Beth made up the suite for you." "No thanks, Parsons. I have a heap of maturing to do before I earn the right to sleep in Mandra's bed. It's her house, and always will be."

Parsons smiled, warmly. "It's nice having you home again." Jeneil patted his arm and went to Bill's back door.

"Amy Farber!" She moaned as she rang the bell, remembering how she had set Bill up the day the Boy Scouts attacked.

Jake answered, stunned to see Jeneil at the back door. She stepped inside. "Is Bill free to visit with an old friend?" She asked.

"Jake. Was that somebody from the Pike place? I just saw their car leaving." Bill walked to the kitchen carrying some papers. He smiled broadly when he saw Jeneil.

"Hey, beautiful." He said and hugged her off the floor. Jeneil caught glimpses of a blonde standing near the door as Bill whisked her around. He set her down. "Where's that good looking surgeon husband of yours." He smiled. Jeneil could tell that Bill was spreading on the status symbols for Amy's sake.

Jeneil smiled. "I left him at the airport back east."

"Are you here for a Christmas visit?"

"No, Steve and I are coming in for New Years." I'm here for a painting to give as a gift."

Bill raised his eyebrows. "Must be special to rate airfare."

"My Grandfather." Jeneil said.

Bill kissed her. "You look sensational. You hair looks great, I love it that length." He hugged her and then put his arm around her. "Come into the den. They turned and faced Amy Farber. "Jeneil." Bill smiled, looking straight into her eyes, meaningfully. "You remember Amy Farber, don't you? Well, I guess it's not Amy Farber anymore. Let me get this right." He said. "Amy Farber Atkins, Wooley, Densley."

"Amy Densley will be fine, Bill." Amy grinned. "And if I had Jeneil's brain, it would have stayed Farber. How are you, Jeneil?"

"Just fine Amy. Thanks." Jeneil was surprised she didn't remember Amy's blonde hair looking so brash and she always had the latest hairstyle. It was unstyled now and tied up in back, plainly. Jeneil was stunned. They sat in the den and Bill got drinks.

"Don't you age?" Amy said, looking Jeneil over.

"Who doesn't?" Jeneil shrugged.

"Well that Pike money must help. I'd head for a spa myself if Ms. Pike had left me that boodle."

Bill set bourbon plain before Amy and club soda with lemon juice for Jeneil, then he sat down on his leather chair and grinned. "Jeneil hasn't touched the Pike money Amy; she opened a branch of Alden-Connors in the east and made it pay."

Amy smiled. "You always were smart. I've invested in men. They're a lousy return on your effort." She took a drink and Jeneil thought it went down too easily. Amy was hurting and Jeneil felt the pain.

Bill grinned. "Oh now Amy we're not all bad."

"Very few aren't." She grinned. "And they should clone you." She giggled and took another drink. Bill looked at Jeneil and winked. Jeneil felt torn in her loyalties. Bill was obviously enjoying having the upper hand in some game he had going, but Amy's pain was real and Jeneil felt bad that her life had soured her at such an early age.

"What are you doing now, Amy? Raising a family?" Jeneil asked.

"No. I've been growing up myself, Jeneil and I'm not there yet. My talent was never brainpower." She sighed. "No, my talent if I charged for it, I'd get arrested." Jeneil was impressed. An honest and forthright Amy Farber was never something she'd expected to see. "Right now, I'm trying to expand my talents. I just finished Junior College and I'm opening a boutique in Loma. At least I hope I am if Bill here will invest some money in me."

Bill sighed. "I don't think so, Amy." Jeneil felt the disappointment. Amy was stricken, she could see that.

Amy held up her glass in a toast. "Then we don't expand my talents and I'll try to find a job at Clausen's as a buyer."

"What's the problem, Amy? Why aren't conventional moneylenders interested?" Jeneil asked.

"They're really picky, Jeneil. They want collateral and experience. If I had collateral, I'd sell it and use the money to open the place without high interest loans on my back. The banking business shits. Oops." She shrugged, apologetically.

Bill frowned. "Well, your attitude won't help get you a loan, either."

Amy grinned. "Oh Bill, I snipped and tucked myself into a real image when I went money shopping. Those warthogs are so stiff-necked, they can't see the future. I got four no's and one maybe if I change the name from boutique to clothes store or Shoppe and one yes if you'll sleep with me. If he'd put that in writing, I might be tempted. A blindfold is cheap enough." She made a face. "And I'd need one to live through the ordeal."

Bill grinned. "Well Amy, maybe you're paying for past sins. All those loan officers are the nerds you wiped your feet on in school. Maybe they're getting even."

Amy raised her eyebrows to their limit. "Oh hell, what a major bummer. I have to be punished here by toads and by God later for the fun I had with fake Princes, who were toads, too. Doesn't seem hardly fair, does it?" She said to Jeneil.

"Not hardly, Amy." Jeneil agreed.

Amy smiled. "You were always the smart one. You kept your life to yourself. The boy's were drooling to go out with you. Your figure made them hyperventilate, but you used your brain and went to school then caught yourself a rich doctor. No wonder you don't have to worry lines on your face. You don't know pain. You've kept your life in a neat little package. Not me, every damn piece of hell raisin I did shows up on me," She sighed, "and boy none of the memories are worth it." Jeneil saw her eyes get moist. The lump in Jeneil's throat surprised her, because she thought she hated Amy Farber, but she could feel a commraderie with her. They had both been disappointed in love.

Bill watched her. "Amy, I'll make you an offer."

"Yes," Amy smiled, "and I won't need a blindfold." Jeneil laughed, shocking Bill.

Bill ignored Amy's remark "Get a job at Clausen's and keep it for a year, then come back and ask for a loan with more than this research behind you." He said, holding up papers. "Go back to school at night and study business management."

Amy sighed. "That doesn't leave time for hell raisin Bill."

"What do you want with useless memories anyway Amy?" Jeneil said. "When you can end up with a grown up Amy Farber in just one short year."

Amy grinned. "You two." She said, pointing at Bill and Jeneil. "You two were always the shrewdest of the whole bunch of us. You never let life touch you. Clever sons of guns, the two of you." Bill and Jeneil looked at each other, not believing that Amy Farber actually said that life never touched them.

Bill walked Amy to the door and Jeneil paced before the fire in Bill's den. He watched her for a second and then went into the room. "You look a little edgy."

"The plane was crowded." She replied. "Amy was certainly a jolt. Is she that bad a risk?"

"Yes." Bill answered. "I don't think this marriage will last much longer, and if she follows her previous pattern, she'll drink heavily for a while and then find someone else. I hope she turns it around, but who's going to risk sizable money on her?"

"Too bad." Jeneil mused. "The business success might help her self image." She shook her head. "Amy Farber with a self image problem. Boy where life does toss us."

Bill chuckled. "Well I wouldn't know Jeneil, you heard Amy, we don't let life touch us."

Jeneil smiled. "I'll bet she doesn't even remember the incident in the barn and its aftermath."

"They don't." Bill smiled. "Bob Borren works in the mill and everytime I go there; I get a pat on the back from my old buddy Bob Borren." Bill shook his head. "No conscience. None of them."

Jeneil sighed remembering Bob Borren as the Boy Scout who pulled Bill's clothes off to expose him. Jeneil paced. "Well looking at Amy, I can believe the scripture about reaping what you sow."

Bill laughed. "But she doesn't understand that, Jeneil. No conscience, I'm telling you. I must be losing my taste for blood revenge. I guess. I should have made her squirm, but I didn't and I promoted Bob Borren to supervisor. He's good. He's been good for years. I've just been getting even."

Jeneil smiled. "Is revenge any fun if they don't know why they're being punished?"

"Yes." Bill grinned. "I've loved every minute of holding the jackass back and knowing he couldn't quit. Where could he get a job paying as much so I paid him so he'd stay under my thumb? You should try taking some swipes at a few of them."

Jeneil shrugged. "I've carried my anger around too, but seeing Amy Farber…" She shook her head. "I couldn't think of more punishment than she's heaping on herself in life. I was surprised to feel as much sympathy for her as I did. She reminds me of one of your father's quotes. The one where he says. Help me to forgive my trespasses Father for they know not what they do."

Bill smiled and kissed her cheek. "My father's right. If you became a nun, you'd achieve sainthood."

Jeneil laughed. "Aren't you supposed to say, Meet Jeneil, the Pollyanna Goody- two shoes? That's what you used to say when I got too sickening sweet."

Bill smiled. "I've lost my taste for teasing, too. Come and have some dinner with me. I had Anna set a place for you. Just sit with me if you've already eaten."

"I'm starved." She smiled. "I was going to ask if I could raid your cupboards. But a hot meal, I must live right."

Bill laughed. "Maybe sickening sweet pays off." He put his arm around her shoulder. Jeneil put her arm around his waist and walked to the diningroom with him feeling very glad that she had made the trip.

Bill watched her as they ate and talked, studying her closely. They returned to the den with coffee. Jeneil stood near the fire watching the flame. "I can't believe you came all the way here after a Christmas present for your Grandfather."

Jeneil shrugged. "He's part of my past Thanksgiving Conscience Searches. I'd like peace between us for my parent's sakes. I think they'd like that."

Bill laughed. "You still do Thanksgiving Consciences Searches?"

She nodded and smiled. "I guess Amy and I are late bloomers. We grow up slowly."

Bill chuckled and then watched her. "How's the marriage?" He asked.

Jeneil sipped her warm cider. Bill watched her closely. She sat on a hassock near the fire. "I think I made a mistake." She said, quietly.

Bill watched her. "Sleep with him, Jeneil." She looked up quickly, startled by the comment. "Make it a real marriage, Honey. That's what the struggle is about isn't it? The path got cloudy so you came back to your roots."

She sighed. "Am I that transparent?"

"To me." He grinned. Jeneil stood up and walked around the room. Bill watched her. "You and Steve looked like a good combination."

"I thought we were." She said. "But the marriage is destroying a very good friendship, we had going for us."

"Then save it. Move into his bedroom or let him move into yours."

"You noticed. The marriage was a fake?" He nodded. "Two bedrooms were hard to miss."

"I know." She sighed. "Others are noticing too. That's part of the problem."

"Then close down one bedroom, Honey." Bill replied and watched her carefully.

"It's not that easy." She said, wringing her hands.

"Why not?" Jeneil paced silently and Bill watched her. "Why not Jeneil?" Bill asked again. "Is Peter still in the way?" She nodded. "You can't have a real life living with memories."

"I know." She sighed. "But Peter is only part of it."

"What else?" Bill asked. Jeneil paced wringing her hands. "What's wrong, Jeneil, did you misplace the door to the ivory tower?" Bill asked, concerned.

"Ivory tower?" Jeneil questioned.

"Yes, you usually climb the tower to rise above the hurt in order to avoid it. Have you forgotten to get out?"

Jeneil thought about the question. The observation made her curious. She stopped pacing. "It's all a little confusing from this point on."

"Try me." Bill answered.

Jeneil sat on the hassock and rested her chin on her hand. "I'm not in love with Steve."

"You married him."

"But we were good friends; I thought we could make it work."

"I'm your good friend too. You didn't marry me. You married Steve. You have other good friends, but you married Steve. "If he's your good friend then you achieved half a good marriage. It sounds like it just needs a little freedom for the chemistry formula to work."

"But is it fair if I don't love him?"

Bill smiled. "Jeneil, you love everybody. Is that your problem, ethics? You're an Amy Farber with a strong conscience."

She shrugged. "Maybe, I'm not really sure."

"You are different." He chuckled. "I know a male and female who romp after some business deals are closed just to relieve the tension, no strings attached at all."

"It can be that easy?" She asked, surprised.

Bill chuckled. "The chemistry just needs nudging, but I usually give in after I stop worrying that we'll get too serious and I couldn't replace her if she quit." Jeneil smiled and then laughed, lightly.

"Is there a problem about the chemistry?" He asked, watching very closely. "You should be able to tell by now; you've lived with him for two months."

Jeneil wrung her hands nervously "No." She answered, quietly. "The chemistry is nudgeable. Not easily, but possible."

Bill smiled broadly; glad to have heard that answer. "Then why are you hesitating?"

She sighed and rubbed her face gently with both hands. "Bill maybe I'm odd, but I'm scared to death. I don't begin relationships easily. They're awkward and tense and the last thing I feel is sexy."

Bill was confused. "But you and Peter."

"That was different." She said. "He's as offbeat as I am. I seduced him when we went camping. It was comical, but Peter handled it." Bill recovered from his shock quickly and wanted to laugh. "I'm proud of you, kid." He grinned.

She smiled, sheepishly. "Poor Peter, I shocked him completely."

Bill put his coffee cup down, smiling. "Well, Steve doesn't look backwards to me don't you think he'll handle it?"

Jeneil's face got serious. "He's not backwards, Bill. He's fast. Very fast lane. His nickname at the hospital was the White Stallion. Bill was stunned that his shy and gentle childhood friend had a White Stallion agree to marry her and keep his hands off and then he realized how much Steve must love her. He was torn about his promise to Steve not to tell her. Jeneil sighed. "I'm not his speed, Bill. I won't be able to please him and the marriage will end anyway because it'll be based on just sex." She stood up and paced. "It was a mistake." Bill watched her beginning to understand that Steve hadn't told her how he felt yet and he wondered why.

"Have you and Steve talked about any of this?"

Jeneil shook her head. "Bill, we never talked really. We didn't even think. We just agreed to get married, we got married, and I ran out the night we got married scared that I was expected to sleep with him. He came to my apartment the next day and said he understood that I still loved Pete and he didn't expect a physical relationship. We talked about where we would live and life went on from there becoming more and more awkward. I've just faced reality about the marriage needing to be physical or ended." She took a deep breath.

"You should talk to Steve." Bill said, growing in admiration for the man Jeneil married and his stamina, knowing that after two months of living with her he'd have thrown her over his shoulder and then taken her to bed in caveman fashion from hormone havoc alone.

Jeneil sat down again. "I needed to think." She said. "He wanted to talk. He has said that a few times now that I think about it. Bill it isn't easy. A part is still deeply in love with Peter and the rest of me is a combination of sexual ignorance, childhood insecurities and romantic fantasies. I can't have just sex; it reminds me of the snickering the boys did about me because of the gossip. I'd feel dirty." She got up quickly and paced. "It's just easier to not be married."

Bill watched her, knowing that she had been deeply hurt and confused from the gossip. "Jeneil, talk to Steve."

"I'd have to no matter what my decision is won't I?" Jeneil went to the fire. "Bill, I'm not capable of being a real wife to the White Stallion. I've seen the women he's been involved with."

Bill shook his head. "Jeneil will you please put more trust in Steve. He agreed to marry you that should tell you something."

"We both wanted out of the singles game and out of the sex race." She said.

"Well then, doesn't that mean that the White Stallion is only trotting now? You're selling yourself short. Do you want to be single?"

"No." Jeneil sighed. "No. I want to be married and I want to be married to Steve. I've enjoyed the marriage. He's romantic and caring, sensitive and patient and much more." She said, wistfully.

Bill smiled, listening to the compliments of Steve that so easily filled her mind. "Then don't be afraid of the White Stallion, Honey."

Jeneil sat down and looked at Bill. "Maybe you're right. Peter and I didn't separate because of incompatibility and he was called the Chinese Stud."

Bill couldn't stand it any more; he put his head back and laughed. "Oh my gosh, Chinese Stud, White Stallion. Is this the girl who stomped on my foot for pinning her against a tree in the woods once when we were younger?"

Jeneil grinned. "Well, I told you, Bill, Amy Farber and I are late bloomers, we're growing up slowly.

Bill laughed. "Jeneil, Honey. There's not a thing wrong with you. It's just your same old song. You see life differently, that's all. So whatever you did that allowed you to seduce Peter, do it again."

*****

Jeneil got into bed feeling less tense. Her visit with Bill was exactly what she needed, a chance to talk and hear herself express her feelings. She missed Steve. "How to tell him about physical?" She groaned. The idea seemed difficult but she was determined that marriage was what she wanted and real marriage needed physical. "Steve dear, I don't love you in the romantic sense, but let's sleep together." She groaned. "Oh that sounds so brutal." She turned over. "Oh courage please rise with the sun in the morning." After turning several times, she slept. Jeneil was up early in the morning going through her mother's paintings. The homestead canvas was wrapped and Bill took her to breakfast. Parsons drove her to the airport and she boarded the plane for home.

*****

Steve sat in the den listening to the emptiness of the house wishing Jeneil would call. Their goodbye was so hurried that he never asked when she was returning. He missed her. "I wish the whole thing was as easy as just saying Jeneil, I love you as much as any man can love a woman and maybe more, give me a chance to prove it." He got up and added some wood to the fire. "Boy Bradley I don't recognize you talking like that." He watched the flames lick the new wood. "I don't recognize me feeling like this either. I can't take much more of this craziness. I can't pretend much longer but I don't want to push her. She doesn't like being pushed or smothered or she gasps for freedom and air. He sighed, "So I'll wait, I guess, and I'll pretend because at least we're together. I hate it when she bolts from me. I hate it when she turns away. What will it take to bring her to me?" The telephone rang. "Jeneil let it be you." He said, going to it quickly.

"Steve its Sheldon Taft. I'm calling to thank you for covering the seminar for me. my parents would like to show their appreciation for the favor so they've offered the home in Oyster Bay to you while they're in Switzerland."

"That isn't necessary, Sheldon." Steve replied.

"Let them do it, Steve. You really pleased them jumping in like that. I'd like to go there myself. The cabin cruiser glides over the water and then you anchor in the cove for swimming. Boy after Friday's ice storm I could take that very easily."

Steve began to soften. "Sheldon the offer sounds tempting."

"Take it Steve really. It would please my mom and dad."

"Can you sleep on the cabin cruiser?"

"Four romantically and six to ten on a beer party."

Steve laughed. "How long does it take to get there?"

"Three hour flight and a half hour drive to the bay. The marina is ten minutes from the house."

"I wouldn't mind a weekend." Steve smiled.

"That's all?"

"I can't get away any longer. The seminars have taken their toll on my surgical schedule. At best I could take a Friday or Monday off for a long weekend next week."

"Then do it Steve. I want you to."

"Let me talk to Jeneil. But I wouldn't mind the trip even alone. I need a break from the pace. A vacation sounds great."

"You got it. This coming weekend?" Sheldon asked, "I'll let dad know and get back to you."

"Okay." Steve replied, "And thanks."

"It's my thanks Steve I mean that sincerely. My mother was thrilled to have Christmas all together."

Steve went back to the den. "I haven't been scuba diving since I dated Linda, what's her name? Man what that girl could do underwater. This sounds good." He smiled and picked up his mug to get more coffee. Going through the freezer he saw a packet labeled chocolate chip cookies. "Lunch." He smiled and took it out. He looked at his watch, "And maybe dinner too." The telephone rang again. Steve reached for it thinking Sheldon don't you dare cancel my weekend vacation now. It's in my blood. He answered.

"Hi Steve."

Steve smiled broadly, "Jeneil. I was hoping you'd call. You didn't tell me when you were coming back. I was going to give you until six tonight and then call you. Are you okay?"

"I'm okay." She said, "I'm okay."

"Have you had time to think?"

"Yes, I have."

"So everything's better now?"

"Just fine." She smiled.

"When are you coming home, Honey?" He waited hoping to hear soon.

"I'm back, Steve."

"What?" He stood up straight. "You're here? Now?"

"Yes at the airport. I was going to rent a car but then I realized that we'd only have to return it. Are you free to come for me?"

"I'll be right there." He smiled, "I'm on my way."

"I'll wait out front so you won't have to park."

He ran to the garage. "Fantastic!" He smiled. "Not even two days of withdrawing this time. Anthony you and your parakeet are worth a mint to me. That's the answer Steve, you wait and don't push, don't rush her. Pretend if you have to. There's progress being made I can see it." He smiled and he pulled out of the driveway.

Jeneil bit the tip of the index finger on her leather glove absentmindedly as she waited, and wondered where to begin. "With me." She said, "Totally with me. Bill's advice was good. Whatever I did before do it again. So I'll prepare myself to be part of a harem and I'm even taking exotic dancing lessons." She pulled off her gloves. "Never in a million years would I wear that outfit except for lessons." She saw the SX7 pull to the curb and she picked up her luggage and painting. Steve got out of the car smiling broadly.

"Hi." He said and kissed her lips lightly. She smiled. He looked different to her now that she looked at him as someone she'd have to sleep with. Taking her luggage, they walked to the car. He got in. "I'm glad you're home." He said and he pulled away from the curb.

"Sheldon Taft's parents have invited us to stay at their vacation home in Oyster Bay, Florida while they're in Switzerland as a thank you for taking his place at the seminar in Minnesota. How about flying down next weekend and spending it on their cabin cruiser? I haven't been scuba diving in a long time."

The thought panicked her. "I won't scuba dive okay?"

He smiled. "The cabin cruiser is a lot bigger than the sea urchin. Can you take that on water?"

"Will we sleep on the cabin cruiser?" She asked.

He nodded, "Having trouble aren't you?"

"No. Well yes, but I'll be fine. I'll handle it." Determination was becoming a good part of her courage.

Jeneil saw the package of chocolate chip cookies on the counter when she went to prepare dinner. Steve had waited for her to unpack. She was quiet on the drive home and he was concerned. "That was going to be my lunch and dinner." He said, seeing her holding the package of cookies.

She chuckled. "Men are so fascinating. Dr. Vance can make baked stuffed shrimp and you can defrost chocolate chip cookies."

He smiled, "I can broil steak and make a salad. You taught me."

She smiled and went to the freezer. "Sheldon called while you were unpacking. The house in Oyster Bay is clear for us this weekend."

"House?" Jeneil asked. "I thought it was a cabin cruiser."

"They have a house. But I want to stay on the cabin cruiser." He grinned. "You can stay in the house if you want to."

"No." Jeneil answered, "The cabin cruiser is fine with me too." She said, unwrapping some chicken to defrost. The weekend was becoming very important to her too. It was an opportunity for her to make the marriage real. She had decided to spend the week working on herself for the Sultan. She knew that it was impossible for her to discuss the situation with Steve. She thought it would be much better to just approach him as a wife would since he didn't seem opposed to making the marriage real anyway. All his actions lately seemed to indicate that. The thought of having to tell him she didn't love him the way she thought a wife should paralyzed her every time it entered her mind. She had convinced herself that it would be far easier to just drift into a real marriage naturally than to be in with a cold analytical discussion which contained brutal truth. She smiled, "It was difficult for her to imagine Steve as a Middle Eastern sultan. He looked more like a Swedish Prince with his blonde hair and blue eyes."

"What's so funny?" Steve asked interrupting her thoughts.

"Funny?" She asked.

"Yeh, you were smiling like something was very funny to you."

"Don't mind me." She chuckled and took the pan of chicken to the microwave.

He watched her, "She's different." He thought. "She's involved in her own thoughts a lot since I picked her up. That's what makes her so difficult to reach. She has her own world in her mind somewhere and she enjoys being there. Don't push." He cautioned himself. "Just be patient." He contended himself remembering that she bolted but returned by herself the next day. He didn't have to go to her this time. He watched her, "What the hell is it about her that makes me so crazy. The whole situation is a pain in the ass if you look at it squarely yet I stand here feeling grateful that she came back to me." He grinned as he watched her seeing part of what the magic was, she looked all soft and gentle and she was in his house making his dinner. She was his wife. That made him crazy. Electricity stirred in his chest. He went to her as she cut some vegetables and he put his arm around her shoulder. "I'm glad you're home." He said. She smiled at him and nudged him gently. He kissed her cheek and moved away before the electricity got too serious.

"I didn't know that you could scuba dive. Did you take lessons?"

"No a friend taught me, that and boating too."

She nodded, and went to wash the cut vegetables. A thought surfaced. "Was the friend a girl?" She asked with a sinking feeling.

"Yes." He answered taking a cookie.

Her stomach tensed. "A girl who was a friend or a girlfriend?" She asked.

He swallowed the mouthful of cookie wondering why she'd ask such a question. "What difference does it make?"

"None, I guess." She answered but it made a lot of difference to her as she compared herself to the kind of self assured woman who was able to take him on a boat and play the role of teacher to him which was a superior role, than jump over the side weighted down by air tanks and flippers still feel like a woman and survive all of it. Jeneil drained the vegetables and got the pot. "You are kidding yourself here." She thought. "Look at what he's used to. You will have to take Dramamine and chloroform to just get on the boat." She felt her courage weaken about being his wife. She sighed.

"Hey what's happening in your head now?" He laughed.

"What?" She turned to him.

"You're running through all kinds of emotions. Something was funny before and now you look so down."

She took the pot to the stove.

"I'd like to pay a penny for your thoughts." He smiled.

She turned on the burner. "You'd be getting cheated."

He watched her return to the sink to clean up the vegetable scrapings. "You live there don't you?" He asked.

"Where?" She asked putting the scrapings into the disposal.

"In your mind."

She smiled, "Yes, that's why I have to be careful about eccentric. I don't want to make a left turn into the twilight zone. Where do you live?" She asked leaning against the counter near him and wiping her hands.

"Right here in this house." He shrugged.

"That's it?" She said surprised, "That's the total dimension?" She took the cookie from his hand took a bite then returned it to him. She went to the cupboard for dishes, "That sounds so wonderfully uncomplicated. I live right here in this house." She sighed as she repeated his answer. He smiled as he saw more of her magic. She was hopelessly entangled in tilt. She struggled with it and it made her vulnerable which in turn made her look fragile to him like she needed protecting. He went to her. He wanted to hold her watching her struggle. She turned holding the dishes, "Let's eat in the kitchen." She said and went to the table.

"Fine." He said, stopping short seeing that she was out of fragile now and into decisive. He chuckled, "She's crazy and I think it's cute." He laughed to himself. "Honey your mind is the twilight zone."

*****

Jeneil had changed her hours at the office to accommodate her "other life" as she called it. She was serious about following all the interests that riddled through her. The studio was finished and needed to be set up and she had to concentrate on preparing for a harem. Leaving the car in the driveway, she ran upstairs to change from her office clothes to her exotic dance outfit since she was a little late getting away. The doorbell rang as she came down the stairs. "Wonderful just when I can't spare the time." She went to the closet as the doorbell rang again. "Wait I can't answer looking like this." She looked down at herself through the filmy material of her costume that consisted of chiffon pantaloons over briefs of a deeper shade of red. The instructor called the top a jacket but it looked like a glorified bra to Jeneil. She slipped her coat on and went to the door. Dana Tulson and Merrill Landers, wives of two doctors from Steve's office, were bobbing up and down in the cold air dressed in a powder blue and light pink sweat suit jogging outfits. Vapor from their breaths puffed in rhythms.

"Hi." Dana smiled, continuing to run in place. "We're starting a running club would you like to join? We think America needs to be healthier so we're doing something about it."

Jeneil smiled warmly, "That's a great cause." She said. "I believe in exercise too. I was just leaving to do some."

Merrill Landers, the more shy of the two, looked at Jeneil's legs. "Won't you be cold? That's an awfully thin jogging suit?"

Jeneil laughed, "I don't jog. I'm on my way to dance class."

"Oh," Merrill smiled. "That sounds so nice. My knees and ankles kill me from jogging."

"You're a cream puff Merrill," Dana said, continuing to run and puff in place. "I'm glad I found you."

"Dana." Merrill grinned, "Let's go with Jeneil. Can we?" Merrill asked, smiling sweetly. "Does your teacher allow visitors?"

Jeneil was speechless as the situation began to steamroll.

"What kind of dancing is it?" Dana asked, "I like feeling like I've worked out."

"Well exotic dancing works me out." Jeneil smiled.

Dana stopped running in place, "Exotic dancing?" Jeneil nodded.

"What's exotic dancing?" Merrill asked.

Dana raised her eyebrows and shook her head. "She's a home "ec" major. Merrill you know exotic dancing. Duh, duh, duh duh." Dana said waving her arms and wiggling her hips.

"Oh my gosh." Merrill chuckled. "You really do that stuff Jeneil?"

Jeneil laughed, "That stuff is hard work and it's more than just belly dancing. The class covers a lot of cultural ceremonial dances."

Dana laughed, "What a kick. Count me in. Can we go dressed like this?"

"Sure." Jeneil smiled.

"Oh my gosh." Merrill giggled as she got into Jeneil's car. "My mother would die if she knew."

They drove onto the street and toward the Rand's house. "We should ask Sondra to come." Dana said. "She's too bookish. She needs to run."

"She's into lib." Jeneil said, "I doubt this would please her."

Dana shrugged, "Let's ask anyway. At least we've done our part to make her healthier."

Jeneil smiled, "You're into causes, Dana."

She stopped at the Rand driveway. Sondra was hanging suet on an evergreen tree for the birds. She came to the car. Dana waved, "We're forming and exercise club, Sondra. Right now we're on our way to visit an exotic dance class. Want to come?"

Sondra looked at all three slowly, "Who's into exotic dancing?" She asked.

"Jeneil is." Merrill smiled, "It sounds like fun."

Sondra covered her mouth to hide a grin. "Ladies thank you, but I'd rather have both hands amputated than to lower myself to the level of sex object to please male hormones."

"Well we jog too." Dana added.

"Good," Sondra said, "try books, they jog the mind. Don't neglect exercising the brain, that's just as important. Thank you for stopping and inviting me." She smiled, "But I'll pass." She bent down to look at Jeneil, "You surprise me Jeneil. You seemed more liberated than that."

Jeneil shrugged, "Well some of us grow more slowly than others. We still appreciate those who have fought for the freedoms. At least I can leave the kitchen now and take dance lessons. Any kind I want, not just ballet or the waltz."

Sondra smiled broadly. "Class act Jeneil. You have supportive sisterhood buttoned down very well. I'm impressed." Jeneil smiled.

Dana was undaunted, "Join us Sondra. You can run the book exercise part. I'll take the running and Jeneil will take the dancing and cultural."

"What about me?" Merrill asked.

"You can bring refreshments." Dana smiled.

"I hate home "ec" major jokes." Merrill frowned.

Sondra smiled impressed with the warmth of the group, "Look I really appreciate you stopping for me, but I've learned that if you get into too many causes you don't serve any of them really well. I prefer to specialize. When equality is cemented then I'll take time for fun. But thanks for asking I mean that sisters."

"Okay, Sondra." Dana smiled, "See you at the Christmas Party."

"Plural." Sondra groaned, "Parties. There's a rash of them."

She waved and stepped back to let them drive off. Dana shut the car window as Jeneil drove away. "She is too deep into the movement. Militant isn't stable either, I don't think."

Merrill smiled, "Oh I don't know, Dana, Sondra isn't too militant and is a great cook. She can make a Braised Duck á l`Orange without looking at the recipe.

Dana looked at Jeneil and smiled, "Merrill is older than I am and she feels like my younger sister. I wish I could have tolerated Home Ec. Life sounds so simple."

"I'm not insulted Dana." Merrill chuckled.

"I was expressing admiration, Merrill." Dana replied.

Jeneil smiled enjoying both of her unexpected companions. Dana looked at Jeneil. "You're pretty good handling Sondra. She sometimes fires heat seeking missiles."

"She does," Merrill agreed, "and I don't think exotic dancing is making yourself a sex object, but I know I won't tell my mother or I'll hear that "Ladies don't do that.""

Jeneil grinned, "That's why what Sondra is doing is so important. We at least know now that a lady is a woman with good manners, but first she's a woman; her own woman."

Dana clapped her hands, "Right on." She said.

Merrill smiled, "I like that. I'll remember that definition for when my mother finds out. She finds out everything."

Dana laughed, "You must tell her. How else could she find out?"

Merrill chuckled, "You're right, but she has the piercing stare that makes me want to confess to everything including not having taken my vitamins regularly." Jeneil and Dana laughed.

"Maybe Sondra will teach us how to liberate ourselves from our mothers." Dana chuckled.

"I'll go to that class." Merrill said, "Doug would insist on it, I'm sure. He keeps telling me that he married me not my mother so I should think for myself. I don't know what he's complaining about though. She told me to marry him." Dana slapped her knee and laughed hysterically. "Well don't make fun I was sharing a sensitive feeling." Merrill said.

"I'm not." Dana laughed holding her stomach.

Jeneil looked at Merrill in the rear view mirror and smiled. "We love you Merrill. Your simplicity is refreshing. Dana loves fun and laughing. She's complimenting you."

"Sometimes I'm not sure with Dana, thanks Jeneil."

Jeneil pulled into the parking lot of a two story office building. All three got out of the car and went to the building.

"Oh there's Mary Tyachz." Dana said stopping.

"Her name is Mary-Elizabeth." Merrill smiled.

Mary-Elizabeth Tyachz stopped looking anxiously at them. "Hi Merrill, Mrs. Tulson, Mrs. Bradley." Jeneil saw Mary-Elizabeth look at her chiffon covered legs.

"Dance class." Jeneil smiled.

"Oh." Mary-Elizabeth nodded, "I'm late for an appointment so I hope none of you will think I'm rude if I just run on in."

"Go ahead!" Dana replied, "We understand."

"Thanks." Mary-Elizabeth said disappearing into the building.

Dana sighed, "She is one person I'd love to get into the club." She said.

Merrill frowned, "I don't think so, Dana. She shouldn't jog right now."

Dana looked at Merrill, "You mean?"

Merrill nodded, "Her appointment's with Dr.Vandiver OB-GYN."

"She's pregnant." Dana sighed. "I thought she looked kind of blue green around the edges. Oh poor Mary-Elizabeth." She said sadly.

"Why poor Mary-Elizabeth?" Jeneil asked. "Pregnancy isn't usually fatal."

Dana and Merrill looked at each other and then at Jeneil, "It's probably an attempt to save her marriage." Merrill frowned.

"I don't understand." Jeneil said as they walked toward the dance studio door.

Dana shook her head. "George is...is, oh damn he's cheating is what he's doing." Dana said angrily.

"Shhhh." Merrill said. "You can't be sure where there are ears."

"Oh that's too bad." Jeneil said.

"I'd like to ring Barbara Barnard's neck." Dana snapped.

"Dana, please, shhh." Merrill looked around nervously, "Jeneil don't pass any of this on will you? She is your next door neighbor and all."

"Oh damn. That's right." Dana said covering her mouth.

"Don't worry about me." Jeneil said. "I seldom see her. Are you sure about Barbara, though?" She added. "She and Drexel seem pretty solidly married."

Merrill and Dana looked at each other. "You belong in Sayard with us, Jeneil. You're not very fast. Neither am I." Merrill said.

Dana smiled, "Jeneil, Tecumseh has some pretty strange people living in it. Barbara Barnard is a nymphomaniac."

Jeneil put her hand to her throat. "Oh," She said. "I hope that's true, because that's pretty ugly gossip.   It could ruin her marriage."

Dana and Merrill looked at each other again. Dana chuckled. "Your husband must be pretty tight lipped, Jeneil. Drexel Barnard is into troism in any combination so Barbara's quark is a turn on for him."

"Oh really?" Jeneil said, "Well it's great that they found each other then isn't it?"

Dana and Merrill chuckled. "You have a great attitude." Dana said. "We wondered how you would get along in Tecumseh, you look so straight, but you're sophisticated. You live and let live. That's really true, I guess. It's really more of my business is it? I just hate seeing Mary-Elizabeth suffer that's all."

"I'd better get to class." Jeneil said, "The teacher might let you participate instead of just watch. He claims that you have to feel the dancing in order to appreciate it."

"Oh good." Dana smiled following her.

"Yes." Merrill said following quickly.

Jeneil hung up her coat wishing she had a dictionary so she could look up the word troism. "I'll go talk to the teacher." Jeneil said and walked away.

Dana looked at Merrill, "Wow, I'm signing up for this class. If I can get to look like she does in that outfit from exotic dancing."

"I know what you mean. She's usually so modestly dressed that her figure is hidden completely. No wonder her husband is so crazy about her. She is a woman and a lady."

Dana looked at her. "You don't believe what they're saying about all her trips out of town then?" Dana asked.

"No I don't." Merrill insisted. "Darcy said Steve Bradley has changed a lot and I watched him at the last associates' dinner with her. He's crazy about her. I'd love to have my husband look at me like that. She knows what she's doing. She's one very smart lady. Let life live around you and make yourself an inevitable for your husband. She's now and today. I'm glad we stopped when we saw her car. I like her a lot."

"Me too." Dana smiled, "She seems so normal for such a big business woman."

Merrill smiled, "I know what you mean. Her head is probably full of stock quotes, but I feel comfortable talking to her about anything. She's got her life completely together. I envy that. I wish I did." Dana nodded agreeing with her.

Both women enjoyed the class and signed up. Jeneil took them to lunch at a vegetarian restaurant which fascinated Merrill and pleased the health conscious Dana. After dropping them at their homes Jeneil went to hers pleasantly surprised that she had enjoyed herself so much with women. She liked the way her "other life" was beginning. She spent the next hour reading poetry and listening to classical music as part of her training for a harem. She found that she had to work into it again at a lower level of sensuousness. Her level of cerebral surprised her and she knew that Bill was right; she was in an ivory tower. She reviewed her harem program and decided to leave the concentration on the Sultan's qualities for closer to the weekend, remembering that the exercise was very potent and became very stimulating.

Twenty-Seven

Dinner was eaten by candlelight which surprised Steve who wasn't sure what to make of the woman sitting at the table with him. He chuckled to himself whenever he caught her watching him. "Another mind study." He thought, "I'd pay a dollar for her thoughts." He was completely thrown off center when she breezed into the den after dinner with strawberries out of season and melted chocolate for desert. She poured brandy into a swifter and placed it near the fire place to heat for him and apple juice for her while she lit some candles. They were red and had holly at the base. He assumed it was a Christmas thing she was doing. He liked it. She wasn't very talkative as she sat next to him on the sofa reading a book and he got into studying for a surgical case. He assumed the warmed brandy was getting to him when he became aware of her perfume and her presence near him. He was surprised to find her leaning closer to him sprawled along the sofa. The whole mood of the room was getting to him. "Would you like more brandy?" She asked dipping a strawberry slowly into the chocolate.

"I don't think so." He said running his fingers through his hair and taking a deep breath. She sat up and then moved closer to him as she handed him the strawberry. He watched her puzzled by the sensuousness of the whole move. If he was with anybody else but her he'd would make a move. he took the strawberry and she smiled at him. She was getting to him and he knew he was in trouble because he felt she was being deliberate which he knew was ridiculous. He looked at his watch. 9:00. "I need to call Dr. Sprague about a case tomorrow. He's probably home by now." He said standing up.

"Bye." She smiled and slowly licked the chocolate from the strawberry she was holding.

He caught his breath as he watched her. "She can't be doing this deliberately. It's way beyond the realm of what she even knows probably. The damn warmed brandy is getting to me." He thought. "Bye." He said and left the room going upstairs quickly to get away from the high powered den.

Jeneil grinned and bit into the strawberry. "Poor Steve. American men just don't understand how to be a proper sultan. They're not trained for it." She thought, "I'll have to teach him." She grinned and took another bite of the strawberry. He stayed in his room after his call not trusting himself to understand what was happening in the den or to resist it. He felt there was no way he was going to mess up his relationship with her now just because her holiday mood was romantic and sensuous to him. She knocked at his door at 10:30.

He sat against the headboard reading with his shirt completely unbuttoned. "What?" He called.

She opened the door surprising him. "Was Dr. Sprague in?" She asked, leaning against the door as she held the doorknobs in her hands.

"Yes." He said wondering why she just didn't say her usual quick goodnight.

"Is everything settled for the case tomorrow?"

He nodded.

"Good." She smiled. "Can I get you anything?"

He shook his head.

"Then I guess I'll go to bed." She smiled again.

"Okay." He nodded.

"I'll see you in the morning." She said and waved gently then closed the door quickly behind her.

He covered his mouth with one hand; "Holy shit her "other life" is going to kill me if this is what it's going to be like around here.

She had a different type of robe on at breakfast which they both ate standing in the kitchen since Jeneil was going to the office very early in order to spend some time in her "other life." Steve went to the garage after breakfast wondering how come the kitchen seemed sensuous too. The image of her standing there in the soft blue robe with her hair tussled and falling over one eye was close to irresistible, but there was something about the way she was smiling and saying "Bye" lately that was jolting his whole rib cage. He sighed and drove off glad to be in the cold air. He had a full morning of surgery and he stopped to buy a bowl of soup for lunch and brought an apple with him to eat at the Group Associates Staff Meeting. He walked in after the younger members were there, but the older doctors hadn't arrived. The seating usually divided itself at the long rectangular table with the older at one end and the younger at the other which also divided into Sayard, Tecumseh and Other. Steve sat at the dividing line between Sayard and Tecumseh home owners and he noticed that Morgan Rand always did the same at the opposite side of the table from him. "Human behavior." He thought putting his briefcase down and taking his seat. Taking a bite of his apple he noticed that some of the doctors at the Sayard end were talking and smiling and looking at him. "What have I missed?" He asked.

Bob Tulson grinned, "What were you doing last night at 9 o'clock?"

Doug Landers smiled broadly and the others were chuckling.

Steve thought about the previous night, "Talking to Dr. Sprague about the Kincaid surgery. Why?"

Doug Landers, smiled. "Fool."

"What?" Steve asked confused.

"You missed your Christmas present then."

"Didn't your wife tell you what she did yesterday?"

"What did she do?" Steve asked.

Drexel Barnard became interested in the goings on from his Tecumseh seat and Morgan Rand looked up from his papers.

Bob Tulson grinned, "My wife and Doug's jogged to your house to invite Jeneil to join a jogging club. You wife was already going to an exercise class and took our wives along."

"Bless her heart." Doug Landers sighed happily.

The Sayard doctors chuckled, and Bob chuckled, "Our wives signed up too and they decided that at 9 o'clock last night they'd put on their dance outfits and show us what they learned in class as a Christmas present for us."

Doug laughed, "Merrill told me that neither she nor Dana are as good at it as Jeneil. Merrill thinks she's fantastic."

Bob nodded, "Dana said Jeneil has the instructor impressed."

"With what?" Steve asked.

"Her expertise in exotic dancing."

"What?" Drexel Barnard laughed. Morgan Rand dropped his pen. Steve put his apple in the trash basket as all the other doctors sat forward and became interested in the conversation. The Sayard group all chuckled.

Bob Tulson smiled, "My wife said that the instructor started Jeneil on a ceremonial fertility dance and couldn't believe her ability to do pelvic thrusts so easily. Jeneil told him she learned it studying yoga."

There was soft chuckling all around the table. Doug Landers contentedly sighed, "Merrill showed me a pelvic thrust, Steve. It was deadly and Merrill wasn't doing it right." He laughed, "So I taught her how, my way." Everyone laughed. "I warned her that if she confesses to her mother that she's taking exotic dance lessons, I'll divorce her. The mother-in-law has lived her life and wants to live Merrill's too. Jeneil gave her a taste of thinking for herself and Merrill's excited, to say nothing of her husband."

Morgan Rand smiled, "I wish they'd stop at my place. Sondra needs to get involved in more things in order to balance her life."

"They stopped for Sondra, Morgan, but she said she'd rather have both hands amputated than make herself a sex object to satisfy male hormones."

Morgan sighed, "That sounds like a direct quote."

Everyone laughed except Steve who was still struggling with the shock.

Bob Tulson smiled at Steve, "You know Dana is into physical fitness and health. She has been since she was a teenager and she thought she had her body pretty limber, but Jeneil impressed her. She said the control Jeneil has of her torso is outstanding." Bob smiled warmly, "Dana's energy and no fuss approach to herself has always impressed me I like it. But last night she was different. She did her hair all girlie and put on makeup to do the dance. She said exotic dancing was very rhythmic and graceful and makes you feel different about yourself." He sighed, "Viva la difference."

The doctors laughed or wolf whistled. Steve shook his head. "Jeneil's a crazy combination of things. She's never boring, that's for sure."

Doug Landers agreed, "Merrill wrote down a definition Jeneil told her and she put it on our refrigerator. Now Merrill's rehearsing it for when she sees her mother. She keeps saying "A lady is a woman who has learned good manners, and what's expected of her, but first she's a woman, her own woman.""

The doctor's around the table applauded and whistled. Dr.'s Young, Tyler and Sprague filed in and the tumult subsided. "What's all the excitement about, gentlemen?" Dr. Young asked standing tall and dignified at the head of the table.

The doctors all looked at each other grinning. Doug Landers grinned, "Mrs. Bradley took some of our wives to lunch yesterday that's all."

Dr. Tyler furrowed his brow, "And that rates an applause?" He asked.

Dr. Sprague smiled, "Jim we're getting old. They're leaving out important descriptive sentences as a sign of respect to our grey hair. Someday let's tell them how we got this way."

"Can they take the shock Warren?" He laughed.

The younger doctors laughed as a show of respect for the three older doctors who they knew had earned it.

*****

Steve drove home from the office still thinking about the exotic dancing story. He felt awkward not having known what the other doctors were talking about. For a brief moment he wondered if that was why Jeneil seemed different the night before and then he discarded the idea as ridiculous. He knew she'd never do something like that as a surprise, it wasn't her style, but something in him wished it was. He wished his wife had given him the Christmas present and a memorable evening of fun too. Sometimes the pressure of the pretend marriage made him weary. He showered quickly in order to get energized and headed to dinner. Jeneil had a long dress on and had a Christmas candle burning on the kitchen table where they were having a light dinner. She was humming merrily as she set the food on the table. She looked great and the fact that he was held back from enjoying it openly added to the weariness. He knew he needed the weekend vacation. "I'll be picking up Morgan, Drexel, George Tyachz and Everett Tufton." He said finishing his coffee. "Would you mind if I took the Torrance? There's more leg room in the back."

"Fine." She answered watching him and noticing the slight tension. He got up and took his topcoat from a nearby chair. "Is something wrong?" She asked.

He sighed, "I need the weekend vacation." He said fixing his collar.

"Life closing in on you?" She asked sympathetically.

He looked at her. "In a way yes." He said. "Jeneil the next time all the wives plan to give their husbands special Christmas presents, would you at least tell me so I won't look so stupid when they're talking about it?"

"Then Dana and Merrill did go through with it."

"Oh yes." Steve said. "They're husbands loved it Jeneil. I heard about my wife being the ringleader at a staff meeting. I should be back at 10:30." He said heading toward the door.

She watched him, "Well that's very interesting. I even get yelled at when I hang around with women. Maybe you could chain me to a wall in the cellar and give me a fresh supply of food and water daily so I won't cause you trouble."

He stopped and turned around grinning. "Now I know that's a left hook to my stomach because I don't hear an ounce of sorrow in your voice."

"Shall I cry?" She smiled.

He chuckled. "I deserve the jab to the stomach."

She nodded and folded her napkin, "Yes you do. You're acting like a jerk."

"Hey that's my line." He smiled and walked back to her.

She chuckled, "You can add the word again."

He stopped beside her grinning, "You're a smart mouthed bitch."

She fixed his tie, "I accept your sweet apology."

He smiled, "Brainy as all hell too."

She touched his cheek tenderly surprising him then leaning forward she kissed his lips softly shocking him and taking his breath away. He stared at her for a second and then he stood up turning red. "I'll be back at 10:30." He said clearing his throat.

She nodded and smiled, "Bye." Jolting his rib cage.

"Bye." He said going to the door and putting on his gloves. The door closed and Jeneil smiled. "Mr. Husband, you really do need the weekend." She sighed.

Steve took a deep breath as he got behind the wheel and rested his head back, "Jeneil, sweetheart, you kiss me as a friend and I want you as a wife a real wife. How much more can I take?" He sighed and started the engine, "Life doesn't wait." He said, backing out of the garage.

Steve's schedule wouldn't allow him to take more than a half day on Friday for the weekend, but he didn't complain. He was ready to get away even without Friday at all. His main concern was Jeneil. She was behaving so differently that he had to spend more time in his room than he cared to just to be away from her and stable his blood pressure. By Thursday he began to wonder about her seriously thinking that maybe she was trying to let him know that she could accept a real marriage. The thought frightened him knowing that if he was wrong and he made a move, irreparable damage could be done. The idea that she was clinging and snuggling and sensuous because of the vacation and the holiday was a possibility even though it wasn't like Jeneil to be coy. He was confused and having a difficult time dealing with his feelings for her. She had been into some high powered moves that were leaving him speechless and he hoped the weekend would run smoothly. The thought of the two of them all alone, a cabin cruiser, dressed for water fun had him very concerned. His only hope was if she was serious about a real marriage, that she would be more explicit about it, although he couldn't' imagine how. In all his experience with women never once were the words spoken first and he couldn't imagine Jeneil saying the words "lets sleep together" or "let's make the marriage real," it was too out of character for her. Yet, he knew that she would have to be the one to approach him in order to minimize the risk of his misreading her behavior. He gloved for early surgery planning to leave at noon to get Jeneil and catch a two o'clock flight.

*****

Jeneil lingered at the jewelry counter of a large department store in the mall. She was finished buying Christmas presents now. She had gone shopping for personal items for the weekend trip and stopped in for two gifts that completed her shopping. She lingered not wanting to go home where she would get nervous. The weekend felt like a honeymoon to her and she needed to keep busy in order to stay calm. So she browsed, planning to leave in another 15 minutes. A crying child caught her attention and she looked up to see what might be wrong. Its mother was carrying it quickly to an exit door while the child insisted that he wanted to stay with Santa. Jeneil smiled as she watched the woman head for the exit embarrassed by the looks she was getting. A man held the door for her as the mother got to it and Jeneil's whole body became numbed by shock impulses when she recognized Peter as he walked into the store after the woman left. Her breathing became shallow and then seemed to stop altogether as Peter went to the far end of the long network of glass display cases with lamps positioned every 4 yards or so on the counter. Jeneil felt her heart thump violently in her chest and she forced herself to take a deep breath as she felt the tightness begin in her throat. "He's lost weight." She thought watching him from the far section at a lamp. She smiled noticing his woolen top coat and leather gloves. He was wearing a suit and tie. "He's all grown up into a doctor now." She smiled and then she felt her lip quiver and tears sting her eyes. She swallowed hard and then inhaled deeply trying to keep herself from giving in to crying. She missed him, with every cell in her whole body, she missed seeing him. Nebraska, Jeneil and Irish all missed him as she stayed positioned behind the lamp and glimpsed from behind its shade. The sales clerk brought several scarves to show Peter placing them on the display counter for him. He touched one gently.

"That's a very lovely one." The salesclerk smiled. "Would you like that one?"

Peter looked up, "No." He said. "I knew someone who had one like it. I'll take the green one."

The clerk nodded and took his card to the register. He touched the burgundy printed scarf again thinking of Jeneil. He was thinking of her a lot as the holiday got closer that's why he was going to spend Christmas like he had spent Thanksgiving. There was no way he would be able to pretend that he was in a holiday mood. Leaving town was the best way to survive. She was so much a part of him that he felt like she was near him. He looked around half expecting to see her, not knowing what he would do if he did. Jeneil slipped behind the lamp lowering her head when she saw him look up afraid he might see her. Waiting a few minutes she glimpsed past the shade and saw him leaving the store into the foyer of plants and carolers. Disappointment filled her. She had wanted more time to just look at him. Tears filled her eyes and she struggled with a lump in her throat. She took her handkerchief and dabbed at the tears. Her temples were throbbing she massaged them gently.

"Are you alright Miss?" A salesgirl asked.

"Yes." Jeneil answered forcing a smile, "I just have a sinus headache starting I guess."

"There's no time for headaches this time of year." The clerk smiled.

Jeneil nodded, "You're so right." And she gathered her packages to leave.

"Merry Christmas." The sales girl said.

"Thanks. Merry Christmas to you." Jeneil answered going toward the exit feeling far from merry. She sat in her car breathing just to calm down. She needed to drive the car. Her husband would be getting home soon so they could leave for their weekend vacation. She burst into tears. She had driven home with the car window wide open hoping to dry her eyes. Rushing to her room to repair the damage from tears she looked in the mirror. She had stopped crying by thinking of Steve and how anxious he was to get away. She packed her purchased items quickly and was putting on fresh makeup when she heard the SX7 drive in. As she put her luggage in the hallway, Steve reached the top of the stairs.

"Ready Honey?" He asked smiling.

Jeneil nodded aware that something in her resented him calling her Honey. He put his arms around her and held her. She wanted to push away from him go to her room unpack her bags and let him leave by himself. She shut her eyes tightly. "Oh my gosh!" Her mind screamed, "How am I going to manage this."

Steve's excitement gave her some privacy as he busied himself getting the luggage in the car and locking the house. They took the Torrance to the airport and the bustle of the crowds and numbered gate ways and tickets allowed her more privacy. She closed her eyes and pretended to be sleeping on the plane which allowed her privacy again and soon the pretense became real. She awoke by Steve kissing her cheek. "We're here." He said softly, "Are you okay?" He asked.

"Yes. Why?" She gathered her carryall and purse.

"You've slept for almost three hours. You won't sleep tonight." He said getting up.

"Want to bet?" She thought and the anger in her scared her. She wasn't prepared for the sunshine and warm air as she got off the plane. It felt good. She let Steve handle the luggage details while she sat on a bench grateful to have some time to herself.

The weekend on the cabin cruiser loomed before her with a heavy depressive pall. She knew there was no way she could let Steve or anyone touch her. She didn't even want to be there now.

"Jeneil?" Steve stooped before her, "What's wrong?" He asked looking concerned. He took her hand gently. She wanted to pull it from him angrily and tell him to stop touching her and to keep his hands to himself. He smiled gently, "Honey, don't spend the weekend scared. Try the cabin cruiser. If you can't handle it, Sheldon gave me the key to the house. Its 10 minutes from the marina. I'll take you to the house and I'll go out on the boat alone." He smiled and touched her cheek lovingly, "You look so upset. A vacation should be pleasant even for landlubbers."

She watched him. His gentle words calmed her anger. His words out on the boat alone relaxed her as she realized that he had no romantic intentions about the weekend. None at all. She chocked up and stayed silent.

He chuckled, "Are you catatonic?"

She smiled and shook her head.

"Then let's go, Mrs. Bradley. Times a wastin!"

The name Mrs. Bradley sounded very foreign to her and she realized that she was heading for some serious trouble if she allowed herself to coast emotionally any longer. He rented a car and studied a map Sheldon Taft had given him then he pulled away from the airport. Jeneil folded her arms and stared out the window oblivious to the flowers and foliage passing her window as her mind recalled the image of Peter in the store. In her mind she saw him walking away into the mall corridor and she felt tears begin to surface.

"Jeneil?" She turned her head to look at Steve. He looked concerned. "I called you three times and you never answered. Are you feeling well?"

She nodded, "Why were you calling me?"

"I'm going to turn back. There was a large market a short way back there. Provisions will cost less. Can you hold out for food for a while?"

"I'm not really hungry." She said, "I can wait."

He looked at her for a second and then back at the road frowning.

He parked the car, "Come in with me." He said looking at the list. "I don't want to mess up. You have everything all organized with menus." Steve watched her as they shopped still concerned about her. She seemed out of it somehow. "Jeneil, have you taken any medication for air sickness or sea sickness?"

"No. I don't want to unless the water is rough." She answered getting some juice.

He nodded and continued watching her. "Why so many eggs?" He asked two aisles later.

"You eat three eggs when you do eat them and they don't sell ½ dozens." She said.

"You have two dozen Jeneil."

She looked surprised and then impatient with herself. She put one dozen back and sighed. Steve was becoming concerned.

The marina lay before them, a small city in itself with an expanse of water behind it. Steve smiled and shrugged, "I'm ready. Oh man I am ready. Why don't we change into sea clothes and then go to dinner?" He said showing every bit of the excitement he was feeling. She nodded.

Jeneil found the cabin small and stuffy and she changed into white slacks with a navy top quickly as the stale air began to feel suffocating. The window wouldn't open and she sighed wanting to cry. Her surroundings were unfamiliar and uncompromising making her tense. She longed for some peace and privacy. Steve knocked. "Can I come in?"

"Yes." She said backing away from the window which was above the bed staggering as the boat bobbed.

Steve walked in. "What are you up to?" He laughed.

"The window won't open!" She snapped, "The air in here is unhealthy. Do you expect me to hold my breath all weekend?"

He studied her face surprised by her tone of voice. She got off the bed and Steve checked the window. He looked at her. "Jeneil you're supposed to unlatch it first. See." He opened the porthole easily; he stepped off the bed and went to her going to put his arms around her. She moved away. Her behavior was totally opposite of what he'd been used to all week. "Ready for dinner?" He asked letting the incident pass as jitters.

Jeneil brushed her hair. "Well I'm not really hungry, but I heard somewhere that you're safer to eat at sea to avoid seasickness. I'm ready." She said taking a white jacket.

They walked to a small seaside restaurant. Steve noticed that Jeneil kept her arms folded unlike her usual routine of holding his hand. She was also very silent. The waiter poured the wine and left.

"Honey maybe you should stay at the house. You look very tense."

"I'll be fine." She said sounding guilty, "Just allow me some space and I'll be okay." She said rubbing her temple.

He nodded. The sky was beginning to darken into evening as they walked back to the boat and got on board. Steve changed to cut offs and took his shirt and socks off then went on deck. "I'm going out to the cove and anchor for the night." He said going to her.

Jeneil wrapped her jacket around her body and folded her arms tightly. Steve noticed. "Do you need anything from land? Last call?"

"No, nothing." She answered.

"Okay then I'll start the engine."

Jeneil looked around and found a seat expecting a takeoff jolt. The smooth glide surprised her and she stood up to watch the marina grow smaller in the distance. Her stomach tensed and she got a full glimpse of her fear of water as it surrounded her on all sides. She looked around and swallowed hard. She had taken two cruises with Mandra but they were on large ships which had given her the idea that she could deal with her fear now, but the cabin cruiser was smaller and she wasn't used to that much water surrounding her. She concentrated on the deck itself and calmed down somewhat.

They secured the boat in the cove and sat on the deck watching the red and orange brilliance at the horizon. The air was cool and a steady breeze soothed the face. Steve sat checking the scuba equipment and looked at Jeneil from time to time knowing that something was very wrong. She was deep into her own thoughts and her expression showed a sadness. Steve expected her to cry several times, but she hadn't. He was completely baffled about why her cheerful, excited mood at breakfast was so damaged. She had said she wanted some space so he just watched with concern. Steve flipped the lantern switch and the deck was bathed in light forcing the surrounding area into blackness.

"I'm tired." Jeneil said standing up, "I'll think I'll go to bed."

"The light switch is on the right."

She nodded and went to the cabin stairs. A wave lapped at the boat causing a strong bobbing movement. Steve heard the rolling thump of something falling. "Jeneil!" He grabbed the lantern and ran to the stairs. Jeneil was sitting down. He was at her side. "Are you hurt?" He asked.

"No something in the cabin toppled. I just sat down so I wouldn't." She.

Steve smiled, "You have ship sense." And he went to kiss her cheek. She turned her head and stood up. Steve's luggage had been thrown from the perch. "I thought I had secured that. Loose objects can be dangerous around here if they're tossed hard enough." The window had been slammed shut. He opened it again. "Jeneil what's wrong?" He asked concerned and he put his hands to her shoulders.

"I'll be fine." She said. "I'll get some sleep."

He nodded. "Goodnight." He said and left the cabin having felt her stiffen as he touched her shoulders. Her reaction hurt. It felt like bolting to him. Both were rejection and he knew it.

*****

Jeneil awoke in a sweat and sat up. She was thirsty and she felt feverish. The window had slammed shut again. She felt around the rim for the latch trying to get it to work. She couldn't. Taking the flashlight, she went to the small refrigerator for water. It was wet but not satisfying. She felt too hot. Steve was sleeping soundly, his bed unfolded from the built-in sofa in the main cabin. Not wanting to wake him, Jeneil made her way past him quietly going up the stairs to the deck. The sky was clouded and the night air was cool. She had put on a pair of shorts and a blouse as pajamas since she had brought only two very nice nightgowns thinking the trip was going to lead in another direction. She sighed as she thought of the turn of events. "I'm in trouble." She said, knowing that after seeing Peter she had rushed back into the ivory tower and slammed the door, locking it tightly with cerebral. Sitting on the deck against a cushioned bench she breathed in the refreshing coolness of the night. "I have to pull myself together." She thought. She sat listening to the water around her slap against the sides at the boat. Blackness surrounded Jeneil and the slapping of the water against the boat seemed more intense, reminding her of her fear. Her stomach knotted. She concentrated hard on the solidness of the deck with both hands, balancing the flashlight on her lap. She began to calm down. A wave lapped at the boat sending it into a strong bobbing action and thrusting the flashlight from her lap. It hit the deck hard causing the light to go out. She felt around on the deck with her hand for the flashlight. The boat bobbed again shifting her off balance spilling her against some equipment. Not having looked at the deck that closely she had no idea of the layout and couldn't get her bearings as the blackness disoriented her. The water on one side sounded very close and fear pulsed through her body as she wondered where she was. She felt around with her hand heading back in the direction towards what she thought would be the cushioned bench. She knew it was a straight line to the cabin door from there. She kept inching her way and she began to think that she was going in the wrong direction entirely since it was taking so long to get to the bench. The water sounded very close again and she knew she must be near a railing. The boat heaved shifting her against the side. She reached up and felt the metal and ropes of the railing and it sent a shiver through her knowing how close she was to the water. It was too close. "Where is the cushioned bench?" She sighed. She crept away from the railing feeling with her hands as she inched her way. Her knees were hurting now and she felt tired from being tense and confused. Another strong bobbing action spilled her against what felt like equipment and her arm felt some rope. She couldn't find an end to it. Taking the rope she made a flattened loop and tied it around her waist in a knot. "What if the rope isn't secured to something," she thought. She felt around and her hand hit a metal ring attached to the deck. Making another loop she knotted the rope again onto the ring. "Well I won't be going too far on the next bob." She said and she pulled herself onto the pile of rope since it was softer than the deck. She laid there to wait for light to break through the blackness.

*****

Steve opened the doors to the cabin and walked onto the deck. The sky was clear and the day looked like it promised to be good. He steadied himself as the boat bobbed. A flashlight rolled across the deck coming to rest against his foot. He wrinkled his brow wondering where it came from. Picking it up, he saw that the switch was on and the bulb was out. "Was Jeneil out here last night?" He went to her cabin and knocked. There was no answer. He opened the door and looked inside. Empty. "Oh shit! No!." He ran back to the stairs and onto the deck as fear began to seize him. He ran to the railing and caught sight of her curled up on a pile of rope on the deck. The rope was tied around her waist and tied to the ring latch of the tool compartment on the floor. He sighed with relief and then laughed silently. "What the hell was she doing?" and then he understood that she had tied herself there from fear. The pathetic side to the scene reached him as he realized that she never called to him or had she? "You'll never learn to come to me will you?" He sighed as he stooped down to wake her. She looked blurry eyed as she sat up and looked around. She had crawled diagonally across the deck. The cushioned bench had been only two yards to her left. She was smudged from the rope and her knees and hands were dirty from crawling.

"What were you doing on the deck?" He asked.

She rubbed her face smearing dirt under her eye. "My cabin got hot and I came up here. The flashlight got tossed to the deck and I lost my way."

"Why didn't you call me?"

"I didn't think." She shrugged, "I don't know really."

He helped her to her feet and undid the rope around her waist. "You must be stiff from sleeping there."

"I am." She said, moving her neck. "A little, I'm a mess." She sighed looking at herself. "I'll get cleaned up." She went into the cabin feeling like she hadn't slept and washed herself in the small lavatory. She changed her clothes and left her room. Steve had made breakfast. She sat and drank her juice.

"I'm taking you to the house." He bit into his toast not looking at her. She didn't argue.

While he headed back to the marina, she cleaned up the breakfast things. "I'll be back for you at lunch around twelve or one." He said, leaving her inside the house. He seemed annoyed or upset but she was too tired to care. She watched him drive off and then went to find a bed to sleep on.

When she awoke it was two o'clock in the afternoon. She went to the living room thinking Steve was there. The car wasn't out front. She made the bed and took a shower. It was 3:30. She walked to the marina. The boat wasn't there. The car was. Steve had the keys. She paced on the dock. Going into a small diner, she bought a cheese sandwich and a glass of milk. She returned to the dock. "Four o'clock." She said, looking at her watch. Climbing the wall across the street, she scanned the bay not really knowing where to look and she sat under a tree to keep cool.

She was worried. "I should call the police." She said, standing up and heading back to the dock to ask directions.

She passed their rented car and saw the note on the windshield. *"Mrs. Bradley, Engine trouble. Details at Marina office."* The uniformed man smiled when she introduced herself. "We're leaving you notes all over town. There's another one on the Taft house door."

"I've been pacing on the docks. What has happened?" She asked, concerned.

"The engine quit when your husband was starting back. He radioed us and we sent our mechanics out. He's out past the cove near Clintock Reef so it took time to get there and then fix the engine."

"Oh, poor Steve, a weekend boating vacation and he gets engine trouble."

"No Problem." The man smiled. "When our mechanics got there your husband went scuba diving again. He's still on vacation."

Jeneil laughed. "Well that's good to hear. He's been so excited about this trip."

"You don't like the water?" The man asked.

Jeneil shook her head. "Only swimming pools."

The man nodded. "Me too. The closest I get to the ocean is in this office right here and a Tuna Sandwich." Jeneil laughed.

"When are they expected back?"

"Probably in half an hour." The man replied.

"I'll walk on the docks then."

He nodded and Jeneil left the office.

The crowd level at the beach was thinning and Jeneil went to walk there. The white sand felt warm and soft to her bare feet. She sat on the piling and watched the water roll onto the shore. She thought of Peter and then her mind remembered what he was doing at the store. "The scarf is probably for Uette." She said and her heart felt the pain the ache and hurt of the words. "Stay in reality Jeneil. He chose to stay married. Get on with your life. Not a real one. Not yet. I just can't switch my feelings so fast." She thought of Steve. "He needs a wife. A real wife. He's such a nice guy and he's got such a klutz for a wife."

She walked back to the dock quickly having stayed too long at the beach. The boat was back. Looking around she noticed that the car was gone. "I did it again." She sighed and headed back to the Taft house on foot. She could see the rental car as she approached the house and she relaxed glad that things hadn't gotten too complicated again. Steve was lying on the lawn chair under a tree with his eyes closed. She was glad to see him and she approached quietly. Picking some leaves from a box elder, she dropped a couple on his face. He brushed them away without opening his eyes. She dropped another and he did the same again. She dropped more and he opened his eyes looking around.

"Hey." He smiled broadly, sitting up. She sat on the lawn looking around at the surrounding grass.

"What are you looking for?" He asked.

"Snakes." She said.

He chuckled, "Jeneil you're afraid of water and snakes. I never knew how much courage it took for you to just get out of bed everyday."

"Well, this is poisonous snake country. Better safe than sorry." She smiled.

"I messed up your vacation." He said, going to touch her hand, but stopping himself.

"No. It's been a fine vacation for me; it's been what I've needed." He studied her face, noticing that she looked better, less disconnected.

"Let's have an early dinner and I'll spend some time with you, then go out on the boat again." He opened the car door for her and got in on his side.

"No." She said, as soon as he got behind the wheel. "Don't leave me here. I want to go back on the boat too." Steve avoided looking at her.

"Jeneil, I can't take you on the boat." He frowned. "You scared me this morning when you were missing. Whatever you're working through has you too distracted. Your mind isn't clear."

She nodded. "I have been distracted, but I promise I'll be fine, now."

He turned to face her putting his arm on the car seat behind her. "Jeneil, I know I'm only a pretend husband, but legally I am your husband and maybe it's time I started acting like one." She watched him wondering what he meant. "We're married; Jeneil and we confided more in each other when we were just friends than we do now. I miss your friendship and our closeness. I want to know what tipped you over so badly." Tears filled her eyes. "Cry Honey, but I still want to know."

His show of strength and concern touched her deeply.

"You are such a nice guy." She sniffed, reaching for a tissue. He touched her hair and smiled.

"Good, then it should be easy to tell me."

She wiped her tears. "I saw Peter yesterday." Steve's heart stopped. Jeneil drew a deep breath. "I was shopping at the mall and he was too." Steve was speechless as he remembered how she had been pulling away from him and avoiding him since yesterday. His heart sank wondering what might have happened between her and Peter. She dabbed the corners of her eyes. "We didn't talk. I didn't have the courage. Just seeing him unraveled me." She said, softly.

Steve relaxed grateful that they hadn't talked and decided that they were meant for each other after all. His heart beat rapidly at the thought. He put his arm around her shoulder and she moved closer to him to be comforted. He smiled, noticing that she did. "It's understandable, Honey." He answered softly, kissing her temple.

His attitude surprised her. She looked at him. "Do you really mean that?" She asked. "You honestly believe my reactions are understandable? You actually understand that?"

"Of course." He smiled. "It's not too hard to understand. Part of you will always love him. It's what makes you Jeneil."

She stared. "And as your wife, you can accept that in me?"

He wrinkled his brow. "Why not?"

Jeneil was amazed as she saw clearly the biggest difference between Steve and Peter. Clearly Chang had to know that a woman was his completely, while Steve had a more sophisticated attitude, a less idealistic approach. Jeneil was astonished as she understood that the White Stallion, the person she disliked with such vehemence, when she first met Steve was exactly the right person to accept her as a wife. The White Stallion who shook her confidence in herself as a woman was the only man she knew who was worldly enough to understand and accept her lopsided heart. Even Robert Danzieg had admitted that he couldn't accept her torn loyalties, and she thought he was very sophisticated. "I'm stunned." She said, indicating it in her voice.

He laughed. "I don't know why. What else can anyone expect of you?"

"And it's as easy as breathing to you?" She marveled staring at him in disbelief.

Steve watched her. "Whoa, Jeneil. I don't want to be a hero or a 12th century saint. I'm a man. I'm comfortable with that."

She smiled gently, and nodded. "True greatness usually isn't aware of itself."

"Oh my gosh." He laughed, putting his head back. "You don't believe me." She smiled as she watched him, sensing that her love for him had just moved slightly past friendship. He was a man, she knew that, but she now felt it, too. He kissed her cheek and chuckled, calming down from the humor he saw in the situation.

"Boy, I'd better take you to dinner before I fall off that pedestal you're building for me and break my clay feet." He snickered and faced the steering wheel putting the key in the ignition.

"I love you, Steve." She said, softly. His heart nearly burst through his chest as he heard the difference in the way she said it. It wasn't how he hoped it would sound eventually, but she was changed, he heard it in her voice. He smiled at her and then turned the key in the ignition, wanting to move away from the moment before he proved to her how much of just an ordinary man he really was.

She was silent as he drove to a restaurant that Sheldon Taft had recommended for seafood, but he didn't mind her silence because she hadn't moved away from him. She was still beside him and he knew that she was letting him know that she needed him.

They stopped at the marina after dinner to get fresh water and juice. Steve took care of the air tanks then they boarded and set out for the cove. Steve wanted to scuba dive at Clintock Reef again and the cove was mid-point to the reef before having to leave for the 3:30 flight home. They played backgammon on deck for a short while and then went to bed wanting to be up very early the next morning to take full advantage of all their time left. Jeneil got into bed feeling tired and she hoped she would sleep right through the night this time. The sleeping compartment was not her favorite spot on the ship, because it lacked good ventilation, but she was determined to be less trouble as Steve couldn't regret bringing her along. She thought about the weekend and couldn't believe how really simple a life Steve lived. He never even suggested going to a pub. All his time had been spent on the boat alone or with her. She smiled. "Is the White Stallion out to pasture or was he just a myth."

*****

Steve stirred awake slowly the next morning. All the physical exercise he had gotten had him very relaxed and he had slept soundly. He couldn't remember stirring once. He ran through the day's schedule in his mind groggily and then became aware that something felt different. He sat up jolting awake as he saw Jeneil curled up at the bottom corner of his bed asleep. He grinned understanding that her cabin must have been too hot again and he was pleased that she had come and slept there. He chuckled trying not to laugh as he saw her curled up almost in a circle to fit on the corner. "Now if I can teach her that she's not my pet kitten and that she's allowed to sleep beside me under the covers, we may have something here." He slipped out of bed carefully not wanting to wake her.

She was sitting on the bed cross legged when he came out of the lav. She held a hand up in a wave and yawned. "My bed was too hot." She said, pushing the hair from her eye. He held back a remark and hoped someday he'd get a chance to say it.

"Okay." He smiled, heading toward the refrigerator to get juice for them. "I don't know, Jeneil. I keep finding you in my bed, maybe you should just sleep there. He held his breath putting the juice glasses down, shocked that he had said that. He turned, slowly. She was staring at him from under her tousled hair. He pointed at her. "I uh..., I didn't mean anything by that. I swear." He held up his hand swearing to his word.

She got off the bed and walked to him picking up a juice glass. "Maybe I will." She said, quietly, turning and walking away. She stopped and turned around pointing at him. "I uh..., I didn't mean anything by that. I swear." She held up her hand, mimicking him. She drank some juice and turned around again, picking up her blanket from the corner of his bed and continued to her room. "I'll be right back to help with breakfast." She said, closing the door.

Steve stayed staring, trying to catch his breath. "Maybe I was wrong. Maybe that wasn't a pet kitten sleeping on the corner of my bed. Maybe it was a full grown She Cat." He picked up his glass of juice and drank it down in a gulp.

No mention of the incident was made after that. Steve was pleased that it had happened, but he knew that she had been tripped over pretty badly from seeing Peter and it would take time to get her steadied again. He kept to his original plan of letting her decide.

Steve took the boat out of Clintock Reef and anchored. Jeneil watched him suit up and strap on his diving gear. The whole outfit looked so heavy and awkward that she wondered how divers didn't just sink to the ocean floor and stay there. She got out her book on fishes and plants of the ocean and Steve promised to bring samples of seaweed and anything he could manage to show her. Kissing her cheek, he went over the side and disappeared under the splashes of foam and ripples. She watched as long as she could see him clearly and wondered why he seemed to have a proclivity to being out of his natural element by sky diving and scuba diving. She shook her head. "Average life can't hold him. He should have become an astronaut." She thought and smiled.

*****

The sun was merciless as it glared down in the boat with blistering intensity. Jeneil went inside and changed into her swimsuit for relief. Drudging some ocean water with a bucket, she poured it over herself and was about to refill the bucket when she saw the three fishes swim past. She stepped back from the railing shivering with horror. "Uhgh, they are big." She shivered again, going to her fish book. "Cod," She said, looking at a glossy picture that matched the swimmers she saw. She went to the railing again. "How can Steve stand being around neighbors that don't look like him? You can't reason with them in a debate over territory if it should be necessary. Oooo it's unnatural." She shivered. "He's in there domain using manufactured gills. Maybe it's a tribute to man's ingenuity, but it's not a tribute of sensibility. Why does he insist on stretching past common bounds?" She sighed and dipped the bucket in again since she was nearly dry from the last dousing. "This is too hot." She said, pouring the ocean water over herself and putting the bucket aside. She looked around at the scenery. There wasn't any. Just water. Blue water that met the blue skies. "It's all wasted on me." She said. "The water would be more impressive to me viewed from the moon when it makes the earth look like a big blue marble. Up close it's too expansively monstrous and smothering." A sense of her aloneness filled her. "I don't know anything about survival here." She thought. "I don't even know how to work the radio if I needed help. If a monsoon or a hurricane hit, I'd have to raft to Japan on a piece of the cabin roof. This is dangerous." She thought feeling her vulnerability. "For Steve too. If a shark decided to spit pieces of him onto the deck, I wouldn't know how to get him help." She shivered, at the thought. "Jeneil you're getting morbid. Go study the radio and get out of the sun." Taking the booklet posted by the radio set, she sat down to study enjoying learning the parts to the radio so much that she wanted to talk to someone. She read the frequencies then buzzed in, curious to see if what she had learned was right.

"This is marine Coast Guard Cutter 2599. Come in." Jeneil looked shock. "The Coast Guard?! Oh my gosh." She thought. "Can they arrest civilians for playing with the radio? I wonder?" She thought. "Come in, please. This is Marine Coast Guard cutter 2599. We read your signal. Can you answer? Is this an S.O.S? Are you unable to speak?"

"S.O.S.!" Jeneil gasped. She pushed the button for transmit. "Uh, no it isn't marine coast guard cutter 2599. I'm on board a cabin cruiser alone while my husband is scuba diving and I just wanted to make sure I knew how to work the radio if I needed to. This is all new to me."

"Very good, ma'am." The officer responded, chuckling. "Make a note of the frequency you are transmitting on if you should need to call us. Now look at your boat's control panel." Jeneil did. "You should have some discs that indicate compass readings."

"I see them." Jeneil said.

"Well if you should be in emergency, you would signal us and give us those readings. We would then stay in touch by radio to help and dispatch a cruiser to you for assistance."

"Oh very good. Thank you." Jeneil smiled. "I feel better knowing that. Thank you again, that's all I needed."

"Signing off then." The marine operator said and the radio was silent.

"I did it." Jeneil smiled, proudly.

The radio bleeped and a male voice was heard. "Velvet Voice cabin cruiser, come in, please. If you'll give me your readings, I'll stop by to help you learn your way. Just a quick study of your equipment will be all that's necessary for some expert service."

Jeneil wrinkled her eyebrows. "What does that mean?" She said, staying away from the radio.

The voice continued. "29.5 and answer please, Velvet Voice. Set the knob marked readings on your radio, Velvet Voice, please."

"Danny is that you?" Another male voice asked.

"Yeh Skip, did you hear her?"

"Yeh, I did. Who is she?" Skip asked in a sexy voice.

"I'm trying to find out. Come in Velvet Voice, come in. Push the transmit button. Don't leave me now just when I've found you at last." Jeneil looked at the set, looking surprised.

A third male voice interrupted. "All right Danny Bryson and Skip Davies, that's enough. Close it down."

"No. Mr. Standbridge, No." Danny pleaded. "She's the girl of my dreams. I've been waiting all my life for her."

"Oh cripes." The older voice said. "All your life. You're only fourteen"

"Shut up." Danny yelled. "Don't listen to him, Velvet Voice." He's joking.

"That's right, Velvet Voice." Skip said. "Mr. Standbridge is a real kidder."

The older man laughed. "Oh sheez, one lies and the other one swears to it." Jeneil smiled. "Velvet Voice." The older man continued. "This is Standbridge at the Oyster Bay Marina Office. You can get rid of this voice by turning the button marked "Off" on the radio."

"No." Danny screamed. "Don't listen to him, Velvet Voice. Talk to me."

"Pipe down." Standbridge ordered. "Go do your homework. Mrs. Bra…I mean Velvet Voice." Standbridge said. "These two minnows are harmless, but if they should slip past their babysitters on their paddleboats, you have flare guns in the tool compartment. I have a mechanic's boat nearby. Just shot one off and he'll be there."

"He knows her." Danny answered, excitedly. "He knows her."

"I heard." Skip answered.

"I'm coming for you with a club, Mr. Standbridge. Right now." Danny threatened.

"Clear the air waves, boys." Standbridge ordered, and laughed.

Jeneil turned off the radio laughing and went to the deck feeling very proud of herself. Steve was packing the diving equipment. "You're back! I didn't hear you get on board."

Steve smiled. "Learned the radio, huh?"

"Yes." Jeneil beamed. "I did. Did you find any sharks?"

Steve chuckled. "Not as many as you did, Velvet Voice."

Jeneil laughed. "Weren't they funny?" Steve smiled and locked the equipment compartment.

They packed all their gear and closed their belongings from the cabin bringing them to the deck. "I've enjoyed this weekend." He said. "I have had a ball." Going to the cushioned bench, he picked up something from the deck and brought it to her.

"Here are samples of what's growing down there."

"Oh thanks." Jeneil smiled. "This one is kelp. I know that much. I'll get my book." She went to her carryall.

Steve watched her and smiled. "Books on a boat." He thought, shaking his head.

Jeneil sat on the bench looking through the pages and comparing the Samples Steve had brought. He went to her and placed a reddish brown rock on the book.

Jeneil took it. "Oh how cute! It looks like a turtle. Did you find it on the ocean floor?"

Steve sat on the bench beside her. "Ocean floor?" He laughed. "Honey, I had air tanks, not a mine sub. I was on the reef."

"I like it." She smiled, looking the rock over.

"It's a remembrance of our second trip together."

He smiled watching her. She was slightly sun burned and her eyes were a bright rust color from the strong sunlight. Her hair had a copper tinge to it which surprised him. He had always thought of her as deep brown, a true brunette.

She looked at him and grinned. "Thanks for the turtle."

He nodded and smiled. "Glad you like him."

She kissed his cheek. "Have you had your fill of diving now?"

"No." He replied. "Jeneil you should come down with me sometime with a camera. It's beautiful like nothing you've have ever seen on land."

"Is it?" She asked. He nodded. She sighed. "I don't think so; I saw three cod and the sight of them sent me to the radio to make sure I could get help if I had to."

He chuckled. "Well cod is vicious." He teased.

She snickered. "I don't have your compulsion to shake my fist at life."

"Do I do that?" He laughed.

She nodded. "Being in the human dimension doesn't seem to be enough for you. You take to the sky like a bird and to the ocean like a fish. If the principle of reincarnation is true, I'd love to hear what you've been up to before this life." He smiled.

"I've never known anyone as afraid of life as you are."

"I'm not afraid of life."

"You're afraid." He grinned. "Face the truth honestly."

"I face life honestly, Steve. Even in other dimensions, but not the way you do."

He smiled. "I think I'll teach you to be less afraid. That's my goal as your husband."

She smiled at him gently and kissed him. "Thank you for caring enough to want to." She said, seriously.

"I care a lot." He said, just as seriously. They looked at each other, both sensing that something was different between them. There had been a change in the past two days and their closeness was different now. Seeing Peter had been damaging but the recovery had been good for their relationship. They were stronger. Jeneil could see that and she was grateful that the weekend hadn't gone as she had planned since the new difference felt like the possibility of more than just sex.

He kissed her cheek, not trusting himself to kiss her lips. The moment was volatile. "Let's go to the house and get ready for our trip to the airport from there."

She nodded. "That's a good idea. The boat is fun, but it's not civilized and we're going back to civilized now."

"Sometimes I wonder Jeneil. Nature seems more civilized to me than the society man has designed."

Jeneil nodded. "I know what you mean, but I don't think man designed it Steve. It seems to be the principle of natural selection in reverse. We're not evolving."

"Whatever." Steve grinned. "But it's called home and we're due back to it, so I'll get to the engine." He stood up and went to the wheel. It was obvious to Jeneil that Steve really had gotten totally away on his short vacation and she had never imagined the White Stallion thinking his philosophical thoughts. "He's really more of the White Stallion type.

There are layers of his inner-self still very hidden." She smiled. Her husband was still fascinating her even after almost two months of marriage. She liked that. She liked that a lot.

They reached the marina and Steve grinned as he saw two teen boys watching eagerly as his boat and another just ahead of him docked. "I think your sharks are circling." He laughed, helping her with her luggage. Jeneil looked up and saw two boys at another boat watching eagerly as the passengers stepped onto the dock. "They're looking for Velvet Voice."

"Oh great!" She sighed. "My long shirt is at the bottom of my luggage. It's the only thing that will cover my swimsuit.

Steve smiled. "Don't cover up, make their day. Hey, they're working hard to find Velvet Voice. Let them see that the body matches the voice. Unless boys have changed since I was one, they're hoping like hell it does." Jeneil raised her eyebrows. Steve noticed. "Jeneil you're body isn't a "2", you must know that."

"I can't." Jeneil said, holding her hand to her throat. "They're the ages of the boys in Loma who snickered at me because of gossip. It makes me feel dirty. I'll unpack my bag."

He held her arm. "No, you won't. Those two kids aren't snickering because of gossip, Velvet Voice stirred them. It's only natural they want to see the rest. Face the fear, Jeneil. These two aren't kids from Loma, and neither are you anymore."

Jeneil began to feel irked. "Well, that's an odd attitude for a husband isn't it?"

Steve smiled. "I married a "10", why is it odd that I don't care if the world knows it?" Worded that way Jeneil couldn't find a defense that didn't make her sound like a dried up prune. The boys headed toward their boat.

"Hi." One said. "We're thinking of going out to dive. Have you done any today?"

"I have." Steve smiled, impressed with their subtleties.

The two boys glanced at each other and raised their eyebrows. "How was the water? Any undercurrent trouble?" One asked.

"Diving, yes." Steve replied. "My wife stayed on the boat."

The boys looked at each other grinning excitedly. "Where's your wife?" The boys asked.

Steve turned around to look behind him wondering why they even asked. Jeneil had gone into the cabin.

"Jeneil." Steve called. "We've got to leave. Let's go, Honey."

"What's her name?" One boy asked.

"Jeneil." Steve replied, smiling.

"That sounds pretty."

"Jeneil." Steve called again as he put the luggage on the dock. "What are you doing, Honey?"

"We forgot to leave the refrigerator door open, I'm coming."

The boys raised their eyebrows smiling at each other and nodding as they heard her voice and recognized it. Steve grinned pretending not to notice. "What color is her hair?" One boy asked. Steve wanted to laugh wondering if they had a bet going.

"Well you heard her voice, what's your guess?" He asked them.

"Dark – a brunette, soft and velvety." One smiled.

"No, a redhead, daring and fiery." The other grinned.

"Oh yeah?" Both boys smiled and then stared past Steve as Jeneil walked to the railing gate.

The boys looked her over slowly almost gaping and Steve felt sure that neither one was disappointed. Steve helped Jeneil to the dock and she held his hand tightly.

"Honey, these boys are thinking of going diving. They just wondered what the water was like." Steve played along with their charade.

Jeneil looked at each one as they stared at her face and then her legs alternately.

"Do either of you know two men named Danny Bryson and Skip Davies?" She asked.

They nodded slowly. "Yeah, we do." They fidgeted, nervously.

"Well, they were on the radio today while I was on the cabin cruiser alone for the first time in my life. I really felt less alone out there listening to the fun they were having. When you see them, would you tell them that Velvet Voice said thank you." Both boys had been staring intently and when she mentioned their names, went to a grin and then a full smile.

"We'll tell them." One said.

"We sure will." The other, agreed.

"Thanks." Jeneil smiled at them forgetting her own nervousness. Steve and Jeneil walked toward the rental car and Steve was aware of the looks Jeneil was getting from some of the men along the way. "I have a question." Jeneil said. "How come I get two 15 year old boys and you're getting women who aren't 15. No 15 year old girl can look at a man like they're looking at you." Steve grinned.

"Looks like the world has noticed I married a "10"." Steve said smiling, seeing that his wife was becoming quite adept at being a woman. Jeneil just smiled. She was still fascinating him after almost two months of marriage. He liked that. He liked that a lot.

Twenty-Eight

The weekend vacation was a memory to be shared at work as each explained their sun burned skin, and then shared again at dinner hoping to make the memory last as they returned to the pace the civilized world was keeping. Steve had a meeting one night during the week and the Barnard's Christmas Party was lined up for Friday. The studio began to be furnished inside with what Robert Danzieg called a creative no-fuss decor.

Jeneil was settling into it and had a telephone installed since she seemed to spend so much time there. Robert called it, "The Cloud" because most of all four sides were windows floor to ceiling with white draw drapes. You had to reach it by temporary wooden stairs or by Robert's installed method of a large marine rope knotted every foot for climbing. He would call "Rapunsel, Rapunsel let down your hair" and Jeneil would drop the knotted rope off the deck for him to climb. Robert had two reasons for calling to her that way. One was for the rope and the other was his way of encouraging her to listen to the jungle drums that he felt sure were beating loudly inside of her. Steve had been in the studio once when Robert called for the rope. He beat Jeneil to it and tossed it over the deck wondering if Robert would ever come up. Steve was surprised at how quickly Robert scaled the knotted rope, but his resentment of Robert was deep so he attributed Robert's agility to a close kinship with a lower order of primate who was skilled on climbing trees in jungle for bananas. It was Steve's private joke especially after he had tried and could only get halfway to the deck using the rope.

Steve had noticed that Jeneil was very quiet since the weekend. She had installed photography lamps and was spending most of her days and nights working on a painting. He found the painting very odd. It was done in shades of grey, white and black, and it looked like an animal of some kind except nothing but the eye and the surrounding fur, were visible, not even a nose so it was difficult to tell just what animal it might be. But it was the eye that had Steve curious. It was the most detailed thing on the canvas and the glare of light that would usually be reflected from the eye was done in white in an odd shape like someone dancing giving the portrait an abstract look. Robert had liked the painting, especially the fur, where Jeneil had textured the paint in different levels, and he had asked why she had painted White Fang, a wolf-dog from literature. Jeneil had only replied that it was something that needed expressing and so she had expressed it, but Steve was very curious about the eye because to him it looked very Asian making him wonder if there was a connection between Jeneil's quietness and having seen Peter. The painting was put aside unsigned after it was completed. It sat in a corner of the studio facing a wall and Jeneil went on to another small canvas using vibrant colors, in sweeping lines that when combined looked very happy, very free, and Steve liked it a lot. It was a jolt from the sadness of the other, but he felt that it was a huge improvement if both paintings had reflected her mood,. She put it all aside to get ready for Christmas and the Barnard's party.

*****

The kitchen smelled of spice and baking when Steve arrived home on Friday and there were several gingerbread cookie people on racks. Two trays of Christmas cookies were on the counter and some loaves of bread and a light cake filled with fruit. "This is ultra-baking." He smiled wondering if he'd be allowed to sample. Jeneil walked in dressed in her terry cloth robe which she wore after showering.

Steve looked at her and grinned. "Grease and oil day, huh?"

"How did you know?" She chuckled.

"You're shining and glowing."

"I'm going dressed as a Christmas decorated tree." She said, going to the oven.

Steve stared. "You're kidding right? We need costumes?"

Jeneil laughed and turned around. "Are you afraid, I'm not?"

"Well, with all the expressing yourself you've been doing these days, I wasn't sure how far the artistic path was going."

Jeneil grinned. "You'll love the necklace I've made. Its mini-blinking plastic lights, just like a Christmas tree. I think it's very clever. Its battery operated and I've glued silver tinsel into dangle earrings. I love the way it feels brushing over my shoulders and the shiny silver reflects the lights. I just finished the bracelet that matches." Steve stared. "I'll wear a cluster of Holly in my hair with a Christmas ornament hanging from a red ribbon bow. I had fun designing that. Holly is so Christmassy. I was going to wear a flashing star for a tree top kind of look, but then I decided not too. That would be too garish with a blinking necklace." She had set their dinner on the table as she talked and Steve continued to stare as he sat down.

"Jeneil, you're kidding aren't you?"

She pouted. "Oh now you're getting that, but I'm–a-conservative-dark-suited-surgeon-and-your-my-wife, look. Don't you dare kill my fun Mr. Husband? I feel like a Christmas tree today and I've worked hard to express that."

Steve tasted his food. "Jeneil swear that you're kidding." He pleaded.

"Relax, Steve." Jeneil insisted. "Wait until you see that outfit. It's colorful, but tasteful, very art nouveau."

"Art nouveau?" Steve said, Jeneil swear you are only kidding."

She held up her hand. "Steve, I swear to you that I made the outfit for the party. Stop looking so worried. I felt really Christmas treeish this morning and I was going to spray paint toilet brushes green and tack them to the skirt of the dress to look more authentic, but I dropped the idea in favor of conservative good taste. After all, by an art expression, it's not a costume."

"Conservative?" Steve said. "Blinking tree lights are conservative? This is Danzieg's fault." Steve sighed. "Him and his "Rapunsel, let your hair down shit." Jeneil wear the dress you wore for the open house. That's Christmassy enough."

"No, everyone has seen that dress already. Do you want your colleagues to think you're cheap? I'm wearing the outfit I made. I know it's different from my usual, but I wanted to experiment. I want to be me. Besides, it's almost time to leave and I just need to put on my dress and jewelry."

Steve was having trouble finishing his dinner. Jeneil got up and cleared her place. "You're really slow tonight. I have to get ready." She left quickly.

Steve tried to chew the fork full of rice he had just put into his mouth. "I may kill Robert Danzieg after I see this outfit." He cleared his dishes from the table. "I'll just refuse to go, if it's too outrageous. How can blinking lights not be outrageous?" He said, rinsing his plate and putting it into the dish washer.

"Here I come." Jeneil called from the stairs. "Are you ready?" Steve rinsed his glass and put it in the dishwasher, not wanting to look.

"So what do you think?" Jeneil said, standing in the kitchen.

Steve turned slowly. "Cute! Very cute bitch!" He laughed, seeing the black dress and Jacket. "You set me up! And you even swore that you weren't kidding. You're such a liar."

She smiled. "I didn't lie. I swore that I made my outfit for tonight and I did." She said, going to him.

He put his arms around her waist and kissed her cheek. "You scared the shit out of me." He chuckled.

She laughed. "Well really there was a method to my madness. I didn't know if you'd go for me wearing a homemade outfit and this is my two dollar necklace from the second hand store, so when the kidding begun I decided to set the stage so outrageously that this outfit would look great to you. I even had a real pearl and two small diamonds put into the necklace hoping to redeem my place in your status symbol world. Do I look okay?" She asked. "Is it politically acceptable?"

He was still holding her and the jacket felt very flimsy to him. He stepped back to look more closely. She had been right. Once he didn't see blinking lights, tinsel and toilet brushes, she looked great to him. He looked her over. The jacket was more like a blouse with full sleeves. It was see through and covered a black dress with only thin straps holding it up.   "This is different for you."   He said, looking surprised.   "More sophisticated."

"I made this outfit as a frame for the necklace. You don't like this outfit?" She asked.

"Yes, I do." Steve replied. "It's just more sultry."

She raised her eyebrow. "Is this the same husband who didn't care if the world saw his "10" wife in a swimsuit?"

He smirked. "Well damn, they were only 15 year old boys. The people at this party are grown men who live next door or in the neighborhood."

Jeneil smiled. "Will you put that logic in an essay for me? Right now. I'm ready and we're leaving.' She handed her fake fur jacket to him to hold so she could put it on.

He watched her as she put on her leather gloves. "Hey." Steve smiled. "If you wear a fake fur jacket so you can preserve animals, how come you wear leather gloves?"

Jeneil grinned.   "The Preservation League serves meat at their fundraisers, too. I've decided that the whole movement was begun by the oil industry so the price of plastic and acrylic fibers would soar. Mark my words, eventually a good fake fur jacket will cost more than the natural fibers, even the Russian Sable where animals are bred especially so there's no danger of extinction." She shrugged. "But the movement has merit; I think we need to have a conscience about endangering any species of life and inhumane slaughter isn't necessary, so I can live with the paradox, just like the one where a husband will allow his wife to wear a swimsuit for 15 year old boys but not for grown men." She smirked.

"Clever wench." He smiled, looking her all over. "You look 15 right now."

"Is that a score or an age?" She asked.

He laughed, opening the front door for her. "Honey, no 15 year old girl can do that to a dress neckline."

She punched his stomach gently as she walked by him. He laughed and put his arm around her shoulder as they walked next door to the Barnard's who were already receiving a steady stream of guests.

*****

The black Brandon pulled up to them and the tinted window eased open. Kirk Vance smiled. "Hey Bradley's, parking is outrageous around here, can I use your driveway."

"Sure." Steve said.

He looked Jeneil over slowly. "Mona Lisa, I think I like black on you, too. Fur is for you all right. Great look." Clumsily like a little girl on heels for the first time, Jeneil curtsied and Kirk Vance laughed. "Wait for me."

"I'm in a party mood." Jeneil said, putting her arms around Steve's waist. "Let's dance or sing or something." She kissed him lightly.

He smiled. "I like the "or something" better."

"Merry Christmas." She chuckled.

"Kissing without mistletoe." Kirk Vance said, joining them. "Keep it up and the neighbors won't believe you two are really married to each other."

Steve took Jeneil's hand as all three got in step and headed for the Barnard's Christmas party. Steve grinned, thinking about her mood. He noticed that she had come out of her quietness after the wolf-dog was finished. He still wasn't sure what it meant and the painting had even disappeared. Jeneil had given it to Robert for a bazaar, one of his many charity organizations was having. She refused to sign it or allow them to put her name on it claiming that her expression on canvas was to be anonymous or not at all. Robert complied reluctantly understanding the artistic temperament.

Steve was glad to see her quietness and the painting disappear feeling that both were somehow tied to Peter. She was getting comfortable around him again and he was very hopeful that she would soon take the last step to a real marriage. He had to stop keeping the thought uppermost in his mind though, since it interfered with celibacy. He decided to forget about it and wait until she was ready to plainly express her move to being a real wife. Life was easier for him that way.

"Steve?" Jeneil called to him.

"What?" He asked, leaving his thoughts.

"Dr. Vance just asked you about scuba diving."

"Oh, what about it?" "

"Forget it Steve." Jeneil laughed.

Kirk Vance chuckled. "Jeneil, your kisses must be a new form of mind alteration." He rang the Barnard's doorbell.

Drexel answered showing surprise at seeing the three in combination.

Drexel smiled as they walked in. "Oooo Jeneil, give me the jacket fast before my wife sees it."

"Too late, Drex." Barbara laughed.

"Merry Christmas all of you." She kissed Kirk Vance's lips and Steve's and hugged Jeneil.

"Some men know how to treat their wives." Barbara cooed at her husband as she held Jeneil's jacket.

"It's fake fur, Barbara." Jeneil said. "Try it on. The Presentation League is promoting it as an alternative."

Barbara twirled in it hugging herself. "It makes you "heady." I want one."

"I knew it." Drexel sighed.

"It's reasonable." Jeneil assured him.

Drexel laughed. "Honey, your level of reasonable and mine are not the same, I'm sure."

"Oh Drexie." Barbara pouted. "Stop being so old money. It's Christmas."

Drexel laughed. "Barbara thinks Christmas is an excuse to flirt with poverty. She wanted to hire the catering company you two used for the open house. You're not nice Jeneil. They're expensive even at half the crew and food. I know you can afford more but you really should keep in line with what's being spent at the poverty level of your neighbors or you'll make us look bad." He teased.

Jeneil smiled. "The party was supposed to be simple until extra people started responding. And the use of the company personnel is part of my salary. The party was my Christmas bonus. But because last minute food and liquor had to be gotten, I spent more than I would have, now Steve and I are living on beans and greens to recoup the cost."

"Oh stop." Drexel laughed. "You'll have me crying with that sad fairytale."

"It's true." Steve defended Jeneil. "Honest, she loves and could live on macrobiotic food. We have been eating beans and grains. We're repaying our bank account like a loan company until the cost of the open house is replaced."

Drexel put his head back and laughed. "I love you, Jeneil. I love you. Give Barbara those recipes." He hinted.

Barbara stared at Jeneil. "You sound like you've had old money training. Drex's parents are wealthy tightwads."

Jeneil nodded. "I can understand that. Once money starts to slip past you, it can roller coaster."

Barbara frowned deliberately. "Jeneil, please don't agree. Drex will have me sewing my own clothes if you keep it up. His mother knits for an orphanage and loves it so much she makes her family sweaters, too.

"Barbara, mother's sweaters are excellent. I love mine. I've asked for one every Christmas."

"You see." Barbara shook her head. "These are money people, can you believe it?"

Steve laughed. "Well, Jeneil sewed her outfit."

Jeneil covered her face, embarrassed that Steve had told them. "You weren't supposed to tell anybody that." She whispered, hoarsely. Kirk Vance laughed. Drexel looked her over smiling and Barbara was speechless. "Look, it's a hobby." Jeneil replied trying to get out of the situation gracefully. "I don't sew as much anymore really. I only made this to frame the necklace. I love the necklace."

"Aha." Barbara smiled. "I know that's a real pearl and I'll bet two real diamonds. It looks expensive, like it's a really old piece of jewelry. She has extravagance, Drex."

Steve couldn't resist tossing Jeneil into the spotlight. "She bought it for $2.00 in a second hand store. And had the pearl and diamonds set."

"Oh my gosh!" Jeneil moaned.

"I love it. Jeneil's a tightwad!" Drexel laughed, hysterically.

Barbara covered her mouth. "You did that to a piece of costume jewelry?"

"Well you thought it looked more expensive until you heard the truth." Jeneil grimaced.

Kirk Vance smiled. "You have style Mona Lisa, real style. Not a trace of carbon copy in you. I like it a lot."

"Keep my secret, please." Jeneil pleaded.

"Count on it." Barbara laughed. "There's no way I'd want that catching on. I hate sewing and cooking."

The doorbell rang; someone took Kirk Vance's arm and walked away with him. Jeneil and Steve headed to the living room where the largest group of people were gathered and they wished the season's best to them and began the rounds of conversation that were a part of groups. Jeneil became thirsty from the exercise of being personable and walked herself to the diningroom where the refreshments were set up. A round of wolf whistles began from the doctor's at Steve's office. Jeneil looked behind her to see who they were whistling at. "Oh boy, Jeneil's here." Larry Gaines yelled. "We've been waiting for you to show up, we want to see some of your exotic dancing and don't you dare leave out one pelvic thrust." Their were hoots and wolf whistles and applause. Jeneil stared not believing what was happening.

Sondra Rand patted her shoulder. "Congratulations dear, now you know what the movement is up against and these are educated men. Can you imagine what it's like at zoo level?" She walked away shaking her head.

"Come on Jeneil, we hear you're pretty good." Ron Towers, smiled.

"We want a dance." Larry Gaines started chanting and was joined by some others. Jeneil felt herself getting red.

Glenn Tufton was standing near her. "Aw come on guys ease up, she's shy. Look at her, she's turning red." He put his hand to her face, gently. "What incredibly soft skin you have. You are a beauty." He grinned and kissed her cheek, smoothing his lips on her skin. She stared at him.

"Maybe she'll do a private performance then." Larry Gaines said. "Lottery system guys, six at a time. Is that too many Jeneil, sweetie." Jeneil stared not knowing what to say hoping that she was right about this all being a joke.

"Feel her white skin." Glenn Tufton said, taking her by the shoulders to another doctor. "You won't believe it."

Larry Gaines laughed. "Oh get the dermatologist and plastic surgeon copping a free feel of her skin." Everyone laughed.

Jeneil felt herself getting shaky inside. Being surrounded by the men reminded her of the time in Loma after the gossip began when she went to the Library and a group of boys were sitting on the lawn. They surrounded her looking her over from head to foot and started to hold on to her as she tried to get past them. Mr. Bartlett the librarian had come out and rescued her. The boys claimed that they were only fooling with her because she was so serious, but she ended up in the lady's restroom crying and shaking thinking that they believed the group. Mr. Sheldon had been very sympathetic, being one of the people who hadn't believed the group. They were good friends. She had been going to the library for years, and he being a widower, would bring him food as she learned to cook.

Everett Rowe touched her face as Glenn Tufton held his arm around her shoulder. "Jeneil you really look after your skin. It has a beautiful moisture balance and tone." She told herself that they were just being doctors, but she still felt shaky inside and then she felt two hands at her waist behind her and the surrounding wasn't funny to her anymore.

"What are you guys doing to my wife?" Steve laughed lightly, squeezing her waist. Jeneil grabbed his hand at her waist, holding tightly. He kissed her temple. "It's okay, Honey, they're kidding." He whispered. Glen Tufton and Everett Rowe released her.

"We're admiring her skin. It's fantastic. Do you have salon treatments, Jeneil?" Glen asked.

"No, I give myself facials at home." She answered, feeling herself starting to relax. Steve was rubbing her arm gently as he held her and he felt her lean against him.

Everett Rowe smiled. "Well, you've found a good routine. Stay with it. Do you diet with your skin in mind too?"

"No, I just diet to stay healthy and weight control."

Glen Tufton smiled. "You have gorgeous skin, you can be proud of it."

"Come on, Jeneil." Larry Gaines called. "First class starts in the den in ten minutes."

Steve smiled. "Sorry guys she's signed to me in a personal contract. I have exclusive rights to all the dances."

"Oh you are a sorehead, Bradley." Larry Gaines grinned. "I even collected seven handkerchiefs so she could do the dance of the seven veils for us." Jeneil laughed, surprising Steve.

"Handkerchiefs?" Jeneil said. "You men are too wicked. One veil is larger than seven handkerchiefs. The dance of the seven veils is an art form not a skin show performance."

"But aren't they see-through?" One doctor asked.

Jeneil smiled impishly. "We…maybe."

"Aw Steve, you're a traitor. Let her go get her costume and model it at least." Another said.

"I can't." Jeneil smiled. "I'm not qualified to dance for anyone. I haven't graduated yet. I could get expelled from dance class." The doctors laughed.

Steve laughed lightly and hugged her to him with the arm he held around her loving her comeback and for facing her fear.

"Well how come Steve watches?" Larry Gaines asked, tauntingly.

Jeneil shrugged. "My teacher never gave me any rules about homework." The men laughed and some hooted and applauded. Several said they wanted her talk to their wives about the class. Jeneil smiled and confidently cut a path through them to the drinks area to pour some club soda with lime for herself and Steve.

Kirk Vance had been watching and listening from near the wall. He held up his glass and lowered his eyelids. "Mona Lisa you are a fascinatingly sexy woman." He said in his deep affected voice. All of them were smiling, some hooted and some agreed.

Jeneil held up her glass, looking at him with a studied sensual gaze, matching his. "Dr. Vance, all women are fascinatingly sexy for the guys' man enough to unleash it in us." She said in a breathless, throaty voice matching his sensuousness.

Steve raised his eyebrows. "Oh my gosh." He mumbled going to her quickly. The room was filled with wolf whistles. Some of the women had joined them wondering what all the fun was and they smiled holding their drinks up to Jeneil saying. "Listen to her guys." They laughed.

Steve put her arm around her shoulder. "Boy I'm glad you're allergic to liquor, Honey. You get drunk on the banquet alone. Let's get you some food." The room filled with laughter and Steve kept her close to him as he edged to the buffet table.

"That's one hell of a deadly look and voice you've developed there." He whispered near her ear.

"Thank you Stevie." She said in a pretend little girl's voice. "It's one of my fun favorites, too."

He laughed and shook his head, getting a plate for her. She kissed his cheek and smiled as he leaned to the cracker tray. "Merry Christmas."

He kissed her lips, lightly. "You're beautiful." He said, seriously.

Larry Gaines watched them as he stood next to Kirk Vance. "Too bad the White Stallion insists on a personal contract. She looks like she'd be on hell of a kick on Friday nights."

"Tell me about it." Kirk Vance answered.

Some of the women asked Jeneil about the dance class and why she was taking it. With all the attention on the sexiness of it. Jeneil was glad to have a chance to explain. She explained the cultural study and exercise part of it in detail avoiding the idea that exotic dancing was sexy. Steve was shocked but proud of her for the way she dealt with the men in the diningroom. He could tell that she really was trying to face her fears. She could show her spitfire side at times and get away with it because the role seemed so opposite for her. The role spitfire seemed twice as funny since she was usually so quiet and shy. Jeneil left the group of women to look for Steve. It was getting late and she was hoping to leave soon.

Kirk Vance appeared in the hallway as she walked toward the living room. She **stopped** when she saw him. "Dr. Vance was Steve in the den?"

"When will you call me Kirk?" He asked in his husky voice.

"When you stop talking to me in your nyphistopilean voice."

He laughed slightly holding his hand to his chest. "I'm wounded, pained clear through. I've worked hard on that voice."

"Why?" Jeneil asked, "Your natural voice is very deep, why change it? Doesn't that hurt your throat?"

"You mean the resonance doesn't reach you?" He asked.

She shook her head, "No, my brain intercepts yelling insult, insult."

He chuckled and stood closer to her. "Have dinner with me sometime."

She looked at him steadily, "I'll check with Steve to see when he's free."

"I invited you, Mona Lisa."

Jeneil was openly stunned by his boldness. "Well sucks," Jeneil said in a southern drawl. "That would hardly be a propah thing for a wife to do, but ah'll take the invitation as flattery from a gentleman because you haven't proven your not one yet and you're not leadin that way are you now?"

He smiled and watched her eyes gazing deeply, "I'd like to, boy would I like to."

Jeneil raised her eyebrows. "Well I'm leavin real quick then suh, the thought that you're not a gentlemen is too painful." She put her hand to her forehead dramatically.

He chuckled and folded his arms watching her. "Has that gimmick ever worked on anyone?"

"It does on true gentlemen." She drawled, "Isn't it working on you?" She asked backing away.

He laughed, "Come to a Friday party sometime." He added.

"I don't like your temple room." She said being totally honest.

"I'll teach you to."

"I doubt it." She replied.

He smiled. "You'd be a natural there with your ability to abandon yourself to your senses."

"I'm not very fond of parties."

"I could teach you that too." He grinned.

Jeneil felt dirty.

"Teach her what?" Steve asked coming up behind Kirk Vance.

"To like parties." Kirk answered.

Steve felt his jaw tighten. "No, Kirk. Those Friday parties are not for her."

Kirk grinned, "Who are you insulting, the parties or Jeneil?"

Jeneil was surprised by Kirk's ability to manipulate. "You know what I mean Kirk." Steve answered.

Kirk smiled, "It's been too long since you've attended one White Stallion. Your memory falls short. Those parties started out at her level and believe it or not there are still some devotees to the true sensual arts. There are still a handful of people who can tell the difference between a nude and a naked body, love and lust, fad and art. Don't put down the whole party just because others there ricochet into lesser levels along the way. You can't raise the level of conscious appreciation in others if they're not allowed to be around it. That's snobbery. You should know that White Stallion you studied at all levels with remarkable ease and skill."

Jeneil watched and listened marveling at how skillful Kirk Vance was at dissecting truths into dimensions. She felt that Robert was right when he said that Kirk Vance could make bizarre sound sane. "He should have been a lawyer." She thought.

"Steve I'm going to ignore the offense to me personally in your influence that I wouldn't appreciate Jeneil's level. I don't have to prove that I'm capable of perceiving first magnitude star quality, my reputation is near flawless to those who know me well."

Steve smiled, "You can still dish out bullshit better than anyone, I know. That's an art with you too."

Kirk Vance shrugged slightly and grinned, "It's all in perception Steve. To one what is truth may be the opposite to another."

Steve laughed, "You're right it is all in perception and yours is very faulty or you wouldn't be inviting Jeneil to a party. But I won't take any offense either, Kirk. You don't know her that well obviously. I realize that."

Jeneil watched as Steve held his own with Kirk Vance even mastering Kirk's style though with less grace. Jeneil was impressed.

Kirk grinned mischievously, "Will you allow me to know her better, White Stallion?"

Steve looked at Jeneil and slipped his arm around her smiling. "At her level, I would Kirk. Only at her level." Steve answered confidently.

Having heard Kirk's defense, Jeneil began to wonder about the Friday parties. "Dr. Vance how did the story about a girl having a drug slipped into her drink at one of your parties get started?"

Kirk's face showed the startled reaction he felt. He laughed lightly, "You have quite a level of directness there, Jeneil."

"Is that your explanation? No comment." She asked completely without guilt.

He studied her face and smiled slightly, "You're a fascination," he said, "Robert Danzieg's right and that's where you got the story I'll bet."

"Is that your answer?" She asked not moving from her original question.

Kirk Vance grinned, "No that's not my side of the story. I investigated the whole thing when I heard about it. The girl is Bethany Rogers of the Rogers family. She was a regular at the Friday parties, and she even came in sometimes having popped her own happy pills before getting there. She swore to me before witnesses that she was clean, but I should have tested her for myself instead of trusting her. The girl is a flake. I was suspicious and low dosed her to be safe. I do that sometimes like for someone who can't hold liquor, you water down the drink to slow them down. Her stuff and mine set her very free and she spun out. What happened to her on film was her doing not mine. Those rooms are private for that reason. She wanted a copy of the film. I sent her the film when it was developed. The only copy. I develop the film and I always check with the women a month later to see if they want them at all. Time can change things. I never keep copies of her style of fun anyway. She was running with a cinematographer at the time and he got the film. He drove me crazy for a copy, she sent it to him after he broke up with her so he'd remember her fondly. He showed me the note from her. He kept it as a legal document because he sold the film to a porno producer. Then as it often happens in the life of debutante's, the family whirled her through the circuit of eligible men hoping to settle her down with her kind and one turned her head. Marriage was planned and a copy of the film turned up somewhere amongst her fiancé's friends. She needed a reason for what she was doing on film. My party was convenient."

Jeneil nodded, "I understand the paths of gossip. Steve had defended you in that lie and I was curious about how it happened. Aren't you concerned about the narcotic squad showing up uninvited?" She asked.

Kirk chuckled, "Not as long as government executive officers keep showing up too. And not everyone at the parties is tripping. I meant exactly what I said. There are true aficionados there."

Jeneil needed the clarification, "Aficionados of what?"

"Truth, beauty, pleasure. Consciousness raising. Its popularity only seemingly died out as the full drug problem in society overshadowed it. Like alcohol, drugs got ruined by people who abuse it."

"Abuse? It's a foreign substance unnatural to the body. Isn't that abuse?" Jeneil raised her eyebrows, "Dr. Vance there are some people who feel that one aspirin is nearing drug abuse level."

Kirk smiled, "Society will always have fanatics."

Jeneil watched him for a second. "Dr. Vance you and I sound like polar extremes and yet we both deal in fictions."

Kirk grinned, "I don't think so Mona Lisa. I really don't think so. I'd like a chance to prove it."

Steve smiled, "Well polar extremes or not. We won't know for sure. I'm taking my wife, Mona Lisa, home now." He emphasized the words my wife.

"I would too if she'd go with me." Kirk replied watching Jeneil.

She looked down at the floor embarrassed. Kirk smiled enjoying her shyness.

Steve shook his head and chuckled, "Kirk, I'll have to tell you that you've met your match with her." He began walking away.

"No offense, Steve." Kirk said, "My fascination with her is intended to be complimentary to both of you. I hope you know that."

"I remember, I remember." Steve smiled as he took Jeneil's hand.

"Mona Lisa." Kirk said in his natural voice, "You will attract lovers of beauty. Don't run from it." He touched her face gently enjoying the feel of her soft skin.

She watched him steadily, "Dr. Vance, I understand the compliment, but most galleries won't allow the public to handle its treasures. Steve owns the painting."

Steve broke into quick laughter and Kirk Vance smiled broadly removing his hand from her face. "You're a work of art, every facet of you." He said kissing her lips lightly.

"Merry Christmas to you too." She smiled.

Kirk sighed and shook his head. "You're right Steve, I have met my match." He grinned sensuously. "But I love a challenge, Mona Lisa."

"Goodnight Kirk." Steve laughed pulling Jeneil along behind him by her hand.

"Merry Christmas you two." Kirk grinned.

Jeneil waved goodnight to the guests as she followed behind Steve who pulled her steadily toward the door. "Well that's a clear message." Larry Gaines laughed watching Steve pulling Jeneil. "Very primitive."

"Bye Larry." Steve laughed not stopping.

"Merry Christmas." Jeneil smiled continuing caboose style behind Steve.

"I'm taking exotic dance lessons." One women standing in a group of wives said as they watched Steve pulling Jeneil through the hall.

"Uh huh," another smiled watching Steve put Jeneil's coat on quickly and push her out the door.

"I think I'll have my husband take the lessons." Another added. "My pelvic thrust is fine. He needs to learn the beat."

They all laughed. "Well those two look like they have the dance steps mastered."

"Don't they just." Another oooed. "It's electrical."

Steve listened to Jeneil humming a Christmas carol softly as they walked back to their house and he smiled thinking about all the different kinds of women she was. He thought it was comical that she was so high powered but she didn't really realize it.

Jeneil straightened the bow on the wreath as Steve unlocked the door. She went to the den quickly and turned on the Christmas tree lights. Standing back, she absorbed the glow of the tree. Steve watched her enjoying the feeling of Christmas. They had eaten dinner while trimming it one night. It had felt like a party. He joined her.

"Have some Christmas with me." She smiled, "I'm not ready to sleep."

Steve wondered about whether he should, he was already very physically aware of her from the party, but he wasn't ready for sleeping either, "Okay." He said. She hugged his arm showing gratitude, then slipping her jacket off she tossed it to the chair and headed to the kitchen.

Steve picked up her jacket and held it to him closely caressing the pile as he went to the closet to put his coat away too.

Sitting back on the sofa, he watched a tree light twinkle rhythmically. Jeneil sat beside him with a small tray and a plate of cookies with two glasses of milk. Steve took a Christmas tree cookie and bit off the top. Jeneil took a wreath and broke it in half and broke a half into another smaller piece. "Steve why wouldn't I fit in at Dr. Vance's Friday parties?" She put the cookie piece into her mouth.

He was surprised by her question. "Why are you asking?" He furrowed his brow and watched wondering if Kirk Vance had reached her.

She shrugged, "Well it just seems like the rest of the world goes to them, but you don't think I would fit in. The White Stallion fits in at all levels, but his wife doesn't seem to be quite up to par at the bottom rung. That doesn't make us very compatible does it?"

Steve felt the pulse beat through his chest as he heard her looking for compatibility with the White Stallion. He put the cookie on the tray and sat back turning to face her hoping he would handle it well. "Honey you're life, your standards, your sensitivities wouldn't have a place there. You wouldn't be comfortable. The White Stallion is gone. You're married to Steve Bradley. He doesn't want his wife there which proves that. He wouldn't be comfortable there either."

She had been watching him steadily as he talked. She nodded slightly and looked away staring at the Christmas tree. Steve watched her closely realizing that her thoughts might be about them as a couple. She felt every bit a wife to him at the party, in every possible way. He almost believed that after getting home they would get into bed and make love like most of the other couples there would probably do. She felt that close to him in his mind. He watched her now as she sat thinking. "Do you want to go to a Friday party?" He asked.

She turned her head and smiled at him gently, "Not really, I just don't like hearing that I wouldn't fit in. I'm not a freak. I just grew along a different path, that's all. I can't be as free physically as some people. Especially groups."

Her honesty and openness touched him. She probably never would catch up to what she missed learning through dating in her teen years. He could tell that she knew very little about physical relationships with men and sex wasn't something she studied that's what was causing the look of innocence, the look of vulnerability the virginal quality in her. It all added to the soft and gentle aura that made her Jeneil. Steve smiled as he realized that if within the next year she slept with seven different men, she would be wide eyed about each relationship. Since she saw each person as an individual each relationship would be a first for her. She lived by instinct and sensitivity keeping them tempered by order. "Robert and Kirk saw it clearly. She is fascinating," Steve smiled to himself, "and she's my wife," He sighed, delighted. "and at the moment she's trying to define that role in her mind." Steve's heart raced through five beats as he saw how close she was to putting all the pieces of the marriage in place. He was surprised and pleased with her trust in him. "She's like a jungle animal. Something wild and undeterred that you can't rush at or she would bolt from fear of losing herself or from being overwhelmed. Her raw instincts and sensitivities were the scramblers in her life, order was her balance which allowed her to live at tilt. That's why she was so many different combinations of qualities. The different path she grew in was the jungle of emotions that she tasted and tested at her own pace in her own way. Irish is the jungle in her animal, the one roaming free and unadulterated by group limits and society's narrow rules. The electricity took his breath away as he glimpsed Irish in her. "Sensitive, passionate Irish who smolders." He thought. He wanted to hold her to let her know that he understood her, but he knew that like the true instinctive, sensitive jungle animal she had to come to him. She had to be the initiator. He could only wait. She would work it through. He could see that as she sat deep in thought before him. "Steve owns the painting." She had told Kirk and Steve could see that Jeneil was working her way toward belonging to him. He didn't even dare touch her at the moment even lightly not wanting to disturb the smoldering and searching she was going through. It was enough for him to know that she was searching at least. And he understood why she married him. Trust. For whatever reason she sensed trust in him. "You've got it, sweetheart." He whispered in his mind. "I'll never do anything to cause you to lose that trust. Including rushing you. That's a promise." He thought to himself. She turned her head and smiled at him.

"I like being married to you." She said softly. "I feel secure and safe. You're a great husband."

He smiled as she touched her cheek lovingly to the hand he had resting on the back of the sofa. His heart beat wildly as he realized that he had discovered the door to the ivory tower. He kissed her forehead and she nestled into the arm he rested near her for comfort. "There are all kinds of ways of making love, Mrs. Bradley and you're only beginning here, I understand that. I'll wait for superlative level whenever you're ready for it."

*****

On Sunday Peter stopped to get his grandfather who with two other friends were going to the International Arts League. He had avoided going inside the house for them when he saw Karen's car. He avoided Karen because of the deep anger he felt toward her. His mother had waved to him from the aluminum storm door and he had returned a casual wave too. There was still a strain between them. He had felt closest to his mother when he was with Jeneil. She seemed to explain his mother to him and the explanations usually made sense. He talked to her even though he never stopped at the house. They didn't war with each other like they once had. Her meddling in his life about Uette had been a great lesson for her. She saw his sadness now. She called him once a week or so and was sending food regularly out of concern for how tired and thin he looked when he had once stopped by the China Bay to get his grandfather. He appreciated it. Therapy was taking its toll on him as he struggled to face truths in his life. Cooking food or cleaning his apartment were unpleasant chores to him. It was easy to heat what his mother sent or eat it cold. He had hired a woman to clean his apartment and that ended his concern for his surroundings. He could scramble eggs which he learned by trial and error from having ruined some along the way. Having stood next to Jeneil while she made brunch for them so often had given him the basic idea of it. He missed her BBQ'd chicken though and the freezer full of goodies that he could microwave whenever he felt like it. Nobody could make carrot cake the way she did. He smiled remembering that as he bought a small carrot cake at the table in the International Arts League fund raising Christmas Shop. He was glad he had stopped in instead of just dropping his Grandfather and his friends off. The bakery table had some home made Jewish bagels for sale and he had a patient in the hospital now recovering from hip surgery who would probably enjoy them. Since hurting her hip, she hadn't been able to do much in her kitchen. She and her husband both missed her cooking. He had promised her that she would be cooking after the surgery and she had promised him some chicken soup and a loaf of homemade bread when that happened. She thought he was too thin too and she told him to marry some nice Chinese girl who could make a decent soup to nourish him. That it seems he could easily do right now since the Chinese community was scrambling over itself subtly offering daughters as wives for him. It was a real switch from his years as the Chinese Stud in New York where fathers would whisk their daughters off the streets if he was walking past. He was resisting it all. He didn't even know himself anymore as a result of therapy let alone seriously consider getting involved in a permanent relationship. He even avoided dating hoping the tumult inside him would ease up enough for him to take on more of his personal life. He couldn't believe that he was being thrown so far back in his development every time he wrestled with the feelings of dissatisfaction. He hadn't had these feelings since his early residency years just before meeting Jeneil and her conveyor belt strangulation theory. Life made sense to him with her. He was coming together personally as solidly with her as when he was with the Dragons. He knew who he was with them and with her, but not now. Therapy had him opening doors and facing facts that he never even thought existed and some didn't even sound like truth. The only person he was sure of at the moment was the doctor in him and he clung to that like air, water and food. He caught sight of his grandfather at a table of knitted and hand sewn clothing. "Find something?" Peter asked.

"Yes." His grandfather smiled, "a nice sensible wool scarf. Nothing keeps me as warm as the wool shirt Jen…" He stopped his sentence and frowned displeased with himself.

"It's alright grandfather." Peter said, "You can say her name. The wools shirt Jeneil made for you when you caught the flu. I remember."

"Are you sure you can handle it?" The older man asked.

"She was what was good in my life, that's a very pleasant memory for me. I always did like the sound of her name. I like thinking about her and I like talking about her."

The grandfather watched him, "You've never gotten angry at her have you?"

Peter shook his head, "Why would I? She hasn't done anything. She's the only innocent one in the whole mess. I knew that, Chang reminded me of it often enough and if anyone knew Jeneil at all it was Chang." Peter glanced at the next table and something caught his eye. "I'll be back." Peter said staring at the next table and walking away.

The grandfather watched him as he left, "I don't know Peter." He sighed to himself, "It is true that Jeneil is innocent but without your anger you won't separate from her. You can't live with memories alone. You need a real life, feeling real feelings for a real woman. You can't live alone with memories of Jeneil." He watched his grandson saddened by the lack of progress he seemed to be making in his personal life. "He hasn't faced the deep hurt from her loss yet and without that he won't heal. I think I'd rather have you angry at her Peter. As undeserving as it is at least your wound would heal." The older man sighed as he thought of Jeneil, "The Songbird caused deep love in him. The anger and hurt will be powerful too when it starts. Yen and Yang Peter. The innocent Songbird must have faced her hurt too. She loved him deeply too. There's a mystery to all this a part that's missing and yet it must be so minor because it's so undetectable." The older man wrinkled his brow remembering Jeneil's panic to have their souls married. "Is there a purpose to all this?" His curiosity grew as the thought evolved and germinated in him. He watched Peter and wondered.

Peter lifted the painting from its makeshift tripod on the table. "White Fang?" His mind asked as he looked at the grey white and black brush strokes that looked like fur. From a distance it had looked like an animal like a wolf or a dog, but up close it looked different. Would it be that the eye made it difficult to know for sure. The eye was odd. Peter studied it and then realized that the glare of light in the eye had form and shape. It appeared like it was someone dancing, a girl. "Yes." Peter thought looking at it closely, "There's a long hair flowing behind her in the wind." In the wind. The sentence caused his mind to flash the image of Jeneil on the beach the first time he saw her there. He touched the glare of light on the painting. "That's how she looked." His heart skipped a beat. He studied the painting for a name even turning it over and checking the back of it. There wasn't one. As he turned the canvas to the painted side again the eyes suddenly looked Asian to him. "Soul?" His mind questioned. "Is someone painting soul?" He asked himself. His grandfather noticed him with the canvas and went to him.

"What is it Peter?"

The woman in charge of the table joined them after finishing with a customer. "That's an unusual painting." The woman smiled. "It tricks the eye like an optical illusion. Do you see an animal in it?" She asked.

"Yes." Peter answered, "Do you know where the painting came from? It's unsigned." He asked.

"We thought that was unusual too. Sometimes we get them with only initials, but whoever did that one is someone who loves being anonymous, I guess."

Peter stared at the woman and remembered Jeneil. "Anonymous." He thought. "Could it be Jeneil's painting?" He asked himself.

"We don't know where it's from. It's hard to keep track when so many people donate items. Unless they ask for a receipt for taxes we don't keep records. The only thing we are sure of is that it was just painted recently. Smell the canvas."

Peter held it to his nose. It smelled of new paint.

"See." The woman said.

Peter nodded.

"We guess it's no more than a month old maybe less. That painting's a mystery, even the subject. We're not sure if it's an animal or not."

"How much is it?" Peter asked.

The woman shrugged, "We left our paintings unpriced feeling that whoever was touched by them should have them and there seems to be some message involved in this one. Did you see a person in the eye if that is an eye? Someone made the comment that they even looked like entrances of some kind." The woman laughed, "Well I've heard that the eyes are the entrance to the soul. I don't know. I just think it's an interesting painting. We left it unpriced so whoever it touched could give what they could afford. Art seems to be elite only for the rich. I don't believe that and we wanted our canvases to go home with people who love them." She smiled.

"I'll take this one." Peter said taking out his wallet.

The woman looked at him. "Isn't that odd? I've felt the eyes looked Asian and here you are buying it. I love antiques and sometimes I wish objects could talk. What fascinating stories they could tell."

"I know what you mean." Peter replied wondering very much about this new painting of White Fang, a girl dancing in the wind and soul. "She's been married for almost three months. If it's her painting why did she paint it?" Peter wondered as he handed the woman the money.

"Oh this is generous." The woman smiled looking at what he gave.

"I like the painting." Peter answered.

"Thank you." The woman said, "I hope it brings you years of enjoyment. Merry Christmas."

"Thanks, Merry Christmas to you." Peter said walking away from the table.

"The painting touched you Peter, why?" His grandfather asked.

"Grandfather, it's the weirdest thing. Jeneil gave me a book called White Fang, a wolf dog. It was important to her she saw me connected to the story. She used to do that in the wind." He said pointing to the glare in the eye. "That's what she was doing when I first met her on the beach. She was dancing in the wind. And soul Grandfather. She did a thing called soul. It involved the eyes."

"Do you think she painted it?" The grandfather asked not believing what was turning here.

Peter sighed, "Boy I wish I could find out because if this is a new painting I'd like to know why after three months of marriage to Steve she's painting something that's connected to me."

The grandfather was concerned, "Peter is that wise. You don't' know that she painted it. Maybe it's time to move on Peter. Get on with your life."

"My memories of her hold me together grandfather. I haven't told you but I'm in psychotherapy."

The grandfather looked concerned, "Because of Jeneil?" He asked.

"No, because of me. Look at what I've asked myself. A tough ethnic street kid who nearly died with his best friend in an alley then pushed himself to become a surgeon. Now that I've reached my goal the merry-go-round pace of college, studying and pushing has stopped and I'm left with making sense of it all. Add to that a weird marriage and the truth about my father after all these years. Jeneil made life make sense to me. Losing her just left me alone with the situation. She seemed to know who I am more than I did. More than I do now. Her and her Chang." He smiled. "She found me when I was showing signs of needing help. Damned if she didn't know that too. 'Scars, Peter, we found each other because of scars', she said. She's uncanny. I'm going to put the painting in my car. Take your time looking around, grandfather. I'll come back and browse too." Peter walked away smiling cheerfully.

His grandfather watched him with deep concern. "Peter you don't even know that it's her painting." The old man sighed, "He grasps for anything like he's drowning. I'm glad he's getting help this is all very strange." The germinated thought surfaced again. "My gosh if that is her painting and it's found its way to him does that mean this isn't over? That can't bring anything but more hurt for all three of them. They were such strong energies. I felt it. I saw it. And their lives got so strangely entwined. None of them needs to be hurt any more than what's already happened, especially the songbird. If that is her painting then that would mean she isn't free of Peter either. Does Steve know that? How is she able to pretend? And why is she married to Steve then?" He rubbed his face as the confusion made him weary. "My gosh if the paths of their lives cross again seriously then one of them could end up torn from it surrounded by chaos and struggling for survival. I don't know which of the three is a strong enough energy for that kind of turmoil." He felt a chill as he thought of them. "Wind, fire and earth." He sighed, "what is life requiring of them." The old man shook his head deeply concerned, "There is no way he'll know for sure if that's her painting and maybe that's for the best." His grandson now had him very worried.

Twenty-Nine

Cutting the ends from the red bow, Jeneil fastened it to the package. "Done." She said and Steve looked up from his cup of coffee.

"You're dragging your feet on this visit aren't you?"

Jeneil nodded, "My grandfather doesn't really like me. If he cared enough to talk to me, he'd probably tell me that, so it's been hard to motivate myself to visit him especially with the painting. It could explode in my face if he gets upset over it. He's 97 maybe I should just let the man live out his days uncluttered instead of pushing sour memories at him hoping for peace. Rachel said she'd talk to him and prepare him as much as she could."

Steve got up from the kitchen table and went to her. "Get your jacket on, honey, so you can put the visit behind you and be left in peace. You've been telling me for days that it's the right thing to do. You thought it would bring peace between him and his daughter. It can go either way. If he's soured by it, what have you lost? If it softens him then you've gained."

She smiled and hugged him, "You're right, you're right. I love your brain. I'm glad you're going with me."

He kissed her cheek, "You'll see he'll be charmed by it. What are the other packages?"

"A painting for Aunt Rachel and a woolen shirt jacket I made for her to wear in the house. We've had the insulation checked, but it's a big house and hard to heat. My mother felt the cold air penetrate her bones. I made one for my grandfather too. The small red container is applesauce for him. I found the recipe in my mother's cookbook. It was her mother's. And it was called Mother Alden's applesauce. It's very sour but I followed the recipe exactly maybe that's how my grandfather likes it if he grew up on it. Mother Alden must be his mother, I'm guessing." She sighed, "This could all be for nothing. The last time I went to visit him he pretended I wasn't there. My Aunt said he's not very receptive to her children either." Jeneil shrugged, "The man is naturally sour I guess."

"Too much of his mother's applesauce." Steve said jokingly.

Jeneil chuckled and slipped her arm into the sleeve of her jacket. Steve put his overcoat on having decided to visit in a suit to make a good first impression as a husband for Jeneil. "I'm a little nervous." He said. "All these generations of family and me a kid the stork really delivered." He laughed. "He'll probably toss me out the window with the painting for not knowing my parents."

"We'll feed him the applesauce first." Jeneil smiled and they headed to the garage.

The parking lot of the nursing home was full of people making Christmas visits. Jeneil hoped her grandfather wouldn't cause a scene with such a crowd around. It still pained her to think of her father being literally chased from the Alden house and having obscenities shouted at him. She sighed and held Steve's hand grateful that he was along. Jeneil conscience appeared when she entered the building. The surroundings were cheerfully decorated and a holiday spirit could be felt. She was glad that she had moved her grandfather here. If this visit didn't work she thought she could at least relax and know that she had tried to improve her grandfather's life if not resolve the bitterness. Rachel was coming from his room with a group of four people. One girl had purple spiked hair. Rachel smiled warmly when she saw Jeneil. "You look stylish." Rachel said taking in her cashmere coat and leather boots. "You have some cousins to meet." She said.

"Aunt Rachel this is my husband Steve."

Rachel extended her hand. "Dr. Steve Bradley, very nice to meet you." She smiled looking Steve over too. "This is my daughter Nedra and my son Tom. This is Tom's son Rocko. It's really James but he calls himself Rocko. And this is Nedra's daughter Krystaline. Family this is Jeneil, Aunt Jennifer's daughter, and her husband."

Nedra and Tom smiled thanking her for the help she was giving their mother. Their children nodded and sneered which Jeneil felt sure was intended to be a grin since they didn't seem hostile just into the teen years where identity was important, but could never be stabilized. The group left after chatting sociably for a few minutes, and Rachel sighed.

"I'm sorry, I had no idea they would visit this afternoon. Krystaline's hair upsets father and Rocko looks like his mother which father finds unforgivable." She shook her head, "Tom's wife is French. They've been here in America for years, but she's French to my father. And poor Nedra she married an Italian boy. Again they've been here for years a warm loving and giving family who even include me for holidays so I won't be alone, but father won't allow them to visit." She shrugged, "He's probably in his room getting steamed up."

Jeneil sighed, "Shall we just leave the packages then?"

Rachel thought for a second. "No you both look so nice and normal, father might like that."

Jeneil found herself irritated at trying to please the man's pettiness. They followed her into the room. Rachel was right, the old man was sitting in his chair scowling. Rachel sat on the bed as the man looked at Steve and Jeneil. "Father. Jeneil has come to visit with her new husband, Steven Bradley. He's a doctor, a neurosurgeon. They've driven a long way to visit you and you should thank Jeneil for paying for this nursing home. You've told me how much nicer this place is than the hospital. It's really very kind of her to care about you so much."

Jeneil felt sickened by Rachel's pleading for good behavior from him on her behalf. The grandfather stared at Jeneil looking her over and then at Steve doing the same. Jeneil held her breath. "Get my glasses." He grumped hoarsely. Rachel obeyed quickly not wanting to irritate him. He put them on with shaking hands and looked them over again. Steve fidgeted and Jeneil felt her stomach get tense. "Steven." The old man said studying him, "That's a good bible name. Not like Krystaline and Rocko. They even made up her name. He pointed to Jeneil. Damn crazy world nowadays. Are you any relations to Pawcatuck Bradleys?"

"No sir." Steve answered, "I'm from Western New York State."

The old man nodded, "My mother's name was Bradley. Pawcatuck Bradleys. Good people. You got Scandinavian in you?" He asked, "You're as blonds as the sun, good strong blue eyes too. Swedish are you?"

Steve looked at Jeneil. "Austrian. Grandfather Alden with a sprinkling of Norwegian." Jeneil lied just to protect the good mood that was so evident. Rachel was stunned by her father's pleasant behavior.

The old man smiled and nodded. "You've got an Austrian chin. Bring chairs and sit." He added and then took a breath. Steve looked around. Putting the Christmas packages on the bureau, he brought two both straight chairs to the group. Holding one for Jeneil as she sat. The old man noticed. "Now that's breeding. Comes from good bloodlines." He grumped to Rachel. "Not like those Europeans your two married."

"Yes father." Rachel replied lowering her head.

Jeneil's back stiffened. "Aunt Rachel I've brought some applesauce. The recipe said Mother Alden's applesauce."

Rachel looked excited. "You have it! I must have lost ours and I haven't been able to make it like mother for him. Could you send me the recipe?" She turned to her father. "Did you hear that?" She asked him.

"No, she's an Irish mouse, didn't speak up enough."

"She has a copy of Grandmother Alden's applesauce recipe. She made some for you. I'll go get a spoon." She got up and patted Jeneil's shoulder excitedly as she left.

The old man looked at Jeneil. "Where'd you get my mother's recipe?"

"My mother had it written in her cookbook."

"My wife and Jen…" He stopped and scowled, "and your mother were the only two women who could make it like my mother did. Even Becky and Rachel couldn't."

Jeneil just nodded. Steve put his arm on her chair. "You learn to cook from your mother?" He asked.

Jeneil nodded again wondering why all his questions sounded so harsh.

"Is she a good cook?" He asked Steve.

"Very good." Steve smiled.

"Good wife too?" He asked.

"The best." Steve said.

"Minds your house. Looks after your needs with no sassin?" He asked.

"Good as gold." Steve replied wondering if needs really meant what he thought it did.

The old man looked at Jeneil, "Well I'm glad to see that your mother didn't lose her Alden training even though she tramped all over."

Jeneil wasn't sure of the word tramped, but she forced herself to be silent to honor her parents. He looked at Steve. "Her mother was sassiest of all three girls. Broke more saplings on her to break that wild streak in her. Done no good at all. She was hell bent for trouble that one. Kicked her out so she wouldn't disease the other two. Can't have one bad apple ruining the rest."

Jeneil choked up and stayed silent. She resented her mother being called diseased because she was free spirited. "Look for one like her mother in your kids. Seems to skip a generation. My wife's mother was a sassier. Almost didn't marry my wife, scared her mother's mouth was in her. Turned up in her mother." He pointed at Jeneil. "Serena all over, that was her mother. She don't' look none too sassy this one." He said looking Jeneil over, "Looks quiet like my Sarah. Nothin rattles the nerves more than a wife who don't know her place."

Jeneil began to appreciate the suffrage movement and women's liberation far more than she had before. Rachel returned with two spoons and a small dish. Jeneil got the container for her. Rachel served the treat to her father. He savored the first spoon carefully. He looked at Jeneil. "You got your mother's touch with food. She was real good. Softest biscuits and crispiest chicken. Made gravy that nobody could copy even my Sarah who was a blue ribbon cook."

Jeneil began to understand that "my Sarah" wasn't intended to sound possessive. He meant it as a term of endearment. She found herself unable to talk to this man. She just smiled. Her grandfather watched her. "Rachel: her mother taught her to be a lady. You can see it in her face."

Steve smiled to himself. "Fragile and vulnerable are written all over her and he thinks it's being a lady. Boy have men changed too. I couldn't stand the kind of woman he thinks is perfect."

The old man concentrated on eating the applesauce showing his enjoyment with each spoonful. He looked into the large container. "Enough for three meals. You got a generous nature too. You been taught the bible?" He asked.

Jeneil nodded.

"Your father's?" He scowled.

"Both." Jeneil answered, "But I went to the protestant church on Sundays and I sang in the youth choir there." Jeneil couldn't believe that she was dragging out facts about herself that she hoped would please the old man. She began to understand her mother's rebellion.

The grandfather chuckled, "Bet that ripped that heathen father of yours to shreds. You got Alden blood alright."

Jeneil clasped her hands tightly as annoyance stirred. "My father drove me to youth choir practice every Wednesday night. He and the minister were very good friends."

The grandfather was surprised, "Well maybe your mother done that anti-Christ some good. God will forgive her then and your mother has done a good job with you. Hasn't she Rachel."

Rachel warmly smiled, "She really has father."

The grandfather smiled, "Girl has good manners, she's generous, behaves like a lady, cooks and Steve was telling me that she's a proper wife."

Rachel smiled at Jeneil and looked at her father. "You can be very proud of her mother. She's raised a child that honors the name of her grandparents." Rachel winked at Jeneil.

"Did you ever have purple hair?" The old man asked studying Jeneil.

"No sir."

The old man nodded. "See Rachel it does skip a generation. Nedra has Serena's sass in her daughter Krystaline and Jennifer got my Sarah in her daughter Jeneil. Saplings don't do nothing. It's bloodlines."

Steve smiled wondering what a geneticist would do hearing Jeneil's grandfather's theories or what the old man would say if he knew that Jeneil was a spitfire. Jeneil smiled and decided not to tell her grandfather that her middle name is Serena and she thought she was like her. His world was too compact and he was too old to have his narrow theories disproved now. Peace was far more important and so she stayed silent letting the old man believe what he wanted as truth. Jeneil realized that it wasn't the applesauce, or her perseverance in the situation that was softening her grandfather. The solitary successful influence was the fact that her husband was blond blue eyed and a doctor, but possibly his career didn't matter either. The old man looked contented after his treat and Rachel smiled at Jeneil appreciatively. "It was very thoughtful of you to make the applesauce. The visit is a pleasant one for him. I'm glad you stayed." She watched her father rest his head back tired from the cheerfulness of his animated conversation with this granddaughter who had pleased him by achieving what her mother hadn't, a marriage to a man of whom he approved.

Jeneil got up and went to the bureau for the Christmas gifts. She handed two to Rachel. "Merry Christmas, Aunt Rachel." She smiled handing the holiday wrapped packages to the surprised woman.

"Oh Jeneil, you are so very sweet. Besides all the help you give me already, you've done this too." The woman's eyes moistened as she held Jeneil's hand. "You are exactly what I would have chosen as a niece. I'm so glad you took the time to find me."

Jeneil hugged her Aunt aware that her grandfather had raised his head and was watching her. "May I open them now?" Rachel asked.

"Whatever suits you." Jeneil replied taking her seat again.

The grey wool tweed shirt jacket pleased her Aunt when she saw it. "This is wonderful. My sweaters just don't keep out the cold anymore." She said feeling the material to her face.

Jeneil nodded, "My mother had the same problem. Wool seemed to help."

"Thank you, Jeneil. You made this didn't you? There's no tag in it and it looks sturdy."

Jeneil nodded again. "Family rule. One gift had to be made personally."

Her Aunt smiled warmly, "It's nice that you continue the tradition."

"It feels like Christmas when I'm making gifts. I enjoy it. This tray of cookies is for you too."

Rachel looked at her father, "Jennifer kept the Alden traditions father, she's taught them to Jeneil."

The old man watched Jeneil steadily. She decided not to tell them that she also had Connors traditions that she celebrated, since the visit was going too smoothly to jeopardize peace. She felt sure that her father who was a pacifist would understand. Rachel reached for the second Christmas package and opened it carefully. Jeneil was glad that she had given her the painting her mother called three sisters. Her Aunt seemed to recognize something in it right away that touched her deeply. Rachel wiped the tears that spilled down her cheeks and held the framed painting close to her. "Thank you very much, Jeneil. At this point in my life, there is nothing that could mean more to me than this painting done by my sister. Thank you for understanding that. I miss them both." She said taking her handkerchief and going to the window. The old man watched his daughter, and then he reached for the painting that was lying on the bed. His weakened and shaking hands struggled to bring it to him. Jeneil reached for it helping him to rest it on his chair. She watched him wondering what his reaction would be. He looked up at Rachel who still had her back to them as she dealt with the emotions the gift had stirred in her and then he studied the painting. Jeneil wished she could hear his thoughts, but all she saw was the quiet expression on her grandfather's face as he looked the painting over carefully.

"The girl could always draw good. Spent hours sittin under the lilacs with her paper and pencil. It's the only thing that quieted her especially after I took a sapling to her for sassin! Must have got that from her grandmother too. Serena's embroidery could be framed it was that good. Those two always did understand each other without talking! My Sarah was jealous of Serena and Jennifer together. They were more like mother and daughter. Like two good friends. It was Serena who begged us to let Jennifer go to France to school and even helped with the money to pay for it. Sarah asked me to allow it. She thought Jennifer would settle down as an art teacher once she got her roamin done with. I knew it would only bring trouble and I was right. Should of listened to my own thoughts. The girl would have been different. But I kept thinking that I should keep up with the changing world. Hhmph, if tain't changing for the better then tain't no sense a chagin with it is there? But the girl was good. Drawin was a natural thing with her." Jeneil watched him fascinated by his admission and understanding that her concern for bringing peace between her mother and her grandfather was groundless almost egotistical. She could have little affect on the situation except to be an extension of her parents. As she watched her grandfather she could see that the real work of peace was being handled by her mother through her artwork. The feelings her mother so sincerely expressed on canvas were speaking to her sister and echoing to her father now. Jeneil felt she understood immortality a little better now and she felt more confident about giving the grandfather his painting. She went to the bureau and brought the painting to him. He looked up at her holding the package, "I have one too?" He asked surprised.

Jeneil smiled and took Rachel's painting from him. As she handed the gift wrapped painting to him she felt like she was delivering the letter from her mother that he had returned unopened and peace settled within her. Again, she felt the "high" that Mandra and her parents would describe when you've done something for the side of truth and the improvement of the human condition. They called it an oneness with Universal good or positive energy. She held the weight of the painting as the old man unwrapped it. The harsh lines on his face seemed to soften as he uncovered the canvas called "Home for the Harvest." The painting was better than delivering the unopened letter, there would be no regrets for not reading and responding to what had been written. The painting expressed the love her mother felt for the farm where she grew up. It was a message her father could grasp easily. The painting was a bond between him and his daughter now since the farm of her mother's memory was only a memory to him as well. Time had given them a common appreciation, a memory of a homestead where their lives were once shared. Jeneil felt that her mother had really captured the feeling of harvest on the canvas. From the farmer filling his barn with crates of picked produce and the cow with a heifer by its side to the trees heavily laden with fruit. All reaping rewards of their hard work in the cycle of life. "It's better than a snapshot." The old man said in a voice hoarse from emotion.

"It's the farm in the fall that's certain." Rachel said standing by her father's arm to see the painting.

The old man sighed. "I didn't know she had the feelin for harvest that I did. I guess it's what came as natural to me as drawin did to Jennifer." He said. "The waitin the watchin and then pickin and cratin! The land was good to me."

Jeneil sensed his love for the land and she understood because she had the same feeling for it. For the energy of the earth that made a seed sprout and grow and the taste of life that was part of that whole cycle. "My mother told me that you loved the land. She had a garden every year that fed us well. A lot of her paintings are of landscapes and nature. She must have inherited your love for it."

The old man watched and listened. "Did Jennifer sell her paintings?" He asked.

Jeneil nodded. "Especially in Nebraska. The people there shared her love of the land and nature. These are paintings from our home. Paintings that she did for herself or for us as gifts. I think she can be considered a successful artist."

"That's good." The old man commented, "That's good."

Jeneil was pleased. She felt the vibrations of peace as she noticed her grandfather saying her mother's name more easily now. She bent down and kissed his cheek lightly. "Merry Christmas grandfather Alden." She smiled. The old man seemed startled by her action.

"Merry Christmas." He faltered with the words stumbling through the sentiment. When Jeneil and Steve left the grandfathers room he was wearing the shirt jacket Jeneil had made for him and holding the painting of his farm. Rachel had walked to the foyer with them smiling happily about the way the visit had gone. She hugged the two of them and wished them both the best making Jeneil promise to keep in touch.

Steve settled in behind the wheel of the SX7 noticing Jeneil staring out the window. "You're not concerned are you?" He asked. "Everything went well. Even I got all caught up with the feelings going on in that room. You all sort of resemble each other and I looked at you, your aunt and your grandfather thinking that you represented almost a hundred years of life in one family. Family didn't really register until I saw it in the three of you together."

Jeneil smiled at him, "Family as I define it doesn't really apply to us. Mr. Chang felt more like my grandfather than my own grandfather does. I was in that room lying and pretending in the hopes of bringing peace between him and my mother." She chuckled, "How successful do you think I'd have been visiting as Mrs. Peter Chang? He raged about Krystaline's purple hair. If he only knew that I had lived with a man who is Chinese, he'd have refused to admit I'm his granddaughter. But I married the right man: blondie." She shook her head, "How does it feel to have doors open magically simply because you're white, blonde, blue eyed and male?"

Steve snickered, "Hey woman don't get to none of your sassin or I'll tell your grandfather and have him take a sapling to you. He looks like he could still swing a mean sapling!"

Jeneil laughed.

Steve smiled and started the motor. "Look sweetheart pick on me for things I've done. I had nothing to do with how I look; I got dumped here like this same as you. I don't know what the lottery system is that decides these things."

Jeneil patted his arm, "Thanks for lying for me in there."

"No problem kid. Even I resented the questions about you." Steve said.

Jeneil smiled, "I believe that. I'm sure you did. The visit did go well and I think he has softened toward his daughter now. I can rest. I'm glad you visited with me. There was no way he'd have even listened to me without you there."

Steve smiled, "It's okay. We white supremacists can be sensitive to the needs of the less fortunate around us. It's what makes us superior."

Jeneil chuckled and then laughed, "Don't push it. You ain't seen the kind 'o sassin I'm capable of. Serena and my mother were mute by comparison."

Steve grinned, "I lied to your grandfather for the sake of peace, but I want you to know that I like fiery women and you are a spitfire." He avoided looking at her, aware that she was watching him closely. He wanted her to know that he approved of her. It was his way of clearing the path from her bedroom to his which he felt that she was considering lately. He was keeping his distance so he wouldn't appear to be rushing her.

*****

With Christmas only four days away their evenings had been a flurry of activity with two Christmas concerts, a Christmas play and visits to her friends to deliver Christmas gifts and then to the Tecumseh and Sayard people to deliver gourmet trays and bottles of wine. Steve was weary of it all and made her swear an oath that Christmas Eve would be theirs since they were spending Christmas Day with the Spragues. He was tired of running and getting in late, then going to bed. They were facing a weekend seminar in New York between Christmas Day and New Year's Eve. It was a tradition with the medical group to take the wives along to this seminar so they could shop and see the glitter of Manhattan decorated for the holidays. It was their annual Christmas party. Jeneil had been excited about it when she heard. Steve was concerned about the sleeping arrangements. It would be different to hide the two bedroom marriage. He had hoped to excuse Jeneil with an out of town trip, but she insisted that she'd like to see New York again and so he had reserved a room with two double beds hoping to have as much room as possible so she wouldn't feel uncomfortable about sharing a bedroom. The whole situation seemed too risky to him since knowing that at other seminars peopled wandered in and out of each others rooms, the possibility of the whole medical group learning about the arranged marriage was very likely. He felt pressured to the point of almost discussing the problem with Jeneil, but the pace of their lives never seemed to leave enough time or the right atmosphere lately. It was his hope to approach her with the problem on Christmas Eve. The atmosphere could possibly be right, they would be alone and he hoped the subject itself would help her to at least discuss being together in a real marriage relationship. He almost wished he had saved the Oyster Bay trip as a Christmas treat for them having remembered how close they had become on the boat, but he also knew that the trip had made her closer to him as a result of having seen Peter. There were moments since Oyster Bay that he felt certain she wanted to approach him, but she always looked like she felt awkward. The risk that he might be misreading her always made him hesitate to reach out to her since he remembered feeling so sure that her behavior before the Oyster Bay trip was a preparation for truth on the boat. He had been wrong then, he felt he couldn't risk being wrong now or the damage to their relationship might be very serious. She had to be the one to make the first move in order to avoid real trouble. Christmas Eve had to be special and he worked toward the goal as he shopped for her gifts. Shopping for her had been the real holiday delight for him this Christmas. She was his this time. Last Christmas he had been so much in love with her that he was afraid his choice of gifts would indicate that. Christmas was different this year, he was free to buy her anything he felt he wanted to. He had shopped and brought home the gift wrapped packages without concern for how it looked and that freedom felt great to him. He felt certain that she couldn't be blind much longer to his feelings for her. Life for them was nearing real and normal for their marriage, he sensed that strongly.

*****

Peter packed his weekender slowly and watched the new painting hanging on the wall in his bedroom. He went to it and touched the image of the girl dancing in the wind. "I know this is yours, baby. What is it all about? Why are you painting memories of me if you're married to Steve? Is something wrong?" He sighed thinking of the possibility that the marriage wasn't working. "What then?" He asked himself, and he knew that he'd just have to hear of the slightest chance that she was still his and he'd move on it. The thought surprised him, even shocked him that Chang could accept the idea. "She's married to Steve." He ran his fingers through his hair. Knowing full well what that meant, but Chang didn't care. "This is me." He said touching the painting again. "Damn it. What's happening? What is it? Is she still mine?" He asked himself, "Then why did you marry Steve baby? Why?" He smiled at the painting. "Is it soul, honey? The marriage on the balcony was real, I know it was. Will you always belong to me like we promised?" He sighed, "I'm going to find out honey, I promise. We should have talked, my grandfather was right."

*****

Jeneil paced anxiously watching the clock on the mantle and then she heard the delivery truck pull into the driveway. She went to the front door quickly. "You scared me." She smiled at the driver as he came to the door. "I didn't think you would get here today."

"Sorry, lady." He said opening his book for her signature, "Christmas Eve slows us down. Nothing and nobody is where they're supposed to be. Parties everywhere, last minute shoppers and travelers clogging the streets. I'm glad it's all over tonight." He sighed handing her the book to sign.

"I hope it's in working order." She signed her name quickly.

"They tested it before it left the warehouse." He assured her.

"Oh good!"

"Where do you want it?"

"In the den. Do you want to bring it through the garage? There may be fewer steps that way."

"I'd appreciate that, Lady. This is no small gift."

"I know." She laughed, "I'm feeling embarrassed about it now."

"Nah." The driver laughed looking at the house and neighborhood, "What the hell can you give to somebody who's got it all? My helper and I will back the truck to the garage door."

Jeneil covered her mouth staring at the size of the gift as it sat near the tree. "It's enormous." She chuckled, "I must have been crazy to have bought it."

The mantle clock chimed the hour and Jeneil grabbed the folds of material and began the job of wrapping the gift before Steve got home. She laughed to herself for her silliness in buying fabric to wrap it so she could reuse the material to decorate the studio. "The whole gift is a silly extravagance and you worry about throwing out so much wrapping paper." She hurried knowing that the late delivery didn't leave her too much time to wrap it before Steve arrived. She heard the SX7 and pinned the last corner quickly. Grabbing the large red bow she had made for the SX7 she pinned that onto the top of the box and looked up as Steve walked in.

"What is that?" He asked looking shocked.

"A Christmas present that every neurosurgeon needs." She said stepping down from the chair.

"My own portable operating room?" He laughed, "Look at the size of the box." He said touching the side. "What is it?"

"Can't tell it isn't Christmas yet." She smiled and went to him for a hug.

"You got crazy, kid. I can tell." He laughed holding her gently.

"You're right, I did." She admitted quickly, "But like it anyway okay?"

He kissed her lips lightly and smiled. "Merry Christmas, Mrs. Steve Bradley."

"Thank you, Dr. Bradley and the same to you." She said undoing the buttons of his overcoat. "Are you ready for dinner?"

"Not really." He replied. "The medical group had a buffet lunch brought in and we picked at it all afternoon."

"What!" She gasped, "You asked me to make the pot roast dinner." She hit him gently with his scarf.

"I'll eat it." He laughed. "But there's no rush is there? We have all evening don't we?"

"Yes." She smiled. "and I'm going to change into my Christmas Eve duds right now to begin the evening."

"Aw, honey. I wanted to relax in jeans and a comfortable shirt."

"That's fine." She smiled, "You get comfortable your way and I'll get comfortable my way. Meet you back here in a few minutes."

He watched her run up the stairs, "Boy she's easy to live with." He smiled, "No fuss life she just lets it happen the way it happens sometimes." He put his coat in the hall closet and walked upstairs to change. Steve returned to the den before Jeneil did and filled the fireplace with wood. Striking the match to the kindling and tinder he waited for the flames to work through the crevices.

Jeneil joined him and reached for the matches, "I'll light the candles and then let the merriment begin."

Steve looked at her in the long green dress. "Honey you look fantastic. Now I feel bad. I'll change."

"Don't you dare." She held his arm, "I'm dressed like this so I can slouch or lie on the floor in comfort. This isn't formal. I don't like being bound in slacks and I would have to sit ladylike in a shorter dress. I'm dressed for comfort, believe me."

He smiled, "Well you look beautiful really beautiful."

"Thank you." She kissed his cheek and then went to light the red and green candles that were in clusters all about the room with boughs of greenery and holly tied with burgundy velvet bows. Steve watched her. The room looked festive, she looked gorgeous he was hopeful that the evening would be good for their relationship. "Don't rush," He cautioned himself, "You have the whole evening with her. Just let it happen. Give her a chance to be less awkward." He thought watching her. "Oh man, she's incredibly beautiful."

Jeneil put a tape of Christmas music in the player then disappeared into the kitchen returning with eggnog and nibbles for them. "Let's toast to something." She smiled, "There aren't too many chances in life to make wishes."

"To our marriage." He said.

"Yes." She smiled, "May the happiness continue."

"To improve." He pointedly added not looking at her as they both sipped egg nog.

"This feels like Christmas." She said taking a marinated shrimp.

"You've made it feel that way." He smiled at her.

She took a shrimp for him. "What would you like to do? We can sit and talk, play backgammon or watch a movie from my father's collection?"

"Let's dance."

Jeneil was surprised, "Dance to Christmas music?"

"No of course not. We can make it something slow and soothing to help us unwind. It feels great to be having a quiet evening at home."

She patted his arm nodded and went to the music case. Steve watched her feeling the electricity stirring in his chest. She returned and held her arms in the dance position for him to hold her. Putting his cup of egg nog down he went to her and slipped his arm around her bringing her to him. Taking her hand he kissed her fingertips lightly as he held them. She snuggled to him resting her cheek next to his causing his heart to skip a few beats. He clenched his jaw afraid he'd tell her everything he was feeling at the moment. Her earlobe seemed so close to his lips. He wanted to kiss it. Her earlobes had always driven him crazy and it was the first time he could ever remember being attracted to a woman's ears. Forcing himself to slow down the electricity racing through him he kissed her forehead lightly. She smiled at him gently, "This was a good idea. I love dancing with you. It's a real enjoyment. You chose your dates well. They've taught you to scuba dive and dance. What did Marsha teach you?"

He smiled, "That I had lousy manners and I talked like a gutter rat. Oh yea, I also learned not to trust women from her."

Steve saw the compassion in her eyes, "Well I was thinking that I was probably the only woman in your life who hasn't taught you anything, but I'd rather have my rating of teaching you nothing than Marsha's, I guess." She patted his shoulder and hugged him.

"You've taught me something, Jeneil. Something I never thought I'd learn."

"Oh what's that?" She asked looking into his eyes and smiling.

"To trust, honey. I'd trust you with my life."

Jeneil was deeply touched and very surprised. "I've done that/" She asked, showing she was sincerely pleased with the compliment.

He smiled. "Yeh, Mrs. Bradley, You've done that. You've done that in spades. Why do you suppose I married you?"

"I don't know. Except for saying that we wanted out of the dating marathons. We've never really talked about us. Friendship isn't really such a bad beginning for a marriage, is it?"

He shook his head, "No, I haven't found it to be."

She smiled happily and snuggled to him, "That makes me a pretty good wife then doesn't it? If I've taught you to trust women."

"Not all women. I trust you, Jeneil. Just you."

"Oh." She answered quietly. "Well I'm still pretty pleased with myself. At least I've taught you something. Now I'm like the other women you've known."

Steve squeezed her gently and kissed her cheek wishing he could tell her that she has also taught him to love and care about someone so deeply that it's a part of his inner self that belongs to her. "Someday." He thought to himself. "Someday soon, I'd like her to know that."

They danced in silence enjoying the closeness that moment had brought. Jeneil's stomach rumbled loudly from hunger. "Excuse me." She chuckled, "But I haven't been nibbling on a buffet lunch all afternoon."

"I'm sorry honey." He said, "You're starved. I should have realized that. You were waiting for me to eat."

She smiled. "I was fine until I ate that shrimp. My stomach is letting me know it didn't appreciate being teased."

"Let's eat then." He said releasing her and taking her hand, "I'll help get it to the table."

"Where did you learn to be such a good husband?" She squeezed his hand.

He watched her. "Do you really want to know?"

"Yes, do you know?"

He nodded. "Yeah, Marsha taught me."

"Marsha?" Jeneil replied showing her surprise.

Steve nodded again, "I figured out that she dumped me because I didn't measure up, so I've been killing myself trying to be the perfect man for women. I think that's why it was so easy for me to slip into the White Stallion role. Boy, I was out of control back then. Probation was the greatest thing for me. It forced me to become a real person."

Jeneil smiled at him and touched his cheek lovingly with her hand. "Well you're at a superlative level now, White Stallion. You're a very nice real person."

The moment had such personal honesty to it that Steve was left vulnerable and he watched her quiet brown eyes showing approval of him. He touched the hand she held to his cheek and moved his head pressing his lips to her palm. Jeneil was watching him steadily as he turned back to look at her and for the first time Steve felt the electricity between them. It was real. The moment was volatile and as close to being perfect as it had ever gotten. The doorbell chimed and someone used the brass knocker loudly. Steve felt anger begin.

"I'll get it." Jeneil said quietly still watching him steadily for a moment and then she went to the hallway.

Steve heard Robert Danzieg's voice wishing Jeneil Merry Christmas and resentment surged through him for the intrusion. Robert explained that he'd just driven in from Fairhaven and that he wanted to bring a gift by. Steve sat on the sofa and braced himself for Robert's torment.

"Hi Steve." Robert smiled, switching a large flat package to his other hand.

"Robert." Steve mumbled in return. He hadn't seen him since their argument.

"I brought a gift by for you two."

Steve watched him and stayed expressionless. Robert looked at Jeneil handing her the package. She smiled warmly as she steadied it. "Why aren't you in sunny California this Christmas?"

"I can't spare the time. The Fairhaven job is sizable and I've already gotten two other commissions as a result. There'll be a break after the New Year. I'll fly out and visit then."

"We were about to have dinner. Can you stay for a short visit at least?"

Steve felt his heart drain.

Robert grinned sheepishly, "Could I stay for dinner? I drove straight through to get here early enough to visit friends. I'm bunking with Dennis tonight."

Jeneil hugged his arm and smiled. "We'd love to have you stay for dinner. In fact, we insist on it." Steve wondered why Jeneil said "we".

"What are you having not that it matters?" Robert smiled.

"Steve's favorite, pot roast, mashed potatoes and gravy."

Robert shrugged grinning boyishly. "I knew I was right stopping here first. Your pot roast is one of my favorites too. I was hoping to scrounge some leftovers from you and if I'm intruding kick me out with a food bag."

Jeneil smiled at him. "You're family silly. Steve will you get Robert a glass of wine?"

"Sure." Steve replied getting up from the sofa.

"Robert I know this is a canvas." Jeneil said, "Is it all right if we open it now? I'd like to see what you've done."

Steve smiled as he poured the wine and listened to Jeneil saying "we". He noticed that Robert wasn't being sarcastic; he smiled again appreciating Jeneil having supported him as her husband. His love for her filled him as he poured the wine into a goblet and he felt every bit the husband of a beautiful wife in a home comparable to his associates celebrating Christmas. He took a deep breath as the electricity raced through him. He loved it all, Jeneil marriage a home and his career, he found that he could even feel kindly toward Robert at the moment. "Season's best to you." Steve smiled as he handed Robert the glass of wine.

"Thanks." Robert replied holding his goblet to a short toast and then sipping. "Ooo. Chablis French." Robert said tasting the wine. "I guess you've forgiven me."

Jeneil looked up from the unwrapped canvas. "Oh Robert it's wonderful! What sensitivity this expresses. The muted colors seem so perfect for the subject."

"I call it New Love." He said going to her side smiling appreciatively.

"Yes. The title is perfect too. Both the man and the woman do express the electricity of a new love between them. I can see it clearly. I can feel it. Why did you paint this?"

"I do my fantasies now and then. It keeps my libido happy."

Steve joined Jeneil and Robert to view the canvas. He liked the painting too. There was a lot of sensitivity between the woman lying on the grass by a stream and the man sitting by her gazing steadily into her eyes as he handed her a flower. The woman was reaching for the flower and the two hands almost touching felt electrical. Steve grinned and sipped some wine as he recognized a close resemblance to Jeneil in the woman. The thick dark hair was hard to miss and the dress was the one she bought in Mirahesh. It looked soft and skimmed the contours of the body. In reality Jeneil's only draped. The man leaned over the woman resting on one hand that he had placed on the ground near the thigh and buttocks of the woman. The woman's other hand was placed on her chest drawing attention to her well-shaped body. Steve also noticed that the man in the painting had Robert's color brown hair and he had to wonder why Robert hadn't painted the man with blonde hair if the canvas was intended as a gift for him and Jeneil.

"I tried making the guy a blonde, but the brightness distracted from the subtlety of the other colors. Sorry Steve, I took artistic license there."

Steve fidgeted uncomfortably at having even thought the question. "Is that us?" Jeneil asked.

"Well it's my fantasy, but I decided it would apply."

"Well that's nice of you. Thank you Robert." Jeneil leaned toward Robert to kiss his cheek.

Robert put his arms around her holding her close to him. "Merry Christmas Jeneil."

Steve noticed Robert squeeze her. Steve could tell that Robert's feelings for Jeneil were sincere and he was surprised to feel compassion for him. He remembered Jeneil with Peter and how it felt to choke on the truth of his own feelings for her as he wished her a Merry Christmas the previous year. "She's a killer." He thought as he sipped his wine. Robert kissed her lips lightly and released a surprised Jeneil.

"I missed you too Robert." She said.

Robert smiled, "You noticed that did you?"

She nodded and grinned, "I'll get dinner." She patted his arm.

"I'll help." Robert said following her.

Steve sighed and went to sit on the sofa resting the painting against the low table nearby. He studied it as he sipped his wine and he heard the laughter from the kitchen. "We don't laugh like that together anymore, Jeneil." He thought. "The celibacy of our marriage has us so serious. I want what's in this painting, honey." His mind added. He felt the hand lightly on his shoulder and he jumped startled by it.

"I'm sorry." Jeneil said, quietly watching him closely, "Dinner's on the table."

"Right." He said getting up.

Jeneil watched him as he walked to her. "It's okay about Robert isn't it?" She asked.

"Sure." Steve smiled chucking her chin gently.

"Thank you." She said feeling very grateful. "A person needs friends when they're alone at Christmas."

"I know." Steve replied, putting his arm around her shoulder.

"You are a great husband." She said, almost in a whisper. The electricity pulsed through him and he kissed her warmly pleased that she never tensed up and that she never pulled away even gently. He sat at the dining table feeling very encouraged about the way Jeneil was behaving toward him.

Jeneil served dinner and conversation fell into a light chatter that was very pleasant. Steve really appreciated Robert's new attitude, and considering he was alone on Christmas Eve, he accepted the intrusion more calmly feeling strongly that he and Jeneil were on a solid path now. She was allowing him to be physically closer to her which would give him the chance to initiate the move toward a full relationship between them since she seemed to feel awkward about dealing with it. Again the perfectness of the situation filled him. The lighted Christmas candles in the dining room created a mellow glow that accentuated the mellowness of his own mood and he began the meal his wife prepared completely happy. The doorbell rang and all three looked at each other.

"Santa Claus?" Robert joked.

"We'll see." Steve said getting up.

Jeneil went to put coffee on and returned to the dining room to find Kirk Vance with Drexel and Barbara Barnard. "Jeneil," Barbara smiled, "You're home looks so warm and festive. The truckload of candles really works a magic spell and you look so holidayish special."

Drexel laughed. "Steve looks like he's going to a basketball game you two are mismatched."

"Thanks Drex." Steve smiled falsely.

Robert watched the group as he took a taste of his potatoes. Jeneil smiled, "We've just begun dinner, can you stay and visit? Join us with coffee or something?"

Kirk Vance smiled, "You're a sweetheart, Mona Lisa, unexpected company and you just keep adding chairs to the table."

Jeneil shrugged, "Well you're welcomed to wait in the den if you'd like, but I thought we could all just gather here. You all know Robert." She added.

Drexel cleared his throat, "Actually, Jeneil, I've had nothing all day except pickings and drinks from buffets and visits to friends. This meal looks so damn wholesome, I wouldn't mind a small plate of it."

Steve was concerned that there may not be enough he looked at Jeneil. "I made enough for six people, Drex. I freeze meals ahead for busy days. If you'll all just set your own places from the hutch, I'll add more food to the serving dishes. All three responded readily and Robert smiled watching Steve who was looking stunned as he took his seat.

Jeneil brought the food and placed it on the table to be served family style so she could return to her own meal. The conversation went on in easy chatter again. Everyone cleared his place and added the dishes to the dishwasher while Jeneil got coffee together in a server along with a plate of Christmas fruit cake, cookies and tarts. Robert excused himself as the group adjourned to the den wishing everyone a good holiday and taking Jeneil to the door with him. Kirk Vance went to the painting.

"Nice," He commented, "Jeneil and Robert Danzieg isn't it?"

Steve turned quickly, annoyed by the remark, adding wood to the fire. "Now how do you even see Robert Danzieg in the man except for the hair color?" Jeneil responded as she walked into the room having picked up on Kirk's observation and wanting to take the heat off of Steve. "It's a stylized painting. Robert tried the man as a blonde, but the colors conflicted so Robert added darker shades to the hair. That's hardly me either. The picture is titled "New Love." I think it shows Robert's sensitivity very well. His paintings all but speak don't you think?"

Steve smiled at Jeneil loving the way she maneuvered the conversation to an intellectual level.

"Yes his boldness is still evident in this painting too." Kirk Vance added, "He's quite a talent. How did you meet him?"

"At a gallery show of his work." Jeneil replied, "I had been an admirer and I owned some of his work. He's photography is very striking. He's been working on the Viking Complex in Fairhaven lately. His admirers have multiplied."

"I know." Barbara smiled. "A lot of our friends have at least one of his paintings. Was this one a Christmas gift?"

Jeneil nodded. "Who would like coffee now?" she asked going to the serving table and again Steve was impressed with how easily Jeneil could direct the conversation away from herself and her personal life. Jeneil poured the first cups of coffee and then everyone was on his own after that as she settled on the hassock near Steve's chair. He noticed and squeezed her hand gently. She responded with a slight smile. Between wine and the ambiance of the room the conversation turned to reminiscence of how they all met.

"Jeneil what were you doing in that nothing hospital job?" Barbara asked.

"Avoiding going home."

"You're a complete shock from the person who worked in records. You were such a mystery to us."

"We all are," Jeneil added, "Does anyone know anyone else really well?"

Barbara chuckled, "No, no I suppose that's very true except for maybe the White Stallion. His life was an open book and an active one."

"But even some of the White Stallion legend was hype." Jeneil defended. "These were stories circulated about him that weren't even true."

Barbara laughed. "And some others that never even described the whole truth. He was quite the flirt at Kirk's Friday parties."

"Barbara let the White Stallion enjoy being buried." Steve replied becoming uncomfortable.

"But we miss him." Barbara pouted for emphasis.

"We sure do." Drexel agreed.

Kirk Vance grinned. "There was no one before or since as creative as he was in groups on Fridays."

Steve got up and poured more coffee for himself. "Anyone for a refill on anything?" He asked.

"Why don't you two come to a party some Friday?" Drexel smiled at them both.

Steve shook his head, "The White Stallion is gone."

"So you come instead." Barbara smiled, "Maybe we can jog your memory and resurrect the White Stallion." She raised her eyebrows seductively and Jeneil's spine stiffened as she watched and listened causing a thought to surface. She fidgeted and became quiet.

"Why did you ever get tangled with that redhead? She turned you into a recluse, and you lost her anyway? You'll pardon the cattiness but she looked pretty stiff, you're lucky you lost her she looked ice cube to me."

Jeneil knew they were talking about Sienna and she could feel the annoyance welling up in her.

"It takes all kinds to make up a world, Barbara." Steve smiled.

"Well you seem more natural now thanks to Jeneil." Barbara added.

Jeneil looked up, "Don't give me the credit. Steve is his own person. Who and what he is has been achieved on his own. He's not so easily manipulated." Steve leaned to her and kissed her cheek. "Thank you." He smiled and squeezed her shoulder.

"You two look so natural together and yet I would never have paired you with each other at the hospital. How did you two develop a relationship without the hospital knowing about it?"

"We ran into each other after she had left and became good friends." Steve answered quickly and Jeneil relaxed.

"You look like good friends." Drexel commented. "It's nice to see that in a couple."

"It is." Barbara agreed.

"It is nice." Kirk smiled watching Jeneil. "And I'm trying to convince them to share the friendship."

Barbara looked at Kirk. "Oh I'd like that too." She chuckled causing Jeneil to stiffen as the thought surfaced in her again.

Drexel yawned and apologized. Standing up and returning his wine goblet to the serving tray he looked at his wife, "Right now we should let them get on with their evening or what's left of it. Jeneil, thank you for dinner. I feel human again since eating. The holidays are a marathon at times. It was pleasant just stopping to be human with some nice neighbors."

Jeneil smiled at him not adding any sentiments of her own feeling that she wouldn't be sincere.

Steve got up wanting to support Drexel's idea that they leave. "Thank you for the burgundy." He said. "And Kirk that's a nice dinner rose."

"Invite me over to share it." Kirk smiled getting to his feet. "Do you cook Italian?" He asked Jeneil.

"Probably not as well as you do." She replied.

Kirk kissed her lips lightly, "I make a mean marzipan sauce that I'd be happy to bring to dinner."

Jeneil nodded, "Before the next party, how's that for you?"

"Deal." Kirk said, "Thanks for dinner tonight. You have a smooth touch creating warm atmospheres, but that doesn't surprise me at all." He touched her cheek gently and took the coat that Steve was holding for him.

Kirk's attention to her was wearing thin on Jeneil. She was left wearied from the visit and was glad to hear the door close on the evening. Steve returned and watched her standing before the fire. She seemed deep in thought. He went to her and put an arm around her shoulder. "You did make this a warm evening." He said squeezing her to him.

"That's good." She replied, continuing to watch the fire.

He kissed her cheek gently, "Let's sit on the sofa and talk."

She nodded and followed him.

He thought she seemed distant. "Honey are you okay? Is something wrong?"

She was silent for a moment and then she looked at him. "Have you slept with Barbara Barnard?"

Steve felt the blood drain from him. "Honey, it's really best to not ask about life before. It's not fair to anybody."

"I thought so." She sighed.

Steve could feel the panic begin in his stomach.

"Others in Tecumseh too, I guess." She added looking at the hands she clasped tensely.

Steve was desperate for a defense, "Jeneil those Friday parties were crazy. I told you that my life was out of control."

"Yes you did and yet you moved to Tecumseh right into all the memories of that era in your life."

"You chose Tecumseh, Jeneil, not me and I don't have any memories here. The parties were so crazy I can't remember faces and names."

She stared at him and he saw the shock the sentence caused in her.

"You're shocked, I can see it." He sighed. "Jeneil maybe we'd better talk about all of it in detail."

She got up quickly. "Oh please don't." She said, "Right now I'm not sure if it's better for me to just assume that everyone in Glenview is involved or not. Maybe it is better not knowing for sure." She went to the fire rubbing her temples. He got up slowly not sure what to do or say as fear for their relationship took hold on him.

He touched her shoulder lightly and she moved away from him. "How could you allow that in your life?" Steve heard her struggling with anger.

"Jeneil you told Robert that you had heard all the stories about the White Stallion."

She turned sharply. "Yes but I never expected to face your victims at my dinner table." She put her fingers to her lips struggling to not cry.

"Victims?" Steve was stunned, "Jeneil I never forced anybody and I never took advantage of anybody. Why is all the blame on me?"

"What do you want a medal for helping to satisfy her nymphomania." Jeneil flared and then turned away. "Oh my gosh listen to me even my accusations sound disgusting." She sighed heavily.

"You don't understand those Friday parties obviously." Steve said.

"And I don't want to." Jeneil replied sharply, "But they keep intruding on my life through you."

"You don't understand." He pleaded.

She glared at him. "Probably not and I hope I never will." She headed toward the door.

He grabbed her arm. "Jeneil don't do this. You're resurrecting the White Stallion for trial. I can't win, the guy's as guilty as hell, but I'm not that guy anymore. I'm not. This isn't fair to me. Doesn't this past year of my life count for anything at all?"

The question struck her and she stared at him, looking puzzled, "This is all rushing at me. I need some space and time." She moved away from him and ran up the stairs. He heard her bedroom door close hard.

"Shit!" He raged at himself, "Where the hell did you get the nerve to think you could be married to her? She's not the White Stallion's kind and she's Steve Bradley's fantasy. I can see it clearly now this whole marriage is a huge fairy tale. It can never be real. Every time I turn around I hit the button marked "shit." He went to the liquor cupboard and poured some gin than drink it down quickly.

Thirty

Morning lightened his room and Steve turned over sighing. He hated the thought of facing Jeneil. He wondered how they could even go to the Sprague's for dinner. He hadn't seen Jeneil since she left the den so upset on Christmas Eve. Hitting his pillow he stuffed it under his head resenting the way their first Christmas together had gotten ruined. He shook his head and the lump in his throat began to hurt, "Our first and last Christmas together probably." He swallowed hard and brushed his hair back with his hand. "How the hell can I win? The White Stallion keeps trucking shit into her life. I'll never be free of his crazy past."

There was light knocking on his door. He stared at it shocked that she was there. "Come in." He called.

"Good morning." She said, putting her head inside the room, "Merry Christmas." She added.

He stared, not believing that she was actually standing there being cheerful.

"I brought some juice." She walked into the room with a small tray balancing two glasses. "I thought you'd never wake up. Are you hung over?"

"No, why?"

"I saw the bottle of gin out of the cupboard, I just wondered."

"I had a shot." He studied her face, "Jeneil is everything okay?"

"I'm working on it." She answered quietly, sitting on the edge of the bed.

"Jeneil I'm sorry. I really am."

She handed him a glass of juice, "Let me work it out Steve. I'm dealing with a lot of pettiness right now. Things that can't be changed so my attitude has to."

"Why don't we talk about it?" He suggested.

She shook her head. "No not on Christmas day, Steve. We've both planned for today, let's not allow it to be ruined."

He felt encouraged. "Well as long as the end result is that we stay married." He said. "Jeneil I want the marriage to work, I really do."

"To our marriage, remember?" She held up her juice glass reminding him of Christmas Eve toast and smiled gently.

He grinned and nodded loving her attempt at salvaging the day. He wished he could just take the glass from her and pull her under the covers with him ending the celibacy between them and hopefully every awkward moment forever. She took his empty juice glass and got off the bed. "I'll meet you under the Christmas tree." She said cheerfully and closed the door.

He sighed, "We're back to square one again. Damn that White Stallion and the people who won't let him stay buried." He got up and headed to the shower discouraged about the setback but still hopeful about their relationship. Jeneil had a small breakfast buffet waiting on the serving table in the den when Steve walked in. "Mmmm it smells good in here." He went to the table where Jeneil was sitting on the floor in a green velvet robe and he sat near her. "Now what?" He asked.

"Eat fast I want my loot. I've been up for hours." She joked.

Steve broke into laughter and kissed her cheek. "You're a nut." He kissed her again and felt the resistance in her. He backed off realizing that she was really struggling and she did need some space. Jeneil reached for a china plate with a Christmas design on it and handed it to Steve. "I'll pour your coffee."

He was still eating his country eggs when she put her empty plate back on the serving tray and watched him.

"I'm eating as fast as I can." He grinned, "Have seconds or take larger portions while you wait!"

She smiled, "Well maybe a melon slice."

"Good, you're a pest when you want something." He said, biting into a biscuit.

Dipping two fingers into the yogurt and fruit spread; she took the glop and smeared it across his cheek.

"Hey!" He moved his head, "What the hell. Are you crazy?" He took his napkin and cleaned his cheek.

She smirked. "Don't call me a pest."

He shook his head. "For that I'll eat slower."

"Go ahead, I'll throw out my gifts to you and open mine."

"Sure you would." He chuckled and continued eating. Putting the melon slice on her plate, she wiped her fingers and started crawling toward the gifts under the tree.

"Jeneil." He said watching her wondering just how reckless she was feeling. "Jeneil don't get crazy." He put his plate down as she reached the tree and began piling his gifts. "What are you doing?" He asked watching her put them into a plastic garbage bag.

"Getting your gifts ready for the trash compacter."

He got up and went to the tree quickly kneeling by her. "Cut the comedy." He said and watched her continue putting gifts inside the bag. "Two can play reckless you know and if you don't stop, I'll stuff you in there with the gifts." He warned.

She stopped, "You and what army?" She began filling the bag faster.

"Good call my bluff. I'm in the mood." He said and he grabbed the bag from her. She moved away slightly and he grabbed her hand. She wrenched free and turned over quickly to get away. "Oh no you don't." He said, getting to her as she was kneeling to stand up. "In the bag for you wise guy. You like tormenting me so much now pay the price." The bag wouldn't lift easily over her from the weight of the gifts inside and he struggled with the opening.

She giggled, "I thought so, you do need an army, wimp."

"Wimp!" He raised his eyebrows at her insult as she got to her knees again. He pushed her over sending her backwards causing her to lose one leather slipper. "You smart mouthed bitch, now you will pay." He said emptying the gifts from the bag by turning it upside down. They spilled onto the rug.

Jeneil watched, "Cheater, you threatened to put me in there with the gifts. That's the easy way out. Cheater. Fake." She said, backing away.

"I'll put the gifts in after you." He said heading for her.

"That's still cheating, but I'll handle it." She challenged, confidently. "Come on." She said sitting up and pushing the sleeves to her robe up to the elbows. "But I'm not promising I won't hurt you." She said, pushing the hair from her eye.

He stopped to laugh finding her threat funny, which gave her time to get to her feet. She faced him holding her hands on her hips. "Okay tough guy, we're at face off now what?"

He watched her and smiled slightly, "Be right back." He said, mischievously and headed toward the door.

"Oh yes of course, I'll wait." She giggled, "Some war strategist you are."

He turned. "I don't need strategy, woman you're the weaker sex. I'll prove it when I get back."

"Well you'll have to find me first and your gifts too." She chuckled. "What women may lack in might we make up for in mind." She said, tapping her temple with her index finger.

"We'll see." He grinned and ran down the hallway. Jeneil began gathering the scattered gifts quickly and stuffing them into the garbage bag. Grabbing the load by the twisted top of the bag she headed out of the room and toward the stairs. Steve appeared at the hallway and rushed toward her.

"You're too slow woman. I'm back and you're finished." He grabbed her around the waist and pulled her down the two stairs she had already climbed. She wriggled and then leaned forward to toss him over her hip in a ninja move, but he had hold of the banister and she couldn't budge him.

"Oh well." She sighed relaxing in his arms. "I guess you're right, women are weaker. You win." She said.

He laughed as he held her tighter. "Do you think I'm falling for that "oh gosh, gee whiz" routine of yours; you crazy wench, I've seen you in action before. My army doesn't take hostages, sweetheart. You're going to get what I promised you." She wiggled frantically in his grasp and he held her tightly with two arms enjoying the fun of the game and holding her so close to him. She stopped struggling and relaxed against him panting from the struggle.

"I give up." She said. "I give up."

He held her closer, "I don't want you to give up. I don't care if you give up. You're going inside the garbage bag."

"I'll even climb into it myself." She said, sounding tired.

"Sure, sure." He chuckled, "I know you." He bent down and picked up the rope he'd gotten from the garage and dropped the stairs. "Sit on the floor." He said.

"Why?" She asked, "I've already quit. Do you want an apology too? Okay I'm sorry."

"Sit on the floor." He insisted.

"No." She replied stubbornly.

Dropping the rope to the floor, he then pushed against the back of her knees causing them to buckle from under her then he placed her gently on the floor with her arms behind tying her quickly at the wrists and then at the ankles. He went to the kitchen and returned with another garbage bag which he slipped onto her, over her feet. Tearing the second bag he slipped it over her head stopping to tie it at her neck leaving only her head exposed. He leaned over her and pushed the hair from her eye gently as he smiled. "Gotcha, wise guy." He kissed her cheek and stood up. Leaving her lying on the hallway floor, he picked up some of his packages and took them into the den. He returned for the rest. "Merry Christmas woman. I'm going to open my gifts and if you behave I won't throw yours away. See you." He smiled and returned to the den.

Jeneil lay on the hallway floor not believing she was there. She kept expecting him to come back and untie her. She heard wrapping paper rustling. "Oh Jeneil what a nice gift. I really like it." Steve called to her. She wiggled frantically, "Let me out of here." She yelled. "I want to watch you open your gifts that's the fun in shopping. Come here and untie me now you brute."

"Behave yourself." He warned, "Or I could get angry."

More wrapping paper wrestled. "Oooo nice." He said.

"Steve!" She yelled. "This isn't fair. Untie me." She pleaded.

"You don't sound sorry enough."

She sighed, "Please, Steve. I'm really sorry."

"That's a little better, but not quite."

Jeneil heard voices nearing the front door. Straining to turn her head, she glimpsed Drexel Barnard through the narrow window and she wickedly grinned. "Help!" She shouted. "Please someone help me." She screamed, "Help! Please help."

Steve ran from the den, "What's wrong honey?"

Jeneil screamed loudly, scaring Steve. "Help!"

"What's the matter with you?" He asked puzzled. The bell rang several times and fists pounded on the door. Steve was shocked. "Jeneil shut up. There are neighbors at the door."

"Help!" She yelled and the visitors began pounding and calling to Jeneil who looked at Steve and stuck out her tongue.

"Jeneil don't." He grinned. "I know you're mad at me but this could be serious."

She screamed again. Someone pushed heavily at the door trying to break through. "Jeneil for gosh sakes! Shut up." Steve said going to the door and opening it.

Kirk Vance burst through the door past Steve. "What's wrong with Jeneil?" He stopped with his mouth gaped as he saw her lying on the hallway floor covered in garbage bags.

"What the?" He knelt beside her. Drexel and Barbara Barnard had followed Kirk in and were staring just as shocked.

"Steve felt foolish. This isn't how it looks." Jeneil began shaking, "Please Dr. Vance untie me. Help me, please." She pleaded in a shaky voice.

"Jeneil!" Steve went to her. "Jeneil don't clown around, honey."

"Don't touch me!" She said, struggling to move away from him. "Please Dr. Vance. Please untie me." She nestled her face to the hand he had near her.

"Untie her?" He looked at Steve questioningly.

"Take the bags off me, you'll see." She said looking scared and anxious.

Steve kneeled next to her. "No! Don't touch me. I'm sorry I made you angry."

"Jeneil please for gosh sakes tell the truth." He said, tearing the garbage bag as Kirk Vance stood up looking wide eyed at the Barnards.

"Don't go please." Jeneil struggled to see where Kirk Vance had gone. "Don't leave me here with him. I made him angry. Untie me, please."

"Jeneil." Steve touched her face gently, "This isn't funny sweetheart. Don't fool around." He looked at them. "She's mad at me." He said weakly.

"I don't blame her." Barbara said as Steve tore through the second bag exposing Jeneil's bound hands and feet.

"It's a joke." Steve said.

"She's not laughing." Kirk answered seriously stooping next to Jeneil again trying to untie her hands, as Steve untied her feet.

"Oh thank you, Dr. Vance. Thank you." She said as her hand separated she leaned on her elbow waiting for her feet to be free moving away from Steve as soon as the last knot was loosened. She sat on the floor rubbing her wrists and Kirk took her pulse.

"What is all this?" He asked her.

"I made him angry and he was teaching me a lesson." She said quietly.

Kirk looked at Steve. "Is that true?"

Steve rubbed the back of his neck, "Well yes, but it's not the way she's saying it. Jeneil, honey, enough now tell the truth."

"I just did." She answered.

"The whole truth, Jeneil." Steve pleaded.

She looked at Kirk Vance, "I made a breakfast buffet and I finished eating before he did. He said I was a pest because I was anxious to open the gifts so I began teasing by taking back all my gifts to him then he went to the garage to get this rope and he caught me as I was trying to run up the stairs to get away from him."

"Is that true?" Kirk asked Steve.

Steve covered his face. "Oh shit it sounds worse and worse as she explains it."

"That isn't the truth?" Kirk asked.

Steve sighed, "It's true but not honest."

"What the hell does that mean?" Kirk asked, looking puzzled.

Steve looked at Jeneil who sat huddled near Kirk Vance with her head bent. "Yeah it's true." Steve said with resignation realizing he couldn't win.

Jeneil put her head back laughing, "Gotcha! Wise guy, gotcha. Caught you in your own game." She laughed and leaned against Kirk for support. "Tell me how women are the weaker sex." She laughed searching in the garbage bag for her slippers. Kirk Vance and the Barnards looked from one to the other.

"Well who's telling the truth?" Drexel asked Steve.

Steve held up his hands in surrender. "I quit." He said, "She's a spitfire totally beyond me."

Jeneil laughed as she put on her slippers. Walking on her knees, she went to Steve who was kneeling on the floor and she put her arms around his neck lovingly. "Poor Stevie B." She kissed his cheek and hugged him as the visitors watched.

Steve shook his head, "You got me good, sweetheart." He grinned.

"I know." She laughed, "You made the web and I snared you in it." She laughed into his shoulder and he slipped his arms around her smiling as he held her.

Drexel grinned, "What is this some kind of kinky fun?"

Jeneil pulled away from Steve laughing hysterically at Drexel's remark sitting on the floor and holding her stomach. "Steve's right." She said trying not to laugh anymore. "I was telling the truth but I wasn't being honest. It was only a joke and I was getting even with him."

"But tying you up is a little extreme isn't it?" Barbara asked with raised eyebrows.

Jeneil burst into laughter, again hugging Steve. "I can't save you Steve. It's hopeless. They won't believe me." She smoothed back his tousled hair and held his face in her hands. "I'm sorry, you poor darling!" She said between laughs, "I'm sorry I made you look like a pervert."

He held her to him and chuckled as she rested against him laughing.

Drexel laughed, "You two are a weird combination; I want you to know that. I'd like a video of your life together."

Kirk Vance watched Jeneil. "Mona Lisa." He said in a deep voice, "You are a spitfire, a real hellion. Another facet that skyrockets." He smiled, enjoying Steve who held her in his arms.

"Why are you here?" Steve asked the three as he held Jeneil.

Drexel laughed, "Because we're nosy. We wanted to know what's in that big box of a Christmas present. We thought it would be unwrapped by now."

Jeneil stood up and helped Steve to his feet. "We've been to busy playing gotcha." She chuckled. "Why don't' you unwrap it now." She suggested. Everyone gathered around as Steve undid the seam pins and slipped the fabric from the box. Taking a sturdy knife, he tore through the side of the box and pulled the corrugated covering away. He put his head back and laughed as he saw the huge arcade video game. Drexel and Kirk pulled the rest of the pieces off the machine to get a better look.

"Well I'll be." Drexel chuckled.

Steve smiled, "I played this game one weekend when Jeneil and I were away. It's therapeutic. I got lost in it." He looked at her smiling. "You are a nut." He kissed her cheek.

"Plug it in." Kirk said helping to uncover the rest of the huge game. All three men became involved in putting the video game together.

"Who's got a quarter?" Kirk asked going through his pocket change.

Jeneil brought Steve his Christmas stocking. "Take that package." She said pointing to a red cloth pouch tied with green yarn.

He undid the tie and uncovered fake coins designed for the machine.

"Hey." Drexel chuckled, "What a great idea. Who's first?"

"Me." Steve said.

Barbara Barnard joined Jeneil at the fireplace as she nibbled a slice of melon. "They never get too old for toys, do they?"

"Apparently not." Jeneil smiled watching Steve work the game flanked by Drexel and Kirk who were waiting for their turns. "How about some coffee?" Jeneil asked.

"Might as well." Barbara sighed, "Drex looks like he's entrenched. We may even forego his parents Christmas brunch and dinner for the video game." She smiled watching the men at Steve's elbow kibitzing as she sat with Jeneil on the sofa drinking coffee. "What's so fascinating about a lot of bleeps and squeaks?" She asked, getting up and joining the men at the video game. Jeneil was relieved that Barbara had left. She found she didn't have the pretense to make conversation with her. She was still rattled since discovering Barbara's involvement with Steve. Jeneil poured some grapefruit juice and sipped it slowly watching the group and feeling irritated that Barbara knew Steve better than she did. "In the biblical sense anyway." She thought chuckling to herself, "only in the biblical sense." She sighed, watching Barbara nest amongst all the men and Jeneil admired the ease and confidence Barbara possessed dealing with them. Her eyes widened as she realized that Kirk had spent the night at the Barnards. "Two at the same time?" She gasped as her mind tossed out the thought. "Good grief how?" She drank more juice to help close her mouth and then found that she could accept Barbara and Steve more easily now as she remembered that there was Barbara and Kirk, Barbara and Drexel and also George Tyachz. Jeneil passed the cool glass across her lower lip thinking how life seemed to deal so oddly with people. Barbara had her problems because she could deal physically with men too easily and she had her problems because she couldn't. "Well physical was easy for me with Peter." She thought defensively and then she felt the pain pass through the center of her as his name passed through her mind. She drank more juice hoping to dissolve the lump in her throat. She sighed and wondered if life had always been this complicated or was she losing stamina for the crazy race life demanded. Finishing the juice she watched the low fire turn a log red hot. Steve sat down beside her and she turned her head to look at him. Noticing the look of concern on his face, she smiled slightly and patted his arm. "I'm glad I saw you open that one."

"I never opened any." He grinned, "I was teasing."

"You're good at gotchas." She said, returning the glass to the serving table and smiling.

"All right men." Barbara Barnard grinned at her husband and Kirk, "and right now I use the term loosely." She laughed, "Let's leave so the Bradleys can get to their Christmas.

We've intruded long enough." She pulled the two men away from the game. "Look at all the presents that are still wrapped."

Kirk chuckled. "Hell I'd forget all my presents too if Santa Claus left her wrapped and tied in my front hall."

The group laughed merrily as they headed toward the door. "Bye spitfire." Kirk called as the front door closed.

Jeneil sat on the sofa and grinned remembering the fun of the whole joke and she was grateful and comforted that she had Steve in her life especially on a Christmas morning that could easily have found her alone. "He's the only one I know who could handle such a crazy marriage." She sighed as she watched the fire. She looked up to see Steve watching her and the feeling of gratitude for him as a husband filled her. She got up and went to him quickly nestling to him for a hug. His arms felt strong and secure as they wrapped around her. He felt so good to her there holding her. "My husband." She thought to herself, "My husband." She thought again changing the inflection of the phrase, "I think it's time for me to grow up." She added mentally. "I have a husband who deserves to be more than pretend and pretend was part of Camelot apparently. Tecumseh is stark reality. I have to get on with life, a real one." She snuggled to him relaxed by the thought that she didn't need another gift, because she has an outstanding husband who cares about her. "I can see it in the way he looks at me." She smiled as she rested her head against his cheek.

Steve held her, surprised and thrilled at her display of affection. He had seen her drifting into her own thoughts and he had begun to worry, but she was in his arms now and not for comfort he sensed that. "Everything's okay isn't it? I mean the White Stallion mess and all." He whispered. "You got rid of it didn't you?"

She nodded, "Everything's okay." She replied softly.

He held her closer and kissed her cheek, "I'm glad." He sighed with relief. "I'm so damn glad." He smoothed a kiss across her cheek gently and slowly. She smelled so good and her skin felt so soft, he continued and pressed his lips to her neck in a light kiss. The warmth of her skin was intoxicating and he smoothed his face against her neck enjoying the smooth warmth not realizing that she had tilted her head to allow him the freedom. Jeneil closed her eyes as the electricity stirred within her at the touch of his light beard against her skin. His heart pounded in his chest as he noticed how she was responding to him. "Oh shit!" He moaned to himself, "Of all the damn times I've wanted her like this and it happens now!" His watch alarm signaled and he sighed knowing that it was time to get ready to leave for the Sprague's and they hadn't even opened their gifts. There wasn't even time to pass on the gifts and continue. He didn't want whatever was happening to rush through their first time together if that was happening. "Why now, damn it?" He thought angrily.

"We're so far behind schedule today." She said softly and he nodded and continued holding her. She chuckled, "You don't let me get away with too much. I couldn't believe that you actually tied me up and stuffed me into a garbage bag." She chuckled again and Steve was surprised that she had drifted from the moment so easily.

"Everything distracts her." He thought, "But that's okay, honey. Now that I know you'll allow me this, I'll handle it if I have to smash through the whole damn ivory tower that you're wrapped in."

He smiled at her lovingly, "I think it's a matter of pride and ego with me. You seem to bring out macho in me."

She grinned, "That's all right, I love Neanderthal." She blurted out the honest statement shocking herself. He laughed and hugged her not daring to kiss her knowing that at that moment he wouldn't stop.

"I'd like you to open a gift." He said, releasing her reluctantly and going to the Christmas tree. Jeneil followed. Reaching toward one of the tree branches, he lifted off a small red package tied with green ribbon that held the wire ornament hanger attached to the spiked limb of the evergreen.

"I've never noticed it there." She smiled loving the idea.

"I put it there last night." He said handing her the small package.

She took it and unwrapped the shiny paper carefully. The box was unmistakable and she was pleased even before she opened it. Curiosity filled her and she smiled at him as she pulled open the hinged cover wondering what kind of ring he had chosen. The diamond stunned her as it glistened from its deep blue base. "Oh Steve, it's fantastic, beautiful. It's really gorgeous." She gasped studying the workmanship of the filigree on the setting. "It is so beautiful." She whispered.

He reached for the ring, "Well I thought that since we're married it might be a good time to get engaged."

She smiled as tears filled her eyes.

"Honey don't get mushy on me now, I've never done this ceremony before, I was sort of counting on you to guide me through it." He said taking the ring from the box. She brushed the tears away quickly.

"Well you'll have to propose." She smiled. "Put the ring on my finger and ask me to marry you." She directed holding her left hand out for him. She felt his hand shaking as he slipped the ring on her finger and she smiled. "I seem to remember that you shook when you put the wedding band on too. Having trouble with the corrals White Stallion?" She teased.

He looked into her eyes steadily, "No, no trouble at all." He said seriously, and took her hand, "Jeneil will you marry me?" He asked not flinching or wavering and sounding so sincere that Jeneil felt her heart stop for a second.

"Gladly." She replied softly. "I want to be your wife." She added and Steve felt that they had now reached an attitude of commitment in their relationship that wasn't there before. She spoke the words of a commitment to a real marriage and his heart raced.

"I want you to be my wife. I want the chance to be your husband, Jeneil."

She nodded and moved to him to be held as her heart pounded with excitement. She slipped her arms around his neck and hugged him tightly.

"I love you, Jeneil." He said enjoying how the words felt.

"I'm so glad I'm married to you." She replied, "Sometimes being with you seems so overwhelmingly right to me, so natural. Like I belong here."

He smiled and held her closer. "It's almost confusing."

She moved away from him slightly. "I think we should be married soon. There doesn't seem to be any sense to a long engagement since we're already married." She said grinning.

He touched her cheek tenderly and nodded. Moving closer to her he kissed her lips lightly and she responded to him gently. There was magic in the kiss and Steve held her feeling for the first time since they'd been married that he had a real wife. He stopped the kiss as the electricity began to fill his chest wanting to wait so that their first time together would be handled right. "I love you." He whispered.

"I love you too." She smiled at him gently taking his breath away.

The other gifts were unwrapped and the new feeling of commitment lasted. Steve noticed Jeneil would hold her hand out to admire the ring from time to time and then she would hug him. Life was at last settling in for them as a couple. He now relaxed as hopes of the weekend seminar in New York becoming a great get away surfaced for them. He watched her opening a package and he smiled to himself. "Maybe you and I should get married tonight," He thought, "since Friday would bring the hectic pace of leaving for New York. Being together for the first time all that rushing wasn't how he wanted to begin his marriage with her."

She looked up from the silk blouse she had just unwrapped. "You have chosen such wonderful gifts. It's positively eerie how well you know me after only a short time being married." She kissed him and smiled warmly folding the blouse carefully to return it to the box. He grinned thinking how natural it was for him to know her so well after being in love with her for so long. He knew her every mood from having watched her with Peter. He had studied her likes and dislikes so much that he thought for a while it was the real reason she felt that their marriage seemed so right. But to him the feeling of her being his was deeper than that and having heard her say it too was what he found eerie. He leaned toward her kissing the side of her head gently loving the feeling of her soft hair.

"We're going to be good together." He thought. That much of the White Stallion was still alive in him, he had a sense about physical being great before an actual encounter and he had often wondered if it was biochemical since the vibrations were usually strong. He had known that about Rita having only once met her at a Friday party at Kirk's place. The vibrations with Jeneil were beyond anything he could remember with anyone else which surprised him since she had only responded for brief moments with him. He had always thought it was the electrical charge caused by anticipation between two people responding simultaneously that caused the vibrations but that wasn't the case with Jeneil. Most times she was locked in her ivory tower completely unaware of him as a man and yet his sensitivity of the vibrations was unmistakably strong and clear without her response. He kissed her head again and she leaned into the kiss gently in response. He smiled noticing that she had automatic responses to physical touch which she performed with ease. Snuggling, hugging, and nestling were simple routines to her like breathing. Passion didn't surface in her too easily, but he felt that her level of passion must be more intense since all the steps that usually aroused passion in others were only mild stirrings to her. He had always sensed that she just smoldered and then probably ignited spontaneously and he was looking forward to learning more about her. His other gifts were a complete blur to him as he sat admiring the gift that life had given to him for whatever strange reason that only life would probably ever know. The woman he had fallen so deeply in love with so many months ago was his wife this Christmas and about to become his wife in reality. Life was perfect for him. There was nothing else he needed or wanted with her in his life.

Thank you for taking the time to read
"The Songbird / Volume Four - Author's Limited Edition."

In The Songbird/Volume One we introduced the main characters of the story. Jeneil and Peter were able to keep their relationship private and a secret and as such were able to establish a firm foundation with promises for a bright future together.

In The Songbird/Volume Two outside forces have loomed it's ugly head. Protecting the Songbird is not easy for Peter as Jeneil continues to expand her search for superlative in her life. Is Peter up to the task? And what about Steve? Is he really Peter's best friend? Will Peter and Jeneil survive?

In The Songbird/Volume Three we are introduced to a new character, an "Evil" girl named "Uette". In the dictionary "Evil" is defined as (1) morally bad or wrong; wicked, (2) harmful; injurious, (3) unlucky; disastrous (4) wickedness, sin. (5) anything that causes harm, pain, etc. Is Uette really an "Evil" person or is she just plain desperate???

In The Songbird/Volume Four Peter and Steve try to protect Jeneil from the dangers surrounding her. Peter's search for truth and dignity has disastrous consequences.

In The Songbird/Volume Five (The final volume in the series) Beverly is able to tie the loose ends together to bring the story of The Songbird to it's happy conclusion.

Your views would be most welcome and appreciated. Feel free to post your thoughts and comments on our website at:

http://www.TheSongbirdStory.com
OR
Search "The Songbird Story" on Facebook

"The Songbird"
by
Beverly Louise Oliver-Farrell

Author's Limited Edition / Five Volume Series

This unedited version of "The Songbird/Volume Four" is as the author intended it to be read. Only a limited numbers of copies will be available for the family and her friends. (A more condensed offering of "The Songbird Story" with be made available for the public at a later time along with a screenplay version.

We invite you to visit "The Songbird Story"website at:

http://www.TheSongbirdStory.com

Register your Email address to receive information on the final volume.
The Songbird /Volume Five
This last Volume in the series will be available in November of 2012.

For Further Information and Inquiries Contact:

Brian B. Farrell
4844 Keith Lane
Colorado Springs, CO 80916

Tel / Fax: (719)380-8174

Email: farrell_family@usa.net

BUY DIRECT FROM THE FAMILY AND SAVE

Made in the USA
Charleston, SC
04 October 2013